Baltic Mission

For Regine and Neil

Richard Woodman was born in London in 1944 and crewed in a Tall Ships race before becoming an indentured midshipman in cargo-liners at the age of sixteen. He has sailed in a variety of ships, including weather ships, lighthouse traders and trawlers, serving from apprentice to captain. He is the author of twenty-three works of fiction and non-fiction, a member of the Royal Historical Society, the Society for Nautical Research, the Navy Records Society and the Square Rigger Club. In his spare time he sails an elderly gaff cutter with his wife and two children.

'This author has quietly stolen the weather-gauge from most of his rivals in the Hornblower stakes' *Observer*

'Packed with exciting incident, worthy of wide appeal to those who love thrilling nautical encounters and the sea' *Nautical Magazine*

Also by Richard Woodman

Nathaniel Drinkwater Series

AN EYE OF THE FLEET
A KING'S CUTTER
A BRIG OF WAR
THE BOMB VESSEL
THE CORVETTE
1805
UNDER FALSE COLOURS
THE FLYING SQUADRON
BENEATH THE AURORA
THE SHADOW OF THE EAGLE
EBB TIDE

WAGER
THE DARKENING SEA
ENDANGERED SPECIES
WATERFRONT
UNDER SAIL

THE FIRST NATHANIEL DRINKWATER OMNIBUS
THE SECOND NATHANIEL DRINKWATER OMNIBUS
DEATH OR DAMNATION: THE FOURTH NATHANIEL
DRINKWATER OMNIBUS
DISTANT GUNFIRE: THE FIFTH NATHANIEL
DRINKWATER OMNIBUS

Blaze of Glory!

The Third Nathaniel Drinkwater Omnibus

Baltic Mission
In Distant Waters
A Private Revenge

RICHARD WOODMAN

timewarner
paperbacks

A *Time Warner* Paperback

This omnibus edition first published in Great Britain by Warner Books in 2001
Reprinted by Time Warner Paperbacks in 2003

The Third Nationel Drinkwater Omnibus Copyright © Richard Woodman 2001

Previously published separately:

Baltic Mission
First published in Great Britain in 1986 by John Murray (Publishers) Ltd
Published by Sphere Books Ltd in 1988
Reprinted by Warner Books in 1991
Reprinted 1995
Copyright © 1986 by Richard Woodman

In Distant Waters
First published in Great Britain in 1988 by John Murray (Publishers) Ltd
Published by Sphere Books Ltd 1989
Reprinted 1987, 1988, 1990, 1991
Reprinted by Warner Books 1992
Reprinted 1995
Copyright © 1988 by Richard Woodman

A Private Revenge
First published in Great Britain in 1989 by John Murray (Publishers) Ltd
Published by Sphere Books Ltd 1990
Reprinted 1990
Reprinted by Warner Books 1993
Reprinted 1996, 1997, 1999
Copyright © 1989 by Richard Woodman

The moral right of the author has been asserted.

A CIP catalogue record for this book is available from the British Library.

ISBN 0 7515 3174 X

Typeset in Palatino by M Rules
Printed and bound in Great Britain by Clays Ltd, St Ives plc

Time Warner Paperbacks
An imprint of
Time Warner Books UK
Brettenham House
Lancaster Place
London WC2E 7EN

www.TimeWarnerBooks.co.uk

Contents

PART ONE: THE SHIP

    Eylau 1
1   The Kattegat 10
2   An Armed Neutrality 24
3   The Shipment of Arms 34
4   A Stay of Execution 44
5   News from Carlscrona 60
6   A Perfect Opportunity 72
7   Nielsen 87
8   Friedland 102
9   Mackenzie 112
10 The Mad Enterprise 124

PART TWO: THE RAFT 135

    Napoleon 137
11 The Road to Tilsit 140
12 Ostroff 156
13 The Waters of the Nieman 163
14 The Meeting of Eagles 172
15 The Secret 181

PART THREE: THE POST-CHAISE 191

    Accord 193
16 The Return of Ulysses 195
17 The Vanguard of Affairs 204
18 News from the Baltic 215
    Copenhagen 223
    Author's Note 224

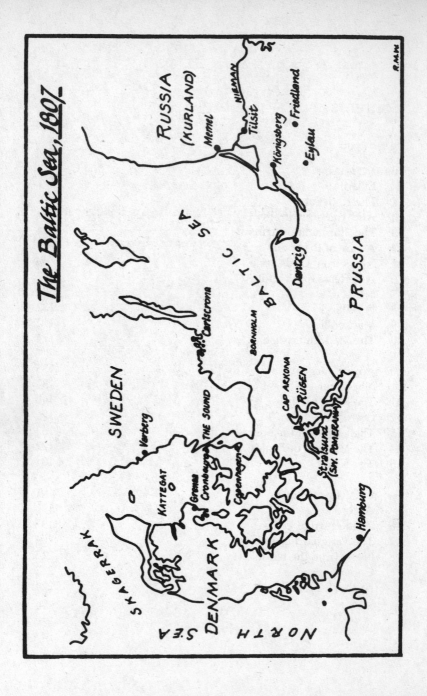

The Baltic Sea, 1807

SKAGERRAK
NORTH SEA
DENMARK
SWEDEN
Varberg
KATTEGAT
Grena
Cronburg
THE SOUND
Copenhagen
Hamburg
BALTIC SEA
Carlscrona
BORNHOLM
CAP ARKONA
RÜGEN
Stralsund
(Sw. POMERANIA)
PRUSSIA
Danzig
Königsberg
Eylau
Friedland
Tilsit
NIEMAN
Memel
RUSSIA
(KURLAND)

R.MAN

PART ONE
The Ship

'I was born on a battlefield – what are the lives of a million men to me?'

Napoleon, Emperor of the French

Eylau

8 February 1807

The horses of the two squadrons of Cossacks were labouring as they breasted the low ridge dominating the shallow valley and the frozen river behind them. They were almost blown by the speed of their recent charge and the violence of their clash with the enemy along the line of the river. As the officer at their head caught sight of the red roofs of the village of Schlöditten, he threw up his blood-stained sabre, stood in his stirrups and ordered the fur-swathed cavalry to wheel their shaggy mounts. They reined in, faced about and halted as their officers trotted back to their posts.

'Well done, my children!' the Russian officer called with patri-archal familiarity, smiling and nodding his clean-shaven face to the swarthy and bearded troopers who grinned back at him. The Cossack horses tossed their heads in a jingle of harness, edging their tails round into the biting northerly wind. Breath erupted in clouds from their distending nostrils and the snowflakes that were again beginning to fall melted on contact with their steaming flanks. Lowering their lances across their saddle-bows, the Cossacks exchanged ribaldries and remarks, incongruously cross-ing themselves as they called the unanswered names of men they had left behind them in the valley. A few bound each other's wounds, or ran their filthy hands gently down the shuddering legs of horses galled by the enemy. Most remained in their saddles, reaching under their sheepskins for flasks of vodka, or for car-casses of chickens that hung in festoons from their belts.

Reaching his post at their head, the clean-shaven officer aban-doned the dialect of the Don. 'Hey, my friend! Come!' he called in French to another officer. Sheathing his sabre he fumbled in a pis-tol holster for a flask which he beckoned the other to share.

'What does the esteemed representative of the staff think of today's work?' He held out the flask, his blue eyes intently observing him. 'We made short work of those French bastards, didn't we, eh?'

The staff-officer grinned, but his eyes kept returning to the valley below them, into which they had charged twenty minutes earlier.

'They were Lasalle's bastards, you know, Count. The best light cavalry in the Grand Army.'

'And we beat them, by Almighty God.' The count crossed himself piously and his companion raised a sardonic eyebrow at the practice.

'We haven't finished the business yet,' he said, pointing to the southward, where the little town of Preussisch-Eylau lay engulfed in smoke. Only its church belfry showed above the pall as, house by house, it crumbled beneath the storm of shot from two massive Russian batteries close to its eastern outskirts. Beyond the town and spreading out over the gently rolling snow-covered countryside of East Prussia, the dark masses of the Grand Army of France and her allies attempted to roll up the Russian left wing.

Four miles away to the north, just beyond the frozen river at the other extreme of the contending armies and immediately in front of the Cossacks, Lasalle's repulsed hussars were re-forming. Between them the bloody corpses of two dozen men were already stiffening like the trampled and frozen reeds of the river margin. To the south of the French cavalry, the dark swirl of Marshal Soult's Fourth Army Corps had been thrown back from their own assault upon the Russians. The Cossack commander slapped his thigh and laughed with satisfaction.

'Ha! You see, my friend, they *are* beaten! And was it not us, the squadrons of Count Piotr Petrovich Kalitkin, that took the very orders of the great Napoleon himself from the hands of his courier? Eh? Well, wasn't it?'

'Indeed, your Excellency,' said his companion with exaggerated courtesy, 'I think we may take a measure of credit for today.' He returned the vodka flask amid an outburst of indignation.

'Measure of credit! Measure of credit!' spluttered Kalitkin. 'As a result of *us*, Marshal Bernadotte never received his orders, and . . .'

he waved his gloved hand over the battlefield, 'is not here to support his Emperor.'

The staff-officer nodded, his expression of amused irony altering to one of concern. It was quite true that Napoleon's courier had fallen into the Cossacks' hands at Lautenberg, but the staff-officer had a wider appreciation of events than Count Kalitkin.

'You are quite right, Count, but Ney is not here either, and that worries me.'

'Bah! You know too much and it makes you worry too much.'

'That,' said the staff-officer, levelling a small telescope to the north where snow was falling thickly from a leaden sky, 'is my business, Count, and the reason for my attachment to your brilliant command.'

'Ah, you and your damned reports. I know you are a spy; though whether you spy for Bennigsen on me, or for St Petersburg on Bennigsen, I have not yet determined.'

The staff-officer lowered his telescope and grinned at the Count. 'You are too suspicious, Count, and too good a light-cavalryman to need a nursemaid.'

'Bah!' repeated Kalitkin good naturedly, apparently unconcerned at the purpose of the staff-officer's attachment to his squadrons. 'You are an impudent rascal and I should have you whipped, but you would report me and I should be reduced to a troop again, damn you.'

'If I were you, my dear Count,' said the staff-officer, staring again through his glass, 'I should forget about whipping me and send a patrol to find out who is approaching from the northward; if it's Ney we shall be outflanked.' He passed the glass to Kalitkin whose manner was immediately transformed.

'I'll go myself.' He turned in his saddle. 'Hey! Khudoznik, stop doing that and mount up with your men!' A score of Cossacks fastened their saddle-bags and slung their lances, detaching themselves from the main body and forming a loose column. Kalitkin turned to the staff-officer. 'I shall leave the fate of Holy Russia in your hands and save Bennigsen's reputation again.' Kalitkin threw the vodka flask to his friend and kicked his horse to a trot. In a few moments he was no more than a blur in the swirling snow.

The staff-officer edged his horse forward to catch a glimpse of the battlefield before more snow flurries obscured it. To his left a battery of 60 cannon kept up a ruthless fire into the re-forming battalions of Soult. Beyond, the orange flashes of a further 120 guns pounded Eylau; but in the far distance heavy columns of French infantry could be seen advancing to attack. For a while the snow curtained everything, even deadening the concussion of the guns, but when it cleared again the French attack seemed to have failed.

Nearer at hand a greater drama was unfolding. About a mile away from the ridge a huge column of Russian infantry, grey-coated and with feet muffled in sacking, hurled themselves forward against the houses of Eylau. Six thousand peasant soldiers followed their officers with the obedience of small children and fought their way into the town like furies. Unseen by the distant Cossacks, Napoleon was driven from his post in the church belfry and only escaped by the self-sacrifice of his bodyguard. But the Cossacks observed his angry response to this insolent bravery; they shook up their horses' heads and grasped their lances, in case they were called upon to react to the great counterattack that burst out of the French position.

The snow cleared completely, torn aside by the biting wind as swiftly as it had come, and this lull was accompanied by a sudden brightening of the sky as Napoleon's brother-in-law, Marshal Murat, led forward more than ten thousand horsemen to burst through the Russian line. Wheeling in its rear and repeatedly breaking the centre, they sabred the indomitable gunners and cut up the devoted Russian infantry that had so recently threatened their Emperor. Behind Murat's cuirassiers and dragoons, Marshal Bessières followed with the Horse Grenadiers of the Imperial Guard, big men on huge black horses who trampled the remains of Bennigsen's frontal assault beneath their hooves. But the tide of cavalry had reached its limit. It was unsupported and ebbed inexorably back towards Eylau. The guns of the Russian centre were remanned and began to pour shot into the enemy as they retreated. Then another curtain of snow closed over the mass of dying and mutilated men, so that their cries and groans were unheard.

The staff-officer finished the flask of vodka and tucked it into the breast of his coat. He nodded companionably to a subaltern who rode up from the Cossack flank.

'Well, young Repin, this is a bloody business, but a sweet revenge for Austerlitz, eh?'

'Indeed, sir, it is.'

'Count Kalitkin should rejoin us soon . . . ah, here he comes, if I'm not mistaken . . .' Kalitkin rode up and reined in, his eyes gleaming with triumph, his horse steaming.

'Well, my friend, I have done it again! I have found your Ney for you. *Voilà!*' Kalitkin pointed behind him where some of Lasalle's hussars were moving out to form a screen behind which the head of a marching column could just be made out through the snow. 'And also I have found our valiant ally, or, at least, what remains of him . . .'

'General Lestocq's Prussians?' asked the staff-officer sharply.

'Exactly, my dear wiseacre. Lestocq and his Prussians, and we must move to the right and cover their march across our rear.' Kalitkin suddenly drew his sabre with a rasp and pointed it across the shallow valley. 'There! See, those French pigs are ahead of us! They will try and harry the Prussian flank . . .'

'I told you they were the best light cavalry in the Grand Army.'

'You go and tell Bennigsen that the squadrons of Piotr Kalitkin have saved Mother Russia again . . . and if he gives me a division I will win the whole damned war . . .' He stood in his stirrups and bawled an order. This time the whole mass of the Cossacks moved forward and the staff-officer wheeled his horse aside to let them pass. For a moment he remained alone on the ridge to watch. The trot changed to a canter and then to a gallop; the lance points were lowered, the pennons flickering like fire as the dark wave of horsemen swept over the frozen marshes bordering the river, and crashed into the ranks of the French hussars. The enemy swung to meet them, their breath steaming below their fierce moustaches and their hair braided into dreadlocks beneath their rakish shakos. The staff-officer pulled his horse round and spurred it towards the headquarters of the Russian army at Anklappen.

*

5

Night fell early, the short winter afternoon expiring under heavy clouds and the smoke of battle. The French attack failed, largely due to the timely arrival of General Lestocq's Prussians and the late appearance of Ney: Napoleon had received the worst drubbing of his career, but Lasalle's hussars had had their revenge, and Kalitkin's Cossacks had been pushed back beyond the village of Schlöditten, to bivouac and lick their wounds. It was past midnight when Kalitkin had posted his vedettes, rolled himself in his cloak and lain down in the snow. A few moments later he was roused as one of his men brought in a strange officer, wearing an unfamiliar uniform and raging furiously in a barbarous French at the Cossack trooper whose sabre point gleamed just below the prisoner's chin.

Kalitkin sprang to his feet. 'Mother of God! What have you there, Khudoznik? A Frenchman?' Kalitkin addressed the prisoner in French: 'Are you a French officer?'

'God damn it, no, sir!' the man exclaimed. 'Tell this ruffian to let me go! I am Colonel Wilson, a British Commissioner attached to General Bennigsen's headquarters. I was reconnoitring when this stinking louse picked me up. Who the devil are you?'

Kalitkin ordered the Cossack Khudoznik to return to his post and introduced himself. 'I am Count Piotr Kalitkin commanding two squadrons of the Hetman's Don Cossacks. So, you are a spy of the British are you?' Kalitkin grinned and made room round the fire.

'You Russians are a damnably suspicious lot,' said the mollified Wilson, rubbing his hands and extending them to the warmth of the fire.

'But you have come to see we don't waste your precious English gold, eh?'

'To liaise with the headquarters of the army, Count, not to spy.'

'It is the same thing. Where are your English soldiers, Colonel, eh? Your gold is useful but it would have been better if some English soldiers could have helped us today, would it not? There would be fewer widows in Russia tomorrow.'

'My dear Count,' replied Wilson with a note of tired exasperation creeping into his voice. 'I am plagued night and day with pleas for which I can offer no satisfaction until the ice in the Baltic thaws and His Majesty's ships can enter that sea. Until then we shall have to rely upon Russian valour.'

'So, Colonel,' said Kalitkin, still grinning in the firelight, 'you are a courtier *and* a spy. I congratulate you!'

'I hope,' said Wilson with a heavy sarcasm, 'that I am merely a diplomat.'

A stir on the outskirts of the firelit circle among the half-sleeping, half-freezing men caused both Kalitkin and the Englishman to turn.

'And,' exclaimed Kalitkin triumphantly, 'here is another spy. Welcome back, my friend. I expected you to spend the night in a whore's bed at headquarters. Are there no women with General Bennigsen?'

'Only pretty boys dressed as aides,' said the staff-officer emerging from the night, 'in accordance with the German fashion. Besides, I came back to bring you . . . *this*!' The staff-officer produced a bottle from the breast of his cloak with a magician's flourish.

'Ah! Vodka! Next to a woman, the best consolation.'

'One can share it with more facility, certainly . . . I see you have company.'

As Kalitkin laughed, snatching the bottle and wrenching the cork from its neck, the staff-officer's expression of cynical levity vanished at the sight of the British uniform.

'Yes, my friend,' explained Kalitkin after wiping his mouth, 'a spy like you. He is an English officer; a *commissioner* no less.'

In the firelight the staff-officer's mouth set rigid, his eyes suddenly watchful. 'I am Colonel Wilson,' said the Englishman again, waving aside the vodka that Kalitkin companionably offered him after liberally helping himself, 'His Britannic Majesty's representative at the headquarters of His Imperial Majesty's army.'

'Colonel Wilson . . .' the staff-officer muttered under his breath, his eyes probing the face of the English officer.

'Count Kalitkin has introduced himself,' said Wilson, referring obliquely to Kalitkin's failure to introduce the staff-officer. 'Whom have I the honour of addressing?'

The staff-officer hesitated, looked down and with a muddy boot kicked back a piece of wood that had been ejected from the heart of the fire by a small explosion of resin deep in its core.

'Tell him, my friend,' said Kalitkin, swigging again at the vodka. 'Tell him who you are.'

The staff-officer's obvious reticence combined with the scrutiny to which he had been subject to awaken suspicions in Wilson's mind. Kalitkin's flippant allusions to espionage had been initially attributed to the subconscious reaction to excessive centralisation that Wilson had encountered in his dealings with the Russians. Watching the staff-officer's face he was aware of a quickening interest in this man.

'Come, sir,' he prompted, 'you have the advantage of me.'

'I am Captain Ostroff, Colonel Wilson, aide-de-camp to Prince Vorontzoff and presently attached to Count Kalitkin's squadrons of the Hetman's Don Cossacks.'

But Wilson paid little attention to the details of the staff-officer's status. What interested him far more was the way in which this Ostroff had pronounced Wilson's own name. For the first time since his secondment to the Russian army Wilson had heard his surname without the heavy, misplaced accent upon its second syllable. In a flash of intuition he realised he was talking to a fellow Englishman.

'Your servant, Captain Ostroff,' he said, bowing a little from the waist and holding the other's eyes in a steady gaze. But Ostroff's expression did not alter, not even when a sharp crack at their feet ejected another sliver of wood from the bivouac fire.

'How interesting,' went on Wilson with the smooth urbanity of the perfect diplomat, 'I have not had much opportunity to study the Russian tongue of your *muzhiks*, but if I am not mistaken, your name is the Russian word for . . .'

'*Island*,' snapped Ostroff suddenly and it was not the abruptness of the interruption that surprised Wilson but the fact that where he had been about to employ the French noun, Ostroff had chosen to head him off with a sideways glance at Kalitkin and the use of a definition in plain English.

As the two men strolled with an affected nonchalance away from the recumbent Kalitkin and his bivouac, the Count lounged back on his sheepskin. 'Spies,' he muttered to himself, 'spies, the pair of them . . .' and he stared up at the stars shining through the rents in the clouds, aware that their motion had become suddenly irregular.

1   The Kattegat

March 1807

His Britannic Majesty's 36-gun, 18-pounder frigate *Antigone*, commanded by Captain Nathaniel Drinkwater, lay at anchor off the Swedish fortress of Varberg wrapped in a dense and clammy fog. Her decks were dark with the moisture of it; damp had condensed on the dull black barrels of her cannon, giving them an unnatural sheen, and her rigging was festooned with millions upon millions of tiny droplets like the autumn dew upon spiders' webs. Wraiths of fog streamed slowly across her deck, robbing the scarlet coats of her marine sentries of their brilliance and dulling all sounds.

The duty midshipman leant against the quarterdeck rail with one foot upon the slide of a carronade and contemplated the dark oily water and the ice-floes that bumped and scraped alongside. Fifty yards out from the ship's side he could see nothing and the view from the deck was too familiar to engage his slightest interest.

Not that the slowly swirling ice-floes were worthy of study in themselves, for they were fast melting and puny by comparison with those he had seen in the Greenland Sea, but they were hypnotic and drew all active thought from the brain of the idle young man. They set him to dreaming aimlessly and endeavouring to pass the time as pleasantly as possible without the tiresome need to exert himself. For the past forty minutes Midshipman Lord Walmsley had been the senior officer upon the upper deck and in that capacity he saw no reason to exert himself. The sentries were at their posts, the duty watch fussing about routine tasks, and he was perfectly content to leave them to the supervision of the petty officers and their mates. Besides, Walmsley had been cheated of the prospect of an early repast and the trivial sense of grievance only reinforced his inertia. In the absence of the captain ashore, the first lieutenant, Mr Samuel Rogers, had repaired to the gunroom for a meal he felt he was more entitled to than the midshipman.

Lord Walmsley did not seriously dispute the justice of the contention, for to do so would have involved far more effort than he was capable of. So he let the silly sense of grievance paralyse him and dreamed of a distant milkmaid whose willing concupiscence had long since initiated him to the irresponsible joys of a privileged manhood.

Inertia was endemic aboard the *Antigone* that morning. Captain Drinkwater had zealously pushed his frigate from the Nore through a succession of gales and into the breaking ice of the Baltic to reach Varberg as soon as he could. The whole of *Antigone*'s company was exhausted, and they had lost a man overboard off the Naze of Norway: a sacrifice to the elements which seemed determined to punish them for every league they stole to windward in a searing succession of freezing easterly gales. It was, therefore, scarcely surprising that once the anchor had bitten into the sea-bed off the coast of Sweden and the captain departed in his barge, the mood on board *Antigone* should have been one of euphoria. As if confirming the frigate's company in their own merit, the elements had softened, the wind dropped, and within an hour of Captain Drinkwater's departure the fog had closed down on them, wrapping them in a chill, damp cocoon.

'Well now, d'you intend to spend the entire day in that supine way, laddie?'

Walmsley straightened up and turned. Mr Fraser, the frigate's second lieutenant, crossed the deck to stand beside him.

'I was merely ascertaining whether I could hear the captain's barge returning, Mr Fraser, by removing my ears from the sounds of the deck and leaning over the side.'

Fraser raised a sandy eyebrow. 'Your lordship is a plausible liar and should have his ears removed from the sounds of the deck to the masthead. A spell of sky-parlour would cure your impudence . . . but cut along and have something to eat . . . and send young Frey up in your place,' he added, calling after the retreating midshipman.

The Scotsman began a leisurely pacing of the deck, noting the

11

other duty-men and sentries at their places. A few minutes later Midshipman Frey joined him.

'Ah, Mr Frey,' remarked Fraser in his distinctive burr, 'you well know how my flinty Calvinist soul abhors idleness. Be so kind as to pipe the red cutter away and row a guard around the ship.'

'Aye, aye, sir.'

Fraser regarded the activity that this order initiated with a certain amount of satisfaction. His mild enjoyment was marred by the unnecessary appearance of Rogers, the first lieutenant. Fraser had just left Rogers at table, his big fist clamped proprietorially around the neck of the gunroom decanter as though it was his personal property. Rogers's face was flushed with the quantity of alcohol he had consumed.

'What the devil's all this fuss and palaver, Fraser?'

''Tis nothing, Mr Rogers. I'm merely hoisting out a boat to row guard about the ship while this fog persists . . .'

'You take a deal too much upon yourself . . .'

'I think the captain would have . . .'

'Damn you, Fraser. D'you threaten me?'

Fraser suppressed mounting anger with difficulty. 'Reflect, sir,' he said with frigid formality, 'we have a considerable sum in specie under guard below and I think the captain would object to its loss in his absence . . .'

'Oh, you do, do you? And who the hell's going to take it? The Swedes are friendly and the Danes are neutral. There isn't an enemy within a hundred leagues of us.'

'We don't know there isn't an enemy a hundred *yards* away, damn it; and as long as I'm officer o' the deck there'll be a guard pulled round the ship!' Fraser had lost his restraint now and both officers stood face to face in full view of the men at the davit falls. Fraser turned away, flushed and angry. 'Lower away there, God damn you, and lively with it!'

Rogers stood stock-still. His befuddled mind recognised the sense in Fraser's argument. He was aware that he should have sent off a boat as soon as the fog settled that forenoon. Knowledge of his own failure only fuelled his wrath, already at a high pitch due to the amount of wine he had drunk. And his mind was clear enough to realise that Fraser had committed the unforgivable in losing his temper and answering a senior insolently. 'Come here, Fraser!' Rogers roared.

Fraser, supervising the lowering of the cutter, turned. 'D'you address me, sir?' he asked coldly.

'You know damn well I do! Come here!'

Fraser crossed the deck again slowly, grasping the significance of Rogers's new attack. Once again the two officers were face to face.

'Gentlemen, gentlemen, this is no time for such discordant tomfoolery . . .'

Rogers's colour mounted still further as he spun round on the newcomer who, called by the sudden interest stirring between decks, now arrived on the quarterdeck.

'You keep out of this, Hill,' snarled Rogers at the sailing master.

'No, sir, I will not.' He lowered his voice. 'And you are making damnable fools of yourselves. For God's sake stop at once!' Hill's warning ended on an urgent hiss.

'And I suppose, Hill, you'll feel obliged to inform the captain of this matter?' Rogers snarled.

'I'll hold my tongue if you'll hold your temper,' Hill snapped back sharply, fixing the first lieutenant with a stare. Rogers exhaled slowly, his breath strong with the odour of liquor. He turned abruptly and went below. Hill walked forward.

'Coil down those slack falls! Bosun's mate, chivvy those men and put some ginger into it! By God, you're as slack as the drawstrings of a Ratcliffe doxy!'

Normality settled itself upon the ship again.

'Thank you, Mr Hill,' said Fraser somewhat sheepishly. 'The old devil had me provoked there for a moment . . . it would never have happened if the captain had not been out of the ship.'

'Forget it. Fortunately that is a rare occurrence. I must confess to a certain uneasiness, considering the contents of the hold, the fog and the absence of the captain.'

'Mr Frey is at least a diligent young man . . .'

'Boat 'hoy!' The midship's sentry's call stopped the conversation dead and the two officers rushed to the rail while the suspicious marine cocked his musket. The bow of a boat emerged from the fog.

'*Antigone!*' came the coxswain's Cornish accent.

'By God, it's the captain returning!' Fraser flew to the entry, aware that fog and anger had caused him to fail in his duty and that Captain Drinkwater would reboard his ship with less than half a side-party because of his own inattentiveness. To his chagrin the captain's barge had not even been challenged by Frey's guard-boat which was still on the other side of the ship.

As Captain Drinkwater's head came level with the deck, Fraser set his right hand to the fore-cock of his own hat. He was relieved to hear the squeal of a pipe in his right ear. The marine sentry presented arms and the side-party, though not complete, was at least presentable.

Drinkwater swung his weight from the baize-covered man-ropes and stood on the deck, his eye taking in the details of *Antigone*'s waist even as his own right hand acknowledged the salutes.

'Mr Fraser,' he said, and Fraser braced himself for a rebuke.

'Sir?' The captain's sharp grey eyes made him apprehensive.

'My compliments to the first lieutenant and the master, and will they attend me in the cabin . . .'

'Aye, aye, sir.'

'And Mr Fraser . . .'

'Sir?'

'Mr Mount is to come too.'

'Very well, sir.'

'Damn this fog.'

'Aye, sir. We were not expecting you so soon.'

'So I perceived,' Drinkwater said drily, 'but the t'gallant masts are clear above the fog from the ramparts of Varberg castle.' He reached beneath his boat-cloak and fished in the tail pocket of his coat. 'I took the precaution of taking this.'

Fraser looked down at the folded vanes of Drinkwater's pocket compass.

'I see, sir.'

With a dull knock of oar looms on thole pins the guard-boat swung clear of the bow and pulled down *Antigone*'s starboard side.

Drinkwater nodded his satisfaction. 'A wise precaution, Mr Fraser,' he said and made for the ladder below, leaving the second

14

lieutenant expelling a long breath of relief. Fraser turned to the boatswain standing beside him, the silver call still in his hand.

'I'm indebted to ye, Mr Comley, for your prompt arrival,' Fraser muttered in a low voice.

'Wouldn't like to see 'ee caught atween two fires, Mr Fraser, sir,' said Comley, staring after the young Scotsman as he went off on the captain's errand. Then he turned and put the call back to his lips. Its shrill note brought silent expectation to the upper deck again.

'Man the yard and stay tackles there! Prepare to 'oist in the barge!'

Captain Nathaniel Drinkwater took off the boat-cloak and unwound the muffler from his neck. He handed them, with his hat, to his steward, Mullender.

'A glass of something, Mullender, if you please.'

'Blackstrap, sir?'

'Capital.' Drinkwater's tone was abstracted as he stared astern through the windows at the pearly vapour that seemed oddly substantial as it swathed the ship. He rubbed his hands and eased his damaged shoulder as the chill dampness penetrated the cabin.

'Damn this fog,' he muttered again.

Mullender brought the glass of cheap blackstrap and Drinkwater took it gratefully. He relaxed as the warmth of the wine uncoiled in his belly. He could hear the creaks of the tackles taking the weight of the barge, felt the heel of the ship as she leaned to it, then felt the list ease as, with half-heard commands, the heavy boat swung inboard. A dull series of thuds told when it settled itself in its chocks amidships. The guard-boat swam across his field of vision, rounded the quarter and vanished again.

He was recalled from his abstraction as a knock at the door announced the summoned officers. Turning from the stern windows he surveyed them. Hill, the sailing master, he had known for many years. Fifty years of age, Hill was as dependable as the mahogany he appeared to be carved from. Balding now, his practical skill and wisdom seemed undiminished by the passing of time. Like Drinkwater himself, Hill bore an old wound with fortitude, an arm mangled at Camperdown ten years earlier.

15

Drinkwater smiled at Hill and addressed Rogers, the first lieutenant.

'All well in my absence, Mr Rogers?' he asked formally.

'Perfectly correct, sir. No untoward cir . . . circumstances.' Rogers's reply was thick. Like Hill, Rogers was an old shipmate, but he was showing an increasing dependence upon drink. Disappointed of advancement and temperamentally intolerant, his fine abilities as a seaman were threatened by this weakness and Drinkwater made a mental note to be on his guard. For the moment he affected not to notice that Rogers had over-indulged at the dinner table. It was not a rare occurrence among the long-serving officers of the Royal Navy.

'Very well.' Drinkwater diverted his attention to the third officer. Mr Mount was resplendent in the scarlet, blue and white undress uniform of the Royal Marines. His inclusion in the little group was pertinent to *Antigone*'s purpose here, off Varberg. It was Mount who, in addition to his customary duties of policing the frigate, had had in his especial charge eighty thousand pounds sterling, and whom Drinkwater was anxious to keep abreast of the latest news.

'Well, gentlemen, I wished that you should be informed of some news I have just gleaned from the Swedish authorities at Varberg. About five weeks ago, it seems, the Russians administered a severe check to the French army under Napoleon. No,' he held up his hand as Mount began to ask questions, 'I can give you little more information, but that which I can tell you would be the more convivially passed over dinner. Please pass my invitation to the other officers and a few of the midshipmen. Except Fraser, that is. It'll teach him to keep a better lookout in future.'

An expression of satisfaction crossed Rogers's face at this remark and Drinkwater was reminded of the burgeoning dislike between the two men.

'That will be all, gentlemen, except to say that there is, as yet, no news of our convoy. They have not yet come in after the gale but that is not entirely unexpected. Neither Captain Young's nor Captain Baker's brigs are as weatherly as *Antigone*, but we shall make for the rendezvous at Vinga Bay as soon as the wind serves and disperses this fog.'

They left him to his glass, Mount chattering excitedly about the news of the battle, and Drinkwater dismissed the preoccupations of the ship in favour of more important considerations. The bad weather had separated him from the two brigs whose protection he had been charged with. He had every confidence in locating Young and Baker at Vinga Bay. The Swedes had told him the ice was breaking up fast and The Sound was clear, except for the diminutive fragments of the pancake ice that spun slowly past them towards the warmer waters of the Skagerrak and the grey North Sea. Carlscrona was already navigable and he might have landed his diplomatic dispatches there, closer to Stockholm than the Scanian fortress of Varberg. However, the Swedish governors had assured him that was unimportant. He had personally guaranteed their swift delivery to King Gustavus who eagerly awaited news of support from London.

Drinkwater drained the glass. Exactly how accurate the news was of a check to the French he did not know, but he was acutely aware that the events of the coming summer were likely to be vital in the Baltic.

As the cabin door opened to admit the officers the noise of a fiddle came from forward where the hands had been piped to dance and skylark. Drinkwater stood and welcomed his guests as Mullender moved among them with a dozen glasses of blackstrap to whet their appetites.

'You ordered the purser to issue double grog to all hands, Mr Rogers, I trust?'

'Aye, sir, I did.' Rogers had made some effort to sober up from his injudicious imbibing earlier that day.

'That is as well. I am conscious of having made all hands work hard on our passage. Despite the disappearance of the convoy, which I don't doubt we shall soon remedy, it was necessary that we deliver the Government's dispatches without delay.' Drinkwater turned to a tall, thin lieutenant who wore a hook in place of his left hand and from whose pink nose depended a large dewdrop. 'I see you have come from the deck, Mr Q. Is the fog still as dense?'

Lieutenant Quilhampton shook his head, sending the dewdrop flying. 'Doing its damnedest to lift, sir, though I cannot depend on half cannon-shot at the moment. But a dead calm still and no sign of any merchantmen.'

17

'And unlikely to be, Mr Q. They'll have snugged down and ridden out that gale like sensible fellows, if I don't mistake their temper.'

'Rather an unusual convoy for a frigate of our force, sir, wouldn't you say?' put in Midshipman Lord Walmsley. 'I mean two North-country brigs don't amount to much.'

'I don't know, Mr Walmsley,' replied Drinkwater who from their earliest acquaintance had avoided the use of the young man's title on board, 'their lading is almost as valuable as our own.'

'May one ask what it is?'

'One hundred and sixty thousand stand of arms, Mr Walmsley, together with powder and shot for sixty rounds a man.'

Drinkwater smiled at the whistles this intelligence provoked. 'Come gentlemen, please be seated . . .'

They sat down noisily and Drinkwater regarded them with a certain amount of satisfaction. In addition to the three officers he had summoned earlier, James Quilhampton the third lieutenant, Mr Lallo the surgeon, and four of *Antigone*'s midshipmen were present. Mr Fraser was absent on deck, pacing his atonement for failing to sight the captain's barge that forenoon, an atonement that was spiced by Rogers's passing of the instruction, leaving Fraser in no doubt of the first lieutenant's malicious triumph.

In the cabin Drinkwater paid closest attention to the midshipmen. Mr Quilhampton was an old friend and shipmate, Mr Lallo a surgeon of average ability. But the midshipmen were Drinkwater's own responsibility. It was his reputation they would carry with them when they were commissioned and served under other commanders. Their professional maturation was, therefore, of more than a mere passing interest. This was the more acutely so since most were protégés of another captain, inherited by Drinkwater upon his hurried appointment to the corvette *Melusine* during her eventful Greenland voyage. By now he had come to regard them as his own, and one in particular came under scrutiny, for he had both dismissed and reinstated Lord Walmsley.

Midshipmen Dutfield and Wickham were rated master's mates now and little Mr Frey was as active and intelligent as any eager youngster, but Lord Walmsley still engaged Drinkwater's speculation as, laughing and jesting with the others, he addressed himself to the broth Mullender placed before them. Despite Walmsley being a dominating, wilful and dissolute youth, Drinkwater had discerned some finer qualities in him during the sojourn in the Arctic. But the boy had abused his powers and Drinkwater had turned him out of the ship for a period, only taking him back when Walmsley had gone to considerable lengths to impress the captain of his remorse. There were still streaks of the old indolence, and touches of arrogance; but they were tempered by a growing ability and Drinkwater had every confidence in his passing for lieutenant at the next available Board.

Drinkwater pushed his soup plate away and hid a smile behind his napkin as he watched Walmsley, at the opposite end of the table, talking with a certain condescension to Mr Dutfield, some three years his junior.

'A glass of wine with you, sir?' Sam Rogers leaned forward with exaggerated cordiality and Drinkwater nodded politely, raising his glass. The conversation swelled to a hubbub as Mullender brought from the little pantry the roast capons and placed them before the captain. The homely smell of the meat emphasised the luxury of this fog-enforced idleness and combined with the wine to induce a comfortable mellowness in Drinkwater. He felt for once positively justified in putting off until tomorrow the problems of duty. But Mr Mount was not of so relaxed a frame of mind.

'Excuse me, sir,' put in the marine lieutenant, leaning forward, his scarlet coat a bright spot amidst the sober blue of the sea-officers, 'but might I press you to elaborate on the news you gave us earlier?'

'I did promise, did I not, Mr Mount?' said Drinkwater with a sigh.

'You did, sir.'

Drinkwater accepted the carving irons from his coxswain Tregembo, assisting Mullender at the table. He sliced into the white meat of the fowl's breast.

'It seems that a pitched battle was fought between considerable forces of French and Russians at a place near Königsberg called . . . Eylau, or some such . . . is that sufficient, Mr Rogers? Doubtless,' he continued, turning again to Mount, 'it is noted upon your atlas.'

A chuckle ran round the table and Mount flushed to rival his coat. He had been greatly teased about his acquisition of a large

Military Atlas, purporting to cover the whole of Europe, India, North America and the Cape of Good Hope to a standard 'compatible with the contemplation, comprehension, verification and execution of military campaigns engaged in by the forces of His Majesty'. Armed with this *vade mecum*, Mount had bored the occupants of the gunroom rigid with interminable explanations of the brilliance of Napoleon's campaign in Prussia the previous year. The double victory of Jena-Auerstadt, which in a single day had destroyed the Prussian military machine, had failed to impress anyone except James Quilhampton who had pored over the appropriate pages of the atlas out of pity for Mount and was rewarded by a conviction that the likelihood of a French defeat was remote. The completeness of the cavalry pursuit after Jena seemed to make little difference to the naval officers, though it had brought the French to the very shores of the Baltic Sea and reduced the Prussian army to a few impotent garrisons in beleaguered fortresses, and a small field force under a General Lestocq. Mount's admiration for the genius behind the campaign had led him to suffer a great deal of leg-pulling for his treasonable opinions.

'And the outcome, sir?' persisted Mount. 'You spoke of a check.'

'Well, one does not like to grasp too eagerly at good news, since it has, in the past, so often proved false. But the Russians gave a good account of themselves, particularly as the French were reported to have been commanded by Napoleon himself.'

Drinkwater looked round their faces. There was not a man at the table whose imagination was not fed by the prospect of real defeat having been inflicted on the hitherto triumphant Grand Army and its legendary leader.

'And the Russkies, sir. Who was in command of them?'

Drinkwater frowned. 'To tell the truth, Mr Mount, I cannot recollect . . .'

'Kamenskoi?'

'No . . . no, that was not it . . .'

'Bennigsen?'

'You have it, Mr Mount. General Bennigsen. What can you tell us of him?'

'He is one of the German faction in the Russian service, sir, a Hanoverian by birth, something of a soldier of fortune.'

'So your hero's taken a damned good drubbing at last, eh, Mount?' said Lallo the surgeon. ''Tis about time his luck ran a little thin, I'm thinking.' Lallo turned to Drinkwater, manifesting a natural anxiety common to them all. 'It *was* a victory, sir? For the Russians, I mean.'

'The Swedes seemed positive that it was not a French one, Mr Lallo. It seems they were left exhausted upon the field, but the Russians only withdrew to prepare positions of defence . . .'

'But if they had beat Boney, why should they want to prepare defences?'

'I don't know, but the report seemed positive that Napoleon received a bloody nose.'

'Let us hope it *is* true,' said Quilhampton fervently.

'And not just wishful thinking,' slurred Rogers with the wisdom of the disenchanted.

'Napoleon's the devil of a long way from home,' said Hill, laying down his knife and fork. 'If he receives a second serious blow from the Russkies he might overreach himself.'

Drinkwater finished his own meat. The uncertainty of speculation had destroyed his euphoria. It was time he turned the intelligence to real account.

'I believe he already has,' he said. 'Those decrees he issued from Berlin last year establishing his Continental System will have little effect on us. Preventing the European mainland from trading with Great Britain will starve the European markets, while leaving us free to trade with the Indies or wherever else we wish. Providing the Royal Navy does its part in maintaining a close blockade of the coast, which is what the King's Orders in Council are designed to achieve. I daresay we shall make ourselves unpopular with the Americans, but that cannot be helped. Napoleon will get most of the blame and, the larger his empire becomes, the more people his politics will inconvenience.' He hoped he carried his point, aware that a note of pomposity had unwittingly crept into his voice.

'So, gentlemen,' Drinkwater continued, after refilling his glass, 'if the Royal Navy in general, and you in particular, do your duty, and the Russians stand firm, we may yet see the threat to our homes diminish. Let us hope this battle of Eylau is the high-water mark of Napoleon's ambition . . .'

'Bravo, sir!'

'Death to the French!'

'I'll drink to that!' They were all eagerly holding their glasses aloft.

'No, gentlemen,' Drinkwater said smiling, relieved that his lecturing tone had been overlooked, 'I do not like xenophobic toasts, they tempt providence. Let us drink to our gallant allies the Russians.'

'To the Russians!'

Drinkwater sat alone after the officers had gone. Smoke from Lallo's pipe still hung over the table from which the cloth had been drawn and replaced by Mount's atlas an hour before. He found the lingering aroma of the tobacco pleasant, and Tregembo had produced a remaining half-bottle of port for him.

He had watched the departure of his old coxswain with affection. They had been together for so long that the demarcations between master and servant had long since been eroded and they were capable of anticipating each other's wishes in the manner of man and wife. This uncomfortable thought made Drinkwater raise his eyes to the portraits of his wife and children on the forward bulkhead. The pale images of their faces were lit by the wasting candles on the table. He pledged them a silent toast and diverted his thoughts. It did not do to dwell on such things for he did not want a visitation of the blue devils, that misanthropic preoccupation of seamen. It was far better to consider the task in hand, though there was precious little comfort in that. Locked away beneath him lay one of the subsidies bound for the coffers of the Tsar with which the British Government propped up the war against Napoleon's French Empire. Eighty thousand pounds sterling was a prodigious sum for which to be held accountable.

He drew little comfort from the thought that the carriage of the specie would earn him a handsome sum, for he nursed private misgivings as to the inequity of the privilege. The worries over the elaborate precautions in which he was ordered to liaise with officials of the diplomatic corps, and the missing shipment of arms in the storm-separated brigs, only compounded his anxiety over the accuracy of the news from Varberg. There seemed no end to the war, and time was wearing away zeal. Many of his own people had been at sea for four years; his original draft of volunteers had been reduced by disease, injury and action, and augmented by those sweepings of the press, the quota-men, Lord Mayor's men and any unfortunate misfit the magistrates had decided would benefit from a spell in His Majesty's service.

Drinkwater emptied the bottle and swore to himself. He had lost six men by desertion at Sheerness and he knew his crew were unsettled. In all justice he could not blame them, but he could do little else beyond propitiating providence and praying the battle of Eylau would soon be followed by news of a greater victory for the armies of Tsar Alexander of Russia.

Occasional talks with Lord Dungarth, Director of the Admiralty's Secret Department, had kept Drinkwater better informed than most cruiser captains had a right to expect. Their long-standing friendship had given Drinkwater a unique insight into the complexities of British foreign policy in the long war against the victorious French. All the British were really capable of doing effectively was sealing the continent in a naval blockade. To encompass the destruction of the Grand Army required a supply of men as great as that of France. 'It is to Russia we must look, Nathaniel,' Dungarth had once said, 'with her endless manpower supported by our subsidies, and the character of Tsar Alexander to spur her on.'

He had one of those subsidies beneath him at that moment; as for the character of Tsar Alexander, Drinkwater hoped he could be relied on. It was rumoured that he had connived at the assassination of his own sadistically insane father. Did such acquiescence demonstrate a conviction of moral superiority? Or was it evidence of a weakness in succumbing to the pressure of others?

Wondering thus, Captain Drinkwater rose, loosened his stock and began to undress.

2   An Armed Neutrality

March 1807

'Here's your hot water, zur,' Tregembo stropped the razor vigorously, 'and Mr Quilhampton sends his compliments to you and to say that we'll be entering The Sound in an hour.' Tregembo sniffed, indicating disapproval, and added, 'And I'm to tell 'ee that Mr Hill's on deck . . .'

Drinkwater lathered his chin and jaw. 'And my presence isn't necessary, is that it?'

Tregembo sniffed again. 'That's the message, zur, as I told it.'

Drinkwater took the razor and began to scrape his lathered face, his legs braced as *Antigone* leaned to the alteration of course. 'Huh! We're off Cronbourg, Tregembo, and the Danes are damned touchy about who goes through The Sound. Where are the two brigs?' he asked after a brief pause, pleased that he had located his charges at Vinga Bay as predicted.

'Safely tucked under our larboard beam, zur.'

'Good. We'll keep 'em on the Swedish side.' He concentrated on his shave.

'You'll pardon me for saying, zur,' Tregembo pressed on with the familiarity of long service, 'but you've been under the weather these past two days . . .'

'You talk too much, too early in the day, damn you . . . God's bones!' Drinkwater winced at the nick the razor had given him.

'You'd do better to take more care of yourself,' Tregembo persisted, and for a second Drinkwater thought he was being insolent, referring to his own bloodily obvious need to keep his mouth shut. But a single glance at the old Cornishman's face told him otherwise. Tregembo's concern was touching.

'You cluck like an old hen,' Drinkwater said, his tone and mood mellowing. He had to admit the justice of Tregembo's allegation, although 'under the weather' was an inadequate description of Drinkwater's evil humour. He wiped off the lather and looked at Tregembo. It was impossible for him to apologise but his expression was contrite.

"'Tis time we went ashore, zur. Swallowed the anchor, in a manner of speaking.'

'Ashore?' Drinkwater tied his stock, peering at himself in the mirror. 'Ashore? No, I think not, Tregembo, not yet. I don't think I could abide tea and gossip at the same hour every day and having to be polite to the train of gentlewomen who infest my house like weevils in a biscuit.'

Tregembo was not so easily diverted, knowing full well Drinkwater's exaggeration only emphasised his irritability. "'Tis time you purchased a bit of land, zur. You could go shooting . . .'

Drinkwater turned from the mirror. 'When we swallow the anchor, as you quaintly put it, Tregembo,' he said with a sudden vehemence, holding his arms backwards for his coat, 'I pray God I have done with shooting!'

Tregembo held out the cocked hat, his face wearing an injured look.

'Damn it, Tregembo, I've a touch of the blue devils lately.'

'You know my Susan would run a house fit for 'ee and Mistress Elizabeth, zur.'

'It's not that, my old friend,' said Drinkwater, suddenly dropping the pretence at formality between them. 'Susan and Mistress Elizabeth would both be full of joy if we went home. But d'you think they'd tolerate our interfering indefinitely?' He made an attempt at flippancy. 'D'you think you'd be content to weed the onion patch, eh?' He took the proffered hat and smiled at the old Cornishman.

'Happen you are right, zur. There's many as would miss 'ee if 'ee took it in mind to go.'

Drinkwater hesitated, his hat half raised to his head, sensing one of Tregembo's oblique warnings.

'I know the people are disaffected . . .'

'It ain't the people, zur. Leastways not as cause, like. They be more in the nature of effect.'

'Meaning, Tregembo?' asked Drinkwater.

25

'Mr Rogers, zur, is shipping a deal of the gunroom *vino*. 'Tis a fact 'ee cannot hide from the people, zur. They hold 'ee for a fair man, zur. 'Twould be a pity to see Mr Rogers become a millstone, zur, if 'ee takes my meaning.'

Drinkwater jammed the hat on his head. He should be grateful for Tregembo's warning, yet the old man had only revealed the cause of his own recent ill-humour. Carrying eighty thousand pounds around in an explosive corner of the world with one hundred and sixty thousand muskets tucked under his lee for good measure was bad enough, but to have to contend with a pot-tossing first lieutenant to boot was well-nigh intolerable.

'Belay that infernal prattle,' he snapped and threw open the cabin door. Ducking through with a nod to the marine sentry he sprang for the ladder to the quarterdeck.

Behind him Tregembo shook his head and muttered, 'Jumpy as a galled horse . . .' He rinsed the razor, dried and closed it, nodding at the portrait of Elizabeth on the adjacent bulkhead. 'I did my best, ma'am.'

Lifting the bowl of soapy water he threw it down the privy in the quarter-gallery where it drained into *Antigone*'s hissing wake as she sped past the fortress of Cronbourg at the narrow entrance of The Sound.

On deck, Drinkwater's sudden arrival scattered the idle knot of officers who stared curiously ahead at the red-brick ramparts and the green copper cupolas of the famous castle, above which floated a great red and white swallow-tailed flag, the national colours of neutral Denmark. Drinkwater took Hill's report and left the master in charge of the con. He stopped briefly to stare at the two trim brigs with their cargoes of arms that they had found two days earlier in Vinga Bay, just as predicted; then he fell to pacing the starboard rail, watching the coast of Denmark. The shreds of conversation that drifted across to Drinkwater from the displaced officers were inevitably about the great expedition, six years earlier, which had culminated in Lord Nelson's victory at Copenhagen. Although he had distinguished himself both before and during the famous action, Drinkwater's already morbid humour recalled only a dark and private episode in his life.

It was here, among the low hills and blue spires already slipping astern, at the village of Gilleleje, that Drinkwater had secretly landed his own brother Edward on the run from the law. Edward had had a talent with horses and drifted into the life of a gambler centred on the racing world of Newmarket and the French *émigrés* who had settled there. His entanglement with a young Frenchwoman had resulted in his murdering his rival. Drinkwater had always felt his honour had been impugned by the obligation Edward's ties of blood had held him to. Even at this distance in time, even after Drinkwater had discovered that in murdering his rival, Edward had inadvertently killed a French agent, Drinkwater was still unable to shrug off the shadows that had so isolated him then. Nor did it seem to mitigate Drinkwater's personal guilt that Edward had found employment as an agent himself. For after landing at Gilleleje and going to Hamburg, Lord Dungarth had sent him eastwards, relying on his ability to speak the French he had learned from his faithless mistress. Drinkwater knew that Edward had been at the battle of Austerlitz and was the origin of accurate intelligence about the true state of affairs in the Russian army after that bitter and shattering defeat. The news, it was said, had killed Billy Pitt; and this too seemed full of a dark accumulation of presentiment. With an effort, Drinkwater cast aside his gloom. Sunshine danced upon the water and they were rapidly approaching the narrowest point of The Sound commanded by the Danish guns in their embrasures at Cronbourg. It was, he thought with sudden resolution, time to make a show, a flourish. He spun on his heel.

'Mr Rogers!'

The first lieutenant's florid features turned towards him. 'Sir?'

'Call all hands! Stuns'ls aloft and alow! Then you may clear for action!'

'Stuns'ls and clear for action, sir!' The order was taken up and the pipes twittered at the hatchways. Drinkwater stood at the starboard hance and watched the temper of the hands as the watches below tumbled up. Topmen scrambled into the rigging and Comley's mates chastised the slower waisters into place as they prepared to send up or haul out the studdingsails. Drinkwater's gaze rose upwards. Already the agile topmen were spreading out along the

27

upper yards on the fore- and main-masts. Out went the upper booms thrust through their irons at the extremities of the topsail and topgallant yardarms. At the rails by the fore-chains, the lower booms were being swung out on their goosenecks. Festoons of guys straightened into their ordered places. He watched with satisfaction as the midshipmen, nimble as monkeys in their respective stations, waved their readiness to the deck. The upper studdingsails, secured to short battens, were stowed in the tops. At the signal first the weather and then the lee studdingsails were run up to the booms next above. They fluttered momentarily as the halliards secured them, then their lower edges were spread to the booms below. On the fo'c's'le two large bundles had been dragged out of their stowage in the boats. They were similarly bent onto halliards and outhauls stretched their clews to the guyed ends of the lowest booms which were winged out on either side of the frigate's fore-chains. In a minute or so *Antigone* had almost doubled the width of her forward sail plan.

Rogers, satisfied with the evolutions of the ship's company, gave the men permission to lay in. Watching, Drinkwater knew that there had been a few seconds' hesitation before the nod to Comley had brought the bosun's pipe to his mouth and the topmen had come sliding down the backstays. Rogers crossed the deck and knuckled the fore-cock of his hat.

'Very well, Mr Rogers, you may beat to quarters.'

As Rogers turned away, Drinkwater caught again that slightly malicious grin that he had noticed when he had ordered Fraser to keep the deck off Varberg. Whipping a silver hunter from his fob, Rogers flicked it open as he roared the order. Again, and with a mounting disquiet that he could not quite place, Drinkwater watched the motions of the men. To a casual glance they appeared perfectly disciplined, tuned to the finest pitch any crack cruiser captain could demand but . . . that element of perplexity remained with him.

The marine drummer doubled aft, unhitched his drum and lifted his sticks to his chin in a perfunctory acknowledgement of the pre-scribed drill; then he brought them down on the snare drum and beat out the urgent ruffle. The frigate, alive with men still belaying ropes and laying in from aloft, suddenly took on a new and more sinister air. Along the length of her gundeck the ports were raised and round each of twenty-six 18-pounder cannon and the ten long 9-pounder chase guns the men congregated in kneeling and expectant groups. Others mustered elsewhere, the marines at the hammock nettings and in the tops, the firemen unreeled their hoses and worked the yoke of their machines to dampen the decks. Boys scattered sand or stood ready with their cartridge boxes. The activity died to an expectant hush. Each gun-captain's hand was raised. Rogers lifted his speaking trumpet.

'Run out the guns!'

The deck beneath Drinkwater's feet trembled as the gunners manned their tackles and hauled the heavy cannon out through the gun-ports.

With every man at his station, her yards braced to catch the quartering breeze and her charges safely tucked under her lee, *Antigone* entered The Sound. Drinkwater indulged Rogers in a final look round the upper deck while he studied the ramparts of Cronbourg less than a mile away. Through his glass he could see the tiny dots of heads beneath the gigantic swallow-tailed standard which rippled gallantly in the breeze. At this distance those men could not fail to remark the belligerent preparedness of the British cruiser. Denmark was a neutral state, but not therefore without influence upon international affairs. Her trade, particularly in the matter of naval stores, if directed towards the beleaguered fleets of France, could be damaging to the war-efforts of Great Britain. And since Napoleon had decreed that no European country, whether under the control of his legions or attempting to maintain a precarious neutrality, might trade with Britain, the British must treat her with suspicion.

'Ship cleared for action, sir.' The snap of Rogers's hunter made Drinkwater lower his glass.

'Very well. An improvement?'

'About the same, sir,' replied Rogers non-committally, and in a flash Drinkwater knew what he had been witness to, what had been going on under his very nose. He fixed his keen glance on the first lieutenant.

'I thought they were a trifle faster that time.'

He saw a hint of uncertainty in Rogers's eyes. 'Well, perhaps a trifle faster,' said Rogers grudgingly, and Drinkwater was certain his instinct was right. Between first lieutenant and the hands there existed a state of affairs exactly analogous to that between Britain and Denmark: a neutrality in which each warily sought out the weakness and the intentions of the other. Rogers, the first lieutenant, the all-powerful executive officer, was always ready to punish any gun-crew, yardarm party, or individual, whose standard was not in his opinion of the highest. Against him were pitted the people, hydra-headed but weak, vulnerable to some simple, silly slip, yet knowing that they had only to wait and the bottle would destroy the first lieutenant. The certainty of this knowledge came as a shock to Drinkwater and the colour drained from his face, leaving his eyes piercing in the intensity of their anger.

'By God, Sam,' he said softly through clenched teeth, 'I will not have you judge, lest you be judged yourself.' Rogers's glance fell as they were interrupted.

'I think we have not bared our fangs in vain, sir,' said Hill, stumping across the deck to draw Drinkwater's attention to the events unfolding on the starboard bow. Hill paused, sensing an open breach between captain and first lieutenant where he had anticipated only an exchange of remarks concerning the ship's internal routines. He coughed awkwardly. 'Beg pardon, sir, but I . . .'

'Yes, yes, I see them,' snapped Drinkwater and raising his glass once more, affected to ignore Rogers.

Standing out from Elsinore Road to the south of Cronbourg was a two-decked line-of-battle-ship, and astern of her a small frigate. They too were cramming on sail, coming in at an angle to *Antigone*'s bow as though to intercept her.

'Their bearing's opening, sir,' offered Hill, coolly professional again, 'only slowly, but they'll not catch us.'

'Very well, Mr Hill, but we ought not to outrun our charges.' Drinkwater nodded at the brigs, now some distance astern of them. The Danish warships would pass between *Antigone* and the two British merchantmen.

'Notified of our approach from the castle, I'll warrant,' remarked Hill.

'Yes.' Drinkwater subjected the two ships to a further scrutiny through his glass. The Danes had proved tough opponents in 1801, reluctant to surrender and forcing from Lord Nelson the remark that they played the hottest fire he had ever been under. The two Danish ships broke out their own studdingsails. He watched critically. It was well done.

'I thought we had buggered their damned fleet for them,' said Rogers with characteristic coarseness in an attempt to defuse the atmosphere between himself and Drinkwater.

'Apparently not,' Drinkwater replied as if nothing untoward had occurred, watching the ships as their respective courses converged. But Hill was right, the bearings of the Danes were drawing aft, showing that the *Antigone* was the faster ship. 'They've had six years to right the damage,' he said, turning to look again at the lumbering brigs on the larboard quarter. 'I don't like exposing our charges like this and I'm rather disposed to test their mettle . . . Secure the guns where they are, Mr Rogers,' he said with a sudden sharpness, 'and get the stuns'ls off her!'

Rogers began bellowing orders. Again *Antigone* seethed with activity. Whatever discontents might be running through her people, the chance of demonstrating their superiority as seamen before a mob of tow-haired Danes animated the ship. In a few minutes her studdingsails fluttered inboard.

'Clew up the courses!' Drinkwater ordered sharply, for he had not wanted anything to go wrong, or the Danes to put a shot across his bow, turning a voluntary act into a submissive one.

'Lower the t'gallants on the caps!' *Antigone*'s speed slowed, yet she held her course and the hands were sent back to their battle-stations as the Danish warships came up, the frigate ranging out to larboard so that they overtook on either quarter.

Hill was looking at him anxiously.

'My God,' said Rogers to no one in particular, 'if they open fire now they will . . .' His voice trailed off as he wiped the back of his hand across his mouth. It was, Drinkwater noted, the gesture of a thirsty man.

'They are neutrals, gentlemen,' he said. 'They dare not fire upon us without provoking an act of war. They simply wish to demonstrate their readiness not to be intimidated on their own doorstep . . . Just keep the men at their stations in silence if you please, Mr Rogers, and perhaps we may yet surprise 'em,' Drinkwater added as an outbreak of chatter started up in the waist.

Drinkwater strode forward as the line-of-battle-ship ranged up on their starboard beam, her two tiers of guns also run out so that they dominated the much lower deck of the British frigate.

'Mr Mount!' Drinkwater called to the marine officer.

'Sir?'

'Form your men in two divisions, facing outboard on either side, then bring 'em to attention.'

'Very good, sir.'

As the quarterdecks of the three ships drew level the marines stood rigid. Drinkwater casually mounted the starboard rail in the mizen rigging. He turned back inboard. 'Have the hands piped aloft to man the yards, Mr Rogers.' He ignored the puzzled apprehension in Rogers's eyes and turned to the Danish ship, not two hundred feet away and stealing their wind. He doffed his hat in a wide sweep.

'Good day, sir!' he shouted.

A line of Danish officers regarded him and there was obviously some conferring going on on her quarterdeck. After a pause a junior officer was pushed up onto her rail.

'Gut morning, Capten. Vat ship is that, please?'

'His Britannic Majesty's frigate *Antigone*, upon a cruise with merchantmen in company, sir,' Drinkwater bawled back cheerfully.

'Ve hope you do not vish to stop Dansk ships, no?'

'My orders are to stop all ships carrying cargoes of war material to His Majesty's enemies. This policy is clearly stated in His Majesty's Orders in Council, sir, copies of which have been delivered to your Government's representatives in London.'

The Danish officer bent down, obviously in consultation with a senior, for he stood again. 'You are varned against stopping Dansk ships, Capten.'

'I shall carry out my orders, sir, as I expect you to maintain your neutrality!' He turned to Rogers: 'I want three hearty cheers when I call for 'em.'

He heard Rogers mutter 'Good God!' and turned again to the Dane. The big battleship was drawing ahead now and he could read her name across her stern: *Princesse Sophia Frederica*.

'Three cheers for His Majesty the King of Denmark! Hip! Hip! Hip!'

'Hooray . . .' The three cheers ripped from over his head and Drinkwater jumped down from the rail.

'Now, Sam, let fall those courses, hoist the t'gallants and reset the stuns'ls!' He turned to the sailing master, standing by the wheel. 'Hold your course, Mr Hill . . . Bye the bye, did you get the name of the frigate?' Drinkwater nodded to larboard.

'Aye, sir, *Triton*, twenty-eight guns.'

'Very well.' Drinkwater clasped his hands behind his back and offered up a silent prayer that his pride was not to be humbled in front of such witnesses. But he need not have worried. It was not merely his own pride that was at stake; some of the defiance in his tone had communicated itself to the hands. This was no longer a petty internal matter, no empty evolution at the behest of the first lieutenant, but a matter of national pride. Now the captain was handling the ship and they behaved as though they were in action and their very lives depended upon their smartness.

Antigone gathered speed as she again spread her wings. Her long jib-boom swung across the great square stern of the two-decker as she pointed closer to the wind. She began to overhaul the Danish ship to windward and with an amiable insouciance Drinkwater again waved his hat at the knot of officers who stared stolidly back at him.

The cheering provoked no response from the Danes.

'Miserable bastards,' remarked Rogers sullenly, coming aft as the studdingsail halliards were coiled down. In their wake the Danish battleship hauled her wind and put about, turning back towards her anchorage off Elsinore.

Triton kept them company as far as the island of Hven, then she too put about and the incident was over. To larboard the Scanian coast of Sweden lay in the distance, while closer to starboard the coast of Zealand fell away to a low-lying, pastoral countryside dotted with church towers and white farms. Astern of *Antigone* the two brigs followed in their wake, while ten miles ahead, faintly blue in the distance, the spires of Copenhagen broke the skyline.

The British frigate and her small convoy entered the Baltic Sea.

3   The Shipment of Arms

April 1807

Mr James Quilhampton peered over the ship's side and watched the little bobbing black jolly-boat, from the nearer of the two brigs, hook neatly onto the frigate's main chains. The man in her stern relinquished the tiller, stepped lightly upon a thwart and, skilfully judging the boat's motion, leapt for the man-ropes and the wooden battens that formed a ladder up the frigate's tumblehome. He was met by midshipman Lord Walmsley and Quilhampton straightened up as the man, hatless despite the cold and in plain civilian dress, strode aft.

'Good morning, Lieutenant,' he said in the rolling accent of Northumbria.

'Good morning, Captain Young,' responded Quilhampton civilly. 'I have informed Captain Drinkwater of your approach and here he comes now.'

Drinkwater mounted the quarterdeck ladder and cast a swift and instinctive glance round the horizon. *Antigone* and the two brigs lay hove-to on a smooth grey sea which was terminated to the north and east by an ice-field that seemed at first to stretch to the horizon itself. But beyond it to the east lay the faint blue line of land, a low country of unrelieved flatness, almost part of the sea itself.

'Captain Young,' said Drinkwater cordially, taking the strong hand and wincing with the power of its grip. His right arm already ached from the cold seeping into the mangled muscles of his wounded shoulder and Young's rough treatment did nothing to ease it. 'I give you good day. I take it that you and Captain Baker and your ships' companies are well?'

'Why aye, man. As fit as when we left London River.'

'What d'you make of this ice?' Drinkwater disengaged his arm from Young's eager, pump-handle grasp and gestured eastward.

'The Pregel Bar is not more than two leagues distant, Captain Drinkwater. It is unlikely that the ice will last more than another sennight.' He smiled. 'Why, man, Baker and I'll be drinking schnapps in Königsberg by mid-month.'

'You think the ice in the Frisches Haff will have cleared by then?'

'Aye, man. Once thaw sets in 'twill soon clear.'

'In view of the presence of ice I think it better that I should remain with you. You might have need of my protection yet.'

'As you wish, Captain.'

'You have your instructions as to the formalities necessary to the discharging of your arms and ammunition?'

'Aye, Captain.' Young smiled again. 'You may allay your fears on that score. They will not fall into the wrong hands.'

'Very well. But I could wish for more positive assurances. News from the shore that Königsberg is not in danger from the French . . .'

'No, Captain, I doubt there's any fear o' that. At Vinga we heard that Boney's had both his eyes blacked proper by them Russians. You've no need to fear that Königsberg's a French port.'

'Let's hope you are right,' said Drinkwater.

'What about your own cargo, Captain Drinkwater?' Young asked.

'Eh? Oh. You know about that do you?'

'Of course,' Young chuckled, 'have you ever known a secret kept along a waterfront?'

Drinkwater shook his head. 'I have to deliver it to Revel but, as you can see, the ice prevents me for the time being.' He attempted to divert the conversation. He had no business discussing such matters with Young. 'What will you do once you have discharged your lading at Königsberg?'

'Coast up to Memel and see what Munro has for us.'

'Munro?' asked Drinkwater absently.

'A Scottish merchant who acts as my agent at Memel. He and I have been associates in the way of business for as many years as I've owned and commanded the *Jenny Marsden*. The rogue married a pretty Kurlander at whom I once set my own cap.' Young grinned and Drinkwater reflected that there was a world as intimately connected with the sea as his own, but about which he knew next to nothing.

'The trade and its disappointments seem to keep you in good humour, Captain Young.'

'Aye, and in tolerable good pocket,' Young added familiarly.

'We had better anchor then . . .'

'Aye, Baker and I will work our way inshore a little, if you've a mind to close in our wake.'

'It won't be the first time I've worked a ship through ice, Captain,' said Drinkwater returning Young's ready smile. 'Mr Q! Have the kindness to see Captain Young to his boat.' He could not avoid having his wrist wrenched again by the genial Northumbrian and felt compelled to dispel his anxiety by more of the man's good-natured company. It would do him no harm to learn more of the Baltic for he might yet have the convoy of the whole homeward trade at the close of the season. 'Perhaps you and Baker would do me the honour of dining with me this afternoon, Captain. 'Tis a plain table, but . . .'

'None the worse for that, I'm sure. That's damned civil of ye, Captain Drinkwater. And I'll be happy to accept.'

'Very well. Ah, Mr Q . . .'

As the little jolly-boat pulled away, Drinkwater raised his hat to Young and then, his curiosity aroused after the conversation, he fished in his tail-pocket for the Dollond glass and levelled it at the distant smudge of land. The sand-spit that separated the open sea from the great lagoon of the Frisches Haff was pierced at its northern end, allowing the River Pregel to flow into the Baltic. Twenty miles inland lay the great fortress and cathedral city of Königsberg, once the home of the Teutonic knights and later a powerful trading partner in the Hanseatic League. Now it was the most eastern possession of the King of Prussia and the only one, it seemed, that contained a Prussian garrison of any force to maintain King Frederick William's tenuous independence from Napoleon. As such it formed an important post on the lines of communication between Russia and the Tsar's armies in Poland, a depot for Bennigsen's commissariat and the obvious destination for one hundred and sixty thousand muskets, with bayonets, cartridge and ball to match.

'Beg pardon, sir, but the brigs are hauling their mainyards.'

Mr Quilhampton recalled Drinkwater from his abstraction. He shut the glass with a snap, aware that he had seen nothing through it apart from grey sea, ice and the blue line of a featureless country. It seemed odd that history was being made there, among what looked no more substantial than a streak or two of cobalt tint from Mr Frey's watercolour box.

'Filling their sails, eh, Mr Q? Very well. Do you do likewise. And you may pass word to rouse up a cable and bend it onto the best bower. We shall fetch an anchor when those two fellows show us some good holding.'

Captain Young's forecast proved accurate. Within a few days the ice began to melt and disperse with dramatic rapidity. A soft wind blew from the south-east, bringing off the land exotic fragrances and stray birds that chirruped as they fluttered, exhausted, in the rigging. From here the boys were sent aloft to chase them off and prevent them fouling the white planking of *Antigone*'s decks. The relative idleness of the enforced anchorage served to rest the men, settling those new-pressed into a more regular routine than the demands of passage-making allowed, and Drinkwater detected a lessening of tension about the ship. His warning to Rogers seemed to have been heeded and he felt able to relax, to consider that their earlier problems had been part of the inevitable shaking-down necessary to the beginning of every cruise.

As the ice broke up, the three ships moved closer to the estuary, and ten days after their first anchoring, Drinkwater began to send boat expeditions away to determine the effect of the thaw upon the fresher waters of the Frisches Haff. A few days later local fishing boats appeared and then there were signs of coastal craft beyond the sand-spit that was in sight of them now. And then, quite suddenly and with unexpected drama, proof came that confirmed that navigation was open up the Pregel to the quays of Königsberg itself. While Drinkwater was breakfasting one morning an excited Midshipman Wickham burst into his cabin with the news that a large and 'important-looking barge' was coming off from the shore. Hurriedly swallowing his coffee, Drinkwater donned hat and cloak and went on deck.

Lieutenant Fraser had already caught sight of the unmistakable flash of scarlet under a flung-back grey cape and the ostentatiously upright figure of a military officer standing in the big boat's stern. He had had the presence of mind to man the side, Drinkwater noted, as he joined Fraser at the entry.

'My congratulations, Mr Fraser,' he said drily. 'Your vigilance has improved remarkably.'

'Thank ye, sir,' replied the Scotsman, sensing the captain's good humour, 'but to be truthful I think yon gentleman was of a mind to draw attention to himself.'

'Yes.' Drinkwater nodded and stared curiously at the approaching stranger. 'He seems to be British, and in full regimentals,' he remarked as the boat came alongside below their line of vision.

A twitching of the baize-covered man-ropes, and then the cockerel plumes, bicorne hat and figure of a British colonel rose above the rail to a twittering of pipes, stamp of marines' boots and the wicked twinkle of sunshine upon Mount's flourished hanger. The officer saluted and Drinkwater tipped his own hat in response.

'Good morning, sir. This is an unlooked-for pleasure. Permit me to introduce myself. Captain Nathaniel Drinkwater of His Britannic Majesty's thirty-six-gun frigate *Antigone*.'

The newcomer managed a small, sharp bow. 'Your servant, sir. Robert Wilson, Colonel in His Britannic Majesty's Service, attached to the headquarters of His Imperial Majesty's armies in Poland and East Prussia.' He held out a paper of accreditment taken from his cuff and stared about him with an intelligent and professional interest.

Drinkwater gave the pass a cursory glance and said, 'Perhaps we should adjourn to my cabin, Colonel Wilson . . .'

'Delighted, Captain . . .'

The two men went below leaving an air of unsatisfied curiosity among the men on deck.

In the cabin, as Mullender poured two glasses of wine, Drinkwater checked Wilson's pass with more thoroughness. 'Please be seated, Colonel Wilson,' he said and then handed back the document with a nod. 'Thank you. How may I be of service?'

'You have two brigs with you, sir. The *Nancy* and the . . . *Jenny*

Marsden. They are filled with a consignment of arms and ammunition for the Russian army, are they not?'

'They are indeed, Colonel,' said Drinkwater, relieved that Wilson had come off to assume responsibility for them. 'Are you intending to see them to their destination at Königsberg?'

'I shall do what I can, though Russian methods can be damnably dilatory.'

'Then I am doubly glad to see you.' Drinkwater smiled, 'And I'd welcome reliable news of the action we heard had been fought in February. I have been concerned as to the accuracy of the reports I had from the Swedes and the safety of such a shipment if left at Königsberg.'

Wilson stretched his long legs and relaxed in his chair. 'You need have no fear, Captain. The Russian outposts confront the French all along the line of the Passage. They have not moved since Eylau . . .'

'So they *were* held . . .'

'The French? Oh, good God, yes! Had they been under Suvoroff, well . . .' Wilson sipped his wine and shrugged.

'Were you there?'

'At Eylau, yes. The Russians fought with great stubbornness and although Bennigsen left the field the French had been fought to a standstill; Boney himself had had the fright of his life and the Grand Army were dying in heaps *pour la gloire*. Their cavalry were magnificent of course, but even Murat was powerless to break the Russkies.'

'Will Bennigsen complete the matter when you come out of winter quarters?'

'Bennigsen? Perhaps. He's a German and unpopular with many of the Russian-born officers who will want some of the credit if a victory's to be had; but they're only too happy to blame a scapegoat if they're defeated. Bennigsen's competent enough, and he's close to the Tsar.'

'How so?' asked Drinkwater, fascinated by Wilson, whose close contacts with the Russians were interesting to him on both a professional and a personal level.

'Bennigsen was one of the officers present when Alexander's father, Tsar Paul, met his end in the Mikhailovsky Palace. It is said that Bennigsen was the first man to lay his hands on the Tsar. Outside the room was the Tsarevich Alexander, who happened to be Colonel-in-Chief of the Semenovsky Regiment which stood guard that night. Not an attractive story, but Alexander's complicity is well known. Paul was a highly dangerous man. Apart from his secret accord with Bonaparte, he *was* a vicious and cruel monster. Alexander, on the other hand, nurtures ideal views on kingship.' Wilson tossed off his glass and Drinkwater refilled it.

'Your post is a curious and fascinating one, Colonel. Tell me, what is your candid opinion of the likelihood of the Russians finally trouncing Bonaparte?'

Wilson raised his eyebrows in speculative arches. 'I know that's what your friend Lord Dungarth wants, hence the arms and the specie you have below . . .'

Drinkwater coughed into his wine and looked up sharply. 'You know a great deal, Colonel Wilson. What the devil makes you say Lord Dungarth is my friend?'

'Well, he is, ain't he?' replied Wilson. 'That's why *you* are here, Captain Drinkwater, as I understand it.'

Drinkwater assumed an air of sudden caution. Stories of murder and intrigue from St Petersburg were all very well, but Colonel Robert Wilson figured nowhere in his instructions from the Admiralty. 'I have my orders, Colonel Wilson, respecting the specie about which you seem to know everything. I am directed to hand it over at Revel to Lord Leveson-Gower in his *diplomatic* capacity as Ambassador to St Petersburg and not to yourself.'

'My dear sir,' said Wilson smoothly, crossing his legs, 'that ain't what I mean at all, damn me. I assumed that it was you as had been given this assignment in view of your unusual personal connections hereabouts.'

Drinkwater felt the colour leave his face. Surely Wilson could not know about his brother? The feeling that, in some way, providence would make him expiate his guilt for Edward's escape from justice suddenly overwhelmed him. It was an irrational fear that had haunted his subconscious for six years. 'What the devil do you mean?'

Drinkwater's extraordinary reaction had not escaped Wilson, but he had not thought it caused by guilt.

'Come, Captain Drinkwater, I think you need not alarm yourself. I have myself been, if not directly employed by Lord Dungarth's Secret Department like yourself, connected with it in view of my duties here. I am frankly amazed that my presence surprises you. Were you not told? Is it not part of your orders to liaise with any British agents in the field?'

'In so far as I am permitted to discuss my orders, Colonel, I can only shake my head to that question,' Drinkwater said cautiously.

'Some damnable back-sliding between the Horse-Guards and the Admiralty I don't doubt. A confounded clerk that's forgotten to copy a memorandum, or lost a note he was supposed to deliver.' Wilson smote his thigh with a relatively good-natured and contemptuous acceptance. 'Still, that's as may be. Then your orders, after you've turned your convoy and your specie over, are those usual to a cruiser, eh?'

Drinkwater nodded. 'Watch and prey is the formula off Brest, but here 'tis tread the decks of neutrals without upsetting anyone. A difficult task at the best of times.'

'Then you had better know more, Captain, in case we want you . . .'

'We?'

'Yes. Doubtless Lord Leveson-Gower will have something to say to you, but there are men in the field whom I will advise of your presence on the coast. Should they want swift communication with London they will be looking out for you. Often a frigate is the best and safest way. Chief among them is Colin Mackenzie. Whatever names he uses in his work he is not ashamed to own Ross-shire ancestry on his father's side, though what his mother was only his father knows. I would advise you offer him whatever assistance he might require. There is another man, a Captain Ostroff, in the Russian service. Both these fellows use a cryptogramic code for their dispatches – I am sure you are familiar with the type of thing – and all are sent to Joseph Devlieghere, Merchant of Antwerpen . . .'

'The clearing house . . .'

'Yes. And for all I know, where Bonaparte's people open 'em up before popping them into a Harwich shrimp-tub together with a keg or two of Hollands gin. The way Paris seems to know what's going on is astounding. That man Fouché is diabolical . . . You smile, Captain. . .'

'Only because he outwits us, Colonel,' said Drinkwater drily. 'If he was one of our fellows he would be considered brilliant.'

'True,' said Wilson smiling.

'I understand. I shall, of course, do what I can, but I assure you I have had no direct orders from Lord Dungarth, nor have I executed any commission for him since April last year.' Drinkwater refilled the glasses, then went on, 'But tell me, if you are confident about Russian prospects, why all this anxiety about agents? Indeed you did not fully answer my question about the military situation.'

'No more I did.' Wilson sipped his wine, considered a moment, then said, 'It is not entirely true to say the situation is static. With Napoleon in the field any thoughts of immobility can be discounted. Colberg and Dantzig have been invested and may fall to the French any day; that much we must expect. Marshal Mortier is occupying our supposed allies, the Swedes, before Stralsund, in Pomerania . . .' Wilson shrugged, 'Who knows what might happen. As to the main theatre here, well . . . I will give Boney one last throw. He is a damned long way from Paris. He's been absent for a year and when the cat's away we all know what the mice get up to. Bennigsen gave him a drubbing. He can't afford to retreat, either politically or militarily. But then he can't risk a defeat which the Russkies are quite capable of giving him. My guess is a battle of his own choosing and a big stake on a single hand.'

Drinkwater digested this. 'I should not care to bear such a responsibility,' he said slowly.

'No more would I,' said Wilson tossing off his glass and making to stand. 'The Russians are a rum lot, to be sure. Touchy, secretive and suspicious, but brave as lions when it comes to a fight.' He rose and looked pensively round the cabin. 'You seem to have a little piece of England here, Captain.'

Drinkwater smiled and drained his own glass. 'The other man's grass always appears a little greener.'

Wilson rose. 'The sooner you deliver your specie to Revel, Captain, the better. My stock at Imperial headquarters may rise a little and I may be less importuned and accused of British lassitude.

The Russians are constantly asking why we do not send troops to their assistance. Money and arms seem to disappear without effect.'

'God knows it costs enough without our having to fight their battles for them!' Drinkwater said indignantly.

'Ah, the pernicious income tax!'

'I was not thinking merely of the money, Colonel.' Drinkwater gestured vaguely around him. 'It is not merely ships that make up the navy. It takes many men. Do the Russians not appreciate that?'

Wilson raised his eyebrows, his expression one of amused cynicism, and, pulling himself upright, caught his head on the deck beam above. Wincing, he said, 'They are a land-power, Captain. We cannot expect them to understand.' He extended his hand.

'Let us hope,' said Drinkwater, shaking hands, 'that you and Bennigsen finish the business. Then we can enjoy our next glass together in London.'

'A cheering and worthy sentiment, Captain Drinkwater, and one that I endorse with all my heart.'

Drinkwater accompanied Wilson on deck and saw him over the side. He watched as the barge was pulled across to Young's brig, the *Jenny Marsden*. Wilson looked back once and waved. Drinkwater acknowledged the valediction then turned to the officer of the watch. 'Well, Mr Fraser . . .'

'Sir?'

'Not all the lobsters strut about St James's. Now do you prepare to get the ship under weigh.'

4   A Stay of Execution

April 1807

'It comes on to blow, Mr Q!' Drinkwater clamped his hat more securely on his head. 'You were quite right to call me.' He staggered as *Antigone*'s deck heeled to the thump of a heavy sea. The wave surged past them as the stern lifted and the bow dropped again, its breaking crest hissing with wind-driven fury as it was torn into spume.

'We must put about upon the instant! Call all hands!'

'Aye, aye, sir!' Quilhampton shouted forward and the bosun's mate of the watch began to pipe at the hatchways, then he turned back to the captain who had crossed the heeling deck to glance at the compass in the binnacle. 'I've had Walmsley aloft this past hour and there's no passage as yet . . .'

Drinkwater moved to the rail, grasped a stay and stared to leeward as *Antigone* lay down under the sudden furious onslaught of a squall. Through his hand he could feel the vibration of the wind in the frigate's rigging, feel the slackness in the rope as it bowed to leeward. He wiped his eyes and stared across the white-streaked water that heaved and boiled in the short, savage seas that were the result of comparatively shallow water and a quickly risen gale. The rim of the sea terminated, not at the skyline, but in a line of ice.

'Damned unseasonable,' Drinkwater muttered – unconsciously rubbing his shoulder which ached from damp and the chill proximity of the ice – while he considered the effect of the gale on the sea. It occurred to him that it might bring warmer air to melt the ice, and the thought cheered him a little, for it was clear that until the ice retreated further northwards any hope of reaching Revel was out of the question.

Drinkwater left Quilhampton to tack the ship. The frigate came round like a jibbed horse, her backed fore-yards spinning her high-stabbing bowsprit against the last shreds of daylight in the west.

'Mains'l haul!' The blocks clicked and rattled and the men hauled furiously, running the lee braces aft as the main- and mizen-yards spun round on their parrels.

'Pull together there, damn you!' Comley roared, his rattan active on the hapless backs of a gaggle of men who stumbled along the larboard gangway.

'That's well with the main-braces! Belay! Belay there!'

'Fore-braces! Leggo and haul!' The fore-yards swung and *Antigone* gathered headway on the starboard tack.

'A trifle more on that weather foretack there! That's well! Belay!'

He stepped up to the binnacle, then looked at the shivering edge of the main-topsail. 'Full and bye now, lads,' he said quietly to the four men at the frigate's double wheel, and the overseeing quar-termaster acknowledged the order.

'She's full an' bye now, so she is.'

'Very well.' He turned to Drinkwater. 'She's holding sou' by east a quarter east, sir.'

'Very well. Mr Q! Do you shorten down for the night. We'll keep her under easy sail until daylight.'

'Aye, aye, sir!'

Drinkwater watched patiently from his place by the weather hance, one foot on the little brass carronade slide that he had brought from the *Melusine*. The big fore-course, already reefed down, was now hauled up in its buntlines and secured, forty men laying out along the great yard to secure the heavy, resistant can-vas. When they came down it was almost dark. They were waiting for the order to pipe down.

'Mr Quilhampton!'

'Sir?'

'Pass word for Mr Comley to lay aft.'

'Aye, aye, sir.' The lieutenant turned to Walmsley. 'Mr Walmsley, cut along and pass word for the bosun to lay aft and report to the Captain.'

'Aye, aye, sir.'

Lord Walmsley made his way along the lee gangway to the

fo'c's'le where Mr Comley stood, the senior and most respected seaman in the ship, at his post of honour on the knightheads.

'Mr Comley!'

'Mr Walmsley, what can I do for you?'

'The Captain desires that you attend him on the quarterdeck.'

'Eh?' Comley looked aft at the figure of Drinkwater, shadowy in the gathering gloom. 'What the devil does he want me on the King's parade for?' he muttered, then nodding to Walmsley he walked aft.

'You sent for me, sir?'

Drinkwater stared at Comley. Hitherto he had never had the slightest doubt that Comley's devotion to duty was absolute. 'Have you anything to report, Mr Comley?'

'To report, sir? Why . . . no, sir.'

'The four men at the lee main-brace, Mr Comley – Kissel, Hacking, Benson and Myers, if I ain't mistaken – are they drunk?'

'Er . . .'

'Damn it, man, you'd do well not to try and hide it from me.'

Comley looked at the captain, his expression anxious. 'I, er, I wouldn't say they was drunk, sir. Happen they slipped . . .'

'Mr Comley, I can have them here in an instant. They are all prime seamen. They didn't slip, sir. Now, I will ask you again, are they drunk?'

Comley sighed and nodded. 'It's possible, sir. I . . . I didn't know until . . . well when they slipped and I got close to 'em. I could smell they might be in liquor, sir.'

'Very well, Mr Comley.' Drinkwater changed his tone of voice. 'Would you answer two questions without fear. Why are they drunk and why did you not report it?'

Even in the twilight Drinkwater could see the dismay on Comley's face. 'Come, sir,' he said, 'you may answer without fear. And be quick about it, the watch below are waiting for you to pipe 'em down.'

'Well, sir, beggin' your pardon, sir, but the men ain't too happy, sir . . . It's nothing much, sir, we ain't asking no favours, but we . . . that is the old *Melusines*, we was volunteers, sir, back in the year three. Now we're all shipped with pressed men an' quota-men, men that ain't prime seamen, no, nor don't take no shame from that fact, sir; and the length of the commission and there bein' no pay

46

last time at the Nore, sir, and the men beginning to run . . .' His voice faded miserably.

'Personal discontent is not a crime, Mr Comley. I too should like to go home, but we have not yet destroyed our enemies . . . Be that as it may, you have not answered my question. Why did you not report it?'

Drinkwater could see a gathering of pale and expectant faces staring aft, waiting to be dismissed from the tasks they had been called on deck to carry out. All hands were witness to Mr Comley's talk with the captain.

'I don't want no trouble, sir . . . that's all . . .'

'I understand that, Mr Comley . . .' Drinkwater saw Comley's eyes slide across to the figure of the first lieutenant whom, he realised with a sharp feeling of guilt, he had not noticed on deck until that moment. Comley's predicament was obvious. He was supposed to report all misdemeanours direct to Rogers, but Rogers had not been on deck. No doubt Comley, if he really had intended to report the four men, would have let the matter blow over, since the first lieutenant had failed to answer the call for all hands. Rogers's strictness was well known and in that game of each trying to catch out the other, first lieutenant and crew had developed a subtlety of play that Drinkwater was only just beginning to grasp. Even now Comley's stuttering excuses, although they might be understood as the genuine, if ill-expressed, discontent of the best and oldest hands on board, were evidence of a game that became increasingly deadly with every round.

Drinkwater thrust his own culpability out of his mind for a moment or two. Although Rogers's absence had compromised Comley in the strict line of his duty, it had given a round to the hands. That much was obvious to all of them as they stood there in the twilight watching. And now Rogers was compromising Drinkwater, for it was clear that the first lieutenant was the worse for drink. In a second Drinkwater would be compelled to take very public notice of Rogers's condition; and at the moment he wanted to avoid that. He affected not to have noticed Rogers.

'Mr Comley,' he said with every appearance of ferocity, 'I'll not have the ship go to the devil for any reason. D'you clearly understand me?'

His tone diverted Comley's eyes from the person of Rogers to himself.

'Aye, aye, sir.'

'I hold you personally responsible. It's your duty to report such things, and if you can't I'll turn you forrard and find someone who can!' He paused, just long enough to let the words sink in. 'Now have those four men confined in the bilboes overnight and pipe down the watches below.'

'Aye, aye, sir.'

Drinkwater left the deck as Comley put the silver call to his mouth. The captain was raging inwardly, furious with Rogers and himself, himself most of all for his self-delusion that all was well on board. The marine sentry held himself upright at what passed for attention on the heeling deck as Drinkwater stalked past him.

'Pass word for the first lieutenant and the marine officer!' he snapped, banging the door behind him.

Mullender was fussing about in the cabin. 'Why aren't you on deck, Mullender? Eh? Ain't the call at every hatchway enough for you? Don't you hear properly, damn it? The call was for *all* hands, Mullender!'

'But, sir, the first lieut . . .'

'Get out!' It was no good Drinkwater making Mullender the surrogate for his anger. The unfortunate steward fled, scuttling out through the pantry. Drinkwater flung off his cloak, massaged his shoulder and groaned aloud. The damp was searching out the old wound given him long ago by the French agent Santhonax in an alley at Sheerness and made worse by a shell-wound off Boulogne. It reminded him that his cross was already heavy enough, without the added burden of Rogers and the fomentation of an exhausted crew. The pain, resentment and momentary self-pity only fuelled his anger further and when Mount and Rogers came into the cabin they found him sitting in the darkness, staring out through the stern windows where the heaving grey sea hissed and bubbled up from the creaking rudder and as suddenly dropped away again.

'Gentlemen,' he said after a pause and without turning round, 'the men are in an evil mood. The grievances are the usual ones and most are justified. Mr Mount, your own men must be aware of the situation, but I want them to be on their guard. Any reports of meeting, combinations . . . the usual thing, Mr Mount. Make sure the sentinels are well checked by your sergeant, and change their postings. I know they've enough to do watching the specie but I'll not have a mutiny, by God I'll not!'

He turned on them, unwilling to let them see the extent of his anger. A light wavered in the pantry door and Mullender stood uncertainly with the cabin lamps he had obviously been preparing when Drinkwater threw him out. 'Yes, yes, bring them in and ship 'em in the sconces for God's sake, man!' He looked at Mount, 'You understand, don't you, Mr Mount?'

'Yessir!'

'Very good. Carry on!'

'Sir.'

Mullender and Mount both left the cabin and Drinkwater was alone with Rogers who remained standing, one arm round the stanchion that rose immediately forward of the table.

'Well, sir,' said Drinkwater, looking upwards at Rogers, 'it was ever your dictum to flog a man for every misdemeanour. I have apprehended four men drunk at their stations tonight. Had you been on deck you might have attended to the matter yourself, as you are in duty bound. Had you brought those men to the gratings tomorrow I would have had to flog 'em. But now your conduct has ensured that if I am to flog them I must, in all justice, flog you, sir! Yes, you, sir! And hold your tongue! Not only are you in liquor but you prevented my steward from mustering on deck as he should have done. Why that was I'll forbear enquiring, but if it was to obtain the key to the spirit-room, by God I'll have you broke by a court martial!'

Drinkwater paused. There was a limit in the value of remonstrance with a drunken man. Either rage or self-pity would emerge and neither was conducive to constructive dialogue. Rogers showed sudden and pathetic signs, not of the former, as Drinkwater had expected, but of the latter. Drinkwater had had more than enough for one day and dismissed Rogers as swiftly as possible.

'Get to bed, Mr Rogers, and when you are sober in the morning, be pleased to take notice of what I have said.'

Rogers stepped forward as though to speak, but the ship's

movement, exaggerated here at the stern, checked him and the lamps threw a cautionary glint into Drinkwater's grey eyes. In a sudden access of movement Rogers turned and fled.

Samuel Rogers woke in the night, his head thick and his mouth dry. He lay staring into the creaking darkness as the ship rose and fell, riding out the last of the gale under her reefed topsails and awaiting the morning.

The events of the previous evening came back to him slowly. The pounding of his headache served to remind him of his folly and, once again, he swore he would never touch another drop. He recalled the interview with Drinkwater and felt his resolve weaken, countered by his deep-seated resentment towards the captain. They were of an age; once a few days had differentiated them in their seniority as lieutenants. Now there was a world of difference between them! Drinkwater a post-captain, two steps ahead of Rogers and across the magic threshold that guaranteed him a flag if he lived long enough to survive his seniors on the captains' list.

It was convenient for Rogers, in the depths of his misery, to forget that it was Drinkwater himself who had rescued him from the gutter. Samuel Rogers was no different from hundreds of other officers in the navy. He had no influence, no fortune, no family. Fate had never put him into a position in which he could distinguish himself and he lacked that spark of originality by which a man might, by some instinctive alchemy of personality, ability and opportunity, make his own luck. To some extent Rogers's very sense of obligation fired his steady dissolution; his jealousy of Drinkwater's success robbed him of any of his own. In his more honest moments he knew he had only two choices. Either he went to the devil on the fastest horse, or he pulled himself together and hoped for a change of luck. In the meantime he should do his duty as Drinkwater had advised and the consideration that he was on a crack frigate under an able officer seemed to offer some consolation. But after that one drink that was all he needed to settle himself, the axis of his rationality tilted. After the inevitable second drink it lost its equilibrium, leaving him ugly with ill-temper, inconsiderate and tyrannical towards the gunroom, cockpit and lower deck.

As he lay in the darkness, while above him the bells rang the middle watch through the night, he knew that some form of turning-point had been reached. Up until that moment his drunkenness had not come to Drinkwater's attention. Until that had happened, Drinkwater was simply the captain, a man of influence and advantage, one of the lucky ones in life's eternal lottery seen from the perspective of one of its losers. Now, however, the captain assumed a new role. His power, absolute and unfettered, could confront Rogers and demolish his alcoholic arrogance with fear.

For although the service had disappointed him, Rogers had nothing beyond the navy. If he was broken by a court martial as remorse said he deserved to be, he would have only himself to blame. The penury of half-pay in some stinking kennel of lodgings alongside the whores and usurers of Portsmouth Point was all that disgrace and dismissal would leave him with.

He lay in his night-shirt, sweat sticking it to his body, staring into the darkness of his tiny cabin. Loneliness possessed him in its chill and unconsoling embrace as he knew that, come the morning, he would be unable to resist the drinks that even now he swore he would never touch again.

Drinkwater was on deck at dawn. He, too, had slept badly and woke ill-at-ease. He had not liked humiliating Rogers any more than discovering four men turned-up drunk from their watch below. It was manifestly unfair to expect men who had more than a liberal amount of alcohol poured into them by official decree to off-set the deficiencies of their diet, to remain as sober as Quakers, particularly in their watch below. But, Drinkwater reasoned, four drunkards probably indicated that a hardened group had illicit access to liquor. In addition to these men, Rogers was obviously abusing his own powers to gain access to the spirit-room. The addictive qualities of naval rum were well known and many a man, officer and rating alike, had died raving from its effects upon the brain. Furthermore it was possible that whoever was aiding and abetting the first lieutenant was probably taking advantage of the opportunity to plunder an equal quantity for the hardened soaks among the crew.

The thought tormented Drinkwater as he lay awake, shivering

slightly as a faint lightening of the sky began to illumine the cabin. He abandoned his efforts to sleep, swung his legs out of the cot and began to dress. Ten minutes later he was on deck. The wind had eased during the night and the approaching daylight showed it to be backing. They would have to tack again soon, and stand more to the west-north-westward. Hill had the morning watch and, having passed instructions to tack at the change of watch, Drinkwater fell to pacing the quarterdeck.

His mind was in a turmoil. He loathed using the cat-o'-nine tails except for serious crimes. For most minor punishments, public humiliations and loss of privilege served to make a man regret his folly. Besides, it was Drinkwater's firm belief that a strong discipline, strictly enforced, prevented most men from overstepping the mark. At home he tired of debates with Elizabeth upon the subject. She considered his rule illiberal, but failed to understand the cauldron of suppression that a man-o'-war on a long commission became: some ten score of men whose only reason for existence was to pull and haul, to hand, reef and steer, to load and ram and fetch and carry and fight when called upon to do so, in the name of a half-witted old king and a country that cared more about the nags and fillies of Newmarket than their seamen.

Drinkwater's anger grew as he paced up and down. It was Rogers's business to manage this motley mixture of seamen, this polyglot collection of the 'jolly-jack tars' of popular imagination, who were everywhere shunned once they got ashore among the gentry of the shires. It was a simple enough matter, if attended to sensibly. The might of the Articles of War stopped the poor devils from being men and turned them into pack-animals deserving of a little attention. God knew they asked little enough! Damn Rogers! He had no business behaving like this, no business prejudicing the whole commission because he could not leave the bottle alone!

Little Midshipman Frey skidded across the deck on some errand for the master.

'Mr Frey!' he called, and the lad turned expectantly. 'Mr Frey, give my compliments to the surgeon and ask him to step on deck as soon as he can.'

'Aye, aye, sir.'

Drinkwater stared grimly after the retreating figure. It was not yet time for Mr Lallo to be called. He was one of the ship's idlers, men whose work occupied them during daylight hours and absolved them from night duty except in dire emergencies. From his eventual appearance it was obvious Drinkwater's summons had called him from the deepest slumber. Drinkwater was suddenly touched by envy of the man, that he could so sleep without the interference of troublesome thoughts.

'You sent for me, sir?' Lallo suppressed a yawn with difficulty. 'Is there something amiss? Are you unwell?'

Drinkwater turned outboard, inviting Lallo's confidence at the rail. 'The matter is not to become common gossip, Mr Lallo.'

Lallo frowned.

'The first lieutenant . . . I want you to have him confined quietly in his cabin for a day or two, starve him of liquor and convince him it is in his own best interests. Tell the gunroom he is sick. D'you understand?'

'Yes, I think so, sir. You want Mr Rogers weaned from the bottle . . .?'

'And quickly, Mr Lallo, before he compels me to a less pleasant specific. I cannot hold my hand indefinitely. Once I am forced to recognise his true state then he is a ruined man. Quite ruined.'

'I cannot guarantee a cure, sir, I can only . . .'

'Do your best, yes, yes, I know. But I am persuaded that a few days reflection may bring him to his senses. Do what you can.'

'Very well, sir.' Lallo sighed. 'I fear it may be a violent business . . .'

'I am sure that you will see to it, Mr Lallo. And please remember that the matter is between the two of us.'

'The three of us, sir,' Lallo corrected.

'Yes, but it is *my* instructions that I want obeyed, damn it! Don't haze me with pettifoggin' quibbles and invocations of the Hippocratic oath. Rogers is half-way to the devil unless we save him,' Drinkwater said brusquely, turning away in dismissal.

'Very well, sir, but he is a big man . . .'

'Just do your duty, Mr Lallo, if you please.' Drinkwater's exasperation communicated itself to Lallo at last and he hurried off. Drinkwater watched him waddle away then stared again over the sea. The waves were no longer spume-streaked. Fluttering up into

53

the wake a bevy of gulls hunted in the bubbling water where the tiny creatures of the deep were caught up in the turbulence of *Antigone*'s passing hull. The crests broke infrequently now and the vice had gone out of the wind. He watched the pattern of quartering gulls broken up by the predatory onslaught of a sudden swift skua. The dark bird selected its quarry and hawked it mercilessly, folding its neck beneath one wing until the gull, terrified into submission, evacuated its crop in one single eructation. The skua released its victim and rounded on the vomited and part-digested food, folded its long dark wings over its back and settled in the frigate's wake.

He was startled by someone at his elbow.

'Beg pardon, zur, but your shaving water's getting cold in the cabin.'

Drinkwater nodded bleakly to his coxswain. He thought that Tregembo already knew of the strong words that had been passed between captain and first lieutenant the previous evening. Doubtless Mullender had let the ship's company know too, but that was unavoidable. He led Tregembo below.

Taking off cloak, coat and hat, and unwinding the muffler from his neck, he began to shave. 'Well, Tregembo . . . what do they say?'

'The usual, zur.'

'Which is one law for the officers . . .'

'And one for the hands, zur.'

'And what do they expect me to do about it, eh?' He pulled his cheek tight and felt the razor rasp his skin. The water was already cold. He swirled the blade and scraped again.

'They are content that you are a gennelman, zur.'

Drinkwater smiled, despite his exasperation. It was a curious remark, designed to caution Drinkwater, to place upon him certain tacitly understood obligations. Only a man of Tregembo's unique relationship could convey such a subtlety so directly to the commander of a man-o'-war; while only an officer of Drinkwater's stamp would have taken notice of the genuine affection that lay beneath it. 'Then I am content to hear it, Tregembo.'

'There *are* four men in the bilboes, zur . . .'

'Quite so, Tregembo.' The eyes of the two men met and

Drinkwater felt forced to smile again. 'Life is like a ship, Tregembo.' He saw a puzzled look cloud the old man's face. 'Nothing ever stays still for long.'

Picking up the napkin he wiped the remaining lather from his face and held his hands out for his coat.

Drinkwater looked down at the faces of the ship's company assembled in the waist. They were the usual mixed bag, some thirteen score of men from all four corners of the world, but most from Britain and Ireland. There were the prime seamen, neat in their appearance, fit and energetic in their duties, those men for whom, in the purely professional sense, he had the highest regard. Yet they were no angels. Long service had taught them all the tricks of the trade. They knew when to 'lay Tom Cox's traverse' and avoid work, how to curry favour with the petty officers and where to get extra rations, tobacco or spirits in the underworld that flourished aboard every King's ship. Neither were they exclusively British or Irish. There was at least one Yankee, on board a British ship for a reason he alone knew though many suspected. There was also a Swede, two Finns and a negro whose abilities aloft were, within the little world of the *Antigone*, already part of legend. But the bulk of the frigate's people were made up of 'ordinary' seamen, waisters and landsmen, in a strictly descending order of hierarchy as rigid as its continuation upwards among the officers. It was a social order imposed by the uncompromising nature of the sea-service and extended in its inflexible formality from Drinkwater to the stumbling, idiotic luetic whose only duty consisted of keeping the ship's lavatories clean. Each man had a clearly defined task at sea, at anchor, in action and during an emergency in which the strength of his arm and the stamina of his body were the reason for his existence.

They spread right across the beam of the ship, no further aft than the main-mast. Some ships bore a white line painted across their deck planking there, but not the *Antigone*. She had been acquired from the French and no such device had ever been added. They were perched in the boats on the booms, up on the rails and sitting on the hammock nettings. Men crowded into the lower ratlines of the main shrouds and all wore expressions of expectancy.

Between the untidy mob of 'the people', the midshipmen, master's mates and warrant officers occupied the neutral ground. Abaft them the files of marines made a hedge of fixed bayonets, cold steel ready for instant employment in defence of the commissioned officers.

The murmur of comment that noted the absence of Rogers subsided the instant Drinkwater's hat began to rise in the stairwell, but he heard it, as he was meant to. He strode to the binnacle and looked at the men and took his time, opening the punishment book with great deliberation, gauging the mood of the hands. He looked about him, checking that the helmsmen, quartermaster, sentinels and look-outs were at their stations.

'Bring up the prisoners!'

The ship's corporal guarding the four seamen with a drawn bayonet shoved them forward from the companionway. They stood miserably after a cramped night in the bilboes, their ankles sore from the chafing of the irons. They could expect, by common custom, three dozen lashes apiece. Drinkwater turned to Fraser and raised an eyebrow. 'Mr Fraser . . .' he reminded.

'Off hats!'

'Benson, Hacking, Kissel and Myers . . .' Drinkwater read their names and then fixed the four guilty men with a baleful grey eye. He was not in the mood for the lugubrious formalities of the Articles of War with their dolorous recital of the punishment of death for each and every offence, scarcely suggesting that 'such lesser punishment' was ever employed in mitigation. 'You four men were drunk last night at the call for all hands . . .' Drinkwater pitched the words forward so that they could all hear. 'If you had been topmen such conduct might have caused you to fall to your deaths. Indeed you might have killed others. Understand that I will not tolerate drunkenness . . .' he looked from the four wretches in front of him and raked the whole assembly, officers included, with his eyes, ' . . . from anyone, irrespective of station. At the next occurrence I shall punish *to the very extremity* of the regulations.'

He turned to the four prisoners. 'You four men are stopped all grog until further notice. Mr Pater,' he turned to the purser, 'do you see to it: no grog.'

'Aye, aye, sir.'

A murmur broke out amidships, but this time Fraser needed no prompting. 'Silence there!'

'Very well. Dismiss the ship's company, Mr Fraser, and send Mr Comley aft.'

Drinkwater stalked away and, tucking the punishment book in his pocket, grasped the taffrail with both hands and stared astern. Behind him Fraser ordered the ship's company to disperse and they did so in noisy disorder, only the measured tramp of the marines' boots conveying the impression of discipline. A few minutes later Comley appeared.

'You sent for me, sir?'

'Yes.' Drinkwater turned and faced the bosun. 'I shall flog on the next occasion, Mr Comley, be quite certain of that.'

'Yes, sir.'

'You must see to it that it ain't necessary.'

'Very well, sir. Them four men'll suffer more from loss o'grog . . .'

'A flogging still hurts 'em, Mr Comley, and I'd not have any of them thinking I've no stomach for it. You do understand, don't you?'

Comley looked at the captain. He was not used to being intimate with Drinkwater twice in two days, preferring his daily encounters with the first lieutenant. He had the measure of Mr Rogers who was no different from half-a-hundred first luffs in the navy. He had seen the captain in action and heard more of him from his old Cornish coxswain. For all that a shrewd cockney knew that a Kurnowic man could spin a lie like an Irishman and make it sound like the unvarnished truth, there was something in Drinkwater's eyes that bade Comley take care.

'I understand, sir,' he said hurriedly.

'Very well. And now, Mr Comley,' said Drinkwater more brightly, 'I want you to put it about the hands that there'll be a good-conduct payment at the end of this cruise, payable in cash . . . do close your mouth there's a good fellow.'

Comley did as he was bid, but stared after the retreating figure of the captain as he was left standing thunderstruck by the taffrail.

'Did you hear that, soldier?' he asked the marine whose sentry post was across the frigate's stem, ready to hurl a lifebuoy at any man who went overboard.

'Does that include the sojers, Bose?'

'I dunno,' ruminated Comley.

'He's a rum bastard,' offered the marine.

'He is that,' said Comley, going forward with the extraordinary news.

Mr Lallo stared unhappily at the snoring figure in the cot. Inert, Lieutenant Rogers seemed even larger than the surgeon remembered him when standing. If he woke now, what the devil did one say to him?

'Please, Mr Rogers, the captain says you're a drunken oaf and would you be so kind as to keep quietly to your cabin for a day or so. After you have rested and your body has acclimatised itself to no rum, you'll be fit as a fiddle to resume your duties.' It was impossible. For days Rogers would toss and rave and drive himself to the edge of sanity. Lallo shook his head. In his younger days the surgeon had eaten opium. It had only been a mild addiction, but the memories of those hallucinations still haunted him.

''Ere ye are, Mr Lallo . . .'

He turned, his finger to his lips, as his loblolly boy, Skeete, entered the first lieutenant's cabin. Skeete wore an expression of impish glee that revealed a mouth full of carious teeth. Lallo took and shook out the heavy canvas strait-jacket.

'Very well, work your way round the cot and if you wake him I'll have you at the gratings.'

Rogers stirred as Lallo moved forward and Skeete moved round the cot. 'What the . . . what the devil?'

'Hold him!'

'I *am* holding him!'

'Let me go, damn you! Help, murder!'

Lallo thrust a rag into Rogers's gaping mouth and knelt upon his struggling body, trying to avoid the halitosis of Skeete. They passed the lashings of the jacket, rolling Rogers over and avoiding his thrashing feet. In that position it was easy to secure the leather gag and, wiping the sweat from their eyes, roll him face upwards once again.

'There! It is done.' Skeete grinned, his face hideous. ''Tis like trussing a chicken . . .' His pleasure in so dealing with a person of Rogers's importance was obvious.

'Hold your tongue!' snapped Lallo as the man's stinking breath swept over him yet again. 'Help me settle him a little more comfortably.'

The fight had gone out of Rogers. The skin on his forehead was pallid and dewed with drops of heavy perspiration. His eyes were wide open, the pupils unnaturally dilated and expressive of a bursting sense of outrage.

'Get out . . . and Skeete, try and keep your damned mouth shut about this, will you?'

'Anything to oblige.'

Lallo stared disgustedly at his assistant. His manner had the sincerity of a Jew proclaiming a bargain. The surgeon sighed and turned to Rogers when they were alone. He and Skeete were guardians of the frigate's most arcane secrets. Mostly they consisted of who was receiving treatment for the clap or the lues, but now Rogers's infirmity was to be included, under disguise, since the whole ship knew he was 'indisposed'. Such an open secret had to be treated with due form, in accordance with the ritual that maintained the inviolability of the quarterdeck.

Rogers grunted and Lallo gave his patient his full attention. 'Now, Mr Rogers, please try and behave yourself. You have been drinking far too much. Your liver is swollen and enlarged, man. You are killing yourself! You know this, don't you?' Rogers's eyes closed. 'You have got to stop and the captain has ordered you be confined for a day or two, to see you over the reaction . . . now you try and relax and we'll see if we can't dry you out, eh? Until I'm sure you'll behave, I am compelled to restrain you in this way. Do you understand?'

Rogers grunted, but the malevolent glare from his eyes was full of a terrible comprehension.

5   News from Carlscrona

April–May 1807

Drinkwater laid down the pencil and stared at the little column of figures with a sense of quiet satisfaction. With only a one per cent commission on the specie in the strongroom, to which as captain he was entitled, he would be able to pay a 'good conduct' bounty of three pounds per man and still have a few guineas left over for himself. Not only that, he had acquired another form of punishment: that of cancelling the bounty if an individual deserved it.

It was true that his own fortune would be the poorer, but he was not a greedy man. The days of being an indigent midshipman and making free with gold taken aboard a prize or two were behind him, thank God. A small bequest by an old and bachelor shipmate had rescued him from the poverty of reliance upon pay and his home was comfortable if modest. Although he had withered Tregembo's suggestion that he purchase a gentleman's estate, the idea occasionally occupied his thoughts, but in a sense he thought the money better spent this way. Commissions on specie were a perquisite of which his puritan soul did not wholeheartedly approve. Besides, he knew Elizabeth would have appreciated his action and that she, unlike so many post-captains' wives, did not measure her husband's success by the number of horses that drew her carriage.

Drinkwater's mood of self-esteem was ruptured by the sudden appearance of Midshipman Frey. 'Beg pardon, sir, but the look-out's reporting a sail . . . '

A few minutes later he stood beside the master, levelling his glass and focusing upon the newcomer. 'What d'you make of her, Mr Hill?'

'Swede, sir . . . naval dispatch vessel, from Carlscrona probably . . . ah, that's interesting.'

Drinkwater saw it at the same time. In addition to the yellow and blue of the Swedish national colours at her main peak, the schooner had broken out a flag at her foremasthead as she altered course towards them. The flag was the British Union.

'She wants to speak to us. Heave to, Mr Hill, and a whip and a chair at the main-yardarm.'

Half an hour later a damp civilian gentleman in a caped surtout stood uncertainly upon *Antigone*'s deck and looked curiously about him. Drinkwater approached and extended his hand. 'May I present myself. I am Captain Nathaniel Drinkwater of His Britannic Majesty's . . .'

'I know, Captain,' the stranger cut him short, 'and damned glad I am to have found you.' He laughed at Drinkwater's surprise. 'Yes, I'm British. Straton, British Resident at Stockholm.' They shook hands. 'May we adjourn to your cabin? I have something of the utmost importance to communicate.'

'Of course, Mr Straton.'

'Would you be so good as to hoist in Johansson, the pilot?'

'Pilot? Why should I need a pilot? Where is he for?'

'Carlscrona, Captain. Come, let me explain in your cabin.'

'Very well. Mr Hill, you are to hoist in another person. It seems you are right about Carlscrona. Come, sir, this way.' He led Straton below.

In the cabin he indicated a seat and sent Mullender for a bottle of wine.

'Our present position is about twenty miles south-east of Gotland, I believe, Captain,' said Straton non-committally as Mullender fussed around.

As soon as the steward had gone Drinkwater said, 'Well, sir?' expectantly.

'Well, sir. To be brief, you are not to deliver your consignment of specie to the Russians.'

'The devil I'm not! And on whose instructions, may I ask?'

'Those', said Straton, drawing a slim leather wallet from a voluminous pocket in his greatcoat, 'of His Majesty's Government . . .' He handed a paper to Drinkwater who took it and examined it closely. As he did so Straton studied the captain.

Grey eyes were masked by his eyelids, one of which was

61

freckled by blue powder burns, tattooed into the soft skin like random ink-spots, his tanned face was disfigured by a thin scar that ran down his left cheek and the mop of brown hair bowed over the paper was shot with grey and tied at his nape in an old-fashioned queue. The epaulettes, Straton noticed shrewdly, were not level, betraying an inequality in the height of the shoulders, the evidence of a serious wound. It was obvious to Straton that Captain Drinkwater had seen a deal of service, but to his courtier's eye the captain still seemed something of a tarpaulin officer, perhaps too set in his ways to appreciate the tangled diplomacy of the Baltic. He would have preferred a younger man, in his late twenties perhaps, and from his own class. The captain looked up and returned the papers.

'You must forgive me my suspicions, Mr Straton.'

'They are quite understandable.'

'The truth is I am astonished at the change in my orders, but they are dated recently.'

'Yes, they arrived by fast cutter at Helsingborg and were delivered overland by a courier. I received them less than a fortnight after your own dispatches from Varberg. All I can tell you is that there is some doubt as to the wisdom of forwarding further subsidies to the Tsar at the moment.'

Drinkwater frowned. 'Why is that? Not many days ago Colonel Wilson sat in that very chair and emphasised how important they are to the continued maintenance of the alliance. Besides, from what I hear, Sweden is scarcely a safe haven for such a sum.'

Straton dismissed his doubts about the political capacity of Captain Drinkwater.

'You are concerned about the reliability of the King, no doubt, Captain. Well, it is common knowledge that His Majesty King Gustavus Vasa is quite mad, but he isn't insane enough to lose sight of reality. This situation creates a state of uncertainty which keeps even his court guessing! Although he has foolishly quarrelled with Berlin and petulantly withdrawn troops from Stralsund as a consequence, he is unlikely to fall out with us. It is true that internally Sweden is in trouble, for Gustavus has no interest in the welfare of his people, hates the French and therefore hates the reforming faction of his own nobility who are Francophile in sentiment. The people of Sweden are opposed to the King's foreign policy, concerned about their ruined economy and apt to contrast their plight with their prosperously neutral neighbours in Denmark whom they used to regard as inferior.'

'On the face of it then, hardly a place for eighty thousand pounds . . .'

'Government instructions are explicit, Captain Drinkwater,' Straton said and Drinkwater shrugged. It was no concern of his, but he remained curious.

'But why deny Russia the money?'

'I believe it is only a temporary delay.'

'What on earth for?'

'As an inducement, I assume. You have heard of the action at Eylau?'

'Yes.'

'Well, there has been some agitation in St Petersburg to have General Bennigsen removed, a court intrigue you understand, probably related to the fact that certain people do not want a German to reap the credit for the death-blow to Napoleon.'

'Let them argue about that when they have secured the victory. At least the Russian rank and file have proved themselves the equals of the Grand Army . . .'

'Exactly, Captain, and the removal of Bennigsen would be a disaster. The campaigning season is already open. If the Tsar is swayed by the anti-German lobby then the damage to the Russian army may be incalculable. A large number of officers of German extraction occupy key posts; Bennigsen's dismissal would unsettle them and reduce the chances of success in the next, vital, clash with the French. A brief withholding of your subsidy is the British Government's caution to the Tsar to maintain the status quo. Bennigsen's army did well at Eylau and he has it in his power to deal the fatal blow to the over-extended divisions of France. Then . . . ' Straton brought the edge of his hand down on the table like the blade of a guillotine, *'c'est fini, n'est-ce pas?'*

'It seems a devious and damned risky gamble to me,' replied Drinkwater uneasily, 'but then it doubtless would to a sailor.' He paused and drained his glass. 'So I am to accompany you to Carlscrona, eh?'

'Exactly, Captain.'

'Then perhaps I can offer you the hospitality of my cabin while I go and pass the requisite orders.'

As the south-westerly gale blew itself out, the warm air it had drawn into the southern Baltic cooled on the distant ice-edge and *Antigone* became shrouded in rolling banks of damp fog. To the north the ice began to melt rapidly but, in the open sea south of Gotland, the fog and the calm kept the British frigate and her smaller Swedish consort immobilised for almost two weeks. Then, quite suddenly, as if impetuously relenting, the long northern winter metamorphosed into summer and on a day of brilliant sunshine, on a sea as blue as the Mediterranean ruffled by a light easterly breeze, the *Antigone* closed the Swedish coast. Only the islands littering the approaches to Carlscrona remained gloomy, hump-backed under their dense mantles of fir trees.

Johansson, the pilot, stood at the weather rail and guided their course as they wove between the islands. All hands were on deck, trimming the yards as the frigate followed the schooner towards the Swedish naval arsenal of Carlscrona. Drinkwater remarked the dark spikes of the fir trees and the scent of the resin they gave off, sharp in his nostrils. Under her three topsails and a jib, *Antigone* ghosted through the still water, the hiss and chuckle of her wake creaming out from under her round bows.

'You seem to have a most expertly drilled company, Captain, though I am no judge of such matters.'

'You are very kind, Mr Straton, but I daily wonder how long they can be kept at this ceaseless task. Many of these men have not seen home for four years.'

'Yours is not an enviable task.'

'Nor yours, sir.'

'We must both stand to our posts, Captain,' Straton said sententiously, 'and bring this damnable war to an advantageous conclusion.'

'I should rather you had said "victory", Mr Straton. "Advantageous conclusion" smacks too much of half-measures for my liking now.'

Straton laughed. 'You are right, Captain Drinkwater. I have been too long at the Swedish court!' He pointed ahead to where, beyond a rocky point, the citadel and anchorage of Carlscrona was coming into view. There were men-of-war anchored in the road. 'And here we are. The nearest vessel is the *Falken*. She flies the flag of a rear-admiral which you should salute as we arranged. It is into her that you are to turn the specie.'

Drinkwater nodded. 'Mr Fraser! Have the chasers manned and prepare to make the salute. Mr Hill, you may bring the ship to her anchor under the lee of yonder man-o'-war.'

A few minutes later the hands were away aloft to stow the topsails and the surrounding islands flung back the echoes of *Antigone*'s guns as she paid her respects to her Swedish allies.

Drinkwater leaned over his chart of the Baltic Sea. He was tired and the candlelight played on features that betrayed his anxiety. He had fondly imagined that, once the specie had been discharged and he had Straton's signature for it, he would be free. But one responsibility had exchanged itself for another and he was now faced with the unnerving problem of what to do next. Once free of his convoy and the Tsar's subsidy his orders were far from explicit. He was instructed to act 'with discretion, bearing in mind the paramount importance of His Majesty's Orders in Council'. Theoretically the duties of blockading were simple enough, but during his brief stay at Carlscrona he had learned that in the tangled diplomacy of the Baltic states, where the very crisis of the war seemed to be developing, the discretionary part of his orders might place far greater demands upon him. He recalled Wilson's surprise that he had no specific instructions from Lord Dungarth and now he studied the chart as if, like Mount's Military Atlas, it would provide him with all the answers.

Along the southern shore of the Baltic lay the coast of Germany, mostly the territory of Frederick William of Prussia but now under the control of the French. The large island of Rügen was still in Swedish hands, as was the town of Stralsund, now under siege by Marshal Mortier's army corps. Drinkwater's gaze moved east, along the coast from Pomerania towards another port holding out against a French force: Dantzig. Beyond this allied outpost and its bight, the coast swept northwards, past the Frisches Haff and Königsberg to Russia beyond and the Kurland ports of Memel and

Revel. Somewhere near Königsberg the main armies of France and Russia faced each other along the line of the River Passarge.

Straton had made it clear that the British Government was now meditating moves which not only could influence Drinkwater, but also be significantly affected by his own operations in this period of uncertainty. This was the nub of his own dilemma.

A knock at the door interrupted his deliberations. 'Enter. Ah, come in, Mr Hill.'

'She's under easy sail for the night, sir.' His eyes fell on the chart.

'Very well.' Drinkwater studied the face of the master. 'What the deuce d'you make of it, Mr Hill, eh? Do we sit here and stop neutrals or d'you fancy a spar with Johnny Crapaud?'

Hill grinned. 'I don't understand, sir.'

'Would to God that I did,' said Drinkwater, 'but Straton came off to see me again before we left Carlscrona. He told me his instructions from London, just arrived, are to urge King Gustavus to reinforce his troops in Rügen and Stralsund . . .' Drinkwater laid his finger on the chart. 'Gustavus insists our subsidies are too small and wants British troops to help him. The problem seems to be that if London sends troops, Gustavus insists on commanding them personally.'

'Good God,' Hill chuckled, 'then he's as mad as they say!'

'Yes. But that ain't all. There's a considerable faction at his court which is pro-French and wants reform. In short, the threat of a revolution is simmering in Sweden.'

'What a mess!'

'My head aches with the complexity of it all.' Drinkwater looked up and, catching Hill's eye, appeared to make up his mind. 'Damn it, we can't dither like this, Hill. We're like a couple of old women! The men are spoiling for a fight . . .' He bent over the chart and Hill leaned over with him. Drinkwater's finger traced a strait of water between the island of Rügen and the mainland where it ran past the engraved outline of the town of Stralsund.

'Let's see what is to be done against Marshal Mortier.'

'Beg pardon, sir . . .'

Fraser turned at the waft of malodorous breath. The obscenely grinning features of Skeete, Lallo's elderly loblolly boy, were thrust expectantly into his face.

'Skeete, what the de'il d'you want on the upper deck?'

'Mr Lallo's compliments, sir, and would you step down to the first lieutenant's cabin.'

'The first lieutenant?'

'Mr Rogers, sir.'

'I know fine well who the first lieutenant is, damn your insolence.'

'Aye, aye, sir.' Nothing seemed to wipe the grin from Skeete's face. He had been too long an intimate with death not to find most situations in life full of morbid amusement. He followed Lieutenant Fraser below.

The door to Rogers's cabin swung ajar with the roll of the ship and from inside Lallo beckoned him. The surgeon closed the door against Skeete. After the upper deck the cabin was dark, the air stale and for a second he did not see the trussed figure of Rogers lying in the cot. His dislike of Rogers had not encouraged him to enquire too eagerly into the nature of the first lieutenant's 'indisposition'.

As his eyes focused he saw a pale face, the hollow cheeks slashed by the cruel line of the gag, and was unable to master an over-riding feeling of revulsion at the harshness of the surgeon's treatment.

'Dear God, Lallo, take that thing off him!'

'I cannot, Mr Fraser . . . the captain . . .'

'The captain did not tell you to gag him. Take it off, I say.' Fraser leaned forward and began to fumble.

'No, sir! Don't, I beg you!' Lallo put out his hands to prevent Fraser's loosening of the gag. 'I asked for you to come down in the hope that you might help . . .'

'Sweet Jesu, Lallo, how much of all this does the captain know?' Unable to get the gag off, Fraser gestured round the tiny cabin.

'Look, Mr Fraser, I have no mind to confine him a moment longer than I have to . . .'

'Then let him out of that . . .'

'For God's sake, sir, do me the favour of listening,' hissed Lallo, suddenly very angry. 'I have twenty-eight men on the sick list and cannot mollycoddle one who's over-fond of the bottle. There are the usual bruises and ruptures, three consumptives, an outbreak of the flux, a man with gravel and one with a paraphimosis, plus the usual clutch with clap. Rogers can only be treated by Procrustean methods and I'm damned if I'm prepared to have *you* interfere like this!'

'Away with your blather, man! What the de'il d'ye want with me then?'

'I do want your assistance to enable me to get him out of that thing as fast as possible.'

Now that his active participation was required Fraser was suddenly cautious.

'In what way?' Fraser looked at the first lieutenant, whose eyes seemed unnaturally large and held his own in a glare of intensity.

'I am prepared to release him today, but if I do I need you to stand surety for me.'

'Why me?'

'Because,' said Lallo, a note of weary contempt entering his voice, 'you are the next senior lieutenant and I am concerned that he may attempt to revenge himself.' Lallo spoke as though Rogers was not there, but his worry was clear enough to Fraser.

'Look, Mr Lallo, if the captain ordered you to confine the first lieutenant, why must you drag me into the imbroglio?'

'The captain didn't order me to truss him up.'

'He didn't? But you just claimed he did!'

'No, he ordered me to keep the first lieutenant quiet for a day or two . . . Mr Fraser, where the hell are you going?'

But Fraser had gone. Uncertain of the correct course of action, he thought it proper to inform Captain Drinkwater. Much though he disliked Lieutenant Rogers, the thought of a man of Lallo's stamp having the power to truss up a commissioned officer like a pullet appalled him.

Lallo shook his head over his patient. 'Another young pipsqueak with all the answers, Mr Rogers,' he said, putting the palm of his hand on the lieutenant's sweating forehead, 'and I thought we might have you quietly out of there today.'

Fraser found the captain poring over Mount's atlas and the charts spread out on the cabin table.

'Ah, Mr Fraser, and what brings you rushing in here?' Drinkwater asked, looking up.

'It's the first lieutenant, sir. The damned surgeon has him trussed like a lunatic!'

Drinkwater frowned. It was in his mind to enquire how Fraser had come by this knowledge, but he knew it had been a vain hope to expect the confinement of the first lieutenant to be kept a secret. He recollected he had given Lallo a free hand and had thought the surgeon would have used the powerfully sedative properties of laudanum, but, on reflection, that was Lallo's business.

'Mr Fraser, you are a young man. Your outrage does you credit but I am sure that Mr Lallo was only being cruel to be kind. What was your business in the matter?'

'The surgeon sent for me . . .'

'The devil he did!' Drinkwater snapped. So Lallo had deliberately involved Fraser in direct contravention of his own instructions. 'To what end?' he enquired coldly.

'To stand guarantee for Rogers's good behaviour.'

Drinkwater frowned and felt the sense of affront drain out of him. He had, he realised, been unreasonable in expecting Lallo to work a miracle in secret. Rogers presented them with a problem that only proved their woeful inadequacy to deal with such things. He sighed. 'Well, Mr Fraser,' he said wearily, his thoughts drifting back to the plan formulating in his mind, 'you are the next senior lieutenant. Hadn't you better heed the surgeon?'

'But sir, he's no' a man of much sensibility.'

Drinkwater looked up sharply. 'What the devil d'you mean by that? That he ain't got a commission like yourself? By God, Mr Fraser, you surprise me! Mr Lallo's a professional officer holding a warrant as surgeon, just as Hill holds one as master. Your own status as a gentleman of honour does not entitle you to make such social distinctions among persons of ability! You seem an able and active enough fellow but I'll have none of that damnable cant aboard here! You may save that for the pump-room or Lord Keith's with-drawing room, but not here, sir, not here!'

The unexpected onslaught from the captain took Fraser aback. His face was white and his mouth hung open. Drinkwater cast another look at the papers spread out before him and then up again at the hapless young officer. 'Very well, Mr Fraser; I am aware there is a growing fashion among young men of breeding to consider these matters of some importance, and that may well be the case ashore. However I suggest you might see Lallo at his true worth were a ball to shatter your thigh. Now cut along and pass word to him to get Rogers up here at once.'

Only the direct summons to the captain's cabin prevented the outbreak of rage the surgeon feared from a freshly released Rogers. Pale from his confinement, Rogers entered the cabin and stood menacingly close to Drinkwater, his mouth a hard line, his eyes glittering.

Drinkwater, sensitive to Rogers's fury, ignored it and, after a brief look at the first lieutenant, stared down at the maps and charts.

'Mr Rogers,' he said levelly, 'you're better, I understand. Now I have it in mind to employ you . . .'

'Do you mean to pretend that nothing has happened?' Rogers's voice was strangled as he sought to control himself. 'I have been bound and gagged, you heartless . . .'

Drinkwater looked up, his own eyes blazing. 'What would you have me do? Eh? If I wished, Sam, you'd be going home for a court martial for that remark alone! What was done was done for your own good, and you know it. Lallo says you're over the worst. Hold off the drink for a month and your victory is complete. If I pretend that you've had the flux that's my own business. What would you have me write in the Sick Book?'

Rogers opened his mouth and then shut it again.

'Look,' persisted Drinkwater, 'I'm meditating an attack on the French here. You lead it. Take the post of honour. It's an opportunity. God knows it's one you can't afford to pass up.'

'Opportunity,' Rogers's voice became almost wistful, 'I haven't had an opportunity . . .'

'Well, enough's said then. Come, this will be a boat attack. We are crossing the Greifswalder Bight and will anchor somewhere here, work our way into the strait as far as we can. Then you take all the boats, the marines and a hundred-odd seamen and press an attack against the French lines around Stralsund; do what damage you can and come off again before Johnny Crapaud knows what's

70

hit him. Just the very thing for you. Get you a mention in the *Gazette*.'

Drinkwater smiled encouragingly and met Rogers's eyes. The confusion of the man was plain to be seen. 'A perfect opportunity, Sam.'

6 A Perfect Opportunity

May 1807

'Well, gentlemen,' said Drinkwater, glancing round at the assembled officers, 'when the sun gets high enough to burn off this mist I think we might find some amusement for the hands today.' He kept his tone buoyant. The awkwardness of the officers in Rogers's presence was obvious. The poor fellow was being treated like a leper. A single glance at his face told Drinkwater that Rogers's torments were not yet over. He could only guess at the remarks that had been passed at every mess in the ship: from the gunroom to the cockpit, from the marines' mess to the ratings messing on the berth deck, the scuttlebutt would have been exclusively about the first lieutenant and his mysterious illness. Drinkwater hoped the action today would give them all something else to talk about and, more important, make them act as a ship's company.

Antigone lay on a sea as smooth as a grey mirror in the twilight of the dawn. In the distance, scarcely discernible, a reedy margin could be seen dividing sea and sky. From time to time the quack of ducks came from the misty water's edge.

'From what information we have gleaned,' Drinkwater resumed, 'Mr Hill and I estimate that the French siege lines are no more than about five miles from the ship. They are investing the Swedish town of Stralsund but at present a state of truce exists between Marshal Mortier, commanding the French, and the garrison of Stralsund. No such armistice exists between ourselves and the French, however, while anything we might do to provoke more activity on the part of the Swedes can only be of benefit to the Alliance. So we intend to annoy the French by mounting a boat attack on their lines wherever opportunity offers. The mist offers you good cover for your approach.' He smiled again and felt the mood changing. The officers' preoccupation with the restitution of Rogers was diminishing: fear and excitement were stirring them now. He had only one more thing to say to complete the shift in their thinking.

'Mr Rogers will command the expedition in the launch.' He paused, measuring the effect of his words. Disappointment was plain on Fraser's face, but he ignored it and went on. 'Now, gentlemen, I think you had better break your fasts.' They trooped below and Drinkwater added, 'Perhaps, Sam, you would join me in my cabin.'

In the gunroom, as the burgoo was cleared away and the toast and coffee spread its crumbs and ring-stains upon the less-than-clean table-cloth, the officers deliberated over the coming day.

'Don't look so damned *bereaved*, Wullie,' said Mount, impishly aping Fraser's accent. 'You couldn't expect the Old Man to have done anything else.'

'It's all right for you and your leathernecks,' grumbled Fraser, irritated by Mount's eagerness at the prospect of action, 'you're just itching to get at the enemy. At least you've something to do.'

'So have you.' Mount took up a piece of toast and regarded it with some interest. 'D'you know this looks quite palatable, damned if it don't.'

'Just a bloody boat-minder . . .'

'You might get an opportunity to distinguish yourself,' put in James Quilhampton, pouring himself more coffee. 'I can tell you that poor Rogers will be looking for an opportunity to cover himself with glory.'

'Rogers?'

Quilhampton looked at the second lieutenant. 'You haven't known him as long as I have, Willie. He might be an old soak, but he's no coward.'

'Ah,' said Mount, 'but if he leads, will the men follow?'

The question and the doubt associated with it hung over the table, stirring the cold and personal apprehensions that forgathered before action. Quilhampton shrugged the shadow off first. Like Rogers he too awaited his 'opportunity' and his youth was easily convinced it might be soon. He stood up, his chair scraping in the silence.

73

'Mount,' he said lightly, 'you rumble like a bad attack of borborygmus.'

'Thank you, my young and insolent friend. I suppose I could prescribe myself the carminative of being proved right.'

'I hope you're damn well not,' said Fraser, obviously getting over his pique, 'I haven't written my will this commission.'

'I didn't know you had anything to leave behind you,' laughed Mount.

Fraser made a face, wiped his mouth and looked up. Lord Walmsley stood in the gunroom door.

'What do you want?'

'Mr Hill's compliments, gentlemen,' said Walmsley in his easy manner, 'but the mist's beginning to clear, the first lieutenant is making the dispositions for the boats and the captain's going aloft. Mr Hill is also awaiting the opportunity to come below and have his breakfast.'

'Oh! Damn me, I forgot.' Quilhampton shoved his chair in and reached for his hat and sword. Fumbling with the belt as he made for the door he shouted over his shoulder to the negro messman, 'King! Be a good fellow and bring my pistols on deck!'

In the main-top Drinkwater trained his glass carefully, anxious not to miss the slightest detail emerging from the upper limit of the mist as it hung low over the marshy shore. From their landfall at Cape Arcona they had sailed round the east coast of the island of Rügen, across the mouth of Sassnitz Bay where the Swedish fleet lay at anchor, and round into the Greifswalder Bight. Yesterday they had worked patiently westwards, towards the narrow strait that separated Rügen from the Pomeranian mainland. With a man in the chains calling the soundings they had manoeuvred *Antigone* as far into the strait as wind and daylight permitted, and learned of the state of truce between the Swedes and French from a Swedish guard-boat. As daylight finally faded, and with it the breeze, they had fetched their anchor.

Above the mist, the rising sun behind Drinkwater picked out tiny reflections ahead: the pale gold of a church spire, a sudden flash as a distant window was opened. It was curious how he could see these details twelve miles away, while closer-to there was nothing to see beyond the rounded shapes of tree-tops, elms he thought, and some willows lower down; but that was all that emerged from the nacreous vapour that hung over the water margin. An observer in one of those trees would be able to see *Antigone*'s masts and spars above the mist, while her hull, with its rows of cannon, was invisible. Not that he thought for a moment they had been observed, and the presence of the Swedish fleet in Sassnitz Bay had persuaded him that by flying Swedish colours he would be perfectly disguised.

He heard a distant trumpet and a drum beat, staccato and oddly clear as it rolled over the water, its rat-a-tat-tat mustering Mortier's corps to morning parade. Drinkwater pondered the wisdom of his proposed attack. It was to be made on slender intelligence and he knew his intention had far more to do with the state of his command than any real damage he would inflict upon the enemy. Somehow the unreality was emphasised by the mist and it seemed that the only real danger lay below him in that unhappy relationship between Lieutenant Rogers and the people.

Drinkwater had taken Rogers as his first lieutenant out of pity, knowing him for a dogged fighter and competent seaman. But drink and disappointment had soured the man, and although Drinkwater curbed Rogers's excesses, in his everyday behaviour he had given ample cause for offence and grievance among the hands. He received their daily petitions with an unpleasant contempt, used an unnecessary degree of foul language towards them and provoked a general grumbling. Drinkwater's reluctance to flog was a liberality Rogers disapproved of and which seemed to provoke him to greater unpleasantness towards men whom the iron rule of naval discipline held in a state of thrall.

It was clearly a situation that could not go on. A boat attack under Rogers, Drinkwater had reasoned, gave them all a chance to wipe the slate clean; or at least as good a chance as men in their circumstances were likely to get.

Drinkwater felt the mast jerk and looked down into the waist. Wraiths of mist trailed across the deck but he could clearly see the ordered lines of men straining at the tackles as they lifted the heavy launch off the booms and began to transfer its weight from the stay to the yard tackles. He watched the boat lifted outboard and then lowered into the water. Drinkwater pocketed compass and glass, swung himself over the edge of the top and felt for the futtocks with his feet.

As he jumped down onto the deck, Rogers, Fraser and Quilhampton were telling the men off into the waiting boats. Marines filed along the deck, their muskets slung over their shoulders. Together with the seamen being armed with cutlasses and tomahawks at the main-mast, they scrambled down the nets hung over the ship's side and into their allocated places in the boats.

Drinkwater crossed the deck to where Rogers was stuffing loaded pistols into his waistband. He smiled encouragingly. 'Good luck, Mr Rogers,' he said formally.

Rogers nodded his acknowledgement and paused, as though to say something. But he seemed to think better of it, murmured 'Aye, aye, sir,' and slung a leg over the rail.

'It's up to you, Sam,' persisted Drinkwater, 'you and those men down there.'

Their eyes met and both knew what the other thought.

Then Rogers had gone, and a few minutes later the boats had vanished in the mist.

Lieutenant Rogers, his hand on the tiller of the launch, cocked one eye on the boat-compass at his feet and stole occasional glances at the faint line in the mist that marked the Rügen shore. The surface of the water was as smooth as glass, disturbed only by the concentric and ever expanding rings that marked the progress of the oar blades as they propelled the boats along. Rogers led in the launch followed by Quilhampton in the red cutter, Lord Walmsley in the blue and Lieutenant Fraser in the barge.

Rogers was seconded by Mount and Midshipman Frey, and it was Mount's marines that made up the bulk of the launch's crew, apart from the oarsmen. In the boat's bow, mounted on its slide, a 12-pounder carronade was being fussed over by a gunner's mate.

The boats pulled on in comparative silence, moving in a world that seemed devoid of time or distance, so disorienting was the mist. It hung heavily, close to the water, discouraging speech, so that the only noises were the laboured breathing of the oarsmen, the dull regular knocking of oar looms against thole pins and the dip and splash of the oar blades. Under the bow of each boat a chuckling of water showed as they pulled on for mile after mile. After two and a half hours Rogers drew out his watch and consulted his chart. Then he stood in the stern of the boat and waved the others up alongside. The boats glided together, their oars trailing, their men panting over the looms, dark stains of sweat on the backs of their shirts.

'By my reckoning we must be bloody close to the French lines,' hissed Rogers. 'We'll move across the channel to the mainland side. If we sight a decent target we land and do our worst. Now you buggers keep in close contact, I'll give the order to attack. Understand?'

There was a general nodding of heads.

'Very well. Get your lobsters to fix bayonets, Mr Mount.'

Mount gave the order and the whispering hiss and click of the lethal weapons was accompanied by a sudden twinkling of reflected sunlight from the silver blades.

'There's a bit o' breeze coming up,' observed Fraser and, for the first time, dark, ruffled patches appeared on the water. The heat of the sun was warming the marshes and water meadows on either side of the strait, the rising air sucked in the sea-breeze, a strengthening zephyr which began to disperse the mist in patches.

'Very well, keep your eyes open then.' Rogers waved the boats onward. The oars began to swing again and the boats resumed their passage.

Rogers stared into the mist ahead. He felt the public shame of his recent humiliation like a wound and could still only half comprehend why Drinkwater had sanctioned Lallo's treatment. But he was pragmatist enough to know that, if nothing else, his future hung upon the day's events. He had under his command the greater part of the ship's marines and a large detachment of seamen. He was seconded by most of the officers and had left the frigate almost without boats. What was more, he was alone in a mist and was determined, at any cost, to make an impression upon the enemy. His mouth set in a grim line and, as he looked forward, the eyes of the men tugging at the oars avoided his own. Well, that was as it should be. He was the first lieutenant again, and by heaven they would feel his wrath if they did not do their utmost to secure him a paragraph in the Gazette!

'Boat, sir! Starboard bow!'

Rogers jerked from his introspection and looked to starboard. At the same instant a challenge rang out. A large boat, pulling a dozen oars a side with a huge-muzzled cannon in her bow and the blue and gold of Sweden lifting languidly over her stern, loomed out of the mist. It was a 'gunsloop' rowing guard in the supposedly neutral water of the strait.

Rogers swore and pulled the tiller over, turning to watch the other boats follow in his wake, and headed more directly for the southern bank. Astern he heard shouting and the splash of oars holding water, turning the big gunsloop after them. But after five minutes, despite the gradual dispersal of the mist, they had lost the Swedish boat.

A few minutes later the grey margin of Pomerania was visible ahead and then on the larboard beam as Rogers straightened their course parallel to it. A few cows, brindled black and white, stood hock-deep in the lush grass that swept down to the water. Ruminating gently they stared at the passing boats.

The appearance of the guard-boat had galvanised the oarsmen. Before, the stroke had been that leisurely and easy swing that a practised oarsman could keep up for hours, now the men tugged at their oars and the boats began to leap through the water. Then, quite suddenly, the mist lifted and at the same instant Rogers saw the means of realising his long awaited 'opportunity'.

'By God, Mount!' he said in a low and excited tone. 'See there, ahead! A whole bloody battery with its back to us!'

Ahead of them a sudden bend in the channel brought the Pomeranian shore much closer. A small, low bluff formed a natural feature, a patch of beaten earth which the French had taken advantage of and on it constructed a demi-lune with an earthen rampart reinforced by fascines and gabions. The rampart was pierced by crude embrasures and in each, facing away from the approaching boats towards the town of Stralsund, were eight huge siege guns and a pair of howitzers. A smaller field piece faced across the strait and commanded any approach from Rügen. In quieter times the little bluff had been used as a quay, for behind the battery was a small inlet, the estuary of a stream that wound, willow-lined, inland towards a village. The edge of the inlet was piled with rotten wood staithing from which local peasants had shipped their hay and other produce to the markets of Stralsund. It took but an instant for Rogers to perceive that the inlet and quay gave direct and undefended access to the rear of the battery.

He was standing now and he commanded his oarsmen to pull with greater vigour. Behind him the officers in the other boats had also seen the enemy position and acknowledged his frantic wave.

'Make ready, men,' said Mount quietly beside him.

Rogers looked again at the battery. He could see a pair of artillery-men, each carrying a bucket and wearing fatigues, walking slowly across the beaten earth of the compound. A group of men were gathered round one gun intent upon some task or another and one further man was lounging on the rampart, staring in the direction of Stralsund. Rogers could see quite clearly the puffs of smoke from the indolent sentry's pipe.

'We've got 'em, by God, Mount! The buggers are as good as asleep!'

Rogers put the tiller over and the launch swung in towards the inlet and the quay. He could not believe his luck. 'Come on you lubbers! *Pull!*'

'We are pulling . . .' someone muttered and Rogers's eyes narrowed and he scanned the boat for the insolent seaman. Perhaps he would have taken the matter further but at that instant emerging from the mist astern of them, the Swedish gunsloop hailed them. The cry made the sentry turn. He jerked upright and then began to shout, a hoarse bellow of surprise and alarm. The gunners carrying the buckets dropped them and ran; the group round the siege gun turned and ran also. More men were shouting and appearing from somewhere. Rogers was vaguely aware of trees, horse-lines and a row of limbers, ammunition-boxes and shot piles.

The sight of red coats and the glint of sunshine on bayonets swiftly raised the alarm. Even as the launch closed the last few yards to the quay the French artillerymen were dropping to one knee and levelling muskets fetched from the arms stacks.

'That gun ready?' roared Rogers at his gunner's mate forward.

'Aye, sir!'

'Then clear those bastards out of our way!'

The launch jerked and the carronade roared, recoiling up its slide and flinging its reek back over the gasping oarsmen. The marines were fidgeting and Mount was standing beside Rogers. Most of the canister splattered against the wooden piling, but sufficient balls raked the compound to knock down three or four of the defenders.

'That's the way!' yelled Rogers, drawing his sword.

The next moment the launch bumped alongside the staithe and, as the oarsmen dragged their oars inboard, Rogers leaped from thwart to thwart, closely followed by Mount. Rocking violently the launch spewed its cargo of marines onto the quay as the other boats arrived and more and more men poured ashore.

There were far more soldiers in the demi-lune than had at first been apparent. Hidden by the willows were the bivouacs of the eighty gunners that made up the complement of the battery. They were forming into a rough line, led by a pair of officers on foot. Behind them another officer was struggling into the saddle of a trace-horse.

'Drop that man!' Rogers screamed to Mount, pointing.

Mount turned to a marine who was already levelling his musket, but the shot missed and the officer escaped down a lane that ran alongside the little stream.

'Form line, platoon fire!' Mount was drawing up his men and they began to fire volleys at the enemy. Behind the marines the seamen milled, those of them who had been rowing still getting their breath back.

'Rush the bastards!' roared Rogers impetuously, waving his sword at the other lieutenants, but Mount ignored him. He was advancing his line of marines platoon by platoon.

'Come on, lads, charge them!' Rogers began to run, leading his men through the line of marines.

'Hold on, Rogers!' Mount shouted as the first lieutenant began to block his field of fire, but there was no stopping him. Only a few of the seamen had followed Rogers and there were murmurs among the others, murmurs that, overheard on board, would have earned their makers a dozen at the grating.

'Let the bastard go!'

'Hope he gets a ball in his brain-pan . . .'

'Better his balls . . .'

'Good riddance to him . . .'

Mount stood for a second, furious, and behind him Quilhampton suddenly divined the intentions of some of the men.

'Come on, Mount! Forward! Bayonets!'

'Bayonet charge!' bawled Mount as the artillerymen, taking advantage of the brief pause in the attack, loosed off a well timed volley. Several of the marines dropped, but Rogers, twenty yards from the French, was untouched.

'The devil looks after his own . . .'

They were all running forward now, marines and seamen mixed together, all mad with blood-lust and tripping over their fallen comrades. Then suddenly they clashed with the enemy. The fighting became hand to hand. The artillerymen dropped their muskets and lugged out short swords which each man had slung on a baldric over his shoulder. They were old faces, almost faces they knew, dark with campaigning, slashed by scars, as moustached as their attackers were clean-shaven. They grunted, swore, cut, thrust, killed and died as well as their opponents, but they fell back under the onslaught, out-numbered by the British who fought with a maddened ferocity. For a few blessed moments they were free of shipboard constraints and could swear and stab and hack at anything that stood in their path. With every slash and lunge they paid back the cheating of the purser, the heartlessness of the bosun's mates, the injustice of the lash and the venality of the Dockyard commissioners. In the merciless killing they found outlets for their repressed passions and frustrated desires. It was not the enforcers of Napoleon's Continental System that they killed, but the mere surrogates for the rottenness in their own.

Lieutenant Quilhampton knew this and kept his wits about him. He had heard of men shooting their own officers in the heat of battle and kept a weather eye on Rogers. He did not fear for himself, for the constraints of naval discipline, once they had been laid upon a man, could never be entirely thrown off, even under such circumstances. Intuition told him he was perfectly safe, for he had long ago learned the wisdom of consideration and justice towards the men in his own division. But Rogers was at risk although he seemed safe now, surrounded by Mount and his marines as they swept the last of the gunners out of the battery at the point of the bayonet. The British did not pursue beyond the limit of the rampart. A few of the marines got up on the rough parapet and took pot-shots at the retreating Frenchmen as they ran stumbling over the tussocks of grass and boggy marshland of the water meadows beyond.

'Keep an eye on 'em, Mount. That bloody officer will have gone for reinforcements!'

'Very well!'

All around men panted for their breath. The dead and wounded lay in heaps, their blood soaking darkly into the dry earth. Little Frey with his toy dirk was trying to bandage a cut arm. Other men were attending to the wounded.

'Tom's lost his bonus, then,' said one man, staring down at a dead messmate. Quilhampton recalled the bonus Drinkwater had promised the men.

'You lads start getting the wounded back to the boats now.'

'Aye, aye, sir.'

Rogers was still bawling orders.

'Mr Fraser, bring a party over here! You too, Mr Q! I want those three limbers over to the guns. We'll blow the wheels off! And see here, these Frog bayonets are thinner than ours. You, Walmsley and Frey, gather 'em up and stick 'em in the touch-holes of these guns. Look . . .'

Rogers picked up a French bayonet and stabbed it downwards, into the touch-hole in the breech of the nearest gun. Then he jerked his hand sideways and the narrow blade snapped, leaving the hole neatly blocked. 'See, that should fuck 'em up for a while . . . and stuff those shell carcasses under the guns and they'll blow the whole bloody shebang to kingdom come.'

Officers, marines, midshipmen and men ran about at his bidding, fetching and carrying. Kegs of powder, shell cases and combustibles were placed under each of the siege guns. The field gun close to the strait was rolled into the water and every gun was rendered at least temporarily useless by spiking.

At the height of this activity a strange officer was seen walking slowly across the open space behind the guns. Everyone had forgotten the Swedish gunsloop.

'Excuse . . . you are British, yes? I must protest very much. There is no fighting . . . truce, between the forces of His Majesty King Gustavus and the army under Marshal Mortier.' He approached Rogers who, from his activity and lively direction of affairs, was clearly the senior officer.

'Will you get out of my way . . . hey, you! More powder over here . . . no, no, a keg if you've got one . . .'

'You must not fight . . . not break the truce . . .'

'Will you get out of my way?' Rogers turned on the Swedish officer who suddenly understood he was being rebuffed and drew himself up.

'I am a Swedish officer.'

'I don't give a damn if you're the Grand Turk, fuck off!' snarled Rogers, shoving the Swede aside. The man spun round and reached for his sword, as angry as Rogers.

Quilhampton hurried up. 'Come sir,' he said civilly to the Swede, 'I know you have a truce with the French, but regrettably we do not. I am sure you understand that we mean no offence to yourself.'

The Swedish officer looked down at his sleeve. The point of the iron hook that this tall, gangling English officer wore in the place of a left hand had caught in the fabric of his uniform. It was covered in blood.

Shrugging his shoulders he allowed himself to be led away with as much dignity as he could muster. Quilhampton had hardly seen the intruder into his boat than another crisis occurred. On the rampart a sudden shout from Mount brought both the first lieutenant and Quilhampton running across the compound. Flinging themselves down on the earth beside him, they followed the marine officer's pointing finger.

Jogging towards them, their pennons gay in the sunshine, was a squadron of lancers.

'Jesus Christ!' whispered Rogers and a thrill of pure fear ran through the three men. The thought of being speared by one of those lances was hideous.

'I think it's time for a tactical withdrawal . . .'

'Get your men back to the boats to cover us, Mount,' snapped Rogers.

'I can keep some here and pick a few of those fellows off . . .'

'Do as you're fucking well told!'

'Very well.'

'Mr Q, get the men back in the boats, load up the carronade, tell Fraser . . . where the hell is he?'

'I don't know but I'll find him.'

Rogers ran across the open space. 'Hey, Walmsley, get that last powder keg and lay a trail back towards the boats. Make sure no stupid turd runs in it . . .'

'Aye, aye, sir.' Lord Walmsley picked up a keg and knocked out the bung. He bent over and scuttered backwards, spreading a liberal trail across the earth. 'Mind your confounded feet, damn you!' he shouted at some marines.

'Into the boats, you men!' Quilhampton was shouting at the seamen. 'Get to your oars!'

'They're coming!' Mount was yelling, running back from the rampart. 'One volley, sergeant,' he called, 'then tumble into the boats as quick as you can!'

'Sah!' Sergeant Blixoe lined his men up. 'Steady now, lads. Take partiklar aim and shoot the lubbers' horses in the chest . . . make ready . . .'

The boats were a confusion of legs and oar looms as men tried to sort themselves out. They were stumbling on the wounded whose shrieks and curses lent a nightmare panic to the scene. Somehow the word had spread that they were about to be ridden down by lancers. Round shot and cutlass slashes were one thing. Lances and horses quite another.

Walmsley's powder trail had stopped several yards short of the quay. Rogers stood over him as he tipped the last of the powder out of the keg. 'Get to the launch. Back it off the quay and point the carronade ashore. Leave your cutter alongside for me.' Rogers drew a pistol from his waistband and looked quickly round him. He could feel the earth shaking under the advancing hooves of the horses.

'Get down, Rogers, let me fire over your head,' Mount was shouting at him.

'Damn you, be silent! Fire and get your men in the boats.'

A wild and magnificent feeling swept over Rogers. He stood alone in the middle of the enclosed space. Behind him the boats were full of men and the edge of the quay was lined with Mount's marines, their muskets pointing at the end of the rampart where the little track wound round the battery's defences. All eyes were on him. The humiliation of his confinement, the long-standing and corrosive effects of disappointment and missed opportunity seemed to coalesce in one moment of sublime defiance. Like the men, action had given Lieutenant Rogers the means of defying the system whose injustices had tormented him in proportion to his rank. He was filled with a hysterical disregard for the danger he was in.

The cavalry swept into the battery. Confined to a narrow front of six or seven horses they spread out, their red and white lance pennons lowering. They were in green, wearing tall crested brass helmets, and their horses snorted and plunged as they advanced across the compound.

'Fire!' yelled Mount and then waved his men backwards. A cutter pushed off, so did the barge.

'Come on, sir!' yelled Quilhampton.

Rogers turned. 'Fire that boat gun!' he roared as though bawling out the topmen in a gale. The lancers came on, only yards separating them from Rogers. Mount's men had only succeeded in knocking over one horse, so distracted had they been by the defiant spectacle of Lieutenant Rogers.

'What is the silly bastard *doing*?' agonised Mount as he turned and watched from the safety of a boat.

'Bein' a fuckin' hero, sir,' a man muttered.

'Gettin' 'is name fair an' square in the *Gazette*,' said another, but Mount ignored them.

In the launch the gunner's mate jerked the lanyard of the carronade. Full of men aft and backed off from the quay, the gun took better effect than it had when they had made their approach. The canister tore through the cavalry and threw back three lancers who were within feet of Rogers.

'It's bloody unbelievable,' muttered Mount, half in admiration of the madness being displayed by an apparently fearless Mr Rogers. As if knowing the three men who most nearly threatened his life would be blown away by the shot from the carronade, Rogers bent over the pile of powder, levelled the cocked pistol and pulled the trigger. The spark landed on the powder, grew dim and then suddenly the powder trail took fire. There was a brief searing light but Rogers felt nothing from the burn on his hand. He stood for a second staring at the leaping flame and then seemed aware of the danger round him. He dodged the next lancer who was trying to rein in his horse as he approached the edge of the quay. Rogers ran for the cutter, bending low as the marines stood in the boats and fired over his head. Behind him the powder fired and sputtered and the horses jibbed at the demon under their hooves. There were shouts and plunging horses and then the launch carronade got off another shot. Rogers leapt for the cutter which backed swiftly off the quay.

The cheated cavalrymen were pulling their horses up at the edge of the water. An officer had jumped off his horse and was trying to stamp out the burning train. Some of his men had slung their lances and were levelling their carbines. The little sputter of flame could no longer be seen. Perhaps it no longer threaded its way over that patch of beaten earth.

The shouts and popping of carbine and musket were suddenly eclipsed by the deafening roar which broke into several subsidiary explosions as limbers and carcasses and powder kegs took fire. The redoubt was suddenly transformed into a lethal rocketing of wood, iron and flame among which horses reared in terror and men fell amid the stamping of hooves. Heavy axle-trees, wheels and spokes, even the massive barrels of the cannon themselves were hurled into the air. Pieces of shell-case whistled into the blue sky, then the boats were being showered by black debris which fell into the water alongside them with a hiss.

The boats were swinging into the channel now, the men settling into the rhythm of the long pull back to the ship. They swept past the Swedish gunsloop and Rogers stood and raised his hat in a gesture of arrogant and exaggerated courtesy.

'Bye the bye,' he said to no one in particular as he sat down again, 'did any of you fellows catch a glimpse of Stralsund?'

7   Nielsen

June 1807

Drinkwater sat in his cabin in a happier frame of mind than he had enjoyed for weeks. Although the butcher's bill for the boat action was heavier than anticipated, there was no doubt that the attack had been a success. The real damage to Marshal Mortier's Army Corps was not great, but the unexpected destruction of a battery showed the long arm of the British Admiralty, and could not fail to have its effect upon the general morale of the French corps.

There had been a little necessary diplomacy at the protest they had received from a Swedish officer who had come on board as *Antigone* entered Sassnitz Bay; but it had been passed off easily enough with a glass or two. Most important to Drinkwater was the effect the action had had upon Rogers and the people. He had heard several versions of the affair and gathered that a sneaking admiration had been aroused for Rogers, on account of his coolness under attack. It was undoubtedly only a temporary lull in the hostility between the lower deck and the first lieutenant, but it was a lull nevertheless, and Drinkwater was relieved to see that Rogers himself seemed to have recovered some of his old self-possession.

But it was not merely the raising of the morale of his own ship's company that occasioned Drinkwater his present good humour. On their return to Sassnitz Bay and the Swedish fleet, they had found a flying squadron of British frigates. Supposing at first that he was to place himself under the orders of the senior captain, Drinkwater found to his delight that special orders awaited him. Taking the opportunity to send mails home, including a highly laudatory report on the affair before Stralsund, he had hurried back to

Antigone to digest the import of his written instructions. It was clear that Horne of the *Pegasus* was somewhat jealous of Drinkwater's independence and had wished to include *Antigone* in his flying squadron.

'You seem to enjoy a kind of privilege,' Horne had lisped. 'I have to give you written orders of your own.' Reluctance was written plain on the man's face and even discernible in the way he handed over the sealed package.

'The forward berth ain't always the most pleasant,' Drinkwater replied, happy to escape from the constraints of serving under someone young enough to be his son. Horne would be a rear-admiral by the time he reached Drinkwater's age, but that was not Drinkwater's concern at the moment; he was more interested in the other news newly arrived at Sassnitz Bay.

'I heard one of your officers mention Dantzig when I came aboard,' he prompted.

'Dantzig? Oh, damn me yes, the place has fallen to the French.'

It seemed inevitable that, failing a major Russian victory, the French would mop up the resistance in their rear. Making his excuses as early as he could, Drinkwater had returned to *Antigone*, set a course to the eastward and retired to his cabin to open the package Horne had given him. Slitting the fouled anchor seal of the Admiralty Office, he unfolded the papers and began to read.

His instructions from Mr Barrow, Second Secretary at the Admiralty, were a mere repeat of those he had left the Nore with. The same stock phrases: *You are requested and required to cruise against the enemy . . . to examine all vessels and in particular those of neutral nations . . . detaining those whose cargo is of advantage to the enemy . . .* and so on. In short, there was nothing to suggest that he had earned Horne's envy or that his 'independence' had much advantage to it. But appended to Mr Barrow's formal instructions was another letter, similarly sealed but not signed by the Admiralty's civil administrator; this document bore the scrawled and familiar name of the Director of the Secret Department. It was brief and undated, typical of the writer's economy of style when using plain English.

*

My dear Drinkwater,

    Until you are able to ascertain the outcome of military opera-
tions in East Prussia, you are to cruise to the eastward of the Gulf
of Dantzig and inform London the instant you learn anything of
significance. You should afford any assistance required by persons
operating on the instructions of this Department.

Yours & c
Dungarth

Drinkwater laid the letter down and turned his chair to stare through
the stern windows and watch *Antigone*'s furrowing wake, where the
sea swirled green and white from under the frigate's stern. He saw
nothing of the gulls dipping in the marbled water; his mind was
turned inwards, contemplating the full implication behind
Dungarth's instruction, and it seemed that his independence was no
coincidence. That last sentence, that he should afford assistance to
persons operating on the instructions of Lord Dungarth's Secret
Department, was a clear order. And both Dungarth and Drinkwater
knew that one of those 'persons' was Drinkwater's own brother,
Edward. Drinkwater's frigate was cruising independently for reasons beyond the arbitrary processes of normal Admiralty planning.
Dungarth knew that Drinkwater was the one post-captain on the
Navy List who would take more than a passing interest in 'persons
operating on the instructions of this Department' in East Prussia,
where the Tsar's armies were in the field.

    Drinkwater sighed. Surely this was only a partial truth, and one
that was engendered by his own long-held guilt over the whole
affair of his brother. Colonel Wilson, whose presence in the area
would be well known to Lord Dungarth, had given him almost
identical advice, mentioning in particular a certain Mackenzie.
Nevertheless that strange and fleeting feeling of presentiment
could not be denied. Brief and passing though it was, it had the
reality of one of those glimpses of the hungry gulls quartering their
wake.

    Drinkwater mused on the likely outcome of those military opera-
tions that were obviously preoccupying Dungarth and, by
implication, His Majesty's Government. Horne had told him of the
fall of Dantzig to the French on 26 May. Dungarth could not have

known of that when he had written his letter. Yet Drinkwater knew, as Wilson had told him, the coming weeks of the new campaigning season were vital to the outcome of the long and increasingly bitter war. *Antigone* was to be, for the foreseeable future, the Government's eyes and ears; to learn of the outcome of what promised to be a crucial clash of arms between France and Russia somewhere in East Prussia, Poland or Kurland.

There was a knock at the cabin door; Drinkwater folded Dungarth's letter and slipped it into the drawer.

'Enter!'

Midshipman Wickham's face peered into the cabin. 'Beg pardon, sir. Mr Quilhampton sends his compliments and we shall have to tack, sir. The island of Bornholm is two leagues distant.'

'Very well. Thank you.'

'Aye, aye, sir. And I'm to tell you, sir, that Mr Rogers is on deck.' There was more than a hint in this last remark. It annoyed Drinkwater that a youngster like Wickham should be privy to such innuendo. He frowned.

'Very well, Mr Wickham. Be so kind as to give Mr Rogers *my* compliments and ask him to take the deck and tack ship.'

'Mr Rogers to tack ship . . .' There was a slight inflection of doubt in Wickham's voice.

'You heard what I said, Mr Wickham,' Drinkwater said sharply. 'Be so kind as to attend to your duty.'

The little exchange robbed Drinkwater of some of his former sense of satisfaction. He swore under his breath and, determined not to lose the mood entirely, he reopened the drawer beneath the table, pushed aside Dungarth's letter and drew out the leather-bound notebook and unclasped it. He also took out his pen-case and picked up the steel pen Elizabeth had given him. Uncapping his ink-well he dipped the nib and began to write in his journal.

It would seem that Ld Dungarth's Interest has influenced their L'dships to appoint us to this Particular Service. I am not inclined to enquire too closely into his L'dship's motives . . .

He paused as the pipes twittered at the hatchways. The muffled thunder of feet told where the watches below were being turned up.

There was no need for him to go on deck. Rogers would benefit from any public demonstration of the captain's confidence, though there would doubtless be a deal too much in the way of starting. Drinkwater sighed again. He regretted that, but there was a deal too much of it in the naval service altogether. Shaking his head he continued to write.

I therefore directed our course to the eastward, as far as the wind would admit, intending to try for news at Königsberg; for, with Dantzig capitulated to the Enemy, what news there is will surely be discovered there.

He sanded the page, blew it and put book and pen-case away. Flicking the cap over his ink-well he rose, took his hat from the peg and went on deck.

Antigone was turning up into the wind as he emerged onto the quarterdeck. Rogers was standing by the starboard hance. He looked at Drinkwater but the captain shook his head. 'Carry on, Mr Rogers.'

Clasping his hands behind his back, Drinkwater affected to take little notice of what was going on on deck. Ahead the jib-boom pointed towards the long, flat table-land of Bornholm. Dark with fir trees, it impeded their making further progress to the north-east, and they were in the process of going about onto the larboard tack, to fetch a course of south-east until they raised the low coast of East Prussia, fifty miles away.

'Mains'l haul!'

Rogers's order was given with every appearance of confidence and the hands obeyed it willingly enough. He was not sure that his presence on deck had not toned down the usual activity of the bosun's mates with their rope starters. The frigate paid off on the new tack.

'Fore-yards there! Heads'l sheets! Leggo and haul!'

The fore-yards came round, the sails filled and the ship began to drive forwards again. 'Steer full and bye!'

'Full an' bye it is, sir . . . Full an' bye steering sou'-east three-quarters south, sir.'

'Very well. Mr Frey!'

'Sir?'

'Move the peg on the traverse board, Mr Frey . . . course sou'-east three-quarters south.'

'Sou'-east three-quarters south, sir. Aye, aye, sir.'

A comforting air of normality attended these routine transactions and, much heartened, Drinkwater crossed the deck.

'Very well, Mr Rogers.' He smiled and added with less formality, 'Will you join me for dinner, Sam?'

Rogers nodded. 'Thank you, sir.'

It proved an odd meal. They dined alone and Drinkwater avoided serving wine, drinking the thin small beer that was usually drunk in the cockpit. Its very presence seemed an obstruction to any form of conviviality. Indeed, serving small beer and avoiding any reference to Rogers's recent unhappy experience only seemed to emphasise the matter. Drinkwater tried to fill the awkwardness and attempted an appraisal of the complex state of affairs among the Baltic States. But Rogers was not a man to interest himself in anything beyond the confines of the ship and such had been the mental disturbance he had so recently undergone that he was quite incapable of anything beyond the most subjective thinking. At the end of ten minutes of monologue, Drinkwater's lecture foundered on the first lieutenant's apathy.

'Well, Sam, that is the situation as I comprehend it. Now it remains to be seen who will outmanoeuvre whom. D'you understand?'

'Yes, sir,' said Rogers mechanically, avoiding Drinkwater's eyes.

There was a silence between the two men. It was not the companionable silence of contentment between friends. Drinkwater could sense the hostility in Rogers. Once, long ago on the brig *Hellebore*, it had been open and obvious; now it was concealed, hidden behind those downcast eyes. Drinkwater could only guess at its origins but that letter from Lord Dungarth made it imperative that Rogers suppressed it. He changed the subject.

'You did very well at Stralsund, Sam.'

'Didn't you think I'd be up to it?' Rogers jibbed at the patronisation. 'Look, if you're implying they didn't put up a spirited fight . . .'

'I'm implying nothing of the kind, Sam,' Drinkwater said with a weary patience he was far from feeling. Silence returned to the table. Then Rogers seemed to come to a decision. He pulled himself up in his chair as though bracing himself.

'Did you order Lallo to put me in a strait-jacket?'

Drinkwater looked directly at Rogers. To deny such a direct question would put poor Lallo in an impossible situation and give Rogers the impression that he was dodging the issue.

'I gave orders for the surgeon to restrain you with such force as was necessary, yes. It was for your own benefit, Sam. Now that you are weaned off the damnable stuff and have been recommended in a letter to the Admiralty – oh, yes, I sent it off with Captain Horne's dispatch boat – you have a much better chance of . . .' Drinkwater paused. He knew Rogers craved promotion and the security of being made post. Yet of all his officers Rogers was the one he would least recommend for command. Rogers would turn into the worst kind of flogging captain.

'Advancement?' said Rogers.

'Exactly,' Drinkwater temporised.

Rogers sat back, apparently appeased, looking at Drinkwater from beneath his brows. Drinkwater had told Rogers nothing of the real reason for their new station. The prevailing political situation was one thing, the complexities of secret operations quite another. Nevertheless it was not inconceivable that Rogers might wring some advantage out of their situation. Drinkwater would feel he could encourage Rogers if he could also avoid the man commanding a ship.

'Sam,' he said, 'I have a trifling influence; suppose I was able to get you a step in rank. What would you say to a post as Commander in the Sea-Fencibles?'

Rogers frowned. 'Or of a signal station?' he said darkly.

'Just so . . .'

But Drinkwater had miscalculated. Rogers rose. 'Damn it,' he said, 'I want a ship like you!'

'Damn,' muttered Drinkwater as Rogers withdrew without further ceremony and, reaching for the hitherto untouched decanter, he poured himself a glass of wine.

*

The waters of the eastern Baltic, which two months earlier had presented a desolate aspect under pack-ice, were alive with coasting and fishing craft the following morning. Convention decreed that all fishing boats were free to attend to their business and Drinkwater was not much interested in stopping the small coasting vessels that crept along the shore. But mindful of the underlying task of every British cruiser, Drinkwater's written orders to his officers included the injunction to stop and search neutral vessels of any size. At two bells in the forenoon watch the lookout had sighted a large, barque-rigged vessel of some three hundred tons burthen. As Fraser eased his helm the barque set more sail and Drinkwater was sent for.

Coming on deck Drinkwater heard Rogers remark to Fraser, 'A festering blockade runner, eh?' with enough of his old spirit to dispel any worries as to permanent damage after the previous evening's conversation. He acknowledged the two lieutenants with a nod and a smile. Rogers's face was impassive.

Almost without any conscious effort on anyone's part, the news that the ship was in chase of a possible prize attracted every idler on deck. Gathering amidships were Mount and Lallo, with Pater the purser. Forward, on the triangular fo'c's'le, a score or so of seamen were crowding the knightheads to sight their quarry. James Quilhampton ascended the quarterdeck ladder and touched his hat to the captain.

'Morning, sir,' he said.

'Morning, James,' Drinkwater replied, dropping the usual formalities since Quilhampton not only was a friend but was not on duty. Fraser looked anxiously at the captain. He was eager to crack on sail for all he was worth.

'D'ye wish that I should set . . . ?'

'Carry on, Mr Fraser, carry on. You are doing fine. Just forbear carrying anything away if you please.'

Drinkwater raised his Dollond glass and levelled in on the chase. 'Now what nationality do you guess our friend is, James?' He handed the glass to Quilhampton who studied the quarry.

'Er . . . I don't know, sir.'

'I think he's a Dane, Mr Q; a neutral Dane with a cargo of . . . oh, timber, flax, perhaps, and bound for somewhere where they build ships. We shall have to exercise our right of angary.'

'Of *what*, sir?'

'Angary, Mr Q, angary. A belligerent's right to seize or use neutral property: in our case temporarily, to ascertain if he is bound for a port friendly to the French,' Drinkwater took back his glass and again looked at the barque. Then he turned to Fraser. 'You are coming up on him hand over fist, Mr Fraser. Let us have a bow-chaser loaded, ready to put a shot athwart his hawse!'

In the brilliant sunshine and over a sparkling sea the *Antigone* soon overhauled her deep-laden and bluff-bowed victim. A single shot across her bow forced the barque to bring-to and an hour and a half after they had first sighted her, the blockade runner lay under *Antigone*'s lee.

'Very well done, Mr Fraser, my congratulations.'

'Thank you, sir.' Mr Fraser, looking pleased with himself, acknowledged the captain's compliment.

Drinkwater turned to Quilhampton. 'Do you board him, Mr Q. Examine his papers and, if you think it necessary, his cargo. Take your time. If you consider the cargo is bound for a port under French domination or of use as war material we are authorised to detain him. D'you understand?'

'Perfectly, sir. Angary is the word.' And he went off to the quarter, where the lee cutter was being prepared for lowering.

Rogers and Hill were active about the deck as, aloft, the flogging topgallants were dropped onto the topmast caps and the big maintopsail was backed in a great double belly against the mast. Both courses and spanker were brailed in and *Antigone* pitched, reined in and checked in her forward dash.

'Lower away!' There was a loud smack as the cutter hit the water and a few minutes later she was being pulled across the blue sea towards the barque, her dripping oarblades flashing in the sun.

Drinkwater settled down to wait patiently. The hiatus occasioned by Quilhampton's search could be long, depending upon the degree of co-operation he received from the vessel's master. Drinkwater watched idly as a fishing boat crossed the stern, her four-man crew standing up and watching the curious sight with obvious interest.

'She's Danish, sir,' said Fraser suddenly. Drinkwater looked up and saw that the barque was hoisting the colours that she had studiously avoided showing before. That very circumstance had made her actions sufficiently suspicious to Drinkwater.

'Hm. I thought as much.'

'This'll annoy the Danes,' added Rogers, joining them, and Drinkwater recalled the incident off Elsinore. It seemed an age ago.

'Yes, they are somewhat sensitive upon the subject of Freedom of the Seas,' Drinkwater remarked. 'At least they ain't escorted by a warship.'

At the turn of the century British men-of-war had detained an entire Danish convoy escorted by the frigate *Freya*. The incident had almost caused open hostilities and had certainly contributed to the rupture that had resulted in Nelson's victory at Copenhagen a year later.

'Well, to be neutral during such a war as this carries its own penalties and entails its own risks,' Drinkwater remarked. 'I feel more pity for others whose lives are more deeply affected by French imperialism than a few profitmongering Danish merchants.'

Fraser looked sideways at the captain. Did Drinkwater refer to the widows and orphans they themselves had made in the destruction of the battery at Stralsund? Or was he alluding to the families of the pressed men that milled in the ship's waist?

'Boat's returning,' said Rogers, recalling Fraser from his unsolved abstraction.

'Yes,' said Drinkwater peering through his glass. Beside Quilhampton in the cutter was another figure who seemed by his gesticulations to be arguing.

'Damnation,' muttered Drinkwater, 'trouble.'

'Capten, I protest much! Goddam you English! Vy you stop my ship?'

'Because you are carrying a cargo proscribed by the Orders in Council of His Majesty King George, to the port of Antwerp which is invested by ships of King George's Royal Navy.'

Drinkwater studied the papers Quilhampton had brought him, then looked up at the Danish master. 'The matter admits little argument, sir; Anvers, Antwerpen, Antwerp, 'tis all the same to me.' He held up the papers and quoting from them read, '*Der Schiff*

Birthe, *Captain Nielsen, von Grenaa, Dantzig vor Antwerpen* . . . your cargo is, er, sawn timber, flax, turpentine. They make excellent deals in Dantzig, Captain, and with such deals they make excellent ships at Antwerpen. About a dozen men-o'-war a year, I believe.'

'And vot vill you do now, eh, Capten English?'

'Detain you, sir,' Drinkwater said, folding the *Birthe*'s papers and tucking them in his tail-pocket, 'and send you in as a prize.'

'A prize! *Å for helvede!*'

'To be condemned in due form according to the usages and customs . . .'

'No! Goddam, no!'

Drinkwater looked at the man. He had expected anger and despised himself for hiding this unpleasant necessity behind the jumble of half-legal cant. The Danish mariner could scarcely be expected to understand it, beyond learning that he and his ship were virtually prisoners.

'A disagreeable necessity, Captain, for both of us.' Drinkwater spread his hands in a gesture to signify helplessness. Oddly, the man seemed to be considering something. This suspicion was almost immediately confirmed when Nielsen stepped forward, taking Drinkwater by the elbow and saying in his ear:

'Capten, ve go below and talk, yes?'

'I think that will not be necessary.'

Nielsen's grip on his arm increased. 'It is important . . . ver' important!' He paused, then added, 'Before Dantzig I was in Königsberg, Capten . . .' and nodded, as if this added intelligence was of some significance. Nielsen suddenly stepped back and gave a grave nod to Drinkwater. Frowning, Drinkwater suspected he was to be made a bribe, but something in the man's face persuaded him to take the matter seriously. After all, Königsberg was a Prussian port and Dantzig now a French one. Was Nielsen trying to placate him with some news?

'Mr Rogers, take the deck. Watch our friend carefully. Mr Fraser, this man wants to talk to me privately. I'd be obliged if you'd come as a witness.' And leaving the deck buzzing with speculation, Drinkwater led them below.

'Now, sir,' he said to Nielsen the instant Fraser had closed the cabin door, 'what is it you want?'

The Danish master put his hand up to his breast and reached under his coat.

'If you intend to offer me money . . .'

'*Nein* . . . not money, Capten . . . this,' he drew a package from his breast, 'is more good than money, I tink. I come from Königsberg, Capten, plenty Russians Königsberg.' He handed Drinkwater the sealed packet.

'What the devil is it?'

'It is, er . . .' Nielsen searched for a word, '. . . er, secret, Capten . . . for London from Russia . . . for many times I, Frederic Nielsen, carry the secret paper for you English.'

Drinkwater turned the package over suspiciously. 'You intended taking this where? To Antwerp?' Drinkwater fixed the Dane with his eyes, searching for the truthful answers to his questions. Any fool could wrap up an impressive bundle of papers scribbled in a supposed 'cipher' and try it as a ruse. 'Together with your cargo for the French, eh, Captain. Is that how you trade first with Königsberg and then with Dantzig, eh?'

Nielsen shrugged. 'A man must live, Capten . . . but yes. To Antwerpen. In two days from Antwerpen it can be to London – by Helvoetsluys or Vlissingen – who know? This is not for me. I only make my ship go ver' fast.' He shrugged again. 'Now it is stop by you.'

'Are you paid?'

'Yes.'

'How?'

Nielsen hesitated, reluctant to admit his private affairs. He looked first at Drinkwater then at Fraser. He found comfort in neither face. 'How?' Drinkwater repeated and Fraser stirred menacingly.

'Ven the paper to London, den is money made to me, to Hamburg.'

Drinkwater considered for a moment. 'If I undertake to deliver this, will you get your money?'

A look of alarm crossed Nielsen's face.

'Have a look at the thing, sir,' said Fraser, unable to remain silent any longer. 'He's trying to get you to let his cargo through on the pretext o' this cock-and-bull story.'

'What is the news in here, Captain Nielsen?' Drinkwater tapped the packet.

Again Nielsen shrugged. 'I do not know. Is some good news for London I hear at Dantzig.'

'Good news! At Dantzig?'

'Yes. French have battle at Heilsberg. Russian ver' good.'

Drinkwater frowned. 'You say the Russians beat the French at Heilsberg?'

Nielsen nodded. Drinkwater made up his mind, turned to the table and picked up the pen-knife lying there.

'No, Capten, I tell good, if you cut paper I not get money! *Gott!*'

It was too late. Drinkwater had slit the heavy sealing on the outer, oiled paper and unfolded the contents. They consisted of several sheets of handwriting at the top of which was a prefix of seven digits. The message was meaningless in any language and was either in cipher or an imitation cipher. Drinkwater looked up at Nielsen.

'Any damned fool could write a few pages of gibberish,' said Drinkwater. He lifted the final sheet. At the bottom was a signature of sorts. At least it was a series of signs in the place one would write a signature. They seemed to be in Cyrillic script whereas the body of the thing was in Roman handwriting; Drinkwater could make nothing of them, but then his eye fell on something else that stirred a memory of something Colonel Wilson had said. When he had mentioned Mackenzie, the British agent to whom he should offer assistance, he had also spoken of a Russian officer, a lieutenant whose name he had forgotten. Were those Cyrillic letters this man's signature? Both men used a cryptogramic code, Wilson had said, and both sent their reports to Joseph Devlieghere, Merchant of Antwerpen. He did not have to recall the Flemish name: it was written at the bottom of the page.

'Capten, if you take my ship prize, you make London ver' angry. Frederic Nielsen help you English . . .'

'For money!' said Fraser contemptuously.

'No!' Nielsen was angry himself now and turned on Fraser. 'Why you not to trust Nielsen, eh? You English not like business of oder people! Only for English it is good. Yes! But I tell you, Capten,' here he rounded on Drinkwater, 'if Nielsen not bring paper, sometimes London not know what happen in Russia, Sweden an' oder place.

You English send gold . . . much gold . . . but not keep it good . . . Ha! Ha! Ver' funny! You English crazy! You lose much gold but stop poor Frederic Nielsen to take some deals to Antwerpen . . . bah!'

Drinkwater had only the haziest notion of what Nielsen meant and was only paying partial attention to the Danish master for there was something else about the papers he held that was odd; not merely odd but profoundly disquieting. Something had tripped a subconscious mechanism of his memory. Now he wanted Nielsen and Fraser out of his cabin.

'Take Captain Nielsen on deck, Mr Fraser. I want a moment to reflect.'

'Don't be misled by such a trick, sir,' Fraser said anxiously.

'Cut along, Mr Fraser,' Drinkwater said with sudden asperity, waiting impatiently for the two men to leave him alone. When they had gone he sat and stared at the document. But he could not be certain and gradually the beating of his heart subsided. He cursed himself for a fool and began to fold the letter, then thought better of it and opened his table drawer, drew out journal, pen-case and ink-well. Very carefully he copied into the margin of his journal the strange exotic letters of the document's 'signature': НСЛАН᷅ .

Then he stowed the things away again, stuffed Nielsen's dispatch into the breast of his coat, strode to the cabin door and took the quarterdeck ladder two steps at a time.

'Mr Rogers!'

'Sir?'

'Be so kind as to have Captain Nielsen returned to his ship.' Drinkwater turned to the Dane. 'Captain, I apologise for detaining you.' He handed the dispatch back. 'You must re-seal it and please tell Mynheer Devlieghere the news of the defeat at . . .'

'Heilsberg,' offered Nielsen, visibly brightening.

'Yes. Heilsberg. Good voyage and I hope you have good news soon from Hamburg.'

Nielsen's face split in a grin and he held out a stubby hand. 'T'ank you, Capten. You English are not too much friend with Denmark, but this,' he wagged the dispatch in the air, 'this is good news, yes.' He strode to the rail where a puzzled Quilhampton waited.

'You are not going to let the bugger go, are you?' asked Rogers with some of his wonted fire, seeing a plum prize slipping once again beyond his grasp.

'Yes, Mr Rogers,' said Drinkwater, fixing the first lieutenant with a cautionary eye, 'for reasons of state . . .' Then he turned to the master. 'Mr Hill, be so kind as to resume our course for Königsberg when the boat returns,' he said and added, by way of a partial explanation, 'we must investigate the nature of a French defeat at a place called Heilsberg.'

'Aye, aye, sir,' replied the imperturbable Hill.

'And Mr Mount?'

'Sir?'

'Can we locate Heilsberg on that atlas of yours?'

'I should hope so, sir,' said the marine officer with enthusiasm as Drinkwater led him below.

Lieutenant Rogers strode to the lee rail and watched the boat pulling back towards *Antigone*.

'Reasons of state!' he hissed under his breath, and spat disgustedly to leeward as the Danish barque made sail.

8 Friedland

June 1807

'No, Mr Rogers, no wine, I beg you.' Lallo put out a restraining hand.

Rogers, his fist clamped around the neck of the decanter which he had ordered the negro messman to bring, looked from one to another of the gunroom officers. They returned his stare, watching his pale face with its faint sheen of perspiration showing in the dim light of the gunroom.

'God damn and blast you for a set of canting Methodisticals,' he said. 'God damn and blast you all to hell,' and drawing back his arm he sent the decanter flying through the air. It smashed on the forward bulkhead and in the silence that followed they could hear Rogers's laboured breathing.

'Mr Rogers . . .' began Fraser, but he was instantly silenced by Lallo. They watched as Rogers calmed himself. After a pause Rogers ceased to glare at them all, picked up his knife and fork and addressed himself to his plate. In an embarrassed silence the others dutifully followed suit. For fifteen minutes no one said a word and then Rogers, flinging down his utensils, rose from the table and stumped out. His exit provoked a broadside of expelled breath.

'Phew! How long will he go on like this?' asked Fraser. 'If he isn't damned careful he'll end up with the other irredeemable tosspots in Haslar Hospital.'

'That was what I tried to tell you, Mr Fraser,' said Lallo, 'when you interfered.'

'I'm damn sorry, Mr Lallo, but I couldna tolerate him being trussed like a chicken for the table.'

'I was not aware,' said Lallo archly, 'that there was any love lost between you.'

'Nor there is, but . . .'

'The captain ordered me to restrain him. It was out of kindness, to avoid too public a humiliation for the man.'

'But was all that really necessary?'

'In my opinion yes. Despite being anorexic, which was attributable to his reliance on strong drink, he was quite capable of doing himself and myself a great deal of damage in his ravings. The aboulia . . . the loss of will-power associated with addiction, disturbs all the natural processes and inclinations of the body. He was by turns lethargic and extremely violent. At times he was almost cataleptic, but at others his strength was amazing.' Lallo paused, then added, 'I'd say the treatment, though drastic, was successful.' He turned and looked down on the deck where the broken decanter lay amid a dark stain on the planking. 'At least he resisted the stuff.'

'Well, it was a damnable thing . . .' said Fraser.

'It was a damnable thing that you had a man gagged yourself for the use of strong language the day before yesterday . . .'

'That's preposterous . . .'

'And furthermore,' Lallo interrupted, 'I'd diagnose your own condition . . .'

'For goodness sake, gentlemen,' put in Quilhampton, raising his voice to overcome the rising argument, 'I conceive Mr Rogers to be upset because we let the Danish ship go. He has never enjoyed much luck in the way of prize-money.'

'There would have been nothing very certain about making any out of that Dane,' snapped Fraser. 'Condemning neutrals usually turns upon points of law. It isn't the same thing as taking a national ship or a privateer.'

Lallo was grateful for the changed mood of the conversation. 'What *did* happen in the cabin, Mr Fraser? Did the scoundrel offer the captain money?'

'No,' said Fraser after a pause. 'The Dane, Frederic Nielsen, claimed he was carrying secret papers for London, or some such nonsense. The fellow was adamant and I don't think the captain believed him. Then . . .'

'Go on . . .'

Fraser shrugged. 'Well, he suddenly looked closer at the papers and appeared to change his mind. Bundled Nielsen and myself

103

out of the cabin and a few minutes later came up, handed the papers back to the Dane and let him go.'

'Just like that?' asked Lallo.

'Yes. Or that is how it seemed to me.'

'I wonder . . .' mused Quilhampton, attracting the attention of the other two.

'You wonder what, James?' asked Fraser. 'Have you any idea what's afoot?'

'The captain's been mixed up in this sort of thing before.'

'What sort of thing?' asked Fraser.

'*This* sort of thing.'

'*What* sort of thing, for God's sake?' Fraser repeated in exasperation.

'Well, secret operations and suchlike.'

'*Secret operations?*' said Lallo incredulously. 'Are we bound on a secret operation? I thought we were on a cruise against blockade runners.'

'Can't you be more specific, James?' Fraser's curiosity was plain and almost indignant.

Quilhampton shrugged. 'Who knows . . .?' he said enigmatically.

'Oh, for Heaven's sake, James!'

'Well, ask Hill. They were both on the cutter *Kestrel* years ago, doing all sorts of clandestine things . . . Oh, my God!' Quilhampton jumped up.

'What the devil's the matter?'

'It's Hill! I've forgotten to relieve him again!' Quilhampton grabbed his hat and trod in the broken glass from the smashed decanter.

'Damn! Hey, King! Come and sweep up this damned mess, will you?'

Drinkwater paced up and down the deck as the hands went aloft to stow the sails. *Antigone* rocked gently in the swell that ran in over the Pregel Bar. The desolation of two months earlier was scarcely imaginable in the present lively scene. The sea, now clear of ice, was an enticing blue. The distant line of coast was a soft blue-green and, above the long yellow spit that made it a lagoon, the Frisches Haff was dotted with the sails of coasting craft and fishing vessels. There were others in the open sea around them and the activity seemed to indicate that events ashore were having little effect on the lives of the local population who were busy pursuing their various trades. Perhaps Nielsen had been right and the French had been badly mauled at Heilsberg. Perhaps another battle had been fought and the Russians had flung back the Grand Army. Perhaps the French were in headlong flight, a circumstance which would explain all this normality! Drinkwater checked his wild speculation. He was here to gather facts without delay. He would have to send to Königsberg as soon as the ship was secured and a boat was prepared. He contemplated going himself. Properly it was Rogers's prerogative to command so important an expedition but, despite his success at Stralsund, Rogers's lack of interest in political matters did not recommend him for the service. On the other hand, if he sent Fraser, the next in seniority, a slight would be imputed to Rogers. He did not wish to risk a reversal to the first lieutenant's progress back to normality. But that left Hill or Quilhampton, and Hill could not be sent because the same imputation attached to the dispatching of the sailing master as the second lieutenant. It would have to be Quilhampton.

Drinkwater, irritated by all these trivial considerations, swore, consoled himself that Quilhampton was as good a man as any for the task, and made up his mind. He passed orders for the preparation of the launch for a lengthy absence from the ship and summoned the third lieutenant to his cabin.

'Now, Mr Q,' he said, indicating the chart and Mount's borrowed atlas. 'See, here is Königsberg. You are to take the launch, which is being provisioned for a week, and make the best of your way there. I shall provide you with a letter of accreditment to the effect that you are a British naval officer. Your purpose is to ascertain the truth and extent of a report that the French suffered a defeat at Heilsberg.' Drinkwater placed his finger on a spot on a page of the atlas. 'You *must* get the best information you can and try to determine if anything else has occurred. Was the French army routed or merely checked? Have there been any further engagements? That sort of thing. Do you understand?'

'Yes, sir.'

'Very well. Now, I suggest that initially you search out a British merchant ship. There will almost certainly be at least one in the port. Do that first. Do not land until you have made contact and obtained advice from a British master. The port is Prussian and there may be Russian troops there. You would do well to avoid any problems with language and your best interpreter will be the master of a British ship who will have an agent and therefore someone acquainted with local affairs.' Drinkwater remembered Young and Baker and added, 'Sometimes, I believe, these fellows have quite an effective intelligence system of their own.'

'What force will I take, sir?'

'Twenty-four men, James; no marines, just seamen.'

'Very well, sir . . . May I ask a favour?'

'Well?'

'May I take Tregembo, sir?'

'Tregembo?' Drinkwater frowned. 'You know I dare not expose him to any unnecessary danger, I shall never hear the last of it from his wife . . .' Drinkwater smiled.

'Well, Königsberg is supposed to be a friendly port, sir. I cannot see that he can come to much harm.'

'True. Why do you want Tregembo?' Drinkwater paused and saw Quilhampton's hesitation. 'Is it because you do not trust the temper of the men?'

Quilhampton shrugged, trying to pass his concern off lightly. 'One or two may try and run, sir. They are still somewhat mettlesome. With Tregembo there they will be less inclined to try. Besides, I shall have to leave the launch.'

'You will take two midshipmen, Dutfield and Wickham.'

'I should still like Tregembo.'

Drinkwater raised his voice. 'Sentry! Pass word for my coxswain!'

A minute or two later Tregembo arrived. 'You sent for me, zur?'

'Aye, Tregembo. Mr Q here wants you to go in the launch with him to Königsberg. To be particular, he has requested you go. I'd like you to accompany him.'

'Who'll look after you, zur?' Tregembo asked with the air of the indispensable.

'Oh, I expect Mullender will manage for a day or two,' Drinkwater replied drily.

Tregembo sniffed his disbelief. 'If you'm want me to go, zur, I'll go.'

'Very well.' Drinkwater smiled. 'You had better both go and make your preparations.'

An hour later he watched the launch pull away from the ship's side. On board *Antigone* the men were coiling away the yard and stay tackles used to sway the heavy carvel boat up from its chocks on the booms in the frigate's waist and over the side. Half a cable away the men in the launch stowed their oars, stepped the two masts and hooked the lugsail yards to their travellers. An hour later the two lugsails were mere nicks upon the horizon, no different from half a dozen others entering or leaving the Frisches Haff. Drinkwater settled down to wait.

For two days *Antigone* swung slowly round her anchor. On board, the monotonous routines of shipboard life went on, the officer of the watch occasionally studying the low, desolate shore for the twin peaks of the launch's lugsails. Once a watch Frey or Walmsley climbed to the main royal yard and peered diligently to the eastward, but without seeing any sign of the ship's boat. Then, early in the morning of the third day, an easterly breeze carried with it the sound of gunfire. Sent aloft, Frey brought down the disquieting intelligence that there was smoke visible from the general direction of Königsberg.

All the officers were on the quarterdeck and Mount, as if disbelieving the boy's report, ascended the mast himself to confirm it.

'But what the devil does it mean, Mount?' asked Hill. 'Your atlas shows Heilsberg as to the south and west of Königsberg. If the Russkies threw the French back, what the hell is smoke and gunfire doing at Königsberg?' He crossed the deck and checked the wind direction from the weather dog-vane to the compass. 'That gunfire isn't coming from anywhere other than east.'

'It means', said Drinkwater, 'either that Heilsberg was wrongly reported or that the French have counter-attacked and reached Königsberg.'

'Bloody hell!'

'What about Quilhampton?'

And Tregembo, thought Drinkwater. Should he send another boat? Should he work *Antigone* closer inshore? He had no charts of the area accurate enough to attempt a passage over the bar and into the Frisches Haff, and did not relish the thought of grounding ignominiously within range of the shore. A picture of French batteries revenging themselves on him from the shingle spit enclosing the great lagoon presented itself to him. Napoleon would make much of such an event and *Le Moniteur* would trumpet it throughout Europe. No, he would have to give Quilhampton his chance. The man was not a fool. If he heard gunfire he would assume the place was under attack and, as it could only be attacked by one enemy, he would come off to the ship as his orders said. But the officers were looking at him, expecting some response.

'I think that we can do little but wait, gentlemen,' Drinkwater said, and turning he made his way below, to brood in his cabin and fret himself with anxiety. For two hours an uneasy silence hung over the ship, then Frey, suspended in the rigging with the ship's best glass, hailed the deck, his voice cracking with excitement.

'Deck there! Deck there! The launch, sir! It's in sight!' His frantic excitement promised to unseat him from his precarious perch and it was only with difficulty that Hill persuaded him that his own safety was more important than the precise bearing of the launch. But Frey would not desert his post and kept the image of the launch dancing in the lens by lying full length on the furled maintopgallant. It was he, therefore, who spotted the reversed ensign flying from the launch's peak as she approached the ship. 'She's flying a signal for distress, sir!'

Once again all were on deck; the waist and fo'c's'le were crowded with *Antigone*'s people training their eyes to the eastward where the launch was now clearly visible.

'Mr Comley!' Rogers called sharply and with no trace of his former debility. 'Stir those idlers! Man the yard and stay tackles! Prepare to hoist in the launch!'

'Mr Lallo,' said Drinkwater lowering his telescope, 'as far as I can ascertain there is nothing amiss with the launch itself. I can only assume the signal of distress refers to the people in the boat. I think it would be wise if you were to prepare your instruments.' A chilling foreboding had closed itself round Drinkwater's heart.

The launch came running down wind, the men in her hidden behind the bunts of the loose-footed lugsails. She was skilfully rounded up into the wind and, sails a-flapping, came alongside *Antigone*'s waist. With an overwhelming sense of relief Drinkwater saw a dishevelled Quilhampton at the tiller, his iron hook crooked over the wooden bar. Then he saw wounded men amidships: one of them Tregembo.

The fit men clambered from the launch up *Antigone*'s tumble-home. With her sails stowed and masts lowered the boat was hooked and swung up and inboard onto the booms. Here eager arms assisted in lifting the wounded men out and down below to the catlings and curettes of Mr Lallo.

Drinkwater waited until Quilhampton reported. His eyes followed the inert body of Tregembo as, his shoulder slung in a bloodstained and makeshift bandage, he was taken below. He was therefore unaware of a dusty stranger who stood upon the deck ignored amidst the bustle.

'Well, Mr Q? What happened?'

James Quilhampton looked five years older. His face was drawn and he was filthy.

'I have your intelligence, sir, Königsberg has fallen to the French. There has been a great battle, just two days ago. It was disastrous for the Russians. There is chaos in the port . . .' He paused, gathering his wits. He was clearly exhausted. 'I made contact, as you suggested, with the master of a Hull ship. We went ashore to gather news at a tavern much used by British shipmasters. To my surprise Captain Young was there, together with Captain Baker.' Quilhampton shook his head, trying to clear it of the fog of fatigue. 'To my astonishment their ships had still not discharged their lading . . .'

'Good God . . . but go on.'

'The fellows were debating what should be done, as the news had just arrived of the precipitate flight of the Russians. I said *Antigone* was anchored on the Pregel Bar and would afford them convoy. Most felt that with their cargoes not yet completed they could not stand the loss. They affirmed their faith in the garrison and the defences of the city. I tried to tell Young that his cargo *must* not fall into the hands of the enemy. He assured me it wouldn't. The men had had a tiring passage with the necessity of rowing up the river, so I judged that we should remain alongside Young's ship. Her chief mate offered us accommodation and I accepted, intending to see how matters stood in the morning and, if necessary, help to get the *Nancy* and the *Jenny Marsden* to sea. I thought, sir, that if the threat from the French persisted, I might better persuade Captain Young to change his mind. You see, sir, the evening before he had been somewhat in his cups and difficult to move . . .'

'I understand, James. Go on.'

'There is not much more to tell. I slept badly, the town was shaken throughout the night by artillery fire, and the bursting of the shells was constant. In the morning French cavalry were in the town. Young was not on board and I attempted to get his mate to sail and bring out Baker's ship as well. They would not move unless their respective masters were with them. I undertook to return to the tavern where it was thought they had lodged. I got caught in a cross-fire between some infantry, I don't know whether they were Prussians or Russians, and some French sharp-shooters. Tregembo and Kissel were with me. Kissel was hit and Tregembo and I went back for him. As we dragged him towards the *Jenny Marsden*'s jolly-boat we were ridden down by French dragoons. They dispatched Kissel and wounded Tregembo . . .'

'Go on. What happened to you?'

'Oh, nothing, sir.'

'He unhorsed a dragoon, Captain, pulled the fellow clean out of his saddle . . .'

Drinkwater turned and was aware of an unfamiliar face.

'And who, sir, are you?'

The stranger ignored the question. 'Your officer unhorsed the dragoon with that remarkable hook of his. You see, sir, they were pursuing me. I had evaded them in an alley and they took their revenge on your officer and men. However, as I swiftly made him out to be a seafaring man as well as an Englishman, I made myself known to him and assisted him in getting his wounded comrade into the boat.'

'I doubt I could have done it alone, sir,' explained Quilhampton, 'before the other dragoon got me. Fortunately the fellow missed with his carbine and we were able to get to the *Jenny Marsden* without further ado, but I could not get either of them to unmoor and, with shot flying about the shipping and this gentleman here insisting on my bringing him off, I decided that discretion was the better part of valour . . .'

'What is the extent of Tregembo's wound?' Drinkwater cut in.

'A sabre thrust in the fleshy part of the shoulder, sir. I do not believe it to be mortal.'

'I hope to God it ain't.' Drinkwater turned on the stranger. 'And now, sir, who are you and what is your business?'

'I think, Captain,' said the stranger with that imperturbable coolness that was rapidly eroding Drinkwater's temper, 'that this should be discussed in your cabin.'

'Do you, indeed.'

'Yes. In fact I insist upon it.' His cold blue eyes held Drinkwater's in an unblinking gaze. The man made a gesture with his hand as if their roles were reversed and it was he who was inviting Drinkwater below. 'Captain . . .?'

'Mr Q, get below and turn in. You, Mr Frey, cut along to the surgeon and tell him to debride those wounds immediately or they will mortify.' He turned to the stranger. 'As for you, sir, you had better follow me!'

Drinkwater strode below and, shutting the door behind the stranger, rounded on him.

'Now, sir! Enough of this tomfoolery. Who the deuce are you and what the devil d'you mean by behaving like that?'

The stranger smiled coolly. 'I already have the advantage of you, Captain. Your lieutenant informed me that you are Captain Drinkwater. Captain Nathaniel Drinkwater, I understand . . .' A small and strangely threatening smile was playing about the man's mouth, but he held out his hand cordially enough. 'I am Colin Alexander Mackenzie, Captain Drinkwater, and in your debt for saving my life.'

9 Mackenzie

June 1807

Drinkwater felt awkward under Mackenzie's uncompromising scrutiny. He hesitated, then took the outstretched hand. Everything about the stranger irritated Drinkwater, not least his proprietorial air in Drinkwater's own cabin.

'Mr Mackenzie,' he said coldly, 'Colonel Wilson mentioned you.' Drinkwater was not ready to say the British Commissioner had urged him to offer this cold-eyed man as much assistance as he required. The manner of Mackenzie's arrival seemed to indicate he already had that for the time being.

'So,' Mackenzie smiled, 'you have met Bob Wilson. I wonder where he is now?'

Drinkwater indicated a chair and Mackenzie slumped into it. 'Thank you.'

'A glass?' Drinkwater asked.

'That is very kind of you. What did Wilson say?'

Drinkwater poured the two glasses of wine and handed one to the Scotsman. He did not hurry to answer, but observed the man as he relaxed. After a little he said, 'That I was to afford you such assistance as you might require. It seems we have already done so.'

The two men were still weighing each other up and Drinkwater's manner remained cool. Now, however, Mackenzie dropped his aloofness.

'I'm damn glad you did, Captain. I had to ride for my very life. I am almost sure those dragoons knew who I was . . .' He shrugged, passing a hand over his dust-stained face. 'The Russians were smashed, you know, on the fourteenth, at a place called Friedland. Bennigsen got himself caught in a loop of the River Alle and, though the Russians fought like bears, the French got the better of them. Bennigsen was forced to retreat and Königsberg has fallen. The Russians are falling back everywhere to the line of the Nieman. I was lucky to get out . . . and even luckier to find you.' He smiled, and Drinkwater found himself feeling less hostile. However he did not pass up the opportunity to goad Mackenzie a little.

'What exactly is your function, Mr Mackenzie? I mean what was it you feared the French dragoons took you for?'

Mackenzie looked at him shrewdly, again that strangely disquieting smile played about his mouth, again Drinkwater received the impression that their roles were reversed and that he, in goading Mackenzie, was in some obscure way being put upon.

'I am sure you are aware of my function as a British agent.' He paused and added, 'A spy, if you wish.'

Drinkwater shied away from the dangerous word-game he felt inadequate to play. This was his ship, his cabin; he switched the conversation back onto its safer track.

'I heard that the French were defeated at a place called Heilsberg. After Eylau we were expecting that the Russians might throw Boney back, once and for all.'

Mackenzie nodded tiredly, apparently equally relieved at the turn the conversation had taken. 'So did I, Captain. It *was* true. The Russians and Prussians moved against the French at the beginning of the month when Ney's Corps went foraging. *Le Rougeard* was caught napping and given a bloody nose. But Napoleon moved the whole mass of the Grand Army, caught Bennigsen ten days later at Friedland and crushed him.'

'I see.' Drinkwater considered the matter a moment. He did not think that the news left him much alternative. The retreat of the Tsar's Army beyond the Nieman, the French occupation of Poland and East Prussia, the fall of Dantzig and now Königsberg, left Napoleon the undisputed master of Europe. In accordance with his orders, London must be informed forthwith.

'Well, Mr Mackenzie, having rescued you and rendered that assistance required of me, I must now take the news you bring back to London. I take it you will take passage with us?'

Mackenzie hesitated then said, 'Captain Drinkwater, how discretionary are your orders?'

'Those from their Lordships are relatively wide.'

'You have, perhaps, orders from another source?' Mackenzie paused. 'I see you are reluctant to confide in me. No matter. But perhaps you have something else, eh? Something from the Secret Department of Lord Dungarth?'

'Go on, Mr Mackenzie. I find your hypothesis . . . intriguing,' Drinkwater prevaricated.

'The Russians are defeated; the shipments of arms in the two merchantmen at Königsberg have fallen into enemy hands. In commercial terms the Tsar is a bad risk.' Mackenzie smiled. 'Sweden is led by an insane monarch and on the very edge of revolution. Now, Captain, what is the victorious *Napoleone* going to do about it all? He has destroyed Prussia, driven the Russians back into Mother Russia itself, he is suborning the Swedes, threatening the Danes. He has the Grand Army in the field under his personal control, his rear is secured by Mortier at Stralsund and Brune's Corps of Hispano-Dutch on the borders of Denmark. Austria is quiescent but . . .' and Mackenzie paused to emphasise his point, 'he has not been in Paris for over a year. The question of what is happening in Paris will prevent him sleeping more than anything. He has a few more months in the field and then,' he shrugged, 'who knows? So what would you do, Captain?'

'Me? I have no idea.' Drinkwater found the idea absurd.

'I would conclude an armistice with the Tsar,' said Mackenzie evenly.

Drinkwater looked sharply at him. The idea was preposterous. The Tsar was the sworn enemy of the French Revolution and the Imperial system of the parvenu Emperor, and yet such was the persuasion of Mackenzie's personality that the cold, cogent logic of it struck Drinkwater. He remembered Straton's cautionary removal of the Tsar's subsidy, and his own now-proven misgivings. He said nothing for there seemed nothing to say.

Then Mackenzie broke the seriousness of their mood. His smile was unsullied and charming. 'But then, 'tis only a hypothesis, Captain Drinkwater . . . and it is my business to speculate, intelligently, of course.'

'And it's not my business to verify the accuracy of your speculations, Mr Mackenzie,' said the captain brightening, 'but to take this intelligence back to London as quickly as possible.'

'Have you heard of any preparations against the Baltic being made at home?'

'Yes,' said Drinkwater. 'Horne of the *Pegasus* mentioned some such expedition to be mounted this summer in support of Gustavus at Rügen. There were problems of command: the King of Sweden wanted to command British troops in person . . .'

'They would walk into a trap,' said Mackenzie, his voice a mixture of contempt and exasperation.

'Well then,' said Drinkwater, 'the sooner we prevent that, the better.'

'I think you are mistaken, Captain, to think our news would stop His Majesty's ministers from acting in their usual incompetent manner. Hypotheses are not intelligence. Lord Dungarth would be pleased with the news, but not ecstatic. They will know of the Battle of Friedland in London in a day or so, if they do not already. There are other channels . . .' Again Drinkwater was confronted by that strange, ominous smile.

'Well,' expostulated Drinkwater, feeling his irritation returning, 'what do *you* suggest I do?'

'I know what we *should* do, Captain Drinkwater. The question is, *can* we do it?' Mackenzie's eyes closed to contemplative slits, his voice lowered. 'I am certain that there will be an armistice soon. The French dare not overextend themselves; Napoleon must return to Paris; yet, if he withdraws, the Russians will follow like wolves. There *must* be an accommodation with the Tsar.'

'And will the Tsar agree to such a proposal, particularly as it reveals Boney in a position of weakness?'

Mackenzie chuckled. 'My dear Captain, you know nothing of Russia. There is one thing you must understand, she is an autocracy. What the Tsar wills, is. Alexander professes one thing and does another. The Tsar can be relied upon to be erratic.'

Drinkwater shook his head, still mystified. 'So what do you advise I do?'

'You already asked that question.'

'But you did not answer it.'

'We should eavesdrop on their conversation.'

'Whose?' asked Drinkwater frowning.

'Alexander's and Napoleon's.'

115

'Mr Mackenzie, I am sure that you are a tired man, that your recent excitement has exhausted you, but you can scarcely fail to notice that this is a ship of war, not an ear trumpet.'

'I know, I know, Captain, it is only wishful thinking.' Mackenzie's eyes narrowed again. He was contemplating a scene of his imagination's making. 'But a frigate could take me to Memel, couldn't it?'

'Is that what you want?' asked Drinkwater, the prospect of returning Mackenzie to the shore a pleasing one at that moment. 'A passage to Memel?'

'Yes,' said Mackenzie, seeming to make up his mind. 'That and somewhere to sleep.'

Drinkwater nodded at his cot. 'Help yourself. I must get the ship under weigh and see the wounded.'

Picking up his hat Drinkwater left the cabin. Too tired to move suddenly, Mackenzie stared after him. 'Captain Drinkwater,' he muttered, smiling to himself, 'Captain *Nathaniel* Drinkwater, by all that's holy . . .'

In the dark and foetid stink of the orlop deck Drinkwater picked his way forward. *Antigone* listed over, and down here, deep in her belly, Drinkwater could hear the rush of the sea past her stout wooden sides. Here, where the midshipmen and master's mates messed next to the marines above the hold, Lallo and his loblolly boys were plying their trade.

'How are they?' he asked, stepping into the circle of light above the struggling body of a seaman. Lallo did not look up but Skeete's evil leer was diabolical in the bizarre play of the lantern. Drinkwater peered round in the darkness, searching for Tregembo, one hand on the low deck beam overhead. The prone seaman groaned pitifully, the sweat standing out on his body like glass beads. His screams were muted to agonised grunts as he bit on the leather pad Skeete had forced into his mouth. With a twist and a jerk Lallo withdrew his hand, red from a wound in the man's thigh, and held a knife up to the dim light. The musket ball stuck on its point was intact. Lallo grunted his satisfaction as the man slipped into a merciful unconsciousness, and looked up at the captain.

'Mostly gunshot wounds . . . at long range . . . spent . . .'

116

'They came under fire getting out of the river. Where's Tregembo?'

With a grunt, as of stiff muscles, Lallo got to his feet and, stepping over the body that Skeete and his mate were dragging to a corner of the tiny space, he led Drinkwater forward to where Tregembo lay, half propped against a futtock. Drinkwater knelt down. Tregembo's shirt was torn aside and the white of the bandage showed in the mephitic gloom.

'A sabre thrust to the bone,' explained the surgeon. 'It would have been easier to clean had it been a cut. It is too high to amputate.'

'Amputate! God damn it, man, I sent particular word to you to ensure you debrided it.'

Lallo took the uncorked rum bottle that Skeete handed him and swigged from it.

'I took your kind advice, sir,' Lallo said with heavy irony, 'but, as I have just said, the wound is a deep one. I have done my best but . . .'

'Yes, yes, of course . . .'

Tregembo opened his eyes. He was already on the edge of fever, slipping in and out of semi-consciousness. He made an effort to focus his eyes on Drinkwater and began to speak, but the words were incomprehensible, and after a minute or two it was plain he was unaware of his surroundings. Drinkwater touched his arm. It was hot.

'The prognosis?' Drinkwater rose, stooping under the low deck-head.

Lallo shook his head. 'Not good, sir. Uncertain at best.'

'They spent a long time in the boat after the wounding.'

'Too long . . .' Lallo corked the rum bottle and wiped his mouth with the back of his hand.

'Mr Lallo, I will risk the chance of offending you by saying that, when I was a prisoner aboard the *Bucentaure*, I observed a method of dressing a wound that was considered highly effective.'

'A *French* method, sir?'

'Yes.'

'Humph!'

'Soak a pledget in sea-water or camphorated wine and add a few drops of lead acetate. D'you have any lead acetate? Good. Bind the wound firmly with a linen bandage in which holes have been cut. Do not disturb the dressing but have the purulent matter which seeps through the holes wiped away. A compress of the same type is bound tightly over the first dressing and changed daily.' Drinkwater looked at the men groaning at his feet. 'Try it, Mr Lallo, as I have directed . . . and perhaps you will have less need of rum.'

He turned and made for the ladder, leaving Lallo and Skeete staring after him. On deck the fresh air was unbelievably sweet.

Mackenzie woke among unfamiliar surroundings. He tried to get out of the cot and found it difficult. When he got his feet on the deck *Antigone* heeled a little, the cot swayed outboard and in getting out he fell, sending the cot swinging further. Disencumbered of his weight the cot swung back, fetching Mackenzie a blow on the back of the head.

'God!' He got to his feet and stood unsteadily, feeling the bile stirring in his gullet. Casting desperately about he recalled the privy and reached the door to the quarter-gallery just in time. After a little while he felt better, and being a self-reliant and resourceful man he diverted his mind from his guts to the matter in hand. He carefully crossed the cabin and stood braced at Drinkwater's table, staring down at the chart and the open pages of Mount's Military Atlas. The latter attracted his interest and he swiftly forgot his seasickness.

'By God, that's providential,' he murmured to himself. After a moment or two his curiosity and professional interest turned itself to Drinkwater's desk. The left-hand of its two drawers was slightly open. Mackenzie pulled it out and lifted Drinkwater's journal from it. He flicked the pages over and, on the page on which the neat script ceased, he noticed a strange entry in the margin. It consisted of a short word in Cyrillic script: **NСЛ АНй** .

'So, I was right . . .'

'What the devil d'you think you're doing?'

Mackenzie looked up at Drinkwater standing in the doorway, his hat in his hand. He was quite unabashed.

'Is this how you abuse my hospitality?' Drinkwater advanced across the cabin, anger plain in his face. He confronted Mackenzie across the table; Mackenzie remained unruffled.

'Where did you come across this?' he pointed to the strange letters.

In his outrage Drinkwater had not seen exactly what Mackenzie had found. He had assumed the spy had been prying. Now the sudden emphasis Mackenzie put on those strangely exotic letters recalled to his mind his own, intensely personal reasons for having written them. He was briefly silent and then suddenly explosively angry.

'God damn you, Mackenzie, you presume too much! That is a private journal! It has nothing to do with you!'

'Be calm, Captain,' Mackenzie said, continuing in a reasonable tone, 'you are wrong, it has everything to do with me. What do these Russian letters mean? Do you know? Where did you learn them?'

'What is that to you?'

'Captain, don't play games. You are out of your depth. This word and the hand that wrote it are known to me.' He paused and looked up. 'Do you know what these Cyrillic letters mean?'

Drinkwater sank back into the chair opposite to his usual one, the chair reserved for visitors to his cabin, so that their roles were again reversed. He shook his head.

'If you transpose each of these letters with its Roman equivalent you spell the word *island*.'

Drinkwater shook his head. 'I do not understand.'

'If you then translate the word *island* back into Russian, you have the word *Ostroff*. It is a passably Russian-sounding name, isn't it?'

Drinkwater shrugged. 'I suppose so.'

'Do you know who *Ostroff* is?'

'I haven't the remotest idea.'

'Oh, come, Captain,' Mackenzie remonstrated disbelievingly. 'You went to the trouble of making a note of his name and in a book that was personally significant.'

'Mr Mackenzie,' Drinkwater said severely, 'I do not know what you are implying, but you have obviously invaded my privacy!'

But Drinkwater's anger was not entirely directed at Mackenzie, furious though he was at the man's effrontery. There *had* been a reason why he had noted that incomprehensible Russian lettering down in his journal; and though he did not know who Ostroff was, he had his suspicions. He resolved to clear the matter up and settle the doubts that had been provoked by the sight of Nielsen's dispatch.

'Who the devil *is* this Ostroff then?'

Mackenzie smiled that tight, menacing smile, and Drinkwater sensed he knew more than he was saying. 'A spy. An agent in the Russian army. And now perhaps you will trade one confidence for another. Where did you get these letters from? Are you in correspondence with this man?'

Drinkwater's heart was thumping. Mackenzie's words closed the gap between speculation and certainty.

'From a dispatch intercepted in the possession of a Danish merchantman which I stopped a week or two ago.'

'What was the name of the ship?'

'The *Birthe* of Grenaa, Captain . . .'

'Nielsen?' interrupted Mackenzie.

'Yes. Frederic Nielsen.'

'And what did you do with Nielsen and his dispatch?'

'I let him go with it. I was satisfied that he and it were what they said they were.'

'But you copied out the name by which the dispatch was signed?'

'Yes.'

'Why?'

Drinkwater shrugged.

'Captain, you say you were sure of the authenticity of a dispatch carried by a neutral and you let the vessel go. Yet you were not sure enough not to note down the signatory. Odd, don't you think? Where was the dispatch bound?'

'I do not think that a proper question to answer, Mackenzie. I am not sure I should be answering any of these questions. I am not sure I ought not to have you in irons . . .'

'Captain,' said Mackenzie in a suddenly menacing tone, 'mine is a dangerous trade in which I trust no one. I am curious as to who you thought this man was; why you copied out this signature. It is almost inconceivable that any obviously trusted servant of their lordships of the Admiralty should behave traitorously . . .'

Drinkwater was on his feet and had leaned across the table. He spat the words through clenched teeth, beside himself with rage:

'How dare you, you bastard! You have no right to come aboard here and make such accusations! Who the hell are you to accuse me of treason? Get out of my seat! You stand *here* and make *your* report to *me*, before I have this ship put about for The Sound and confine you in the bilboes!'

'By God, Captain, I apologise . . . I see I have misjudged you.' Mackenzie stood and confronted Drinkwater. 'I think you have reassured me on that point at least . . .'

'Have a care . . .'

'Captain, you must hear me out. It is a matter of the utmost importance, I assure you. I know you have had previous contact with Lord Dungarth's Secret Department; I assume from what you implied earlier that you have some freedom in the interpretation of your orders, perhaps from his Lordship. I also assume that you let Frederic Nielsen proceed because he had a dispatch addressed to Joseph Devlieghere at Antwerp . . . Ah, I see you find that reassuring . . . Tell me, Captain, did you ever know a man called Brown?'

'I saw the Dutch hang him at Kijkduin.'

'And do you think the Dutch were responsible?'

Drinkwater looked sharply at Mackenzie, but he did not answer.

'Come, Captain, have you not come across a French agent named Edouard Santhonax?'

Drinkwater strode across the cabin, pulled out his sea-chest and from it drew a roll of frayed canvas. He unrolled it.

'Identify this lady and I'll believe you are who you say you are.'

'Good God!' Mackenzie stared at the cracking paint. The portrait showed a young woman with auburn hair piled upon her head. Pearls were entwined in the contrived negligence of her classical coiffure. Her creamy shoulders were bare and her breasts just visible beneath a wisp of gauze. Her grey eyes looked coolly out of the canvas and there was a hint of a smile about the corners of her lovely mouth. 'Hortense Santhonax, by heaven!'

'A celebrated beauty, as all Paris knows.'

'Where the devil did you get it?'

Drinkwater nodded at the portrait of Elizabeth that had not been done with half as much skill as that of Madame Santhonax. 'It used to hang there. This ship, Mr Mackenzie, was once commanded by Edouard Santhonax when she was captured in the Red Sea. I was one of the party who took her.' He rolled up the portrait. 'I kept it as a memento. You see, I rescued Madame Santhonax from a Jacobin mob in ninety-two . . . before she turned her coat. She was eventually taken back to France. I was on the beach with Lord Dungarth when we released her. . .'

'And he didn't shoot her,' put in Mackenzie, shaking his head. 'Yes, he has told me the story.' He looked about him. 'It's incredible . . . this ship . . . you. Captain, I am sorry, I acted hastily. Please accept my apologies.'

'Very well. It is of no matter. I think you have provided proof of your identity. We had better sink our differences in a glass of wine.'

'That is a capital idea.' Mackenzie smiled and, for the first time since meeting him, Drinkwater felt less menaced, more in control of the situation. He poured the two drinks and behind him he heard Mackenzie mutter 'Incredible' to himself.

'This man Ostroff,' said Drinkwater conversationally, seating himself in his proper place at last, 'is he of importance to you?'

'He will be invaluable if my hypothesis proves accurate.'

'You mean if an armistice is concluded between Alexander and Napoleon?'

'Yes. Whatever terms are agreed upon, they will clearly be prejudicial to Britain. Ostroff is the one man in a position to learn them. Now, with the loss of Königsberg, Ostroff's communications are cut. The situation is serious but not fatal. We still have access to Memel, at least until the two Emperors meet, hence my request that you carry me there. You see, I am Ostroff's post-boy. I forwarded his dispatch through Nielsen.'

'You . . . you know him well then, this Ostroff?' Drinkwater's heart was thumping again; he felt foolishly vulnerable, although Mackenzie's manner towards him had so drastically altered.

'Oh yes, I know him, Captain Drinkwater. That is why I could not understand your attitude.'

'I do not understand you.'

Mackenzie frowned. 'You mean you really do not know who Ostroff is?'

'No,' he said, but he felt that his voice lacked conviction.

'You share the same surname, Captain Drinkwater . . .'

The blood left Drinkwater's face. So, he had been right! Despite the cipher, despite the years that had passed, he *had* recognised the hand that had penned Nielsen's dispatch.

'So Ostroff is my brother Edward,' he said flatly.

'It is a chain of the most remarkable coincidences, Captain,' said Mackenzie.

'Not at all,' replied Drinkwater wearily, rising and fetching the decanter from its lodgement in the fiddle. 'It is merely evidence of the workings of providence, Mr Mackenzie, which rules all our fates, including those of Napoleon and Alexander.'

10   The Mad Enterprise

June 1807

'How did you discover the connection between us?' Drinkwater asked at last, after the two men had sat in silence awhile. 'I understood my brother to be living under a *nom de guerre.*'

'Oh, it isn't common knowledge, Captain Drinkwater; you need have no fear that more than a few men know about it. Dungarth does, of course, and Prince Vorontzoff, your brother's employer and a man sympathetic to the alliance with Great Britain, knows him for an Englishman. But I think I am the only other man who knows his identity, excepting yourself, of course.'

'But you have not said how you knew.'

'It is quite simple. He told me once. He was sent to me from Hamburg. I introduced him to the elder Vorontzoff and, one night, shortly before I left St Petersburg, we got drunk . . . a Russian custom, you see,' Mackenzie said and Drinkwater thought that Mackenzie had probably ensured Edward's loose tongue by his own liberality. 'He had reached a turning-point. A man does not put off the old life overnight and he seemed over-burdened with conscience. He made some thick allusions to drinking water. The joke was too heavy for wit and he was too drunk to jest, yet his persistence made me certain the words had some significance . . . but it was only when I learned your name from Lieutenant . . .'

'Quilhampton.'

'Just so, that I began to recall Ostroff's drunken pun. Then, having had my professional curiosity aroused, I felt it was necessary to,' Mackenzie shrugged with an irresponsible smile, 'to invade your privacy, I think you said. And my effrontery was rewarded; you had inscribed Ostroff's Russian signature in your journal. *Quod erat demonstrandum.*'

'I see.' It was very strange, but Drinkwater felt an enormous weight lifted from him. Somehow he had known for years that he must atone for his own crime of aiding and abetting Edward's escape from the gallows. It was easy to excuse his actions, to disguise his motives under the cant of reasons of state. The truth was that his own rectitude made him feel guilty. Edward was a man who drifted like a straw upon the tide and who, through some strange working of natural laws, managed to float to the surface in all circumstances. To Edward, and probably Mackenzie, his own misgivings would seem utterly foolish. But he knew himself to be of a different type, a man whose life had been dogged by set-backs, wounds and hardships. Perhaps the atonement would still come but he could not deny the relief at Edward's identity no longer being quite so hermetic a secret.

He looked at Mackenzie. A few moments earlier he had been ready to consign the man to the devil. Now they sat like old friends sipping their wine, bound by the common knowledge of Ostroff's true identity. It occurred to Drinkwater that, yet again, Mackenzie had a superior hold over him; but he found the knowledge no longer made him angry.

'I knew my brother to have found employment with Prince Vorontzoff, on account of his abilities with horses, but I do not fully understand how he serves you and Lord Dungarth.'

'He is a brilliant horseman, I believe, and on account of this he formed a close friendship with Vorontzoff's son. Good horsemen are much admired in Russia and the younger Vorontzoff, being appointed to the army in the field, got some sort of commission for Ostroff. That sort of thing is not difficult in the Tsar's bureaucracy. Ostroff was at Austerlitz and attached to the Don Cossacks at Eylau, though what he has been up to lately I do not know. I was trying to make contact with him and Wilson when I was chased into Königsberg by those French dragoons.'

'And now you want to make another attempt at reaching him through Memel?'

'Yes. And I would wish you to wait there for my return.'

'And then convey you to London with all dispatch?'

'I see, at last, that we are of one mind, Captain Drinkwater,' Mackenzie smiled.

'Then we had better drink to it,' Drinkwater said, rising and fetching the decanter.

'A capital idea,' replied Mackenzie, holding out his glass.

Drinkwater woke sweating and staring into the darkness, trying to place the source of the wild laughter. He had been dreaming, a nightmare of terrifying reality, in which a white-clothed figure loomed over him to the sound of clanking chains. The figure had been that of Hortense Santhonax, her beauty hideously transformed. The Medusa head had laughed in his face and he had seemed to drown below her, struggling helplessly as the laughter grew and the breath was squeezed from his lungs.

In the darkness of the cabin, surrounded by the familiar creaking of *Antigone*, he found the laughter resolve itself into a knocking at the cabin door. He pulled himself together. 'Enter!'

'It's Frey, sir.' The midshipman's slight figure showed in the gloom. 'Mr Quilhampton's compliments, sir, and we've raised Memel light.'

'Very well. I'll be up shortly.'

Frey disappeared and he lay back in the cot, seeking a few minutes of peace. The nightmare was an old one but had not lost its potency. Usually he attached it to presentiment or times of extreme anxiety, but this morning he managed to smile at himself for a fool. It was the unburdening of the secret of Edward that had brought on the dream; a retrospective abstraction haunting his isolated imagination while he slept.

'Damn fool,' he chid himself and, flinging back the blankets, threw his legs over the edge of the cot. Five minutes later he was on deck.

'Mornin', Mr Q.'

'Morning, sir. Memel light three leagues distant, sir.' Quilhampton pointed and Drinkwater saw the orange glow. 'It's supposed to rival the full moon at a league, sir.'

'I'm pleased to see you have been studying the rutter, Mr Q,' said Drinkwater drily, amused at Quilhampton.

'To be fair, sir, it's Frey who has studied the rutter. I merely picked his brains.'

'Tch, tch. Most reprehensible,' Drinkwater laughed. 'Incidentally, Mr Q, I will want you to put our guest ashore later.'

'Mr Mackenzie, sir?'

'Yes.'

Drinkwater could almost hear Quilhampton's curiosity working. He considered the wisdom of revealing something of Mackenzie's purpose. On balance, he considered, it would not hurt. It was better to reveal a half-truth than risk stupid speculation growing wild. He had known a silly rumour started on the quarterdeck reach the fo'c's'le as a hardened fact magnified twentyfold. It had caused a deal of resentment among the hands, and even a denial by the first lieutenant had failed to extinguish it. The old saw about there being no smoke without fire was murmured by men starved of any news, whose days were governed by the whims of the weather and the denizens of the quarterdeck, and by whom any remark that intimated yet greater impositions upon them was accepted without question. In the end it was better that the people knew something of what was going on.

'I expect you are wondering exactly who, or what, Mr Mackenzie is, eh, James?'

'Well, sir, the thought had crossed my mind.'

'And not just yours, I'll warrant.'

'No, sir.'

'He's an agent, Mr Q, like some of those mysterious johnnies we picked up in the Channel a year or two ago. We shall put him ashore in order that he can find out what exactly the Russians are going to do after Boney beat 'em at Friedland.'

'I see, sir. Thank you.'

Drinkwater fell to pacing the quarterdeck as, in the east, the light grew and the masts, rigging and sails began to stand out blackly against the lightening sky. By the time the people went to their messes for breakfast they would know all about Mr Mackenzie.

A few hours later the barge was swung out and lowered as, with her main-topsail against the mast, *Antigone* hove to. It was a bright summer morning and the port of Memel with its conspicuous lighthouse was no more than four miles away. Mackenzie came aft to make his farewells.

'I rely upon you to cruise hereabouts until my return, Captain,' he said.

'I shall maintain station, Mr Mackenzie; you may rely upon it. I may chase a neutral or two for amusement,' Drinkwater replied, 'but my main occupation will be to ensure the ship is in a fit state for a swift passage home.'

Beyond Mackenzie, Drinkwater saw the word 'home' had been caught by a seaman coiling down a line. That, too, would not hurt. It would brighten the men's spirits to know the ship was destined for a British port.

'Do you wish me to keep a boat at Memel to await you, Mr Mackenzie?'

'No, I think not, Captain. In view of the possible results of our . . . hypothesis, I think it unwise. I can doubtless bribe a fishing boat to bring me off.' He smiled. The cupidity of fishermen was universal.

Mackenzie held out his hand and moved half a pace nearer. 'Do you have a message for Ostroff?' he asked in a low voice.

'Yes . . . wish him well for me, Mackenzie . . . and ask him if he is still afraid of the dark.'

Mackenzie laughed. 'He does not strike me as a man who might be afraid of the dark, Captain.'

Drinkwater grinned back. 'Perhaps not; but he was once. Good luck, Mackenzie.'

'*A bientôt*, Captain . . .'

For two days Drinkwater kept *Antigone* under weigh. He was merciless to the entire crew, officers and men alike. The British frigate stood on and off the land, first under easy sail and then setting every stitch of canvas she possessed. When ropes parted or jammed, he chastised the petty officers and midshipmen responsible with verbal lashings from the windward hance. It brought him a deep inner satisfaction, for junior officers were rarely blamed for the many small things that went wrong on board. They buried such failings more often than not by starting the unfortunate hands, a practice that usually assuaged the quarterdeck officers. Midshipmen had the worst name for these minor malpractices which caused such resentment among the men, and it did them good to be chased hither and thither and called to account for their failures in full view of the ship's company.

As the studdingsails rose and set for the eighth or ninth time, as the topgallant masts were struck and the yards sent down, the men worked with a will, seeing how at every misfortune it was a midshipman, a master's mate or a petty officer that was identified as being the culprit. The hands were in high glee for, with the captain on deck throughout the manoeuvres, there was little revengeful starting carried out by the bosun's mates who well knew Drinkwater's aversion to the practice. It was one thing to start men aloft in an emergency or when faced with the enemy, when the need to manoeuvre was paramount; but quite another to do it when the ship was being put through her paces.

Even the officers bore their share of Drinkwater's strange behaviour, Rogers, as first lieutenant, in particular. But he bore it well, submitting to it as though to a test of his recovery. At the end of the second day, as the men secured the guns from a final practice drill, Drinkwater pronounced himself satisfied, ordered a double ration of three-water grog served out to all hands and brought the ship to anchor a league from Memel light.

'Well, Mr Rogers, I think the ship will make a fast passage when she is called upon to do so, don't you?'

'Yes, sir. But a passage where, sir?' asked Rogers, puzzled.

'Well, if we get the right slant of wind, we shall make for London River!'

Rogers's smile was unalloyed. 'Hell's teeth, that's good news. May I ask when that might be?'

'When Mr Mackenzie returns, Sam, when Mr Mackenzie returns. '

Mr Mackenzie returned shortly before noon three days later, hailing them from the deck of a fishing boat and obviously in a state of high excitement. Drinkwater was on deck to meet him and found Mackenzie had lost his air of cool self-possession. His dust-stained clothes flapping about him, he strode across the deck, his face lined with dirt which gave its expression a compulsive ferocity.

'Captain, your cabin at once.' He seemed breathless, for all that he must have been inactive during the boat's passage.

'Prepare to get under weigh, Mr Rogers,' Drinkwater ordered, turning towards Mackenzie, but the agent shook his head.

'No . . . not yet. There is something we must attend to first. Come, Captain, every second counts!'

Drinkwater shrugged at the first lieutenant. 'Belay that, Mr Rogers. Come then, Mr Mackenzie.' He led the way below and Mackenzie collapsed into a chair. Pouring two glasses of black-strap Drinkwater handed one to the exhausted agent. 'Here, drink this and then tell me what has happened.'

Mackenzie tossed off the glass, wiped a hand across his mouth and stared at Drinkwater with eyes that glittered from red-rimmed sockets.

'Captain,' began Mackenzie, 'I need you to come with me. I have returned to persuade you. It is imperative. It is a mad enterprise, but one on which everything hangs.'

'Everything?' Drinkwater frowned uncertainly.

'Yes, everything,' Mackenzie insisted, 'perhaps the history of Europe. You are the one man who can help!'

'But I am a sea-officer, not a spy!'

Drinkwater's protest roused Mackenzie. 'It is precisely because you are a sea-officer that we need you . . . Ostroff and I. You see, Captain Drinkwater, my hypothesis has proved correct. Napoleon and Alexander are to meet in conditions of the greatest secrecy, and to gain access we need a seaman's skills.'

The British spy made out a desperate case for Drinkwater's help and he had to concede the justice of the argument. What Mackenzie demanded was incontrovertibly within the latitude of Dungarth's special instructions. Whatever the bureaucrats at the Admiralty might think of him leaving his ship, he felt he was covered by Lord Dungarth's cryptic order: *You should afford any assistance required by persons operating on the instructions of this Department.* Now he knew why the old, recurring dream had woken him a few mornings before; he had felt a presentiment and he knew the moment for full atonement had come.

'Damn these metaphysics,' he growled, and turned his mind to more practical matters.

Mackenzie had suggested they took a third person, someone with a competent knowledge of horses, for they had far to travel, yet one who would play up to the fiction of Mackenzie masquerading as a merchant and Drinkwater as the master of an English trading vessel lying in Memel. For this there was only one candidate, Midshipman Lord Walmsley, the only one of *Antigone*'s people who was familiar with horses, and who spoke French into the bargain. His lordship showed a gratifying willingness to volunteer for a 'secret mission' and was ordered to remove the white patches from his coat collar and to dress plainly. His preparations in the cockpit spread a sensational rumour throughout the ship.

For himself Drinkwater begged a plain blue coat from Hill, leaving behind his sword with the lion-headed pommel that betrayed his commissioned status. Instead he packed pistols, powder and ball in a valise together with his shaving tackle and a change of small clothes.

'You will not need to worry about being conspicuous,' Mackenzie had yawned, 'the countryside is alive with travellers all going wide-eyed to see their Little Father the Tsar meet the hideous monster Napoleon.'

The hours of the afternoon rushed by. He had left instructions with Quilhampton to execute his will should he fail to return, and had attempted to write to Elizabeth but gave the matter up, for his heart was too full to trust to paper. Instead he went to the orlop to see Tregembo who was recovering well, and passed on a brief message to be given in the event of his disappearance. It was inadequate and ambiguous, but it was all he could do.

'I wish I could come with 'ee, zur,' the old man had said, half rising from the grubby palliasse upon which he lay. Drinkwater had patted his unhurt shoulder.

'You be a good fellow and get better.'

'And you look after yourself, boy,' Tregembo had said with a fierce and possessive familiarity that brought a sudden smile to Drinkwater's preoccupied face.

Finally, he had written his orders to Rogers, placing him in temporary command. Should he fail to return within ten days, Rogers was to open a second envelope which informed their Lordships of the state of affairs Mackenzie had so far discovered and his own reasons for leaving his ship. As the dog-watches changed, Mackenzie woke, and half an hour later they left the ship.

Lieutenant Quilhampton commanded the boat, making his second trip to Memel to land agents and scarcely imagining why the captain found it necessary to desert them like this. The mood in the boat was one of silent introspection as each man contemplated the future. Drinkwater and Mackenzie considered the problems ahead of them while James Quilhampton and the oarsmen gazed outboard and wondered what it would be like to be under the orders of Samuel Rogers. The only light heart among them was Lord Walmsley who had a thirst for an adventurous lark.

The long northern twilight offered them no concealment as they pulled into the river, past the lighthouse tower and its fire. The quays of Memel were still busy with fishing boats unloading their catches. Drinkwater tried to assume the character of Young, master of the *Jenny Marsden*, as typifying the kind of man he was trying to ape. He tried to recall the jargon of the merchant mariners, mentally repeating their strange terms in time with the oars as they knocked against the thole-pins: loss and demurrage; barratry and bottomry; pratique and protest; lagan and lien, jetsam and jerque notes, flotsam and indemnity. It was a bewildering vocabulary of which he had an imperfect knowledge, but in the event there were no Custom House officers to test him and with a feeling of anti-climax Drinkwater followed Mackenzie up a flight of slippery stone steps onto the quay, with Walmsley bringing up the rear.

There were no farewells. Quilhampton shoved the tiller over and the bowman bore off. Ten minutes after approaching the quay the barge was slipping seawards in the gathering darkness. Quilhampton did not look back. He felt an overwhelming sense of desolation: Drinkwater had deserted them and they were now to be subject to the arbitrary rule of Samuel Rogers.

Lieutenant Samuel Rogers sat alone at the captain's desk. His eyes looked down at the table-top. It was clear of papers, clear of Mount's long-borrowed Military Atlas, clear of everything except a key. It was a large, steel key, such as operated a lock with four tumblers. A wooden tag was attached to it and bore the legend: SPIRIT ROOM.

Rogers stared at the key for a long time. He was filled with a sense of power quite unattached to the fact that he was now in effective command of the *Antigone*. This was something else, something strange stirring in a brain already damaged by alcohol and the horrible experience of being lashed in a strait-jacket. Rogers was quite unable to blame himself for his addiction. He blamed fate and bad luck and, in a way, that obligation to Drinkwater which had become a form of jealousy. And Lallo's justification for his treatment had rested on Drinkwater's own instructions. He had been 'confined quietly' . . . the meaning was obvious. That it had been done for his own good, Rogers did not dispute. Disagreeable things were frequently done for one's own good and a streak of childishness surfaced in him. Perhaps it was a weakness of his character, perhaps a by-product of his recent chronic alcoholism, but it was to darken his mind in the following days, worsened by the isolation Drinkwater's absence had placed him in and the position of trust that he now occupied. That, too, was attributable to Drinkwater, and it was this sense of being in his place and having to act in his stead that suffused Rogers with an extraordinary sense of power. In this peculiar and unbalanced consummation of a long aggrieved and corrosive jealousy, Rogers found the will to reject his demon.

With a sweep of his hand he sent the spirit-room key clattering into a dark corner of the cabin.

PART TWO
The Raft

'I hate the English as much as you do!'

ALEXANDER TO NAPOLEON, 25 JUNE 1807

Napoleon

June 1807

General Edouard Santhonax, aide-de-camp to His Imperial Majesty Napoleon, Emperor of the French and Commander-in-Chief of the Grand Army, completed his verbal report. He watched his master pace slowly up and down the beaten earth floor of the low wayside inn which was serving briefly as Imperial Headquarters. The Emperor's polished half-boots creaked slightly as he walked between the two crude tables and their attendant benches at which sat his secretaries and crop-headed Marshal Berthier, the Grand Army's Chief-of-Staff. Their heads were bent over piles of documents taken from dispatch boxes.

The Emperor was dressed in the dark green undress uniform coat of the Horse Chasseurs of the Guard and his plump hands were clasped in the small of his back. He spun round at the end of the tavern, his head bowed, the fine brown hair swept forward in a cow-lick over the broad forehead. He paced back, towards the waiting Santhonax.

Santhonax stood silently, his plumed hat beneath his arm, the gold lace on his blue coat a contrast to the Emperor's unostentatious uniform. Napoleon stopped his pacing a foot in front of the tall officer and looked up into Santhonax's eyes.

'So, my General, we have an emissary from the Tsar, eh?'

'That is so, Sire. He waits for your command outside.'

Napoleon's face suddenly relaxed into a charming smile. His right hand was raised from behind his back and pinched the left cheek of General Santhonax, where a livid scar ran upwards from the corner of his mouth.

'You have done well, *mon brave*.'

'Thank you, Sire.'

Napoleon turned aside to where a map lay spread on the rough grey wood of the table. He laid a plump finger on the map where a blue line wound across rolling country.

'Tilsit.'

A shadow of hatching lay under the ball of the Emperor's finger, indicating the existence of a town that straddled the River Nieman.

'You say the bridge is down?'

Santhonax stepped forward beside the Emperor. 'That is so, Sire, but there are boats and barges, and the transit of the river is not difficult.'

'And you are certain that Alexander seeks an armistice, eh?'

'That is what I was led to believe, Sire.'

The Emperor hung his head for a moment in thought. At the end of the table Berthier stopped writing, pushed aside a paper and sat poised, as though sensing his master was about to dictate new movements to the Grand Army. A silence hung in the long, low room, disturbed only by the scratching of the secretaries' pens and the buzzing of a pair of flies in the small window of the inn, for the June heat was oppressive.

'Very well!' The Emperor made up his mind and began to pace again, more rapidly than before. Santhonax stepped back to make way for him.

'Write, Berthier, write! The town of Tilsit is to be declared a neutral zone. On the acceptance of our terms by the Tsar, orders are to be passed to the advance units of the Grand Army that have already crossed the Nieman, that they are to retire behind the line of that river. An armistice is to be declared. General Lariboissière of the Engineers is to requisition boats and to construct a pontoon or raft surmounted by pavilions, two in number, one to accommodate their Imperial Majesties, the other their staffs.' The Emperor paused and looked at Santhonax.

'It is fortunate, General, that you were formerly a frigate-captain. We shall put your maritime expertise to good account.' Napoleon smiled, as if pleased at some private joke, then he addressed himself to Berthier again. 'General Santhonax is to liaise with General Lariboissière as to the method of mooring this raft in midstream and to be responsible for the complete security and secrecy of the meeting between ourself and the Tsar.'

The Emperor swung suddenly round on Santhonax and his eyes were ice-cold.

'Is that clearly understood, my General? Secret, utterly secret.'

'Perfectly, Sire.'

'The Russian court is a sink of iniquitous intrigue, General Santhonax, a fact which should be uppermost in your mind.' The Emperor's mood had mellowed again; he seemed suddenly in an almost boyish good humour.

'Of course, Sire,' replied Santhonax dutifully.

'Very good! Now you may show in this Russian popinjay and let us set about the wooing of Alexander!'

11   The Road to Tilsit

June 1807

Captain Drinkwater woke from a deep sleep confused and disoriented. For several moments he did not know where he was. The unfamiliar smell of his bedding, the whitewashed ceiling and the chirruping of sparrows outside the small window all served to perplex him. Slowly he recalled the rapid train of events that had taken place since they landed from the barge and took their unceremonious farewell of Quilhampton.

Led in silence by Mackenzie, Drinkwater and Walmsley had walked swiftly into a maze of small, narrow streets reminiscent of an earlier age, with overhanging buildings and rickety roofs. Despite a lingering light in the sky, the omnipresence of the shuttered houses threw them into darkness as they followed the spy. Then abruptly they stopped and Mackenzie knocked imperiously on a nail-studded door. After a moment it opened, there was a quick exchange of what Drinkwater took for sign and countersign and then he and Walmsley were drawn inside, the door was closed behind them and they stood in a large, partially lit room, their presence and necessities being explained by Mackenzie to the occupant of the house. A sense of curiosity filled Drinkwater. The street smells of Memel had been odd enough, but those of the house seemed almost diabolical and this impression was heightened by what he could see of the room. Low and overhung with beams, it was largely lined by shelves, drawers and cupboards. On the drawers he could see vaguely familiar lettering and in the cupboards, behind glass, the owner's lantern shed highlights on jars and sorcerers' retorts. On the shelves, however, were even more sinister exhibits: a monstrous foetus, a coiled snake and a diminutive mermaid. Beside him he felt Walmsley shudder with apprehension and utter a low expression of repulsion. Drinkwater recognised the lettering on the little wooden drawers as the abbreviated Latin of the Pharmacopoeia.

'We are the guests of an apothecary, I believe,' Drinkwater whispered to the midshipman. Both men were fascinated by the ugly mermaid whose wrinkled, simian face stared at them, the dancing light of the lantern flame reflected from her glass pupils.

Mackenzie and their host turned at this moment. 'Ah, so you like my little mermaid do you, gentlemen?' The apothecary was of middle age and held the lantern for them to see the piece of cunning taxidermy. His accent was thickly Germanic, but his command of English appeared good. Mackenzie smiled.

'Well, gentlemen, our host will show you to your rooms. It is already late. I advise you to retire immediately. I have some business to attend to and we must make good progress tomorrow.'

There were no introductions and in silence Drinkwater and Walmsley followed the apothecary to an attic bedroom where two low beds were prepared by a silent and pretty blonde girl with a plait like a bell-rope down her back. The two Englishmen stood awkwardly with the apothecary while the girl bustled about. Then, as she left, he gestured to the beds.

'Thank you,' Drinkwater said. The man bowed and withdrew. Mackenzie had already disappeared and as the door closed Drinkwater heard the lock turned. 'It seems we are prisoners for the night, Mr Walmsley,' he remarked with an attempt at a reassurance he was far from feeling. To his surprise Walmsley grinned back.

'Perhaps it's just as well, sir.'

'Eh?' Drinkwater was puzzled, then he remembered the blue eyes of the girl and her last, frankly curious glance as she bobbed from the room. 'Ah, yes . . . well, I think we must sleep now.' And despite his misgivings, despite a gnawing reaction of having deserted his post, Drinkwater had fallen into a deep, dreamless and wonderful slumber.

His confusion on waking was less comforting. He lay for a long time wondering if he had made the right decision in leaving *Antigone*; his thoughts alternated in a wild oscillation between a patient argument in favour of co-operating with the mysterious

Mr Mackenzie and a swift panic that he had acted with insanely foolish impetuosity. In the opposite corner Midshipman Lord Walmsley still snored peacefully, sublimely unconcerned and probably dreaming of the blonde girl.

There was a sudden grating in the lock and the door opened. The apothecary came in and wished them good morning. The girl followed, a tray in her pink hands from which coffee, fresh bread and a species of black sausage sent up a pungent and appetising aroma. Drinkwater saw Walmsley stir and open his eyes. He looked at the pretty face, smiled and sat up.

'Herr Mackenzie requests that you be ready in half an hour, gentlemen,' the apothecary said, then chivvied the girl out and closed the door.

'I will shave while you pour the coffee,' Drinkwater said in an attempt to preserve a little of the quarterdeck dignity in the awkward and enforced intimacy with the midshipman. While this curious little ritual was in progress Mackenzie made his appearance.

'Good morning, gentlemen. You must forgive me for having deserted you last night. There were certain arrangements to make.'

He waited for the two naval officers to complete their preparations and when they were both ready said, 'Now, gentlemen, when we leave here we assume our new identities. I am a merchant, a Scotsman named Macdonald. You, Captain, are a merchant master. I leave you to choose your own name and that of your ship. Mr Smith here,' he nodded at Walmsley, 'is a junior mate. I have a chaise below.' He smiled at Drinkwater. 'By great good fortune you are not compelled to ride. Lord Leveson-Gower arrived here last night. He is no longer persona grata at the Tsar's court. Fortunately the chaise he used for amusing himself in St Petersburg bears no arms. I have the use of it.' He made a gesture to indicate the door. 'Come, we must be off. We have twenty leagues to cover before night.'

They clattered down the stairs and emerged into the apothecary's room which looked less terrifying in the daylight that slanted in through the narrow windows. The mermaid was revealed as a hybrid sham, a curiosity of the taxidermist's art designed to over-awe the ignorance of the apothecary's customers. They passed through into the street.

'The box please, Smith.' Mackenzie nodded Walmsley to the driver's seat and opened the door of the chaise for Drinkwater. 'A steady pace,' he said to the midshipman. 'We don't want the horses blown.'

Walmsley nodded and vaulted up onto the seat. Drinkwater climbed in and settled himself. Mackenzie lifted their meagre baggage in with them and then climbed in himself. He tapped Walmsley's shoulder and the chaise jerked into motion. Drinkwater turned to take his farewell of the apothecary, but the studded door was already closed. Only a small, pretty, blue-eyed face watched their departure from a window.

For the first quarter of an hour Drinkwater attended to the business of settling himself in comfort as the chaise moved over the uneven road. Mackenzie was kneeling up on the front seat, giving the midshipman directions as they drove the equipage through the narrow streets, round innumerable corners and out onto what passed in Lithuanian Kurland for a highway.

'A sea of mud in the autumn, a waste of ice and snow in winter, a mass of ruts in the spring and a damnable dustbowl at this time of the year,' explained Mackenzie at last, 'like every damned road in the Tsar's empire.'

In the June heat the dust clouds rose from the horses' hooves and engulfed the chaise so that Drinkwater's view of the countryside was through a haze. The road ran parallel to the wide and shining expanse of the Kurische Haff, the huge lagoon which formed the ponded-back estuary of the Nieman. On either side, slightly below the level of the highway, the marshy grassland was grazed by cattle.

'A somewhat monotonous landscape, Captain,' observed Mackenzie conversationally, 'but I assure you, you are seeing it at its best.'

'You know it well?' prompted Drinkwater, enforced leisure making him anxious to discuss with Mackenzie more than the appearance of the hinterland of Memel.

Mackenzie, with an infuriating evasion, ignored the question. 'I believe that it was the great Frenchman De Saxe that wanted this country for his own. A bastard aspiring to a dukedom, eh? And now, in our modern world, we have an attorney's son aspiring to an empire . . . That, my dear Captain, is progress.'

'He has done more than aspire, if what you are saying is true.'

'You prefer "acquire" then?'

'It would be more accurate . . . Mackenzie.'

'Macdonald.'

'Macdonald, then. This chaise, you say it belongs to our ambassador, Lord Leveson-Gower, and that he arrived in Memel last night?'

'Yes. The Tsar let it be known that his lordship was no longer welcome about His Imperial Majesty's person. He confirms what I had already learned, that emissaries have been received with every appearance of cordiality from French Headquarters and that Prince Czartoryski has left for a preliminary interview with the French Emperor to arrange a secret meeting.'

'So your worst fears are indeed justified.'

Mackenzie nodded. 'And now we have the leisure, I can offer you a full explanation of what has happened, and how your help is essential.'

'Anything that lessens my doubts about the folly of this journey would be welcome,' said Drinkwater grimly, suddenly clutching at the side of the chaise as it heeled over, its offside wheels running off the road while they overtook a heavily laden ox-cart trundling slowly along. He gestured at the pair of plodding peasants who trudged at the head of the team and the man and woman who sat on the cart.

'I am still unconvinced about your lack of secrecy,' he said frowning. 'I am at a loss . . .'

Mackenzie laughed. 'This business of spying,' he said, still smiling, 'is not always a matter of cloaks and daggers. I move about quite openly for the most part. For me the subterfuge of disguise is of little use. I am well known in high places in Russia. The Tsar himself might recognise me, for I have served in the Caucasus with a commission from himself.'

Mackenzie's eyes drifted off, over the flat landscape that was such a contrast to the precipitous peaks of those distant mountains. 'General Bennigsen knows me too. In fact we shall be sharing lodgings with him.'

'Good Lord!'

'Let me explain, Captain. There is no hurry, we have a long way to go. To allay your fears of being discovered you will observe before we go very much further that the whole country is turning out. Tilsit, the town on the Nieman whither we are bound, is attracting all the country gentry for miles about. It has been declared a neutral zone and will be seething with soldiers and squires by tonight. It was already filling when I left. Nothing like this has happened in this backwater since De Saxe came to Mitau to wrest Kurland from the Tsars. We shall be like a drop in the ocean. Sometimes a bold front is the best concealment.' He nodded at Walmsley's back. 'I have told your young friend there to cluck to his horses in French, and am glad that he knows enough of the tongue to manage tolerably well.'

'You think of everything.'

'It is my business to. Now, as for me, I proceeded directly towards Tilsit when your lieutenant landed me the other day. As soon as I encountered the outposts of the Russian army I made my way to the bivouac of the Hetman's Don Cossacks and found Ostroff. Together we went off to Piktupohen where the Imperial Russian headquarters lay and located Vorontzoff. The Prince is as staunch a believer in a British alliance as his old father and distrusts the French. He told me at once that Alexander has agreed to a secret meeting with Napoleon. Both Vorontzoff and Ostroff undertook to supply whatever information they might learn as to the outcome of this secret conclave, as I told you yesterday. By a stroke of luck Vorontzoff, in his capacity as an Imperial aide, was ordered into Tilsit to commandeer lodgings for the Tsar and his Commander-in-Chief, General Bennigsen. As a result, I was able to apply a little influence and General Bennigsen and his staff will be quartered in a large house on the Ostkai, having a good view of the Nieman and the French across the river. It is an ancient house, built round a courtyard, and the ground floor consists of stables and a large warehouse. The owner is an old Jew who proved characteristically amenable to gold. I secured a tiny attic, locked and barred from the inside and obviously a well-used hiding place during the frequent persecutions of the Hebrews. Here I prepared to hole-up until it became clear what had been arranged between Alexander and Napoleon. I was ideally placed. If my hypothesis proved true and Alexander and Napoleon combined, then it was likely that

Bennigsen would fall from grace. He is already in disfavour, having lost at Friedland. Such are the suspicions at the Tsar's court that the fact that he was born a Hanoverian and hence a subject of our own King George is held against him, and there is, in any case, a rising tide of resentment against German officers, who are held largely responsible for the recent military disaster.'

'But I thought the Tsar owed Bennigsen some obligation due to the part he played in the murder of his father,' put in Drinkwater, as Mackenzie drew breath.

Mackenzie smiled with a sardonic grin. 'There is little honour in this world, least of all among thieves and murderers, despite the proverb,' he said. 'No, I think Bennigsen will be quietly sacrificed when the time comes. Alexander is unpredictable in the extreme, and an autocrat's foreign policies are apt to be as erratic as the tacking of your own frigate.'

It was Drinkwater's turn to grin at the simile. 'So, you were ensconced in the attic of the Jew's house,' he prompted.

'Yes. And I could rely upon Bennigsen's disaffection and consequent disloyalty if things went against us. Part of Bennigsen's staff arrived, a coterie of drunken young officers whose behaviour would disgrace a farmyard. But they brought with them some of the finest bloodstock in Russia, stabling them in the warehouse. My own mount was quartered some distance away and this ready form of transport further satisfied me in my choice of post.'

'And yet you deserted this secure bolt-hole, risked everything and returned to Memel to fetch me. Yesterday you mentioned boats and secret meetings and the presence of a seaman as being vital.'

'My dear Captain, I spavined a good horse because, without exaggeration, you are truly the only man who can help effect this thing.'

'That much you already said, but you also said my brother . . .'

'Ostroff.'

'Ostroff, then, was not likely to be able . . .'

'Not without you, Captain, hence your unique importance in the matter. You are, as it were, of a dual value.'

'I do not follow.'

Mackenzie leaned forward, his face a picture of urgency. Gone were the traces of yesterday's exhaustion. 'Captain,' he said,

'Napoleon has ordered that his meeting with Alexander shall take place exactly midway between their two armies, in conditions of such secrecy that no one shall be privy to the settlement between them.'

'I understand that; and that you intend, with my help, to eavesdrop on them.'

'Exactly, Captain. You will help devise the method by which it shall be done, but there is also the question of who shall do it. I myself cannot undertake the task since it is for me to ensure that the intelligence is got out of this benighted land and back to London. Vorontzoff is out of the question since he has his duties to attend to, is of more use in other ways and is far too well known to be passed off in disguise. The only candidate for the post of danger is Ostroff, but Ostroff protests it is impossible, despite the money he has been offered, and only you, as his brother, will be able to persuade him of the absolute necessity of attempting this coup.'

Drinkwater sat for some moments in silence. The whirring of the wheels on the road, the heat and the dust suggested an illusion of peace, yet every revolution of those soothing wheels took them nearer a situation as desperate and risky as any he had yet faced in his life. He was penetrating deep into territory that would soon be abruptly hostile, dressed in plain clothes on a mission of such danger that he might end his life before a firing squad, shot as a spy. He passed a hand wearily over his face and looked up at Mackenzie.

'You have me on a lee shore,' he said ruefully as Mackenzie smiled thinly. 'So I have to convince Ostroff that he must spy on the two Emperors as well as devise a means by which it may be done?'

'Exactly,' replied Mackenzie, leaning back against the buttoned leather of the chaise, his face a picture of satisfaction.

'Has it occurred to you that the thing might indeed be impossible?'

'No. Difficult, yes, but not impossible.'

'You have a great deal of faith in my inventiveness . . . something I'm not sure I share with you.'

'Come, come, Captain, I'm certain that you have sufficient resourcefulness to devise a means of concealing a man in a raft!'

The morning rolled by in a cloud of dust. The broad and shining

Nieman wound its way through increasingly undulating country of low hills. Here and there the river ran close to the road, undercutting a red clay cliff before it swung away in a great loop. The coppices of willow gave way to birches and scattered elms that reminded Drinkwater of home and they passed through the occasional village with its low steadings and slow, incurious peasants. Above the noise of the horses, the creak of harness and the thrum of wheels on the dirt road, the soaring song of larks could still be heard. At one point, where the river swung close to the road, Mackenzie bade Walmsley pull over and into a side lane which led down to a ferry.

'We'll water the horses and take a bite to eat,' he said and they pulled up beside a sunken hovel and a box-like pontoon provided with chains that formed a crude ferry across the Nieman.

As Walmsley tended the horses and Mackenzie provided black bread, sausage and a bottle of kvass from his saddle-bags, he nodded to the ferry.

'Take a look at it,' he muttered. 'They've one just like it at Tilsit, hauled out on a slipway and being prepared for the secret meeting.'

Drinkwater walked casually down to the rickety wooden jetty alongside which the ungainly craft lay moored. He ignored the ferryman who emerged from the hovel and approached him, concentrating his attention on the raft. It was a 'flying bridge', or chain ferry of large size, clearly intended to transport cattle and carts across the broad river, and he spent several minutes studying the thing intently. Mackenzie shouted something incomprehensible at the ferryman which made the Lithuanian swear and retire gesticulating behind a slammed door.

Twenty minutes later they resumed their journey. Mackenzie had briefed Walmsley as to the dangers they might now encounter, leaving Drinkwater to consider the problem of the raft. When they were fairly on their way Mackenzie leaned forward.

'Well, can it be done?'

Drinkwater nodded. 'In theory, yes . . . but we need to consider tools, how we get to the thing . . . you must let me think . . .'

Mackenzie leaned back, permitting himself a small, secretive smile of satisfaction. From time to time he cast a surreptitious glance at Drinkwater, but for the most part he dozed as the chaise rolled on. Ahead of them smoke blurred the horizon and there were an increasing number of travellers on the road. The carriages and open chaises of the gentry, blooming with the light colours of women's dresses and hats, were moving towards Tilsit, while coming in the contrary direction a thin stream of peasants accompanied by the occasional bandaged soldier made their weary way. Mackenzie roused from his nodding.

'The wealthy and curious travel with us,' he said, 'the indigent poor escape the rapacity of the military who will be busy consuming every hidden bushel of stored grain, every chicken and pig in every poor steading, and requisitioning every house, hovel and pigsty for their billets.'

As the afternoon wore on, Mackenzie's assertion was proved true. For now, along the road were encamped green-and-grey-clad infantry, milling in bivouac, their cooking fires sending a smoke pall up into the blue sky. Lines of tethered cavalry horses stood patiently as troopers distributed fodder, and the regimental smithies stood by the roadside and made good the ravages of the campaign. Here and there lines of unlimbered guns were pulled off the road, their gunners sitting on the heavy wooden trains smoking, drinking or playing cards. Along the riverside a party were duck-shooting and, at one point, they were over-taken by a wild group of young officers racing their Arabs, to the complete disregard of all other users of the highway.

They passed through a village deserted by its inhabitants. In the duck-pond an entire battalion of nakedly pink Russian soldiers splashed and skylarked, bathing themselves clean of the red dust. The plain was filled with men and horses, and it seemed impossible that this vast multitude had suffered a defeat. Such numbers seemed to Drinkwater to be invincible.

They breasted a low hill and were met by a great wave of sound, that of hundreds of deep voices intoning the chants of the Russian Orthodox liturgy. Amid the gaudy trappings of war the summit of the knoll was crowned with the gilded panoply of the church. The priests' vestments gleamed in the sunshine as they moved through a long line of bare-headed men beneath banners of gold and red. The gilded chasubles, the waving banners and the sacred images borne aloft by acolytes were accompanied by wafts of incense and the intense, low, humming song of the soldiers of Tsar Alexander at their devotions.

Mackenzie leaned over and tapped his knee: 'You see now why Napoleon wants them for allies, and why we must not let them go. I know them, Captain, I have served with them.'

As they slowed to force their way through the worshippers, Drinkwater thought that at any moment their progress would be challenged. But nothing happened. There seemed to be hardly a man posted as a sentry. In company with other equipages they travelled on, Walmsley on the box, making sheep's eyes at the prettier of the women in the neighbouring conveyances.

The sun was westering when Mackenzie pointed ahead and Drinkwater craned around to see.

'*Voilà*, Tilsit.'

The Nieman was narrower now, and wound less wildly between the water-meadows of lush green that were dotted with the bright gold of buttercups. More cows grazed its banks and stood hock-deep in its waters among the reeds, their tails lazily flicking off the flies and mosquitoes that abounded. On the rising ground to their left the ripening wheat and rye was trampled, but ahead of them the red roofs and towers of a substantial town lay hazy in the sunshine.

'And look there!' said Mackenzie suddenly, pointing again, but this time across the river.

A score of horsemen were watering their horses. They wore rakish shakos and pelisses, their two vedettes clear against the skyline.

'French hussars!' Mackenzie declared.

Drinkwater's curiosity was terminated abruptly when Walmsley pulled back on the reins and applied the brake, so that the wheels locked and the chaise skidded. He turned in his seat as Mackenzie put a cautionary finger on his knee.

'I'll do the talking,' he said, nodding reassuringly as Walmsley looked round anxiously from the box.

Ahead of them, drawn up in a rough line across the road, was a dark mass of cavalry; shaggy men on shaggy horses whose fierce eyes glared at the passengers in the carriages and moved over reluctantly to let the gentry through. Drinkwater looked at them with undisguised curiosity, for these were undoubtedly the Cossacks of which he had heard. They scarcely looked like cavalry; they wore baggy blouses and their trousers were stuffed into boots, it was true, but their waistbands and sheepskin saddles were strung about with the products of looting and plunder. Those few who were on foot waddled bowlegged with a rolling gait that reminded Drinkwater of grotesque seamen. Wicked-looking lances were slung across their backs and sabres gleamed in metal scabbards at their hips.

One great bearded giant, whose legs seemed to drag low on either side of his diminutive pony, kicked his mount close to the chaise. Peering at Drinkwater he made some comment which excited laughter from his compatriots. Drinkwater smelt the animal odour of the man, but Mackenzie, undaunted, riposted in Russian. The Cossack's face altered and his friends roared again at the man's obvious discomfiture.

The man was about to reply when his pony was shoved aside by a magnificent bay horse ridden by an officer. He appeared to recognise Mackenzie.

'Ah, Alexei, where the devil did you spring from?' he said in the French that was the lingua franca of the Russian nobility. 'I thought you had gone into Tilsit with Ostroff.'

Drinkwater recognised the last word and felt his heart hammering painfully under his ribs.

'Indeed, Count, I did, but I returned to Memel to fetch this gentleman here,' Mackenzie said in the same language, gesturing towards Drinkwater. 'He is the master of an English brig.'

'An Englishman, eh?' The Cossack officer stared at Drinkwater. 'I doubt he'll be welcome in Tilsit. But, to you merchants and the English, business is business, eh?'

'If the rumours are true, Count, and an armistice is declared, the Captain here wants his cargo out of Tilsit and Memel. But the rascally Jews won't sell at the prices they had agreed because the place is stuffed full of fools who might buy at a higher rate.'

'Tell him to hurry then,' said the Cossack officer and added, 'you'll be lucky to find lodgings in the town unless, like the Blessed Virgin, you are satisfied with a byre.' He crossed himself as he laughed at his blasphemous joke, then he peered into the chaise.

Drinkwater looked with sudden apprehension at Mackenzie, but the 'merchant' grinned and reached under the seat.

'Would a bottle be welcome to help us past your unspeakably stinking ruffians, Count?'

'As the Blessed Virgin herself, M'sieur Macdonald.' The officer grinned and caught the bottle of vodka. 'I shall toast you, Alexei, when I rest my ignoble centaurs tonight.' He turned and shouted something to the great bearded Cossack who had taken such an interest in Drinkwater. 'Hey, Khudoznik . . .!'

The man was looking curiously at Lord Leveson-Gower's horses in the shafts. At the Count's remark he looked up and growled something in reply, at which the whole squadron, its commanding officer included, roared with laughter.

'On your way, Alexei, and *bon voyage*, Captain!' he said, and Walmsley, seeing the road ahead clear, whipped up the horses.

Drinkwater wiped his face with relief. 'Who the devil was that? You seemed uncommonly intimate.'

Mackenzie laughed. 'That, believe it or not, was Ostroff's superior officer, Count Piotr Kalitkin, commander of two squadrons of the Hetman's Don Cossacks. He knows me for a Scottish merchant, Alexander Macdonald, and we have been drunk several times in each other's company. He thinks you are going to Tilsit . . .'

'Yes, I got the drift of it: to find out why my cargo has not been brought down river to Memel.'

'Excellent!' laughed Mackenzie, in high good humour after the incident.

'What was that exchange between the Count and that malodorous fellow?' asked Drinkwater.

'It was an obscenity. The Count asked the man, Khudoznik, if he wanted to bugger our horses before he stood aside and let us through. Khudoznik replied there was no need for he had found a farm where the farmer had a wife, a daughter and forty cows!'

'Good God!'

'I doubt they're any worse than your own seamen . . .'

'Or some of the officers,' agreed Drinkwater, jerking his head in Walmsley's direction, 'but those fellows looked born in the saddle.'

'Indeed. Their Little Father, the Tsar, exempts them from taxation in exchange for twenty to forty years of military service. And they will literally steal the shirt from your back, if you let them.' Mackenzie nodded at Drinkwater's open coat.

'It seems I had a lucky escape in several ways,' remarked Drinkwater.

It was dark by the time they reached the town and here they encountered sentries. They were the third in a little convoy of carriages that had bunched together on the road, and by the time the sergeant had got to them he paid scant attention to the pass Mackenzie waved under his nose.

'I doubt if the fellow can read,' Mackenzie said, as Walmsley urged the exhausted horses forward, 'although, if he could, he would find the pass in order and signed by Prince Vorontzoff.' Mackenzie stood and tapped Walmsley on the shoulder. 'Pull in over there,' he ordered in a low voice, and the chaise passed into the deep shadow of a tall building. Mackenzie and Walmsley exchanged places and the chaise rolled forward again.

'How do you do?' Drinkwater asked Walmsley in a low voice.

'Well enough, sir,' replied the midshipman, stretching tired muscles. 'Where are . . .?'

'No questions until we are safe.'

'Safe, sir?'

'In hiding.'

'I don't think I'll feel safe until I'm back on the old *Antigone*.'

'We are of one mind then. Now be quiet.' They had pulled into a side turning which bore no resemblance to what Drinkwater had imagined the Jew's house looked like even in the darkness. Mackenzie dropped from the box, opened the door and motioned them down. Taking the saddle-bags from the chaise he handed them to Drinkwater.

'Wait here,' he said and moved round to the horses' heads. He led the chaise off, and left the two Englishmen standing in the darkness. They pressed back into the shadows and listened to the noises of the night.

Kalitkin's news of an armistice was affirmed by the noise of revelry around them. Every window they could see was ablaze with candlelight. The strains of violins and balalaikas, of bass and soprano voices were added to raucous laughter and the squeals of women. Beside him Drinkwater heard Walmsley snigger nervously and their proximity to a bawdy house was confirmed by Mackenzie who approached out of the shadows without horses or chaise.

'The more people, the easier the concealment,' he whispered. 'I've left the chaise at the brothel full of officers' horses.' He led them back the way they had come and into the comparative brilliance of the town square.

The place was full of people milling about, women giggling on the arms of officers, the curious gentry and their outraged womenfolk hurrying past the licentious soldiers. Beggars and whores, vendors and street musicians filled the open space and occasionally a horseman would ride through, or a carriage escorted by lancers trot by to be wildly cheered in case it was the Little Father, the Tsar.

Drinkwater began to see what Mackenzie meant. The crowd, hell-bent on pleasure, took no notice of them. Within minutes they had entered beneath a low arch, reminiscent of an English coaching inn, and found themselves in a courtyard. Two or three orderlies lounged about, smoking or drinking, but no one challenged them. Even the tall sentry at the door snapped to attention as Mackenzie, walking with an air of purpose, threw open the door and led the trio inside.

Crossing the courtyard Drinkwater had been aware of stable doors and upper windows flung open, from which candlelight and the noise of drunken revels poured in equal measure. Inside, the stairs were littered with bottles, an officer in his shirt-sleeves, his arm round the waist of a compliant girl, lounged back and ignored them. A half-open upper door revealed a brief glimpse of a mess-dinner, a table groaning under food, bottles, boots upon the table-cloth and a whirling dancer kicking out the *trepak* to the wild and insistent beat of balalaika chords.

On the next floor the doors were closed. A woman's chemise and a pair of shoes and stockings lay on the landing. Above the shouts and cheers from below, the shrieks of drunken love-making came from behind the closed doors and were abruptly drowned by the concerted tinkle of breaking glass as, below, a toast was drunk to the dancer.

A flight higher they encountered the Jew, his family behind him, peering anxiously down from an upper landing. Mackenzie addressed a few words to him and he drew back. Drinkwater saw the dull gleam of gold pass between them.

They passed through a further door, dark and concealed in the gloom. It shut behind them and they stumbled up bare wooden steps in total darkness. At the top Mackenzie knocked on a door; three taps and then two taps in a prearranged signal. There was the noise of a bar being withdrawn and a heavy lock turning. Drinkwater followed Mackenzie into a tiny attic, the rafters meeting overhead, a dormer window open to the night and from which the quick flash of lamplight on water could be glimpsed. Mackenzie stood aside, revealing the single occupant of the attic.

'Let me introduce you, Captain, to the man called "Ostroff".'

12 Ostroff

24 June 1807

'By God, it *is* you . . .' Edward came forward, holding up a lantern to see his brother. 'Mackenzie said he would force the issue one way or another. It never occurred to me he would bring *you* back. You've come a damned long way to collect your debt.'

Edward's poor joke broke the ice. Drinkwater held out his hand and looked his brother up and down. The jest about the money was characteristic; Edward was still the gambler, the opportunist. He was heavier of feature than Drinkwater remembered, his face red with good living and hard drinking, and he wore a Russian uniform unbuttoned at the neck. His feet were stuffed into soft boots and he had the appearance of a man who was about to settle. As if to confirm this he took off his tunic and loosened his stock.

'By God, it's hot up here, under the eaves. Who's this, Mackenzie?' He indicated the midshipman.

'Our driver, who has done a fine job and deserves some reward. Have you a bottle?'

Edward reached under a truckle bed and produced a bottle of vodka. 'There are glasses on that chest.'

They drank and Drinkwater performed the introduction, explaining that Ostroff was a British officer in the Russian service. Fortunately the looks of the two brothers were too dissimilar to excite suspicion as to the true nature of their relationship and Walmsley, tired and slightly overawed by the situation he found himself in, maintained a sensible silence. As they finished the vodka Mackenzie motioned to the midshipman.

'You and I will go and forage for something to eat, and leave these gentlemen to reminisce over their last encounter.'

They clattered down the steps and left a silence behind them. Drinkwater peered cautiously from the window, but he could see little beyond the black and silver river, the tall houses of the quay opposite and the sentries pacing up and down in the lamplight.

'You can't see much, but the raft is to the right. You'll see it clearly in daylight.'

'You know why I'm here, then?'

Behind him Edward sighed heavily and Drinkwater turned back into the attic. Edward had sat himself on the truckle bed and Drinkwater squatted on the chest.

'Yes. Mackenzie, a remarkable wizard, assured me he would bring back the one man who could accomplish this thing.'

'You sound doubtful.'

'It's impossible, Nat. Wait until you see the bloody raft. They've got one of those flying bridges . . .'

'I know, I saw one lower down the river.'

'And you think it can be done?' Edward asked doubtfully.

Drinkwater shook his head. 'I don't know yet. Let us make up our minds in daylight.'

'Here . . .' Edward held out the bottle and refilled their glasses. 'To fraternity.'

Their eyes met. 'Do you remember my taking you aboard the *Virago*?'

'I found the life of a seaman far from pleasant.'

'I'm sorry,' said Drinkwater curtly, 'I had no option. You recall Jex, the purser who discovered who you were?'

'Christ yes! What happened to him?'

'He was providentially killed at Copenhagen . . . But tell me about yourself. You look well enough. Mackenzie tells me that you live *chez* Vorontzoff.'

Edward smiled. 'Oh yes. The life of an exile is a good one when well-connected. Your Lord-at-the-Admiralty pays me well enough and I still trifle a little at the tables . . . I'm very comfortable.'

'Are you married?'

Edward laughed again. 'Married! Heavens, no! But I've a woman, if that's what you mean. In Petersburg, in Vorontzoff's palace . . . I do very well, Nat, that's why you will find me unwilling to risk myself under that raft.'

'I understand that Mackenzie has promised you a very handsome sum if you can pull it off.'

Drinkwater saw the expression of greed cross Edward's face; a small narrowing of the eyes, the quick lick of the tongue across the lips. He had always been a slave to money, easy money in large amounts. Edward suddenly looked askance at Drinkwater.

'You haven't come to reclaim your debt, have you?' The irrelevant question revealed the extent of Edward's corruptibility. Drinkwater smiled sadly.

'Good heavens, Ned, I cannot remember how much I loaned you.'

'Neither can I,' Edward replied with dismissive speed and occupied himself with refilling the glasses. 'You know, Nat,' he continued after a moment, 'I owe neither you, nor Mackenzie, nor Great Britain any allegiance . . . Despite my association with Vorontzoff, I am my own man . . .'

'That begs the question of whether you will get under this raft,' said Drinkwater, the problem vexing him again and intruding into his mind so that he half-stood, cracked his head on the eaves and sat down again. 'Besides, did you know who you killed at Newmarket?'

A shadow passed over Edward's face.

'I have killed since,' he said with sudden aggression, 'mostly Frenchmen . . .'

'It was a pity about the girl, Ned, but the man was a French agent.' Dawning comprehension filled Edward's face.

'Is that how you managed to protect me?'

Drinkwater nodded. 'And myself . . . and if you were to carry out this task, Ned, I fancy that I might persuade my "Lord-at-the-Admiralty" to obtain a Royal Pardon for you.'

Edward stared at his brother, his expression of incredulity gradually dissolving to amusement and cracking into stifled laughter. 'My dear Nat, you do not change! For God's sake . . . a Pardon! I would rather have two thousand pounds in gold!'

Mackenzie woke Drinkwater from his place of honour on the truckle bed at dawn. Drinkwater's head ached from the vodka and his mouth was dry. Mackenzie indicated a jug of water and, as

Drinkwater vacated the bed, he rolled into it. Walmsley still slept, rolled in a blanket, on the rough boards of the attic floor. Edward was not there.

'Where's . . . Ostroff?'

'Don't worry,' muttered Mackenzie, his eyes already closed, 'he'll be back.'

Drinkwater stared for a moment at the extraordinary man. Edward had called him a wizard and doubtless had good reason for doing so. Mackenzie's quick-wittedness had clearly proved invaluable and he was as at home in the presence of the Tsar as on this present strange campaign. For Drinkwater himself, separation from his ship, the horrible responsibility of his task and the risk of capture filled him with fretful gloom. But he addressed himself to the matter in hand. Edward had said the raft was visible . . .

He fished in the tail-pocket of Hill's coat and brought out his Dollond glass. Cleaning the lenses carefully with a pocket handkerchief whose stitched monogram brought a painfully poignant reminder of his wife, he peered from the dormer window whose casements stood open against the summer dawn.

The Nieman was perhaps a hundred yards wide. On the opposite bank a stone quay, similar to the one on which the Jew's house stood, was lined with tall old buildings, their storeys rising up above the storage for merchandise at ground level. They had Dutch gables and mansard roofs pierced by dormers such as the one from which he peered. On the quay, the Westkai, he could see the blue and white figures of the sentries, French sentries!

The thought made him ease forward gently so that he could see almost directly below him. Their Russian counterparts lounged on their muskets along the Ostkai and he withdrew into the shadow of the room. Then he saw the raft.

It was drawn up on a gravelled hard where the Westkai was recessed to facilitate the repair of the river barges. Drinkwater levelled his glass and studied it. It was identical to the flying bridge he had examined the day before, except that upon its rough boarded surface the railings had been removed and carpenters had begun the erection of a framework. He made his examination carefully, his heart beating with a mounting excitement as the possibility of success grew. Every supposition he had made after his examination of the chain ferry seemed borne out by the scrutiny of the pontoon opposite. It was impossible to be sure at this distance, but, as he went over and over his plan, he could find no major flaw in it. It would be difficult, but if he could lay his hands on some simple tools and a little luck . . .

He pulled back into the attic and put away his glass. 'The game must be worth the candle,' he muttered to himself. He cast a look at the extraordinary man who snored softly on the truckle bed and who had so disrupted his life.

'You could be the instrument of my undoing, damn you,' he murmured ruefully. When he turned again to the view of the Westkai the rising sun was gilding the gables opposite and a clock in Tilsit was striking five.

The day that followed was one of an intolerable imprisonment. The June heat upon the roof tiles made that attic an oven. Mackenzie left them during the forenoon to glean what news he could, and to see if he could acquire the few tools that Drinkwater wanted. Behind him, forbidden to show himself near the window, Walmsley fretted and fussed like a child. Ostroff made no appearance and Drinkwater became increasingly worried. From time to time he watched the raft. French engineers, under the direction of an officer of high rank, were assisted by local craftsmen. The pavilion rose steadily during the morning and began to be draped during the afternoon.

Drinkwater's anxiety reached fever-pitch when he realised there was one vital matter that, in his study of the pontoon, he had completely overlooked. It was a piece of the most idiotic stupidity yet, after his realisation that he had overlooked it, the desperate need for quick improvisation was a solace for his over-active mind.

Drinkwater's problem was simply how to get across the river. To swim was too risky; besides it exposed Edward to a long period of immersion. The rowing-boats on the river had all been withdrawn to the French side, apart from a large barge moored almost directly below their window. A solution defied him until about mid-afternoon when, after a shouted parley across the Nieman, a small boat put off from the west bank. In its stern sat two officers.

160

They disembarked just out of sight. Drinkwater heard the sound of talking men striding below the window. He guessed the two French officers had been met by some Russians. Unable to see much he realised the group had stopped directly underneath them. Wriggling back from the window he beckoned Walmsley. The bored young man came forward.

'I want you to see if you can hear what they are saying below,' Drinkwater whispered, pointing frantically downwards. Walmsley nodded and eased himself up under the sill of the open window. Drawing back into the attic Drinkwater stood and stretched. For perhaps ten minutes the hum of voices came up to them and Walmsley's face was contorted with concentration, but at last the impromptu conference broke up and Walmsley moved back into the room.

'Well?'

'I couldn't hear well, sir; but it was something about getting the barge across the river tonight . . . something about . . .' he frowned.

'Go on!'

'Well, I thought he said a "pavilion", a "second pavilion" . . . but I don't understand what that had to do with a barge . . .'

'Never mind, Mr Walmsley,' said Drinkwater suddenly grinning like a fool, 'you do not know what a signal service you have just rendered your country, by God!'

'Indeed, sir, I do not . . .'

'Never mind. When we return to the ship I shall tell you, but for the time being I must urge you to be patient and . . .'

He never finished the sentence, for the coded knock came at the door. Drinkwater motioned Walmsley to unlock it and lift the bar, while he picked up and cocked the loaded pistol left by Mackenzie when he had departed.

Mackenzie slid inside, his eyes shining with excitement.

'Bennigsen's below. The Tsar's given him the devil of a drubbing, and in public too. Bennigsen's furious at the humiliation and muttering God knows what . . . and there's more,' he took a draught at the vodka Walmsley passed him and unhooked his coat. 'The meeting is set for tomorrow.'

Kicking off his boots, Mackenzie padded cautiously to the window and stared at the raft. He gave a low whistle. '*Le théâtre de*

Napoléon,' he said with an appreciative grin. It occurred to Drinkwater that Mackenzie throve on such high excitement. 'Hullo, what have those fellows been over for?' He nodded across the river and Drinkwater eased himself alongside. The small boat had returned to the Westkai and the two French officers were disembarking up an iron ladder.

'General officers,' murmured Mackenzie, 'by the look of them.'

The two men exchanged remarks, the sunlight reflected off their highly polished thigh-boots, and began to stroll along the quay towards the slipway and the bedizened raft. They were resplendent in the blue and gold of field officers, their great, plumed bicorne hats tucked under their arms. One of them, the taller of the two, wiped his forehead with a handkerchief. Some primaeval instinct beyond curiosity prompted Drinkwater. He drew out the Dollond glass again and focused it on the two officers. He drew his breath in sharply and Mackenzie turned.

'What the devil is it?'

'God's bones,' said Drinkwater, his face drained of colour. 'Santhonax!'

13   The Waters of the Nieman

24–25 June 1807

Mackenzie snatched the glass from him. 'By God, you are right!'

'It's uncanny,' Drinkwater said, his mouth dry. He accepted the glass of vodka Mackenzie held out. 'Our paths have crossed so many times . . .'

'No matter,' said Mackenzie, suddenly resolute, 'I have brought the things you wanted. A farrier's axe was the nearest I could manage to a hammer and it can be used instead of a spike.'

Drinkwater looked at the axe which was similar to a boarding axe with a blade and spike. 'What about nails?'

'Here,' Mackenzie fished in his pocket, 'horseshoe nails.'

'It reminds me of the nursery rhyme,' Drinkwater said, regaining his composure. It was quite impossible that Santhonax posed a threat to the success of the enterprise. 'Now what about Ostroff? Where the hell is he? I want to move at dusk, if not before . . . and Mackenzie, have you been in contact with Bennigsen's staff?'

Mackenzie nodded and both men listened to the hubbub that floated up from lower in the house. 'Somehow you've got to find out which of them met those two over there,' he jerked his head towards the window. 'They'll be detailing someone off to move that barge across the river. Local watermen, I expect. You're a merchant, an ingratiating fellow. Tell them you'll arrange it.'

'I'll get the Hebrew to do it. It's his barge.'

'No, Ostroff and I will get the barge over.'

Comprehension dawned in Mackenzie's eyes and he smiled appreciatively.

'And get us some rags and soot from the Jew.'

'I see I was not mistaken in you, Captain,' Mackenzie said.

'It'll come to naught if Ostroff ain't found!' said Drinkwater sharply. 'And now I want some food!'

'I shall attend to those matters forthwith.'

Midshipman Lord Walmsley heard the departing footsteps of Captain Drinkwater and Ostroff fade down the stairs. The strange Russian officer had returned only a few minutes earlier, in time to receive his instructions from an impatient Drinkwater. He had protested a little and was then coerced by the captain and Mr Mackenzie into agreeing to change into loose-fitting peasant's trousers, felt boots and a coarse cotton blouse. Both men put on hats and were given tobacco tubes such as were smoked by the Lithuanian peasantry. Walmsley had heard Captain Drinkwater mention that his capture in such clothing would guarantee his being shot as a spy and Ostroff, in a curiously unaccented English, denied it, saying the smell would drive off the most officious French officer. The grim joke shared between the two men sent a shiver of fear for his own safety up his spine. And then they had gone, leaving Walmsley hot, bored, yet strangely fearful, alone with the enigmatic Mr Mackenzie who ignored him in his eagerness to observe the departure of the barge from the Ostkai.

Walmsley lolled back in his corner of the attic and gave his mind up to the only thing a young man of his tastes and inclination could think of in such stultifying circumstances: women. The apothecary's daughter and the pretty young women in the carriages that had accompanied them on their journey had awakened desires which had been further titillated by the occasional squeals of pleasure or protest from below. He lay imagining the activities of the young bloods on Bennigsen's staff and brooded on his own long deprivation.

At last he could tolerate inactivity no longer.

'Do you mind, sir,' he hissed at the back of Mackenzie's head, 'if I take the opportunity to empty the bucket and get a breath of air?'

Mackenzie turned from the window and wrinkled his nose at the pail they had been using as a privy. 'If you are careful, no. You may walk about a bit . . . seek crowds, you are safer in a crowd.' He turned again to look down into the river.

Walmsley could scarcely contain his excitement and, picking up the bucket, he unbarred the door.

Drinkwater forced himself to resist the nausea that swept over him as he tried to master the art of smoking tobacco. The nausea was replaced by an odd lightheadedness. The disgusting import brought back by Russian armies serving in the Caucasus revolted him almost as much as the filthy workman's clothing in which he was clad. He cleared his throat and spat with unfeigned gusto into the brown waters of the River Nieman. Above their heads the west-ward-facing glazings of the dormer window blazed with the reflected sunset, masking entirely the watching face of Mackenzie.

Edward, similarly malodorous but smoking with ease, came up to him. 'This is bloody ridiculous!' he muttered in English.

'We've no alternative,' his brother replied. Drinkwater was ter-rified of the need to speak, despite an hour's coaching in a few words of Lithuanian by Mackenzie. Edward, for whom languages presented little difficulty and who had learned sufficient patois from his campaigning, was to speak if speech were necessary. Drinkwater began to cast off the mooring ropes under the curious gaze of a tall Russian sentry.

As the semi-darkness of the northern twilight began to close over them, Drinkwater handed the end of the rope to his brother. He had told Edward exactly what to do: to hold on with a single turn until he gave the word. Drinkwater walked aft to where the sweeps poked their blades outboard, their looms constrained by grommets round single thole pins on either quarter. Drinkwater bent and ran the long sweeps out. It was going to be far from easy. He gritted his teeth, braced his feet and called 'Los!'

Edward cast off and pushed the stone facing of the Ostkai with a booted foot. The current began to move the barge as the bluff bow fell slowly off the quay. Drinkwater began to move the sweeps.

Edward came aft. 'Can I help?'

Drinkwater shook his head. Edward was no expert and it was only necessary to get a little headway on the barge and let the cur-rent do the rest.

'I'll get the line ready then.'

Drinkwater nodded and strained with the effort necessary to

make an impression on the massive inertia of the barge. He stared down into the hold, thankful that it was empty, as he thrust at the oar looms with every sinew he possessed.

He began to get the swing of it. They were thirty yards out from the Ostkai now, but fifty downstream. He threw his weight back and dragged the blades out of the water, dipped them and fell forward, his breast against his fists, his calf muscles bulging as he heaved his body forward against the resistance. The blades drove through the water slowly and he dragged them out again to repeat the process over and over, keeping the barge pointing upstream, angled outwards slightly against the current, so that they crabbed across the river.

The sweat rolled off him and he felt his head would burst. He clenched his eyes shut to prevent the perspiration stinging them. He drew breath in great rasping gasps and the unaccustomed effort set his muscles a-quiver. He became blind to everything but the need for constant effort and it seemed that he had been doing this for ever.

Then, through eyes that he opened briefly, he glimpsed the looming gables of the houses of the Westkai. Ten long minutes later, Edward jumped ashore with the bow line. The gentle nudge with which the barge brought up against the quayside almost knocked Drinkwater off his feet as he dragged the sweeps inboard. Breathing heavily and his heart thumping painfully, he caught the stern line through a heavy ring and walked forward to see that Edward had secured the bow. In accordance with their plan, and in view of the sentries on either bank, they sat down on the hatch-coaming of the barge and broached a bottle of vodka. Both men took a small swig themselves and let some dribble down over their chins and onto their clothes. Edward lit another of the disgusting cheroots while Drinkwater sat and scratched himself. The red haze was beginning to disperse from his eyes when suddenly they focused on the French sentry who came forward to stare down at them.

Edward looked up and said something in Russian. Weakened from his strenuous exertion Drinkwater sat panting, trying to still the thundering of his pounding heart. He felt quite powerless to confront the danger they were in and left the matter to his brother. The Frenchman shrugged uncomprehendingly so Edward held out the bottle. The soldier hesitated, looked round and then grabbed it and swigged at it twice before handing it reluctantly back. Edward laughed and made a guttural comment and the two men grinned, the soldier wiping a hand across his mouth. Suddenly the sentry turned, as though hearing something, and disappeared from view. A few seconds later two French officers gazed down at them and enquired what they were doing.

Edward embarked on a pantomime of pretended explanation, gesturing first to the east bank of the Nieman and then to the west, interspersed with grunted interrogatives aimed at the two officers. At their lack of understanding he launched into a repeat of the whole thing until one of them cut him short.

'*Très bien, mon vieux, nous savons* . . .' He turned to his compatriot and Drinkwater heard the name General Santhonax used twice. He felt his blood run cold and prayed to heaven that it was not their intention to verify the arrival of the barge with Santhonax. Not that he thought Santhonax would recognise him, unshaven, dirty and so totally unexpected in such a place, but the very presence of the man filled him with apprehension. His heart had stilled now but the worms of anxiety were writhing in his guts.

Edward managed a loud belch and ostentatiously swigged the vodka again. Passing the bottle to Drinkwater he reached up and dragged himself up onto the quay. His sang-froid seemed to dispel any remaining suspicions the French officers might have had. They drifted away and Edward bent to give his brother a hand up.

'Phew!' Drinkwater grunted his thanks and Edward replied by giving an exaggerated and pointed belch, reminding him of the necessity of appearing tipsy. They approached the end of the quay where the small gravel slipway ran into the river. Another sentry stood on the corner of the quay.

'*Qui va là?*'

They both began babbling incoherently, pointing down at the slipway, and indicating their intention to sleep on the pontoon that lay there.

'*Non.*'

Edward uttered an obscene dismissal. The sentry, a young man, cocked his musket but Edward slapped him on the shoulder and hung upon his arm. The man shrugged him off, wrinkling his nose in disgust, and nodded them past. They slid down onto the gravel and settled themselves under the growing shadows of the raft, lolling together and allowing their heartbeats to slow.

Twice the young sentry came to look at them but they lay still, two drunks inert and indistinguishable from the surrounding gloom. The clock in the town struck eleven then midnight. There was a crunch of boots as a patrol, led by a corporal, came by to change the guards. Words were spoken as the man going off duty indicated the two pairs of felt boots that were just visible from the quay. The corporal spat, an eloquent attestation of the superiority of the French military over a pair of drunken Kurlanders, and the patrol marched on. The silence of the night settled over them, the noises of debauch muted beneath the low chuckle of the River Nieman as it made its way to the Baltic Sea.

'Let's begin,' whispered Drinkwater as soon as the sound of the marching feet had faded. Edward eased himself up and located the new guard. He was a more experienced soldier and had made himself comfortable against a bollard on the corner of the quay. A cloud of tobacco smoke was faintly illuminated from the red glow of his pipe bowl. Edward leaned down and tapped the all clear on Drinkwater's shoulder, remaining on the look-out while his brother crawled under the pontoon to begin work.

The flying bridge, or *pont volant*, was built on a heavy timber frame. The main members of the sides ran the length of the craft. These were crossed by beams on which the rough planking of the decking was laid. Such a craft would have floated very low without proper buoyancy and this was provided by two large box-like floats to which the main members were fastened. Watching the preparations from the attic window Drinkwater had observed some attention being paid to one section of these flotation chambers and had suspected one of them was giving cause for concern. Almost immediately he found fact and conjecture had spliced themselves neatly. Beneath the pontoon the new planks were identifiable by their slightly lighter colour and the rich smell of resin from them. The raw wood was unpayed and Drinkwater investigated further. His heart leapt for he was in luck.

Reaching down to his waistband he drew out the farrier's axe. His eyes were adjusted to the darkness and he worked the spike of the axe under the end of the upper plank and began to lever it off. The rot that had necessitated the renewal of the planks had already spread into the frame so the nails drew quite easily. He got the top plank off and then he dragged himself through the gap and slumped inside. The raw pine resin could not disguise the stench of the rotten wood and stagnant water which seeped into his clothes and felt cold against his sweating skin. Twisting round, he felt about in the roof of the chamber for any opening which would allow a man to receive sufficient air to breathe and, most important, to hear. He discovered a split between two planks and enlarged it with the axe. Rubbing his hand in the foul slime of the bottom, he smeared it over the raw wood to hide his work from a casual glance. When he had finished, he drew himself out of the chamber. Even beneath the pontoon the night air smelt sweet. He lay on the damp gravel, panting heavily; the clock in the town struck two.

Dragging himself along he pulled himself out from beneath the pontoon close to his brother. Edward was shivering from the chill. 'Well?' he hissed.

'Get under when you can. It's all ready.'

Edward cast a look round and Drinkwater sensed his reluctance, but the hesitation was only momentary. The two brothers crawled below the pontoon and Drinkwater tugged Edward until he was aware of the opening. He put his mouth close to Edward's ear. 'You won't drown, even if it fills partially with water. I have cut holes in the top, you should have no trouble breathing or hearing.'

Drinkwater patted Edward's shoulder and drew back. He felt Edward shudder and then begin to work his way through the narrow gap, which gave him more trouble than his slimmer brother. A hiss of disgust told that Edward had discovered the stink and damp of his prison.

'Christ, this is madness. Why did I let you talk me into it?'

'You can get out by kicking away the ends of the planks.'

'Leave me the axe.'

'I need it for hammering home the nails.' Drinkwater paused. Edward's face was a pale, ghostly oval in the Stygian darkness. 'Do you have your bottle?'

'Of course I bloody well do.'

'Good luck.' Drinkwater moved to put the first board into

place, fishing in his pocket for the stock of nails provided by Mackenzie. Holding the head of the axe he had Edward grip the bottom plank, found the nail hole with some difficulty, inserted a nail and pushed it with the end of the axe. He felt the nail drive part way into the rotten framework. Then he drew back his right hand and smacked it hard with the open palm of his left. After repeating this process a few times he felt the nail drive home. He managed the next nail at the other end of the plank in a similar fashion, but the third proved less easy. He knew he would have to give several hard bangs with the whole axe haft. He rolled quickly across and peered from under the pontoon. There was no sign of the sentry.

With feverish impatience he returned to the hole and, holding his breath, gave a few quick, sharp taps with the axe. In seconds the plank was secure. Edward's face peered from the narrowed gap as Drinkwater returned from a second look for the sentry. There was still no sign of the man. He must have strolled off to the far end of his beat. Drinkwater lifted the second plank. Edward resisted it being put into place.

'Nat.'

'What is it?' Drinkwater asked in a desperate whisper.

'Will you get me out of here if I cannot make it myself?'

Drinkwater remembered a small boy who was afraid of the dark and the shadows in the corner of the farmhouse bedroom. 'You'll have no trouble, I promise you.' He hissed reassuringly. 'Brace your back and simply kick outwards with your heels.'

'But promise.'

'For God's sake, Ned, of course . . .'

'Your word of honour.'

'My word of honour.' He pushed the plank and Edward vanished behind the faint grey of the new wood. As he tried to locate a nail, his hands shaking with the tension, the plank was pushed towards him. He choked down an oath with difficulty. 'What?'

'We may never meet again.'

'Don't be foolish. We shall meet when you get out, at the Jew's house tomorrow.'

'But it will not be the same.'

'For God's sake . . .'

'I *must* tell you something. I want you to know I repent of the murder . . . not the man, but I loved the girl . . .'

Drinkwater expelled pent-up breath. 'I am sorry, Ned . . . Now for God's sake let me finish.'

'And I know I owe my life to you.'

'No matter now.'

'But all debts will be paid when this thing is done, eh?' Edward's voice was barely a whisper now, but Drinkwater was beside himself with anxiety. Once again he bore the burden of an elder brother. He comforted Edward's fear of a greater darkness.

'All paid, Ned, all paid.'

To Drinkwater's infinite relief Edward withdrew and Nathaniel began to fasten the last plank. It was the upper one and the nails went home with difficulty. In the end he was forced to bang hard, several times. The noise seemed deafening and as he drew back he heard the scrape of boots on gravel as a man jumped down onto the hard from the quay. He uttered a silent prayer that Edward would not react and rolled away from the buoyancy chamber, retreating further into the blackness beneath the raft.

As he lay inert, his eyes closed, trying to still his breathing, he could hear the sentry move round the pontoon, the crunch of his boots close beside him on the wet gravel. Beyond the shadow of the raft Drinkwater was aware of the first flush of dawn, a pale lightening of the river's surface. He could hear the man muttering and knew that he would be looking for the two drunken Kurlanders. For a second Drinkwater hesitated. Then, knowing he must leave Edward in no doubt of his successful escape, he acted.

Rolling from under the raft he found himself suddenly at the feet of the sentry.

'*Qui va là?*' snapped the astonished man unslinging his musket.

With one eye on the lowering bayonet Drinkwater grunted and rose on one knee. Tucking in the filthy breast of his blouse he gripped the boarding axe more firmly and staggered to his feet. If he allowed himself to be kept at bayonet point he was lost. The sentry growled at him.

Sucking in his breath he tore the axe from his breast and then, expelling air for all he was worth, he swung his arm with savage ferocity, twisting his body at the same time. With such sudden impetus the axe whirled and struck deep into the skull of the French soldier. With a dull thud the man fell, stone dead.

Drinkwater paused for an instant to catch his breath again, then he rounded on the raft and pressed close to the timber side of the float.

'Can you hear me?' he hissed.

'Yes,' he heard Edward's low reply.

'You're quite safe. I'm going now.'

Edward tapped twice and Drinkwater turned back to the gravel slipway and the dead sentry that lay beside the lapping water of the river. Slinging the musket he grabbed the man's heels and dragged him quickly into the water beneath the overhang of the quay. After the gloom beneath the raft it seemed quite light, but the dawn was delayed by rolling banks of heavy clouds and no cries of alarm greeted his panting efforts. He let the man's feet go and pushed the body out into the river. Unslinging the musket he let it fall to the muddy bottom of the Nieman. In the town the clock struck a half hour as he lowered himself into the water. He paddled out into the stream, nudging the body of his victim until he felt the current take it, then let it go. The water bore the thing away from him and he rolled on his back and peered back at the Westkai. He could see a party of sentries marching with a corporal, bringing the relief guard: he had left not a moment too soon. He began to swim with more vigour, the freedom of the river almost sensual after the strain and activity of the night. A light rain began to fall. Drinkwater rolled onto his back and let the gentle drops wash over his face.

By the time he floundered ashore on the opposite bank the rain had become a steady downpour.

14   The Meeting of Eagles

25 June 1807

Drinkwater found himself in shallow water a mile below the town where the Nieman's banks were reeded. Lush green water-meadows lay beyond, rising slowly to low hills clear in the grey light. A windmill surmounted one of these and he remembered passing it as they had approached Tilsit. He lay for some time, gathering his strength and no longer sustained by the vodka. The rain had drawn a heavy veil of cloud across the sky and a smoking mist hung over the river. He had come a long way downstream, to be met by a herd of piebald cows whose steaming muzzles were turned suspiciously towards him. He would have to make for the road and knew that the next hour was, for him, the most danger-ous. He had been unable to think out any strategy for his journey back, hoping that he would land in darkness only a short distance below the Ostkai.

'You are grown too old for this lunatic game,' he muttered wearily to himself and rose to his feet. Squelching through the reeds he reached a place where the river bank was trodden down by countless cattle hooves. The raindrops plopped heavily into each tiny lake and the mud dragged at his feet. He struggled through cow-pats and sodden grass, making towards the windmill and the road. He was within a few yards of the mill when the bugle sounded reveille. With a sudden panic he realised the place was a billet and full of soldiers. He fell back towards a ditch on his left. Then he saw the boat.

With ineffable relief he turned to it. It was a crude, flat-bottomed punt, meant only for river work, but it had a pair of oars across the thwarts and offered Drinkwater the only satisfactory means of re-entering Tilsit. He was dressed as a lighter-man and here was a boat, presumably belonging to the mill, and a downpour to explain his soaking condition. With renewed heart he clambered aboard and untied the frayed painter from a rotten stake. He got out the oars and worked the boat out of the dyke. Ashore he could hear shouts as men assembled for morning roll-call. He entered the main river, the rain hissing down, the smooth grey water an infinity of concentric circular ripples. Keeping close to the bank he found the counter-current and pulled easily upstream. Despite his lack of sleep he found his lassitude evaporate; the demands of pulling the boat sent new life into his chilling limbs and the rain seemed warm upon his tired muscles.

Edward Drinkwater lay on his back in the solitary darkness and fought successive waves of panic that swept over him, manifesting themselves in reflexive spasms of nausea. Despite the pale sliver of sky that showed through the slits his brother had opened in the float, the surrounding darkness had a threatening quality, a sentient hostility that caused him to imagine it was contracting upon him. So strong was this awful sensation that twice he found himself stuffing a fist into his mouth to prevent himself from screaming, while a cold sweat broke out all over his body. But these periods of terrifying panic waned and were replaced by a slow acceptance of his situation which was aided by the bottle of vodka. After an hour or two he floated in a kind of limbo: the stinking bilge-water and the damp clothes that wrapped him seemed bearable.

He was jerked from his reverie by the noise of approaching feet scrunching the gravel and his heartbeats thundered in the clammy darkness as men resumed work on the raft. The hammering and sawing went on for what seemed hours, resonating throughout the float so that his former silence seemed heavenly by comparison. He lay on his back, twisting about from time to time to keep his circulation going, watching the narrow strip of sky periodically obscured by the boot-soles of the French soldiers and diverting himself by practising eavesdropping on their conversation. Sometime later he smelt a curious smell and recognised it as it grew stronger for the odour of Stockholm tar. He knew then that it was almost time for the pontoon to be dragged down the slipway and into the river.

*

'They are heating tar,' observed Lord Walmsley, taking his eye from Drinkwater's telescope and turning towards Mackenzie lying on the truckle bed. 'D'you think the Captain and Ostroff are all right?'

'Uh?' Mackenzie rubbed the sleep from his eyes and rolled off the bed to join Walmsley at the window. 'I hope by now Ostroff is – what d'you sailors say? – *battened down* in that *pont volant* and the Captain already in the stable below. What o'clock is it?'

'Seven has struck, and the half hour. D'you want me to look in the stable?'

'Yes, take my cloak. Bennigsen's lot sleep late; they gave a dinner last night for some French officers. Just act boldly, there are too many comings and goings for anyone to take any notice, and the sentries are too ignorant to stop anyone with an air of authority.' Mackenzie gave a short, contemptuous laugh. 'Good men in a fight but deprived of any initiative . . . the Jew will notice you . . . take a rouble from the gold on the bed and slip it to the burgher if you see him.' Mackenzie's voice became weary, as though the corruptibility of men bored him. Behind him the doorlatch clicked and the stairs creaked as Walmsley descended to the stables. Mackenzie focused his attention on the distant pontoon. The final touches were being put to the decorations, a wooden monogram placed over each of two draped entrances. He saw two men, wearing the regulation aprons of pioneers, emerge from under the pontoon with a steaming pot of pitch. The men worked doggedly but without enthusiasm as the rain continued to fall. He shifted his glass to the barge that the two brothers had moved across the river the evening before. Already a group of labourers had brought piles of sawn deals from an adjacent warehouse where they had been awaiting shipment, and were laying them across the lighter's open hatch to make a platform. Mackenzie took the glass from his eye and rubbed it, yawning. A movement on the extreme right of his field of vision caught his eye. A man was rowing upstream in a small boat. He would soon become involved with three other boats, anchored to moorings which they had been laying in midstream. There was more movement too, on the Westkai. They were changing the guard opposite. The sentries from a line regiment were being replaced by the tall bearskins and red plumes of the French Imperial Guard.

175

'*Grand tenue*, by Jupiter,' he muttered sardonically to himself. 'Pity about the rain.'

He peered cautiously below him where, on the Ostkai, a similar ritual was in progress. Instead of bearskins the Russian Guard wore great brass-fronted mitre-caps that had gone out of vogue in every other European army a generation earlier.

'*Touché*,' chuckled Mackenzie, almost enjoying himself, as the brilliance of the preparations was muted by the heavy downpour. The man in the small boat had pulled alongside and was making his painter fast.

Lord Walmsley could find no sign of Captain Drinkwater in the stable, but he found something else, something he had failed to find in his walk of the previous night. The naked leg of a girl hung from the hayloft. Walmsley felt a stab of lust and cautiously peered through the gap in the stable doors. Several orderlies lounged under the overhanging roof of a balcony on the opposite side of the courtyard. They were smoking and drinking tea, and clearly unwilling to rush into the business of grooming officers' chargers while their owners slept off the excesses of the night. The stable was heavy with the smell of horses, dung and hay. The magnificent animals reminded him of his father's stables, and the naked ankle of a girl he had once laid in the straw there.

There was a ladder close to the bare foot and he climbed it, taking care not to wake its owner. The horses stamped and pawed the ground and whickered softly to each other, but he ignored them and climbed up to the sleeping girl. She was a maid in the Jew's service and lay prettily asleep, her red mouth half-smiling and her dreams full of the love-making of the Prince who had had her the night before. She had escaped when his drunkenness became violent, and found her refuge in the hayloft. Walmsley was aroused by the sight and scent of her. He slid a hand over her leg. She turned languidly, her body responding, and opened her eyes. Walmsley smothered her surprise with his kisses, his urgency meeting her own awakened lust half-way, and with the intemperate passion of their youth they were swiftly entwined in each other's arms.

*

Drinkwater flicked the painter through the ring set in the face of the quay, shipped his oars and steadied the boat at the foot of the steps. It was too late to turn back. The military activity on the Ostkai would have to be brazened out. He climbed the steps and found himself face to face with a giant of a man in a huge brass-fronted hat. The man stood immobile in the continuing rain and, without the slightest hindrance, Drinkwater shuffled past him. No one took the slightest notice of so disreputable and so familiar a sight as a dirty, stinking peasant. Even the orderlies smoking in the yard of the merchant's house ignored him. He was able to slip into the stable as arranged. From here Mackenzie was to arrange his return to the attic when the coast was clear.

He found Midshipman Lord Walmsley standing at the top of a ladder, buttoning his breeches. Wisps of straw clung to his clothing and beside him the face of a girl appeared. He caught the gleam of gold tossed to her, saw her bite it and lie back giggling. Neither of the lovers had seen the sodden beggar at the doorway. Then Walmsley turned and spotted Drinkwater, who scowled at the midshipman and, catching sight of Mackenzie's cloak that Walmsley had carelessly draped over one of the stalls, pulled it round himself. Walmsley joined him in silent embarrassment and led him into the house.

Mackenzie turned as they regained the attic. 'Ah, he found you all right. Good. Welcome back. Did everything pass as planned?'

'Well enough,' said Drinkwater shortly. He rounded angrily on the midshipman. 'What the hell are you playing at, you fool? Was that English gold you gave that trollop?' he asked savagely. 'If it was you'll likely have us all damned for your stupidity.'

'You gave that gold piece away? To a girl, or the Jew?' Mackenzie asked curtly.

Walmsley went pale under the inquisition of the two men.

'He gave it to a whore!'

'Who was she? That trull that skivvies for the Jew?'

Walmsley nodded.

Mackenzie chuckled. 'Calm yourself, Captain. It was Russian gold and I expect the trull has given him something for small change. It is of no account, she has been laid by most of Bennigsen's killbucks and I doubt she can tell the difference between an Englishman and a Russian in the throes of love!' Mackenzie dismissed the matter.

Drinkwater was dropping with fatigue. He sank on the low bed and, within moments, was asleep.

It was past noon when Mackenzie shook him awake. 'You should come and look. Great events are in progress. There is some bread and sausage . . .'

Drinkwater rose with a cracking of strained muscles. His shoulder ached with a dull, insistent pain, but he stripped the filthy rags from his body and drew on his own breeches and shirt, joining Mackenzie at the window.

'You smell better in your own clothes,' observed Mackenzie, making way in the open casement. There was no need for concealment now for nearly every window was occupied by a curious public. Both quays were lined by the massed ranks of the Imperial Guards of both Emperors, row upon row of splendid men in the impressive regalia of full-dress, their officers at their posts. A handful of staff-officers, more youthful than useful, dashed up and down on curvetting horses, their hooves striking sparks from the cobblestones. The heavy rain of the morning had stopped and a watery sun peeped occasionally through gaps in the clouds, lighting up bright patches of red roof tiles, the green leaves of trees and the gaudy splendours of military pomp.

But it was the river that was the cynosure for all eyes. A musket-shot from the watchers in the attic, roughly level with the slipway from which it had been dragged that morning and moored in the centre of the Nieman, the flying bridge lay at anchor. It was festooned with a profusion of drapery, red and blue and green, laced with gold tasselling, and on the side facing them the drapes had been looped back to form an entrance surmounted by the initial letter 'A'. Twenty yards downstream lay the less gaily appointed barge.

'Impressive, eh?' Mackenzie was grinning like a schoolboy on holiday and both knew a sense of triumph at their success. Two boats had now arrived, one on each side of the river waiting at the steps there. On the far quay a cavalcade of horsemen had appeared, riding through the ranks of soldiers. On a white horse sat the unmistakable figure of Napoleon Bonaparte, Emperor of the French, wearing the green and white of the Horse Chasseurs of the Guard. He was followed by a glittering bevy of marshals, one of whom ostentatiously caracoled his horse.

'That vainglorious fellow is Murat,' whispered Mackenzie.

They watched Napoleon dismount and walk to the steps. In the boat below him an officer stood and Drinkwater drew in his breath, for it was Santhonax. He pointed him out to Mackenzie and they watched the emperor and some of his entourage embark. People on either bank were cheering. A minute later and the French marines were plying their oars as the boat swung out for the caparisoned raft. The distant batteries began the ritual discharge of the imperial salutes.

Mackenzie pointed downwards and they craned their necks. Almost exactly below them a similar scene was being enacted and another boat was pulling out from the Ostkai. Sitting in the stern were several officers of exalted rank.

'Ouvaroff and Count Lieven have their backs to us,' explained Mackenzie in a low voice, 'the gentleman with the unpleasant countenance is the Grand Duke Constantine, next to him is Bennigsen . . .' Drinkwater looked at the snub-nosed, stubborn features of the Hanoverian. He was answering a query from a fifth man, a tall, erect, red-haired officer in an immaculate, high-collared tunic.

'The Tsar.'

Drinkwater stared at the profile of the man who was said to be composed of a confusion of liberal ideals and autocratic inclinations. Surrounded by the pomp of the occasion it was difficult to imagine that the handsome head knew anything but the certainty of its own will. A reputation for erratic decisions or total apathy seemed undeserved. The bizarre sight of the Tsar chatting to a man who had engineered the death of his own father, whom he had the day before humiliated in public and who, Mackenzie thought with his amazing prescience, might turn his coat in the next hour or two, reminded Drinkwater that he was in Kurland, a remote corner of a remote empire whose alliance with his own country was in jeopardy.

Beside him Mackenzie's mood ran in a lighter vein. 'Trust Boney to work for a meeting on equal footing and then upstage Alexander.'

The French boat arrived at the raft first. It pulled away to disembark the French staff on the barge, downstream. As the Russian boat arrived alongside the raft and Alexander stood to disembark, Napoleon appeared in the entrance on the Russian side, his hand outstretched. A great cheer went up from the massed soldiery on either bank. As the Russian boat dropped downstream, Napoleon let the curtains of the pavilion down with his own hands.

As if at a signal of the combined imperial wills, the concussions of the salutes faded into echoes and from a lowering sky the rain again began to fall.

In total secrecy, two men decided the fate of Europe.

15   The Secret

25 June 1807

Edward Drinkwater found the water rose no more than four inches about him once the pontoon had been launched. He found his situation uncomfortable but was less anxious once he felt the raft moored. He had suffered a brief, heart-thumping fear as the water rose about him, but his brother had been right, though to what properties of hydrostatics it was due, Edward was quite ignorant. The clumsy vessel found a sort of equilibrium, presumably supported by the other chambers, or perhaps due to its attitude to the stream of the river, once it had been moored. At all events the inrush of water soon ceased and he lay awash, awake and alert.

He heard the cannon and the cheers and the bumps of the boats. A few indistinct words of French, a rapid series of footsteps overhead, and then a voice asked: 'Why are we at war?'

It was quite distinct and clear, even above the rush and chuckle of the water to which his ears had become attuned, a question posed with some asperity and emotion. The reply was equally charged and candid: 'I hate the English as much as you do!' Edward recognised the Tsar's voice.

There was the small sharp slap of clapped hands and a brief barked laugh. 'In that case, my dear friend, peace is made!'

Lord Walmsley was denied much of a view of this historic event by Drinkwater and Mackenzie. The delights of the morning, despite the embarrassment of their conclusion, had not satisfied his desire. Mackenzie's gold still lay on the bed where it had been taken from the butt of one of his pistols. The girl might be a whore, as Captain Drinkwater and the mysterious Mr Mackenzie had alleged, but the captain was prone to a certain puritan narrowness. Walmsley had lain with whores before and he had been far too long without a woman. It was true he owed Captain Drinkwater a great deal, but not his moral welfare; that was his own business. Besides the girl had been good. Walmsley sat on the bed and supposed it had been hers before Mackenzie had seduced her Jewish master with his limitless gold. Desire pricked him again and he knew he would not be missed for a while. As the bellowing of the Guards again broke out, Walmsley slipped from the attic unnoticed. On the raft, the two Emperors had reappeared, smiling publicly. Renewed cheering greeted this concord and echoed through the streets of Tilsit.

General Santhonax dismounted from his horse and threw the reins to an orderly. It was already evening and the volleys from the two armies which signalled a general rejoicing had at last died away. He was tired, having been up since just after dawn, when the report of the missing sentry had been brought to him. It was the fourth such desertion of the night and with the armistice declared he was not surprised. He greeted a fellow officer with a tired smile.

'Ah, Lariboissière, His Imperial Majesty requires you to start immediately to throw a pontoon bridge across the river. He is desirous of impressing our late enemies with the superiority of our engineering. You may withdraw the rafts when you have finished.'

'*Merde!*' Lariboissière and his men were tired out, but an order was an order. 'Was His Imperial Majesty satisfied with today's arrangements, General Santhonax?'

Santhonax remounted and settled himself in the saddle. 'Perfectly, my friend,' he said urbanely, tugging his charger's head round. 'It went better than I anticipated.'

Edward had had enough. His head still buzzed with the news he had gleaned and he was eager to escape confinement. He had heard the town clock strike six and could wait no longer. Twisting round he got his shoulders against the plank-ends that Drinkwater had nailed down and pushed hard. He felt something give, and kicked. The plank-end sprang and light entered the chamber. He forced the other end free. The plank dropped into the water and he repeated the performance with the next. More water began to lap into the chamber. He took a deep breath and forced his body through the gap, rolled into the water and submerged. When he came up he was clear of the raft. Over his head arched the blue of the evening sky. He felt a supreme elation fill him and kicked luxuriously downstream.

General Santhonax pulled up his horse at the end of the Westkai and stared down at the slip where the *pont volant* had spent the previous night. The trampled gravel was covered with sawdust, wood offcuts and a few pieces of cloth where the drapery had been trimmed. One of the men had left a tool behind. The polished steel gleamed dully in the muck where it lay half-buried by a careless foot. It looked like a cavalry farrier's axe.

The professional curiosity of a former secret agent made Santhonax dismount and jump down onto the hard. He pulled the axe out of the mire and looked at its head. A feeling of disquieting curiosity filled him. He returned to his horse, tapping the grubby object thoughtfully with one gloved hand. Lithuanian workmen had been employed in raising the pavilion, but they had been civilians. What then was a Russian farrier's axe doing there? He looked down again. The thing had stained his white gloves with mud. But there was something else too: the spike on the vicious weapon was sticky with blood and hair.

A sudden alarm gripped General Santhonax. He recalled the post of one of the missing sentries and his eyes flew to the gaudy and deserted raft in midstream. A sudden flash came from just below the raft, a plank upflung and yellow with new wood reflected the low evening sunlight that had replaced the day's rain. And was that a head that bobbed and was gone behind the barge? He kicked his horse into motion, leaving the quay and riding along the raised bank that was topped by a narrow path. He fished in one holster for his glass.

Then he was sure. Downstream on the far bank he saw a man crawl out of the river. His blood ran cold. That man had to die, die secretly without the Emperor ever knowing that Santhonax had failed in his duty.

Tilsit was *en fête*, celebrating the peace. Candles lit every window again, the streets were thronged and cheers greeted every person of consequence who appeared. The Tsar was wildly applauded as he prepared to cross the river and dine with Napoleon. Edward made his way through the crowd to the rear of the Jew's house unnoticed, for it was abandoned by Bennigsen and his suite, and the orderlies had taken themselves off to celebrate in their own manner, leaving only the sentries at the main entrance. Edward reached the attic and was helped out of his stinking rags while both Mackenzie and Drinkwater waited eagerly for his report. In the excitement no one was concerned by Walmsley's absence.

'Well,' said Mackenzie as Edward devoured a sausage and a quantity of vodka, 'our luck cannot last for ever, we are in hostile territory now by all accounts.'

'You are indeed,' said Edward swallowing the vodka, standing naked in a tin bath. 'But another thousand . . .'

'Damn you, Ned!'

'Five hundred,' said Mackenzie coolly, picking up the pistol from the bed, 'and not a penny more.' Mackenzie brought the pistol barrel up and pointed it at Edward's groin.

Edward realised he had chosen a bad moment to bargain; a man rarely impresses when naked. 'Very well, gentlemen,' he said grinning sheepishly and attempting to pass off the matter lightly.

'The truth, mind,' warned Mackenzie, the pistol unwavering.

'Yes, yes, of course,' agreed Edward testily, reaching for his breeches as if insulted that he was suspected of real perfidy.

'Well?'

'There are to be long negotiations, but Napoleon is a master of deceit; he played Alexander like a woman. I have never heard flattery like it. He sold his ally Turkey to the Tsar, promised him a free hand against the Porte, guaranteed him the same in Swedish Finland, told him that he was a true child of the liberating ideals of the French Revolution and that the two of them would release the new renaissance of a resuscitated Europe! I could scarcely believe my ears. Why such a tirade of flattery and promises should be made in such secrecy is for you to judge.'

'One always seduces in private,' observed Mackenzie, ironically, 'but go on. What of Great Britain?'

'That came last, though I distinctly heard Alexander declare his hatred of the English at the start, but he was much less easy to hear . . .'

'Go on, we have little time. . .'

'Britain is to be excluded from all trade with Europe or Russia. The Tsar agrees to chastise anyone who trades with a nation so perfidious as yours.' Edward paused, his choice of words significant. 'Your navy is to be destroyed by sheer weight of numbers. Napoleon said your navy is exhausted, your sources of manpower drying up, and that you cannot maintain a blockade for ever. He told the Tsar, who made some remark at this point, that your victory at Trafalgar was a narrow one and that this is proved by the death of Lord Nelson. He claimed the tide would have gone the other way but for the Spaniards deserting the French. Had the French had the Russian fleet with them that day the trident of Neptune would have been wrested from Britannia and with it the sceptre of the world!'

'What eloquence,' remarked Mackenzie.

'So the Russian fleet is to break out of the Baltic, eh?' asked Drinkwater.

'Yes. The Baltic is to be a *mare clausum* to Britain, supine under Russian domination, and to outnumber you the Portuguese fleet is to be seized at Lisbon and the Danish to be commandeered at Copenhagen.'

'God's bones!' exclaimed Drinkwater, his mind whirling with the news. With France and Russia allies, Napoleon's power in Europe would be absolute. The Russians would be free to expand into Turkey, the French to mass their great armies on the Channel shore once more for a final descent upon England. Napoleon would be able to summon the combined navies of every European power to add to his own. There were ships of the line building at Toulon, at Brest, at Antwerp; the Portuguese navy and the Danish navy would add a powerful reinforcement to the Russian squadrons already at sea, cruising as allies of Great Britain. Against such a force even the battle-hardened Royal Navy would find itself outgunned by sheer weight of metal! And, as Drinkwater well knew, the Royal Navy, that reassuring bulwark of the realm, was wearing out. Its seamen were sick of endless blockade, its officers dispirited by stalemate, its admirals worn with cares and its ships with sea-keeping. Such an outcome negated Drinkwater's whole life and he was filled with a sudden urgency to be off, to leave this stifling attic and regain the fresh air of his quarterdeck and a quick passage home with this vital intelligence.

'You have done well,' Mackenzie was saying, spilling into his palm a shower of gold. He held it out to Edward who was now fully dressed. 'Here, this is on account, the rest within the month in the usual way.'

Edward pocketed the cash. He was again the Russian officer, Ostroff. He held out his hand to Drinkwater. 'The parting of the ways, then, Nat?'

Drinkwater nodded. 'Yes . . . it would seem so.'

'I have discharged all my obligations today.'

'With interest,' said Mackenzie drily as the two brothers shook hands.

'Where's Walmsley?' Drinkwater asked suddenly as their minds turned towards departure. The three men exchanged glances.

'He can't be far away,' said Mackenzie. 'It isn't the first time he's wandered off.'

'No, but it will be the last,' snapped Drinkwater anxiously.

'He's gone a-whoring,' said Edward as he bent to pick up his gear. Mackenzie slung his saddle-bags over his shoulder and Drinkwater put a pistol in his waistband.

'We cannot wait,' said Mackenzie, looking at Drinkwater. 'Perhaps he's down below.' Mackenzie unbarred the door and led them out down the steep and narrow stairs.

The only person they met in their descent through the eerie silence of the house was the Jew, who was on an upper landing. Mackenzie passed more money to him and the three men walked into the courtyard, shadowed by the late afternoon sunlight.

'I have a horse quartered here,' said Edward, turning aside.

'Where do you go now?' asked Drinkwater.

'To Vorontzoff,' Edward replied, entering the stable. Drinkwater followed to see if Walmsley was repeating his performance of that morning: a brief look showed the hayloft empty.

'Come on . . .' said Mackenzie.

Drinkwater hesitated. 'I must have a look for Walmsley.'

Mackenzie swore and, for the first time since they had met,

Drinkwater saw irresolution in his face. 'Damn it then, a quick look, but hurry!'

General Santhonax had searched the warehouses of the lower town as unobtrusively as possible. The thought that a soaking man could not vanish without accomplices beat in his brain. He reached the Ostkai with its tall houses where the previous evening he had selected the barge. Lariboissière's men, with whose help he had crossed the river, were already stretching the first cable of the bridge Napoleon had ordered thrown over the Nieman. Angrily he turned away. Perhaps the inns round the town square might have offered concealment.

Lord Walmsley smiled down at the girl. The bed of the Russian prince was rumpled by the wanton violence of their combined lust, but Walmsley knew he had to leave, to see if the strange, English-speaking Russian officer, Ostroff, had returned to the attic. He emerged onto the landing, hearing a noise on the stairs. Below him someone went out into the courtyard. From a window he could just see down into the deepening shadows of the yard. Captain Drinkwater was there and he was joined by Ostroff, leading a grey horse out of the stable. At the same time Mackenzie appeared, shaking his head. It was obvious that departure was imminent. Behind Walmsley the girl appeared and wound her arms around him.

Below in the courtyard the three men were holding a hurried conference.

'Nothing. It means we'll have to search the place thoroughly.'

'He may have wandered off anywhere,' said Mackenzie. 'I let him go for a while yesterday . . .'

'You'd best forget him,' said Edward, putting one foot in the stirrup. 'I will keep an eye out for him and spirit him away if I can.'

'And if you can't?' asked Drinkwater, at once furious with the midshipman for his desertion and in a quandary as to what to do.

'Come, this is no time to delay, we must make the best of our separate ways now,' Mackenzie said, taking Drinkwater's elbow. 'Come on, it is only a short walk to Gower's chaise and we have little to fear. It will not be very surprising if a Scottish merchant and an English shipmaster evacuate Tilsit in the wake of the day's events.'

Edward looked down from his horse. 'Goodbye, Nat, and good luck. Forget your young friend, I'll do what I can.'

'Very well, and thank you. Good fortune.'

The two men smiled and Edward dug his heels into the flanks of the grey and clattered out of the yard. At the arched entrance his horse shied, skittering sideways as a tall military officer almost collided with them. Edward kicked his mount forward.

As the big grey horse trotted away Santhonax looked under the arch. He saw two men walking towards him carrying bags over their shoulders; they had the appearance of travellers on the point of departure, yet he could see no reason for men to leave a town that was so full of wild celebration. With sudden caution he drew his pistol as they entered the covered passage and moved towards him.

Drinkwater saw the man under the arch and caught the movement of the drawn pistol.

'Look,' he hissed, sensing danger at the same moment as Mackenzie.

Drinkwater's hand went to his own pistol, Mackenzie strode forward.

'*Bonsoir, m'sieur,*' he said. In the gloom the man turned and Drinkwater recognised Santhonax. Without a moment's thought he swung his heavy pistol butt: the steel heel of the weapon caught Santhonax on the jaw and he crashed against the wall. Drinkwater hit him a second time. Santhonax sprawled full length, unconscious.

'It's Santhonax,' hissed Drinkwater as both men stared down at the French general, their thoughts racing. 'Do you think he was looking for us?'

'God knows!'

'Do we kill him?'

'No, that might raise a hue and cry. Take his watch, make it look like a theft.' Mackenzie bent over the inert body and wrenched at Santhonax's waist. He straightened up and handed a heavy gold watch to Drinkwater. 'Here . . .' Mackenzie rifled Santhonax's pockets and then turned back the way they had come. 'Leave him.

To hell with the chaise. I smell trouble. For all I know he's already discovered Walmsley . . . there is not a moment to lose.'

Drinkwater ran back, following Mackenzie into the stable. In a lather of inexpert haste Drinkwater tried to get a horse saddled in imitation of Mackenzie. The other came over and finished the job for him. They drew the horses out of the stable and mounted them. Drinkwater hoisted himself gingerly into the saddle.

'Are you all right?' hissed Mackenzie.

'I think so . . .' Drinkwater replied uncertainly as the horse moved beneath him, sensing his nervousness.

'Listen! If we are pursued, get to Memel and your ship! Go direct to London. Ostroff and I will take care of Walmsley . . . Come, let's go!'

They rode across the yard and through the archway.

Behind them General Santhonax stirred and groaned.

Santhonax got slowly to his feet, clawing himself upright by the wall. His head throbbed painfully and his jaw was severely contused. He staggered forward and the courtyard swam into his vision. He looked dazedly about him. A young man was staring at him and then seemed to vanish. Santhonax frowned: the young man had been wearing something very like a seaman's coat.

His head cleared and then it came back to him. The two men, the sudden guilty hesitation and the deceptive confrontation by one of them while the other struck him with a clubbed pistol. The apparition of the youth and the smell of a stable full of horses spurred him to sudden activity. He crossed the yard and met Walmsley at the stable door.

'What's happening?' asked Walmsley in English, mistaking his man in the gloom. Santhonax smiled savagely.

'Nothing,' he replied reassuringly, his own command of English accent-free.

'Is that you, Ostroff?'

'Yes,' lied Santhonax, silhouetted against the last of the daylight.

'Have they gone then?' Santhonax heard alarm awaken in the question. 'Are they getting the chaise?' Guilt had robbed Walmsley of his wits.

'Yes . . .' Santhonax pushed Walmsley backwards and followed him into the stable.

'Why, you're not Ostroff! That's a French uniform!'

'*Oui, m'sieur*, and who are you?' Walmsley felt the cold touch of a pistol muzzle at his chin. 'Come, quickly, or I'll kill you!'

Walmsley was trembling with fear. 'M . . . midshipman, British navy!'

With this information Santhonax realised the extent of his own failure to keep the Emperor's secret.

'You are not wearing the uniform of a British midshipman, boy! Where are your white collar-patches? What the hell are you doing here?'

'I was acting under orders . . . attending my captain . . .'

'What captain? Where is your ship?'

Walmsley swallowed. 'I surrender my person . . . as a prisoner of war . . .'

'Answer, boy!' The pistol muzzle poked up harder under Walmsley's trembling chin.

'My frigate is off Memel.'

'And the captain?' asked Santhonax, lowering his pistol and casting an eye for a suitable horse. Walmsley sensed reprieve.

'Captain Drinkwater, of the *Antigone*, sir,' he said in a relieved tone.

Santhonax swung his face back to his prisoner and let out a low oath. 'You are a spy, boy . . .'

Walmsley tried to twist away as Santhonax brought up the pistol and squeezed the trigger. The ball shattered the midshipman's skull and he fell amid the straw and horse dung.

Among the rearing and frightened animals Santhonax grabbed Walmsley's saddled horse and led it through the doorway, then mounted and dug his spurs into the animal's sides. The terrified horse lunged forward and Santhonax tugged its head in the direction of the road to Memel.

PART THREE
The Post-chaise

'It is their intention to employ the navies of Denmark and Portugal against this country.'

GEORGE CANNING, FOREIGN SECRETARY,
to the House of Commons, JULY 1807

Accord

25 June 1807

The two Emperors sat at the head of an array of tables that glittered with silver and crystal. The assembled company was peacock-gaudy with the military of three nations. The sober Prussians, humiliated by the indifference of Napoleon and the implied slight to their beautiful queen, were dour and miserable, while Russians and French sought to outdo one another in the lavishness of their uniforms and the extravagance of their toasts.

General Bennigsen, still smarting from the Tsar's rebuke, sat next to the King of Prussia whose exclusion from the secret talks had stung him to the quick. His lovely Queen displayed a forced vivacity to the two Emperors, who sat like demi-gods.

'She is,' Napoleon confided slyly to the Tsar, 'the finest woman in the whole of Prussia, is she not?'

Alexander, beguiled and charmed by his former enemy, delighted at the outcome of the discussions which gave him a free hand in Finland and Turkey, agreed. The man he had until today regarded as a parvenu now fascinated him. Napoleon had shown Alexander a breadth of vision equalling his own, a mind capable of embracing the most liberal and enlightened principles, yet know-ing the value of compulsion in forcing those measures upon the dark, half-witted intelligence of the mass of common folk.

'I hope,' Napoleon's voice said at his side, 'that you are pleased with today's proceedings?'

Alexander turned to Napoleon and smiled his fixed, courtly and slightly vacant smile. 'The friendship between France and Russia,' he said to his neighbour, 'has long been my most cherished dream.'

Napoleon smiled in return. 'Your Majesty shows a profound

wisdom in these matters,' he said and Alexander inclined his head graciously at this arrant flattery.

Napoleon regarded the banquet and the numerous guests, his quick mind noting a face here and there. Suddenly his benign expression clouded over. He leaned back and beckoned an aide. Nodding to a vacant place on a lower table he asked the young officer, 'Where is General Santhonax?'

16   The Return of Ulysses

June 1807

Drinkwater clung to his mount with increasing desperation. He was no horseman and the animal's jerking trot jolted him from side to side so that he gasped for breath and at every moment felt that he would fall. It was years since he had ridden, and want of practice now told heavily against him. The thought of the long journey back to Memel filled him with horror.

Equally anxious, Mackenzie looked back every few yards, partly to see if Drinkwater was still in the saddle, partly to see if they were pursued.

As they left the town and found themselves surrounded by the bivouacs of the Russian army they passed camp-fire after camp-fire round which groups of men played cards, drank and smoked their foul tobacco tubes. There were other travellers on the road, officers making their way to the celebrations at Tilsit; but the news of peace had removed all necessity for caution and the horsemen continued unopposed along the Memel road.

At last they drew away from the encampments. It was dark but the sky had cleared, and a silver crescent of moon gave a little light, showing the dusty highway as a pale stripe across the rolling countryside. As Drinkwater jogged uncomfortably in his saddle it occurred to him that as he became accustomed to the horse, he became less able to capitalise on his improvement, for his buttocks and inner thighs became increasingly sore.

Drinkwater grunted with pain as they rode on, passing through a village. The road was deserted but the noise of shouting, clapping and a guitar came from its inn. A few miles beyond the village Mackenzie looked back at his lagging companion. What he saw made him rein in his horse. They were in open countryside now.

The Nieman gleamed a pistol shot away, reflecting the stars, and the road lay deserted before them.

Drinkwater looked up as he saw Mackenzie stop and heard him swear.

'I'm doing my damndest. . .'

'It's not that . . . Look!'

Drinkwater pulled his horse up and turned. A man was pursuing them, his horse kicking up a pale cloud of dust, just discernible in the gloom.

'Santhonax!'

'Can you remember the content of Ostroff's report?' Mackenzie asked sharply.

'Of course . . .'

'Then ride on . . . go . . . get back to your ship. I'll do what I can to stop him, but do not under any circumstances stop!'

'But you? What will you do?'

'I'll manage . . . get to London overland, Captain, bringing your midshipman with me, but you go *now*!' And Mackenzie brought an impatient hand down on the rump of Drinkwater's horse.

'God's bones!' Drinkwater lost the reins and grabbed the animal's mane, his sore knees pressed desperately inwards against the saddle. He dared not look back but he heard the pistol shots, and the image of Santhonax still in hot pursuit kept him riding through the night as if all the devils in hell were on his tail.

Lieutenant James Quilhampton lay rigid and awake in the darkness. The scratching sound came again, accompanied by a sibilant hiss. He swung his legs over the edge of the cot and, crouching, pressed his ear against the cabin door.

'Who is it?'

'Frey, sir.'

Quilhampton opened the cabin door and drew the boy inside. He was in shirt and breeches, a pale ghost in the darkness.

'What the devil d'you want?'

'Sergeant Blixoe sent me, sir. Roused me out and sent me to wake you and the other lieutenant. He says there's a combination of two score of men in the cable tier. They're murmuring, sir . . . after the day's events . . .'

Quilhampton began tearing off his nightshirt. 'Get Mr Fraser and Mr Mount, quickly now, while I dress, no noise . . . then double below and tell Blixoe to call out all his men!'

He began to dress, cursing Rogers. The first lieutenant had flogged two men the previous day with the thieves' cat. Their offences were common and had not warranted such severity. One had neglected his duty, the other was judged guilty of insolence towards an officer. What made the event significant was that the man who had not jumped to his allotted task with sufficient alacrity to satisfy Rogers had not done so because he had been flogged for drunkenness only the previous day. This circumstance had sown a seed of genuine grievance among men whose usual tolerance of the navy's rough and summary justice had been overstretched during Rogers's brief tenure of command. The surgeon's claim that the man was not fit to receive punishment had encouraged a seaman to speak up in support of the protest and he had been judged guilty of insolence by an infuriated Rogers.

Before nightfall one of the men was dead and the news spread quickly through the ship. Shortly after midnight, word had gone round the berth deck of a meeting of delegates from each mess in the cable tier. It was this disturbance that had prompted Sergeant Blixoe to action.

Quilhampton checked the priming of his pistol and belted on his sword. His anxiety at Drinkwater's absence had increased with every abuse and loss of temper that had marked Rogers's behaviour. For the last few days every motion of the ship's company had been accompanied by ferocious criticism and vitriolic scorn as Rogers continued to exercise the crew remorselessly.

Drinkwater's regime had been too lax, their performances too slow. The bosun's mates were too gentle with their starters and Rogers, in a paroxysm of rage, had grabbed the rope's end from the hand of one man and laid about him in a fury, sending the topmen scampering aloft. When he was satisfied with their performance he had brought them down again, then started the bosun's mate for 'lenience' and disrated him. Quilhampton knew Rogers was exercising considerable will-power over his craving for drink. But his ungovernable rages and transports of savage injustice had become intolerable.

He emerged from his cabin and turned forward, ducking under the men still in their hammocks. There was no sentry at the midships companionway and he stood and looked down into the cable tier. The space was capacious, but filled with the great coils of ten-inch hemp, so that the huge ropes formed miniature amphitheatres, lit by lanterns, their sides lined with thirty or forty men in vehement but whispered debate.

'But the captain ain't 'ere, for Chris' sakes . . . and that blackhearted bastard'll kill more men before 'e gets back . . .'

'*If* 'e gets back . . .'

'If we rise, do we take 'em all?'

'Yes,' a man hissed, 'kill all the buggers, for they'll all flog you!'

'Aye, an' we're men, not fucking animals!'

'Let's act like men then!'

'Aye!'

'Aye!'

They began to stir, resolution hardening in their faces, an impression heightened by the lamplight. Quilhampton realised he had to move fast. He cocked the pistol and descended the ladder.

The silence that greeted his appearance was murderous. He stared about him, noting faces. 'This is mutinous behaviour,' he said and judging a further second's delay would lose him the initiative added, 'the Captain's due back imminently.'

'That may be too late for some of us,' a voice said from the rear. It found an echo of agreement among the men.

'Go back to your hammocks. No good can come of this.'

'Don't trust the bastard!'

Quilhampton uncocked the pistol and stuck it in his belt. 'The marines are already alerted. Mr Mount and Mr Fraser are awake. For all I know they've called Mr Rogers . . .'

'We are betrayed!'

Quilhampton watched the effect of this news. Fear was clear on every man's face, for they knew that once Rogers identified them, each man present would likely die. They had only two choices now, and Quilhampton had already robbed them of their weapon of surprise.

'Get to your hammocks, and let me find this place deserted.'

They remained stock still for a second, then by common consent they moved as one, slipping away in the darkness. Quilhampton waited until the last man had vanished, stepped forward into the encirclement of the cable and picked up the lantern. Reascending the companionway he walked aft. A few of the hammocks swung violently and he caught sight of a retracting leg. He ascended to the gundeck and met Lieutenant Mount. He was coming forward with his hanger drawn, his marines behind him in shirtsleeves but with their bayonets fixed. Fraser was there with the midshipmen and the master.

'James! Where the hell have you been, we've been looking for you?' Fraser asked anxiously.

'I went to check the cable tier.'

'You *what*?'

'Have you informed Lieutenant Rogers?'

Fraser and Mount looked at each other. It was clear they had been debating the point and had decided not to.

'Because if you have, you had better tell him it's a false alarm. The cable tier's quite empty . . . except for the cables of course . . .'

'This is no time to be flippant!' snapped an irritated Mount, lowering his hanger.

'This is no time to be wandering around,' said Quilhampton, with affected nonchalance. 'Good night, gentlemen!'

General Santhonax recovered consciousness aware of a great weight pressing upon his leg. His skull, sore from the pistol blow on the left-hand side of his head, now bore a second lump on his forehead where he had struck it as his horse fell. The animal was dead and it took him several minutes to assemble his thoughts. In the east the first signs of daylight streaked the sky and he recalled the urgent need for pursuit. Then, triggered off by this thought, the events of the previous night came back to him. He swore and pulled his leg painfully out from beneath the horse.

He needed another mount, and would have to go back to the horse lines of the nearest Russian cavalry regiment for one. He began unbuckling his saddle. Should he then ride on to Memel? Or was he already too late?

He paused, forcing his aching head to think. Drinkwater would be within ten miles of Memel by daylight. Pursuit was pointless, but return to Tilsit risked disgrace or worse.

Dawn showed the road ahead of him, a thin ribbon beside the grey shimmer of the Nieman, with only an early peasant and an ox-cart upon it. The devil alone knew how he could face the Emperor again, for it was certain his absence would have been noticed. A furious anger began to boil within him – he had been outwitted and by his old antagonist Drinkwater, of all people!

He had forgotten how many times their paths had crossed. He only recalled in his bitterness that he had twice passed up the opportunity to kill the man. How he regretted that leniency now! Napoleon's secret would be in London as fast as Drinkwater's frigate could carry it and she was, as Santhonax had cause to know, a fast ship. He smote his saddle in his frustration and then calmed himself and resolved on the only course now open to him. His anger was replaced by the desperate courage of absolute necessity. Dragging himself to his feet, Santhonax turned his footsteps back towards Tilsit.

It was mid-morning when Drinkwater reached Memel. His horse was blown and he slid to the cobbles of the quay, his legs buckling beneath him. The flesh of his thighs was raw and his whole body was racked with an unbelievable agony. He had covered fifty-odd miles in twelve hours and almost certainly outrun pursuit. He had no idea what had become of Mackenzie beyond knowing that he had thwarted Santhonax by some means. Pain made him light-headed and he sat for a moment in the sunshine of early morning, mastering himself and trying to think clearly. Whatever had happened to Mackenzie or Walmsley his own task was clear enough. Standing unsteadily he walked along the quay, looking down at the boats tied alongside. An occasional fisherman mended nets. None looked in condition to sail imminently. Only one man stared up at him, a broad-faced man with a stubby pipe who smiled and nodded.

Drinkwater felt in his pocket and his fist closed on some coins. He drew them out and pantomimed his wishes. The man frowned, repeating the gestures of pointing, first at Drinkwater, then at him-self and then a quick double gesture at the deck of his boat and then the horizon. He seemed to ask a question and Drinkwater thought he heard the word 'English': he nodded furiously, pointing again at himself and then directly at the horizon.

Comprehension linked them and Drinkwater held out the gold for the man to see. There was a pause in the negotiation, then the man agreed and beckoned Drinkwater down onto the deck. Sliding back a small hatch, he called below, and a moment later a younger version of the fisherman appeared. Drinkwater made himself useful casting off and tallied on a halliard, within minutes they had hoisted sail and were moving seawards.

As Memel dropped astern and the Nieman opened into the Kurische Haff and then the Baltic Sea, his anxiety waned. He had avoided pursuit and for a while he enjoyed the sensation of the brisk sail as the fishing boat scudded along before a moderate breeze. It was good to feel the sea-wind on his face and see a horizon hard-edged and familiar. He relaxed and smiled at the pipe-smoking Kurlander at the tiller.

'A good boat,' Drinkwater said, patting the low rail.

The man nodded. '*Gut. Ja, ja . . .*'

Soon Drinkwater could see the masts and yards of the *Antigone*. His last fear, a childish one that the ship would not be on station, vanished. His problems were almost over. He could shave and bath and soak his raw flesh, and then sleep. . .

'All hands! All hands! All hands to witness punishment!'

Quilhampton looked up from the gunroom table where he had the midshipmen's journals spread out before him. He met the look of incredulity on Mount's face.

'Christ, not again. . .'

The two officers hurried into their coats, and left the gunroom buckling on their swords. As they emerged onto the upper deck they were aware of the ground-swell of discontent among the people milling in the waist. Rogers, in full dress, was already standing on the quarterdeck, Drinkwater's copy of the Articles of War in his hands.

'I should think he knows the Thirty-Sixth by heart,' Quilhampton heard someone mutter but he ignored the remark. Quilhampton took his now familiar place and cast a quick look over the marines. There might be a need for them shortly, but even among their stolid files there seemed to be a wavering and unsteadiness. He caught Blixoe's eye. The man's look was one of anger. Blixoe had acted to forestall mutiny in the night and Quilhampton had made a fool of him. Now the advantage of warning no longer lay with the officers and marines. With the whole ship's company assembled and every man except Rogers aware of what had transpired in the middle watch, a sudden explosion of spontaneous mutiny might result in the officers and marines being butchered on the spot.

'Silence there!' bawled Rogers, opening the book and calling for the prisoner.

It was Tregembo, his shoulder still bandaged, and pale from the effects of his wound. Quilhampton could only guess at Tregembo's crime and as Rogers read the charge it seemed to confirm his supposition. It was insolence to a superior officer. Tregembo had clearly spoken his mind to Rogers. The first lieutenant did not even ask if any officer would speak for the man. Once again he was lost to reason, consumed by whatever fires were eating him, possessed only of an insane hatred that had no meaning beyond expressing his own agony.

'Strip!'

Quilhampton was surprised to see the faint scars of previous floggings crossing Tregembo's back. Then Lallo stepped forward and declared the man unfit to undergo punishment. It was an act of considerable courage and so riveting was its effect on Rogers that no one saw the fishing boat swoop under the stern, nor paid the slightest attention to a fluttering of sails as it dropped briefly alongside.

'Stand aside!' roared Rogers, stepping forward.

Lallo fell back a pace and Rogers rounded on the bosun's mates standing by the prisoner. 'Secure him!'

They crucified Tregembo across the capstan, lashing his spread-eagled arms along two of the bars. A thin trickle of blood started down his back from beneath the bandage of his wound. Flogging against a capstan was a barbarism that refined an already barbaric custom; to flog a wounded man was a measure of Rogers's depravity. What he did next he must have conceived as an act of humanity. As a murmur of horror ran through the ship's company at the sight of Tregembo's reopened wound, Rogers nodded to the bosun's mate holding the cat.

'Strike low! And do your duty!'

202

By avoiding the shoulder, the cat would not do further damage to the wound. But it would lacerate the lower back and could damage the organs unprotected by the rib-cage. The bosun's mate hesitated.

'Do your duty!' Rogers shrieked.

'Mr Rogers!'

The attention of every man swung to the rail. Teetering uncertainly at its top, a hand on each stanchion, an unshaven and dirty figure clung. The hatless apparition repeated itself.

'Mr Rogers!'

'It's the cap'n,' said Quilhampton and ran across the deck.

'Get the ship under way at once!' Drinkwater ordered, before falling forward into Quilhampton's arms.

17   The Vanguard of Affairs

June–July 1807

Drinkwater stood immobile by the starboard hance, leaning against the hammock netting and with one foot resting on the slide of a small brass carronade. It seemed to the watches, as they changed every eight bells, that the captain's brooding presence had been continuous since they had broken the anchor out of the mud of Memel road four days earlier.

In fact the truth was otherwise, for it was Rogers who got the ship under weigh and Hill who laid off the first of the courses that would take them home. The captain had vanished below, exhausted and, rumour had it, wounded as well. It was a measure of Drinkwater's popularity that when the nature of his indisposition was properly known it did not become the subject for ribald comment. Nevertheless, as soon as he was rested and the surgeon had dressed his raw thighs, Drinkwater was on deck and had remained so ever since. He moved as little as possible, his legs too sore and his gait too undignified, atoning in his own mind for the sin of absence from his ship and the troubles it had caused.

The reassuring sight of Drinkwater's figure calmed the incipient spirit of revolt among the people. The fact that they were carrying sail like a Yankee packet and were bound for England raised their hopes and fed their dreams like magic. The dismal recollections of their period off Memel faded, and only the unusual sight of a marine sentry outside the first lieutenant's cabin served to remind the majority. But there were men who had longer memories, men who bore the scars of the cat, and, while the news of Lord Walmsley's disappearance seemed to establish an equilibrium of sacrifice in the collective consciousness of the frigate's population, there were those who planned to desert at the first opportunity.

For Drinkwater there was a great feeling of failure, despite the importance of the news he carried. It was compounded from many sources: the high excitement of his recent sortie; the intense, brief and curiously unsatisfactory reunion with his brother; the death (for such he privately believed it to be) of Lord Walmsley; his uncertainty as to the fates of either Mackenzie or Santhonax; and finally, the tyrannical behaviour of Rogers and the maltreatment of Tregembo. All these had cast a great shadow over him and it took some time for this black mood to pass. It was in part a reaction after such exertion and in part a brooding worry over what was to be done about Samuel Rogers. There was a grim irony in contemplating the future of the first lieutenant; Rogers had failed worst where he had succeeded best. The effort of will and the strength of his addiction had combined to produce a monster. He had been placed under arrest and confined to his cabin where, so the surgeon reported, he had fallen into a profound catalepsy.

The only bright spots in Drinkwater's unhappy preoccupation were the continuing recovery of Tregembo and the value of the news from Tilsit. As the days passed these grew in strength, gradually eclipsing his misery. At last his spirits lifted, and he began to share something of the excitement of the ship's company at the prospect of returning home. He thought increasingly of his wife and children, of Susan Tregembo and the others in his household at Petersfield, but the heavy gold watch he carried in his waistcoat reminded him that, despite the lofty press of sail *Antigone* bore and the air of expectancy that filled the chatter of her messes, it was the realities of war that drove her onwards.

The fair breeze that allowed them to stand to the westward under studding sails failed them during the forenoon of the last day of June. Chopping slowly round to the west, *Antigone* was forced to be close-hauled and stretch down into the shallow bight east of Rügen, leaving the island of Bornholm astern. By noon of the following day she was five leagues to the east of Cape Arkona and able to fetch a course towards Kioge Bay as the wind backed again into the south-west quarter. They passed Copenhagen through the Holland Deep on the afternoon of 2 July, but their hasty progress was halted the following day as the wind veered and came foul for the passage of The Sound. They anchored under the lee of the island of Hven for two days but, on the morning of the 5th, it fell light and favourable.

Next morning a freshening north-westerly forced them to tack out through the Kattegat, but the sun shone from a blue and cloudless sky and the sea sparkled and shone as the ship drove easily to windward, reeling off the knots. Ahead of them lay the low, rolling, green-wooded countryside of the Djursland peninsula spread out from Fornaess in the east away towards the Aalborg Bight to the west. Astern of them lay the flat sand-cay of Anholt, and the encircling sea was dotted with the sails of Danish fishing boats and coasters – the sails of potential enemies, Drinkwater thought as he came on deck. He leaned back against the cant of the deck, his thighs still sore but much easier now. Aloft, *Antigone*'s spars bent and she drove her lee rail under so that water spurted in at the gun-ports.

'Morning, sir,' said Quilhampton crossing the deck, his hand on his hat and his eyes cast aloft. 'D'you think she'll stand it?'

'Yes, she'll stand it, she goes well, Mr Q, though I could wish the wind fairer.'

'Indeed, sir.' Quilhampton watched the captain keenly as Drinkwater looked about them and drew the fresh air into his lungs.

'The countryside looks fine to the south'ard, don't you think?' He pointed on the larboard bow. 'You know, James,' he said intimately, looking at the lieutenant, 'old Tregembo advised me to retire, to buy an estate and give up the Service. I dismissed the idea at the time; I rather regret it now. I cannot say that I had ever considered the matter before. What d'you think?'

Quilhampton hesitated. Such a notion would deprive him of further employment.

'I see you don't approve,' Drinkwater said drily. 'Well, the matter is decided for Tregembo . . .'

'How is he, sir?' Quilhampton asked anxiously, eager to divert Drinkwater's mind from the thought of premature retirement.

'He'll make a fine recovery from his wound. But he'll not leave his fireside again, and I can't say I'm sorry.'

There was, however, another question Quilhampton wanted

answered, as did the whole ship's company, and he felt he might take advantage of the captain's mood and ask it without impropriety.

'May one ask the reason for your anxiety for a fast passage, sir?' The greater question was implicit and Drinkwater turned to face his interrogator.

'I can tell you little now, James, beyond the fact that I, and others, have been employed upon a special service . . . but rest assured that this ship sails now in the very vanguard of affairs.'

In the event it was all the explanation Quilhampton ever received upon the matter, but the phrase lodged in his memory and he learned to be satisfied with it.

Drinkwater was deprived of his fast passage: in the North Sea the winds were infuriatingly light and variable and *Antigone* drifted rather than sailed south-west, beneath blue skies on a sea that was as smooth as a mirror. For over a week after she passed the Skaw she made slow progress, but towards the end of the second week in July a light breeze picked up from the eastward and the next afternoon Drinkwater was called on deck to see the twin towers of the lighthouses on Orfordness.

'We've the last of the tide with us, sir,' said Hill suggestively.

Drinkwater grinned. 'Very well, stand inshore and carry the flood round the Ness and inside the Whiting Bank and we'll be off Harwich by nightfall.'

'We'll flush any Dunkirkers out of Ho'sley Bay on our way past,' remarked Hill after he had adjusted their course, referring to the big lugger-privateers that often lay under the remote shingle headland and preyed on the north-country trade bound for London.

'No need,' said Quilhampton staring through the watch glass, 'there's a big frigate in there already . . . blue ensign . . .'

They could see the masts and spars of a man-of-war lifting above the horizon, then her hull, rising oddly as refraction distorted it suddenly upwards.

'She's no frigate, Mr Q,' said Hill, 'she's an old sixty-four or I'm a Dutchman.'

Drinkwater took a look through his own glass. The distant ship had set her topsails and was standing out towards them. He could see the blue ensign at her peak and then the relative positions of the two ships closed and the refractive quality of the air disappeared. The strange ship was suddenly much closer and he could see men on her fo'c's'le, fishing for the anchor with the cat tackle.

'She'll be the Harwich guardship, I expect, come out to exercise before grounding on her own chicken bones.' The knot of officers laughed dutifully at the captain's joke. 'Make the private signal, Mr Hill,' he added, then turned to Quilhampton. 'I shall want my barge hoisted out as soon as we've fetched an anchor on the Harwich Shelf. I shall be posting to London directly . . . you had better let Fraser know.'

'Aye, aye, sir.'

Their eyes met. The coast of England was under their lee and it would not be long before Lieutenant Rogers was taken ashore. Fraser would inherit temporary command of the ship, but with Rogers still on board, the situation would be delicate for a day or two in the captain's absence. Quilhampton wondered what Drinkwater intended to do about Rogers and the question lay unasked between them. In a low voice meant for Quilhampton's ears alone Drinkwater said, 'Under last year's regulations, James, a commanding officer is, as you know "forbidden from suffering the inferior officers or men from being treated with oppression". The first lieutenant's conduct . . .'

He got no further. The ship trembled and for a split-second Drinkwater thought they had run aground, then the air was alive with exploding splinters and men were shouting in alarm, outrage and agony. His eyes lifted to the strange ship standing out from the anchorage. The blue ensign was descending, and rising to the peak of the gaff were the horizontal bands of the tricolour of the Dutch Republic.

'Christ alive!' Drinkwater swore, seized by agonizing panic. 'All hands to quarters! Beat to quarters! Rouse out all hands!' He ground his teeth, furious with himself for being so easily deceived, as he waited impotently for his men to rush to their stations, aware that the enemy would get in a further broadside before he was ready to reply. It was too late to clear for action and Hill was altering course to enable *Antigone* to bring her starboard broadside to bear, but it first exposed her to the enemy's fire.

The innocent-looking puffs of grey smoke blossomed from the Dutchman's side before the *Antigones* had cast off the breechings of their own guns. The enemy cannon were well pointed and the shot slammed into the side of the British frigate. Shot flew overhead with a rending noise like the tearing of canvas. Hammocks burst, spinning, from the nettings, splinters lanced across the deck and the starboard side of the launch amidships was shattered. Chips flew from the mainmast and holes appeared in the sails. Aloft, severed ropes whipped through their sheaves and landed on deck with a whir and slap so that unbraced yards flew round and men fell like jerking puppets as langridge and canister swept the deck in a horizontal hail of iron.

'Hold your course, damn you!' Drinkwater screamed above the din, leaping for the wheel. 'She'll luff, else!'

'She won't answer, sir!'

'Bloody hell!'

He looked desperately at the enemy and then, at last, there came from the fo'c's'le an answering gun and Drinkwater saw Quilhampton leaping along the starboard battery. Close to Drinkwater at the hance, little Frey fired one of the brass carronades with an ear-splitting roar and Mount's marines were lining the hammock netting, returning fire with their muskets.

From the waist now came the steady roar of the main guns, the black-barrelled 18-pounders rumbled back on their carriages, snapping the breechings bar-taut as their crews leapt round to sponge, load and ram, before tailing onto the tackles and sending them out through the ports again. Aiming was crude; the instant a gun-captain saw the slightest suggestion of the enemy through the smoke he jerked his lanyard, the flint snapped on the gun-lock and the gun leapt inboard again, belching fire, smoke and iron.

Overhead there was a loud and distinct crack and the maintopmast sagged forward, to come crashing down, tearing at the rigging and bringing with it the foretopmast, enveloping the deck in a heap of spars, mounds of rope and blanketing sheets of grey canvas that were hacked and torn away by the fire-fighting parties in an attempt to keep the guns in action. Smoke rolled over everything and the heat and gases from the guns began to kill the wind. Drinkwater had not lost his sense of impotence: his inattention had denied him the opportunity to manoeuvre, he had made no study of his enemy and all at once found himself pitched into this battle from which there could be no escape. As he stood helpless upon his quarterdeck, it was no comfort to realise the curious refraction in the air had deceived him as to the true range of the Dutch ship, neither did it console him to know that he had failed in this most important mission on the very doorstep of London's river. In a mood of desperation he tried to force his mind to think, to gauge the advantages of striking in the hope that he might contrive to escape with the news from Tilsit. Lieutenant Fraser loomed through the smoke. He was wounded and his expression showed a helpless desire to surrender.

Drinkwater shook his head. 'No! No, I cannot strike. We must fight on!' It was a stupid, senseless order with no chance of success, but Fraser nodded and turned forward again. Behind him the unscathed masts and yards of their persecutor rose up, closing them with a paralysing menace. Drinkwater recalled the large group of men milling on her fo'c's'le, catting her anchor. Realisation of their true purpose struck him like a blow; at any moment *Antigone* would be boarded.

'Fight, you bastards!' he roared as his officers flinched, the shot storming round them. Hill reeled and fell and Drinkwater saw a midshipman carried past him, his face and chest a bloody pulp.

Drinkwater drew his sword and an instant later saw the hull of the Dutch vessel loom athwart their hawse.

'Boarders!' he roared. 'Repel boarders!' He began to move forward, pulling men from the after-guns which had no target now.

'Come on, men! 'Tis them or us!'

Drinkwater felt the jarring crash as the two ships smashed together and to the concussion of the guns was added the howling of boarders pouring into his ship.

'Mr Mount!'

The marine sergeant appeared out of the smoke. 'Mr Mount's wounded, sir.'

'Damn! Get a few of your men, Blixoe. You must guard my person.'

'Guard your person, sir?'

'You heard me!'

'Sir.'

It was not the time for explanations, for he alone knew the value of the news he carried.

A midshipman appeared.

'Mr Wickham, what's happening forrard?'

'We're giving ground, sir.'

'Mr Quilhampton?'

'Down, sir. . . the first wave of boarders . . .'

Drinkwater swung the flat of his sword across the breast of a retreating seaman. That was a rot he must stop. He raised his voice: 'Wickham! Blixoe! Forward!' Drinkwater led the after-guard in a counter-attack that looked like a forlorn hope as it lost itself in the mêlée amidships, where the fighting heaved over the broken ribs of the boats on the booms. Steel flashed in the sunshine and the pale yellow stabs of small-arms fire spurted among the desperately writhing bodies that struggled for supremacy on the deck.

On the fo'c's'le, Quilhampton had been knocked down in the first rush of the enemy boarders. He was not seriously hurt, but his exertions at the guns had left him breathless. By the time he scrambled to his feet the enemy had moved aft and the sight of their backs caused him to pause an instant before charging impetuously upon them. It was clear that things were going badly and he had no idea of the vigour of resistance amidships to the ferocious onslaught of the Dutchmen. He was surrounded by the wreckage of the foremast and the groans of the seriously wounded. He had only to lift his head to see the enemy ship rising above the rail of the *Antigone*.

With a ponderous slowness the two vessels swung together and a second wave of boarders prepared to pour over the Dutch ship's larboard waist, to take the British defenders aft in flank. A few guns continued to fire from both ships somewhere amidships but generally the action had become the desperate slithering, hacking and cursing of hand-to-hand fighting.

It took Quilhampton only a moment to take in these events. Suddenly there appeared above him the muzzle of an enemy gun. He waited for the blast to tear out his lungs, but nothing happened and in a moment of sheer ecstasy at finding himself alive he swung upwards, one foot on *Antigone*'s rail, and leaned towards the Dutch ship. The gun barrel was hot to the touch, but no boarding pike or ramming worm was jabbed in his face; the gun was deserted!

In an instant he had heaved himself aboard the enemy ship and the sudden gloom of the gun-deck engulfed him. Dense powder smoke hung in the air. Further aft a gun discharged, leaping back, its barrel hot, the water from the sponge hissing into steam, adding to the confusion and obscurity. A group of men and an officer ran past and it was clear that everyone's attention was focused outboard and down into *Antigone*'s waist where the issue was being decided. From the shouts it was clear that the Dutch were having their own way.

A battle-lantern glowed through the smoke and Quilhampton made for it. He found himself above a companionway and face to face with a boy. The child had a thick paper cartridge under each arm and looked up in astonishment at the unfamiliar uniform. Quilhampton held out his right hand and the boy docilely handed the cartridges over, his eyes alighting on the iron hook Quilhampton held up. A moment later Quilhampton was stumbling down the ladder. At the foot a sentry stood with musket and bayonet. Before the man realised anything was wrong, Quilhampton had swung his hook, slashing the astonished soldier's face. The man screamed, dropping his musket, and fell to his knees, hands clutching his hideously torn face. Quilhampton pulled the felt curtain aside and clattered down a second ladder.

The wood-lined lobby in which he found himself was lit by glims set behind glass in the deal lining. Another wet felt curtain hung in front of him. Quilhampton had found what he was looking for: the enemy's powder magazine.

Drinkwater's counter-attack was outflanked as the two vessels ground together, yardarm to yardarm. As he stabbed and hacked he felt the increased pressure of the additional Dutch seamen and marines pouring down from the dominating height of the battle-ship.

'Blixoe! Here! Disengage!' He caught the marine sergeant's eye and the man jerked his bayonet to the right and stepped back. As the two pulled out of the throng Drinkwater looked round. The waist was a shambles and he knew his men could not hold on for many more minutes against such odds. His glance raked the enemy rail and then he knew that providence had abandoned him. In the mizen chains of the enemy ship, in the very act of jumping across the gap, was a tall French officer. Their eyes met in recognition at the same instant.

General Santhonax jumped down onto the deck of the *Antigone*, leaping onto the breech of a carronade and sweeping his sword-blade among its wounded crew. Drinkwater brought up his hanger and advanced to meet him.

'Keep your men back, Blixoe!'

'But sir . . .'

'*Back!* This man's mine!'

Then Santhonax was on him, his blade high. Drinkwater parried and missed, but ducked clear. Santhonax cut to the right as they both turned and their swords met, the jarring clash carrying up Drinkwater's arm as their bodies collided. They pushed against each other.

'I have come a long way . . .' Santhonax hissed between clenched teeth.

They jumped back and Drinkwater cut swiftly left. Santhonax quickly turned and spun round. They had fought before; Santhonax had given Drinkwater the first of his two shoulder wounds, a wound that even now reduced his stamina. Had he had a pistol he would not have hesitated to use it but, unprepared as he was, he had only his hanger, while Santhonax fought with a heavier sabre.

Santhonax cut down with a *molinello* which Drinkwater parried clumsily, feeling his enemy's blade chop downwards through the bullion wire of his epaulette. He shortened his own sword and jabbed savagely. Santhonax's cut had lost its power, but Drinkwater felt his blade bite bone and, with a sudden fierce joy, he drove upwards, feeling the hanger's blade bend as the tall Frenchman's head jerked backwards. Drinkwater retracted his arm, fearful that his weapon might snap, and as the blade withdrew from Santhonax's throat the blood poured from the gaping wound and he sank to his knees. Santhonax's eyes blazed as he tried to give vent to his anguish. With lowered guard Drinkwater stood over his enemy, his own breath coming in great panting sobs. Santhonax raised his left hand. It held a pistol, drawn from his belt. Transfixed, Drinkwater watched the hammer cock and snap forward on the pan. The noise of the shot was lost in the tumult that raged about them, but the ball went wide with the trembling of Santhonax's hand. He began to sway, the front of his shirt and uniform dark with blood; his head came up and he arched his back and Drinkwater sensed his refusal to die.

Blixoe's marines closed in round the captain, while all about them men fought, slithering in the blood that flowed from the Frenchman. Suddenly the sabre dropped from his flaccid fingers and he slumped full length. Drinkwater bent beside the dying man; he felt a quite extraordinary remorse, as though their long animosity had engendered a mutual respect. Santhonax's mouth moved, then he fell back dead.

Drinkwater rose and turned, catching Blixoe's eye. The fighting round them was as desperate as ever and the *Antigones* had given ground as far as the quarterdeck.

'Clear the quarterdeck, Blixoe!'

The sergeant swung his bloody bayonet and stabbed forward, bawling at his marines to keep their courage up.

Dropping his hanger, Drinkwater picked up the sabre Santhonax had used and hurled himself into the fight, roaring encouragement to his men. They began to force the Dutchmen backwards, then suddenly Drinkwater was aware of Quilhampton above him, scrambling over the battleship's rail into the mizen chains.

'Get down, sir! Turn your face away!'

'What the hell . . .?'

Quilhampton jumped down among the shambles of struggling men and Drinkwater saw him push little Frey to the deck, then the one-handed lieutenant seemed to leap towards him, thrusting his shoulder, spinning him round and forcing him down.

The next moment Drinkwater felt the scorching heat of the blast and the air was filled by the roar of the explosion.

18   News from the Baltic

15 July 1807

Lord Dungarth rose from the green baize-covered table in the Admiralty Boardroom. He was tired of the endless deliberations, of the arguments veering from one side to another. He stopped and stared at the chart extended from one of the rollers above the fireplace. It was of the Baltic Sea.

Behind him he heard the drone of Admiral Gambier's unenthusiastic voice, raising yet another imagined obstacle to the proposed destination of the so-called 'Secret Expedition' that had been assembled at Yarmouth to carry an expeditionary force across the North Sea to land at Rügen. Dungarth concluded that 'Dismal Jimmy' had so much in common with the evangelical preachers that he professed to admire that he would be better employed in a pulpit than commanding the reinforcements to Lord Cathcart's small force of the King's German Legion already in the Baltic.

'But my dear Admiral,' interrupted Canning, the Foreign Secretary, with marked impatience, 'the Prime Minister has already given instructions to Their Lordships and Their Lordships have doubtless already instructed Mr Barrow to prepare your orders. I don't doubt you will experience difficulties, but for God's sake don't prevaricate like Hyde Parker when he commanded the last such expedition to the area.'

Dungarth turned from the map and regarded the group of men sat around the boardroom table. The 'Committee for the Secret Expedition' was in disarray despite the brilliant arrangements that had assembled in secret a fleet, an army corps and its transports that waited only the order to proceed from the commander-in-chief to weigh their anchors. Dungarth caught Barrow's eye and saw reproach there, aware that his department had failed to produce the definitive intelligence report on the Baltic situation that would have enabled the committee to settle on the point of attack with some confidence. Dungarth knew, as Barrow and Canning knew, that Rügen was a compromise destination, designed to bolster the alliance, a political decision more than a military one. Dungarth sighed, he had hoped . . .

His eyes lifted to the wind-vane tell-tale set in the pediment over the bookcases at the far end of the room. The wind had been in the east for a week now, and still there was nothing . . .

A discreet tapping was heard at the door. Exasperated, Canning looked up.

'I thought we were not to be disturbed.'

'I'll attend to it,' said Dungarth, already crossing the carpet. He opened the door and took the chit the messenger handed him.

'It's addressed to me, gentlemen, I beg your indulgence.' He shut the door and opened the note. Casting his eyes over it the colour drained from his face.

'What the devil is it?' snapped Canning.

'An answer to your prayers, gentlemen, if I'm not mistaken.'

'Well, read it, man!'

'Very well. . .

> HM Frigate Antigone
> Harwich
> 14 July 1807

My Lord,
It is my Duty to Inform His Majesty's Government with the Utmost Despatch that it is the Intention of the Russian Emperor to Abandon His Alliance with His Majesty, and to Combine with Napoleon Bonaparte. Particular Designs are Entered into by the Combined Sovereigns Aimed at the Security of the British Nation which are of sufficiently Secret a Nature as not to be committed to Paper. They are, however, known to,

> *Your Obed.^{nt.} Servt.*
> *Nath^{nl} Drinkwater,*
> *Captain, Royal Navy*

. . . that is all, gentlemen.'

The crinkle of the folding paper could be heard as the astonished committee digested this intelligence.

'It isn't possible.'

'Where is this officer?' asked Canning, the first to recover from the shock. 'Who is he? D'ye trust him, damn it?'

They were looking at Dungarth and Dungarth was staring back.

He was no less stunned at the content of the letter than the others, but he at least had been willing such an arrival for weeks past. 'A most trustworthy officer, Mr Canning, and one whose services have long merited greater recognition by their Lordships.' Dungarth fixed Barrow with his hazel eyes but the point was lost in Canning's impatience.

'If he's kicking his damned heels in the hall below, get him up here at once!'

'At once, gentlemen,' acknowledged Dungarth turning a second time to the door, with the ghost of a smile upon his face.

The sun was setting in a blaze of colour beyond the trees of St James's Park as the travel-stained naval captain and the earl crossed Horse Guards' Parade in the direction of Westminster. As they walked Drinkwater recounted those details of the strange cruise of the *Antigone* in the Baltic that he had not already mentioned in his verbal report to the Committee for the Secret Expedition.

'And you say this Dutch ship was commandeered by our old friend Edouard Santhonax?

'Aye, my Lord, and forced out of the Texel in the teeth of the blockading squadron. I was only thankful that she had not taken on board her full quantity of powder, for if she had, I should not have lived to tell the tale.'

'And your fellow, Quilhampton, boarded her.'

'He is reticent upon the matter, but a determined cove nonetheless. I cannot speak too highly of him.'

'Nor I of you, Nathaniel. So you consider *Antigone* no longer seaworthy?'

'I think not, unless she be doubled all over and she will likely lose her fine sailing qualities. She suffered severely from the blowing up of the *Zaandam*; much of her starboard side was damaged and the first lieutenant was among the victims.'

'I see.'

They walked on in silence. Drinkwater had fought hard to keep *Antigone* afloat as they worked her into Harwich, and she lay now beached on the mud off the old Navy Yard there. Of Rogers he said nothing more, since nothing more need be said. In his own way Rogers had died in the service of his country; it was epitaph enough for him.

'And how is old Tregembo?'

'Like the *Antigone*, not fit for further sea-service.'

They dined at Dungarth's house in Lord North Street, the conversation muted until Dungarth's single manservant had withdrawn and left them with their port.

'Canning is well pleased with you, Nathaniel,' Dungarth smiled, lighting a cigar and leaning back to blow a pale blue cloud over the yellow glare of the candles.

'I suppose I should be flattered.'

'He has had an expedition fitting out for the Baltic for several weeks now. It was destined to support operations in Rügen until your news arrived. I've been warning Canning that something was afoot but until we knew for certain the outcome of events between the Russians and the French we should not show our hand.'

'I thought you must have expected something. When I got your note, I thought . . .'

'What? That I was a necromancer?' Dungarth smiled and shrugged. 'No, but the unusual nature of my duties reveals odd things, and I am not necessarily referring to secrets. For some reason war draws the very best from men who are idle and dissolute creatures else, intent on pleasure, petty squabbling and money grubbing. Give a man a guinea and he will buy a bottle or a whore; give a people freedom and they will turn to riot and revenge . . .' Dungarth poured himself a second glass and passed the decanter. 'And this war . . .' he sighed and watched Drinkwater fill his own glass. 'It is said history imitates itself and men's motives are not always derived, as they would have you think, from their own reason. Some are, I conceive, instinctive, like Santhonax's persistence or your own quixotic abetting of Ostroff. It isn't circumstantial, you know, Nathaniel, and I have always felt that these events are conjoined, like tiny links in a great chain that unwinds down the ages.'

He took the proffered decanter and paused as he refilled his glass again. 'Or like some gravitational pull, which orders our affairs in spite of ourselves and wants only a second Newton to codify it.' Dungarth smiled. 'An odd, illogical fancy perhaps, but then we are all subject to them. Your own fascination with that witch Hortense Santhonax, for instance. No, don't protest your unimpeachable fidelity to Elizabeth. You are as prone to profane thoughts as the next man.'

Drinkwater reached into his waistcoat pocket. 'I did not know you read me so well,' he observed wryly and leaned across the table. His thumb flicked open the back of a gold hunter and Dungarth looked down at the timepiece.

Grey eyes stared up from the pale oval face of the miniature.

'Good heavens! Santhonax's watch?'

Drinkwater nodded, closed it and slipped it back into his pocket.

'It's very curious, is it not?' Dungarth shook his head ruminatively.

'And you, my Lord, you were then moved by the gravity of history to send word, by Horne of the *Pegasus*?'

Dungarth barked a short laugh. 'You turn my metaphor against me. Yes, and no. Perhaps I was and perhaps not . . . I cannot truly tell you.'

'What then will be the destination of this Secret Expeditionary Force – not Rügen, surely?'

'Oh, Lord, no! Not now we know what Napoleon intends. Our most immediate worry is the Danish navy. The French are on the point of occupying the country and the Danish fleet is in an advanced state of readiness.'

'I thought that we had finished that business before, at Copenhagen.'

'Would that we had, but time does not stand still. If the Danes cannot be coerced into surrendering their fleet in return for a subsidy, we shall have to execute a *coup de main* and take it into our safekeeping.'

Drinkwater frowned. 'You mean to cut out the entire Danish fleet?'

'Yes.'

'God's bones! What a savage master this war is become.'

'Like fire, Nathaniel,' Dungarth replied with a nod, 'and like fire, it must be fought with fire.'

'Lord Dungarth has made me privy to the circumstances in which you were compelled to leave your command, Captain Drinkwater.'

Mr Barrow, the Admiralty's Second Secretary, smiled, his pedantic mouth precise in the exact allowance of condescension he permitted an officer of Drinkwater's seniority. He placed his hand palm downwards on the little pile of documents that Drinkwater had submitted. 'I would have thought it your first duty to report to their Lordships but, in view of the importance of the information you have brought, these matters will be overlooked.'

Drinkwater's mouth was dry. After the congratulations of Canning and Dungarth, Barrow's attitude was rather hard to accept. He counselled himself to silence.

'It is also important, I might almost say of *paramount* importance, that the sources of this information are not divulged. I think *you* understand this, Captain. War with Russia is now certain and our agents in that country are in great peril. The matter is therefore a secret of state. You do understand, do you not?'

'I do.'

'Your absence from your ship therefore did not take place,' said Barrow, proceeding like a Domine leading a class through a Euclidean theorem. 'You will surrender your log-books and destroy any personal journals. The death of your first lieutenant is really most convenient.' The thin smile appeared again on Mr Barrow's face. 'I leave an explanation of Lord Walmsley's death for the benefit of his father entirely in your hands, Captain Drinkwater. Lord Dungarth says you have a ready wit in these matters.'

Drinkwater felt a rising tide of anger within him at Barrow's condescension and his self-control slipped further at Barrow's next remark.

'The over-riding importance of secrecy does not permit you much licence. Your people . . .'

'Will gossip, Mr Barrow,' Drinkwater put in sharply, exasperated by Barrow's bland assumption that a man-of-war might be sealed off like some packet of secret orders.

'It is unlikely that your men will have much opportunity to gossip.' Barrow paused to make his effect more telling. 'As for your officers, they are to remain under your command . . .'

'Until death discharges them?' Drinkwater snapped, the sinister and inhuman implication of Barrow's intentions striking him fully.

'Or peace, Captain, or peace. Do not let us be too pessimistic,' Barrow continued smoothly. 'In the meantime I shall see what's to be done about a new lieutenant.' Barrow began to gather up the papers and tie a pink tape around them.

'And the shattered state of my ship, sir, have you considered that?'

'Of course! There are orders for you being prepared in the copy-room. You will turn your ship's company over directly into the *Patrician*, a razeed sixty-four and a particularly fine sailer. She is at Chatham and wants only men . . . your men.'

'And myself, sir?' he asked, numbed by this news but thinking of his wife and Tregembo and the simple desire of a man to go home. 'Am I also affected by this *proscription*?'

Barrow looked up. 'I think it best that you are on shore as little as possible, Captain Drinkwater. The increasing desertions of men are most often noticeable where the commanding officer sleeps out of his ship. You know the regulations.'

Drinkwater stood and gripped the back of his chair in an effort at self-control. 'I had believed that I and my ship's company had earned a measure of respite, having rendered the State a signal service, Mr Barrow. Some of my men have not stepped ashore since the last Peace, God damn it!'

Barrow stared at him and Drinkwater saw with a certain degree of satisfaction that he had at last provoked the man. 'There is no doubt that your service has been most satisfactory, Captain Drinkwater. I thought I had been at some pains to make that clear to you,' Barrow said frigidly, 'but there is no respite for any of us. Every effort will continue to be made . . .'

'I do not think I need to be taught my business, Mr Barrow!'

The two men glared at each other. Barrow's ruthless ability was an admired fact; he was an accomplished administrator with a task of great complexity, but he had little appreciation of a captain's predicament. Duty was obvious, while Drinkwater's sense of obligation to his crew was a tiresome liberality. Nothing of this conflict seemed clear to Barrow.

'No, I am sure I do not, Captain,' Barrow conceded. Then he added, 'But do not forget to forward your logs – privately, you understand.'

Drinkwater stared for a moment at the little heap of Admiralty papers that were now being neatly bundled up in pink tape. How fatuous his conversation with Lord Dungarth now seemed. As Barrow's fingers formed a bow in the pink tape the act was symbolic of dismissal. Tired, angry and disgusted, Drinkwater made for the door.

'One thing more, Captain Drinkwater.'

Drinkwater turned on the threshold.

'The matter of the eighty thousand sterling you conveyed to the Baltic. Unfortunately His Majesty King Gustavus saw fit to impound it for his own use. It never reached the Tsar. Unhappily you will be deprived of your customary percentage . . .' Drinkwater recalled his promise to his men, but Barrow had not yet finished with him.

'One wonders, if it had reached Alexander as intended, whether he might not have remained faithful to the alliance. Good day, Captain.'

Half choking with anger Drinkwater stepped out into the corridor.

Copenhagen

August 1807

Admiral Gambier's fleet of over three hundred men-of-war and transports lay at anchor off the village of Vedboek. To the west of the anchored ships, amid the low wooded hills and red-roofed villages of the island of Zealand, an expeditionary force of the British Army and King's German Legion advanced on the Danish capital of Copenhagen. Field howitzers were already bombarding the city's defences and the thunder of the cannonade, the whistling of the arcing shells and the violent concussions of the exploding carcasses could be heard miles away.

In accordance with his instructions the army commander, Lord Cathcart, had demanded the surrender of the Danish fleet in exchange for an annual payment to be made for as long as was necessary. The Danes had refused the terms, voluntarily submitting their capital to bombardment rather than their honour with their ships.

When darkness fell the night was bright with the traces of shellfire, and over Copenhagen the dense pall of smoke rose into the sky, its billowing under-belly orange with reflected flame.

A few days later the rape of the Danish fleet was completed, and Admiral Gambier sailed homewards with his prizes.

Author's Note

The means by which the British Government learned of the secret articles of the Treaty of Tilsit remain a mystery to this day. Whilst historians may speculate upon probabilities, the novelist enjoys the greater freedom of exploring possibilities. Nevertheless I have tried not to abuse this privilege and have spun my yarn with the few known facts.

The most likely contender for the role of the spy beneath the raft is Colin Alexander Mackenzie, a known British agent who had seen service in the Russian army and was a good linguist. A century after the event his family revealed his close connection with the incident (*English Historical Review*, Vol. XVII, p. 110, 1902). Although this is inconclusive, Canning's steadfast refusal to name his source does suggest a vulnerable individual who remained at large in a suddenly hostile Russia. But Mackenzie was known to the Tsar, and dined with Alexander when he entertained Talleyrand. He may, therefore, have been too conspicuous to have been the actual eavesdropper, though he knew all about it. Circumstantial evidence of his possible arrival in London is not confirmed, but is put *after* 16 July, when Canning wrote his instructions to Gambier and Cathcart for the attack on Copenhagen. Talleyrand himself may have supplied some information, for his betrayal of Napoleon dates from Tilsit, and he occupied the Foreign Ministry of France throughout the transition from Napoleonic to Bourbon rule in 1815, when the French copy of the treaty is alleged to have disappeared. However, he was not under the raft, nor were any of the other Britons known to have been in Russia at the time, such as Lords Leveson-Gower and Hutchinson, Robert Wilson or Dr Wylie, who were kept at a discreet distance.

The intrigues of the Russian court will never be known, but there are several contenders for the role of, at least, accomplice. The Vorontzoff family have been closely connected with the secret, even cited as providing the spy. Leaked information may also have come from Bennigsen, and the British Foreign Office is said to have papers alleging his part in a plot to kill Alexander.

The most intriguingly 'useful' fact is the existence of a letter quoted by Dr Holland Rose, dated 26 June from Memel, from an anonymous officer in the Russian service.

The speed with which the intelligence arrived in London could have been achieved by land or sea. It was a hot summer, 'the labourers fainting in the fields', with little wind and an anti-cyclone over the North Sea. My preference for the frigate *Antigone* is obvious, but lent credence by Richard Deacon's remark in his *History of the British Secret Service* that much information was gathered by cruisers of the Royal Navy. Government secrecy, of course, ensured that *Antigone*'s log book cannot now be found in the Public Record Office!

Much of the credibility of the story rests on the exact nature of the 'raft'. Lariboissière's engineers certainly had a hand in its adaptation and there are hints of the employment of local labourers. The anonymous Russian officer, quoted by Holland Rose, calls the thing a *pont volant*, suggesting the use of an existing 'flying bridge' such as are believed to have been used for moving cattle across the lower reaches of the river. It is this supposition I have favoured in view of the period of concealment and the details claimed by the Mackenzie family.

The free movement of strangers among the military is affirmed by Savary, Duke of Rovigo: 'this meeting attracted visitors to Tilsit from a hundred leagues around.' The opening exchange between Napoleon and Alexander is too widely quoted to tamper with. For, as Napoleon's secretary Bourienne points out, the meeting at Tilsit was 'one of the culminating points of modern history . . . the waters of the Nieman reflected the image of Napoleon at the height of his glory'. Who that reflected image concealed in the water below is here revealed as the mysterious 'Ostroff'.

Wilson's presence at Eylau, the seizure by Gustavus of the Tsar's subsidy and the loss of the arms shipment are all verifiable and the Danes have not yet forgiven us the seizure of their fleet in 1807.

Morality has never been a conspicuous feature of war, and, as Fortescue says, 'it was Denmark's misfortune to lie between the hammer and the anvil' while, on Britain's part, 'the law of self-preservation [was] cogent'. Even as the British struck, Marshal Bernadotte received Napoleon's orders to invade Denmark. Finally, Fouché, Napoleon's Chief of Police, says in his memoirs, 'The success of the attack on Copenhagen was the first thing that deranged the secret article of the Treaty of Tilsit, by virtue of which the fleet of Denmark was to be put at the disposal of France . . . I had never seen Napoleon in such a transport of rage.'

The circumstances under which Edward Drinkwater found himself in Russia are more fully explained in *The Bomb Vessel*.

In Distant Waters

For my brother, Oliver

Contents

PART ONE: LOW WATER 231
The Deserter 233
1 Cape Horn 242
2 The Radoub 255
3 Manhunt 265
4 The Chase 280
5 The Spanish Prisoners 292
6 Of Wine and Women 302
7 San Francisco 310
8 Council of War 323
9 The Leak 330
10 The Labouring of Gentlemen 341
11 Rezanov 351
12 Drake's Bay 360
13 Rubalcava's Revenge 370

PART TWO: FLOOD TIDE 379
14 Débâcle 381
15 The Prisoner 391
16 The Despatch Vessel 402
17 The Virgin of Fair Weather 416
18 The Raid in the Rain 425
19 The Trojan Horse 438
20 Dos de Mayo 451
21 The Night Action 461
Author's Note 469

Alaska   NORTH AMERICA

• MOUNT ELIAS   PACIFIC COAST

• SITKA   1808

Pacific

VANCOUVER   NOOTKA SOUND
ISLAND

COLUMBIA RIVER

• BODEGA BAY
DRAKE'S BAY
PTA DE LOS REYES   • SAN FRANCISCO

Ocean   California

R.M.W.

PART ONE
Low Water

'It is very difficult for history to get at the real facts. Luckily they are more often objects of curiosity than truly important. There are so many facts!'

Napoleon

The Deserter

Although he had been waiting for it, the knock at his cabin door made him start. An unnaturally expectant silence had fallen upon the ship following the noisy tumult of reaction to the pipes and calls for 'all hands'. Beyond the cabin windows the spring ebb-tide and the westerly gale churned the yeasty water of the Great Nore and tore its surface into long streaks of dirty spume. *Patrician* snubbed her cable in the tideway, her fabric creaking and groaning to the interplay of the elements.

Somehow these noises, the working of the rudder stock in its trunking below him, the rattle of the window sashes, the whine of the wind seeking gaps in the closed gun-ports and the thrum of it aloft acting upon the great sounding box of the stilled hull, exploited the strange silence of her company and permeated the very air he breathed with a sinister foreboding.

Beyond the vibrating windows the shapes of the ships in company faded and reappeared in his field of view as squalls swept dismal curtains of rain across the anchorage. At least the weather prevented a close mustering of the squadron's boats about *Patrician*; she could do her dirty work in a measure of privacy.

The knock, simultaneously nervous and stridently impatient, came again.

Captain Drinkwater stood and picked up the paper at which he had been staring. He felt the hilt of his sword tap his hip as he reached with his other hand for the cockaded hat. His chair scraped on the decking with a jarring squeal.

'Come in!'

Midshipman Frey appeared in the opened doorway. He too was in full dress, the white collar patches bright on the dark blue cloth of a new uniform to fit his suddenly grown frame. Above the collar his face was pale with apprehension.

'First lieutenant's compliments, sir, and the ship's company's mustered to witness . . . punishment.' Frey choked on the last word, registering its inadequacy.

Drinkwater sighed. He could delay the matter no longer.

'Very well, Mr Frey. Thank you.'

The boy bobbed out and Drinkwater followed, ducking under the deck beams. Out on the gun deck he raised two fingers to the forecock of his firmly seated hat as the marine sentry saluted, and emerged a few seconds later onto the quarterdeck. The wind tore at him from a lowering sky that seemed scarcely a fathom above the mastheads. In his right hand the piece of paper suddenly fluttered, drawing attention to itself.

'Ship's company mustered to witness punishment, sir.' Lieutenant Fraser, his Scots burr muted by the solemnity of the occasion, made his formal report as first lieutenant. Looking round the deck Drinkwater sensed the awe with which this moment was touched. It was one thing to kill a man in the equal heat of battle, but quite another to cut short his life with this cold and ruthless act that ended the judicial process. Like Fraser, Drinkwater sought refuge in the euphemistic naval formulae under which personal feelings could be hidden, and hated himself for his cowardice.

He met Fraser's eyes. 'Very well.'

He walked forward to stand beside the binnacle and looked steadily around the ship. She was much larger than his last command, but the same faces stared back at him, an old company that was growing tired of war, augmented by a draft from the Nore guardship to bring his crew up to complement. Well, almost . . .

They spilled across the upper deck, perched up on the larboard hammock nettings and across the launch and longboat hoisted on the booms to accommodate them. Only the starboard gangway was uncluttered, occupied by a detail of a dozen men, the ship's most persistent petty offenders against cleanliness and propriety. They stood with downcast eyes in contemplation of their melancholy duty, for the rope they held ran up to the starboard fore-yardarm and back on deck to terminate in a noose.

Beyond the people massed amidships, Drinkwater could see

the anxious face of Midshipman Wickham supervising the men closed up round the heavy carronade on the fo'c's'le. He stared alertly aft, awaiting the signal. Behind Drinkwater, dominating the men in the waist with their muskets and fixed bayonets, the scarlet ranks of the *Patrician*'s forty marines stood rigid, bright against the monotone of the morning. In front of them, still wearing the bandages of his recent wound and with his hanger drawn, Lieutenant Mount stood at his post. His gorget was the only glint of brilliance on the quarterdeck. Alongside Mount, tense with expectancy, his drum a-cock and twin sticks held down the seams of his breeches, was the diminutive figure of the marine drummer.

Close about the captain in a ragged semi-circle were the commissioned and warrant officers, wearing their swords and the full-dress uniform prescribed for their ranks. Above them all the white ensign snapped out, jerking the slender larch staff as the gale moaned through the recently tautened rigging.

'Bring up the prisoner!'

A ripple of expectancy ran through the assembly amidships. Led by the new and lugubrious figure of the chaplain and escorted by Sergeant Blixoe of the marines, the wretched man was brought on deck. As he emerged, Midshipman Frey hoisted the yellow flag to the masthead, Drinkwater nodded, and Wickham fired the fo'c's'le carronade. The short, shocking bark of the 42-pounder thudded out. A brief, acrid stench of powdersmoke whipped aft and Drinkwater saw the prisoner blench at the gun's report. Despite the liberal dose of rum he had been given, the poor fellow was shaking, though his tied hands drew back his shoulders and conferred upon him a spurious dignity.

Clearing his throat, Drinkwater raised the crackling paper and began to read.

'*To Nathaniel Drinkwater, Esquire, Captain in the Royal Navy, commanding His Britannic Majesty's frigate* Patrician *at the Great Nore . . .*

Whereas, Thomas Stanham, Able Seaman, late of His Majesty's Ship Antigone, *hath been examined by a Court-Martial on charges of desertion . . .*'

Stanham had drawn himself up, perhaps, in his extremity, feeling some cold comfort from the tacit sympathies of his old messmates around him. Drinkwater knew enough of the man's history not to feel grave misgivings as to the natural justice of the present proceedings together with a profound sense of regret that Stanham had been tried and sentenced with no one to plead for him. His crime was that of having deserted Drinkwater's last command, HMS *Antigone*, just prior to her departure to the Baltic in the spring. A topman of no more than twenty-one or twenty-two years of age, Stanham had been driven to this desperate course of action by lack of shore-leave and a well-meant letter from a neighbour living near his home in Norwich. According to this informant, Stanham's wife had been 'carrying-on' in her husband's prolonged absence. In company with another Norfolk man Stanham had deserted, slipping ashore from a bum-boat when a marine sentry was distracted. Had he shortly thereafter returned to his duty, Drinkwater would have taken a lenient view of the matter and treated Stanham as a mere 'straggler'. Such things were best dealt with within the ship and the cat-o'-nine tails was a swift justiciar and powerful deterrent. But the enforced and hurried transfer of his entire company from the shattered *Antigone* to the *Patrician* had necessitated the submission of all her books to the Admiralty and the Navy Office.

Drinkwater was sick at heart at the circumstances that had conspired to set Stanham before his shipmates in these last few moments of his life. *Antigone* had returned from the Baltic with the most momentous secret of the entire war. In order to preserve the source of this news, no one connected with the ship was allowed leave, a proscription that included Drinkwater himself. But the *Antigone* had suffered mortal damage to her hull when the Dutch cruiser *Zaandam* had exploded alongside her. As a result she had been condemned and her remaining company transferred to the razée *Patrician*, just then commissioning as a heavy frigate at Sheerness. The tedious and often protracted business of closing a ship's books had been specially expedited on the express instructions of John Barrow, the all-powerful Second Secretary of the Admiralty. Behind this obfuscation, Drinkwater knew, loomed the figures of George Canning, the Foreign Secretary, and Lord Castlereagh, the Secretary for War. Even Lord Dungarth, the Director of the Admiralty's Secret Department, had apparently condoned Barrow's severity and expedition. It only added to

Drinkwater's present mortification to consider his own personal interest in this cloak of secrecy.[*]

But there were other agencies at work conniving against the unfortunate Stanham. Even as the Admiralty clerks examined *Antigone*'s books and discovered the rubric *R* against the name of Thomas Stanham, a letter arrived at Whitehall appraising Their Lordships that acting upon information laid before them, the Norwich magistrates had apprehended Thomas Stanham, a deserter from His Majesty's Service. There was not the slightest doubt to contest the information, affidavits had been sworn accordingly by reliable persons and, to compound the matter, the said Stanham had caused an affray in resisting arrest in which he had maliciously caused one of the constables to be gravely wounded. The magistrates desired to know Their Lordships' pleasure.

Drinkwater knew the scuttlebutt well enough: Stanham had been betrayed by the man who had made him a cuckold. He read on, pitching his voice against the gale.

'Whereas it has been enacted under the several laws relating to the sea-service . . .'

Quite apart from the necessity to get the former *Antigone*s to sea, the Admiralty were increasingly worried about desertions from the ships of the Royal Navy. The long war with the French Empire was dragging on. Russia was no longer an ally, the Prussian military machine perfected by Frederick the Great had been smashed in a single day by Napoleon at Jena and Davout at Auerstadt, while Austrian defiance seemed likely to be the next object of Napoleon's indefatigable attention. It suited Their Lordships to visit the utmost extremity of the Articles of War upon the wronged Stanham, and no plea in mitigation had been allowed.

'. . . Every person in or belonging to the Fleet, who shall desert, or entice others to desert, shall suffer Death . . .'

Drinkwater paused to look up again. That phrase 'in or belonging to the Fleet' bound Stanham like an iron shackle. It ran contrary to the common, canting notions of liberty so cherished by rubicund Englishmen up and down the shires. His eyes met those of the prisoner. Stanham stopped shaking at that terrible final word

---

[*] See *Baltic Mission*.

and his gaze held something else, something unnerving. Drinkwater hurried on.

'And the court hath adjudged the said Thomas Stanham to suffer death by being hanged by the neck at the yardarm. You are hereby required and directed to see the said sentence of death carried into execution upon the body of the said Thomas Stanham.'

There followed the languid flourish of the presiding admiral's signature. Drinkwater lowered the paper and crushed it in his fist.

'Do you wish to say anything, Stanham?'

Again their eyes met, the gulf between them immense. Stanham nodded and coughed to clear his throat.

'Good luck to me shipmates, sir, and God save the King!'

The sudden upward modulation of Stanham's homely Norfolk voice struck Drinkwater as having been the accent of the late, lamented Lord Nelson. He nodded at Stanham as a low rumbling came from the hands.

'Silence there!' Fraser's voice cut nervously through the wind.

'Master-at-Arms! Do your duty!'

Behind Drinkwater there was a snicker of accoutrements at a low order from Mount. The marines' muskets came to the port, forty thumbs resting upon forty firelock hammers. The drummer hitched his snare-drum, brought his sticks up to the chin and then down, to beat the long roll as the master-at-arms led Stanham to the starboard gangway. With a lugubrious expression that Drinkwater found revolting the chaplain brought up the rear. The shamefaced hanging party moved aside to let the grim procession pass.

A short ladder had been set against the rail and the hammock nettings removed just abaft the forechains. Stanham was halted at the foot of the ladder and the chaplain moved closer. While the master-at-arms drew the noose down over Stanham's head and settled the knot beneath his left ear, Drinkwater watched the chaplain bend forward, his lips moving above the open prayer-book, a thin strand of hair streaming out from his almost bald head. Even at a distance Drinkwater felt the inappropriateness of another stilted formula being deployed. He saw Stanham shake his head vigorously. The chaplain stepped back and nodded, an expression of exasperation on his gaunt face. Drinkwater found his revulsion increase at this untimely meanness.

A dark cotton bag was pulled down over the prisoner's head. Stanham's face was extinguished like a candle and a gasp ran through the ship. There was a muffled thump as a small midshipman fainted. No one moved to his assistance; it was Mr Belchambers's third day in the Royal Navy.

Stanham was guided up onto the rail. Beyond the lonely figure Drinkwater could see the rigging of the neighbouring ships dark with their men, piped to witness the example of Their Lordships' remorseless justice being carried out on board *Patrician*.

Drinkwater nodded his head and Wickham saw the signal. The report of the carronade rolled across the water, the brief white puff of smoke alerting the other ships of the solemnity of the moment. Again the sharp stench of powder-smoke stung their nostrils and Drinkwater caught a glimpse of the flaming wadding as it disintegrated in the wind. Beside him the marine drummer stopped his ruffle.

'Prisoner made ready, sir.'

With the gale blowing aft the master-at-arms's voice carried with unnatural loudness. He had done his duty; it extended thus far. To launch Stanham into eternity waited for Drinkwater's own command.

'Mr Comley!' Drinkwater's voice rasped with a sudden, unbidden harshness.

'Sir?' The boatswain stood with his rattan beside the hanging party.

Drinkwater could no longer take refuge in formulae, his honest nature revolted against it. To instruct Comley's party to 'carry out the sentence' would have smacked of cowardice to his puritan soul. The awful implications of power were for his shoulders alone, it was to him that the death warrant had been addressed. In this was some small atonement for his own part in this grisly necessity.

'Hang the prisoner!'

The hanging party moved as though spurred by the vehemence in Drinkwater's voice There was no time for thought, no cause for apprehension to the watching Mount, ready to coerce the party with his muskets.

Comley's men leaned to Stanham's sudden weight as his body rose jerking to the starboard fore-yardarm.

Amidships another man fainted as all watched in terrible fascination. Stanham kicked with his legs, tightening the noose with every desperate movement in his muscles, arching his back as he fought vainly for air. He was a strong man with a powerful neck that resisted the snapping of the spinal cord and the separation of the vertebrae that would bring a quick, merciful end.

Drinkwater found himself willing the man to stop, to submit to the Admiralty's omnipotent will and die quietly as an example to others, but Stanham was not going to oblige. The dark tangle of his blood-choked brain was roaring with the anger of betrayal, of treachery and injustice. The dark shape of his body set against the rolling scud seemed possessed of a protest from beyond the grave. Drinkwater cursed the Norwich informer, cursed John Barrow and his lack of compassion and cursed himself for bringing back such a secret from Russia that men still died for it.

Gradually asphyxia subdued the spasms. Stanham had given up the ghost. It seemed that a collective sigh, audible above the wind and the responding hiss of the sea, came from the *Patrician*'s assembled company.

'Eight bells, sir.'

'Make it so and pipe the hands to dinner.'

The yellow flag fluttered down from the masthead as the four double rings of the bell tolled the hour of noon. Pipes twittered amidships and the men began to move below. Faintly similar noises could be heard from other ships. The rumble of voices grew as the men glanced upwards in passing forward.

'Another good man bin stabbed by the Bridport dagger, 'en . . .'

'No good'll come of it . . . 'tis bad luck . . .'

The mutter was drowned by the crash of the marines' boots as Mount dismissed his guard and reposted his sentries. Frey was bending over the swooning midshipman. Mr Belchambers was not yet thirteen years of age and his name was sonorously inappropriate for so small and insubstantial a figure. It was odd, Drinkwater thought, that men like Stanham had to be hanged while there seemed no lack of foolish boys to come and play at being men.

'We shall get under weigh the instant the wind eases, Mr Fraser,' Drinkwater growled as he turned below. 'I received my orders by the same despatch-boat as brought this . . .'

He held up the crumpled piece of paper.

'Very well, sir . . . and him, sir?' Fraser's eyes jerked aloft.

'Leave him for an hour . . . but no more, Mr Fraser, no more, I pray you.'

Above their heads Stanham's body turned slowly in the wind. Dark stains spread across his clothing and it was subject to the most humiliating ignominy of all; his cuckolded member was engorged with his stilled blood.

1 Cape Horn

December 1807

Drinkwater lay soaked in sweat, aware that it was neither the jerking of his cot, nor the violent motion of *Patrician* that had woken him, but something fading beyond his recall, the substance of his nightmare. Wiping his forehead and at the same time shivering in the pre-dawn chill, he lay back and tugged the shed blankets back over his aching body. The quinsy that had presaged his fever was worse this morning, but the terrors of the nightmare far exceeded the disturbances of illness. He stared into the darkness, trying to remember what had so upset him, driven by some instinct to revive the images of the nightmare.

And then with the unpredictability of imagination, they flooded back. It was an old dream, a haunting from bad times when, as a frightened midshipman, he had learned the real meaning of fear and loneliness. The figure of the white lady had loomed over him as he sunk helplessly beneath her, her power to overwhelm him sharpened by the crescendo of clanking chains that always accompanied her manifestation. As he recollected the dream he strove to hear the reassuring grind of *Patrician*'s own pumps; but he could hear nothing beyond the thrum of wind in the rigging transmitted down to the timbers of her labouring hull. The big frigate creaked and groaned in response to the mighty forces acting upon her as she fought her way to windward of Cape Horn.

Then Drinkwater recognised the face. The white lady had had many forms in her various visitations. Though he thought of her as female, she possessed the trans-sexual ability of phantoms to appear in any guise. This morning she had worn a most horrible mask: that of the hanged man, Stanham. Drinkwater recognised it at once, for after the dead man had been cut down he and Lallo, the

242

surgeon, had inspected the cadaver. It had been no mere idly morbid curiosity that had spurred him to do so, that day at the Nore ten weeks earlier. He had felt himself driven to see what he had done, as if to do so might avert some haunting of the ship by the man's spirit.

Drinkwater had seen again in his nightmare the savage furrow the noose had cut in Stanham's neck. The face above was darkly cyanotic with wild, protuberant eyes. In the flesh Stanham's body had been pale below the furrowed neck, gradually darkening with blotchy suggillations where the blood had settled into its dependent parts. This morning, beneath the horrors of the face, Stanham's ghost had worn the white veils which marked his apparition as a disguise of the white lady.

Full recollection brought Drinkwater out of himself. Unpleasant though the memory was, he was no stranger to death, or the 'blue-devils', that misanthropic preoccupation of naval officers forced to the lonely exile of distant commands. With an oath he swung his legs over the edge of the swaying cot and deftly hoisted himself to his feet as *Patrician* hesitated on a wave crest, before driving down into a huge trough. He half ran, half skidded across the cabin, fetching up against the forward bulkhead as the ship smashed her bluffbows into the advancing wall of the next sea and reared her bowsprit skywards. Drinkwater swore again, barking his shins on the leg of an overturned chair, and bellowed through the thin bulkhead at the marine sentry.

'Pass word for my coxswain!'

As he rubbed his bruised knee and swallowed with difficulty he finally remembered the true disturbance of the nightmare. It was not its recurrence, nor the ghastly transmogrification of poor Stanham, but the fact that the dream was always presentient.

He fought his way aft, across the dark cabin, and slumped in a chair until Tregembo arrived with a light and hot water and he could shave, passing the moments in reaction to the knowledge that came with this realisation. God knew that a great deal could go wrong in this forsaken corner of the world where there seemed no possible justification for sending him, even given the anxieties of the most pusillanimous jack-in-office. In the extremity of his sickness and depression he felt acutely the apparent abandonment of the only man in power with whom he felt he had both earned and enjoyed an intimacy. Lord Dungarth, once first lieutenant of Midshipman Drinkwater's original ship, had treated him with uncharacteristic coolness since he had brought the momentous news of the secret accord between Tsar Alexander and Napoleon out of Russia. It was not the only service Drinkwater had rendered his Lordship's Secret Department and Dungarth's inexplicable change of attitude had greatly pained him, combined as it was with the proscription against shore-leave and the enforced estrangement from his wife and family.

But these were self-pitying considerations. As the *Patrician* fought her way from the Atlantic to the Pacific Ocean, he had gloomier thoughts pressing him. Presentiments of disaster were to be expected and, as he shuddered from his ague, he felt inadequate to the task the Admiralty had set him, not for its complexity, but for its apparent simplicity. It seemed, in essence, to be a mere exercise upon which almost any interpretation might be put by persons anxious to discredit him. So hazy were his orders, so vague in their intent, that he was at a loss as to how to pursue them.

To carry His Majesty's flag upon the Pacific coast of North America on a Particular Service, was all very high faluting; *to make war upon Spanish Trade upon the said coast*, was all very encouraging if one took as one's example the exploits of Anson fifty years earlier. But this was the modern world, and he was not allowed a free hand, being ordered to concentrate his efforts upon the North American coast, far from the rich Spanish trade routed to the Vice-royalties of Peru and the *entrepôt* of Panama. Besides, to any British commander, the Pacific was haunted by the ghosts of a murdered Cook and the piratically seized *Bounty*.

As for what he took to be the core of his orders, the instruction to discourage Russian incursions into that sea and upon the coasts of New Albion, they seemed to Drinkwater to be the most nonsensical of them all, harking back to the dubious claims of Francis Drake and serving to remind him that his Russian connections had landed him in this desperate plight, thousands of miles from home or support. Mulling such thoughts as he fought his quinsy and waited for Tregembo, shaking with the mild fever of an infection, he was in a foul and savage mood. His coxwain's unannounced appearance stung him to an uncharacteristic rebuke.

'Knock before you enter, damn you!'

Sourly he watched Tregembo fuss over the hot water and the glim, whose light was transferred to a lantern and the lashed candelabra, illuminating the cabin with a cheerlessness that revealed the tumbled state of its contents.

'You'll catch your death, zur, sitting like that . . .'

'Don't fuss, Tregembo,' replied Drinkwater, mellowing and seeing in the seams and scars of the old man's highlit face the harrowing of age and service. He opened his mouth to apologise but Tregembo forestalled him.

'The fever's no better, zur, if I'm a judge o' temper.'

Drinkwater stood with the sweat dry on him and drew his nightshirt over his head. He grunted and took the soap from Tregembo's outstretched hand.

'I'll get Mr Lallo to make up some James's Powders, zur . . .'

'You'll do no such damned thing, Tregembo . . .'

'Dover's Powders then, zur, they be a powerful sudorific . . .'

'Damn James and Dover . . . fresh air will cure me, fresh air and hot coffee, be off and find me some hot coffee instead of standing over me like a poxed nursemaid . . .'

'There be fresh air a-plenty this morning, zur,' muttered Tregembo as he left the cabin and the remark brought the ghost of a smile to Drinkwater's haggard face, even as it reminded him of his greatest problem, his crew.

Over four years earlier, in the spring of 1803 and the brief period of peace, he had taken command of the sloop *Melusine*. She had been manned by picked volunteers, men who chose to stay at sea in the Royal Navy, rather than chance their luck in the uncertain world ashore. Many of them had been aboard ship for long before that. The resumption of war had carried them to the Arctic aboard *Melusine*, and to the Atlantic and Baltic in the frigate *Antigone*, into which ship they had been turned over when Drinkwater reached post-rank. Now the process of transfer had been repeated and that core of volunteers still lingered at the heart of *Patrician*'s company.

But men volunteer for perceived goals and these resented being taken advantage of even more than the pressed men. The latter were made up of the victims of the Impress Service, the Quota-men and the Lord Mayor's men, the dregs of debtors' prisons and the hedge-sleeping vagrants that armed parties of officers and seamen had discovered in sweeps made along the ague-plagued coast of Essex, whence Drinkwater had sent his boats. In successive waves these men had made up the deficiencies in number that death and an increase in tonnage had made necessary to man the enlarged complements of Drinkwater's successive ships. What to those eager volunteers had been thought of as a single commission, an Arctic voyage with a bounty at its conclusion, had not yet ended.

The people were divided, the one-time volunteers forming a slowly contracting minority, apt to regard itself as an élite, and suffering from the poor conditions of a Royal Navy on a wartime footing. Earlier that year in the Baltic their mood had become ugly. Lieutenant Quilhampton had suppressed an incipient mutiny by the force of his personality alone, but the news of it had made all the officers wary, heightening the tensions in the ship and drawing again those sharp social distinctions that blurred easily in a happy ship. Inconsequential things assumed new importance. The rivalry between seamen and marines coalesced into something less friendly, more suspicious; and the twinkle of the marines' bayonets lost its ceremonial glitter, fencing the vulnerable minority of the officers from the murmurs of the berth-deck.

For his own part Drinkwater had, that summer, been driven to supplementing the men's pay by a bounty of his own, a circumstance which had imperilled his domestic finances, leaving his wife and dependants at a disadvantage and a prey to the fiscal inroads of inflation and income tax.

Drinkwater scraped his face, nicking his cheek as *Patrician* staggered into another heavy sea. He swore, rinsed his razor and bent unsteadily to his task. The face that stared back at him was drawn with anxiety. The receding hair exposed his high forehead and the streaks of grey at his temples were prominent, even in the half-light of the candle-lit cabin. He still wore a queue, an unfashionable defiance behind, for what nature deprived him of in front. But though his eyes were tired and their lids dotted with powder burns like random ink-spots, though the scar that puckered down one side of his face joined the distortion of his features necessary to the task of shaving, and though he was gaunt from the effects of ague and quinsy, there was about the line of the mouth a determination that marked him for one of the most experienced frigate commanders in the Royal Navy.

Ungraced by much political interest, only his long-standing friendship with Lord Dungarth could be said to have aided his career; but even that had not been without effort on his own part. Dungarth had ensured that all Drinkwater's skills had been fully exploited by his Secret Department, that great coup from beneath the raft at Tilsit, when the two Emperors' conversation had been overheard verbatim, had repaid any debt of advancement his lordship might conceive to be owing.

Drinkwater wiped his chin and called for Tregembo, indicating he had finished with bowl and razor. He tied his stock and drew on soft leather hessian boots. Winding a muffler around his neck he put on his undress uniform coat and a heavy boat-cloak. Tregembo fussed about the cabin, moving quietly in respect of the captain's ominous silence. Picking up his hat Drinkwater jammed it on his head and went on deck.

In the high southern latitude dawn was early. The eastern horizon was suffused with a light still too weak to penetrate the cloud rolling to leeward from the west. On the starboard bow an inky darkness blurred the meeting of sea and sky, and the perceptible horizon was reduced to the crest of the great waves that loomed out of the gloom and roared down upon them, driven by the interminable winds of the Southern Ocean.

As *Patrician* dipped her reefed jib-boom, one such wall of water rose on her bow, its vast face gaining in brightness as it approached the vertical and reflected the growing light from the east. *Patrician* rolled away from it, her topsails, hard reefed though they were, suddenly flapping from want of wind and a hush falling eerily upon her decks. Her hull seemed suddenly inert as the advancing sea sped towards them, its slope streaked with spindrift, debris of a million million successive disintegrations of its toppling crest.

'Hold on there!'

Drinkwater grabbed the nearest hammock stanchion and braced himself as Lieutenant Quilhampton called the warning to his watch. It seemed as if they all held their breath.

And then the frigate began to lift her bow as the trough that preceded the wave passed beneath her and she felt the breasting rise
of that mountainous wave. From a sluggish tremor the angle rapidly increased and then she canted and the bow reared skywards.
Aft, the waterlevel rose almost to the rail, so that the sea squirted in
round the gun-ports and from below came the crash and curse of
men and loose gear tumbling about. Drinkwater prayed that the
double-lashed breechings of the guns had not worked slack during
the night and the dual crash that ended this strange hiatus momentarily persuaded him that he was mistaken. But instinct made him
look upwards to where the wind had reached the topsails. The
maintopsail was already in shreds, pulling at its bolt ropes like
wool caught on a fence, and the foretopsail was bending its yard
like a bow. An explosion of white reared up all along the starboard
rail as they reached the breaking crest and it flung all its fury at the
ship. She rolled to leeward and lay down under the violent
onslaught of the wind. The air, a moment earlier almost motionless
before the advancing mass of water, was now suddenly filled with
the terrible noise of the gale, solid with the particles of water it had
ripped from the surface of the ocean and drove downwind with the
velocity of buckshot.

But the leeward roll saved *Patrician*'s deck from the worst of
the breaking sea, though there was not a man upon it who was not
instantly soaked to the skin. The ship toppled as the wave passed
beyond her tipping-centre and she plunged downwards, into the
welter of lesser waves that scarred the back of the great sea.

'Foretopmast's sprung above the lower cap, Mr Q . . . up helm!
Get the ship before the wind and we'll take that tops'l off her!'

'Aye, aye, sir!' Quilhampton dashed the water from his face
with his one good hand, and swung round, staggering as *Patrician*
lurched; but the huge sea had been the culmination of many, an
ocean-bred monster in whose trail, for a while at least, midgets
would follow. 'Up helm, there!'

The ship's bow paid off to the southward and then to the east of
south. Drinkwater anxiously stared aloft, trying to gauge the extent
of the damage in the growing daylight and irritated at losing distance to windward. He had brought the frigate well south of Cape
Horn, in a great tack to the south and west in order to double the

tip of America as speedily as possible in an area where days of low scud made obtaining meridian altitudes difficult and only a fool would feel confident of his latitude.

'Stand by to take in the foretopsail!'

Quilhampton was bawling at his watch. Their response was slow, they seemed dazed, as if the great wave had some strange effect on them. But that was impossible, a figment of Drinkwater's fevered imagination. He held his peace for a moment longer.

'Man the clewlines and buntlines!'

The men were mustered about the pinrails and Drinkwater was reminded of something he had tried hard to forget; the dilatory action they had fought with a Danish privateer, caught off Duncansby Head, and which had escaped by superior sailing through the rocks off the Orkneys. *By superior sailing* . . . how that phrase haunted him, that sudden failure in performance that had endangered the ship now as it had done before. His patience snapped.

'Call all hands, damn it! All hands, d'you hear there!'

The squealing pipes made little impact on the gale, but the thin noise roused the ship as Quilhampton continued to shout at his men.

'Clewlines and buntlines! Haul taut!'

Drinkwater caught sight of the rise and fall of starters, of a scuffle forward of the boats and a man thrust out of the huddle round the mast.

'Leggo top bowline, there! Lively there! Leggo halliards! Clew down! Clew down, God damn you, clew down!'

'I think we have trouble forrard, Mr Q . . .'

'Aye, sir . . . no, there goes the yard . . . lay aloft and furl . . . aloft and furl!'

Men from the watches below were coming on deck and filling the waist with a worse confusion as another crack from aloft met the violence of a heavy leeward roll. Above the shouting and the orders, the wind screamed with renewed venom and the heeling deck bucked and canted beneath their slithering feet. Green water poured aboard and sluiced aft, streaming over the men at the pinrails and knocking several off their feet.

'Aloft and furl! Mr Comley, damn you, forrard, sir, and hustle the men!'

Perhaps it was the disgruntled look which the boatswain Comley threw at Quilhampton, perhaps the passing of an ague-fit which stimulated Drinkwater to intervene, but he could stand chaos no better than inefficiency and such chaos and inefficiency threatened them all in that wild sea. He began to move forward, along the starboard gangway towards the forechains.

What he found forward of the boats appalled him. The sharp perceptions of a feverish brain, the madness of the morning and the lingering suspicions and doubts about his crew coalesced into an instant comprehension. The few men who had begun to climb into the weather shrouds were half-hearted in their efforts and though no one actively prevented them, there were shouted discouragements thick in the howling air.

'Don't risk yer life for the bastards, Jimmy . . .'

'Let the fucking mast go by the board . . . we'll be home the sooner . . .'

'Oi'll fockin' kill you if you so much as lay that rope on me again, so I will . . .'

A man rolled against Drinkwater, one of the boatswain's mates, his face pale in the cruel, horizontal light of dawn, his eye already dark with bruising.

'Aloft and furl, damn you all!' Drinkwater roared and hoisted himself up into the starboard foremast shrouds. He caught sight of the small, white face of Midshipman Belchambers. 'Take my hat and cloak . . .' The wind tore the heavy cloak from his grasp and thrust it at the boy, who escaped thankfully aft.

'God's bones, d'you want to rot in hell, you damned lubbers? Aloft and furl!' He was aware of sullen faces, the spray stinging them as they looked up at him. The wind tore at his own body and already the cold had found his hands. There was no time to delay. Above them the foretopsail flogged and the mast shook and groaned while something was working loose, its destructive oscillations increasing with every roll of the ship.

He began to climb.

The force of the wind tore at him. *Patrician* was running before it now, throwing away the hard-won windward yards, rolling with an unrestrained ferocity that threatened to tear loose the sprung topmast and send the resulting wrack down on deck. For the preservation of the ship, speed was essential. He did not look down, but the vibration of the thick hemp shrouds told him that men were following him aloft. He fought his way upwards, the thin ratlines twisting beneath his feet and the wind tearing at the bulk of his body, so that his clothing bellied and pulled him forward to where the sea hissed and roared alongside the running frigate. Some active topman drew alongside him.

'That's it, my lad, up you go, up you go!'

He caught a glimpse of a sheepish grin that was instantly lost as more men caught him up, swinging outwards into the futtock shrouds with the agility of monkeys. Captains aloft were such a rare event that even the most discontented topman would be put on his mettle to outdo the intrusion.

Midshipman Frey struggled up.

'Good morning, Mr Frey.' Frey's eyes widened and Drinkwater nodded upwards. 'Have the goodness to pass ahead of me.'

The boy gulped and swung himself outboard, his back hanging downwards as *Patrician*'s hull rolled them out over the sea, then his kicking heels disappeared and Drinkwater took advantage of the return roll and followed him into the top.

Pausing for breath, Drinkwater took stock of the situation. The foretopsail yard, loosed by its halliards, lay roughly over the top of the foreyard, the huge flapping bunt of sail thundered in wild billows only partially restrained by the weight of the yard and the buntlines and clewlines. Drinkwater waved the topmen aloft and out along the yard. He could see Frey already at the extremity of the windward yardarm, his pea-jacket blown over his back and his sparse shirt-tail flapping madly.

'Come on, lads, lay out and furl that tops'l!'

He clung to the topgallantmast heel-rope downhaul and looked aloft. The fore-topgallantmast had been struck, sent down and lashed parallel to its corresponding topmast to reduce the windage of unneeded tophamper. Now, as he stared upwards, his eyes watering and the wind tugging at him, he saw that the housed topgallantmast was acting like a splint to the fractured mast. The latter had sprung badly, the split starting from a shake in the timber. Drinkwater cursed and wondered how long that spar had been pickling in the mast-pond at Chatham. The topmast was almost split in two; whatever he decided to do, it would have to be quick, before both spars were lost. He peered on deck. Morning had broken now, though the sun had risen into a cloud bank and daylight was dimmed. Its arrival somehow surprised him, such had been his preoccupation.

Quilhampton looked upwards anxiously, clearly considering that Drinkwater's action in going aloft was unseemly. Beside him Fraser stood staring up, one hand clapped over his tricorne hat.

The men were laying in from the yard, having passed the reef-points, and Drinkwater called to them to begin to clear the gear away ready to send the topmast down on deck. It would be a long, complex and difficult job in the sea that was running, but he sensed in their changed expressions that the surly disinterest had been replaced by a sudden realisation of the danger they were in. Besides, he had no intention of making life too easy for them; those lost miles to leeward nagged him as he made his way down on deck.

After the clamour of the foretop, the quarterdeck seemed a sanctuary. Fraser began to remonstrate.

'Sir, you shouldn't ha' . . .'

'Be damned to you, Fraser, the men are disaffected . . . in your absence it was necessary I set 'em an example . . . now have the kindness to order the spanker and foretopmast stays'l set . . . just the clew of the spanker, mind you, I want this ship on the wind and then we'll sort out the mess of the foremast . . .'

Fraser nodded his understanding and Drinkwater regretted the jibe at the first lieutenant. It was mean, but he was in a damnably mean mood and meant to ride down this discontent, even if it first meant riding his officers.

'We'll set a goose-winged maintops'l when we've finished, and see if we can't claw back some of the leeway we've made . . .'

Hill, the elderly sailing master summoned on deck at the cry for all hands, nodded his agreement and put the traverse board back by the binnacle.

'It's a damn . . .'

'Deck! Deck there!'

The scream was high-pitched and uttered with such urgency that it carried above the gale. The officers looked up at

Midshipman Frey. He was leaning against the barricade of the foretop, pointing ahead.

'Sir! There's a ship, sir . . . a ship! Right ahead!'

'Impossible!'

That first reaction was gone in an instant. As he scrambled into the mizen rigging Drinkwater's active mind considered the odds of another ship being under their feet in this remote spot. And then he saw her, an irregular, spiky outline flung up against the eastern sky as she breasted a crest. His practised eye saw her hull and her straining sails and then she was gone, separated from them by a wave. She was perhaps three quarters of a mile away.

When she reappeared she was fine to starboard, under close-reefed topsails and beating to windward as *Patrician* had been doing an hour earlier. A curious idleness had filled the hands as they waited for the officers to get over their astonishment. Drinkwater rounded on the latter.

'Gentlemen! You have your orders, kindly attend to them!' They scattered, like chastened schoolboys. Only Hill, his white hair streaming in the wind, stood close to Drinkwater, trying to catch the stranger in the watch-glass.

Fishing in his pocket Drinkwater pulled out his Dollond glass and raised it to his eye, swearing with the difficulty of focusing it on the other ship.

'She's a ship of force, sir,' Hill muttered beside him.

Drinkwater grunted agreement. Her dark hull seemed pierced by two rows of gun-ports and, like themselves, she wore no colours. She beat to windward bravely, passing his own lamed ship as she licked her wound and escaped the worst fury of the storm by running before it. Once again that phrase *by superior sailing* was recalled to his mind.

Although not superstitious, Drinkwater was, like most philosophical sailors, aware of the influence of providence and the caprice of fortune. Nothing had yet happened aboard *Patrician* that persuaded him he was in command of anything but an unlucky ship. Among his ill-educated crew he knew that feeling had developed to a conviction since the execution.

'What d'you make of her, Mr Hill?'

'With that black hull and making for the Pacific, I'd stake my hat and wig on her being a Don, sir . . .'

'Your shore-going wig, Mr Hill?' Drinkwater joked grimly and neither man took his glass from his eye.

'For a certainty, sir . . .'

Drinkwater grunted. He had seen the Spaniards' lugubriously popish fancy for black ships in Cadiz shortly before Trafalgar, but he was recalling the nightmare and its ominous warning. He stared at the ship for other clues, but found none. A minute later she was gone, lost in the bleak and heaving wastes of the Southern Ocean. Captain and master lowered their glasses at the same moment.

'A Don you say, Mr Hill?'

'My life upon it, sir.'

Drinkwater shook his head. 'Rash, Mr Hill, rash . . .'

'You don't agree, sir?' Drinkwater managed a grin at the obviously discomfited Hill.

'I've a hunch, Mr Hill, a hunch . . . nothing more and not worth the trouble of a wager . . . come now, let's get a new foretopmast off the booms . . .'

2 The Radoub

December 1807

Drinkwater swallowed painfully and stared balefully at the first lieutenant. There were moments, and this was one of them, when he would have wished for the return of Samuel Rogers, for all his drunkenness and bullying temperament. Rogers would have understood what was to be done, but Rogers had been blown to the devil with six score others when the *Zaandam* exploded alongside the *Antigone* off Orfordness, and poor Fraser had inherited the first luff's uneasy berth. A quiet, competent Scot, Fraser was an obsessively worrying type, a man who let anxiety get the better of his spirit which was thereby damped and warped. Drinkwater had once overheard Mount referring to him in conversation with James Quilhampton.

'If yon Scot,' Mount mimicked in false North British dialect, 'ever occasioned to fall in the sea, he'd drown.' Then, seeing Quilhampton's puzzled look, he added plainly, 'He possesses no *buoyancy*.'

Drinkwater regarded Fraser, his expression softening. He was a prey to anxiety himself; he was being unjustly hard on a conscientious officer.

'It's high summer hereabouts, Mr Fraser, though it has a damned uncivil way of showing it, but I want the men worked . . . d'ye hear? Worked, sir, and damned hard. Not a single task that ain't necessary . . . I'll have no gratuitous hazing, but I want every manjack of 'em to know that they don't refuse to go aloft on *my* ship!'

Drinkwater drew breath, his anger at his predicament concentrated on the helpless Fraser.

'Aye, aye, sir.' But the first lieutenant hesitated.

'Well, Mr Fraser? What's the trouble?'

'Well, sir . . . such tasks . . . we've sent down the foretopmast . . .'

'Tasks? Are you suggesting your imagination cannot supply *tasks*? Good God, man, was there ever a want of tasks on a man-o'-war?'

It was clear that Fraser's imagination fell somewhat short of Drinkwater's expectation. The captain sighed resignedly as the frigate lurched and trembled. A sea smashed against her weather bow and the spray whipped aft, stinging their faces.

'Turn up all watches, Mr Fraser. I want the people worked until they drop. I don't care that it blows a gale, nor that the ship's doing a dido, or that every manjack of 'em hates my lights by sunset, but we had one brush with an enemy off the Orkneys that I don't want repeated . . . and that ship we sighted this morning, be he Don or Devil, bore *two* decks of guns. If we have to fight her in our present condition, Mr Fraser, I'll not answer for the consequences . . . d'you comprehend my meaning? And I mean the officers to turn-out too . . .'

'The officers, sir?' Fraser's jaw dropped a little further. Anxiety about the unstable state of the crew and the captain's reaction to their behaviour this morning was worming his belly. Drinkwater pressed relentlessly on.

'Now, as to tasks, Mr Fraser, you may rattle down the lower shrouds, slush the new topmast and reeve a new heel-rope. I don't doubt an inspection of the gun-deck will reveal a few of the gun-lashings working and the same goes for the boat gripes. Let's have the well sounded hourly and kept dry as a parson's throat. Have the gunner detail a party to make up more cartridges, the quarter-gunners to reknap the flints in the upper deck gun-locks and overhaul the shot lockers. Turn a party to on scaling the worst-corroded balls and send some men to change all the shot in the garlands. Get an officer aloft with a midshipman and a pencil to carry out an examination of all the spars for further shakes and let me have their findings in writing . . .'

Fraser caught the reproach in Drinkwater's eyes and coloured at his own negligence. He had taken so much of *Patrician*'s gear from the dockyard on trust, since she had been so recently refitted after being cut down to a razée.

'Yes, sir.'

'Very well. You can carry out an inventory of the tradesmen's stores and have a party assist the cooper to stum some casks ready for watering and if that ain't enough, Mr Fraser, do not neglect the fact that we lost two good topsails this morning . . . in short, sir, I want you to *radoub* the ship!'

'Aye, sir . . .'

'And the officers are to take an active part, Mr Fraser . . . no driving the men, I want 'em *led*, sir, *led* by officers so that, when the time comes, they'll follow without hesitation . . .'

'The time, sir . . . ?' Fraser essayed curiously catching a moment of mellowing by the captain.

'Aye, Mr Fraser . . . the time . . . which may catch a ship at a disadvantage and deliver her to the devil in an instant.'

'Or a Don, sir?'

'You comprehend my meaning . . . very well, see to it at once. Pipe all hands . . . Mr Hill and I will tend the deck.'

Drinkwater remained on deck the whole of that day. They set more sail and began to claw back the lost miles to windward. At apparent noon both he and Hill were gratified by twenty minutes of sunshine during which they obtained a perfect meridian altitude and fixed their latitude.

'Fifty-six degrees, fifty-seven minutes south, Mr Hill?'

'Fifty-five minutes, sir . . .'

'Close enough then . . . let us split the difference and lay that off on the chart . . .'

Both men reboxed their instruments, Hill's old quadrant in its triangular box, Drinkwater's Hadley sextant in a rectangular case fitted out with green baize and a selection of telescopes, shades and adjusting tools which gave it the appearance of a surgeon's knife-box. Drinkwater caught the look of satisfaction in Hill's eyes as he handed over the closed case to Midshipman Belchambers.

'I never claimed Hadley's sextant a better instrument than my old quadrant, Mr Hill . . .'

Hill smiled back. 'No, sir, but they say the best tunes are played on old fiddles.'

They made their way below, pocketing their tablets and pencils to allow them to grasp the ropes of the companionways. They leaned over the chart and Hill manipulated the parallel rules, striking the pencil line from west to east on the parallel of fifty-six degrees, fifty-six minutes southerly latitude.

'Well clear of the Horn and the Diego Ramirez Islands.' Drinkwater indicated a group of islands some sixty miles southwest of Cape Horn. They fell silent, both pondering the unspoken question: their longitude?

Were they yet west of the Horn, able to lay the ship's head to the north of west and pass up into the Pacific? Or were they still east of the meridian of the Cape, or Diego Ramirez? That longitude of sixty-eight thirty-seven west?

'Perhaps we will be able to obtain a lunar observation later,' observed Hill. 'The sky shows signs of clearing.'

'Yes,' agreed Drinkwater, 'we might also obtain our longitude by chronometer, though I know your general prejudice against the contrivance.'

Hill looked sidelong at the gimballed clock-face in its lashed box. Cook had proved its usefulness thirty years ago, but Hill preferred the complex computations of a lunar observation to the simpler solution of the hour-angle problem which, he thought, smacked too much of necromancy. Drinkwater smiled wryly and changed the subject as he rolled up the chart.

'I hope to water at Juan Fernandez by mid-January, Mr Hill.'

'Aye, aye, sir . . . we'll have enough casks by then.' Hill referred to the stumming then in progress in the orlop deck where sulphurous smoke emanated from the primitive cleaning process. 'And the labour'll do the men no harm.'

'Quite so.' Drinkwater put the chart and rules away, preparing to return to the deck but Hill stopped him, taking advantage of the intimacy permitted a sailing master and the long familiarity the two men had known.

'Sir . . . that ship, the one we sighted this morning . . . it has been worrying me that you thought my opinion in error . . .'

'I have the advantage of you, Mr Hill.' Drinkwater smiled again, so that Hill was reminded of the eager young acting lieutenant he had long ago known on the cutter *Kestrel*.

'I'm sorry, sir, I didn't intend to pry . . .'

'Oh, the contents of my orders are such that their secrecy applies principally to their comprehension. The truth is that I don't believe that ship was a Don.' He looked up at the old master. Hill was massaging his arm, a wound acquired at Camperdown; his expression was rueful.

'The truth is, I think she was Russian.'

Captain Drinkwater stood at the weather hance regarding the long deck of the *Patrician*. Wrapped in his boat-cloak he ignored the frequent patterings of spray. There was some abatement in the gale and the wind backed a touch, enabling them to claw more westing against wind and the Cape Horn current that set against them at a couple of knots. Midshipman Belchambers hovered near, ready to dash below for sextant and chronometer should the sun appear again. To windward, patches of blue sky punctuated the low, rolling cumulus and it was hard to comprehend the fact that this was the season of high-summer in the southern hemisphere. There was little in the leaden aspect of the clouds, nor the grey streaked and heaving mass of the ocean to suggest it.

Along the deck and aloft men worked in groups and singly. Lieutenant Quilhampton swung about the mainmast with Midshipman Frey and Comley, the boatswain, was overhauling gear on the fo'c's'le and keeping a lively eye on a party of men in each set of weather shrouds who were rattling down. The grim, motionless presence of Captain Drinkwater intimidated them all, for it had slowly permeated the collective consciousness of the hands that their peevish unwillingness to obey orders had not only been let off lightly, but had endangered the ship. To a degree Drinkwater sensed this contrition, partly because he also shared much of the men's embittered feelings. For, notwithstanding their task and the problems which beset it, the voyage had not been a happy one.

From the moment they had run Stanham to the fore-yardarm, it seemed, providence had ceased to smile on them. Ordered north with a convoy to Leith Roads from the London River, *Patrician* had dragged her anchor in an easterly gale in the Firth of Forth. Drinkwater had been dining aboard another ship at the time, in the company of an old friend and messmate from his days as a midshipman.

Sir Richard White had got into Leith Roads three days earlier after his seventy-four-gun *Titan* had been badly mauled in a gale off the Naze of Norway where Sir Richard had been engaged in a successful operation extirpating nests of Danish privateers hiding in the fiords. He had also enjoyed a considerable profit from the destruction of Danish and Norwegian trade, having a broad pendant hoisted as commodore and two sloops and a cutter under his direction for prosecuting this lucrative little campaign.

Sitting in his comfortably furnished cabin, Drinkwater was reminded that there was another Royal Navy to that which he himself belonged, a service dedicated to the self-advancement of its privileged members. He did not blame Sir Richard for taking advantage of his position, any more than he blamed him for inheriting a baronetcy. It was now that the recollection of his old friend's circumstances rankled, as he wrestled with a disaffected crew, a contrary gale and the remotest ocean in the world. But he had enjoyed the conviviality of the distant evening. Sir Richard's officers were pleasant and made much of Drinkwater. He could imagine White's briefing prior to his arrival; his guest was a friend, a seaman of the old school, a tarpaulin of considerable experience, and so on and so forth, all designed to provoke good-natured but superior attitudes. Drinkwater was too old to worry much, though when he thought about such things, they still angered him. At the time he had enjoyed White's company. They had grumbled over the income tax, and agreed on the excellence of the port. They had deplored the standard of young officers and disagreed over the propriety of the new regulation that made masters and pursers equal in status to the commissioned officers. And then the news had come that *Patrician* was making signals of distress and Drinkwater had had a rough and wet return to his ship in his gig, to find chaos in place of an ordered anchor watch and the ship dragging from sheer neglect of the cable at the turn of the tide. The contrast with the well-ordered state of affairs aboard *Titan* was inescapable.

In a fury he had ordered the ship under weigh, only to recall that he had given Lieutenant Quilhampton shore-leave, and been compelled to fetch a second anchor. Poor Quilhampton. Drinkwater looked up at him in the maintop dictating some memorandum to Frey. They were as close to friendship as a commander and his second lieutenant could be, for Drinkwater's wife and Quilhampton's mother enjoyed an intimacy and Quilhampton had been Drinkwater's earliest protégé. He felt a surge of anger against the Admiralty, the war and the whole bloody predicament of his ship at the thought of poor Quilhampton. The young man was wasting the best years of his life, crossed in love by the implacable exigencies of the naval service. Drinkwater wished it was he, and not Fraser, who was first lieutenant.

'Your steward enquires if you wish for some coffee, Captain?'

'Eh? Oh, thank you, Derrick . . .'

Drinkwater roused himself from his reverie and nodded to his clerk. Derrick's face had lost neither its sadness nor its pallor in the months since his impressment by Mr Mylchrist and the cutter's crew. Taken from the banks of the River Colne as he walked from Colchester to Wivenhoe, Derrick had protested his refusal to take part in belligerent operations with such force and eloquence that the matter had eventually been brought to Drinkwater's attention. So too had the strange offender. Drinkwater remembered the man's first appearance in his cabin on that last forenoon at anchor at the Nore, some five days after they had hanged Stanham.

'Take off your hat!' an outraged Lieutenant Mylchrist had ordered, but the man had merely shaken his head and addressed Drinkwater in a manner that brought further fury to the third lieutenant's suffused face.

'Friend, I cannot serve on thy ship, for I abhor all war . . .'

'Be silent, damn you! And call the captain "sir" when you address him . . .'

'Thank you, Mr Mylchrist, that will do . . . I think I know the temper of this man.' Drinkwater turned to the solemn yet somehow dignified figure. 'You are of the Quaker persuasion, are you not?'

'I am . . .'

'Very well . . . I cannot return you to the shore, you are part of the ship's company . . .'

'But I . . .'

'But I shall respect your convictions. Can you read and write? Good, then you may be entered as my clerk . . . attend to the matter, Mr Mylchrist . . .'

And so Drinkwater had increased his personal staff by a clerk, adding Derrick to Mullender, his steward, and Tregembo, his coxswain, and finding the quiet, resigned Quaker an asset to the day-to-day running of the ship. If he had entertained any doubts as to the man infecting the ship's company with his peculiar brand of dissenting cant, he need not have worried. The hands regarded Derrick with a good-natured contempt, the kind of attitude they reserved for the moon-struck and the shambling, half-idiotic luetic that kept the heads clean.

'Thank you, Derrick. Tell Mullender I shall come below . . .'

'Very well, Captain, and I have the purser's accounts fair-copied and ready for your signature.'

Drinkwater took another look round the deck and, as Derrick stood aside, he went below for a warming mug of coffee.

'Deuced if I understand the man.' Lieutenant Mylchrist tossed off the pot of shrub and stared with distaste at the suet pudding the wardroom steward laid before him. His eyes met those of his mess-mates, staring from faces that were tired from unaccustomed exertion. 'He's a damned slave-driver, though why he had to drive us . . .'

'Stuff your gape with that pudding, Johnnie, there's a good fellow,' said Mount, with a note of asperity in his voice. 'Ah, Fraser, here, sit down . . . Steward! Bring the first lieutenant a bottle!'

'Thank you, Mount.'

'Well, there's one consolation . . .'

'And what might that be?' enquired the chastened Mylchrist.

'We'll all sleep like logs tonight.'

'Except those of us with a watch to keep,' muttered Mylchrist.

'You make sure you keep it, cully, not like that episode in Leith Road where you neglected the basic . . .'

'All right, all right, there's no need to go over that again . . .'

'Maybe not, you see yourself as a victim today, but the plain facts are that you'll be a worse victim if you don't take the captain's point.'

Mount stared round the table. He was, with the exception of Hill, the oldest officer in *Patrician*'s wardroom, something of a Dutch-uncle to the lieutenants.

'Well, what exactly is the captain's point?' asked Mylchrist sourly.

'That this ship is a bloody shambles and has no right to be.'

'She's no different from the other ships I've served aboard . . .'

'Bloody Channel Fleet two days from home and a couple of cruises in the Med. For God's sake, Johnnie, don't show how wet you are. Goddamn it, man, Midshipman Wickham was in the Arctic freezing his balls off before you'd heard a shot in anger . . .'

'Now look here, Mount, don't you dare patronise me . . .'

'Gentlemen, gentlemen, be silent!' Fraser snapped, and an uneasy truce settled on the table. 'Mount's right . . . so is the captain . . . it's no your place to strut so branky, Johnnie . . . the men say she's a donsie ship . . .'

'Poppycock, Fraser . . . the ship's not unlucky, for that I take to be your meaning. The trouble is we're out of sorts, frayed like worn ropes . . .' Mount smiled reassuringly at Fraser, 'and that business off the Orkney upset us all.'

'Captain Drinkwater most of all,' said Quilhampton, speaking for the first time. 'I think he feels the shame of that more keenly than the rest of us.'

Quilhampton rose and reached for his hat and greygoe. 'I must relieve Hill . . .' He left the wardroom and a contemplative silence in which they each relived the shame of the action with the Danish privateer. They had chased her for four hours, sighting her at dawn, hull down to leeward ten miles to the east of the Pentland Skerries. The Dane had run, but once it was clear the heavy frigate could outsail her in the strong westerly wind, she had tacked and stood boldly towards the *Patrician*. Unbeknown to the captain on the quarterdeck above, the two lieutenants on the gun-deck had relaxed, assuming the capture to be a mere formality once the intelligence of the privateer's turn had been passed to them. Despite the shot from a bow-chaser the Dane had not slackened her pace, but run to leeward of the *Patrician*, and the sudden broadside that Lieutenant Mylchrist's battery had been ordered to fire had been ragged and ineffectual, only succeeding in puncturing the privateer's sails.

Once to windward the Danish commander sailed his nimble vessel like a wizard. Though Drinkwater turned in his wake, the

Dane beat upwind with an impressive agility. Whenever the *Patrician* closed the range to cannon shot, the Dane tacked, keeping a press of canvas aloft so that the momentary disadvantage he suffered while he gathered way on the new tack was compensated for by the attention the *Patrician* had to pay to going about.

With two hours to sunset the privateer had slipped into Sanday Sound, taking advantage of the weather tide that sluiced through the rocks, islets and Orcadian islands with which her commander was more familiar than either Drinkwater or Hill. In the end, as darkness closed over the *Patrician* and caution forced her to haul off the land, the Danish privateer had escaped.

It was not Hill, but Drinkwater himself who turned the deck over to Quilhampton.

'Well, James, you have the ship.' Isolated by the howl of the wind, Drinkwater unwound with uncharacteristic informality. He fixed the younger man with a perceptive stare.

'Sir?' said Quilhampton, puzzled.

'You have not spoken of it, James . . . the matter upon which you solicited my advice in Leith Road . . .' Drinkwater prompted, 'the matter of matrimony, damn it.'

'Oh . . . no, sir . . . no. But as you said, 'tis likely to be a damnably long voyage.' Quilhampton's answer was evasive and he avoided the captain's eyes, searching the horizon with an expression of despair.

He wondered if it were an accident caused by the violent motion of the ship as Drinkwater went below, or whether the slight pressure against his shoulder had been a gesture of commiseration.

3 Manhunt

February 1808

The islands of Juan Fernandez bear no resemblance to my impression of Crusoe's refuge . . .

Drinkwater wrote in his journal, then laid down his pen, leaned back in his chair and stared rapturously out of the stern windows. The sashes were lifted and the gentle breeze that wafted into the cabin bore the sweet scent of a lush vegetation dominated by the sandalwood trees. He closed his eyes and drew the air in through his nostrils, a calm contentment filling him. For the first time in weeks his cabin bore a civilised air, being upon an even keel. Drinkwater turned back to his journal, rejected the idea of an attempt to rival Defoe and continued writing.

We sighted the peak of El Yunque on the 3rd instant, a fair landfall but occupied by the Spaniards, and, unwilling to advertise our presence upon the Pacific coasts of America, took departure for Farther-out Island, thirty leagues to the westward where we found anchorage in nine fathoms with a sandy bottom, wood and water in plenty, an abundance of pig and goats. There are seals and sea-elephants and several species of humming-bird. The men have been exercised at their leisure, a circumstance which gives me great heart after our recent difficulties . . .

He laid his pen down again and rose, stretching. They lay at anchor within half a mile of the beach and he could see the launch drawn up on the sand, the two boat-keepers paddling like children in the shallows. The warmth of a sun almost overhead lay over the anchorage like a benediction, filling the ship with a languorous air.

'Lotus-eating . . .' he murmured. Leaning his hands on the sill of the window he looked up at the rugged volcanic summit of the island rising precipitously from foothills that were covered in rich

265

vegetation. Unlike the main island of the archipelago, Más-a-Fuera, Farther-out Island, did not possess the anvilpeak of El Yunque, but it was impressively beautiful to men whose eyes had been starved of the sight of green leaves.

An occasional shot echoed up the ravines, evidence of Mount's hunting party flushing the wild pig from the undergrowth. The thought of dining that evening on roast pork brought the juices to Drinkwater's mouth in anticipation and further enhanced his feeling of contentment. They could take a short break here, give the men a run ashore, replenish their wood and water, dine all hands in the very lap of luxury and even, perhaps, if they could find someone among the crew conversant with the process, make some goat's milk cheese.

He returned to his table, picked up a pen and began to write again. The breeze ruffled his shirt and through the skylight the sunshine beat down, warming the old ache in his mangled shoulder.

The mood of the people is much improved since our arrival. Their faces wear smiles this day and I am sanguine that the outbreaks of sporadic drunkenness, of petty-theft and brawling that accompanied our passage of the Atlantic, will cease now that we are brought into better climes and the men become resigned to their task . . .

He looked up and saw the launch coming off, its waist full of filled barricoes of sweet water. Through the skylight he heard orders being given to the watch on deck in preparation for hoisting the casks into the hold. If they worked well today and tomorrow he would give each watch a day's leave of absence and they could scramble about the island like children on holiday.

By noon they had reached the tree-line. Quilhampton in the lead gave a great whoop, like a Red Indian, for it was to be the halting point of the expedition. Drinkwater was panting with the unaccustomed exertion, watching Frey and Belchambers scamper about the increasing number of rocky outcrops that made their appearance as the valley had narrowed and risen.

As behoved the intelligence of naval officers it had been considered necessary to make some purpose of the day. Not for them the wild and aimless wandering of the men, whose liberty infected them like quarts of unwatered rum. Far below they could hear the shouts and laughter of their unconfined spirits as they chased about the ferny undergrowth. Besides, if the men were to give vent to their pent-up emotions, it was incumbent upon the officers to make way for them. So it had been Quilhampton who had decided the walk ashore should become an expedition, and Drinkwater who had suggested they traced one of the streams upwards to its source.

Accompanied by the second lieutenant, the two midshipmen, Mr Lallo the surgeon and Derrick the Quaker clerk, they had set off after breaking their fasts and parading divisions. Those left aboard had worn glum expressions, despite promises of their turn tomorrow, such was the liberating infection of the island upon those destined to run amok today.

The officers began their expedition at the watering place where the stream ran sluggishly out over a bed of pebbles and sand, spreading itself into a tiny delta and carving miniature cliffs and escarpments through the foreshore. But it soon narrowed, its bed deeper and its current swifter, passing beneath a cover of sandalwood trees which already showed evidence of the axe marks of man.

'The oleaginous qualities of this species,' pronounced Lallo, patting one of the dark red tree-boles with a proprietorial hand, 'produce an oil which may, I believe, be substituted for copaiba oil as well as forming an admixture for Indian attars . . .'

'What the deuce is an attar, Lallo?' enquired Quilhampton.

'Perfume, perfume, that fragrance so often necessary to the fair sex in warm weather to render them desirable to men. I should have thought you would have known that, Mr Q, given your strong desire to become a benedick.'

Quilhampton flushed scarlet and Lallo cast a mischievous glance at Drinkwater. 'Is that not so, sir?'

'I fear you embarrass Mr Q, Mr Lallo, but perhaps you would tell me to what use *you* would put such an oil.'

'Well, as for copaiba, it is a specific in certain complaints of the urinary tract . . . it occurs to me that the sandalwood tree might provide us with oleaginous matter with similar properties.'

'Very well. We can gather some chips on our return, but our

young friends here are anxious to continue, I suspect. They are too young for complaints of the urinary tract.'

'Very well, sir. *Adelante!*'

Laughing, they pressed on, ever upwards. The trees thinned to scrub, the ferns that grew prolifically alongside the stream now sprouted from rocks and mosses and the water, no longer dark under the trees, sparkled and ran white, leaping and boiling over rocks and into deep, mysterious pools.

After an hour they came to a waterfall, where the stream dropped almost thirty feet over a sheer lip of grey rock. The silver trail roared downwards, sending up a cloud of spray through which a rainbow curved. On either side dense foliage grew, pierced by the heavy heads of several exotic blooms.

'Sir! Look!'

Drinkwater turned to where Mr Midshipman Belchambers, a bright-eyed and excited child, pointed. Frey was beside him, his pencil already racing over the sketch-block he was rarely without.

'God's bones, a humming bird!' Drinkwater recognised the tiny bird from a print he had once seen in Ackermann's, the extravagant result of the print-maker capitalising on the public interest in such exotic subjects roused by Captain Cook. The blurred whirring of the bird's wings as it held its head motionless at the bell of a flower, was a jewel of pure cinnamon.

For several minutes they stared in wonder at the creature, until the lust for achievement drew them further upwards. When they cleared the undergrowth and the scrub, they emerged onto a steep, rocky scree. Here the grass was sparse, hanging in tussocks, rooted in shallow hollows where rain and humus had collected to produce a soil from the volcanic core of the island. They flung themselves down, sprawling in the sunshine, and broke open the sparse stock of provisions they had brought from the ship.

The view was stupendous. Below them the vegetation spread, giving way to the water of the anchorage, blue-green from the sand and coral reflecting light upwards through it. Upon the limpid water, the frigate sat like a toy, her dark brown sides with the cream strake pierced by the open gun-ports through which fresh air dried out the mildew, damp and rot of the Horn. Her spread sails hung drying in loose festoons. At the stern the white ensign lifted languidly, reflecting the luxurious lethargy of the ship. Beyond the anchorage the ocean spread to the horizon, utterly empty, the pale blue of the sky dotted with an occasional cloud, except to the north-west where a greater massing of cumulus marked the distant peak of El Yunque, dominating Más-a-Tierra (the Nearer Island), mainland of the group.

'D'you intend an attack on the Spanish settlement, sir?' asked Quilhampton, nodding at the distant indication of the island and munching on a slab of purser's cheese that was almost inedible.

'No . . . Ah, Derrick, come sit here with us, man, unless you wish to eschew the company of the ungodly . . .'

They watched the quiet Quaker, awkward in the presence of the officers, squat stiffly with them.

'I knew one of your persuasion, Derrick, when I was in the Arctic. D'you recall Captain Sawyers, Mr Q?'

'The master of the *Faithful*, sir?'

'Yes. A fine seaman and one of nature's gentlemen.'

'I am glad to hear you say so, Captain,' the Quaker replied solemnly.

'Is it to be Panama then, sir?' persisted Quilhampton.

'Ah. The wardroom have sent you to find out my intentions, eh, Mr Q? And I was giving you the credit for wishing to discover the source of this river.'

'Well, sir, I have to admit that curiosity is getting a trifle out of hand . . .' Quilhampton's voice rose at the end of the sentence, so that he left it hanging, like a question. Drinkwater looked round the circle of faces. They were all looking at him expectantly. The mood of the day was too good to spoil.

'Very well, you shall take tablets down from the mountain, gentlemen, beggin' your pardon, Derrick, but you see what curious fellows I am set about with.'

'''Tis a sermon on the Mount that we're getting,' muttered Lallo in a stage-whispered aside that gauged Drinkwater's mood to a nicety.

'Your lese-majestie will be overlooked, Mr Lallo,' he grinned. 'Very well, gentlemen, I will confide in you and parade the hands at sunset, so that your period of privilege is brief.'

'It's a galleon, sir . . . the Acapulco galleon . . . like Lord Anson!'

Lallo's lese-majestie was infectious. Midshipman Belchambers was bolt-upright with excitement. The party laughed indulgently.

'As a matter of fact it ain't, Mr Belchambers. Matter of fact it ain't Panama either . . . at least not directly. Initially we shall strike . . .'

'What the devil's that?' Lieutenant Quilhampton was the first on his feet. They stared down at the ship where the wind carried the disintegrating puff of white smoke gently to leeward. They stood stock-still for an instant and then the second gun came, reverberating up the ravine like the first and prompting them to sudden action. Instinctively, Drinkwater cast a glance round the horizon. The sea was as empty as before; the signal of recall was concerned with some internal matter. They gathered up their odds and ends and began to make their way down the mountain.

'Fine bloody banyan day this turned out to be!' Lieutenant Mylchrist muttered between clenched teeth as Lallo bent over his shoulder. The light from the lamp, held aloft by the elderly loblolly 'boy' Skeete, caught the edge of the catling and Skeete grinned, revealing carious teeth and malodorous breath.

'Now, Mr Mylchrist, d'you care for my rum, or the wardroom's brandy?'

'Get on with it, you damned windbag,' panted Mylchrist, waves of pain spreading from his shoulder where the bruised and rough-edged wound showed the entry point of the musket ball.

'You know, it doesn't do to insult one's physician in such a dependent state, Mr Mylchrist, does it, Skeete?'

''Deed not . . .'

'Damn the pair of you . . .'

'Hold your tongue, Johnnie, and let the surgeon get on with his work.' Mount patted the young officer's shoulder and he lay face down, for the ball had entered his shoulder from the rear.

'You're not the first gentleman to be the victim of a hunting accident,' remarked Lallo, 'now hold still.'

Mount bent, to assist in holding Mylchrist down. Anxiety and responsibility played on his face. 'Trouble is, Bones, I don't think it *was* an accident.'

Mylchrist grunted and Skeete drew the leather pad into his

mouth as the catling began to probe the wound. 'You don't?' asked Lallo without pausing in his task.

'No . . . one of my marines reported his musket missing when we halted and not half an hour later Mylchrist here was shot. As far as I know there was no one near him that belonged to the hunting party.'

'Does the captain know all this?'

'No, not yet.'

'Then I suggest you tell him.'

'Your men to spread out, Mr Mount. They know the two men missing, Hogan and Witherspoon.'

'Sir.'

'Very well. Let's get on with it.'

Drinkwater checked the priming in the pans of his two pistols, loosened his sword and nodded to Quilhampton. The second lieutenant waved the cordon of picked seamen forward. At intervals along their front petty officers and midshipmen were posted to avoid the searchers colluding with the deserters. Thanks to Hogan and Witherspoon this was likely to be the only walk ashore the remainder of the crew were going to have. Captain Drinkwater was in a dark and vengeful mood.

They moved forward, trampling the undergrowth and flushing out birds and small scampering things as they moved inland. Drinkwater looked back to where a party of the gunner's mates carried some sulphur bombs, enlargements of the alchemical concoctions Old Blue Lights made up for stumming the casks; Drinkwater was fairly certain of where his quarry had gone to earth, for he had seen movement on the open scree, spied from his cabin through his glass. He was confident it had been one of the deserters watching the ship for signs of retributive landing parties leaving her. To the right of the spot, overhanging crags opened fissures in the vertical faces of sections of the mountainside and some of these looked large enough to be caves.

It was Drinkwater's party that reached this area and he called up the gunners.

'Let's have a portfire to those sulphur bombs, lively now.'

There was a sputtering of fuse and then an ochreous discharge of acrid smoke.

'Hoy it then, laddie,' coughed one of the gunner's mates, and a pungent missile was hurled into the first cave that seemed to offer sanctuary. Drinkwater moved to the next and bawled his ultimatum into the impenetrable darkness.

'Give yourselves up at once . . . come now, Hogan and Witherspoon, you'll be left otherwise.'

No sound came out of the cave, beyond a disturbed flapping and the emergence of a pair of fluttering bats. Drinkwater nodded to the gunners and a second sulphur bomb was pitched.

'Sir . . .'

They turned and saw Lieutenant Quilhampton pointing. 'There's yellow smoke coming from the hillside above . . . must be a rock fall inside.'

The party began scrambling up beside the cave. On the bleak hillside a hole in its roof had formed a natural chimney, funnelling the sulphur fumes clear. It was an unwitting distraction, for no fugitives ran from the smoke-filled cave.

'Hey! Look!'

Again they turned, this time to the right, looking back downwards to where, some twenty yards away, two men were scrambling down into the cover of the scrub and trees. Drinkwater had guessed correctly. The fugitives had holed up in a cave, but one further along the ledge.

'After them!'

There was a general chase of excited men slithering, scrambling and cursing as they went in pursuit. Drinkwater fired his pistol as a signal to Mount and then forsook his dignity and joined the man-hunt. After ten minutes he recognised the steep valley of the stream they had followed that morning; he could hear the roar of the waterfall somewhere not far below but, apart from broken branches, the fugitives had vanished.

The roar of the waterfall seemed to act as a magnet to the men. They were already thirsty after their climb and there were now sprained ankles and torn skin to add to their moaning. Drinkwater was well aware their hearts were not in the chase, but he could not afford to let Hogan and Witherspoon escape.

'Halt there! Stand easy . . . you may drink. Mr Frey?'

'Yes, sir?'

'Take Belchambers . . . get word to Mr Mount to leave Sergeant Blixoe and his marines at the watering place. He himself is to come up here.'

'Aye, aye, sir.'

Drinkwater watched the two midshipmen scramble down the steep ravine, slashing at the ferns with their dirks. He entertained a moment's apprehension for their safety, they could be hit like Mylchrist . . . then he dismissed the thought. He was almost certain the missing men were now behind him. He looked across the pool. The men were bent over, scooping the water up into their faces. There was about them an air of levity, borne out by suppressed laughter and sly glances cast in his direction. He watched two in particular . . .

Drinkwater turned to Quilhampton.

'Mr Q, I want you to spread the men out and continue down to the beach. Comb this valley and remuster by the boats. We've wasted enough time as it is and it will be sunset in an hour.'

'Aye, aye, sir.' Quilhampton turned and began to shepherd the men down the mountain. 'Come on then, lads . . .'

Drinkwater bent himself to drink from the stream. The two men were watching him, a covert look in their eyes. He stared at them pointedly and, with an obvious and eloquent reluctance, they moved away after the others. With a beating heart Drinkwater remained behind.

Mount found him sitting on a rock, checking the locks of his pistols.

'Sir?' The marine lieutenant was gasping with the effort of his climb.

'Sit down, Mr Mount, take a drink slowly and listen to what I have to say . . .'

Mount sat and drank and listened, looking sharply at Drinkwater as the Captain explained his suspicions, his voice lost in the roar of the waterfall. 'You understand, Mr Mount?'

'Perfectly, sir . . . if you'll give me a moment . . .'

Mount checked his own flintlock, a heavy horse-pistol.

'Why Mylchrist, Mr Mount? D'you know?'

'He's the youngest and most vulnerable officer, sir.' Mount's voice lacked its usual conviction.

'Does he ride the men . . . when I am not there, I mean?'

'I have not noticed so, sir.'

'No . . . and why Hogan and Witherspoon?'

Drinkwater recalled Hogan, a handsome Irish giant whom he remembered now, hearing utter mutinous remarks the night they sprang the foretopmast off Cape Horn; and Witherspoon, by contrast a dark young man, agile as a monkey and one of the *Patrician*'s prime topmen, noted for his daring aloft. Another suspicion came to Drinkwater as he waited for Mount's signal of readiness. It was darker than the first and he cursed himself for not thinking of it sooner, aware that it had been hovering just beyond his consciousness for some time.

'Ready.'

Stooping and moving from rock to rock Mount crossed the stream. On the further bank he looked back at Drinkwater and nodded. Lifting their pistols both men advanced cautiously on opposite sides of the pool. Between them the silver cascade of water fell from above, sluicing over the polished rock lip of the escarpment to fall into the hollow with a roar, the smoking spray of its motion cut by the advancing shadow of the high western bank which terminated the glittering rainbow like a knife.

Ten yards from the foot of the fall, where the rocks were broken, cemented by moss and tiny fern-fronds, and the cliff rose sheer above, both men stopped.

'I command you to come out!' Drinkwater roared above the noise of the fall. The spray was already soaking the two officers whose hands covered the pans of their cocked pistols. Drinkwater's demand produced no response.

'In the King's name . . .'

'Bollocks to your focking King!'

Mount and Drinkwater exchanged glances.

'Come out, Hogan, damn you, otherwise you're a dead man!' Drinkwater's eyes studied the overhang. He could just see the opening in the rock which gave access to the hollow space behind the fall.

'And have ye hang me, Cap'n Drinkwater? I'll not die for your mad raddled King, nor for your damned causes. God damn you, Cap'n Drinkwater, God damn you to hell!'

'Hold your tongue, you Fenian bastard!' Mount roared from the far side of the fall, moving precipitously forward so that Drinkwater was forced to wave him back.

'What about you, Witherspoon? D'you wish to hang? Come, lad, show some sense!'

''E stays with me, so help me!'

'D'you wish Hogan to answer for you, Witherspoon?'

'Aye, sir . . . I do . . .' Witherspoon's voice cracked into a squeak. There was nothing more to be done. Drinkwater nodded and began to edge forward, wondering how much Hogan could see and knowing that, at least, looking from the darkness into the light, the Irishman had the undisputed advantage. He also had a loaded musket.

The base of the waterfall streamed over a rock lip, a great slab of cooled lava that had slipped sideways to form an architrave in the heap of rocks which formed the lower slope of the escarpment. At either end it seemed supported, and softer deposits had been washed out by the water so that, beneath and behind it, a great void opened up, floored by more rock underfoot. Alongside lay the deep pool into which the fall tumbled ceaselessly, its roaring noise buffeting the senses to make thinking difficult. Light entered the cave through the wide silver curtain of the waterfall. Cautiously, Drinkwater moved forward.

As he saw the cave opening up he realised access was obtainable only from his side. Mount could do nothing beyond cover Drinkwater as long as the captain remained outside the fall. But it was too late for such considerations. The deserters knew of their presence; Drinkwater hoped they also thought the area was surrounded by Mount's marines, but, if that were the case, Drinkwater himself was unlikely to be the person sent in to winkle them out.

His eyes were accustoming themselves to the shifting light. The westering sun helped; the rapid tropic sunset was upon them.

Deep within the cave he saw a movement. Instinctively he brought the pistol up and pulled the trigger. The gun kicked in his hand and he saw a scuffle of reaction deep within. Quickly he moved forward, drawing the second pistol from his waistband and finding firmer footing within the cave.

Suddenly he was confronted by Hogan; the man held a levelled musket, its bayonet glittering wickedly in the strange, unreal light.

Drinkwater fired the second gun, but despite having its frizzen on, moisture had seeped from his shirt and been drawn into the powder by its hygroscopic qualities. The hammer clicked impotently and Hogan lunged.

His own gun-lock must have been rendered equally useless for he was relying on cold steel. Drinkwater stepped backwards and reached for his sword. The footing was slippery with slime; both men recovered. Hogan was an immensely strong and powerful man and he had Witherspoon somewhere in the darkness to aid him. Outside Mount was shouting something but Drinkwater paid him no attention, his eyes were fixed on the Irish giant. Somewhere behind Hogan, Witherspoon was suspiciously silent. Drinkwater flicked his eyes into the darkness but could see nothing. Hogan shifted his feet and Drinkwater's attention returned to the Irishman.

'Don't be a fool, Hogan . . . you can't get away with this . . .'

'You're alone, Cap'n . . . that's enough for me. Sure, Oi'll fix me own way to die.'

'What about Witherspoon?' Hogan grinned. It was clear he knew of Drinkwater's fear of the other man.

'Or Oi'll fix yours for you, Cap'n!' Hogan lunged again. His reach was long and Drinkwater fell back, slipped and swiped wildly with his sword. He felt the blade crash against the bayonet and the strength of his opponent as Hogan met the pressure. Drinkwater's mangled right arm was unequal to the contest. He saw victory light Hogan's eyes and felt the resistance of rock against his back.

'Now, you English bastard!'

Hogan drew back the bayonet to lunge, his teeth bared in a snarl that bore all the hatred inherent in his heart. Desperately Drinkwater flung himself sideways, falling at his adversary's feet, the wet slime of the rocky ledge fouling him. He rolled madly, aware that he was somehow in contact with Hogan's feet. He kicked, and suddenly found the edge of the cave. A second later he felt the icy cold of water close over his head. The sudden shock electrified him. An instant later a great, irresistible pressure bore down upon him, punching and bruising him so that for a moment he thought he was being beaten by Hogan until the roaring in his ears proclaimed the source of the pain was the waterfall itself. Then he was subject to an immense rolling motion and vast pressure. Darkness engulfed him as the force of the water thrust him down, rolling him over yet again, but this time in an involuntary way, shoving his aching body so that his lungs began to scream at his brain to let them have air.

He was drowning!

Such were the powerful reflexes tearing at the muscles of his chest that opposition to them was impossible. Blinding lights filled his head, the roaring of the water became intolerable. He could resist no longer. He opened his mouth and dragged water into his lungs.

Mount saw a figure suddenly rise, bursting from the surface of the dark pool some five yards below the fall itself. He levelled his gun, but his finger froze. So far out of the water was the man flung, welled up as strongly as he had just been thrust down, that Mount saw instantly that it was the captain.

A few minutes later Mount had dragged his gasping commander to the side of the pool. Drinkwater lay over a rock, his body racked by helpless eructations as he spewed the water from himself. After a few minutes, as Mount alternately stared from Drinkwater to the ledge beside the waterfall on the far side of the pool, Drinkwater's body ceased its painful heaving. He looked up, pale and shivering, a mucous trickle running down his chin. His shirt was torn and Mount saw the scars and twisted muscles that knotted his wounded shoulder. Instinctively he saw the captain incline his head to the right, indicating the shock of the chill in those mangled muscles.

'Hogan's got your musket . . . his powder's spoiled . . .'

'What about Witherspoon?'

'Didn't see him . . . think I may have winged him with my first shot . . .'

'I'll get support, it's getting dark . . .'

'No! We must . . .'

But he got no further. A loud bellow, a bull-roar of defiance, it seemed, came from the waterfall. Both men looked round and Mount scrambled to his feet.

From behind the silver cascade, glowing now with a luminosity that it seemed to carry down from higher up the mountain where the last of the setting sunlight still caught the stream, Hogan emerged. He bore the musket in one hand and in the other the limp figure of Witherspoon.

It seemed to the still gasping Drinkwater that the darkest of his suspicions had been correct. The bull-roar had not been of defiance, but something infinitely more elemental. It had been a howl of grief, animal in its intensity. The drooping body of Witherspoon was undoubtedly that of a dead lover.

Such was instantly obvious to Mount too. Without hesitation the marine officer raised his big pistol.

'Sodomite!' he snarled, and took aim.

In the almost complete gloom the two officers were quite hidden from Hogan. The Irish giant had no thoughts now, beyond the overwhelming sense of loss. The desperate venture on which he and his lover had set out that morning had seemed worth the hazard. *Patrician* would not stay. Hogan read his commander for a man of resolution, and nothing waited for Hogan over the Pacific horizon beyond the chance of death by wounding, death by disease or death from one or another of the multiple foulnesses that haunted His Britannic Majesty's fleet. The island, though, offered a bold man everything. He could have outwitted fate and lived, like Crusoe, upon such a spot until he met death in God's time, not King George's. It would have worked but for Lieutenant Mylchrist.

His frame was racked by monstrous sobs as he dragged the dead body of his lover out of the cave. It only seemed another paroxysm of grief when Mount's ball shattered his skull, and smashed his brains against the cliff behind him.

Shaking from cold and shock Drinkwater followed Mount gingerly back across the stream. Once again he approached the entrance to the cave. In the last of the daylight the two officers stood staring down at their victims.

'God's bones,' muttered Drinkwater, crouching down before his legs gave under him. His first shot had indeed hit Witherspoon, hit the breast and heart. Witherspoon must have died instantly, so silently that even Hogan himself had not realised until after Drinkwater's escape the damage that single shot had done. For

Witherspoon's breast was exposed as Hogan had desperately sought to stem the bleeding wound. The shirt was torn back and the two officers stared down at the shapely breasts of a young woman.

4 The Chase

March 1808

'I'm damned if I understand why we're not cruising off the Isthmus,' complained Mount as he lounged back in his chair and awaited the roast pig whose tantalising aroma had been permeating the ship for much of the forenoon. 'It is common knowledge, even to Their Lordships, that Panama is the focus of Spanish power.'

'I think you jump to conclusions, Mount,' replied Fraser, cooling himself with an improvised fan fashioned from a sheet of discarded cartridge paper. The wardroom was insufferably hot, even with a windsail ducting air from the deck, and its occupants were as frayed as the end of the canvas pipe itself. 'Besides, preoccupations with opportunities for prize-money are an obstruction to duty.'

'Don't preach to me, Fraser . . .'

'Gentlemen, gentlemen . . . such querulous behaviour . . . it's too exhausting by far . . . be so kind as to leave the preaching to me.'

'God save us from that fate,' said Mount accepting the glass from King, the negro messman, and rolling his eyes in a deprecating fashion at Fraser. Both officers looked at the temporiser in their midst.

The Reverend Jonathan Henderson, chaplain to His Britannic Majesty's frigate *Patrician*, laid a thin, knotted finger alongside his nose in a characteristic gesture much loved by the midshipmen for its imitable property. It invariably presaged an aphorism which its originator considered of importance in his ministry. 'I am sure they know what they are about and it will avail us nothing if we quarrel.'

'What else are we to do, God damn it?' said Mount sharply.

'Come, Mr Mount, no blasphemy if you please.'

'I'm a military man, Mr Henderson, and accustomed to speak my mind within the mess, and I've been too long at sea to have much faith in the wisdom of Their Lordships.'

'If you're referring to my relatively short career . . .'

'*Short?* Good God, man, you've not been at sea for a dog's watch! What the devil d'you know about it.'

'Come, sir, I was chaplain to the late Admiral Roddam . . .'

'Admiral Roddam? He spent the American War swinging round his own bloody chicken bones and port bottles until they had to move the Nore light to mark the shoal . . . Admiral Roddam . . . hey, King, refill my glass and deafen my ears to sacerdotal nonsense'

Henderson looked furiously at the grinning negro and rounded on Mount.

'Mr Mount, I'm a man of God, but I'll not . . .'

'Gentlemen, pray silence . . . you raise your voices too loudly.' Fraser straightened up from the rudder stock cover from which vantage point he had been trying to ignore the petty squabble.

'There has been a deal too much argument since that business at Juan Fernandez . . .'

'There is usually a deal too much argument when empty vessels are banging about.'

'Very well, Mr Lallo,' snapped Fraser at the surgeon who, until that moment, had occupied a corner of the table with his sick-book, 'belay that.' Lallo shrugged and pocketed his pencil. 'Tell us how Mylchrist is.'

'He'll live, but his shoulder'll be damned stiff for a good while.'

'Like the captain's.'

'Aye, like the captain's.'

'But he's over the worst of the fever?'

Lallo nodded and a silence fell as they considered the events on the island. In the days that had followed their departure from Juan Fernandez the echoes of the affair had petered out except when conversation aimlessly disturbed it. Among the people it had lit another portfire of discontent, for two-thirds of the ship's company had not enjoyed the liberty of that first watch-ashore. Nevertheless, the nature of the incident had had less lasting impact on the men than upon the officers. The hands had preoccupations other than sentimental considerations over a pair of love-lorn deserters. In the collective wisdom of the crew there was an easier acceptance of the vagaries of human nature. Their lives were publicly lived, crude in their exposure, and therefore the revelation of Witherspoon's sex came as less of a shock than the vague realisation that they had, perhaps, been made fools of.

Among the officers the reaction had been different. It was to them truly shocking that a woman, even a woman of the lowest social order which it was manifestly obvious that Witherspoon was not, should be driven to the extremity of resorting to concealment on a man-o'-war. Many and various were the theories advanced to explain her action. None was provable and therefore none was satisfactory. To some extent it was this inexplicable nature of the affair that made it most irritating. Unlike the people, the living conditions of the officers were such that they could function as individuals. The solitude of their tiny cabins enabled them to think in privacy and in privacy thoughts invaded unbidden. Of them all James Quilhampton had been most deeply stirred.

It had been Quilhampton who had climbed back up the dark valley and found Mount and Drinkwater, and the dead bodies. It had been Quilhampton who had organised the burial party and stood beside the chaplain as he performed his first real duty since recovering from the sea-sickness induced by the doubling of Cape Horn. The two lovers had been buried that night and the sky above the lantern-lit burial-party had been studded by stars. This involvement had revived thoughts of his own hopeless love affair, left far behind on the shores of the Firth of Forth and long-since repudiated when the news that *Patrician* was bound for the distant Pacific had plunged him into extreme and private depression.

Now he rose from his cot, disturbed by the squabble in the adjacent wardroom, and emerged from his cabin into the silence that had followed it.

'You make as much noise as a Dover-court,' he muttered sleepily, slumping down in his chair and staring at the table-cloth before him, his nose wrinkling to the smell of roast pork.

'You shouldn't be sleeping, James, my boy, when you can be drinking,' said Mount, pushing an empty glass towards him and beckoning King.

'Fill Mr Q's glass, King.'

'Yes sah . . . Missah Q?'

'Oh, very well . . . have you shrub there, King? Good man . . .'

'I was just saying, James, that it's damned odd we aren't attacking the Dons on the Isthmus . . .'

'Oh, for God's sake don't start that again . . .'

'Hold on, Fraser, it's a perfectly logical military consideration, isn't it, James?'

Quilhampton shrugged.

'He's still dreaming of the lovely Catriona MacEwan,' jibed Fraser grinning.

'Well, he's precious little to complain of since he was the last of us to have a woman in his arms,' agreed Mount.

'Except Hogan,' said Quilhampton.

'Ah, you see, he *was* thinking of the fair sex . . . an inadvisable preoccupation in the middle of the Pacific Ocean. What you should be considering is what the devil we're doing so far north . . .'

'If I remember correctly, Mr Q,' broke in Lallo, 'the captain was about to confide in us when the recall guns were fired on the desertion of those two . . .' Lallo hesitated.

'Persons, Mr Lallo?' offered Henderson.

'Exactly, Mr Henderson . . . now tell us . . . that confidence was interrupted, but you are in the captain's pocket enough to get furlough in Edinburgh town . . . What's this about Russians?'

'I've no more influence over the captain than you, Mr Lallo; indeed I've a good deal less, I dare say . . .'

But their deliberations were cut short, for faintly down the cotton shaft of the windsail came a cry: 'Sail . . . sail ho! Two points on the larboard bow!'

They forgot the roast pork and the glasses of shrub and sherry. Even the Reverend Mr Henderson joined the rush for the quarter-deck ladder adding to the clatter of over-turned chairs and the noise of cutlery as the dragged table-cloth sent it to the deck. King stood shaking his head and rolling his eyes in a melancholy affectation. Only Quilhampton remained impervious to the hail of the masthead lookout.

His only reaction was to bring his wooden hand down on the table in a savage blow, bruising the pine board and giving vent to the intensity of his feelings. For underneath his personal misery, below the strange disturbance caused by the desertion on Juan Fernandez, lay the knowledge that most oppressed him and of which he had been dreaming fitfully as he had dozed on his cot. More than any other officer, it was James Quilhampton who best understood the smouldering mood of the men. It had been Quilhampton alone who had defused the incipient mutiny aboard the *Antigone* the previous summer. Very little had happened to placate the men since Drinkwater's bounty, paid out of the captain's own pocket, had eased tension for a while. But the money had been paid to the whores of Sheerness and any good that Drinkwater's largesse had achieved had long since evaporated. Somehow the affair at Juan Fernandez had crystallised a conviction that had come to him as he had held the tawny-haired Catriona in his arms on his departure from Edinburgh, the conviction that *Patrician* was unlucky and that she would never return home.

Captain Drinkwater had been more relieved than otherwise at the discovery of Witherspoon's sex. No captain, particularly one engaged on a distant cruise in the Pacific, relished the discovery of sodomitical relationships within his crew any more than he relished the problem of desertion. The fact that Witherspoon was a woman made Hogan's action understandable and lent a measure of reason to the twin absenteeism that stemmed from passion, not mutiny. What Drinkwater had dreaded when he learned of the failure of two hands to muster was a sudden, unpredictable revolt among the men. His orders were difficult enough to execute without the ferment that such a disorder would cause, a disorder which might threaten not merely his command, but his very life. He was not untouched by the tragedy that had happened beneath the waterfall, but he perceived again the workings of providence and when he had entered the initials *D.D.* against the two names in the ship's muster book, his sense of relief had been very real. In the margin provided for remarks, he had added: *Killed while resisting arrest, having first Run.*

It was a poor epitaph. A poetaster might have conjured up a romantic verse at the tragedy; a venal commander might have kept the two names on the ship's books and drawn the pay himself, or at least until he had repaid himself the cost of the sword he had lost in the pool beneath the waterfall. But Drinkwater felt only a further sadness that Hogan and Witherspoon had gone to join those damned souls who awaited judgement in some private limbo, watched over by the guardian angels of the Admiralty. Such, at least, had been the incongruous core of Mr Henderson's homily on the subject. Drinkwater had begun to doubt the wisdom of Their Lordships in soliciting the aid of the Established Church to subdue the convictions of men forced into His Britannic Majesty's Navy. Drinkwater considered such solecisms foolish; ignorant diversions from the grim realities of the sea-service. He was concluding his private remarks in his journal when he heard the cry from the masthead.

'He has a wind, by God!'

'By your leave, Mr Hill, a rest for my glass on that stanchion.'

'Of course, sir . . . he has a wind . . .'

'So you said . . . a devil's wind, too, what d'you make of him?'

'I reserve my judgement, sir.'

'Eh? Oh, you refer to that fellow we saw off the Horn?' Drinkwater caught the stranger in his image glass. To whatever the sail belonged, it was not a black-hulled two-decker. 'By the spread of her masts and her stuns'ls, I'd wager on her being a frigate . . . and Spanish?'

'Yes . . . yes, I'd not dispute that, sir.'

'Spanish frigate, sir.'

Drinkwater looked aloft. In the mizen top Mr Frey looked down, smiling broadly, and Drinkwater was aware that the deck was crammed with officers and men milling about, awaiting news from the privileged few at posts of vantage or with glasses to their eyes. He caught the ripple of eagerness that greeted the news, saw the smiles and sensed, despite everything, the metamorphosis that transformed his ship at the sight of an enemy.

'Very well, Mr Frey, you may come down and hoist Spanish colours! Clear for action and beat to quarters!' Then he raised his glass again and studied the enemy, hull up now, crossing their bow from the west. 'Mr Frey should know a Don when he sees one, Mr Hill, given his time watching 'em at Cadiz . . . oh, for a breeze!'

'Would to God hers would carry down to us . . . she's seen us, throwing out a private signal.' Hill looked at the masthead pendant and at the dogvanes. They barely lifted in the light airs that slatted *Patrician*'s canvas.

'Shall I hoist out the boats and tow, sir?' asked Fraser, suddenly impatiently efficient.

'No, Mr Fraser, that'll exhaust the men . . .'

The marine drummer was beating the tattoo and the hands were scrambling about the ship. Below, the bulkheads were coming down and aloft the chain slings were being passed, while along the deck sand was being sprinkled and the gun-captains were overhauling their train tackles and their gun-locks. Above their heads fluttered a huge and unfamiliar ensign: the yellow and gold of Spain. Then Drinkwater had a happy inspiration.

'Mr Henderson!' The thin face of the chaplain turned towards him. The fellow was showing a very unclerical interest in the enemy. 'Do you *pray* for a wind, sir.'

Henderson frowned and Drinkwater saw the men pause in their duties and look aft, grinning.

'But, sir, is that not blasphemy?'

'Do you do as I say, sir, *pray* for a wind, 'tis no more blasphemous than to pray for aid on any other occasion.'

Henderson looked doubtful and then began to mumble uncertainly: 'Oh most powerful and glorious Lord God, at whose command the winds blow . . .'

'D'you think it will work?' asked Hill, grinning like the midshipmen. Somewhere in the waist a man had begun to whistle and there came sounds of laughter.

'I don't know, but 'tis a powerful specific against dispirited men by the sound of it . . .'

'How goes the chase, Mr Fraser?'

'To windward, sir, like a wingèd bird.'

'I had no notion you had anything of the poet in you.'

''Tis not difficult on such a night, sir.'

'No.'

'It has a Homeric quality . . . the warm wind, the moon, and a windward chase.'

'Yes.'

They had got their wind, though whether it was attributable to the praying of the chaplain or the whistling that breached the naval regulations was a matter for good-natured conjecture throughout the ship as the men settled down for a night sleeping at the guns. *Patrician* was a big ship, a heavy frigate, a razée, cut down from a sixty-four-gun line-of-battle-ship, but she spread her canvas widely, extended her yards by studding sail booms and hoisted a skysail above her main royal when the occasion demanded.

'Turn!' Midshipman Belchambers turned the glass and the log-party watched the line reel out, dragged by the log-chip astern.

'Stop!' called the boy, the line was nipped, the peg jerked from the chip and the line hauled in.

'Nine knots, sir.'

'Very well . . . like a wingèd bird indeed, Mr Fraser.' Drinkwater smiled in the darkness, sensing the embarrassed flush he had brought to the first lieutenant's cheeks. 'But do we gain on our chase?'

Fraser turned. 'Mr Belchambers . . . my quadrant, if you please.'

'Aye, aye, sir.' The boy ran off.

'How do you find our youngest addition?' Drinkwater asked.

'Eager and agile as a monkey, sir.'

'Hmm. But he's too young. There seems no shortage of such boys with parents eager enough to send 'em to damnation while they are still children. I doubt they can know what their offspring are condemned to endure.'

'Your own son is not destined for the sea-service, sir?'

'Not if I can find him a fat living in a good country parish!' Both men laughed as Belchambers returned with Fraser's quadrant. The first lieutenant hoisted himself up on the rail, bracing himself against the main shrouds, and took the angle subtended by the white shape ahead of them.

Drinkwater watched. The pale pyramid of canvas would be much more difficult to see within the confinement of the telescope and it would take Fraser a moment or two to obtain a good reading. Drinkwater waited patiently. *Patrician* lay over to the breeze, close hauled on the larboard tack. Above him the studding sails bellied out, spreading the ship's canvas and bending the booms.

The sky was clear of cloud, studded with stars and the round orb of a full moon which laid a dancing path of silver light upon the water. The breeze was strong enough to curl the sea into small, breaking crests and these, from time to time, were feathered with phosphorescence.

Fraser jumped down from the rail.

'Aye, sir, I can detect a slight enlargement o' the angle subtended by the enemy.'

'Good; but it's going to be a long chase and this moonlight will discourage him from trying to make a sharp turn . . . 'tis a pity he rumbled us so early.'

'I expect he knew well enough what ships to expect hereabouts.'

'Yes, the Dons are apt to regard the Pacific Ocean as their own.'

They fell to an easy and companionable pacing of the deck. It was astonishing the difference the chase made to the atmosphere on board. All grumbling had gone. Men moved with a new-found confidence and bore themselves cheerfully even in the dark hours. There was a liveliness in the responses of the helmsman, a perkiness about those of the watch ordered to perform the many small tasks as the officers strove in succession to get the best out of the ship. Fraser sought to gain something from the captain's obvious desire to chat.

'Sir . . . I was wondering if you would be kind enough to confide in me. As to our orders, sir . . . if . . . er . . .'

'If anything should happen to me in the next few hours you'd like to know how to act . . . I know, I know . . . damn it, Mr Fraser, the truth of the matter is that I ain't sure myself. We've to damage the Dons and their trade, to be sure, but our main purpose here is to prevent what Their Lordships are pleased to call "incursion into the Pacific" by the Russians.'

'The *Russians*, sir?'

'Ah, I see that surprises you. Well, they have settlements in Alaska, though what possible influence that might have upon the course of the war is something of a mystery . . .'

'And we are making for Alaska now, sir?'

'In a manner of speaking. It seemed the best place to begin exhibiting His Majesty's flag.' Drinkwater felt Fraser's bewilderment. Perhaps he should have confided in the younger man

288

earlier in the voyage, but Fraser had had his own problems and the life of a first lieutenant was, Drinkwater knew, not an easy one.

'You are too young to remember the Spanish Armament in ninety-one, eh?'

'I remember it vaguely, sir. Wasn't war with Spain imminent?'

'Yes, the Channel Fleet were commissioned, a lucky thing as it happened, since, as I recall, we were at war with the French Republic within a year. Let me refresh your mind . . . when Cook's seamen brought high-quality furs from the polar seas off Alaska and Kamchatka and sold them in Canton they attracted the notice of the Honourable East India Company's factors. A former naval officer named Mears . . . a lieutenant, I believe he was, together with a merchant master named Tippin took out two ships across the North Pacific on a fur-hunting expedition. Tippin was cast up on Kamchatka, but Mears wintered somewhere in the islands. The following spring, about eighty-eight or eighty-nine, I forget which, he discovered Nootka Sound, a fine fiord on the west coast of what is now known as Vancouver Island, and he opened a fur trade between the Indians indigent upon the coast and the Company's factors at Canton. In ninety the Spanish sent a naval force, seized the four British ships anchored in the sound, but left two belonging to the United States of America. The British ships were plundered and their seamen sent, on Spanish orders, to Canton in the American bottoms. Once the "haughty Don" had disposed of us, he planted his flag and claimed the whole coast across the whole bight to China!'

'Good Lord!'

'At home we armed for war, but eventually the Dons climbed down. The *sanculottes* obliged us by executing King Louis and depriving His Most Catholic Majesty of the support of His Most Christian ally . . . Their Lordships sent George Vancouver out to receive the surrender of the Spanish commander, a Don Quadra, or some such, and Vancouver spent the next year or so surveying . . .'

'And now we go out to prevent some such measures being repeated by the Russkies?'

'That would seem to be about the size of the thing, Mr Fraser.'

There was a brief silence between them, broken only by the low moan of the wind, the hiss of the sea rushing alongside the frigate, the creak of her fabric and some chatter amidships, where the watch congregated, chaffing the dozing gun-crews.

'That ship we saw off the Horn, sir . . . I believe you expressed the opinion she was a Russian.'

'Ah, Hill's been gossiping again, has he?' Drinkwater chuckled good-naturedly. 'Yes, yes, I believe her to have been bound for the Pacific, like ourselves . . . if she was ordered out as soon as hostilities were declared between Petersburg and London, she would be expected to reach the extremity of America at the same time as ourselves.'

'She was a two-decker, sir.'

'Yes. And if there's close co-operation between the Dons and the Russians . . .' Drinkwater let the import of the sentence sink in by implication.

'I begin to see your problem, sir.'

'Well, Mr Fraser,' remarked Drinkwater drily, 'if I'm knocked up when we overhaul that fellow ahead of us, it'll be *your* problem.'

The wind backed a point towards dawn. Midshipman Wickham came below to where Drinkwater lay on his cot, fully dressed.

'. . . It's increasing too, sir, Mr Quilhampton says, going large we've the legs of him, sir. She reeled off twelve at the last cast of the log.'

Drinkwater yawned. 'Twelve, eh? Very well, Mr Wickham. I'll be up directly.'

Quilhampton was worried when Drinkwater reached the quarterdeck a few moments later.

'She's carrying too much canvas, sir . . .'

Drinkwater gauged the strength of the wind and the feel of the ship beneath his boot-soles. Yes, there was a tendency of the ship to lay down, drowning her lee bow and building up a resisting wave there. He looked ahead. They were overhauling the Spanish ship perceptibly; it would be foolish to risk her escaping by carrying away spars aloft when they might delay the action an hour and break their fasts.

'Very well, Mr Q. Rouse all hands and take in the stun's'ls. Pass the word to the cook to fire up the galley range and boil some skillygolee, and the purser to order "up spirits"; we've a brisk forenoon ahead of us!'

Drinkwater watched the ship burst into life. It was damned odd what the appearance of an enemy did to a ship's company.

'Gives 'em a sense of purpose, I presume,' he muttered to himself, breathing in the fresh air of the dawn and watching the red ball of the sun break the eastern horizon ahead of them, dragging its lower limb like some huge jelly-fish, as though reluctant to leave its resting place, and climb up into the lightening sky.

And then he remembered he had left his sword in the pool beneath the waterfall on Más-a-Fuera.

5   The Spanish Prisoners

March 1808

Drinkwater hesitated in the space his cabin usually occupied. The bulkheads were down, the chairs and table had been removed together with his cot, sea-chest, books and the two lockers that turned the after end of *Patrician*'s gun-deck into a private refuge. Even the chequer-painted canvas that served for a carpet had been rolled away. Only the white paint on the ship's side and the deck-head, gleaming in the reflected light that came in from the gaping stern windows from the ship's wake and sent patterns dancing across it, served to remind its new occupants that it was the hallowed quarters of *Patrician*'s captain. For the purpose of the cabin now became apparent; with the removal of the furniture the obtrusive 24-pounder cannon stood revealed and even the lead sink that served Drinkwater's steward in his pantry was filled with water in readiness to sponge those after guns.

'Where's my cox'n?' he asked of the waiting gun-crews who eyed the unexpected intrusion with some wariness.

''Ere, zur . . .' Tregembo shuffled aft, his old face seamed by a ragged scar, his back stiff from former floggings. 'You'm be looking for this . . .' It was a statement, not a question, and Tregembo held out a sword, a new hanger, by the look of it, with the lion's head pommel of a commissioned officer's weapon.

'Who lent it to you?'

'Mr Mylchrist, zur . . .'

'Ah, yes, thank you, Tregembo. And my pistols?'

'Your clerk's taken 'em to the gunner, zur, for new flints. I tried knapping the old uns but they was too far gone . . . 'ere's your sword-belt . . .'

Drinkwater grinned. He could imagine the Quaker's distaste

for his task. He pulled the sword from its scabbard. Beneath the langets he read the maker's name: *Thurkle and Skinner.*

'I must thank Mr Mylchrist . . . have my pistols taken to the quarterdeck as soon as they are ready.'

'Aye, aye, zur.'

Drinkwater passed through the berth deck to the orlop. In the stygian gloom he found Lallo with his loblolly boys laying out the catlings and curettes, the saws and pincers of his grisly trade. A tub waited to collect the refuse of battle, the amputated legs and arms of its victims. Drinkwater suppressed a shudder at the thought of ending up on the rough table Lallo's mates had prepared. For a moment he stood at the foot of the ladder, accustoming himself to the mephitic air and watching the preparations of the surgeon. Lamplight, barely sustained here, in the bowels of the ship, danced in pale yellow intensity upon the bright steel of the instruments and illuminated the white of Lallo's bowls and bandages. The contrast between these inadequate preparations below for rescuing men from death and the bright anticipation of the gun-deck above struck Drinkwater with a sudden sharpness. He threw off the thought and coughed to draw attention to himself.

'Ah, sir . . . ?' Lallo straightened up under the low beams.

'You are ready, Mr Lallo?'

'Ready, aye, ready, sir,' said Lallo, somewhat facetiously and Drinkwater caught the foul gleam of Skeete's caried grin.

'How is Mr Mylchrist today?'

From the far end of the space Mylchrist lifted a pale face from the solitary hammock that swung just beneath the heavy beams.

'Much better, sir, thank you . . . I wish I could assist, sir . . .'

'You stay there, Mr Mylchrist . . . you've had a long fever and Mr Wickham is doing your duty at the guns, you wouldn't deny him his chance of glory, would you now?'

Mylchrist smiled weakly. 'No, sir.'

'I promise you yours before too long.'

'Thank you, sir.'

'And thank you for the loan of your sword.'

'The least I can do . . .'

Drinkwater smiled down at the wounded officer. Mylchrist had been very ill, avoiding gangrene only by providence and the application of a lead-acetate dressing whose efficacy Drinkwater had learned from the surgeon of the *Bucentaure* when held prisoner on Villeneuve's flagship.

'The employment of your sword guarantees you a share in the day's profits, Mr Mylchrist.'

Mylchrist smiled his gratitude at the captain's jest. If they received prize- or head-money for their work in the coming hours, the third lieutenant's share for a fine Spanish frigate would better his annual salary.

Drinkwater returned to the quarterdeck to find Derrick awaiting him. The Quaker held the two pistols as though they were infected and it was obvious he had tried to leave them in the charge of someone else. The others were enjoying his discomfiture. Fraser was positively grinning and the first lieutenant's levity had encouraged the midshipmen and the gun-crews waiting at the 18-pounders on the quarterdeck. Even the sober Hill, busy with his quadrant determining the rate they were overhauling the Spanish ship, seemed amused.

'Thank you, Derrick.' Drinkwater took the two pistols, checked the locks were primed and stuck them in his belt.

'Mr Meggs loaded them for you, Captain.'

Drinkwater looked at the Quaker. In the months they had been together he had conceived a respect for the man. Derrick had refused to call him 'sir', tactfully avoiding the familiar 'Friend' of his faith, compromising with 'Captain'. Drinkwater did not object. The man was diligent and efficient in his duties and only took advantage of his position in so much as he asked to borrow the occasional book from Drinkwater's meagre library. When he had borrowed Brodrick's *History of the War in the Netherlands*, Drinkwater had raised an inquisitive eyebrow.

'Your interest in that subject surprises me, Derrick.'

'A physician studies disease, Captain, in order to defeat it, not because of his liking for it.'

Drinkwater acknowledged his own defeat and smiled wryly.

'Well, sir,' he said in a low voice, 'the moment has come . . . you had better go below to the orlop. The surgeon has no assistant, only his two loblolly boys, perhaps you might be able to help.'

'I would not have my courage doubted, Captain,' Derrick

flicked quick glances at the inhabitants of the quarterdeck, 'but I thought my post was at your side.'

Drinkwater had never had the luxury of a clerk before and had given the matter little thought, though he recollected Derrick's post in action was 'to assist as directed'.

'Very well, Derrick, but it is glory on the quarterdeck. Courage is a quality you will find at Mr Lallo's side.' He turned and raised his voice, 'Very well, Mr Fraser? Mr Mount?'

'All ready, sir, ship's company fed, fires doused, spirits issued and the men at their battle-stations.'

'My men likewise, sir,' added Mount.

'A little over a mile, sir,' said Hill, looking up from his calculations.

Drinkwater cast an embracing glance along the deck and aloft.

'Very well. Pass the word to make ready. We'll try a ranging shot.'

But there was no need. A puff of smoke shredded to leeward of the Spanish frigate's stern and a plume of water rose close under *Patrician*'s larboard bow. The wind-whipped spray pattered aft and wet them.

'*Olé!*' remarked Mount, dashing the stuff from his eyes.

'We shall make a running fight of it, then,' said Drinkwater, raising his glass.

For the next hours they endured shot from the Spaniard's stern chasers, trying to gauge the weight of metal of the balls. Drinkwater held his hand; to return fire meant luffing to bring a bow-chaser to bear on their quarry; to luff meant to lose ground. The morning was already well advanced by the time they could read the enemy's name across her stern: *Santa Monica*.

Drinkwater spent the time pacing up and down, occupying the leeward side of the quarterdeck where he had a direct view of the Spanish ship and felt no discomfort from the down-draught from the maintopsail in such a balmy climate. From time to time he paused, rested his glass against a hammock stanchion and studied the *Santa Monica*. She was a relatively new ship, built of the Honduran mahogany that made Spanish ships immensely strong and the envy of their worn opponents. Her spars, too, gleamed with the richness of new pine and Drinkwater recalled Vancouver's words about the slopes of the coasts around Nootka Sound 'abounding in pines, spruces and firs of immense height and girth, being entirely suitable for the masting of ships'.

Slowly their view of the enemy altered. As they overhauled her, they began to see the whole length of the *Santa Monica*'s larboard side. Studying the Spaniard, Drinkwater could see her gun barrels foreshortening with a greater rapidity than they overtook. His opponent was preparing a disabling broadside as soon as all his larboard guns bore, while Drinkwater was hampered by his starboard broadside being on the leeward side of the ship. Even with full elevation, the list of the deck was such that his cannon might have trouble hitting their target. In addition there would be the problem of water pouring in through the gun-ports as *Patrician* lay down under the fiercer gusts of a strong breeze that was fast working itself up into a gale. Yet Drinkwater could not reduce the list by taking in sail without losing his chance.

If the Spanish commander succeeded in his design of disabling *Patrician* his escape was guaranteed. If he was a man of unusual energy the consequences might be worse, he could conceivably hold off and rake *Patrician*, for all Drinkwater's superiority in weight of metal. The vision of Lallo's instruments of agony and those empty limb-tubs sprung morbidly into his mind's eye. With an effort of will he dismissed the thought. He would have to think of some counter-stroke and act upon it with a nicety of timing, if he was to disarm the Don's intention. For a moment longer he studied the *Santa Monica* as her bearing opened upon their bow with an almost hypnotic slowness. Then he shut his telescope with a snap.

'Mr Hill! Mr Fraser! A moment of your time, if you please . . .'

He was not a moment too soon. So parallel were the courses of the two ships that the angle of bearing for both of them to fire upon the other with any chance of achieving maximum effect was coincident within a degree or two. Drinkwater had noticed an officer bent over an instrument by the Spaniard's larboard dogvane and made his preparations accordingly.

'Run out the guns!'

When he had passed his orders he heard the rumble of

Patrician's 24-pounders as their forward-trained muzzles poked from the heeling frigate's side. His heart was beating, hammering in his chest as, beside him, Fraser sighted along the barrel of one of the quarterdeck eighteens.

'About two degrees to go, sir . . .'

Drinkwater grunted There had been some movement on the *Santa Monica*'s deck at the appearance of *Patrician*'s guns. Would his opponent react?

For a long moment the question seemed to hang, then he saw the officer by the dogvane bend again. Perhaps they too were waiting in suspense.

Leaning over, the two ships rushed along, *Patrician* ranging slowly up to windward of the Spanish ship, gradually overlapping her larboard quarter close enough to confuse the sea running between them. Above their decks the yards were braced hard-up upon the leeward catharpings, the sails strained against the strength of the wind, driving the foaming hulls relentlessly through the water. From the high-cocked peaks of their spanker gaffs the opposing ensigns of their contending nations snapped viciously, while beneath them the lines of men at their guns, the groups crouching below the rails ready to haul on bowlines and braces, the red-coated marines aiming their muskets from the barricades of the hammock nettings, and the knots of officers on the quarterdecks and at their posts throughout the ships, waited for the orders from the two captains that commanded the destinies of five hundred souls.

'Infernal machines . . .' Drinkwater heard someone whisper, half-admiringly, and smiled grimly when he realised it was Derrick, caught up in the stirring excitement of this insanity.

'Bearing coming on, sir,' said Fraser matter-of-factly, still bent over the dispart sight of the 18-pounder.

Drinkwater saw the Spanish officer by the *Santa Monica*'s larboard dogvane straighten up purposively. Without taking his glass from his eye he gave the order: 'Fire!'

Gun-locks snapped like the crackle of grass as a squall strikes, then came the immense roar of artillery, the trembling rise of the deck as the ship reacted to the recoil and the sudden burst of activity throughout *Patrician* that followed his order. On the gun-deck below, the heavy 24-pounders belched flame and shot, trundling inboard and snapping their tackles together as their crews swarmed round them, sponging and reloading the monstrous things. On quarterdeck and fo'c's'le the 18-pounders and the brutal 42-pounder carronades swept the deck with powder smoke and the enemy with a hail of iron and langridge.

'Up helm!'

Behind Drinkwater, Hill was standing by the wheel, shouting through his speaking trumpet while Fraser, released from his duty bent over the dispart sight, was leaping across the deck whence Drinkwater followed him.

'Smartly there, my lads, stamp and go!'

Patrician's bow swung towards the *Santa Monica* as the Spaniard's hull disappeared momentarily behind the smoke of her own broadside. The fog of her discharging guns would, for a moment, blind her officers to much of his manoeuvre.

Above his head the braces were easing the yards and then there was a rending crash from forward. Drinkwater felt a slight tremble through the hull, but *Patrician*'s turn was unimpeded and then, leaning from the larboard hance, he could see the stern of the *Santa Monica*.

There was a rent in her spanker and her ensign was fluttering down, its halliards having parted as *Patrician*'s jib-boom slashed across her deck. Her stern boat was a wreck and hung down from the davits by a single fall.

'Larbowlines . . . !'

Drinkwater's voice was drowned in the thunder of the larboard guns, fired by their captains as they bore, double shotted and topped with canister they blasted into the starboard quarter of the Spaniard as *Patrician* sliced obliquely across the *Santa Monica*'s stern.

As the smoke cleared Drinkwater caught a glimpse of Comley, the boatswain, wielding an axe on the knightheads, where he fought to free *Patrician* of the obstruction of her smashed jib-boom.

'Hard on the wind again, Mr Hill!'

'Aye, aye, sir, full an' bye it is!'

Patrician turned back to larboard again. She had given ground to the enemy and was now in her lee, but her guns still bore and they were being worked like fury by their crews; flame and smoke roared from her larboard ports as the cannon pointed high. A quick glance aloft showed Drinkwater that barely a shot of the enemy's had told, that their most serious damage had been sustained forward, from their own manoeuvre in crossing the *Santa Monica's* stern to rake her. Drinkwater dismissed that, raising his glass to assess the damage his ruse had effected.

The enemy were hoisting their shot-away ensign into the mizen rigging, and holes were appearing in her sails, but hardly a gun replied to *Patrician* from *Santa Monica's* starboard broadside. Then, as he watched he heard a cheer. Shifting his glass from the enemy's starboard quarter where he could see the splintered remains of her gallery, he caught the toppling maintopmast. For almost a minute it stopped falling, leaning at a drunken angle, held by its rigging to the fore and mizen masts, and then it broke free, crashing downwards and bringing the mizen topgallant with it. The *Patricians* were whooping about their guns and the officers on the quarterdeck wore broad grins. Drinkwater could see they were rapidly shooting ahead of the Spaniard.

'Stand by to tack ship!'

But Drinkwater had no need to range up to windward, subjecting the *Santa Monica* to a further raking broadside from ahead. As he watched, he saw the red and gold lowered from the mizen rigging in token of submission.

'She strikes, sir!'

The news was reported from a score of mouths and more wild cheering broke out from the exhilarated crew of the *Patrician*. All the pent-up frustration of the past months, all the ill-feeling and resentment, the hopelessness of pressed men, the self-pity of dispirited lovers and the petty hatreds of men confined together for weeks on end, seemed burst like an abscess by the violent catharsis of action.

His eyes met those of the sailing master. 'I think our sailing was of sufficient superiority on this occasion, Mr Hill,' Drinkwater remarked, repressing his sudden triumphant burst of exuberance.

'For a Spaniard, sir . . .' replied Hill cautiously and Drinkwater felt the reproach in the older man's tone. He nodded.

'Yes. You are right; for a Spaniard . . .'

*

299

They did not board the prize until the following morning, for the wind threw up too rough a sea for them to launch a boat safely. And when they were successful they discovered their triumph to be short-lived.

Their first broadside had been fired from the starboard guns on a lee-roll. The iron shot had hulled the *Santa Monica*, and damaged her so badly that by the following noon it was clear that her pumps were unable to stem the inrush of water. She began to founder under the feet of her prize crew. Lieutenant Quilhampton, sent aboard the Spanish frigate as prize-master, sent this news back to the *Patrician* by Midshipman Frey.

Reluctantly Drinkwater ordered the prize abandoned and by that evening found himself host to two hundred unwilling and darkly threatening prisoners. They consisted of Spaniards, mission-educated Indians and a large proportion of *mestizos*, a lean and hard-bitten lot led by a tall, gaunt officer who wore the epaulettes of a captain in the Royal Navy of Spain.

'I am Captain Nathaniel Drinkwater, *Señor*, and I compliment you on the gallantry of your defence. I regret the loss of your ship.' He bowed formally and took his opponent's offered sword.

He met the Spaniard's eyes and found in them more than resignation at the fortunes of war. The deep-set expression of anger and hatred seemed to burn out from the very soul of the man, and Drinkwater recognised in the lined and swarthy face the man who had bent over the *Santa Monica*'s rail and whose order to fire Drinkwater had pre-empted by a split-second.

'Don Jorge Méliton Rubalcava . . .' The Spanish commander broke off. Drinkwater had no idea whether Rubalcava understood English from this bald announcement.

'Have I your word that you will not raise a revolt, Captain Rubalcava?' Drinkwater asked, turning the sword-hilt and offering it back to its owner. Rubalcava hesitated and swung to an accompanying officer whom Drinkwater assumed to be his second-in-command. But the other seemed only to be awaiting the completion of the formalities of surrender, before declaring himself a greater man than Rubalcava.

'He was throwing papers overboard, sir,' Quilhampton volunteered, 'a fellow of some consequence.'

Drinkwater was watching the two Spaniards. They seemed to be in some disagreement and Rubalcava's anger was suppressed with difficulty. His companion, however, turned to Drinkwater with an unruffled expression, and addressed him in strongly accented and broken English.

'*Capitán*, Don Jorge he give you his parole and express for him the honour of you give his sword. *Gracias*.' The sentence was terminated by a low bow which Drinkwater awkwardly returned.

'You speak excellent English, *Señor*, perhaps you could tell me whom I have the honour of addressing?'

'I . . . Don Alejo Joaquin Arguello de Salas, aide-de-camp to His Excellency, Don José Henrique Martin Arguello de Salas, *Commandante* for San Francisco . . .'

Again there was an exchange of bows.

'Perhaps, gentlemen,' Drinkwater invited, 'you would do me the honour of dining with me and my officers this evening.'

'*Gracias* . . . what is it you think to do, *Capitán*?'

'We can discuss that matter later, gentlemen. And now, if you will excuse me, I have much to attend to in seeing to the comfortable accommodation of your men.'

There was a further mutual acknowledgement and Drinkwater found himself favouring the simple directness of Derrick's mode of address above this extravagant over-worked charade of elaborate bows. He ordered the incredulous Quaker to see the Spanish officers quartered below and turned to Mount to issue orders for the confinement of their seamen.

Mount concealed his grin with difficulty. The bobbing head and sweeping gestures of the quarterdeck had provoked an outburst of merriment along the deck as ill-concealed as the hostility of Captain Rubalcava.

6   Of Wine and Women

March 1808

'Your allies . . . they make for you good wine . . .' Arguello raised his glass and held it so that the candles shone through the rich, dark Portuguese *bual*. Drinkwater had a few dozen bottles of the Madeira, his only really decent wine, bought from the commander of an East Indiaman which had been lying at the Nore. Its broaching was the culmination of a satisfying meal the main course of which had consisted of the last pig from Juan Fernandez. The unfortunate animal had lived on scraps in the manger forward of the ship's breakwater and been slaughtered before they went into action.

'*Gracias*, Don Alejo . . . you have the same name as the *Commandante* . . .' Drinkwater phrased it as a question.

'*Sí*, 'e is my old brother.'

The wine seemed to have relaxed Don Alejo, though Rubalcava's dark features continued to brood on his defeat. Despite its quality it had been a difficult meal and it was obvious that neither Fraser nor Quilhampton had enjoyed it. Out of courtesy they had drunk toasts to their respective sovereigns and to their own mutual gallantry. There had been a stilted enquiry into the *Santa Monica*'s losses that revealed some difference of opinion between the two Spaniards, and Drinkwater was becoming suspicious about the Spanish frigate's task. He was toying with various expedients as to how to pursue his enquiries when Rubalcava spoke with a sudden, low urgency to Arguello. Don Alejo nodded, leaned forward to light a thin cigar from the candles and blew smoke at the deckhead.

'*Capitán* . . . please, I ask you question . . . what you do with *Capitán* Rubalcava and his men, eh? For you too much prisoner a big . . .'

'Risk?'

'*Sí, Capitán*, a big risk.'

'Of course, Don Alejo, I do not make war upon unfortunate and gallant opponents. Assure Don Rubalcava that I am at his service. To deprive a brave officer of his ship is enough injury to inflict upon any man of spirit . . . where does the good captain wish to be landed?'

It took Arguello a few moments to digest this noble speech, moments in which Fraser writhed in his chair and Quilhampton fixed his commander with an odd, penetrating stare, filling the glass in front of him and hurrying the decanter round the table.

Another low exchange took place between the two Spanish officers. It was clear that Rubalcava had a point of view; it was also clear that Arguello disagreed with it. His exchange with *Santa Monica*'s captain again became sharp, though once the naval officer had been suppressed and had relapsed into a tense and bitter silence, Arguello turned to his host with an air of unimpaired and courtly civility.

'*Capitán* Rubalcava thank you for your much kind express of honour and receive it . . . it is for me to ask you to take us to San Francisco . . .'

Rubalcava drew in his breath, in obvious opposition to this proposal, and there was something tense about Arguello now, something eagerly expectant, as though he wished Drinkwater to answer enthusiastically in the affirmative. Drinkwater met his gaze, as though reluctantly considering his request.

'Of course . . . you will have truce . . . I will, myself, see that you have water . . . anything . . .'

The gesture with the cigar was airily obliging; Drinkwater watched the heavy trail of blue smoke languidly lift in the hot air around the candles. Arguello was begging.

San Francisco; that was where Arguello wished to go. Rubalcava had other ideas. Why? And where had *Santa Monica* been bound when *Patrician* intercepted her?

'Where were you from, Don Alejo? The Philippines?'

'*Sí, Capitán*, Manila . . . excellent for tobacco . . .' He held up the cigar and smoke dribbled from his mouth.

'And where were you bound, Don Jorge?' Drinkwater flung the

question directly at the Spanish captain. It was a phrase which any seaman would comprehend, even in a foreign language, and, while Drinkwater spoke with professional interest, yet he sought to exploit the rift he had detected between the two men.

Rubalcava's dark head came up and his eyes flashed at Drinkwater with a ferocity that reminded Drinkwater of an Arab he had known once in the Red Sea. Rubalcava pronounced his destination with a kind of contempt, as though he had thought no more of it before his capture than he did afterwards: 'San Francisco.'

'And the purpose of your voyage, *Señor*?' Drinkwater thrust the question quickly; he was entitled to ask it.

'*Aviso* . . .' Drinkwater recalled the reported destruction of documents.

'A despatch vessel, with Don Alejo as your courier . . . ?'

'*Qué?* Don Alejo . . . ?' Rubalcava's voice tailed off as Arguello broke in.

'*Sí, Capitán,* I was courier . . . it is my duty . . . I am for the *Commandante* of San Francisco, his chief courier.'

A hiss of dissimulation came from the subsiding Rubalcava.

'You speak excellent English, Don Alejo, please accept my compliments,' Drinkwater coaxed.

'I was prisoner some time, taken off Cadiz but I make exchange. I live at Waltham Abbey.'

'How very interesting . . . perhaps you wish to retire now, gentlemen . . . ?'

Drinkwater rose and his silent officers sprang obediently to their feet. 'Mr Quilhampton, please be so good as to see our guests to their quarters before returning for your orders.'

Quilhampton hesitated, perceived Drinkwater's meaning and acknowledged the instruction. As the Spaniards withdrew from the cabin bowing, Drinkwater motioned Fraser to stay. They were about to leave the cabin when Arguello halted and indicated the portrait of Elizabeth, replaced lovingly by Tregembo on the re-established bulkhead.

'Is this beautiful lady your wife, Captain?'

'Yes . . .' Drinkwater watched Arguello address a remark to Rubalcava and he stiffened, sensing an insult, but it was obvious that it referred to the disagreement that existed between the two men, for Rubalcava's expression bore no trace of that complicity of men sharing a coarse jest at another's expense. Nevertheless Drinkwater bridled at the odd reference to Elizabeth.

'Don Alejo!' he called sharply after the departing Spaniard. Arguello turned in the doorway.

'*Capitán?*'

'It is not permitted to smoke beyond my quarters!'

Arguello shrugged, dropped the stub of his cigar and with an elegantly booted toe, ground the thing into the painted canvas on the deck.

Fraser expelled a pent-up breath as the door closed behind the prisoners.

'Another glass, Mr Fraser, you've earned it by your patience, by God. I've passed word to Tregembo to sling you a hammock in here while Arguello occupies your cabin. Mount has the business in hand?'

'Yes, sir. Mount won't let them move. We've the dagoes battened well under hatches.'

'Good. We should be rid of them in . . .' Drinkwater dragged a chart onto the table from the drawer beneath and cast a quick look at it, 'three days, if this wind holds.'

There was a knock at the cabin door. 'Come in!'

Quilhampton rejoined them and Drinkwater pushed the decanter towards him and re-seated himself. 'Well, gentlemen, what did you make of that?'

'There's bad blood between them. Rubalcava doesn't want to go to San Francisco, that's clear enough.'

'Good, Mr Q. I agree . . . but he didn't want to go to San Francisco *before* they fell in with us, which argues a longer animosity than has been caused by our unexpected appearance in the Pacific.'

'Perhaps they just didna get along too well, sir,' said Fraser.

Drinkwater nodded and refilled his glass. 'But from his latitude and course we can suppose their landfall at least was San Francisco, or the coast thereabouts. Now it is one thing to assume that they were not friends, but let us suppose you are a Spanish officer, bearing despatches from the authorities in the Philippine Islands. Where do you suppose you would be taking them?'

'To the principal naval base in the Americas?' said Fraser.

'Yes, I think so. And that is not San Francisco. That is Acapulco . . .'

'For which he had a fair wind.'

'Correct, Mr Q. Now, to continue the hypothesis, suppose a British frigate appears out of the blue. What would you do, Mr Fraser?'

'If I was running?'

'Yes, as he was.'

'Well, I suppose I would see it as paramount to inform my superiors. From what you told me earlier about the "Armament" of ninety-one they seem to resent intruders in the Pacific.'

'Exactly. And to do that you would lay a course for Acapulco, or Panama, but *not* San Francisco.'

A ruminative silence fell on the three officers which Drinkwater broke.

'So, gentlemen, we have Don Alejo Arguello determined, for some reason, to get to San Francisco *at all costs*, rather than inform his principals at Acapulco that a British frigate is loose in the Pacific.'

'But, sir, though I dinna disagree with your argument, *his principal* is at San Francisco, he said he was aide to the *Commandante* there . . .'

'Who is also his "old brother".' They laughed at the Spaniard's awkward phrase. 'Well, perhaps that argues some collusion, who knows?' Drinkwater yawned. 'It's all pure supposition,' he added dismissively. 'I think it's time we turned in. I suggest you both keep loaded pistols handy. I've no mind to lose the ship while I sleep.'

It was an uneasy three days. Every morning and evening the Spaniards were brought on deck in batches, guarded by the marines and allowed to air themselves in the sunshine. The *Santa Monica*'s officers were herded in sullen little groups and quartered in odd spaces. Curiously, the presence of the Spanish prisoners improved the morale of *Patrician*'s people. The sight of others, more unfortunate than themselves, over whom they could enjoy a sense of triumph, seemed a tonic to their spirits. They did not worry over-much about the loss of prize-money asserting, so Drinkwater heard, that since the proportional loss fell most heavily on the officers, it was a greater hardship to them. There might have been a mutinous component in this dog-in-the-manger attitude, but if there was it was accepted as being part of the black humour of Jack, and to be overlooked. Certainly it amused, rather than alarmed Drinkwater who, as he expressed himself to Fraser, 'had been too much knocked about in the sea-service to do more than acknowledge the rough justice of the men's opinion'.

The officers themselves had little time to dwell on their ill-luck, for the presence of two hundred prisoners left them no time for brooding. Fraser and Quilhampton shared Drinkwater's cabin, a circumstance which exasperated them all despite the curtain that Tregembo had hung about the captain's cot-space, for what men most desire aboard ship is real privacy. No one on board was sorry when the masthead lookout raised the cry of land and an hour later the blue trace of tree-clad hills surmounted by a necklace of cloud lay on the eastern horizon.

Drinkwater was pacing the long quarterdeck, reluctant host to Arguello who walked beside him maintaining a difficult conversation.

'*Capitán* Rubalcava and myself, we were much surprise to see your ship, *Capitán* Drinkwater.' Arguello had been at obvious pains to improve his fluency in English during his captivity. 'You come to make war upon His Most Catholic Majesty's dominions?'

'You did not expect a British ship in the North Pacific, Don Alejo?'

Arguello shrugged. The gesture, though non-committal, was eloquently negative.

'I was five hundred miles from any of His Most Catholic Majesty's dominions, Don Alejo.' Drinkwater stopped pacing and turned to the Spaniard, watching for his response. Again there came the shrug. 'If I wished, I might have devastated the trade of Peru, Panama . . .' It was Drinkwater's turn to shrug and wave his arm to the south, as though the whole Pacific seaboard of America lay at his mercy.

'So, *Capitán*, you come to the Pacific, you do not attack our trade ships, you keep from the land so we do not know you have come.

307

I ask myself why, eh? I think you come to make bigger trouble. I see *Capitán* Vancouver come. I am with Quadra when we made to leave Nootka . . . now you come back.'

Arguello's face was a mixture of dislike, frustration and eager inquiry. It seemed a good fiction to encourage. Nothing as positive came with his orders; as usual governmental parsimony prevented the effort of colonising. All he had to do was to prevent others from accomplishing it, yet such a firmly implanted suspicion in Spanish minds might work to his advantage. He smiled, tight-lipped, and read the gratification in Don Alejo's eyes.

'You may find, *Capitán*, more difficult than you think . . .'

'Perhaps,' Drinkwater said dismissively, 'but tell me about *your* voyage, Don Alejo. What was the purpose of your voyage?' He lowered his voice with the air of a conspirator and saw Don Alejo's glance shift to the figure of Rubalcava, leaning disconsolately against the rail, gazing ahead at the approaching shoreline. 'I see that Captain Rubalcava does not wish to come to San Francisco . . .'

He caught the quick, shifting glance of surprise that Alejo shot him glaze with dissimulation. Then Don Alejo raised his hands in an urbane gesture of helplessness. 'As the French say, *Capitán*, *cherchez la femme.*'

'A woman? Ah, I see, between you . . . I see . . .'

The high-flown theories of grand strategy propounded in his cabin a few nights earlier dissolved in the face of earthier causes. Don Alejo looked puzzled and then laughed, an unfeigned amusement that made Drinkwater slightly uncomfortable and Rubalcava look up from the rail.

'No, no, *Capitán,* not between us . . . *Capitán* Rubalcava does not want to come to San Francisco because of the *hija* of Don José, my brother . . .'

'*Hija?*'

'*Sí* . . . er, I do not know how you say in English, er . . . ?'

A flash of intuition crossed Drinkwater's mind. He recalled the jibe Don Alejo had made at Rubalcava indicating the portrait of Elizabeth on his cabin bulkhead. Arguello had been taunting the Spanish captain. Rubalcava was clearly being put in his place.

'Your brother has a daughter.'

'*Sí*, daughter . . . Rubalcava wishes to marry the Doña Ana Maria Conchita . . . it is impossible.'

'Impossible? The lady is already promised?'

'*Sí, Capitán*, and *Capitán* Rubalcava is not high-born . . .'

Drinkwater looked across the deck at the lounging Spanish officer.

'Rubalcava has much hate in his heart, much hate. And you have destroyed his ship, *Capitán* . . . in Acapulco . . .'

Don Alejo ended his explanation there, the words tailing off into that expressive, Hispanic shrug of immense possibilities and Drinkwater understood. In Acapulco were the means of Rubalcava's revenge.

7 San Francisco

March 1808

Under her huge topsails *Patrician* ghosted inwards between the two great headlands that guarded the entrance of San Francisco bay. Half a league apart the high, tree-clad steeps of Bonita and Lobos Points rose sheer from the sea on either side of the frigate as the onshore breeze wafted her eastwards; the blue water chuckled beneath her round bow and trailed astern. Small seabirds dipped in her wake, screaming and fighting for the minute creatures her passage disturbed, a contrast to the rigidly ordered silence upon her decks.

At her fore-masthead the British ship flew a white flag of truce, but her guns were cleared for action, all but the saluting battery shotted. Slow matches burned in the tubs in case the locks should fail, and every man stood at his post, tense for the slightest sign of hostility from the Spanish ashore.

'They're buggers for red-hot shot, me lads . . .'

'Look, there's a battery below those trees, see . . .'

'And there's two man-o'-war brigs at anchor.'

'Lick those bastards wi' one hand up our arses, Jemmy.'

'Shut your fuckin' mouths!'

The whisper of comment, risen like the beginnings of a breeze in dried grass, died away.

Below, under an even stricter watch, the Spanish prisoners were confined until the proposed terms of the truce were ratified by the Spanish authorities and they could be released. Among them the silence was expectant, for no one ashore could know they were mewed up on board and the authorities might suspect the bold approach of the British cruiser was no more than an elaborate ruse to decimate the merchant shipping loading the hides and tallow, hemp and wheat upon which the fortunes of the settlement depended.

Drinkwater stood at the starboard hance, Fraser and Hill close beside him. The three of them listened to the leadsman, waiting to find the bottom and watching the Spanish lieutenant deputed to pilot them into soundings and the sand of an anchorage as the frigate moved ponderously into the vast embrace of the bay. Señor Lecuna, the Spanish lieutenant, was the only one of the prisoners on deck, both Don Alejo and Rubalcava being confined below until the ship had exchanged courtesies with the fort and established the nature of her reception.

'Fog, sir,' said Hill, sniffing the air like a hound.

It descended upon them like conjuror's magic, suddenly blotting out the surrounding landscape and instantly replacing the warm sunshine with a dripping, saturated atmosphere that darkened the decks and chilled the skin.

'*Pasarán . . . Siga el rumbo!*' said Lecuna. '*Siga el rumbo . . . vigile el compás!*'

'Compass . . . *rumbo*? Ah! Rumb line . . . hold your course, Mr Hill,' snapped Drinkwater in sudden comprehension.

'*Sí . . . sí*, hold course!' Lecuna nodded.

'Aye, aye, sir.'

For ten long minutes *Patrician* held on through the fog, her ropes dripping and the condensation collecting upon the guns.

'Look to your primings,' warned Fraser and prudent gun-captains turned to the match-tubs and whirled or blew on the sputtering saltpetre coils. Above them the sun reappeared, swirling through the nacreous vapour.

'*Caiga a estribor . . . er*, starboard, *Capitán . . .*'

'Starboard helm, Mr Hill, if you please,' amplified Drinkwater, watching Lecuna's hand. The leadsman called out that he had found the bottom, shoaling fast as *Patrician* crept into the anchorage.

'*Sí, bueno . . . arrie las escandalosas . . .*' he pointed aloft, cut his hands outwards in the universal gesture of completion, and then waved them downwards.

'Tops'l halliards, Mr Fraser! Stand by forrard!'

On the fo'c's'le, the grey shapes of the carpenter's party stood ready to let the anchor go. The sea-bed had levelled out and Drinkwater wondered how close Lecuna would anchor them to the guns of the fort.

And then, with the same magical effect and as suddenly as it had come, the fog lifted, rolling away to shroud the great northern bight of the bay, produced by some local anomaly of temperature variation. *Patrician* found herself within the entrance to the southern arm of the huge inlet. A group of islands were visible, one a colony to the extraordinary pelican, while the bay forked, reaching deep inland to the north and the south. San Francisco lay on the slopes and hills of the southern headland, Point Lobos. To starboard, less than long-cannon shot away, rose the first of its green bluffs, a spur of that Point Lobos, surmounted by the white walls of the *Commandante*'s residence and the colours of Castile. Beneath the languidly flaunting red and gold, the ramparts of a fort beetled upon her, muzzles of heavy artillery trained on her decks from their embrasures.

Patrician was turning as she emerged from the fog-bank, her topsails bellying aback against their tops, slowing the ship and imparting a sluggish sternway to her. As she gathered way astern, the anchor was let go, the topsails lowered and the hands piped aloft to stow them. With the cable running through the hawse, the saluting battery opened fire.

Patrician brought up to her anchor as the last echoes of the final gun-shot echoed round the bay. Putting off from a small boat jetty beneath the embrasures of the fort was a smart barge, decorated with scarlet and gold fancy-work. At her stern flew a miniature Spanish ensign and at her bow stood an officer with a white flag.

Drinkwater closed his glass with a snap and nodded his thanks to Lieutenant Lecuna. 'Pass word to bring up Don Alejo and Captain Rubalcava.'

The next hour was going to be difficult.

It had long been a contention of Drinkwater's that contact with the shore was the bane of a sea-officer's professional life and today had offered him no reason to change his mind. Now, as he stood on the wide, paved terrace of the *Commandante*'s residence in the company of Midshipman Frey, awaiting the summons to meet the governor, he tried to relax.

Below them, the bluff was already casting its shadow across the southern arm of San Francisco Bay, the last rays of the sun disappearing over the Pacific behind him, beyond the entrance to the harbour. Skeins of brown and white pelicans flew in to roost, brilliantly lit, for the last of the sunshine illuminated the harbour in a wide swathe from the entrance. He watched the ships in the anchorage preparing for the ceremony of sunset, paying particular attention to his own *Patrician*, and the pair of Spanish brigs-of-war below him. Further away some dozen merchantmen lay off the town, their lower yards cock-billed as they worked cargo out of lighters alongside. Drinkwater could see the stars and stripes of the United States and the diagonal cross of Russian colours. But the big, black Russian line-of-battle-ship he had seen off Cape Horn was not in evidence. He cursed his over-anxiety, aware that he had been too-much worked upon by the cares of the day. And what a day it had been!

A day of constant arguments. First the Spanish officer who had boarded them on arrival had argued with Drinkwater over his blatant disregard for Spanish sovereignty by entering the port with his guns run out, demanding to know, in the name of King Carlos, what the devil he was doing in Spanish waters. Drinkwater had countered these intemperate demands and expostulations by coolly awaiting the arrival of Don Alejo Arguello and Captain Rubalcava.

Captain de Soto, the boarding officer, having made formal apologies for the peremptory mode of his address at the appearance of these gentlemen, then fell to arguing with them, insisting that he was acting on the *Commandante*'s strictest instructions and exploding with rage at the news that the *Santa Monica* had been destroyed. De Soto's anger released a storm of fury from Rubalcava which was incomprehensible to the watching Britons, but which drained the colour from de Soto's face and sent his right hand flying to his sword-hilt. Don Alejo's temporising interruption calmed things down, but it was clear that Rubalcava was a deeply embittered man and the source of his disaffection stemmed from more than a matrimonial disappointment. There was an air of alienation

313

about Rubalcava that seemed to Drinkwater's perceptive eye to go beyond the odium associated with the loss of a ship. Perhaps it was just the fruit of an active rivalry between officers on a colonial station, perhaps de Soto expected command of the *Santa Monica* or had always rated himself higher than Rubalcava; perhaps, Drinkwater thought, his mind running wild as the two Spaniards postured before the calming influence of Don Alejo, it was de Soto who had won the affection and hand of the *Commandante*'s daughter. He gave up the vain speculation with the recollection that Don Alejo had indicated Rubalcava was of low birth. How much that meant in the Spanish colonies, Drinkwater could only guess. He had heard that the results of miscegenation were less frowned upon by the passionate Spaniards than the British in India, and that it was possible for able half-castes to rise in government service. Perhaps Rubalcava was one such man, though in his appearance he seemed to fit the Quixotic image of the Hispanic man of action.

When this purely domestic contention had finally died down, Drinkwater had found himself drawn into further argument following repudiation of his terms. The wood and water promised by Don Alejo were not available, said de Soto; upon that the *Commandante*, Don José Henrique Martin Arguello de Salas, was adamant. The lie of the land persuaded Drinkwater that both were readily available elsewhere, except that the point had become a matter of honour. De Soto's insistence compromised Don Alejo, despite the mandate of the *Commandante*, and Drinkwater sensed the Spanish *hidalgo*'s loss of face before his juniors. He decided to intervene.

'Don Alejo,' he interrupted, 'I am willing to forgo the wood and water.'

Don Alejo's face brightened. '*Capitán*, you are a man of honour . . .'

The indispensable formula of bow and counter-bow threatened to reassert itself and Drinkwater cut it short. 'All I ask, Don Alejo, is a written undertaking that Captain Rubalcava, his officers and the seamen taken out of His Most Catholic Majesty's ship *Santa Monica*, will not bear arms against the forces and possessions of His Britannic Majesty for the duration of the present war.'

'*Qué?*' The vehemence of Rubalcava's interjection suggested he understood the gist of Drinkwater's demand. Rubalcava had been watching Drinkwater closely, knowing him for a wily opponent, and now asked what the heretic commander demanded under the very guns of Spain!

'Otherwise,' went on Drinkwater unperturbed, 'we will have to discuss the terms of ransom. You are my prisoners, Don Alejo, I have treated you as men of honour after you struck your country's colours in the face of superior force. You bear your swords and I offer you your freedom. All I ask is your parole not to serve again in the present war. It is nothing.'

He shrugged, aware that the gesture was catching, and feigned to dismiss further argument. Nevertheless it broke out with renewed violence, but in Spanish and detached from Drinkwater. In the end Don Alejo agreed, but it was clear that Rubalcava did not intend to adhere to whatever the others committed him.

De Soto had departed to confer with the *Commandante*, and the prisoners had resigned themselves to wait. Drinkwater had not agreed to Don Alejo's accompanying de Soto; the muzzles of those Spanish guns were too damned close.

De Soto returned an hour later. He was much changed, an affable, effusive and courtly man who requested the honour of Captain Drinkwater's presence at the *Commandante*'s table that evening. An hour later they had begun to disembark the prisoners. They were still landing them as Drinkwater and Frey looked down into the dark cusp of the bay where, like a giant water-beetle, *Patrician*'s long-boat made its way to the quays of the town.

'You are spared that tedious task, Mr Frey,' he nodded down at the labouring boat.

'Yes, sir.' Spruce in his new coat, its white collar patches bright in the twilight, Frey grinned back from the unaccustomed throttling of his formal stock. He had heard something about meeting a lady tonight. The occupants of the gunroom thought a great deal about meeting ladies.

Drinkwater moved his right shoulder beneath the heavy material of his own full-dress coat, glad of its weight in the evening chill. A touch of mist trailed across the dark foliage of the trees below them and the sudden concussion of the sunset gun made him start. It was echoed smartly by *Patrician* and the two brigs as their colours fluttered down. Night fell on the great bay, the lights of the ships twinkling across the smooth water. Two more beetles crept out from *Patrician's* side and began to circle her darkening bulk languidly.

'And that duty too, Mr Frey,' Drinkwater nodded, and both watched the two cutters begin to row the night's guard round and round the frigate.

The wait was beginning to tell on Drinkwater's patience and he sighed impatiently. He was tired, exhausted by three days of vigilance and today's largely irrelevant exertions. He had wanted only to disencumber himself of the damned prisoners, not to fence endless words, to be caught up in the parish-pump politics of a colonial outpost. He detested such futile activities, longed for the fresh air of the open sea. He straightened his back, eased his shoulder and drew in a long breath of the damp, aromatic evening air.

'Ah, *Capitán*, please forgive . . . His Excellency will receive you . . .'

Don Alejo Joaquin Arguello waved his arm for Drinkwater and Frey to follow.

Lieutenant James Quilhampton nodded a curt farewell to Lieutenant Cesar Lecuna of the *Santa Monica*. Upon these two officers had fallen the duty of co-operation during the landing of the prisoners. He looked briefly at the signed receipt.

'*Adios . . . vaya con Dios . . .*' Lecuna turned to his own men. '*Adelante!*'

Quilhampton turned to walk back along the quay to the waiting long-boat, almost bumping into Midshipman Belchambers who ran up at full tilt.

'Sir! Sir! The men are running!'

'What? God damn! Why didn't you stop 'em?' Quilhampton clapped a hand to his hat and began to run. It was the hour of *corso*, the promenade. The draggle-tailed society of San Francisco was airing its social pretensions. Amid such a crowd, many of whom gathered to hiss and barrack the English sailors, he knew his seamen would melt like snow on a hearthstone.

'We couldn't stop 'em, sir . . . not without firing into this crowd.'

'No, of course not,' Quilhampton replied sourly to the marine corporal whose three men looked down sheepishly. The Spaniards had not liked the presence of the armed marines on their soil and Quilhampton had been obliged to admit they were appointed to the boats for his own protection and to prevent his men deserting. When that news had been communicated to Captain Rubalcava it had brought the first smile to the Spanish commander's face. Doubtless a few dollars had been spread amongst the boat's crew. Now only four men remained on board, studying the bottom boards under Quilhampton's withering glare.

'Did these lubbers try and run too?' he asked, and the question went unanswered. Behind him he felt a stir of hostility among the crowd of idlers. Some unfriendly shouts followed.

'Get in the boat,' he snapped at the marines, 'and take an oar each.'

It was going to be a damnably long pull back to the ship with so few oarsmen, but soon the night would shroud their humiliation. He followed Belchambers and the marines into the long-boat, took his place aft and tucked the tiller underneath his arm.

'Toss oars, bear off forrard!'

The crowd surged to the edge of the quay, abuse rising like a wave behind them. Someone spat, provoking a burst of expectoration and fist-shaking. A stone plopped alongside. A gobbet of spittle struck Quilhampton's neck.

'Pull, you buggers! Put your bloody backs into it!'

The heavy boat moved with ponderous slowness; Quilhampton endured further humiliation, but dared not turn and face his tormentors.

'Pull!'

As he sat hunched and swearing over the tiller his mind ranged over the wisdom of remaining in the harbour an hour longer. It had seemed to him as they had glided into the bay that the *Patrician*'s presence within the dark embrace of those great headlands touched off some primitive suspicion in his mind. Intuition told him that despite her massed cannon, despite her state of readiness and the precautionary guard-boats pulling round the ship, she lay in mortal danger.

He could not explain this theory. The terms of the truce seemed water-tight, and it was unlikely that the Spanish authorities would break their word. But these new desertions combined with his suspicion of the connivance of Rubalcava, triggered off his nervous conviction that the ship was ill-fated, and he doomed with it. It was a far more serious matter than the desertion of the two lovers at Más-a-Fuera, and he had yet to explain it to Captain Drinkwater.

Drinkwater exchanged bows with the *Commandante*, Don José Henrique Martin Arguello de Salas. His Excellency was a tall, heavily handsome man with a thick-set figure that was rapidly running to seed. In contrast to his brother he seemed of a more indolent character. Like Don Alejo he spoke a little English and he had a formally easy manner which, in the circumstances, put Drinkwater on his guard. He disliked being manipulated and Don José seemed an expert in the matter.

'Ah, *Capitán*, Don Alejo speak of his misfortune to meet you. You are come to make trouble for us, no?'

'I have come to do my duty, Your Excellency.'

'And what is your duty, *Capitán*?'

A servant appeared bearing a tray of glasses. Drinkwater took one and sipped from it before replying, meeting the *Commandante's* inquisitorial stare with his own.

'A most excellent sherry, *Señor* . . . I command a cruiser, Your Excellency,' he said slowly, feigning a greater interest in the wine. 'It is the duty of a cruiser to wreck the enemy's trade . . .'

'We 'ave ships of other nations 'ere in San Francisco.'

'You have ships of nations with whom Great Britain is at war, Excellency, nations who until recently were our allies and received payments from our Treasury. You are a man of honour, Your Excellency, and understand such treachery is intolerable.'

'The Russian ships?' Don José asked, frowning, clearly having difficulty with Drinkwater's English.

'That is correct, yes.'

'And the ships of the United States, *Capitán*? Would you fire on the flag of the United States?'

'Great Britain is not at war with the United States, Excellency,' Drinkwater said, noting the quick glance between Don José and his brother, 'but of course,' he added, 'we should find it necessary to search even neutral vessels for contraband cargoes.' He smiled as courteously as he could in the knowledge that they were contemplating such a ruse. 'I would not like to imagine my reactions if I discovered that, for example, a *Spanish* ship was sailing under false, American colours. I am sure you take my meaning.'

The cloud hanging over Don José's brow lifted as Don Alejo hissed a few words of explanation at his elder brother. Don José nodded and met Drinkwater's smile with one of equal falsity. Drinkwater looked about him.

'Is Captain Rubalcava to join us this evening, Your Excellency?' Drinkwater asked. 'He was a gallant enemy . . .'

'No,' put in Don Alejo sharply, 'Don Jorge will not be joining us . . .'

Further enquiry or explanation was cut short by the majordomo's announcement. The gentlemen turned towards a heavy door and Drinkwater and Frey exchanged glances, then imitated the Spaniards' low bows. They were aware of the rustle of skirts and the subtle waft of perfume filling the candle-lit room. As he straightened up Drinkwater heard the faint rasp of sharply indrawn breath from Midshipman Frey. His face was flushed with a sudden wave of long-suppressed concupiscence and Drinkwater smiled, for the object of his sudden lust was overwhelmingly beautiful.

'May I present the lady Doña Ana Maria Conchita . . .' Don Alejo recited the young woman's names and titles, but Drinkwater distilled the information that she was his niece and Don José's daughter. Whilst the long absence from the society of women would have made memorable an hour spent in the company of any young woman with good teeth and a bosom, Doña Ana Maria's presence promised an evening of pleasing enchantment.

Tall, like her father, she wore the wide skirt and tight bodice of Spanish fashion. Her carriage was regal and her bare shoulders rose above the swirl of a shawl which was drawn together below her breasts. About her neck a necklace of Chinese jade reflected the candle-light, rising and falling with her breathing.

But there was far more to her beauty than mere sexual allure, for her face was as intelligent as it was lovely. Her eyes were of such an umbral brown that they appeared bronze in the light from the candles. Her flawless cream skin was unpowdered and her lips were soft, wide and red without the artifice of carmine. Above her

319

straight nose and wide forehead, long black hair was oiled like jet, drawn back in the severe mode of her class, and beneath the swept-back waves at the side of her head, jade earrings depended from the lobes of her ears. Suddenly Rubalcava's embitterment made shattering sense. Drinkwater relinquished her hand and turned to his companion.

'*Señorita*, I have the honour to present Mr Midshipman Frey.'

It was clear that Frey was devastated by the lady, fighting an overwhelming desire fuelled by the gross appetites of the starved, and ready to die for her in the next moment if she had asked it of him. His hand shook as he bent over hers and he straightened up with an idiot look of rapture. She could not fail to be aware of the turmoil she was causing and Drinkwater turned to Don José. Both he and Don Alejo were clearly studying the effect Doña Ana Maria was having on the two British officers. Was there something pre-meditated about this attention?

'My uncle,' she said in an English that contained an elusively familiar inflection, 'tells me you have come to San Francisco with many cannon, *Capitán*.'

She had turned those wonderful eyes on him again.

'I have come on an act of humanity, *Señorita*, to repatriate the gallant Captain Don Jorge Rubalcava and his men, whom the fortune of war made my prisoners.'

There was no trace of reaction to the name of her former suitor, the tiny reactive muscles about the eyes that could reveal the quickening impulses of the brain remained unmoved. Presumably Rubalcava meant nothing to her. 'You speak excellent English, *Señorita*, please accept my compliments.'

'Thank you, *Capitán*. I learn it from my duenna, Doña Helena.' She indicated an elderly woman who wore a *mantilla*, whom Drinkwater had taken for Doña Ana Maria's mother and the *Commandante*'s wife. If his senses had not been so mesmerised he would have recognised the folly of such a supposition. It was inconceivable that he should have entertained it, even for an instant. Doña Helena stared at him from a wizened face with a pair of fiercely blue eyes.

'Your servant, ma'am,' Drinkwater bowed, aware of the ferocity of her scrutiny.

'Aye, honoured ah'm sure, Captain.' There was venom in the reply, a sharp hatred bred in the bone and born of popish origins, and the mystery of Doña Ana's acquired accent was cleared up. In her native Scotland, Doña Helena would have been called Mistress Helen, though it was uncertain when she had last seen her native land.

Only the sombre figure of the priest remained to be introduced. He had come in with the women, an emaciated young Franciscan in a heavy wool habit. His crucifix and rosary chinked gently as he moved and his presence adumbrated the room. There was clearly no Doña José; the *Commandante*, it seemed, was a widower. The Franciscan's introduction as Fra Alfonso terminated the pre-prandial formalities and Drinkwater found himself leading the beautiful Doña Ana Maria in to dinner.

Drinkwater willingly surrendered to the charms of the young woman during the meal as he knew he was intended to do. His host, Don José, was on his left and seemed content to allow his daughter to practise her near-fluent English upon the British captain. There were a few initial questions about Drinkwater's career which he avoided exploiting, paying his host the compliment of reporting on the gallant conduct of the Spanish fleet in the momentous action off Cap Trafalgar, during which he had been a prisoner aboard the French flagship, *Bucentaure*.[*]

'You speak with the Marquis de Solana, *Capitán*, at Cadiz?'

'Yes, Your Excellency, I was received by him several times, concerning the matter of British prize-crews cast up on the coast after the great gale that followed the battle . . .'

The meal passed delightfully, though Midshipman Frey had a less happy time of it, seated next to the Scottish companion, Doña Helena. Yet he would not have traded his place for all the gold in Eldorado, for he could not take his eyes off the beautiful Doña Ana Maria opposite. Aware of Frey's sheep's eyes, Drinkwater began to feel sorry for the young woman, realising she was a victim of her own extraordinary beauty. It was not difficult to see how Rubalcava's proud spirit had been so enslaved. Something of an

[*] See *1805*.

even darker alchemy was brewing in the unholy eyes of the silent Franciscan.

'You have children, *Capitán*?' The timbre of her voice was low and mellifluous.

'Yes, *Señorita*, I have two; a son and a daughter.'

'Ahhh. That is, they say, the choice of kings.' He watched her face as she added, 'I . . . I would like children . . .'

It was an impropriety, an intimacy, a mark of the isolation her beauty caused her, made in a low voice to a complete stranger.

'I understand you are to be married soon, *Señorita*,' he replied quietly.

'Yes . . .' She smiled and he sensed her excitement and the strength of her love for Rubalcava's rival which was prompting these confidences, confidences that were earning glances of disapproval from her duenna opposite. 'As soon as Nicolai arrives,' she ran on, her dark eyes glowing, 'he commands a great ship, like yourself, *Capitán* . . .'

'Nicolai?' Drinkwater was suddenly alert and cast a quick glance to his left where Don José seemed to be speaking in a low voice to Don Alejo.

'Aye, Cap'n, Nicolai Rezanov will be here soon tae clip your wings . . .' Doña Helena's blue eyes were chips of ice, chilled by ancient enmities. Her outburst attracted the attention of the Arguellos and turned them from their private conclave. In the sudden silence Drinkwater exploited the hiatus.

'Rezanov . . . an unusual name for a Spanish officer.'

Don José's face was a mask; Don Alejo made a small gesture to a waiting footman. The door was flung open and de Soto marched into the room and bent to Don José's ear. The *Commandante* looked sharply at Drinkwater.

'*Diablo!*' he muttered, then nodded and, as de Soto straightened up, the *Commandante* said, '*Capitán*, there has been much trouble in the town. Some men from your ship . . . they run away . . . there is a *mêlée* and a woman is killed.'

322

8 Council of War

March 1808

'How many?'

In the light from the candle that stood on the cabin table Captain Drinkwater's face was thrown into dramatic relief. His head was cocked slightly, revealing the damaged muscles of his wrecked shoulder, and the single flame emphasised the intensity of his eyes. He was pale with fury.

'Eight, sir.' Quilhampton had never seen Drinkwater so angry and felt like a chastened midshipman. Beside him Fraser fidgeted nervously.

'Eight? *Eight!* God's bones, man, you had *marines* in that damned boat! Marines with bayonets, for God's sake, and you let *eight* men run!'

'Yes, sir,' Quilhampton mumbled unhappily.

'And do you know what they have done? Do you know what your eight precious liberty-loving English jacks have done, sir?'

'No, sir.'

'They swilled *aguardiente* and ran wild in a whore-house! The upshot of their desertion is that they have been accused of causing the death of a woman and . . . and . . .'

Drinkwater brought his clenched fist down on the table-top so that the candle flame guttered. 'They have entirely compromised me, tied me hand and fist, God damn them!'

'Sir?' Quilhampton frowned, not understanding.

Drinkwater let out a long breath. 'Good God, James, can you offer me nothing in extenuation?'

'Only that there were many people on the quay and to shoot would have endangered the local people.'

'Mr Quilhampton was much abused by the crowds, sir,' put in Fraser, 'much spat upon and the like.'

Drinkwater fell silent and then he asked: 'What became of Rubalcava?'

'He left in the first boat after you and Frey had gone ashore, sir.'

Drinkwater shook his head, then moved round the table and lifted three glasses from the fiddles atop the locker. 'Pass that decanter, Mr Fraser . . . thank you.'

He poured the *bual* into the glasses and handed each of the two officers a glass. 'What's it like on deck?'

'Still foggy, sir, and dead calm. You can hear the guard-boats . . . no fear of a surprise. Mylchrist's up there now, reckons his fever's sharpened all his instincts,' replied Fraser who had not long come below.

Drinkwater grunted. 'We've an hour or two, no more . . . well, your health.'

There was a pause and then Drinkwater looked at Quilhampton. 'Ease your mind, James, 'tis I who am the greater fool.'

'You, sir?'

'Yes . . . I have played right into their damned hands. I suspected something, but could not lay it by the tail . . . damned if I can now, but I'll wager the whore's death was contrived.'

'Contrived? I'm sorry . . . I don't follow . . .'

It had come to him in his enforced idleness, sitting in his barge as the oarsmen brought him back to the ship from the *Commandante*'s boat jetty below the battery. There had been that vague feeling of something passing between the Arguello brothers, that sensation of their using Doña Ana to distract him. Whether she was a party to this he did not know, but it seemed obvious that the news of the brawl had been engineered and it came to him in the boat that those eight seamen had been lured away on promises of safety, promiscuous sex and money.

'Was there much contact between the people and the Spaniards while they were here?' he asked flatly.

'No, sir,' said Fraser, 'no more than one would expect with them cooped up on board.'

'Mount mentioned he caught two seamen and a marine bartering for tobacco,' Quilhampton added.

'Did he indeed?'

'But there is nothing particularly significant in that, sir,' said Fraser.

'Except that ample opportunity existed for a sum of money to pass to disaffected men,' Drinkwater said, 'and God knows it takes little enough to turn the heads of these poor devils. A gold dollar, the promise of a whore and a drink and a pass through the town . . .' Conviction was forming in his mind.

'And they're in an ugly mood, sir . . . simmering below the surface. They fought well enough, sir, but the smell of land . . .'

'Aye, and women,' growled Fraser, and Drinkwater felt guilt fuelling his anger.

'And Don Alejo had gold, sir, a lot of gold.'

'Why d'you say that, Mr Q?'

'He was concealing something on himself when he was compelled to abandon the *Santa Monica*. I thought it was a purse at the time. Then later, when he was quartered in my cabin, I went there by mistake, came below and without thinking, proceeded directly to my cabin. I opened the door before I realised my stupidity. Don Alejo was sitting smoking one of those damned cigars. He was half-undressed, lounging in my chair and on the cot lay his sword, some papers and a leather purse, the same one I had seen aboard the *Santa Monica*. It was bulging, sir, to the extent of revealing its contents . . . gold, sir.'

'Dollars, or pistoles or something very like . . .'

'No, sir, gold nuggets . . .'

'The treasures of the Manila galleon, eh?'

'I think perhaps only a little . . . a private speculation like the nabobs of the East India Company.'

'H'm. How did he take the intrusion?' Drinkwater asked.

'He was not pleased. I told him the stink of his cigar had attracted my attention and that smoking was forbidden below decks.'

'You should day-dream more often of Mistress MacEwan if it leads you into such adventures, Mr Q. Very well, then, it only serves to confirm my suspicions that some of the men were suborned. More may be preparing to desert at the first opportunity, we shall have to proceed warily . . .'

'Sir, Ah'd be obliged . . .' Fraser frowned.

'Yes, Mr Fraser, I'll explain.' Drinkwater motioned them to sit. He was past mere tiredness, the events of the last hours had stimulated him and his active brain was whirling with the problems that suddenly beset him. He passed his hands over his face, seeking a place to begin his explanation.

'Well, gentlemen, the main purpose of our cruise is to dislodge any attempt by the Russians to establish territorial claims northward of the Spanish domain of Nueva Espana. Since the Tsar repudiated his alliance with us last summer, it is believed that it is the intention of the Russian court to settle southwards from Alaska. Some reports, brought into Canada by *voyageurs*, indicated Russian incursions up the Colombia River, further north from here . . . it's all very vague, but as welcome to us as the Spanish claim to Nootka Sound was. Although they have a fur-trading depot at Sitka, in Alaska, the tenuous claims of Captain Vancouver lie between Sitka and here, from whence, if the evidence in the bay is anything to go by, the Russians obtain many necessary supplies.'

'I counted seven Russian vessels in the anchorage, sir, a schooner, three brigs, a barque and a ship, sir.'

'Yes. I saw them last night. They will be expected on the Alaskan coast soon, and now we have arrived, just at the wrong moment for them. Not only have we advertised our presence, but we have destroyed one unit of the Spanish squadron that might have protected their trade.'

'But it's *Russian* trade, sir. I mean, are the Dons that interested in protecting it?' asked Fraser, to whom the matter was still confused.

'I presume they would not want it destroyed,' Drinkwater replied.

'But the Russians, sir, if they are seeking territory, will become a direct threat to the Spaniards, competing for the same length of coast.' Fraser frowned.

'Yes. Eventually they might, once our claims of land and our failure to maintain them are dealt with. But, for the meantime, they are allies of expedience. Besides, this could become a matter of national prestige. I imagine the Dons would like their revenge for the loss of Nootka Sound. They only capitulated before because they lost the French monarchy as a support. Now they have Tsar Alexander. I believe they are about to settle the coast between them.'

'With what force?'

'The destruction of the *Santa Monica* does not draw all their teeth, Mr Fraser. Their main Pacific base is at Acapulco, they will have ships at Panama and, from what I heard tonight, there is a garrison at Monterey. I learnt something else tonight, gentlemen, and this is the reason why we have been compromised. The murder, if indeed there has been a murder, is a prevarication, a means to delay us. The *Commandatore* has agreed to meet me to discuss the return of our men after the murderer has been tried. He has made protestations of not wishing to impugn the honour of our flag after our courtesy to our prisoners. In the same breath he is talking of our breaking the terms of the truce, of referring to Monterey for instructions . . . in short, any damned obstruction that will delay us while we are enmeshed in some specious diplomatic tangle.'

'But sir, they have no *force* to keep us here!' expostulated Fraser. 'We can tow out from their guns in a couple of hours and those toy brigs wouldn't knock the marines' shakoes off.'

'You are correct in your specific, but not your diagnosis. We can tow out, Mr Fraser, but we may well meet a line-of-battle-ship coming in.'

'We can outmanoeuvre a Spanish battle-ship, sir,' said Fraser almost flippantly.

'She will be *Russian*, Mr Fraser, we saw her off Cape Horn and by the certainty with which our friends ashore are behaving, I believe her arrival imminent.'

'*Do* we tow out, sir?' Quilhampton asked, that inchoate sense of foreboding closing round him again. He had found its first physical manifestation at Más-a-Fuera and the second had dotted him with the spittle of hostile Spaniards, half-castes and Indians. Now every moment of delay increased its intensity.

'Yes, make your preparations. Let us slip our cable and use the fog to make a virtue of necessity. In an hour then . . .'

They left him, scuttling out to pass word to the watch and turn out those sleeping below and at the guns. They would all be ragged-nerved and foul-tempered by the time they had laboured at the oars of the boats and dragged *Patrician*'s inert mass clear of the bay. He would have to be patient with them and watch for

327

outbursts of disaffection. In the meantime he would have to wait. He could not sleep, although he was haggard with exhaustion. An hour's sleep would make him feel worse than none at all. He poured the last of the *bual* into his glass and went on an impulse to his sea-chest. Rummaging in the bottom he drew out a frayed roll of canvas. Spreading it on the table he looked down at it. It was the portrait of a woman painted long ago by the French Republican artist Jacques Louis David. In addition to the frayed edges and cracked paintwork, little circles of mould were forming on the canvas, perverting the purity of the colours, and there were three holes, where the tines of a fork had once pierced it.

Hortense Santhonax stared back at him from cool grey eyes. Beneath the studied negligence of her pearl-wound and piled auburn hair, her lovely face held a hint of a smile. He remembered her, years ago, almost as long ago as the Spanish outrage at Nootka Sound, before she married Edouard Santhonax and espoused the Bonapartist cause. She had been a frightened *émigrée* then, Hortense de Montholon, running from the vengeful howl of the pursuing mob, to be rescued by an impoverished master's mate named Nathaniel Drinkwater.*

He had been half in love with her then, before she turned her coat and married his enemy.

He had killed Edouard Santhonax less than a year previously, killed him to preserve the secret he had brought out of Russia. He had widowed her in the line of duty. Or had he and why did he stare at her portrait now? The bare shoulders and the soft breasts were barely concealed by the wisp of gauze artfully placed by the skilled hand of a seductress. She was already rumoured to be the mistress of Talleyrand, a fading beauty he supposed. It made no sense to be subject to so compelling an urge as had driven him to remove her portrait from the obscurity of his sea-chest.

Except that she was providence, an ikon, presentient as his dream and an impulse to be obeyed in those rare moments of hiatus when his tired mind was in revolt. An ikon: an apt simile. He was unable to shake off that old superstition of his destiny. She

* See *A King's Cutter*.

had become the embodiment of the spirit of France, inhabiting the subconscious recesses of his imagination and marrying the man whose fate had become inextricably bound up with his own. The dice had fallen his way last, it had not always been thus as his wrecked shoulder testified; but he was not yet free of Santhonax's ghost. The secret from Russia still haunted him, even here in the Pacific.

'Witchcraft,' he muttered and let the margin of the canvas go. It coiled itself like a spring and he looked up to see the faithful, pale oval of Elizabeth's portrait staring at him from its frame. 'Witchcraft,' he repeated and, hiding the canvas again, he drew on his cloak and went on deck.

In some strange way he felt relieved by the power the portrait of Hortense possessed. There was a reassuring quality of normality about it: a familiar neurosis. He had not been too much overcome by the beauty of Ana Maria.

9 The Leak

April 1808

'If you wish to say something, Tregembo, for God's sake say it and stop fiddling with those damned pistols!' Drinkwater snapped irritably. Mullender's duster and Tregembo's fidgeting had driven him on deck where a sleeting rain had turned him below again. *Patrician* bucked to the onset of the rain-bearing squall and gusts of cold, damp air rattled in through the sashes of the stern windows.

'You'll be needing 'em 'fore long zur, if I ain't mistaken,' Tregembo growled.

'The pistols? Would to God I needed 'em instanter! That damned convoy should have appeared by now . . .'

'I didn't mean for that, zur . . .'

'Eh?' Drinkwater frowned, looking at his coxswain with sudden attention. 'What the devil *did* you mean then?'

Tregembo laid the pistol down in its box and waited until Mullender had gone into the pantry. His old face, lined and scarred as it was, bore every indication of concern. 'Zur . . .' The door to the tiny pantry stood open behind him. Drinkwater crossed the cabin and closed it. 'Well?'

'The people, zur . . . you know they're disaffected . . . 'tis common enough upon a long commission an' they mean no harm to you, zur . . . but . . .'

'Spit it out, Tregembo, I'm in no mood for puzzlements.'

''Tis the men you left behind, zur . . . 'tis scuttlebutt they're to hang, an' such rumouring is having a bad effect, zur . . .'

'For God's sake, Tregembo, those men *deserted* . . .' Drinkwater sat and stared gloomily at the old Cornishman.

'There are stories of women, zur . . . the boats' crews saw women ashore, an' there are grog shops a-plenty . . . those merchant-seamen were three sheets to the wind, they'm saying . . . they be powerful reasons for making a man run, zur.'

Drinkwater nodded. 'I know all this, Tregembo . . . why tell me now?'

'Because it won't be single men, zur. Next time it'll be a boat's crew, zur, an' the word, as I hear it, is to hell with the officers . . .'

There was a peremptory knock at the cabin door. Instantly Tregembo turned away, picked up the pistol case, shut it and slid it into its stowage in the locker.

'Come!'

It was Fraser. He was followed by the elderly Mr Marsden, a wizened and wrinkled man skirted with a leather apron which hid bandy legs but revealed a powerful torso, muscular arms and hands of immense size. The sudden irruption of the first lieutenant and the carpenter into Drinkwater's cabin indicated something serious had happened.

'Begging your pardon, sir, but Mr Marsden has just made an urgent report to me concerning water in the wells.'

Drinkwater looked sharply at the carpenter. 'Well, Mr Marsden?'

'Three feet, sir, in two hours, and making fast.'

'When were the wells last pumped? At the change of the watch?'

'Yes, sir, an' nothink much in 'em bar what you'd expect.'

'Something adrift below, then?'

Marsden nodded. 'Seems likely, sir.'

'Any idea what?'

'No, sir . . .'

'No shot holes . . .'

'Not that I can see, sir . . . 'sides we engaged that Spaniard wi' the larboard broadside . . .'

'Aye, and now we're on the larboard tack! Mr Fraser, put the ship about on the instant! Mr Marsden, pump the wells dry, let's see if the other tack makes any difference.' He rose, perversely relieved in the need for action, potentially disastrous though the news was. For the ship suddenly to make so much water could be due to any one of a hundred reasons, none of them easy to determine, let alone overcome. 'Come, gentlemen, let us be about our business!'

Grabbing hat and cloak Drinkwater hustled Fraser and the carpenter out of his cabin and followed them on deck. Alone in the cabin Tregembo watched the surge of the smooth wake as it rose, bubbling green from *Patrician*'s transom. A long-tailed Bosun-bird slid across his field of view, quartering the wake for prey. 'Don't you forget what I told 'ee,' he muttered after Drinkwater.

On deck the watch were running to their stations to tack ship. Drinkwater took no part in the manoeuvre, instead he fished in the tail-pocket of his coat for his glass then levelled it to the eastward.

Banks of slate-coloured clouds rolled to leeward dragging dull curtains of rain behind them, blotting out sections of the faint blue line of the coastal mountains of California. From one such shroud the low line of Punta de los Reyes was emerging. *Patrician* had spent nine days keeping station off the point round which any convoy from San Francisco must pass on its way to the Alaskan settlements of the Tsar. They had kept well to seaward of the long, low arm of sand-dunes and marram grass, lurking out of sight to avoid either of those two man-of-war brigs that might be sent to see if the coast was clear. Even allowing a week for the tardiest merchant ship to complete her lading, it would be reasonable, Drinkwater argued to himself, for them to have intercepted some trading vessels moving north by now.

Patrician jibbed up into the wind and the foreyards were swung on the word of command.

Unless, Drinkwater mused, those merchantmen were waiting for something more puissant than a pair of brigs; something like a Russian line-of-battle-ship! Not for the first time Drinkwater cursed the brevity of his aptly-styled briefing from the Admiralty. Again he felt that sense of abandonment by Lord Dungarth, the very man from whom he would have expected the most comprehensive elucidation of the state of affairs in the Pacific. He knew his orders originated from British spies in the Russian service, agents whose access to the most secret intentions of the Tsar had been preserved at a prodigious cost, as Drinkwater had good reason to know.

Supposing, he reasoned, he had been utterly mistaken in that glimpse of another man-of-war off Cape Horn. Suppose that brief spectral image had magnified itself in his imagination and the vessel had been, at worst, a Spaniard. He knew that the Russian-American Company, under whose auspices Russian ships traded down the coast from Alaska, had armed vessels at their disposal. He knew, too, that at least one frigate had been built on the Pacific coast of North America for the purpose of reinforcing Russian claims upon the shores of what Drake, Cook, and now the Admiralty, were pleased to call 'New Albion'.

Patrician forged ahead, gathering increasing way on the new tack. The hands were busy coiling the braces on the pins and on the fo'c's'le the weather fore-tack was hauled down to the bowing bumpkin. Shafts of sunlight fanned down through the clouds, dappling the surface of the sea with brilliant patches of dancing water. Off on the quarter a school of dolphins abandoned the chase of a shoal of bonito and gambolled in their tumbling wake. Neither the brightening weather nor the appearance of the cetaceans lightened Drinkwater's gloom. All his ponderous considerations were of little consequence now. Marsden's report postponed them indefinitely. The leak and its cause superseded all other matters and it did not help his temper to realise that the trap he had baited by towing out of San Francisco Bay would now be useless. His nearest dockyard was in the West Indies with the Horn to double to get there. He had only one course of action open to him: Hobson's choice of a careenage.

'Well?'

As Marsden came aft Drinkwater stopped at the after end of the starboard gangway, his cloak flapping round him in the wind, his hands clasped behind his back. The carpenter's face was still clouded by concern.

'She's still makin' water, sir . . . perhaps a little less, but 'tis bad enough, sir.'

'Damn! Very well, Mr Marsden, very well. I'll be below myself shortly. Mr Fraser!'

'Aye, sir?'

'Steer east-nor'-east and fetch me the coast directly.'

Below the waterline the hull was a vast stygian cavern of noise. He followed Marsden and his two mates with their lanterns guttering in the stale, mephitic air, trying to shut out the natural noises of the creaking and groaning space to hear those unnatural sounds the better. It was a hopeless task, one that he was less qualified than Marsden to execute, yet one which demanded his attention. How far below the waterline was this leak? Any remedial action he took depended upon some rough location. To careen *Patrician* properly would render her utterly defenceless should she be taken by surprise, for all her guns and stores would have to come out of her and be safely landed. Drinkwater had himself led an attack on a French frigate in such a supine state, and carried her safely out to sea from her bolt-hole on the Red Sea coast of Arabia. To be served himself in similar fashion, dished-up to an enemy without the chance of defending himself sent worms of apprehension crawling about his belly. But he had to know the worst and he stumbled along the carpenter's walk, a narrow space maintained free of stores just inside the ship's skin, by which access was provided to plug shot-holes and maintain the water-tight integrity of the ship.

'Mind, sir, this grating be a bit loose . . .'

'Yes, thank you . . .'

In the yellow pools of lamp-light he could see the ship's inner skin, discoloured with the traces of mould. The thick air was heavy with the multiple smells of this great warehouse of the cruiser's wants. Here powder and shot were stored in magazines and lockers; locked store-rooms housed spirits and flour, fish and dried peas. Tier upon tier of barrels, stowed bung up and bilge-free, held the potable sweet-water; casks of dubious age contained the salt-pork and cheese provided by a munificent Victualling Board; the oats and dried fruit, the wood-store and oil-room, all fitted below the waterline, above, abaft or forward of the hold proper. The platformed section of the orlop along which they worked their way showed no ingress of water. Amid the creaks and groans of the ship's timbers, the slosh of bilge-water and the hiss of the sea beyond the inner and outer wales and the massive futtocks, they strained their ears for sound of a roar, a spurt, even a trickle of incoming water. But all they could make out above the working of the ship was the squeal of disturbed rats.

Drinkwater escaped to the upper deck, scanning the horizon and again finding the sea bereft of any sign of a ship. A mile to leeward a whale fluked, slapping the water with its gigantic tail before sliding into the depths of the ocean. Somehow that brief appearance of leviathan only served to emphasise the emptiness of the scene.

Slowly *Patrician* approached the coast; the yellow line of Punta de los Reyes spread across the horizon ahead, the clouds hanging over the coastal mountains fused into mist and falling rain. Drinkwater crossed the deck to where Fraser, his odd, sandy features wearing a comic expression that bespoke his anxiety, waited to hear what Drinkwater had to say with as much patience as he could muster.

'Hae ye any luck, sir?'

'Little enough, Mr Fraser.'

'No, I couldna find anything either. I thought it might be the hood-ends . . .'

Drinkwater considered the suggestion. The hood-ends were where the butt ends of the strakes, or planks, met the timbering of the stem. Here, the constant working of the sea round the bow could disturb the fastenings and loosen the planks. Leaking about the stem was very difficult to determine at sea and was increased by the ship continuing to make headway.

'That's an informed guess, Mr Fraser. Whatever the cause we cannot ignore the matter. I intend to get the ship into sheltered water and lighten her. We may have to careen, which will mean the devil of a lot of labour. Whatever expedient we are driven to we'll require a boat guard. If there *is* a Russian battle-ship in the offing we had better lie low. God help us if we are caught.'

'Amen to that, sir.'

'For heaven's sake it'll be like being caught in a whore-house on Judgement Day . . . begging your pardon, Mr Henderson.'

'I appreciate the strength of your metaphor, Mr Mylchrist, and deduce therefrom that we can expect an exceedingly great wrath to descend upon us should the event come to pass.'

'Well, we can't ignore the matter. Three feet in the well ain't a lot, but it came in damned quick and I think something fell out, a trenail, perhaps,' said Quilhampton, leaning on the wardroom table, his head in his hands, 'that's the only logical explanation.'

'D'you think we're up against logic, James?'

335

'What the hell else d'you think we're up against?' Quilhampton jerked up.

Mylchrist shrugged. 'I didn't get my wound from an enemy . . .'

'No . . . no more you did . . .'

Mylchrist's gloomy implication chimed in uncannily with Quilhampton's superstitious foreboding.

'A nail from the hull – another in our bloody coffins . . .'

'Oh, for God's sake, Johnnie . . .'

'Gentlemen, perhaps a prayer is apt while we wait for the first lieutenant.'

'What are you going to pray for, Mr Henderson?' asked Mylchrist sourly. 'Three hundred pairs of feet enabled to walk upon the water?'

'Mr Mylchrist, I am outraged! If God abandons us in our extremity, your blasphemy will give him cause enough . . . happily His mercy is infinite and able to accommodate a miscreant as wretched as you.'

'Ah, I forgot the quality of mercy,' remarked Mylchrist sarcastically, 'the recollection comes as a great relief to me.'

Henderson drew from his nose the spectacles he kept in almost permanent residence there, a habit which intimated he was never far removed from the devout perusal of Holy Scriptures. Such a deliberate and portentous gesture augured ill for the bantering inhabitants of the wardroom as they lounged about, waiting for their orders from the first lieutenant.

'Johnnie, what exactly did you mean just now?' Quilhampton interjected, a preoccupied look on his lean face.

'About what?'

'About the leak. Did you mean to imply someone may have had a hand in the matter?'

'Well , yes, of course . . .'

'Gentlemen, I have your orders . . . pray pay attention. You may require to make notes . . . we're in for the devil of a hard time.' Fraser's burr ended the conversation as the worried Scotsman hurried into the wardroom and waved aside the negro messman and his coffee pot. 'Nae time for that, King, nae time at all . . .'

It was not ground of his own choosing. A light mist trailing in the

336

wake of a rain shower was clearing as they closed the coast. *Patrician* stood shorewards under a single jib and her three topsails, a cable bent to her sheet anchor and a leadsman chanting from the forechains. Balanced on the rail, braced against the mizen shrouds, Drinkwater scanned the littoral ahead. He sought an anchorage beyond the flats that extended northwards from Punta de los Reyes. A long, comparatively low-lying spit of land extended for fifteen miles northward of the headland, behind which, his charts suggested, lay an inlet running deep into the countryside. He had little real knowledge of its suitability, but the preoccupation of a worried mind convinced him that to delay, to seek a more ideal spot, would be foolish.

Ahead of him the mist had resolved itself into a low cloud of spray that hung over the pounding white of breakers where the long Pacific swells toppled and thundered on the sands of the Californian foreshore. Behind the beach low sand-dunes ran to the southward and, somewhere beyond the horizon, terminated at Punta de los Reyes. At intervals along this sand-pit higher eminences rose and, at the distal point, a low but prominent hill marked the termination of the land. The white of breakers pounded on the low bar around which Drinkwater hoped to work *Patrician* and seek an anchorage beyond the spit, in the safety of the long lagoon of Tomales Bay.

The wind had fallen light, a gentle onshore breeze that ruffled the sea. The promise of sunshine earlier in the day had failed and cloud had closed off the heavens and given the sea's surface a leaden colour, as it lifted itself to the easy motion of the incoming swells.

'Noooo bottom!' The leadsman's chant had become monotonous, though they were within a league of the shore and then, sharply insistent: 'By the mark twenty!'

The breakers were suddenly nearer, drawing out on the starboard bow. The gentle pitch of the ship was steepening as she reacted to the shortening of the heaving wave-length compounded of the rise of the sea-bed and the back-swell, beating seawards from the rampart of the land.

'By the mark thirteen!'

Worms of anxiety were crawling in Drinkwater's belly. Hill

came across the deck and stood below him. Without words they shared their apprehension. Tomales Point was opening all the time. A guano-stained rock had detached itself from the land as it changed its appearance with their close approach.

'Bird Rock, sir,' Hill remarked, though Drinkwater knew the comment was an expression of caution, not topographical interest. He felt a swell gather itself under *Patrician's* stern, lifting it and thrusting the ship forward so that her bow dipped sharply. The sudden elevation and clearer view ahead alarmed both captain and sailing master. They were in shoal soundings now, the leadsman chanting the deeps of nine and eight fathoms. Behind the smoking barrier of the long sand-pit, the narrow placid opening of the lagoon stretched away to the southwards. On its far shore the low-lying land rose gradually, hazing into the distance and the rain-covered mountains. But across the entrance to Tomales Bay lay the whitened fury of the thwarted Pacific, roaring and thundering upon the sand-bar that blocked their intended refuge.

Then the swell rolled under them, the stern dropped and the bow reared up, the long bowsprit stabbing almost vertically. Drinkwater felt himself jerked by the mast-whip shaking the mizen shrouds. Ahead of them the smooth back of the swell culminated in a great arch of water, soon to disintegrate in hundreds of tons of roiling water as one more breaker on the coast. It entirely blotted out their view, but both Drinkwater and Hill had seen enough.

'Stand by the braces!' Drinkwater roared, leaping from the rail. 'Down helm! Larboard tack! Hands aloft, let fall the courses and t'garns'ls! Lively there! Afterguard, leggo spanker brails! Haul aft the spanker! Come, Mr Mylchrist, move those lubbers smartly there . . . Fo'c's'le . . .'

'Sir?' Comley stood, four-square, facing aft expectantly.

'Hoist your jibs, sir!'

Hill had moved across the deck to stand by the binnacle. He shot glances at the compass, then aloft at the masthead pendant and at the larboard dogvane.

'Full and bye, Mr Hill . . .'

Patrician began to swing with an infuriating slowness, bringing the swell onto her beam and rolling to leeward. As her bowsprit pointed round to the north it seemed to trace the curved shore of

Bodega Bay. Drinkwater anxiously watched the thundering breakers get closer; the air was full of the roar of them, the air damp with the spray of their destruction upon the sand-bar. Beam-on, *Patrician* lifted on a mighty crest; the huge, oily swell passed beneath her and she rolled violently into the following trough. The sails slatted impotently, slapping back against the masts with a rattle of blocks and slap of buntlines. The wind dropped and, for several minutes, Drinkwater considered the necessity of anchoring, to avoid grounding in such an inhospitable spot. But the ship carried her way and the wind filled her sails sufficiently for her to maintain steerage. Crabbing awkwardly to leeward *Patrician* clawed slowly to the north and westwards, rounding Bodega Head, the far end of the bay, with a cable's length of deep water to leeward.

As the headland dropped astern, relief was plain on everyone's face.

'A damned close thing, sir,' said Hill, shaking his head.

'Yes,' replied Drinkwater curtly. 'Stand the leadsman down now. We'll tack ship and haul to the s'uthard in an hour.'

Drinkwater saw Marsden approaching him, his hat in his hand.

'Yes, Mr Marsden, I presume you have bad news? Troubles never come singly?'

'Yes, sir . . .'

'Well?' Drinkwater could hear the slow, solemn clank of the pumps, sluicing water from below and out through the gun-deck ports. 'How much water is she making?'

''Tis about the same, sir . . . the pumps can cope . . . it's something else, sir?'

'The devil it is!'

'It's an auger, sir . . . there's an auger missin' from my shop!'

'Are you sure?'

'Aye, sir, an' both my mates agree, sir . . . gone missin' recent, like.'

'Anyone else know about this?'

'Well . . . my mates, sir . . . that's all at present but . . .' he looked round helplessly. News such as the theft of a drill-bit from the carpenter's shop following so hard on the discovery of a leak could lead to only one conclusion: the leak was a deliberate act of sabotage.

339

'Very well, Mr Marsden. Tell your men to hold their tongues.' Drinkwater was pale with anger and Marsden happy to quit the quarterdeck under the captain's baleful glare.

10 The Labouring of Gentlemen

April 1808

'Drake's Bay, gentlemen.'

Drinkwater laid the point of the brass dividers on the chart, a facsimile of George Vancouver's survey supplied by an unusually obliging Admiralty whose largesse had been prompted by the desire to see him and his frigate gone from home waters. Captain Drinkwater was, under no circumstances, to have been permitted to plead any of the customary excuses for delay. The folio of copies of Vancouver's and Cook's charts had arrived by special messenger with a smooth but pointed letter from Mr Barrow: *Every consideration is being extended to facilitate the speedy departure of H.M. Frigate under your command . . .*

Drinkwater shook off the obsessive recollection to concentrate upon the task in hand as his officers clustered round. The spur of Punta de los Reyes jutted into the Pacific, doubling back to the eastward in a distal point behind which re-entrant lagoons, sand-dunes and an occasional hill formed the border of a bay within which shelter from the prevailing winds and the Pacific groundswell might be sought. Here, more than two centuries before, driven as Drinkwater now was by necessity, Francis Drake had refitted his storm-battered ship. Drinkwater had rejected the place earlier because there was a danger of its being exposed to view from the south-east, a mere thirty miles from the hostile Spaniards at San Francisco. Now, it offered them their only accessible refuge.

'Ideal, gentlemen,' he said with more confidence than he felt, 'let us hope the ghosts of Drake and his people look kindly upon us, for we have much to do.'

'Why didn't he go into San Francisco, sir?' asked Quilhampton, pointing at the great arms of the harbour as it wound inland amid sheltering hills.

'Because, Mr Q, he sailed right past it, without discovering the entrance. Now, this is what I intend we should do . . .' He paused to get their attention. They straightened up from the chart, coughing and shuffling. Fraser and Quilhampton had notebooks ready.

'Immediately upon coming to an anchor we will hoist out all the boats and lower the cutters. I want Mr Q to land Mount and a detachment of marines with seven days' rations to occupy this hill . . .' Drinkwater pointed to a neatly hachured cone depicting a summit some two miles inland from the eastern side of the bay. 'You will establish a signal station, Mr Mount. We will give you a boat-mast and a few flags and Mr Belchambers with a couple of seamen. I want a daily runner to meet a boat with your report. Understood?'

'Perfectly, sir,' nodded Mount.

'Good. Usual signals for enemy in sight . . . any approaching ship is an enemy.'

'I understand, sir.'

'Very well. When you have landed the marines, Mr Q, I want you ashore here, on the point, with an hour-glass and a tidepole. We know the moon is waxing and the tides with it, but I want to know the maximum rise and fall as soon as possible.'

'Aye, aye, sir.'

'Good. Now Mr Fraser and you, Mr Hill, the greatest burden of the task falls on you. We will send down our topmasts and bridge the boats. I want the spare spars used for that . . . then I want two anchors laid out astern. We will shoe these, for I want no risk of them coming home . . .'

'Your pipe, Mr Comley!'

The boatswain straightened up from the rail and a piercing whistle rolled over the smooth waters of the anchorage. Above the heads of the men in the cutter, all activity aboard *Patrician* ceased. The deck parties getting the topmasts down and the spare spars over the side into the long-boat, launch and barge, the details beginning to shift stores in the hold, the running messengers, the labouring landsmen and toiling cooks all stood stock-still, pending the pipe to carry on.

Under the larboard bow the cutter bobbed, bowsed in to the ship's side by a boat-rope. In shirt-sleeves Captain Drinkwater and Mr Marsden leaned inelegantly over the side, each with a musket ramrod placed against the ship's side; they put the other ends to their ears. The operation had been repeated several times and the men, having been exhorted to work as they had never done before, were heartily fed up with the periodic whistled injunctions to stop and keep silent.

The cutter's crew strove to hold the boat as motionless as possible, the bowman bracing his boat-hook against the downward thrust of the larboard bumpkin, an oarsman stilling the rumble of a rolling loom.

'Got it, sir!' Marsden's eyes gleamed with triumph and Drinkwater withdrew his ramrod, shuffled further forward while the boat lurched dangerously and crouched next to Marsden, his ramrod replaced against *Patrician*'s spirketting alongside that of the carpenter's.

Drinkwater put his ear to the small, expanded bell that was designed to tamp the charge and ball in the breech of a Brown Bess. The dull, formless sound that was part the resonating of the ship, part the blood in his ear was dramatically displaced. It was low and indistinct, but instantly recognisable as the sound of water running through a constriction. His eyes met those of Marsden and he nodded.

'Very well, Mr Marsden, mark it . . .'

Marsden looked at the hull, reached out and scored a mark with a lump of chalk. The problem still remained to discover how far below the waterline the sea was gaining ingress. Not far by the clarity of the noise. Less than a fathom? Drinkwater fervently hoped so. He nodded at Marsden again.

'Well?'

Marsden was looking up at the hull. Above them the curved head-rails swept from the fo'c's'le to the massive stem timbers and *Patrician*'s gilded and painted figurehead. Bright splashes of colour and limned streaks of gilt were encrusted with salt and the chips and chafing of ropes, while overhead stretched the gratings that formed the shitting place for the crew. Suddenly the carpenter turned to Drinkwater, comprehension widening his eyes.

'The shot-locker, sir . . . the forrard shot-locker!'

'By God, Marsden, you're right!' Drinkwater turned and the boat lurched again. 'Haul her back to the ladder there, and be quick about it!'

Neither Drinkwater nor Marsden could contain their impatience as the boat was hauled aft along the ship's side. Noting the sudden flurry of activity below him, Comley leaned over the side.

'Permission to carry on, sir?'

'Yes, Mr Comley, carry on . . . and get two lanterns ready!'

Again the pipe whistled over the placid water of the bay, but now it was not the imperious single note of the 'still'. Now the note hopped down a tone and men swung to work again, cursing and bantering according to temperament and the liberty that the leading hand, or petty officer, midshipman, mate or lieutenant allowed them.

The cutter ground alongside the long-boat and launch which were being lashed into one huge raft, purlined with the spare spars to form a platform for heavy gear and guns. Drinkwater and Marsden scrambled out of the cutter.

'Thank you, Mr Frey,' Drinkwater called to the midshipman in command, 'you had better return to assist the first lieutenant to get that second anchor laid out astern.'

Without waiting for a reply and waving aside a pretended and half-cocked formal welcome, Drinkwater ran below with Marsden waddling in hot pursuit. It had been his strict instruction to his officers, and one which he himself saw no reason to disobey, that the urgency of the work over-rode everything else and that they would borrow the phrase of the English navigator who had first charted the careenage, for the gentlemen should labour with the mariners.

With the activity and eagerness of a man half his age, Drinkwater sped below. Every moment that his ship lay defenceless in the bay cost him agonies of worry; now, with almost certain knowledge of the location of the leak, he was at once nervously eager and apprehensive to see it for himself. If Marsden was right, the leak might not be so very difficult to get at. If it was an act of deliberate sabotage, some ease of access could be assumed; on the other hand anyone contemplating such a deed would run in fear of a discovery that could hang the perpetrator.

'Here, you men,' he hailed a working party hauling cable aft for bending on the spare anchors, 'belay that and come below.'

The shot-locker Marsden referred to was right forward, a deep, narrow, inward funnelling space immediately abaft the massive timbers of the stem. This otherwise useless space was one of several voids about the ship in which iron shot was stowed. In the case of the two shot-lockers at the very extremities of the ship, they served a double purpose and indeed, so wet and corroded did the shot in them become, that it required extensive scaling and was rarely used for action. Instead, while it formed a reserve, its chief purpose was to provide manageable concentrations of weight at the ship's ends by which, with facility, her trim might be altered.

Two or three men might, in such a remote corner of the frigate, shift the contents of the locker and get at the skin of the ship undetected. Drinkwater conceded the lead of the impromptu procession to Marsden who had grabbed a lantern. Dropping from the orlop into the hold they worked their way forward. Now the ship lay tranquilly at anchor, Drinkwater fancied he heard the haunting trickle of water long before they reached the hatch to the forward shot-locker, but there was no doubt half-an-hour later when the seamen he had commandeered sweated below the faint flame of a lantern he held above their labouring heads. The pungent smell of disturbed and powdery rust cut through the thick stench of bilge as the shot was handed up and rolled like reluctant footballs aft, clear of the small square hatch-coaming. Gradually the grunting men worked themselves lower until one swore and suddenly they could see the dark gleam of running water in the lamplight.

'Look!' Marsden hissed. Drinkwater could see for himself. A partially rotten section of the ship's inner skin had been removed, the lighter colour of exposed wood showed clearly. Ten minutes later Marsden and one of his mates had swapped places with the gasping seamen and levered off the broken inner planking. The jet of water that squirted inwards from the outer hit them like a firehose.

They were lucky. Lucky in the mist that lay offshore, shrouding their activities from all but the eyes of a few curious Indians and a drunken *mestizo* that rode, legs swinging, on the swaying back of a decayed *burro*. Lucky in the location of the leak, deliberate though it was, for by discharging only eight guns and shifting stores and cannon aft, they raised it above the waterline where it could be properly repaired. And they were lucky that the wind held light, that no disturbing swells rolled around Punta de los Reyes to dislocate their tender situation.

But luck was something realised in retrospect, or perceived solely by degrees. Nothing at the time could mitigate the excoriating anxiety that churned the pit of Drinkwater's stomach and sent him about the deck to direct, encourage and chivvy. Periodically he cast an eye at Mount's distant flagpole. Once the signal for an enemy in sight lifted limply above the post, and marine runner and midshipman met at the appointed rendezvous to learn that the ship was passing to the south and appeared not to have seen the *Patrician* skulking with lowered masts in the bight of Drake's Bay.

But it was not simply the dread of being caught defenceless with his guard down and the frigate in a state of disorder, as he had once caught Edouard Santhonax in the *sharm* of Al Mukhra, that worried him.[*] Worse was the underlying anxiety of the cause of their predicament, that deliberate act of sabotage about which there was no doubt. He had inspected the hole and it had been drilled with an auger bit and possibly plugged until an apt moment arrived with a coast and refuge to leeward to compel Drinkwater to make for the land.

There was only one explanation for such a calculated act. Whoever planned it, intended to desert. The country about them was empty; a desperate man could lose himself in an hour or two of liberty. In the direction of the distant mountains, the wooded foothills suggested fast-flowing streams, game and freedom. If a few desperate souls succeeded in such a venture it was almost certain that more would follow, that a trickle of stragglers might become a flood. He feared he would be left with a dismantled warship and lack the means of refitting or working her, let alone fighting her.

Such thoughts chased themselves about his weary brain, robbing him of sleep until, when he finally capitulated to exhaustion,

[*] See *Brig of War*.

they inhabited his dreams, assuming nightmarish qualities in which laughing, drunken seamen taunted him as they caroused with dark-eyed Spanish and Indian beauties, or stalked him through the dense woods, as he had once been stalked through the pine-barrens of South Carolina.* He would wake shuddering and sweating, steadying his nerves with a glass and sitting gloomily in his chair, ticking off the precautions he had taken to prevent desertion. Mount had been instructed to watch for a signal from the ship, so that his marines might cut off any men running from the beach; the officers had been instructed in the matter, and the one boat not needed as a platform or for some purpose concerning the refit such as holding stores, rowed a constant night-guard about them.

There had been one farcical alarm when the marine sentry on the fo'c's'le had fired at an innocent turtle, mistaking it for a swimmer, and there had been an inevitable slackening in vigilance as the days passed uneventfully. But there were Irishmen and papists aboard who were less hostile to the thought of Spanish rule, vestigial as it was; and there was a dissenting faction epitomised by the Quaker Derrick with his innocent and simplistic cant about the evils of war.

Lastly, there was Drinkwater himself, by no means unsympathetic to the aspirations of men driven by the protraction of this interminable war. Such sympathy ran contrary to his duty and his sense of the latter had been powerfully reinforced by the wanton act of sabotage, stripping from his consideration the plight of the unfortunate. In the uncompromising light of day he bore the unaltered burden of command: to bring them safe home again having first executed his orders.

'Another heave, there, bullies . . . Waay-oh and belay! Fetch another tackle, Mr Comley, and reeve a bull-rope through the chess-tree sheave and take it to the jeer capstan. We'll get a better lead . . . stand easy a moment there amidships . . .'

Quilhampton wiped his face, smearing his shirt sleeve and feeling the fabric rasp on his unshaven cheek. This was only the third

* See *An Eye of the Fleet.*

gun to be heaved back into position, though they had been labouring since four o'clock in the morning. They had eight more to drag forward from the after end of the gun-deck, 24-pounders, each weighing two and a half tons and each with an inert brutishness that provoked cursing from the tired men. Another eight of the damnable things had been hoisted off their carriages and laid on the impromptu decking of the raft.

They had lifted the bulkheads and deprived the captain and officers of their privacy, rolling guns aft and moving every possible weight towards the stern in order to lighten the bow. The after ends of both the gun-deck and the berth-deck were cluttered, and on either side of her waist amidships, *Patrician* looked like a merchantman loading from lighters.

'Ready there? Very well. Stand-to!' Quilhampton concentrated again, waving up three men with hand-spikes and shouting to set the tackles tight. Slowly the heavy carriage was manoeuvred along the deck, swung through a right angle and its wheels were trundled into the familiar grooves of its station.

Patrician had started life as a small line-of-battle-ship, bearing sixty-four guns according to the establishment of the day. But ten years after her building, when war with France broke out, she was *razée*-ed, cut down by the removal of her upper gun-deck, and converted into a heavy frigate. Her main armament consisted of two dozen of the 24-pounders Quilhampton was engaged in replacing in their ports. Such cannon could be found on the middle gun-deck of first-rates, monstrously awkward things whose movement, even in the tranquillity of a sheltered anchorage, had constantly to be controlled by ropes and tackles.

'A trice more on that bull-rope, there, handsomely . . . handsomely . . . belay! That's well there! Come up!'

Men relaxed, a collective sigh of relief swept the gun-deck and Quilhampton gave them a moment's breather before bawling, 'Next one, lads . . .'

They had started most of their fresh water casks into the bilge and then pumped out the contents to lighten the ship and lessen her draught. That first day Quilhampton had spent hours watching the tide make sluggishly upwards, marking the pole he had driven into the beach. It had risen little more than a fathom, insufficient to persuade Captain Drinkwater to beach the ship. Besides, thought Quilhampton, looking round him as the tackles were over-hauled and hooked into the carriage ring bolts of number nine gun, the leak had been reasonably accessible and a heavy stern cant had brought it above the waterline. They had been lucky. Damned lucky.

'How do you do, Mr Q?'

The unintended rhyme of Fraser's enquiry provoked a ripple of laughter, laughter that the spent officers left unchecked. It was at least a symptom of good nature.

'Well enough, Mr Fraser . . . tomorrow should see the guns back and at least we'll have our teeth again.'

'Aye, then we've only to re-rig, ship spars and boats and dig fifty tons o' ballast out o' yon beach, fill wi' fresh water, rattle down and weigh three anchors an' we'll be as fit as fighting-cocks to combat the world again . . .'

Fraser moved off to inspect the parties in the orlop and the hold, preoccupied and almost as worried a man as his commander.

'Set tight there . . . pass word to the jeer capstan . . . right, heave . . . !'

'Well?' Drinkwater looked up from the charts strewn about the table. Fraser noted they were of Vancouver Island and the Strait of Juan de Fuca. He tried to draw encouragement from Drinkwater's optimism.

'Quilhampton estimates the main batteries back in position tomorrow, sir. He has only the guns overside to hoist inboard now.'

'Good. And the hold?'

'Restowed, but wanting ballast and . . .'

'Water, yes, I know. If we ration we'll have sufficient for a week or ten days, by then we shall fetch a bay to the northwards. There are a hundred watering places on this coast.'

'What about here, sir?'

'Too brackish, I fancy.' Drinkwater tried to encourage Fraser with a smile, aware that he could produce nothing more than a wan grimace. 'And aloft?' he prompted.

'Two days, sir, to be certain.'

'Yes, but I didn't like the temper of tonight's sunset. We may not have too long.'

'No, sir. We've been lucky . . .'

'Damned lucky . . .'

Drinkwater woke aware that he was being shaken violently.

'Sir? Sir, wake up . . .'

'What . . . what is it, Mr Belchambers? It *is* you ain't it?'

'Yes, sir . . . Mr Quilhampton presents his respects, sir . . .'

'Eh? Oh, what's the time?'

'Just before dawn, sir . . .'

The cabin was still dark and Drinkwater felt a surge of irritation. The news of the previous evening that the end of their predicament was in sight had somewhat relieved his mind and the sleep he had fallen into had been profound. 'What the devil are you calling me for?'

'It's a ship, sir . . . a ship coming into the bay!'

11   Rezanov

April 1808

'What kind of ship, Mr Belchambers? Large? How rigged?'

He was awake now, his heart pumping painfully, every shred of anxiety turned over in the previous days now fully justified. This was the Russian ship, advised of their whereabouts and now enabled to catch them half-armed and trapped in the bay. Nicolai Rezanov had paid court to the lovely Doña Ana Maria, languished awhile to recruit his people and relax from the cares of his voyage. Then he must have received reports from the local Indians and Spanish spies that could not have failed to spot the strange ship, or the unfamiliar red coats of Mount's marines at Drake's Bay. Even by the slowest *burro*, news must have reached Don José Arguello of their whereabouts; even, perhaps, their unpreparedness. A sudden violently bilious spasm of hatred towards the anonymous saboteurs jerked him upright from his cot. By God they were going to pay for their treachery now!

'A ship, sir . . . that's all I am able to say, except that Mr Quilhampton is passing word to call the men, sir, quietly . . .'

'Very well, I'll be up directly, pass the word for my coxswain.'

'Aye, aye, sir.'

The midshipman scuttled away as Drinkwater reached for his trousers. Beyond the curtain he could hear the sounds of the ship stirring, the muted groans of tired men dragged early from their hammocks. Where in God's name were his sword and pistols?

'Where away?' Drinkwater hissed, staring into the grey dawn light. Mist trailed away over the water, luminous from an imminent dawn which already lightened the eastern sky.

'Right astern, sir. See where the masts are outlined against the sky?'

'Yes . . . I have her now.' The final fog of sleep dispersed. He could see the upper masts of a ship. How far was she distant from them? How diminished by perspective?

Others were creeping aft. Fraser and Hill joined them.

'I've ordered a spring passed forrard, sir,' said Fraser, 'we can get the starboard broadside to bear . . .'

'Yes,' Drinkwater acknowledged flatly, simultaneously pleased that Fraser had demonstrated his initiative, and irritated that he had not thought of the thing himself.

'What d'you make of her?' he asked Hill, who peered intently through his glass. Daylight grew by the minute and, Drinkwater thought, they were hidden as yet against the land and the retreating night. If the intruder was meditating surprise she had better loose it upon them quickly. 'Well?'

'I don't think it is the Russian, sir . . . at least not that two-decker we sighted off the Horn.'

'Then what the devil is it?' Drinkwater snapped testily, abusing his rank and giving vent to his high-keyed state.

'Want me to take a boat and see, sir?'

'Too big a risk . . . but thank you. No, let us wait for daylight and spend the time getting her under our guns.'

A few minutes later Fraser reported the capstans manned. The cable from one of the two stern anchors had been led forward and a spring taken to the midships' capstan so that by heaving and slacking on the trio of anchors, *Patrician* was turned through almost a right-angle, set within a web of heavy hemp hawsers, her starboard broadside run out and her men at their quarters. In utter silence they waited for daylight to disclose their target.

Details emerged slowly, remarked upon as they were noticed. Her ship-rig, her tall masts and the opinion that she was a Spaniard were followed by other intelligence as to the paintwork and the run of her hull, until the disclosure of a mere six gun-ports confirmed she was only a merchant ship.

The mood changed instantly. Instead of apprehension there was cursing that only a single boat remained to seize her, though they might knock her clean out of the water with a single broadside from the eager guns.

'They must have seen us by now,' said Drinkwater, puzzled at the lack of reaction from the strange vessel. As though this thought had taken wing it was followed by a hail.

'Ahoy there! What ship is that?' The question was repeated in bastard Spanish, but the accent was unmistakable. The newcomer was a citizen of the United States of America, a fact confirmed by the hoisting of her bespangled, grid-iron ensign.

'A Yankee, by God!' remarked Hill, grinning. Drinkwater, seeing them hoisting out a boat and unwilling to reveal the chaotic state of his ship, snapped, 'Get the cutter alongside, *I'll* pay *him* a visit.'

'Well now, Captain . . . sit you down and take a glass. I'm damned if I expected to find the British Navy hereabouts . . . you wouldn't be thinking of pressing my men . . . I might not take kindly to that.'

Captain Jackson Grant replaced the short clay pipe between his teeth and fixed Drinkwater with a grim stare.

'I would not drink with you and then steal your men, Captain.'

'There are those of your party that would, Captain.'

'You have my word upon the matter.'

Grant laughed. 'You think that settles the thing, eh?' He removed his pipe and Drinkwater saw that the man possessed eyes of different colours. The left was dark, the iris brown, while the right was a paler blue. The oddity gave his features, which were otherwise heavily handsome, a curious disbelieving appearance.

'You can rest assured, Captain Grant, that your men are quite safe . . .' Drinkwater recalled the hostile looks that had been thrown in his direction as he had come aboard.

'Here . . .' Grant passed a glass, *'aguardiente*, Captain,' Grant drawled, ' "burning water", made by the Spanish from local grapes. Not to be compared with the cognacs of France, but tolerably agreeable to rough provincial palates.'

'Your health, Captain.' Drinkwater suppressed the shudder that travelled upwards from his stomach in reaction to the fiery spirit. Grant's tone was bantering, hinting at hostility, a hostility that was, for the moment, overlaid with curiosity. They were of an age; Drinkwater put the next question.

'You fought for your independence, Captain?'

Grant grinned, showing yellow teeth. 'Sure. I served under Commodore Whipple and in privateers. Made a deal of money from my service too. British money. And you?'

'Yes. Under Rodney and ashore in the Carolinas. And against privateers. My first command was as prize-master . . . little schooner called the *Algonquin* of Rhode Island.* We caught her slipping into the Irish Sea to stop the Liverpool merchants resting at night . . .'

'God damn! Josiah King's ship?'

'I do not recall the name of her commander . . .'

Grant's curious eyes narrowed to slits. 'You can have been no more than a boy . . .'

'Nor you, Captain . . .'

Grant's hostility began to melt and he grinned, his face relaxing. 'Goddam it no, we were both just boys!' He leaned forward and refilled Drinkwater's glass. The shared memories and the raw brandy loosened their mutual suspicions; both men relaxed, exchanging stories of that now distant war.

'So what *do* you do in Drake's Bay, Captain, with your masts struck and the look of a surprised wench about your ship?'

'Refitting, Captain, a spot of trouble with a leak. And you?'

'A spot of trade.' He held up the glass, closed his brown eye and focused the blue one on the pale amber fluid. ' "Fire-water" sells well, hereabouts. I can't sell it in San Francisco, but *mestizos* and Indians'll be here once they hear Cap'n Jack's anchored.'

'I see,' said Drinkwater wryly, raising one eyebrow. 'And for what do you sell the *aguardiente*?'

Grant grinned again, showing his wolfish teeth. 'California bank-notes, Captain, dried hides, can't you smell 'em?'

Drinkwater sniffed the air. The faint taint of putrefaction came to him.

'Yes . . . and you get the *aguardiente* from where?'

Grant shrugged. 'Monterey, San Francisco, San Diego . . . the damned Franciscans proscribe the trade there, but I find,' he laughed, 'the customers come to me.'

---

* See *An Eye of the Fleet*.

354

'From whom do you buy the stuff, then, if the Franciscans have a hold on the country?'

'Oh, there are plenty of suppliers, Captain. Don't forget I come from civilisation. I can supply bows, buttons, lace and furbelows from Paris faster than the Dons can ship their dull and dolorous fashions from Madrid.' Grant's smile was knowing.

'Does Don José Arguello trade with you?'

Grant shot Drinkwater a shrewd look and his tone was suddenly guarded. 'Oh, no, Captain. Don José is an *hidalgo*, *Commandante* of this vast and idle province. Spanish governors are forbidden to trade on their own or their province's accounts.' Grant tossed off his glass and refilled it. 'Why do you ask?'

'Curiosity.' Drinkwater paused. It came back to him that there had been that atmosphere of hidden secrets about the *Commandante* and his entourage. 'His brother then, Don Alejo?'

'You're very shrewd, Captain Drinkwater, as well as being improperly named . . .' Grant refilled Drinkwater's glass. 'You have heard of the lovely Doña Ana Maria Arguello de la Salas, eh?'

'I have heard something of her . . . and also of a Russian . . .' He let the sentence trail off and sipped the glass. A feeling of contented well-being permeated him. His limbs felt weightless, his energies concentrating on thinking, of gauging this American and divining how much truth he was speaking.

'Oh, yeah . . . I heard the damned Russkies had fallen out with good old King George. Well, he couldn't look after his own, could he? Eh?'

Drinkwater sat quietly, refusing to be drawn, raising his good shoulder in a careless shrug.

'Sure. Now I know why you're here. An' the damned Russkies. Don Alejo encourages them . . . and he trades . . . who wouldn't? A man must take something back to Castile better than button scurvy or mange from this desert of Nueva España. You've heard of Rezanov, Captain, eh?'

'A little, perhaps. I understand he stands high in the favour of the lady you mentioned.'

'Arguello's daughter? Sure, she dotes on him and the match is encouraged by those Spanish apes.' Grant was suddenly serious. 'She's a beautiful woman, Captain, perhaps the *most* beautiful woman. Certainly she's the most beautiful woman Jackson Grant has ever seen. Yes, sir. You haven't seen her . . . by God, she got eyes like sloes, shoulders like marble and a breast a man could do murder for . . .'

Drinkwater stirred uncomfortably, but Grant was oblivious in the fury of his passion. His weird eyes gleamed with an intensity that spoke of the coastal rivalries fired by the unfortunate beauty of Doña Ana Maria.

'Why, a man would pass over a score of these damned flat-nosed Indians, even a brace of the best-looking *Ladinos* from Panama with wanton arses and coconuts for tops'l yards, for an hour in that lady's company for all that she only strummed a guitar and wore the habit of a nun . . .' He wiped the back of his hand across his mouth, poured another peg of brandy into his glass, tossed it back and refilled it again.

'And Rezanov?' Drinkwater prompted.

'Ah, Rezanov . . . Nicolai Petrovich Comte de Rezanov,' Grant lisped the name with an aping of a French accent, his eyes glaring with dislike. Then his face cleared and he laughed, a cruel laugh. 'You have not been in the Pacific long, Captain . . . I consider you should not have come at all . . . you damned British have no right here . . . but neither have the damned Russkies . . .' Grant's voice was slurred, his mind shifted briefly to his Anglophobia and then slid back to a more personal hatred. He waved his hand towards the stern windows. The pale streak of the beach rising to dunes and dun-coloured hills could be seen beyond the anchorage. 'Nueva España . . . New Albion . . . New Muscovy . . . come, Captain, it's not yours, nor Spain's, nor the fucking Tsar's. One day it'll be ours . . . a state of the Union, Californio . . . mark my words, Captain, and Jackson Grant'll be a founding fucking father . . .' Again he held up the glass of *aguardiente* and glared through it with one bright blue eye.

'Oh, Rezanov had his ideas . . . big ideas . . . he came out with an expedition under Captain Kruzenstern, accredited ambassador to the Mikado at Yedo, but the little yellow men kept him kicking his heels at Nagasaki before kicking his arse out of their waters.' Grant chuckled. 'Kruzenstern went on his way and left Rezanov in the *Juno* to inspect the factories, forts and posts of the Russian-American Company . . . now what d'you think the Russian-American Company was, eh? Nothing but a damned front for the bloody Tsar to get his claws on this part of the world. They trap the sea-otter and shoot the grizzly bear, but they can't get the bloody furs to Canton faster than Jackson Grant, and the poor bastards live in squalor in Alasky and the Kuriles. You should see them at Sitka, why it'd make your lower deck scum look like lords . . .

'Rezanov thought he could kill all these ills . . . damned odd lot these Russians. Rezanov thought he was a prophet . . . guess that's why the Doña Ana fell for his line of speaking, her being influenced by the papist church . . . Well . . . he came prospecting down the coast . . . Sitka, Nootka, the Colombia River, Bodega Bay and San Francisco . . . and Doña Ana Maria and her father, *El Commandante* . . .'

'And he secured an alliance to trade?'

Grant shrugged. 'Sure, something of the sort, I guess. They say he bettered that Franciscan corpse that passes for a confessor . . . Don Alejo at least had gold from him . . . Tartar gold, and that's fact . . .'

'And from Doña Ana Maria?'

'A promise of marriage . . .' Grant stared gloomily into his glass, the brown eye lugubrious.

'And Rezanov returned to the north?'

'Yeah. I last saw him at Sitka. I heard later he'd set off for Russia to confirm a treaty with the Tsar . . . get it ratified, or whatever the hell they do with these things. He got his own back on the yellow men, too,' Grant laughed, 'sent men and ships and took the island of Sakhalin from them to please his master, I guess. Reckon a Tsar's signature must be worth an island or two, eh, Captain?'

'And when is he expected to return, this Rezanov?'

Grant frowned, the drink clouding his powers of thought. He seemed to be trying to recall a lost fact. Then, as he remembered, he smiled. 'Never, Captain . . . you see Rezanov's been dead a year . . . just heard the news in Sitka . . . he died like a dog in Krasnoiarsk . . . left the field plum clear for Jackson Grant . . .'

Grant chuckled and Drinkwater considered the import of this news. Apart from altering the life of Doña Ana he did not see that it was of much effect to him. There was still that Russian battle-ship.

'Captain Grant, have you seen anything of a Russian man-o'war on the coast?'

'Sure. The *Juno*'s at Sitka, or was when I left, bound, so word had it, for the Colombia River . . .'

'But the *Juno*'s been in the Pacific for some time, hasn't she?'

'Yeah. She was built on the coast, a frigate . . . maybe thirty, forty guns.' Grant craned unsteadily on one chair leg, staring at the distant *Patrician*. ''Bout the same size as yourself . . .'

'What about a bigger ship? A two-decked line-of-battle-ship with a black hull? Have you seen such a vessel?'

Grant shook his head. 'No . . .'

'And where are you bound from here?'

'San Francisco . . .'

'To tell Doña Ana her lover is dead?'

Grant frowned through his drunkenness. 'They don't know?'

'They were expecting him.'

'What? How the hell do you know that?' Grant attempted to rise, but fell back.

'I was there a fortnight ago.'

'Shit, Captain . . .' He broke off to think, rubbing his hand across his mouth again and then pouring out more brandy. 'How the hell did you get into there and out again without the bloody Inquisition catching you? You're at war with the Spaniards, ain't ya?'

'Under a flag of truce, Captain. I was a cartel . . . returning Spanish prisoners. We took the frigate *Santa Monica*.'

'*Dios!* And Rubalcava? Did you take him a prisoner, or did you kill the bastard?'

'I took him prisoner. I imagine he's pleading his suit with Doña Ana at this moment.'

Grant looked up, fixing Drinkwater with his odd eyes, the one dark and agonised like a whipped cur's, the other flinty with hatred. Drinkwater was surprised at the depth of the wound he had inflicted. 'All's fair, they say, in love and war . . .'

Grant's mouth hung open when suddenly the sound of distant shots came through the open stern windows. Drinkwater rose and peered in the direction of the *Patrician*. Even at this distance he could see the smoke of powder hovering over the deck, and the desperately rowed boat was making for the shore full of men. He grasped the situation in an instant. His men were deserting!

'God's bones!' he hissed through clenched teeth, picking up his hat and making for the door. 'Your servant, Captain Grant, and good luck!'

And the words 'All's fair in love and war' tormented him with their accuracy all the way back to the *Patrician* in the cutter.

12 Drake's Bay

April 1808

'How many?' he asked, aware that he had asked the question before. Last time the answer had shocked him, now it appalled him.

'Forty-eight, sir.'

He looked down the list that Fraser handed him and then at the remnants of *Patrician*'s company assembled in the waist. With Mount absent the bayonets of Blixoe's marines seemed a thin defence against a rising of the rest. Forty-eight men lost in a single act of mutinous desertion. And the remainder were in a black mood. How many of them would have run given the opportunity, seduced by over-long a proximity to the shore yet deprived of even the feel of warm sand under their feet? And he was half-drunk and the day not far advanced . . .

'We were heaving her round, sir, as you said, ready to bring her out of the bay and someone cut the after cable. She swung to the wind and the stern's touching the bottom.'

'Thank you, Mr Fraser.' He looked round the deck and coughed to clear his throat. 'Very well, lads, if there's another man who wishes to go I'll not stand in his way. But I warn you I'll hang any-one . . . *anyone* I catch. Those of you that remain need fear nothing. We shall haul the ship off and complete rigging her. We are better off without unwilling ship-mates. Now let's to work . . .'

Drinkwater turned away, sick with despair, aware of the brandy on his breath and guilt-ridden by his absence at a crucial moment.

'Ah'm sorry, sir, I couldna' gie chase, we had just cast loose the barge frae the raft, an' you had the only other boat . . .'

Fraser's accent was exaggerated by stress. Wearily Drinkwater acknowledged his plight.

'It's not your fault, Mr Fraser, not entirely. We must worry about Mount. I hope to God he does not run foul of those men. Have they arms?'

'Two or three were marines, sir . . . aye, they've a gun or two between them.'

'Get a signal of recall up to Mount and then let us haul her into deeper water.'

Suddenly the danger from surprise attack by Russian battleships seemed a foolishly mythological preoccupation. *Patrician* herself appeared to carry her own ill-luck.

Drinkwater stared down at the rag tied round the hawser. It had definitely crawled aft an inch or two. By a stroke of misfortune the ship had grounded close to high water, and now she was reluctant, twelve hours later, to come off. Above them a full moon hung in the velvet sky and from time to time the ship lifted and then bumped on the bottom as a low swell rolled in from a distant gale somewhere in the vast Pacific.

'Again, my lads.' He could hear the creak of the capstan, the grunts of the straining men and the slither of their bare and sweaty feet on the planking. The rag moved aft another inch. A feeling of hope leapt in Drinkwater's breast. 'Again, lads, again!'

They caught his tone and the grunts came again. He heard Lieutenant Quilhampton's exhortations. Thank heavens they had shoed the anchors, augmented the palms of the flukes with facing pieces of hard-wood, so that they held better and allowed the anchors to bite and not drag home to the ship before they had hauled her into deep water.

The rag jerked again and then began to move steadily. The ship lifted to a swell, the rag surged aft, there was a dipping in the rope and the men cheered, they could feel the tension on the messenger and the nippers ease, someone had fallen over and a ribald laugh came to him. The swell crashed onto the beach and the ship shook with great violence as the entire length of her keel struck the bottom.

'Heave again . . . heave away!'

She was off now, he could feel it through the deck. The next swell passed under her and, though he waited for it, she did not strike in the low trough that followed. Half-an-hour later they had her safe in deeper water.

'Stand the men down, now, Mr Fraser. Six hours below, then turn 'em out again. I want this ship in fighting trim by this time tomorrow.'

They had not finished by the following night, for the long presaged gale burst upon them in the late afternoon. The lurid sunset of the previous evening, green as verdigris, had held its ill-promise by a deceptively mild morning; but gradually cloud had obscured the sun and a damp, misty wind had rolled in from the Pacific. Urgently they had hoisted in the boats and had recovered all but the damaged barge abandoned by the deserters on the distant beach. Even the masts and spars were ready to go aloft again.

As the wind freshened they watched Grant get his ship underway. There was a flamboyant style to the American commander. He loosened his sail and threw his foreyards aback, making a sternboard, until he brought the wind broad onto his starboard bow. Drinkwater watched in admiration, aware that Grant was cocking-a-snook at the British Navy, demonstrating the supreme ability of both himself and his men, men that Drinkwater would fain have had aboard *Patrician* at that moment despite his promises to the American. Grant hauled his foreyards with a nicety that would have delighted even that old *punctilio*, Earl St Vincent, and stood out to sea, heading southeastwards for the better shelter of San Francisco Bay. As Drinkwater watched in his glass the last thing he saw was the American vessel's name, *Abigail Starbuck*, gold letters fading in the grey mist, above which, conspicuous at the taffrail, stood a single figure. Drinkwater could almost imagine Grant winking that pale and sinister ice-blue eye.

'Do you trust him to hold his tongue, sir?' asked Hill, who had also been watching the departure of the American ship. 'Or will he gossip our predicament through every *bagnio* in San Francisco?'

'I mind someone telling me the word "Yankee" is Cherokee Indian for one who is untrustworthy. In Captain Jackson Grant's case I would certainly judge him to be opportunistic.' Drinkwater wondered if Grant might make use of what he knew to gain access to Don José and, through him, to Doña Ana Maria. 'But that, Mr

Hill, is just the opinion of a bigoted Englishman with a deal of things on his mind.'

'Aye . . . the men . . .'

'Or lack of 'em. God's bones, Hill, I wish to God I'd not gone gamming with that damned Yankee!' Drinkwater's tone was suddenly ferocious.

'You'll not go chasing after them, sir?'

Drinkwater turned to the old sailing master. He shook his head.

'Damn it, no. We'll lose the whole festering lot of them once they get ashore. Grant spent yesterday selling rot-gut spirits to the Indians, and I daresay our fellows will soon hear about that. These men will go to the devil if they have half a chance. No, I'll not go chasing after them . . . but damn it, Hill, we've hardly men left to fight. Grant said there was at least a frigate at Sitka . . .'

'But no two-decker . . .' Hill's tone was tolerantly reasonable like a parent leading a wilful child to a desired conclusion.

'You still don't think that ship we saw off the Horn was a Russian, do you?'

Hill shrugged, almost non-committally. 'No, sir, I'm more inclined to think it was a Don and is presently sitting off Panama. And even if it was a Russian, what in the world makes you think it's hovering over the horizon, like Nemesis?'

'You think I am obsessive, eh?'

'You've had a deal of doings with Russia, sir,' Hill said circumspectly, 'I know that . . .' Drinkwater looked at Hill. They shared past clandestine 'doings' on behalf of Lord Dungarth's Secret Department, and Drinkwater saw concern in the older man's eyes. '. . . But here, in the Pacific, surely it's unlikely . . .'

'*Unlikely?* What's unlikely? That the Russians are anxious to dominate the Pacific? Or that I'm off my head about a ship I saw off the Horn? Damn it, Hill, what the deuce d'you think we're out here for but to lick the blasted Russians before they take advantage of the decaying power of Spain? What better time for 'em with Spain a nominal ally, but the whole damned world knowing that the Dons are under the Corsican's tyranny and rotten at the core. D'you think if the Russians land there, that whoremonger Godoy in Madrid is going to lift a finger? Why, he's too busy lifting the skirts of the Queen of Spain!'

Drinkwater's diatribe descended to crudity for lack of better argument. Though he saw Hill could not dismantle it and was reluctantly conceding his viewpoint. He could not explain to the master that he was haunted by fears of a less logical kind.

Hill had not had that prescient dream off Cape Horn, Hill had not been touched by the strangeness of the incident on Más-a-Fuera, nor by the undercurrents of something sinister between the Arguello brothers, nor the beauty of Doña Ana Maria, nor the jealous lusts she excited, nor the ghost of Nicolai Rezanov. Some intuition, born perhaps of the blue-devils, of the isolation of command, of too introspective a nature, or too vivid an imagination, but some powerful instinct told him with a certainty he could not explain that they were in danger.

Its source was, as yet, conjectural, but its reality was as obvious to him as the smell of distant blood to a famished shark.

The gale lasted two days. *Patrician* escaped the worst of it behind the low shelter of Punta de los Reyes, though she snubbed at her cable and rolled in the swells that cart-wheeled into Drake's Bay. They got her topmasts hoisted despite it, and set up her rigging to the upper hounds. A lighter mood settled on the ship as they prepared to face the second night of dismal and howling blackness.

'We're better off without them . . .' said Mylchrist as the wardroom officers relaxed after the day's labours and discussed the matter of the deserters.

'Good God, Johnnie, you ain't going to give us a speech about "we happy few" and "summoning up the blood" are you? For God's sake we're in the Pacific, not on the stage.' Quilhampton slumped in his chair and toyed dejectedly with a biscuit.

'James is right, you know, we're in a damned parlous condition,' observed Mount seriously. He too sat downcast at the table, his fingers fiddling with the stem of a wine glass, rolling it and fitting it over the numerous wine-rings that marked the table-cloth. He had taken the defection of his two marines badly and was angry that his detachment to the observation post had occurred at all. In Mount's opinion, the desertions would not have taken place had he been directly in control of the sentries.

'And now there's a gale . . .'

'And a delay . . .'

Hill came into the wardroom, peeling off his tarpaulin and shaking his head. Water flew from his soaked hair as though from a dog. 'A delay that'll ensure the Dagoes know of our whereabouts . . . give me some shrub, for God's sake, that rain makes a man chilly . . .'

'Have a biscuit . . .' Quilhampton pushed the barrel towards the master who occupied a vacant chair. 'Where's the first luff?'

'Wandering about worried sick . . .'

'Och, an' away,' mocked Mylchrist, but no one paid this puerility any attention.

'And what does the Captain think, Hill? You had his ear all morning?'

Hill looked at Mount, aware that the marine officer held Drinkwater to blame for his absence from the ship at a crucial time.

'You know damned well what the Captain thinks; he's as concerned as the rest of us.'

'And this Russian nonsense? He'd do better thinking the Americans have their greedy eyes on this coast . . .'

'We ain't at war with the Americans,' drawled Mylchrist, eager to re-establish his credibility after his rebuff.

'Doubtless we soon will be,' said Quilhampton, *Britannia contra mundum.*'

'Now who's bleating about "we happy few"?' Mylchrist crowed.

'I think, gentlemen, it's time for sleep . . .' Hill tossed off his pot and rose. 'God grant we're out of this pestilential spot tomorrow morning.'

'Amen to that . . .'

Below his pacing figure the ship slept, exhausted with the seemingly endless exertions of the day. Only the anchor-watch were about, huddled in corners and beneath the boats to avoid the drizzle that hardened from time to time into heavy showers of torrential rain.

The night was black, the wind tugging at the ship and moaning in the lower rigging, rising periodically to a higher cadence as it shifted a point and freshened. But it always fell away again, never sustaining a promise of abandoned violence, though every time it rose, Drinkwater's heart beat faster in anticipation of fresh disaster. In such a state of mind, sleep was impossible.

So he walked his quarterdeck in the time-honoured tradition, between the mainmast and the carved taffrail, for no better reason than it seemed the only way to pass the time of anxiety and to be on hand if the worst of his fears came to pass. He was half-dead with fatigue, his brain had lost the power of coherent thought, yet was too active to permit sleep. In an unending kaleidoscope it reviewed a tumbling series of images, of monstrous black ships in the mighty combers of the Horn, of yawning caverns of water that threatened to suck him down into the bowels of hell, of the laughing mockery of the white-lady of his nightmare who, inexplicably and with a paralysing abruptness, changed into the dark and lovely vision of Doña Ana Maria. And even as he sank fantastically upon her white and ample breasts he found the scimitar smile of Rubalcava and the triumphant eyes of the Arguello brothers. Above these images the imperious shadow of Hortense Santhonax manipulated the wires of a marionette.

In all this waking, walking nightmare he paced the deck, his senses all but dead to anything beyond the fury of his hallucinating brain, his cloak wrapped round him, his eyes stark staring into the windy blackness of the night, until at last he slept, slumped against a quarterdeck carronade.

Lieutenant Quilhampton jumped into the shallows and splashed ashore followed by Sergeant Blixoe, four marines and the bowman of the cutter. As the boat was dragged onto the beach and Blixoe wandered off, following the scuff marks of the deserters' footprints in the sand, Quilhampton strode along the beach to the stove barge. He was joined by Marsden, the carpenter. Both of them stood for a moment looking at the split and holed planks in the side of the boat, the results of a few moments' work with a boarding axe.

'Tomahawk,' opined Marsden, laying the finger of a horny hand upon the splintered wood. 'I can patch it to get her back on board.' He patted the gunwhale of the boat.

'Very well . . .'

'I'll need a hand . . .'

Quilhampton called the cutter's crew over to assist and they lifted her gunwhale and braced her at a practical angle with foot-stretchers and bottom boards so that Marsden could plug the hole with a greased canvas patch covered with a lead tingle. While the work progressed, Quilhampton followed Blixoe up the beach.

The marine sergeant had orders not to proceed out of sight of the ship and Quilhampton followed him to the highest sand-dune in their vicinity.

'Bugger-all, sir,' said Blixoe, turning as Quilhampton came up with him.

'Did you really expect 'em to be in sight, Blixoe?' Quilhampton grinned despite himself, for the marine was itching to fire his musket and dispel the obloquy the returned Mount had heaped upon him. 'No scalps for you, Sergeant, I'm afraid.'

'One 'opes, sir, one 'opes,' Blixoe replied grimly, still searching the desolate locality like a hound sniffing the wind. 'What about there?' He pointed. Beyond the dunes stretched the fingers of an inlet, spreading northwards, cut off from the ocean by a long isthmus which culminated behind them in Punta de los Reyes. An Indian village, a miserable collection of adobe dwellings overhung by the wispy smoke of cooking fires, lay some miles to the northwards.

Quilhampton shook his head. 'No . . . do you ensure none of the fellows that came ashore with us run.'

Blixoe turned and they looked down at the huddle of men round the barge. The rest of Blixoe's men stood about, their stocks loosed in the sunshine that burned warm after the passing of the rain and wind, their loaded muskets at the port, the bayonets gleaming wickedly.

'No bloody fear of that, sir.'

They looked at the ship, silhouetted black against the sun's lambent reflection which danced upon the surface of the sea and was diffused by the watery mist that still lay a league offshore. Already the topgallant masts were aloft and they could see the foretopgallant yard being hoisted, its length slowly squaring against the line of the mast as the lifts were adjusted and its parrel was re-secured.

'Not long now,' Quilhampton remarked, a sense of relief

pervading him. Their luck had held so far. A few more hours . . . nightfall perhaps, tomorrow morning at the latest, they would feel the deeps of the ocean beneath their keel.

'No, sir. We've been lucky.'

'Yes, damned lucky.'

'They say that leak, sir,' ventured Blixoe, taking advantage of Lieutenant Quilhampton's mellow mood, 'well, that it were caused deliberate, like . . .'

Quilhampton looked sharply at the sergeant, but the man was in profile, his bucket hat pulled down over his eyes as he stared at the *Patrician* anchored in her pool of sunshine.

'And what do *you* say, Mr Blixoe?'

Unperturbed, the marine shrugged his white woollen epaulettes. 'How should I know, sir?'

'I'll lay a guinea you've a theory of your own, though.'

Blixoe pulled the corners of his mouth down. 'I reckon we've all got theories, sir. Trouble is, the truth ain't much to do with theories, is it?' Blixoe turned and faced Quilhampton. 'Truth is, sir, that the men are at the end of their tethers. We lost a good prize and we know there's rich pickin's off the bloody Dagoes; there's men as knows the papist's ways, stuffin' their churches with gold and word has it that there is a church somewhere about this coast where they've the bones of some saint all laid out in a casket of jewelled gold . . . and what they're wondering is why, begging your pardon, sir, the Captain ain't batterin' down these bloody Spanish churches, sir . . . by way of an act of war, like? That's the truth of it, sir.' Blixoe paused, then added, 'If you'll pardon me for speaking freely . . .'

'Yes, of course, come, they seem to have finished down there . . .'

They could see the barge being dragged into the water. Men were scrambling into her, ready to pass her painter to the cutter. Quilhampton looked again at the ship. The foretopgallant yard was across.

And then he froze. The heat went out of the sun and his heart suddenly thudded in his chest. 'Look!'

Pointing with one hand he restrained Blixoe with the other. The marine paused and shaded his eyes against the glare. They were insubstantial at first, mere phantoms in the haze, but then their outlines hardened, the sharp, squared edges of topsails, the low hulls of men-of-war standing into the bay. There could be no doubt as to the purpose of their approach.

'Come on!' Slithering in the sand, Quilhampton began an awkward descent.

'Fire those bloody muskets, lads,' Blixoe called to his platoon and a ragged volley of alarm sounded flatly across Drake's Bay.

13   Rubalcava's Revenge

April–May 1808

'God's bones!'

Drinkwater swung round and stared at the beach as the sound of the volley echoed across the bay. He expected to see men running but on the contrary, they stood stock-still around the boats, every attitude suggesting they were as surprised as himself at the shots. Then he saw the tiny white figure of Quilhampton in his shirt-sleeves, running ungainly through the soft sand, his arms waving wildly and with the four marines stumbling after him.

'What the devil . . . ?'

'Deck there!'

They swung to the hail from the foremast where topmen sat astride the newly sent up topgallant yard.

'To seaward, sir!'

Drinkwater and the officers idle on the quarterdeck spun round, following the man's urgently outstretched arm.

'Bloody hell!'

'It's those Spanish brigs!'

'Jesus!'

The two brigs had broken through the vaporous tendrils of the mist and were suddenly recognised as the vessels they had seen last anchored under the shadow of Point Lobos, beneath the *Commandante*'s Residence. They were standing into Drake's Bay, their yards braced and on slightly diverging courses. End-on, Drinkwater did not need glasses to see the bristling lines of cannon piercing their sides.

'Beat to quarters! Man the capstan!'

They had a spring upon their anchor cable; it lay slack in the water and, if they were quick, might give them a moment's advantage.

'Where's my coxswain?'

'Here, zur . . .'

'Sword and pistols, upon the instant! Gentlemen, arm your-selves . . . they will rush us!'

The deck of the *Patrician* presented a spectacle of disorder. Topmen descended from the foremast by the backstays, sliding down hand-over-hand. Officers and men ran, bumping into one another, as they scurried to their posts.

'Man the larboard broadside!'

Drinkwater saw Fraser, his sword drawn, his shirt-tail untucked from some strenuous endeavour at the base of the foremast, run below to command the battery in Quilhampton's absence. Amidships, Hill stood ready by the capstan, pushing spare wais-ters into place about the splayed bars, and then Tregembo was awkwardly hitching his sword-belt about his waist and Derrick was silently offering him his pistols.

He stuck one in his waistband and fisted the other. A thought struck him and he held it out to the solemn Quaker. 'Here, defend thyself, if no one else . . .'

Derrick shook his head and Drinkwater, his mind pressed, dis-missed the man for a high-minded fool.

'Guns are bearing, sir,' squeaked Belchambers alongside him, sent by Fraser.

'Are they loaded, damn it?'

'Mr Fraser says to tell you they're loaded, sir, as best they can be . . . mixed shot and langridge . . .'

'Then run 'em out!'

The boy skittered off and Drinkwater took one last look about the deck. It was a chaos of flung-down hand-spikes, of uncoiled ropes and stoppered sails rolled in grey sausages of resistant canvas. Spars, half-secured and almost ready for hoisting, lay at drunken angles, like pitch-forks left against a hay-cart. But the men at the quarterdeck guns were kneeling ready, though their breasts heaved from their late exertions, and the dishevelled marines, in unprofessional oddities of dress, leaned upon the hammock nettings, their bayonets gleam-ing and their muskets levelled. They had not been utterly surprised and, as yet, the Spanish had not a single gun that could bear. Below his feet he felt the 24-pounders rumble out through their ports.

371

The brigs were close now, perhaps two cables away, and he could hear an angry buzz that came from a dense cluster of men about their twin fo'c's'les. They were dark with boarders, heaped like swarming bees.

'You lads there,' Drinkwater called to the quarterdeck guncaptains, 'mark their boarders,' he raised his voice, 'mark their boarders, fo'c's'le!' A wave of comprehension came from Midshipman Wickham forward. If those three carronades did their business, their spreading langridge would tear a bloody and ragged hole through that cluster of men.

As the noise from the brigs grew louder it seemed a grimmer silence settled upon the *Patrician*. Drinkwater pierced it. He would have to loose his cannon soon, or risk his enemies stretching ahead and astern of him, out of the lines of bearing of his guns.

'Stand by for boarders! Fire!'

The thunder of the cannon erupted in orange flames and the white obscurity of reeking powder smoke. The deck vibrated with the recoil of the heavy trucks and, as the smoke cleared, he could see the gun-crews leaping about their pieces as they reloaded. But, it was already too late. So close were the brigs that the most elevated gun had sent its shot no higher than man-height above their rails. Their masts and topsails, shivering now as they checked way to drive alongside, loomed above the shredding smoke and Drinkwater could see the white circles and interlacing and expanding ripples that showed more than half his shot had plunged harmlessly between, and far beyond, the Spaniards.

But there were bloody gaps in the clusters of men about the beakheads of the enemy, and there were dots in the water, some inert and some waving, where men died and shrove their souls in agony. He could hear the screams and a weird ululating cry as some unfortunate man spewed shock and horror and the dreadful pain of a mortal wound into the air.

It was a moment of the briefest pause. Below a fast-reloaded gun roared again, followed by another and another and then Drinkwater turned. The first brig crashed into the bowsprit, locking her own in a tangle of splitting wood and torn wreckage. He could see the smoke and stab of small arms and a few bold men beginning to scramble across the interlocked spars as the enemy brig, thus entangled, fell slowly off the wind and alongside the British frigate.

Aft, the second brig loomed close alongside. There was a sickening crash as her cathead struck the *Patrician*'s quarter and the impact of the collision sent a second mighty tremble through the ship. A grappling iron struck the rail and its line was belayed, to be cut through by a marine; but another followed, and another, and the marine fell back, clutching his throat, shot through at close range by a pistol ball.

'Get your men on deck, Fraser!' Drinkwater roared below and swung round, his sword drawn, joining the hedge of bayonets and boarding pikes and cutlasses as the gunners abandoned their now useless pieces and fought to defend themselves.

The Spaniards poured over the rails, jumping like reckless monkeys from one ship to another, and Drinkwater knew that the Dons had emptied every stew and calaboose, every tavern and every vessel with men who had a mind to cut the bloody British intruders down to size. And, God, there were enough of them. If every waterfront idler, and every drunken *mestizo* in San Francisco had come, it did not explain the torrent of men that poured, cutting, slashing and stabbing their way across his quarterdeck.

He recognised the uniform of a provincial Spanish regiment, an officer leading a party of the brig's seamen, together with a ragged rabble of 'volunteers', a mixed rag-bag of races, half-drunk and verminous from the desperate look of them.

But as he fought for his life, he recognised something else, something that his heightened consciousness had half-expected. There were men from the *Santa Monica*, men in clear breach of their parole, and at their head, howling with the triumphant bellow of a *conquistadore*, was Don Jorge Méliton Rubalcava.

By the time Quilhampton reached the boats, the brigs were alongside *Patrician*. He splashed through the shallows and fell into the stern of the cutter.

'Leave the barge!' He ordered, panting with exertion, 'Oars! Come on, come on,' he chivvied, 'give way together!'

Shoving the tiller across the boat, he swung the cutter's bow round towards the noise and smoke of desperate battle.

Drinkwater was slithering in gore. His right forearm was cut and blood trickled from the graze of a pistol ball across his skull. He hacked and stabbed with his sword and the clubbed pistol in his left hand was sticky with gore. He was aware of beating off a savage attack, of flinging back the first impetuous rush of the Spaniards. He was aware too that Midshipman Wickham had reported from the fo'c's'le that they had succeeded in staving off the inrush of boarders forward. Slewed on their slides the heavy carronades had cut swathes of death through the enemy and dampened the ardour of their attack.

But Lieutenant Mylchrist had been carried below dangerously wounded, and Wickham feared another rush from the regrouping Spaniards. Drinkwater asked where the first lieutenant was, but lost Wickham's reply as he parried a pike thrust and cut savagely at a swarthy cheek, seeing the bright start of blood and the pain in the glaring eyes of a man.

'Mount, bayonets here!' he bawled and threw himself back into the fight as the Spaniards renewed their attack upon the heavily outnumbered British.

Fraser never got out of the gun-deck. From a boat towing alongside, or by sliding down the bumpkins of the after brig, men squeezed through a loose gun-port as Fraser obeyed Drinkwater's order to reinforce the upper deck with his gun-crews. This small intrusion quickly became a torrent as two, then three ports were opened. Dark, lithe men with short stabbing knives clenched in their teeth and wet from a partial ducking alongside, hauled themselves inboard to confront the gunners. The gun-crews were tired after days of exertion and the recent labour of hauling out their weapons and it seemed this influx of men was endless, a wildly diabolical manifestation rising from hell itself. They were small wiry, half-caste fellows, who wriggled between the guns and seemed utterly at home in the shadows of the gun-deck, as happy as the nocturnal pick-pockets, scavengers, footpads, pimps and thieves they were. They slipped easily inside the long guards of defenders with rammers and pikes, hamstringing and hobbling men who fell howling, only to be disembowelled and eviscerated by the gleaming knives that flashed dully in the semi-darkness.

His hanger flickering desperately, Lieutenant Fraser was fighting for his very life.

Mr Lallo motioned to Skeete and the loblolly boy dragged the twitching body of Lieutenant Mylchrist to one side. Already the pledget they had just secured was darkening with blood.

'Next!' Lallo wiped a reeking hand across his brow and took a pull at the rum bottle he kept propped against a futtock.

Derrick, the captain's Quaker clerk, heaved the next victim onto the canvas spread on the sea-chests. It was one of the topmen, a big, burly man whose legs were curiously drawn up in the foetal position. His eyes were staring wildly and his lips were rimed with dried spittle. The swaying lantern hooked above the operating 'table' threw dreadful shadows across his features, so that his face seemed to be working in convulsive spasms.

Skeete forced fingers into the man's mouth, prised open his jaw and, with the vicious ease of practice, thrust a damp pad of leather into the topman's gape. The jaws snapped like those of a predator.

'Legs down!' Lallo ordered and Skeete jerked his head at Derrick. The Quaker swallowed hard and took the leg opposite to Skeete, while Lallo forced down the man's shoulders.

'Ahhhh . . .'

Lallo slopped rum into the open mouth and deftly replaced the leather pad as the man went slack.

'Not on the wound, for Christ's sake!' Lallo shouted as Derrick, beholding the complete horror of the injury, gagged uncontrollably.

Lallo slopped rum on his hands, wiped them on his apron, and bent over the ghastly ruin of the man's abdomen. The fetid air of the orlop was filled with the stench of blood, urine, rum and vomit and resonated with the groans and whimpers of the wounded.

'He's lucky,' remarked Lallo to the professionally interested Skeete, 'no rupture of the guts . . .' His finger traced the blue outline of a section of intestine, almost caressed the crinkled mass of a protruding curve of bowel and pointed to the smooth darkness of an excrescent organ.

'Aye.' Skeete agreed with his superior.

'Needle and sutures, Skeete . . .' Lallo began tucking the misplaced viscera back into the hollow of the body. He might have been stuffing a cushion. 'You'll have to help,' he remarked, looking up at Derrick, who had come forward again, his forehead pale as wax in the yellow guttering of the lamp-light. 'You should be used to quaking,' he jested, provoking a snigger from Skeete as he produced the prepared needle.

They drew the two sides of the topman's belly together and, with a swift and deft precision, the surgeon looped a line of sutures down the white flesh.

'Missed his wedding-tackle eh, Skeete?' he remarked, finishing the stitches with a flourish.

'By a mile, sir,' grinned Skeete.

'Next,' said Lallo . . .

Midshipman Frey was on the quarterdeck. He was already wounded in the shoulder and feeling light-headed. He felt a terrible blow in his guts, a blow that drove the wind from his body and he felt himself flung back, crashing against a gun carriage and slumping down, hitting his head on the bulwark. For a long time he lay inert, the noise of battle seemingly miles above him while he fought for his breath in an interminable indrawn gasp that seemed like an enormous and unsuccessful paroxysm that would go on until he lost consciousness.

But he did not lose consciousness entirely. He seemed dimly aware of many things; if he did not succeed in inflating his lungs he would die, but the light was bright in his eyes and he remembered the sunshine, diffused by the golden mist. The upper spars that he had been engaged in hoisting seemed drawn with a perfect precision against the sky. He had thought of attempting to paint that effect of the light later, and he thought of the resolution again now, only filled with a sadness that he might never be able to try it. If he did not draw his breath soon, his hand would have lost its cunning for ever.

And then the reflex triumphed and air was drawn painfully into his lungs. Agony radiated outwards like a bomb-burst from his chest, stabbing him with fires of red-hot iron, and it seemed easier to die than to endure.

There were other things troubling him now. The sunlight flickered before his eyes as the dark and sinister shadows of men interposed themselves. He found he resented this and began to try and call them, to tell them to stop standing in the light, that he wanted the warmth of the sun to die by. He could see clearly now, shoes, and bare feet, and a marine's boots, all dancing in a mad figure. He would have to shout louder to make them hear and then they would stop . . .

Drinkwater saw Frey fall and cut his way through between a Spanish officer and a marine, swinging the sword across the neck of the seaman whose pike butt had been driven into the midshipman's guts. The exposure of himself was foolish for, in his concern, he half-turned to see if the lad was alive and received another nick on the forearm for his trouble. But it was the merest pin-prick, the point of a weapon, a long lunge and he saw the triangular blade withdrawn, following it with his eyes until he found its owner, Rubalcava . . .

'You treacherous bastard!' Drinkwater attempted to bind the grinning Spaniard's blade, but a man fell across in front of him stone dead, and he saw it was a marine, and suddenly he was ringed with steel, standing astride the howling, heaving body of Midshipman Frey with a dozen enemies surrounding him. He gasped for breath and read triumph in Rubalcava's eyes.

He saw the Spaniard lower his sword point and stride across the deck. He brandished the long blade in a single side-swipe, severing the halliards of the ensign.

The wind tugged the huge St George's cross and the bright Union in its upper canton. Slowly it fluttered downwards to lie across *Patrician*'s shattered rail. The noise of fighting ebbed away, to be replaced by the silence of defeat.

Quilhampton, willing the oarsmen to reach the ship as soon as possible, was watching events ahead of him in a lather of impatience. He did not recall until they were half-way back to the *Patrician* that he had come ashore unarmed, relying upon Sergeant Blixoe's party to maintain discipline. His chief concern had been to recover the damaged barge. Now he was running full-tilt into action with nothing more than a tiller in his hand.

It was at the moment that this dawned on him that he saw the ensign lowered to the rail in token of submission. Aghast he stood in the boat, staring dumbfoundedly ahead. Seeing him thus, the oarsmen faltered, trailing their oars and looking round.

They were in the shadow of the ship and everywhere swarmed the alien figures of the enemy.

'Fuckin' 'ell, they've taken the fuckin' ship . . .'

'Oh shit . . .'

'Put the helm over, sir . . . let's get the 'ell out of 'ere, for Chrissakes, before those bastards see us . . . come on you lot, back-water starboard and pull like fuck on those larboard oars.'

Quilhampton came to his senses as the boat turned, the jerk of the fleeing oarsmen set him heavily in the stern sheets. He did not interfere with their retreat.

His premonition had been right. They had lost the ship to the enemy.

PART TWO
Flood Tide

'Le trident de Neptune est le sceptre du monde.'

LEMIERRE

14 Débâcle

May 1808

Drinkwater woke in the dawn, disturbed by the throbbing of his wounds and the spiritual nadir of defeat. His cell was a bare room with a small, barred window, a crude table, chair and palliasse, the details of which were just visible in the gloom. The hopelessness that had dominated his thoughts in the night was displaced by the physical discomfort of his body, and this demanded his attention. He was still tired from lack of sleep, but the edge had gone from his exhaustion, and his brain began to seek priorities in the instinctive business of survival.

They had brought him stumbling up what had seemed like thousands of steps before throwing him into this small room. He had no inkling of where he was beyond a vague realisation that Rubalcava had brought his prize into San Francisco Bay. Fatigue, despair and loss of blood had deprived him of rational thought in the aftermath of surrender and it was only just returning to him in the chill of this desolate dawn.

Slowly he dragged himself to his feet and stumbled to the chair, peeling off his coat and laying bare the bloody mess of his forearm. His head ached and he had another wound on his thigh, as well as numerous bruises and a shivering reaction to his plight.

They had left him a plate of bread and a jug of wine. After a mouthful he began to feel a little better. On the table lay the ship's log-book and his journal. He remembered taking them from his rifled cabin. They had also left him tinder and a candle end. He fished in his pocket. His Dollond glass was still there together with a small pen-knife.

He drew out the latter and prised out its tiny blade. Elizabeth had given it to him. For a moment he sat regarding it mistily, fighting off an impulse to weep. He had a second draught of the raw wine and, while the shaking of his hands subsided, he fought to strike flint on steel and catch a light to the candle. It took him several minutes, but he felt much better as he made himself work.

Pulling off his shirt, he removed the tails and tore them into squares, using the wine to clean the superficial head-wounds, scouring them each until some subtle change in their hurt told him no purulent matter adhered to the tissue. Feeling bolder he set to work on his thigh. Like those on his forearm the cut was raised, hot and inflamed. Gritting his teeth he pulled the wound open, releasing a glair flood of matter and shuddering with the pain of the thing. When he had mastered himself he heated the knife blade. He knew he should perform curettage, that much he had learned from M. Masson, the surgeon of Admiral Villeneuve's flagship, the *Bucentaure*. Only thus could all the morbid flesh killed by the weapon be removed. His own surgeon, Lallo, did not believe the theory, pooh-poohing it for Gallic nonsense and regarding, Drinkwater suspected, his own enthusiasm to be verging on the treasonable.

The knife sizzled on his flesh, sending up a disgusting stink as he watched his own body burn. Only when the pain became unbearable did he stop, sweat pouring off him as his muscles contracted into a rigor of agony. He poured wine across the gaping redness and bound his leg with a piece of shirt. Then he turned his attention to his arm.

When he had finished he felt a curious shift in the nature of his pain. The insistent throbbing had eased, replaced by the sharp, almost exhilarating tingling of butchered nerve-ends. The former had throbbed with the rigadoon of death, the latter the invigoration of life.

Daylight had come by the time he had finished. Carefully he edged the table nearer the tiny window and, gritting his teeth, he clambered up on it. He found he could see out quite easily. He knew instantly where he was and the half-acknowledged familiarity of the ascent of the previous evening came back to him.

Between his prison and the distant mountains to the east, the bay of San Francisco harbour lay awash with mist. The summits of the trio of islands, Yerba Buena, Treasure Island and Alcatraz, the island of pelicans, rose like mountain tops above this low cloud. So too did the masts of ships, the half-rigged topgallants of *Patrician* and close on either side, the lower trucks of the Spanish brigs. It seemed to him extraordinary that he did not even know their names. But this realisation was submerged in a greater horror. From the jutting peak of *Patrician*'s spanker gaff the damp folds of bunting lifted lazily in the beginnings of a breeze. There were two flags, the one flaunting above the other; the red and gold of Castile superior to the white ensign. Such a publicly visible token of his abject plight took his spirit to new depths. He could not bear to look, and in shifting his gaze saw other masts, those of the merchant ships anchored off the town, and wondered if the treacherous Grant's *Abigail Starbuck* lay amongst them.

But his eyes were drawn ineluctably back to his ship, emerging steadily from the evaporating mist. Raising the Dollond glass he focused it upon the battered rail and relived that terrible hour.

James Quilhampton woke to the barking of a dog and was instantly on his feet. Rigid with damp and cold he and his men had spent a miserable night beside the cutter. They had watched, in utter dismay, as the victorious Spaniards had carried *Patrician* out of the bay. The shame of the British defeat seemed emphasised by the superior size of the captured ship, but Quilhampton had been granted little time for such fancy philosophising. His party consisted of himself, Blixoe and his three privates, Marsden the carpenter and a boat's crew of eight seamen who had been sent to recover the barge. Their situation was desperate. They had no food or water and the mood of the men was by no means stable. It did not take Quilhampton long to realise that several of the cutter's men were ripe for desertion and that his hold on the leadership of the little band was tenuous. Without a sword he felt naked, and without his coat his wooden arm, its articulation and belting exposed to the gaze of the curious, made him feel doubly vulnerable.

They had escaped from the action unobserved, rowed the cutter deep into the re-entrant lagoon behind the bay and bivouacked after a fashion in the lee of the boat. Blixoe had shot two ducks and they had roasted the carcasses over a miserable fire hidden from observers in a small valley between the dunes. After that they had slept, Blixoe and his marines on their guns. When Quilhampton awoke to the yelp of the dog the first thing he noticed was that the man approaching them did not seem alarmed at their presence. This realisation put him on his guard and he called the others awake.

The newcomer sat astride a plodding donkey, his large, horny feet hanging almost to the ground. He wore a dirty cotton suit, his face grimy and unshaven beneath a battered, wide-brimmed hat. He had a long knife at his belt, carried a gun and, Quilhampton noticed, across his curious wooden saddle-bow a wineskin was slung.

Trying to look casual Quilhampton stood and wished the newcomer good morning.

The man reined in his *burro* and grinned, letting fly a torrent of incomprehensible words and jerking his jutting chin from time to time in the direction of the open sea. He appeared to end his address on an interrogative note. Quilhampton shrugged.

The stranger made the universal gesture of eating and then pointed in the direction of the village they had seen from the summit of the dunes the previous afternoon.

'He's tellin' us we can get food at the village, sir,' muttered Blixoe.

'Yes.' Quilhampton nodded vigorously. The stranger grinned and rubbed his right forefinger tip against the ball of his thumb.

''E wants money.'

Quilhampton shook his head. 'No . . .' He tried to remember scraps of Spanish he had learned as a prisoner at Cadiz, three years earlier, but his memory failed him as the stranger's eyes became less friendly. The man jerked the head of the *burro* round, suddenly suspicious.

Quilhampton had a sudden inspiration. 'Hey . . . *amigo* . . . *agua* . . .' He pointed at his mouth. The mongrel was crouched, as though guarding his master's retreat from these ragamuffin strangers, growling defiance.

But the newcomer was not in a charitable mood. He hefted his gun and kicked the donkey forward. Giving a short bark, the dog turned and followed.

'He had a wine-skin,' said Blixoe, raising his musket.

'No . . .' The powder in the pan flashed and the shot knocked the hat from the *mestizo*'s head. His long legs kicked the donkey wildly and the over-burdened beast broke into an awkward gallop.

'Hold your fire!' Two more of the marines followed their sergeant's lead. The wine-skin, jolted or flung sacrificially from its perch, plummeted to the ground while man, donkey and dog disappeared whence they had come.

A howl of triumph went up and the seamen and marines began running forward. Realising what was happening Quilhampton began to run too. He reached the wine-skin just as a seaman picked it up.

'Give it to me, Lacey.' He held out his hands. The seaman looked around, seeking support among his mates.

'Bollocks,' said someone behind Quilhampton and Lacey tore the plug from the neck of the leather bag and squirted the dark fluid expertly into his open mouth. The act was a signal, the men clustered forward and grabbed at the thing, wine spilled about them and some reached eager mouths, though none were satisfied. Quilhampton, Blixoe and Marsden stood back from this unruly mêlée. Then something inside Quilhampton snapped. He strode forward, swung his wooden arm and scattered the drinkers, catching the wine-skin as someone dropped it.

'Sern't Blixoe, get some order into these men . . . you too, Mr Marsden . . . pull yourselves together and remember you're man-o'-war men, not scum!'

He raged at them and they shamefacedly responded, though one or two remained truculent. Blixoe got his men to shepherd them into a rough line.

'Now then . . . that's better. Let me remind you I'm in command and I shall decide what's to be done . . .'

'Well, what *is* to be done . . . sir?' sneered a man named Hughes.

'That's for me to decide.' Quilhampton faltered. What *was* to be done? There would be food in the village and the inhabitants were, nominally at least, enemies. The marines had their muskets and bayonets, the seamen their knives. Marsden also had his tools, only he himself was unarmed.

'Well . . . I think the first thing to do is to secure some victuals in the village. I'm sure we can persuade our friend to give a quantity of bread as well as the wine.' It was a feeble joke but it brought a laugh to unite them. They turned and began to follow the tracks of the *burro* through the sand.

The Royal Navy had invaded California.

Drinkwater stood as the bolts of his cell were withdrawn. Bread, wine and fruit were brought in and he was reminded of imprisonment in Cadiz in the days before the great battle off Cape Trafalgar. He recognised his guard too, for while the tray bearing his breakfast was carried by a half-breed, de Soto stood in the doorway. His face was expressionless and Drinkwater met his gaze, suddenly feeling his spirit must not submit.

'You are dishonoured, sir,' he snapped suddenly. 'Captain Rubalcava has broke his parole!'

A flicker of anger kindled in the officer's eye as the last word suggested the gist of Drinkwater's outburst. He uttered a word to the *mestizo* who swung a bucket into the cell and retreated, pulling the door behind himself with a crash of bolts.

But Drinkwater felt a renewal of hope. Beyond the confines of the stone corridor he had heard a laugh, a loud, happy laugh and he knew instantly the very curve of the throat from which it had come. He was in a cell below the commandant's residence, a bridewell for special 'guests' of His Excellency, too precious to be mewed up in the common *calabozo* of San Francisco.

'Well, Captain, please sit down.' Captain Jackson Grant, speaking fluent and colloquial Spanish, motioned Rubalcava to a seat. He grinned at the dark and vicious face of the Spaniard. 'You have come to pay me, eh?' Grant laughed.

Rubalcava nodded. 'Yes, I have come to pay you. You are short of men, I have come to pay you in men . . .'

'The devil no! I gave you intelligence of the British . . .'

'You said you were short of men, *Capitán* Grant!'

'Sure, I said I was short of men. I *am* short of men, but I'm damned if I want men for what I told you. I can get my own men in the first cat-house ashore . . .' Grant shouted angrily.

'You will take men, *Capitán* Grant, because that is what you are being paid . . .'

'Damn you, Rubalcava, I don't *need* men. I can sail this hooker from here to Baltimore with a mate and a cook!'

Rubalcava's mouth curved in a sneer. 'You have a great reputation for bragging, *Capitán*. *You* will take men . . . as I give them . . .'

'The hell I will . . .' Grant was on his feet. Rubalcava merely lifted his elegantly booted feet and put the red heels on Grant's table. 'I want gold, Rubalcava, gold . . .'

'We have not yet found El Dorado, *Capitán*, in the meantime, you will settle for men, otherwise . . .'

'Shit, man, there is gold in California . . . what the devil do you mean *otherwise*?'

'Otherwise, *Capitán* Grant, we shall have to inform the authorities that you have been selling *aguardiente* to the natives.'

'The hell you will . . . I *bought* the fucking stuff from the authorities!'

'I think you are mistaken, *Capitán*. At least, the authorities know nothing about the matter.'

Grant expelled a long, frustrated breath. 'You will regret getting the better of me, Rubalcava, damn your insolence . . .'

Rubalcava smiled again. 'Perhaps, *Capitán* . . . anyway I have six men for you. All prime seamen, just as you require.'

'Six. Good God, man, you have a whole frigate's crew imprisoned. You could have let me have more than six!'

'For you to sell to the Russians? No, no, *Capitán*, these are honourable prisoners-of-war. Besides, we need them to work cargo in the merchant ships.' Rubalcava paused, catching the American's eye. 'Or to dig for gold in the hills, *Capitán*, eh?'

Grant laughed, good-naturedly. 'Oh, sure, Captain Rubalcava, sure.'

'It is thirsty work, discussing business, *Capitán* Grant.'

Grant blew out a breath and reached for two glasses and a bottle of *aguardiente*. He slopped a finger of the brandy into each glass and handed one to the Spaniard. 'To what do we drink then? Eh?'

'To the late Nicolai Rezanov, eh, *Capitán* Grant?' And with his free hand Rubalcava piously crossed himself. '*Requiescat in pace.*'

Lieutenant Quilhampton waved Blixoe's flanking party forward, waiting with the main body in a slight hollow in the sand. He watched Blixoe and two of his marines edge forward, approaching the strangely silent village. The smoke of cooking fires rose into the air and the clucking of hens could be heard, but the bark of a dog or the squeal of a child was suspiciously absent.

There was a sudden shout and sand spurted up around Blixoe's party. A haze of smoke hung over the wall of a ramshackle hut and Quilhampton could see the rough timber had been loopholed for small arms. Blixoe began to wriggle back in retreat. There was a second volley and then a whoop. Ragged Indians and half-castes, the tiny population of fishermen, ran out of the hut and launched an impetuous charge across the beaten sand towards them. They waved a few muskets and staves and pikes, and they outnumbered the cutter's crew. Quilhampton turned to his men, but they were already in full flight. He made a violent movement of his good hand to Blixoe, who needed no second bidding, and twenty minutes later they had tumbled into the cutter and were pulling as hard as they could from the desultory shots and the shouted insults of the natives.

When they had opened the range they hung over their oarlooms and, those of them that could, laughed at the comic humiliation of their predicament. Others sat and pondered what was to be done.

'It is God's will, friends, we shall have to make the best of it. It is not the first time we have been torn from our places by the rough circumstances of existence.'

'For Chrissakes, you witless fool, do you not know that a Yankee packet is hell compared to old Drinkwater's barky.'

'Old Drinkwater don't have a fucking barky, Sam, so let's take Derrick's advice and make the best of it. They say these Yankees pay well and sail like witches.'

'And their women is handsome, their land rich and we shall find the streets of Baltimore paved with gold . . . yes, I heard the same kind of crap from a recruiting lieutenant somewheres . . .'

'Well, my lads . . . so you've volunteered for service under the old stars and stripes, the flag of liberty, free trade and sailor's rights and glad we are to welcome you all aboard the old *Abigail Starbuck*.'

Captain Grant came on deck to review his new recruits.

Clucking his tongue and pronouncing himself satisfied, he delivered them to his chief mate.

It was towards evening when the bolts of Drinkwater's cell were drawn back again. Don Alejo Arguello entered the tiny room and swept a bow at his prisoner.

'*Capitán* . . . I am so sorry that you have been the misfortunate victim of the bad luck of war.'

'The misfortunes of war have little to do with it, Don Alejo. I had your words that Captain Rubalcava would not serve again . . .'

'*Capitán*,' Don Alejo protested, his tone exaggeratedly reasonable, 'Don Jorge, he is an officer of, of energy, of spirit . . . he was on board with me, one of the four *fregatas* that your navy attacked without declaration of war four years ago . . . Do not talk of civilisation, *Capitán* Drinkwater . . .'

Drinkwater remembered the incident. Their Lordships had despatched a force of four frigates to intercept a squadron of Spanish cruisers homeward from Montevideo with specie worth over a million pounds sterling. Their force had been so equal that the Spanish commander, Rear-Admiral Don Joseph Bustamente, had been compelled to fight to defend the honour of his flag. A superior force would have achieved the same result (which was to provoke Madrid to declare war) and have avoided the loss of many lives and the explosion of the Spanish frigate *Mercedes*. Governments could forget such things easier than the men whose lives they marked.

'You understand, *Capitán* . . . Doña Ana Maria said you were *simpático* . . .'

'Where are my men, Don Alejo, and my officers? Is the surgeon allowed to attend the wounded . . . ?'

'*Capitán*, I forgot, you are wounded. I will have to send for . . .'

'I am all right, Don Alejo,' snapped Drinkwater, 'it is my men I ask after.'

'My dear *Capitán*,' Don Alejo shed some of his easy humour and his tone hardened, 'we are civilised people. They are being looked after and your officers, they are in the charge of military officers . . . come, I will bring you ink and a pen and send you some meat; we shall look after you. Good night . . .'

And he was gone, leaving Drinkwater alone with his thoughts.

'Belay that sheet and settle down . . . now pay attention. We have only about ten leagues to sail to San Francisco. When we get there we can find out what has become of the ship and our shipmates. Then I will decide what to do. Whatever happens we will have to slip into the harbour unobserved, either at night, or in a fog. I am relying on your loyalty. That's all.'

'I'm hungry . . .'

'Aye and thirsty . . .'

'You can belay that lubberly talk. We're all hungry and thirsty, but tomorrow we will find water at least . . .'

'I bloody hope so . . . for your sake . . . lieutenant . . .'

Quilhampton ignored the sneer. The boat rose and fell on the long Pacific swells that were the aftermath of the recent gale and other, more distant, disturbances. Under its single lugsail the cutter made a good speed and the tiller kicked under his arm. The day was leaching a golden glow across the western horizon behind them as they steered south-east and the first stars were visible against a clear, rain-washed sky.

It was curious, he mused, how the merest chance could comfort a man and how insubstantial a foundation was required for hope. But the disastrous loss of the ship seemed to satisfy some arcane and superstitious foreboding that had haunted him for so long that its fulfilment had come as something of a relief. And so retrospectively ridiculous had the day's events seemed, that their escape was like an *entr'acte*. This instant was reality; this kick of the tiller, this dying of the day and the chuckle of water along the boat's strakes. He sensed a curious and inappropriate contentment, as of one having turned a momentous corner. The episode on the beach had been one of desperation. He was now engaged on something of purpose. The boat's course was his best chance of seeing Catriona MacEwan once again. And as his men dozed James Quilhampton hummed gently to himself, and beat time with his wooden hand upon the gunwhale of the cutter.

15   The Prisoner

May–June 1808

Time hangs heavily upon a lonely man who has suffered a great misfortune. His troubles dominate his thoughts and disturb his attempts at sleep. He relives the hours of his disaster in a knowingly fruitless attempt to reverse time; he attempts to shift blame and then to acknowledge his own responsibility. His mind deploys logic and then rejects it in favour of vague, superstitious emotions which play on the very vulnerability of his isolation. Culpability seems his alone; he has dared too much and providence has cut him down to size. Such solitary pits for the soul are dug by circumstance for every commander of ships. In this, Drinkwater was no exception.

Although logic told him the chain of bad luck began when the leak forced him to seek the shelter of a careenage, superstition sought an earlier explanation: the hanging at the Nore, the loss of the Danish privateer, the sighting of the strange ship off the Horn, the incident at Más-a-Fuera. Even the worthless capture of the *Santa Monica* seemed but another malevolent step in a fantastic conspiracy by fate. Such fears, dominant in the small hours, could have been dispelled by a turn on the quarterdeck at dawn while the watch swabbed down and the smell of coffee blew about the ship. The 'blue-devils' was a misanthropy endemic among sea-officers but against which there were known specifics.

Some men played instruments, some invited company, some diverted their minds by reading, writing, sketching. Some drank. All relied upon the routines of the naval day to ameliorate their obsessive preoccupations. Some carried the dissolution of their lives within their characters, some gave way to jealous fits, some to violent abuses of their powers. Some bickered with their officers, some immersed themselves in trivial matters and disturbed the tranquillity of their ships. Most ultimately coped, because demands were put upon them that compelled them to submit to influences beyond their own passions.

Cooped day after day in solitary confinement, allowed no exercise beyond the tiny cell, Drinkwater went unrescued by routine or any demand upon his expertise with which to patch his spirit. He was left alone with the wild fears of his imagination. Logic told him that he was guilty of misjudgement and incompetence, and every view from his tiny window reinforced this opinion as he looked down upon his captured ship. Superstition told him he had been abandoned to his fate, that dark, unworldly spirits had been released by his actions. From beyond the grave Edouard Santhonax laughed; a great hollow laugh that brought him bolt upright from sleep, and his old enemy melted into the gentle, uncomprehending pity of his own wife's face.

How would Elizabeth feel when she heard? What would Lord Dungarth conclude? What would John Barrow think of him?

'What will they say in England?' he whispered to himself. They had become too used to victory . . .

But that was no good. That was merely another excuse. Discontent had caused the leak and for that he alone was responsible. For several days his mind revolved along this morbid orbit. He sought consolation in the writing of his journal, but after the harrowing experience of recording the events in the log, he could put nothing in his private papers that did not reek of self-pity. He began to dismiss in his mind all mitigating factors. His own culpability began to assume its own stature and grow in his thoughts so that it threatened to unhinge him. But in the end long experience of a solitary existence saved him. The learnt disciplines of combating the blue-devils came to his rescue. At first he stood upon the table and scanned the anchorage, avoiding the sad sight of *Patrician*. He watched the merchant ships, half a dozen of which he could just see. The comings and goings of their boats, the laboriously swept lighters that crabbed out to them like giant water-beetles with the hides and tallow and assorted exports of the colony. He could see among them the *Abigail Starbuck*, a tall-sparred, handsome vessel, as were all the latest American ships. Once he thought he saw

Jackson Grant, and once, quite ridiculously, the figure of the Quaker Derrick upon her deck.

It was that sighting that brought him to the recognition of his self-deception. It was clearly a ridiculous fancy! He would have to take hold of himself. Although he had not mitigated his self-blame, from that moment it ceased to be a passive response to his predicament and began to spur his resolution to transcend his plight. He began to write in his journal and in doing so called up incidents of the previous days that were not directly connected with the loss of the *Patrician*.

. . . I realised the place of my imprisonment when I heard the laugh of Doña Ana Maria . . .

He stopped writing as a thought struck him. If Grant had betrayed him to the Spanish, why had not Grant told Don José of the death of Rezanov? And if he had, why had the news not been communicated to the Russian's betrothed?

That laughter had been full of unalloyed joy, the expectant, irrepressible joy of someone expecting the arrival of a lover. Drinkwater recalled how her eyes had glowed as she had spoken of the Russian. He shook his head. The time for such abstruse preoccupations was over. He wrote on, dismissing the matter, for it made no sense to him and had no bearing on his fate.

He was woken next morning by the concussion of guns. For an instant hope leapt into his heart but the noise, answered somewhere to seaward, resolved itself into an exchange of salutes. He clambered up onto his table. For a long time he could see nothing and then, into his field of view and bringing up to an anchor slightly to seaward of the *Patrician*, was the heavy black hull of a Russian line-of-battle-ship.

James Quilhampton had seen her the previous day from the rocks of a small and insignificant headland a few miles north of the entrance to San Francisco. In the little cove behind him the cutter lay drawn up on the beach, while from the wooded slope that rose behind the strip of sand came the dull sound of an axe. Occasionally the snap of a musket betrayed Blixoe's hunting party.

They had crept into the cove to hide and recruit their strength while Quilhampton decided what to do. Sweet water streamed out of the dense woods and they slaked their thirst and rinsed the salt from their clothes and bodies. That night they bivouacked in the fragrant undergrowth and loafed the following morning away, waiting for the night. In the late afternoon they had sighted the big ship coming down from the northward. From the little promontory, Quilhampton saw she was a two-decked man-of-war, black-hulled and flying the dark, diagonal ensign of Russia.

It seemed the final bar on the stronghold of the enemy, setting awry his carefully made plan. Ordering the men to spend another day in idleness he languished in indecision. But game and water were plentiful, and the fresh meat emboldened him. When the next evening Blixoe came to him for orders, he had decided to throw everything to hazard.

'Very well,' he said as they lay back round the fire, licking their fingers clean of the juice of venison, 'this is what I intend that we do, and if any man will not gamble on the outcome he is free to take his chance . . .'

Quilhampton wanted none but willing spirits with him.

His fears were vindicated; he had no doubt this was the ship they had seen off Cape Horn and now she arrived like Nemesis. Through his glass he saw the twinkle of gold braid upon her quarterdeck, saw her entry manned and the Spanish officer board her. He could hear the faint piping shriek of the calls, given in the British style by officers who had trained with the Royal Navy. Drinkwater remembered Admiral Hanikov's fleet in the North Sea in the summer of 1797 and wondered whether this ship had come direct from Kronstadt or had been detached from Seniavin's Adriatic squadron.

He saw, too, the procession of boats leave the side of the Russian ship and, half an hour later, heard the sound of voices speaking French pass below his window, Russian officers ascending the path that wound upwards to the Residence from the boat jetty and the battery below. Surely now the news of the death of Rezanov would be made known to Doña Ana Maria? To his recovering mind the preoccupation offered a point of focus beyond his own unhappiness.

*

'*Capitán*, I have the honour to present Prince Vladimir Rakitin, of His Imperial Majesty's ship *Suvorov*.'

Drinkwater gave a short and deliberately frigid bow. Although he was curious about the Russian his incarceration had made him angry and he fixed his eyes on Don José.

'Don José, I protest at the dishonour you have done to me. Where are my officers? Why have you not permitted a surgeon to visit me, or allowed me to exercise? What have you done with my people? I had always thought the Spanish a civilised nation. I am mortified to find myself, so recently a guest at your table, treated with every courtesy due an honourable enemy employed on a mission of humanity, suddenly deprived of the courteous formalities of war. You are, sir, guilty of having condoned the breaking of the terms of exchange by Captain Rubalcava and his men.'

Drinkwater felt invigorated by the cathartic effects of this outburst. He felt washed clean of the self-pity that had nearly drowned him in his confinement. Now there were other causes to fight, exposures to make before this newly arrived ally of the Spanish authorities. He turned towards the Russian officer: 'I am sure that His Imperial Majesty's Navy would not have treated the courtesies of war with such disdain . . .'

He bowed with an exaggerated politeness to the Russian officer. Both Don José and his brother were angry. They understood the gist of his wordy accusation although they wore smiles and made gestures of incomprehension. For a moment Drinkwater expected to be conducted peremptorily back to his cell, but it seemed that he had been brought here for other reasons.

'*Capitán*,' said Don Alejo, 'Don Jorge Rubalcava is a zealous officer . . . you see, I know the word from reading your newspapers . . . it is perhaps that he has been,' again the ritual of shrugging, 'much revenge to you . . . but, well, you are our enemy. England is . . .' Don Alejo waved towards the doorway and across the terrace upon which Drinkwater had waited the summons to meet the *Commandante* all those days ago. The gesture was redolent of vast, insurpassable distances.

'And you tell us you come to make war for Russia . . .' Don Alejo smiled and looked in the direction of Rakitin.

'Yes, Captain, you are come to make war on our posts in North America, eh?'

Drinkwater turned. The Russian was a man of middle height, with a powerful physique, deep-set eyes overhung by shaggy brows and a coarse sabre-wound upon his chin. His tight-buttoned blue tunic with its double row of gilt buttons was closed to his chin and heavy bullion epaulettes fringed his shoulders. He wore white breeches and heavy top-boots. His plumed hat was tucked beneath his arm and he was attended by a tall lieutenant and a pair of midshipmen who lounged languidly with the air of bored courtiers, their eyes only casually registering Drinkwater's presence, as though at some minor entertainment offered by a country cousin to visiting townsfolk.

'I have my orders, Captain . . .'

'Yes.' Rakitin turned and with a formally white-gloved hand, patted a small pile of documents on the table beside him. Drinkwater flushed scarlet. He had failed to secure his secret instructions, now they had fallen into the enemy's hands. Suddenly it did not seem relevant that they were imprecise and vague. He had let his orders and instructions, his code and signal books fall into the hands of the enemy! A void opened in his stomach and he made an effort to control himself. Don Alejo was smiling at him; Drinkwater drew himself up and affected to ignore the supercilious Spaniard.

'You speak excellent English, Captain Rakitin. Perhaps I can say that I have found no defence on earth effective against dishonourable men . . .'

The barb went home; Don Alejo's smile vanished, but Drinkwater found little comfort in Rakitin's reply.

'I learnt to speak English in your navy, Captain Drinkwater,' the Russian answered in a chilling bass, 'where I also learned that British officers do not do these things.' Rakitin paused to let the meaning of his words sink in, watching with satisfaction the colour drain from the Englishman's face. 'But you have no further use for them now you are a prisoner. You have failed . . .' Rakitin turned away dismissively. Drinkwater felt as though he had been struck. Shaking violently from a hopeless anger, he was led out of the room. He scarcely saw his surroundings as he stumbled beside his escort across a courtyard to the steps which led to his cell below the stables. A dark shape swam mistily into his vision and then the virago-face of Doña Helena was thrust into his. She wore an expression of triumph, her tiny eyes blue chips of vindictiveness.

'So God has delivered his enemies into our hands . . .'

Her vulturine swoop had halted Drinkwater. He pulled himself upright, suddenly recovering himself before this haggard crone. He mustered all the dignity of which he was capable and, remembering the old woman's office, said, 'Please convey to Doña Ana Maria my sincere condolences upon her tragic loss.'

And as he swept her aside he felt a small satisfaction that the words had come as a surprise and caught her at a disadvantage.

Drinkwater had been imprisoned before. In the hectic days before the great battle off Cape Trafalgar, on his way in a small coasting vessel to command one of Nelson's battle-ships, he had been captured and thrown into a filthy gaol in the Spanish town of Tarifa. From there he had been taken to Cadiz, transferred to the custody of the French and interrogated by Admiral Villeneuve, Commander-in-Chief of the Combined Fleets of France and Spain.* During this period there had been a suffocating sense of frustration at the ill-luck of falling captive, and angry railing against fate in which self-recrimination was absent. But he had been within the orbit of great events, events which were gathering a momentum in which his circumstances might be rapidly altered. Now, however, the hopelessness of his situation was absolute. There was no likelihood of sudden advantage, he could expect no support, no intervention, no miraculous rescue. His ship was taken, his mission exposed, his people scattered beyond recall. He was utterly ruined, having so conspicuously failed in his duty. In his heart he knew that providence had deserted him and that there was only one course of action open to an honourable man. For hours after his humiliating interview with the *Commandante*, Don Alejo and Prince Rakitin, he paced his cell; from time to time his fingers sought the pocketed shape of his pen-knife.

Resolved at last, he tore a page from his journal and began to

* See *1805*.

write. His report to the Admiralty was a model of brevity, recording the essential facts without mentioning the disloyalty of his men, the cause of the leak or the overwhelming numbers of the enemy. Neither did he mention the breaking of their parole by Rubalcava and his men, nor the inhuman treatment he had been subjected to, for fear of Don José's destroying the despatch when it was discovered afterwards. As he wrote the superscription he knew it only necessary to record the end of *Patrician* and his own career. He sealed the folded paper with a blob of candle-wax, tore out another sheet and, dipping his pen, wrote *My Dearest Elizabeth* . . .

Then his nerve failed him and he sat staring into the empty air, fighting back the waves of sick despair that threatened to engulf him. He found he could not conjure the image of his wife's face in his imagination; it seemed their enforced estrangement lay like a great barrier between them. Perhaps, he thought, his death would be the easier to bear. As for his children . . . he threw aside the thought and drew the pen-knife from his pocket, opening the blade and staring at the dull shine of it. He had no idea how long he sat in this cataleptic state. Daylight faded and the cell was in darkness when he heard the lock grind in a cautious tripping of its levers. He was instantly alert to the possibility of treachery. To take his own life as the only recourse open to him was one thing, to be foully murdered by his captors was another, not to be submitted to without a struggle. He gripped the tiny knife and rose to his feet. Beyond the door he heard a whisper. To his astonishment it was a woman's voice.

'*Capitán* . . . please you give your word of honour you will not make to run away . . . I *must* speak with you.'

He knew the voice instantly, recalled her spectacular beauty and felt his heart hammer painfully in his breast. Her tone was insistent, foolhardy.

'*Sí, Señorita*. I understand . . . you have my word.'

How had she obtained the keys? Was she being used and was he about to die in circumstances that had been contrived to compromise not only his professional, but his personal honour? His fist crumpled the unwritten letter to his wife, then the bolts drew and the door swung suddenly inwards. She came inside, a wild perfumed swirl of dark brocade, to lean on the door, swiftly closed behind her.

'*Capitán* . . . ?' Her voice was uncertain in the darkness of the cell. He could see the paleness of her skin and the heaving of her breast as he crossed to the table to strike a flint and steel, slipping the pen-knife into his pocket.

'Pardon, *Señorita*, I was not expecting a guest.'

The sarcasm did him good, driving the gloom from his mind. The tinder caught and he lit the candle stump. The flame rose brilliant and he turned towards her holding it in front of him. She drew in her breath sharply and he realised his appearance was unprepossessing. He rubbed his bearded cheek.

'A razor is not permitted . . .' The incongruity of the remark almost made him laugh, considering what he was about to attempt with his pen-knife blade, and then he saw the state she was in. The candlelight danced in eyes that were full of tears and the heaving of her breast was not due to the excitement of her strange tryst with an enemy officer or the animal stench of his quarters.

'*Señorita*, what is it? What is the matter?'

'*Capitán* . . . what is it that you mean by your words to Doña Helena? It is not true . . . tell me it is not true.'

He frowned, then drew out the chair for her. She shook her head. The candle caught the tears flung from her eyes, the dark shadow of a wave of hair fell across her forehead, too hurriedly put up.

'*Señorita* . . .'

'Prince Vladimir arrived today, but Nicolai is not with him. I ask where is Nicolai and Rakitin says nothing.' She spat the Russian's name as though flinging it from her with contempt. 'But I know his ship has come from the north, he must know about Nicolai.'

She was weeping now. He wanted to comfort her but dare not move. He knew now that he had seen Rakitin's ship off the Horn and that in the interval the Russian had been north to the Tsar's settlements on the coast of Alaska.

'What does your father tell you?' he asked gently. She shook her head, trying to speak through her grief.

'Nothing. Don Alejo promises Nicolai will come on the *Juno* as before,' she threw up her head, 'but I do not believe Don Alejo,' she said in a voice which conveyed the impression that she did not trust her uncle. 'And then you say that thing to Doña Helena,' there was a pause and then she added in a lower voice, a voice that spoke of confidentiality and trust, 'she would not believe you.'

Drinkwater sighed. The honour was one he could have done without at such a moment. '*Señorita*, I do not know that I can tell you the truth, I can only tell you what I have myself been told.' He paused and motioned her again to the chair. This time she moved slowly from the door and sank onto it. There was the faintest breath of air through the cell, reminding Drinkwater that the door was open. For a moment he was a prey to emotions as savage as those which tore at the young woman.

'I was told that Nicolai Rezanov was dead,' he said flatly.

The finality of the word seemed to staunch the flow of tears. Truth was, Drinkwater thought as he held her gaze, always easier to face than uncertainty. 'I may have been misinformed . . . told wrong. I hope, *Señorita*, that I have been . . .'

A ghost of a smile crossed her face and her fingers rested lightly upon his hand. 'Who told you, *Capitán*?'

'An American. Captain Jackson Grant.'

He saw her pupils contract and her nostrils flare with anger and he sensed her resolution. A sudden hope sprang into his mind. 'I know he is not to be trusted. Did he not come here to see your father and betray me?'

'Perhaps,' she frowned, 'yes . . . yes, he was here. I heard he knew where your ship was.'

'Then he is *not* to be trusted,' Drinkwater said hopefully. 'He is a man who seeks for himself . . . one perhaps who would be in Nicolai Rezanov's place,' he added in a lower voice.

She flashed him a look of imperious suspicion, then her expression softened. 'And you, *Capitán*?' she asked raising her fingers from his hand, 'where do you wish to be? Are *you* to be trusted?'

'I can only tell you what I have been told, *Señorita*. I would not cause you distress. I have nothing. All I know is that you expected Rezanov and he has not come. Rakitin is silent, but Jackson told me he died in Krasnoiarsk . . . yes, that was the place.'

'He was a good man, *Capitán* . . . can you comprehend that?'

'Yes. Grant said that.'

But she seemed not to hear him. '. . . A good man, perhaps a saint . . . not like Rakitin.' Again the utterance of the Russian's name disgusted her. It appeared that Rakitin had joined the list of Doña Ana Maria's would-be and unwanted suitors. She let out a long, shuddering sigh. 'And in my heart I know he is dead.'

She crossed herself and Drinkwater put his hand gently upon her shoulder. The warmth of her flesh seemed to sear him. She looked up at him for a long moment so that the temptation to bend and kiss her flared across his brain and then she rose and the moment was gone.

'*Gracias, Capitán*, you have been . . . you have your own misfortune. I shall pray for you.'

Drinkwater recalled the papal attitudes to suicide. 'You do me too much honour, *Señorita* . . . pray for my wife and children.'

She paused in the act of turning for the door. In the gloom of the cell her dark dress and the black pile of her hair merged into the shadows, so that the single light of the candle threw her face into a spectral detachment which seemed to diminish from his vision as in a dream and he stood, long after her departure, with its lovely image imprinted on his retina, unaware of the grind of the bolts or the tumbling of the lock.

' "Whom the gods wish to destroy", ' he quoted softly to himself, ' "they first make mad." '

16   The Despatch Vessel

June–July 1808

He did not go mad. The appearance, or perhaps the disappearance, of Doña Ana Maria saved him from himself. He no longer paced like a lion confined in the Tower menagerie but stood stock-still, held in that cataleptic state familiar to commanders of ships whose duty requires their presence on deck long after the exhausted body is capable of sustaining it. They stand, as Drinkwater stood now, immobilised, faculties reduced to the barely necessary, like a submerged whale, eyes open yet in a strange detachment, all but lost to exterior circumstances so that they endure cold and sleeplessness unaware of cramps or the passage of time, though instantly ready to respond to sudden emergency.

In this condition the mind behaves oddly, ranging over vast plains of consideration, soaring above mountains of fantasy and pausing beside dark lakes of doubt, dispensing with the formality of language and encompassing thoughts and images beyond the powers of expression. Drinkwater's thoughts came and went, slipped in and out of rationality, leapt deep chasms of pure reason and became part of an infinite consciousness beyond himself. In this enchantment Drinkwater slipped the bonds of honour and reaffirmed his faith in providence. All thoughts of suicide left him and it seemed he felt, as he had once before felt when lost in a small boat in the fog of the Greenland Sea, a haunting intimacy with Elizabeth and his family.

He remained in this state for many hours. Even when the candle stump expired with an upward and pungent twist of smoke, he did no more than acknowledge the onset of total blackness without it moving him. In this trance the night passed and grey dawn filtered in through the barred window of his cell before he came to himself, shuddering with the cold and the pain of movement as he returned to full consciousness. But it was more than dawn that had woken him; his seaman's instincts had been stirred by distant noises in the fading night: the splash of an anchor, a few shouts and later the noise of impatient boots upon the steps that ran up from the boat landing somewhere below his cell-window. They echoed in the corridor beyond his barred door and he heard the guard accosted, and then the sounds faded. He dragged the chair to the window and strained to peer below. The harbour was still, the gentle ruffling of the slight breeze had kept the usual morning fog away, enabling the newcomer to work into the anchorage, close under the Residence. She was a schooner, an *aviso*, a Spanish despatch-vessel with tall, raked masts and the look of speed about her. From where had she come? Monterey? San Diego? Panama? And what news did she bring that was so urgent that her commander must bring her in so early and wake the *Commandante*'s household? Did it concern him? Was he perhaps to be taken south, or disposed of in some Spanish oubliette? Inexplicably he felt his long-stilled pulse begin to race.

The noises died away and there followed a silence so full of suspense that it set him to a frustrated and angry pacing in which his mind now boiled with possibilities. For an hour he was a prey to such mental toil that the soothing effects of his catalepsy had evaporated by the time the sun had risen and the blood noise rushed through his ears so that he almost missed the sounds of departure, feet running hastily upon the path below. He reoccupied his spy-post and saw the *aviso*'s boat pull out from the jetty and watched it go, not to the schooner but to the *Suvorov*. Later it returned and he heard the low sinister bass of Rakitin, grumbling at the *Commandante*'s summons and the ungodly hour. Then, a little later still, the hasty retreat of the Russian's boots . . . and silence.

The turning of the lock and shooting of bolts startled him when it came. He half-expected release, so strung were his nerves, but it was only the grimy, sleep-sodden orderly who brought him bread, thin wine and an empty slop pail as he had done on so many, many previous mornings. The familiarity of the ritual, backed by the drawn sword of an officer outside cast Drinkwater's spirit into depression. But he could not eat and jumped upon the chair yet again when the thin, reedy piping of the bosun's calls preceded the stamp-and-go of a hundred feet in the heart-wrenching procedure of departure. Rakitin had learned much from the Royal Navy. Watching from a distance, Drinkwater might have been looking at a British man-of-war getting under weigh and in his mind he could hear the orders passed as the topmen went aloft and the topsails were cast loose in the buntlines, their clews hauled out. On the high steeved bowsprit of the *Suvorov* men scrambled, casting loose the robands that secured the jibs. On the fo'c's'le men leaned outboard, fishing with the cat-tackle for the anchor ring as it broke surface under the round, black bow of the Russian seventy-four. And then he suddenly realised with a pang that sent an actual stab of pain through his guts, his own *Patrician* was also getting under weigh. There were fewer men and it was clumsily done, but within the hour she was slipping out of his view, following in the wake of the *Suvorov*. The last he saw of her as she swung to round Point Lobos was her white St George's ensign: only it was no longer subordinate to the red and gold of Spain. Now above it flaunted the diagonal cross of Russia.

Lieutenant James Quilhampton had intended making the entrance to San Francisco Bay in the last hours of the night. The appearance of a light northerly breeze augured well and they had begun from their refuge in good time to be within the harbour by dawn, intending to hole-up on one of the islands and reconnoitre the shipping during the coming day. But they were turned back by the arrival of a fast schooner, whose commander beat up under the headland of Bonita Point before wearing for the anchorage below the battery near Point Lobos. This obstacle had cost them time, but caution dictated a retreat, and the *Patrician*'s boat was put reluctantly about for the sanctuary of the hidden bay.

. Quilhampton fumed at the delay. He had made his preparations with great care. Although his resources were limited he knew that much depended on success. Everything, in fact, not least his very life and his future. He wished he had not sent that final letter to Catriona. To have someone, however distant, to whose image a man might cling in such desperate moments in his life, seemed to him a most desirable thing. But it would not have been fair to

Catriona and, God alone knew, she had been ill-treated by neglect for too long already.

'I am stripped to the most indigent circumstances,' he muttered to himself as he cooled his heels on the little curve of sand within the cove, 'stripped to the very last resort of the naked . . .'

The phrase pleased him; oddly it comforted him to come face-to-face with absolute desperation. He held his life cheap now, and that meant he could undertake any enterprise. Smiling grimly to himself he looked up, swinging his eyes to rake the small arc of the horizon visible between the two rocky headlands that concealed their hideaway. What he saw destroyed his resolution. Two ships stood out to sea, heading north, their crews making sail as they lay over on the starboard tack. The leading vessel was the big, black Russian two-decker. The other, he was certain, was the *Patrician*.

Quilhampton frowned. What the devil did it mean? Should he go on into San Francisco or follow the two ships? He swore venomously. If Drinkwater and his people were aboard the *Patrician*, it was out of the question for Quilhampton with a handful of men in an open boat to give chase. He was utterly without resources, the mood of his men was not encouraging, in short the mere consideration of such an enterprise was as foolhardy as it was impractical. But was the alternative any better? The plentiful game and easy living of the last few days had prompted muttering from the men. If they had the opportunity of spirits and access to women his control over them would be broken utterly, and any approach to San Francisco, however made, risked that.

And what could he do if he got there? With Captain Drinkwater and some of *Patrician*'s men they might have attempted something, but with the ship and, presumably, Drinkwater himself, carried off under Russian escort, what was the point of running his head into a noose? Sighing, he looked up. Beyond the headlands of the cove the sea-horizon was empty. A sudden, panicky fluttering formed in the pit of his gut and he felt a desperate surge of self-pity. For a moment the horizon misted and then he forced a wave of anger to over-lay the hideous sensation. Reluctantly he turned away from the sea and made his way up the tiny valley behind the cove. There really was no alternative open to him. He would have to give himself up to the Spanish authorities; that way he might survive the mutinous knives of his men.

Some time after the departure of *Patrician* Drinkwater fell into a profound sleep, his exhausted body seeking its revenge upon his shattered spirit. He woke ten hours later, cramped and racked with pain in the mangled muscles of his mauled shoulder, but oddly alert and with his mind calmer than it had been for many days. There was no reason for this feeling beyond a half-remembered fragment of chill philosophy. He could not recall its source; Epictetus, perhaps, or Marcus Aurelius, the only classical reading he had ever found aboard a man-of-war, but the text soothed him. Nothing, the ancient averred, happens to any man which he is not formed by nature to bear.

The pegs upon which men hang their reason are oddly illogical, but Drinkwater put behind him all thoughts of suicide from that moment and sat quietly in the gathering darkness of the approaching night. In such a mood a man might escape, or be shot.

He heard the footfalls on the stone flags of the corridor. There were several of them and they approached purposefully. There was nothing furtive about the way the lock was sprung or the bolts withdrawn. By the time the door was flung open and de Soto entered the cell with a lantern, Drinkwater's heart was pounding. De Soto jerked his head imperiously and Drinkwater rose.

'*Adelante!*' De Soto stood aside and indicated Drinkwater should step outside. Apprehensively he did as he was bidden, the cool, night-fresh air wafting along the corridor sweet in his nostrils. The officer was accompanied by two soldiers bearing muskets with bayonets fixed. They began to walk, Drinkwater with them, to where the corridor turned and joined the entrance gate through which the men from the boats had passed.

But he was not taken to be shot. They crossed the courtyard and entered the *Commandante*'s quarters where once (it seemed so long ago) he had dined in honour and now was brought in ignominy.

He had hoped for an interview with Don José, but it was before Don Alejo that he found himself. From various shreds of evidence, from their first encounter on the *Santa Monica*, to the innuendoes of Don Alejo's niece, Drinkwater had conceived a dislike of the Spaniard. He was as slippery as an eel, interested solely in his own intrigues, whatever they were. If Drinkwater had been hoping for some relaxation in his regimen he was to be disappointed. Don Alejo's remarks were obscure and not reassuring.

'Ah, *Capitán* Drinkwater, I see you are in good health, *buenas . . .*' Don Alejo smiled like a cat, ignoring the stink of his prisoner, the unshaven face, the filthy neck linen. 'We have been waiting for instructions from Panama . . .'

'What the hell have you done with my ship?'

'*Capitán*, please. She is not *your* ship. She fell a prize to the valour of Spain.'

'Where the hell has she gone?'

'Under escort . . . to a place of safety,' Don Alejo's eyes narrowed. 'How do you know about your ship?'

Drinkwater evaded the question. He did not want his tiny window stopped up. 'I am not a fool. You have also received news, Don Alejo, this I know, that an *aviso* arrived this morning . . .'

'Ah, but no news about you, *Capitán*. I regret . . .'

'Don Alejo, I demand that, at the very least, you accommodate me in quarters befitting my rank, that you oblige me by placing me under parole, that you allow me to shave, to see my officers and men . . .'

'*Capitán*, you are not in your quarterdeck, please.' The Spaniard's voice was harsh, cruel. 'It is not possible . . .'

'If I ever have the opportunity to lay even with you, Don Alejo . . .'

The Spaniard had been sitting on the corner of a heavy oak table, one booted leg swinging, his manner disinterested. Now he came to his feet, face to face with his prisoner.

'Do not threaten me, *Capitán*. You have nothing to make me fear. You have no men, no guns, nothing.' He jerked his head at the guards and snarled something incomprehensible. Drinkwater was marched out, still wondering why he had been summoned.

They were crossing the courtyard when they met Doña Ana Maria and her duenna. Seeing him, she smiled sadly. 'A happy day, *Capitán*, for you . . .'

407

He frowned. Was she mocking him? 'For me, *Señorita*? How so?'

De Soto's forbearance snapped and he disregarded the speaker's rank and connections, shouting the girl to silence and propelling Drinkwater suddenly forward with a blow on his shoulder that sent a wave of agony through him. He stumbled and all but fell, the pain blotting out all sensibility until he found himself once more in his cell and heard the heavy, final thud of bolts driving home. It was only then that he tried to make some sense out of the interview and its inexplicable sequel.

'Easy, lads, easy . . .'

The boat ghosted along, only a whisper of water under her bow accompanied by the drip of water from the motionless oar-blades. The dark hull of an anchored ship loomed over them; it was one of the anchored merchantmen and the noise of a squeeze-box and some languidly drunken singing came to them. Lights shone from her stern cabin and a gale of laughter told where her master entertained. The germ of an idea formed in Lieutenant Quilhampton's brain, but this vessel was too big by far, perhaps they would find something smaller, more suitable further into the anchorage. He did not have to surrender; at least not yet.

The need for caution receded now they were in the anchorage. There were other boats about, ferrying liberty-men to and from their ships. It was a contrast to the naval anchorages he was familiar with, where the fear of desertion made every ship row a guard and the passage of boats at night was strictly controlled. He began to relax, to cast about for a likely target, a small ship, like a schooner, easily manageable by a handful of desperate men. If he could strike quickly, divert his men's minds away from the thought of stews and whores he might, he just might . . .

'Sir . . .' the man at bow oar hissed in the darkness.

'What?'

'Listen, sir . . .'

He heard the voice immediately. 'Hold water!' he commanded, and when the boat lay stopped he cocked his ear again, getting his bearings.

The querulous voice was indisputably Yankee.

'Well, Friend, he was here but a minute ago . . . perhaps he pis-
seth against a wall . . .'

'Jesus, I thought you mother-fuckers were supposed to be seamen! I ain't a whit surprised the British are losing ships if they're
driven to manning 'em with canting Quakers . . . you tell him to lay
aft when he's finished for Chrissakes . . .'

'Thou takest too much in vain the Lord's name, Friend . . .'

A snigger of recognition came from the oarsmen, half amused,
half admired at the Quaker's undaunted attitude. If Derrick was
aboard the ship under whose stern they had stopped, who else
might there be? Or had Derrick deserted alone, prompted by those
ridiculous pacifistic views of his? The questions tumbled through
Quilhampton's mind and he leaned forward.

'Give way, easy, lads, and keep deathly quiet,' he whispered, and
the oars dipped into the water again. In the stern, Quilhampton
pulled the tiller hard against his chest and swung the boat's bow
towards the *Abigail Starbuck*.

'Oars . . .'

The men ceased rowing and the boat glided on. A tinkling
sound could be heard and, peering ahead, Quilhampton caught the
faint silver arc of urine falling from the height of a ship's
forechains. As the boat slid under the bulk of the ship's hull he saw,
against the slightly lighter darkness of the sky, the shape of a man
buttoning the flap of his trousers. As the boat got closer and the
man turned inboard his face was suddenly illuminated. Caught
with one foot on the rail as he swung round he paused.

'I heard him,' said a deep-burred and familiar voice, 'a right
bloody bucko bastard of a Yankee Dandy . . .'

Quilhampton drew a breath. If the man holding the lantern was
not Derrick, or there were others within earshot they might be
ruined, but the moment was not to be lost and the occupants of the
boat were all registering recognition and surprise so that their own
silence could not be relied upon.

'Tregembo!' Quilhampton hissed.

Looking up, Quilhampton saw the man turn and peer down,
saw a second head and a lantern.

'Put the fucking light out!' said one of the oarsmen.

'Tregembo, it's me, Mr Quilhampton . . .'

'By Gar . . . quick, Derrick, ower we go, afore that Yankee sees us . . .'

'Wait! Are there more of you?'

'Aye, but don't wait, zur . . .'

Tregembo was already clambering over the side, though Derrick appeared to hesitate. The Cornishman, his legs dangling from the chains, seeking a foot-hold in the boat, looked up.

'Come on, damn 'ee, you can pull an oar if you can't fight!'

Someone stood and reached up. Tregembo fell heavily among grunts from his shipmates and the boat rocked dangerously and then Derrick was following and, a minute later, the long-boat was pulling cautiously off into the darkness.

When sufficient distance had been put between them and the *Abigail Starbuck* Quilhampton ordered them to cease rowing.

'Lay aft, Tregembo, and report.'

'Willingly, zur.' Tregembo struggled down the boat as the men pulled aside for him until his scarred, grizzled and dependable features peered into Quilhampton's face.

'Thank God you came, zur . . . I'd been meditating on swimming ashore once I knowed where they'd got the Cap'n . . .'

'Where *is* he, Tregembo, d' you know?'

'Aye, zur, Mister Derrick, 'e found out. That was the Yankee hell-ship *Abigail Sommat-or-other* and if her mate hadn't had a whore in his bunk we'd not have had the liberty for a piss to remind us we were free men . . .'

'The captain, Tregembo . . .'

'He's a prisoner in the Governor's Residence,' put in Derrick. 'I overheard the mate and Captain Grant discussing the matter when the *Patrician* left harbour this morning.'

'I saw that,' Quilhampton cut the Quaker short. 'Do you know the way to this Residence?'

'It's above the boat jetty, zur, where we was anchored before.'

'Very well . . . stand-by . . . give way together . . .'

As the boat once more gathered way, James Quilhampton turned her in for the shore, conjuring up from his memory the lie of the land above the landing-jetty.

Drinkwater shut the log and doused the candle as he heard the key turn cautiously in the lock. It seemed an age before the bolts were drawn back, by which time her appearance did not surprise him.

'*Capitán* . . . ?'

'Here, *Señorita* . . .'

'You do not know the news? They did not tell you? Not even my father?'

'I have not seen your father, *Señorita* . . .'

'Ahhh . . .' she seemed relieved.

'But what news is this . . . ?'

'Ana Maria?' The voice of Doña Helena rasped anxiously through the night and the hurried tap of her questing feet approached.

'Please, *Capitán*, you go now . . . for our honour, you must go, it is not right . . .'

'But I do not understand . . . you will be in trouble . . . there is no need . . .'

'Please, *Capitán*,' she beseeched him and he heard the prattle of the duenna's voice suddenly louder, rattling something to someone else in quick, urgent Spanish. He heard the lugubrious tone of the Franciscan father and then their shadows leapt large along the wall of the corridor.

'*Vamos!* . . . go quick . . .' She stood aside and the priest loomed in the doorway as Doña Helena screeched something. For the briefest fraction of a second indecision held the four of them in a trance and then Drinkwater acted. The priest held up an imperious hand, but Drinkwater brushed him aside and made for the end of the corridor. The guard was nowhere to be seen. Perhaps too long acquaintance with the English captain had made them careless, perhaps Doña Ana Maria had bribed them, he neither knew nor troubled to think of it, only an iron gate separated him from the terraced garden of oleanders and orange trees through which the path to the boat-jetty led downwards.

It was unlocked. Flinging it open he began to run, his muscles cracking under the unaccustomed strain of rapid descent.

Quilhampton remembered the battery that lay between the boat-jetty and the Residence above. It was not on the direct path, but lay off to the right, occupying a natural bastion, an outcrop of rock behind which earth-falls had filled in a roughly level area which the hand of man had improved with stone flags so that it supported heavy cannon mounted behind embrasures of stone.

He knew it would be guarded and his approach to the jetty was conducted with caution. He was astonished, therefore, when the noises of pursuit, of shouting and brief glimpses of lights came from above and, as the bowman jumped ashore with the boat-painter, he considered immediate withdrawal. But the knowledge that Drinkwater himself was up there somewhere made him stay his hand. He had quizzed both Derrick and Tregembo concerning the disappearance of the ship. They both agreed she had been carried off under Russian colours in full view of all the merchantmen anchored in the harbour; but he was unable to shake them from their conviction that Drinkwater had remained in San Francisco, a prisoner of the Spanish authorities. It occurred to Quilhampton that both men had a personal interest in the fate of the captain, and both were comparatively indifferent to that of the ship herself. If their information was correct and he had judged their motives correctly, then perhaps fortune might be persuaded to turn in their favour.

The noises coming from above certainly indicated that she was not running in the favour of their enemies. A shot rang out, perhaps from the battery, and the string of lights and the noise of pursuit came lower down the hillside. Whoever was running was important enough to warrant a full-scale attempt at recapture.

'Sergeant Blixoe, your best shot to try and hit the leading lantern as soon as he can.'

'Very good, sir.'

There was a stir of excitement in the boat and Quilhampton said, 'Sing, lads, sing loud and clear . . . sing *Spanish Ladies* . . . sing, damn you!'

It was a faltering start and they had no clue as to Quilhampton's crazy idea but something infectiously insane about his own cracked and tuneless voice made them join him.

'Farewell and adieu to you Spanish ladies,
Farewell and adieu to you ladies of Spain . . .'

They could afford to sing in English and indicate their presence to whoever was crashing through the bushes above them with musket balls singing into the night after him. There were enough Americans in port to justify a drunken outburst and no one on a clandestine mission would betray their presence with such impunity. What would happen if they had to suddenly conceal themselves again did not occur to Quilhampton. He had staked all on a single throw, arguing that only one man could be important enough to chase with such energy. It simply never occurred to him otherwise.

Beside him the kneeling marine fired. The snap and flash of the musket punctuated the old sea-song causing a missed beat, but they picked it up again.

'. . . orders to sail for Old England
and we hope in a short-time to see you again.'

Drinkwater heard the singing, taking comfort from the sound of drunken seamen that indicated the probable presence of a boat below. If there had been no boat he would have made for the town where the merchantmen's boats lay, but the sound of so ancient a sea-song beckoned him, and he tripped and stumbled as the first bullet whined past him. It is difficult to hit a target downhill, easier to fire upwards, but the shot that he saw from below made him check his flight. For a moment he was confused, then he heard an anguished roar from above and his heart leapt with hope. It was impossible, but surely whoever fired that lone shot had been aiming at his pursuers. He did not consider the matter an instant longer, but plunged headlong downwards.

Quilhampton saw the figure the second it broke cover from the undergrowth and challenged them.

'Who the hell are you?'

The voice was recognisable, the raw rasp of it familiar to men whom it had commanded for five years and more.

'Friends, Captain, hurry . . . !'

'Mr Q?'

'The same, sir.'

'Well met, by heaven, into the boat, quick . . . why this is *Patrician*'s cutter!'

They tumbled into the boat, Blixoe firing another shot at the Spaniards who were but a few yards behind Drinkwater. The oarsmen needed no special bidding to effort. They had swung the boat round and bent to their task with back-breaking energy that made the oar-looms bend and crack under the strain.

'There's a long-waisted Spanish *aviso*-schooner hard-by, Mr Q,' Drinkwater pointed into the night where two raked masts were just perceptible against the sky, 'and I judge most of her people to be ashore.'

'Aye, aye, sir . . . knives and foot-stretchers, lads, we're almost up to her . . . are you reloaded, Mr Blixoe?'

'We've two cartridges that ain't spoiled, sir . . .'

'Cold steel then . . .' Quilhampton turned to Drinkwater. 'I've no sword, sir . . .'

'Nor me, James . . .'

And then they bumped alongside the low hull of the schooner and were scrambling up her side, finding toe-holds on her gunsills and swinging their legs over the rail.

The anchor watch had been alerted by the shots ashore, no more than two hundred yards away. But they had made the error of going and reporting the matter. The *aviso* had been left in the hands of a young midshipman, newly out from Spain, and her crew were largely *mestizos*, unused to real action on a great ocean that their employers were apt to consider their own exclusive preserve. Only the midshipman put up a fight, to be skewered by Blixoe's bayonet for his gallantry. Within minutes the schooner had changed hands.

There were no boats at the jetty beyond a small dinghy with insufficient capacity for immediate pursuit. But the precise circumstances of Captain Drinkwater's disappearance were somewhat confusing to the pursuers, mixed as they were with treachery within the Residence. Neither did the Spanish immediately appreciate the danger their *aviso* lay in, so that Drinkwater and his companions were able to slip the cable of the schooner and make sail unmolested.

They felt the bow rise to the onshore swell from the mighty Pacific as soon as they rounded Point Lobos. The *aviso* heeled over as they belayed the halliards and Drinkwater came aft to Quilhampton at the helm.

'How does she steer, James?'

'Like a witch!' answered Quilhampton, his eyes dancing in the light from the binnacle.

'Like a witch, eh?' repeated Drinkwater in a lower voice, recalling another face lit from below by a poor glim. How would she fare now, he wondered? And what *was* the fateful news that had caused her to liberate him?

It was then that it occurred to him that had they not killed the midshipman they might have discovered it. 'Too late now,' he muttered sadly.

'Yes,' Quilhampton's voice agreed enthusiastically, 'they're much too late now to catch us.'

Drinkwater opened his mouth to explain, thought better of it and grunted agreement. 'D'you think we can find anything to eat aboard this hooker, Mr Q?'

17 The Virgin of Fair Weather

July 1808

If the vicissitudes of the sea-service had thrown Nathaniel Drinkwater ignominiously out of one of the most powerful frigates in the Royal Navy, then the inexplicable actions of a beautiful woman had restored him to a position of some influence. He had hardly dared hope for such a sudden and apparently fortuitous reversal in his situation as had been precipitated by Doña Ana Maria's actions and consolidated by the appearance of James Quilhampton and his forlorn hope.

The sudden, easy taking of the schooner still struck him as an equally lucky link in the chain of events which had led him to liberty; he had yet to learn that there was more of cause and effect, and less of coincidence in these events than he then supposed. But, for the moment, little could dull the relief and joy that filled him as he watched the dawn over the distant coast and shivered in the fresh westerly breeze that blew onshore and under the influence of which the narrow gutted schooner laid her seething course northwards.

Drinkwater had to acknowledge that she was a smart, fast and rakish craft. Her long, low hull mounted twelve 6-pounder carriage guns, mere pop-guns that could serve to over-awe native craft or a merchantman, but amidships, where traditionally she might have carried her boats, she mounted a heavy carronade, the Spanish equivalent of a 32-pounder, he judged, curiously rigged on a rotating slide somewhat in the manner of the mortars in the old bomb-vessel *Virago*, so that the gun might be brought to bear on a target on either side if due care were taken of the intervening rigging. This powerful weapon gave Drinkwater fresh cause for hope, for with it he might yet achieve something worthwhile and there was only one task that demanded his relentless attention until it was accomplished, the recapture of the *Patrician*.

He looked aloft. The two raked masts carried huge gaff-rigged sails, the after one was capable of bearing a maintopsail which he could set at full daylight when the watch changed. For the time being he was content to act as officer of the watch as well as commander of his pathetically small crew. Still, they seemed happy enough, basking in their change of fortune and making free with the personal effects they had discovered on board. Properly, Drinkwater should have secured these, but he was not kindly disposed towards the Spanish of San Francisco after the breaking of their parole, the shameful way he had been held captive and the mature suspicion that Don Alejo and Rubalcava, at least, were involved in some action which, to them, justified their dishonourable treatment of their prisoners. Besides, the poor devils who had arrived with Quilhampton had only the rags they stood up in, and Drinkwater was far too considerate of his men's welfare to let the conventions of protecting private property stand in the way of their well-being.

'Forward there!'

A man named Lacey stood up from where he had been huddling under the weather rail dodging spray. 'Sir?'

'Ease the foresheets a little . . .'

'Aye, aye, sir.'

Drinkwater eased the helm and the schooner's head fell off the wind a point or two, her long bowsprit pointing at a shallower angle to the line of the coast.

'Ease the mainsheet,' he said to the seaman who stood at the helm beside him.

He felt the pressure on the rudder ease as the sheaves squealed slightly with the strain on the heavy mainsheet.

'She'm a flyer, sir,' said the man conversationally, resuming his post at Drinkwater's side and Drinkwater agreed, reflecting upon the alteration in their circumstances. Aboard the *Patrician* the man would not have dared address his commander in such familiar tones; here, doing duty beside him, it was the most natural thing in the world.

'She certainly is, Potter, and off the wind, on a reach, she'll fly faster than the wind.'

Potter digested this intelligence with a frown, but Drinkwater did not expand upon this curiosity of natural law. Instead he sowed the seeds of his intentions.

'Now we're well out of sight of the Dons, we'll close the coast again. That'll be Point Reyes, where we were cruising when we discovered that leak,' he pointed at the blue line of the Californian shore.

'Ahhh . . .' Potter nodded, pleased to be taken into the captain's confidence.

'Now what I think we should do, Potter, is chase north and find out what those damned Russians have done with our ship and shipmates.' Drinkwater paused and looked sideways at the man, an able-seaman and once rated captain of the foretop. 'What d'you think of that, eh?'

'Few more men'd be handy, sir, begging your pardon for saying so.'

'Yes, they would, but we've got a fair wind, a fast ship and at least one heavy cannon to play with . . . and we've got something else, Potter . . . surprise!'

They fell silent again and then Potter said, 'Sir . . . that leak, sir . . . it were done a'purpose.'

Drinkwater did not take his eyes off the horizon, though he knew Potter was eyeing him sidelong. 'I know,' he said shortly, then turned and smiled disarmingly at the seaman, 'and I'd hang the scum that did it if I had proof, Potter; but that's of no avail now. Do you cut along and call out the watch below. It's time you and I got some rest.' He took the helm and watched Potter scuttle forward.

James Quilhampton came on deck a few minutes later. He was smiling broadly, for it was a beautiful morning with clear visibility and a fresh breeze that made the blue seas turn white as they broke and from which a school of dolphins leapt and gambolled and ran in and out under the cutwater of the racing schooner.

'Morning, sir.'

'Morning, James. We'll set proper watches now. You and Tregembo, Marsden, Blixoe and one marine, together with the four seamen I've just called to form the larboard watch. I'll head the starboard with the rest . . . seventeen of us in all. I'm going to locate the *Patrician* if I can, James, and retake her . . .'

'We could do with a few more men for that, sir,' remarked Quilhampton.

Drinkwater nodded. 'Yes, Potter's just told me that, but what we lack in men we might make up for with stealth and surprise.'

'Not to mention that confounded great "smasher" amidships . . .'

Drinkwater grinned. 'We are of one mind, James . . . here you are, head in for the coast. Keep a sharp lookout for sails or masts. I've no idea what those damned Russians intend to do with the ship, but I don't want to miss her for want of a pair of eyes.'

'Very well, sir.'

'I'm going below to get some sleep.'

They coasted northwards for over a week without the sight of a single sail. The year was well advanced and Drinkwater supposed that merchant ships were either finishing their lading in Alaskan waters and not yet ready to sail southwards, or that Russian ships loading provisions for the hardships of the northern winter had not yet departed from the Spanish settlements of California. Then, as they stood out to sea to round what the English navigators called Cape Disappointment but which on Drinkwater's Spanish chart bore no name at all, they saw the masts of some ships hidden behind a low spit of land to the southward of the Cape.

'The mouth of the Columbia River, James . . . hoist Spanish colours and stand inshore. We'll take a closer look.'

It took them four hours to work their way up into the estuary of the river against a considerable current which, fuelled by the melting snows of distant mountains to the eastward, streamed out into the ocean with an impressive velocity. But the schooner stood inshore and the low point to the southward opened slowly to starboard, to reveal a shallow lagoon and a secondary headland from which the first grew in a long sandy spit. This headland was covered with woods in which a clearing had been made and the stockade of a primitive fort erected. Above the fort flew the colours of Tsar Alexander I, though neither of the two vessels at anchor were larger than brigs.

'A Russian settlement, by Heaven,' muttered Drinkwater,

staring through his looted glass at the group of curious men drawn up by a pair of boats on the beach.

'Fetch us an anchor, James, close alongside the outer of those two brigs.'

'Aye, aye, sir.'

Drinkwater watched Quilhampton go forward, his wooden arm hanging incongruously below the Spanish uniform coat that was far too short for his long, lean frame. He grinned at the young man, and caught the mood of high excitement that infected his men. There were only a handful of them, but they had had time to settle well and, with the single exception of Derrick, were spoiling for a fight.

'Brail all . . .'

Quilhampton passed the agreed order quietly. The jibs fell, fluttering along the bowsprit with a rasp of their hanks on the stays, and a man clambered leisurely out along the spar to restrain them with a roband or two, while the main and foresails were brailed to the masts, their gaffs, standing spars. Against the current the schooner lost way and was brought to an anchor and a short scope of cable. Then they hauled the cutter alongside from its position towing astern. With some show it was manned and a Spanish boat ensign found and its staff stuck in the verdigrised brass ferrule in the cutter's rudder-stock. Wearing an oddly cockaded Spanish bicorne Drinkwater took his place in the stern, a large light-cavalry sabre, that he had found hanging on the schooner's cabin bulkhead, held between his knees. A brace of primed, cocked and loaded pistols lay on the stern sheets beside him, while the oarsmen each had a cutlass from the schooner's capacious arms-chest concealed beneath their thwarts.

They cleared the stern of the schooner and Drinkwater looked up. 'God bless my soul!'

In a beautifully carved scroll worked beneath the cabin windows he read her name for the first time: *Virgen de la Bonanza*. Several men caught the direction of his eye, grinning at the first word which was comprehensible to them. What the rest meant none of them knew. Drinkwater's face stiffened. They were supposed to be masquerading as Spaniards!

The group on the beach had grown by the time they reached it.

About a score of villainously bearded and greasily apparelled men stood idly watching them. He took them all to be Russians, except perhaps one, a late arrival wearing the buckskins and moccasins of a mountain-man, the likes of which he had once seen, long ago in the Loyalist militia in New York. He was clearly something of a wonder to the others, for they looked at him curiously, drawing aside for him as he joined them. Drinkwater was close enough to observe these details, for the next instant the boat grazed the sand and he rose to his feet.

Drinkwater never had any Thespian pretensions, but his lack of familiarity with the Spanish tongue had driven him to an almost risible extreme in an attempt to head off the slightest suspicion that he was anything other than Spanish. 'Needs must when the devil drives,' he said to Quilhampton when explaining his intentions and the men's laughter had been muted by the order that one of them was going to have to carry him, piggyback, ashore. But it was at Derrick's suggestion that he bore the handkerchief, a large, ostentatious square of flowered silk that they guessed was a gift for the *Virgen*'s captain's paramour in Panama. The prominent manipulation of the kerchief alone ensured his disembarkation appeared alien enough and, ironically, he was glad of it himself, when he caught the stench of the Russians.

Potter put him down with a relieved grunt and Drinkwater, the heavy sabre knocking his hip, strode amongst the group of grim watchers and swept his hat from his head.

'*Buenos días, Señors.*' He bowed, placed his hand on his breast and plunged on. '*El Capitán Rubalcava, del barco La Virgen de la Bonanza.*' The name of his assumed identity and that of his ship sounded marvellously authentic and the latter allowed a spate of eloquence that, he guessed, disarmed any suspicions amid the dull-eyed Russians. Of the effect upon the frontiersman he was less sure. He tried to recall the first-person singular and managed only a squeal. '*Eee, er, dos San Francisco . . .*' He allowed himself to peter-out and stare round at the men. Their eyes were blank with incomprehension.

'*No comprendez?*' They stared back. He turned to the mountain-man. He had blue eyes like the others, but there was a narrowing of them, a shred of suspicion in their cold appraisal. Drinkwater leaned forward with exaggerated Latin effusiveness.

'*Señor?*' he asked, directly.

'*No comprendez . . .*' the man said slowly. A spark of understanding formed in Drinkwater's mind and he said quickly before the other revealed a perfect knowledge of Spanish, 'Ahh, *Señor*, *muy amigo*, you spik English, *sí?*'

The man nodded.

Drinkwater straightened, took a step towards him and waved his handkerchief airily, approaching the mountain-man, appearing to dismiss the assembled Russians whose dull, peasant wits watched this show as though it was a visitation by a dancing bear and they would presently be requested to reach for *kopecks*, at which point they would scatter.

'Eet is good, hey?' Drinkwater plunged on, narrowing his eyes and leaning forward again in a mannerism he had copied subconsciously from Don Alejo. 'I come to find Eenglish ship . . . Eenglishmen . . . *comprendez?*' He bastardised the English words by elongation, relapsing into the odd Spanish word for punctuation with a speed he hoped continued to deceive.

The mountain-man regarded him for some time, a ruminative air about him, as though he spoke little, and when he did the words had to be dragged from him.

'Yeah. *Comprendez.* I ain't see'd no ship, but . . .'

Drinkwater drew back in disappointment. With no news of *Patrician* there was little point in risking his neck further; but something about the mountain-man held his attention. He played the charade a step further, aware that beyond the group and walking down from the direction of the stockade a uniformed officer and an escort of armed men were approaching.

'Eenglishmen, *Señor* . . . you see, *qué?*'

'Yeah . . . I see . . .'

"Ow many?'

'Twenty-two . . .' The man became aware of the approach of the officer and he jerked his head. 'Ask him.'

The Russians were falling back; some of them removed their fur hats in the presence of the officer. Drinkwater turned to the newcomer. He wore a uniform of brown cloth with red facings, dark breeches tucked into high boots. His tie-wig was ill-kempt and old-fashioned and the hat he bore in his hands had seen better days.

Drinkwater drew himself up and essayed a low bow, flourishing his handkerchief and never taking his eyes off the face of the Russian officer. It was a cruel face, pock-marked and thin with long deprivation, yet with an imperious pair of eyes deep set on either side of a beak of a nose. The voice, when he spoke, was thin and reedy. The officer was clearly at the opposite end of the social class at whose other extremity Captain Prince Vladimir Rakitin occupied a place.

Taking a deep breath and noticing that his boat's crew had turned the boat round and were standing knee-deep in the water holding it ready for escape, Drinkwater began again.

'*Buenas días, Señor, Ee, er La Capitán . . .*'

"E says he's lookin' for Englishmen, Lootenant . . .'

A look of understanding passed between the two of them and the unpleasant Russian officer fixed his eyes upon Drinkwater. His glance was truly intimidating and, masquerading as he was, Drinkwater felt unequal to the task of staring him down. Instead he bowed again.

'*Niet!* No English. Here, Russia. You go!'

The officer turned on his heel, leaving Drinkwater half-recovered from his bow.

'Now you go, *amigo*,' said the mountain-man, his drawl lingering mockingly upon the Spanish word so that a worm of alarm writhed in Drinkwater's gut. '*Vamos!*'

Drinkwater turned and walked towards the boat. Potter bent his back and Drinkwater waved him aside, splashing through the shallows.

'*Vaya con Dios, Capitán Rubalcava,*' called the mountain-man and then added something which made the Russians around him laugh.

'They were lying, of that I'm certain,' Drinkwater said, accepting the glass of wine that Derrick handed him.

'About the ship, sir?' asked Quilhampton.

'No, about men, Englishmen.'

'Our men, sir?' Quilhampton frowned. 'I don't quite follow . . .'

'There's the rub, James, neither do I.' He felt the wine uncoil its warmth in his belly, relaxing him. 'But I mean to find out. That

Yankee knew something, for he mentioned twenty-odd men and I've already been played false by one American. We'll reconnoitre that fort tonight. Any movement from it?'

'Nothing new. That cove is still spying on us from the platform over the gate.'

'And the brigs?'

'Nothing. They don't appear to be working cargo, though they've tackles rigged.'

'Perhaps we interrupted them.'

'It's possible. What would they be loading?'

'Furs perhaps, jerked meat, other staples, Indian corn, say purchased with iron trinkets. It's a safe enough haven for refitting ships too. They need labour for that, skilled labour . . .'

Comprehension kindled in Quilhampton's eyes. 'You mean English seamen, sir?'

'Yes.'

'You mean men from the *Patrician*, sir?'

'Yes.'

'But we're miles away from Drake's Bay, sir . . .'

'We got here, James, and those brigs looked handy enough craft.'

'Good God!' Quilhampton paused.

'It looks as though the Russians not only took our ship but might be holding our men. Let's get under weigh now and beat a retreat with our tails between our legs. We can return in the cutter after dark.'

18 The Raid in the Rain

July 1808

It began to rain as they left the schooner. Their last glimpse of her pitching in the swell, hove-to in the darkness, was swiftly eclipsed by a hissing curtain of drizzle which seemed to seal them in a hermetic world of sodden misery. It was not cold until those sitting still felt the rain penetrate to their skin and envied the steady labours of the oarsmen. The interminable night passage was accompanied by the steady splash of oars and the occasional staccato chatter of teeth.

But the rain killed the wind and flattened the sea to a greasy swell that, at last, thundered on the low sand-spit ahead of them and signalled their proximity to the estuary. Drinkwater swung the tiller and skirted the breakers, edging round the northern extremity of the spit until they knew by the feel of the boat that they were in the mouth of the river and could feel the bite of the seaward current.

'Oars.'

The men ceased rowing and bent over their looms. Drinkwater ordered a tot passed to each man. It was *aguardiente*, Spanish fire-water, but none the worse for that. They would need all the courage it put into their bellies, for their powder was soaked and whatever they might achieve would be by cold steel.

'Stand-by . . . give way together . . .'

They pressed on until they could see the dull leap of orange flames from behind the Russian stockade. They paused again and Drinkwater gave his final instructions. A few moments later the cutter's stem grounded on the shore of the Columbia River for the second time, only on this occasion there was to be no masquerading. Leaving the boat keepers, Drinkwater led Quilhampton and

Blixoe, Tregembo and a handful of seamen inland. The rain still fell and they felt their feet sticking in the ooze which sucked tenaciously on the well-trodden path up from the landing place. After a few yards they reached the tideline where low scrub, grass and trees began.

Drinkwater led them off to the left, keeping between the river and the fort, but working round behind it, guided by the red glow of the fire within the stockade. The seething hiss of the rain on the sea and mud became a low roar as they moved beneath the trees, dripping in huge droplets upon them. Despite the discomfort it covered their approach and they were close enough to make out the dancing of flames through the interstices of the pine-log rampart. Motioning them to stop, Drinkwater edged forward alone to peer through one of these slender gaps.

By now his night-vision was acute. He could see the upper outline of the stockade against the sky and, except by the gate, it appeared to be unpierced by guns, although there was doubtless a walk-way behind it to allow defenders to fire over the top. For some yards clear of the fort, the trees and brushwood had been cleared, but the nature of the night allowed him to slip across this glacis undetected. Pressed against the resinous pine trunks he peered into the fort.

The interior of the post was roughly circular, a number of buildings within it provided quarters and stores. Outside what he supposed to be the main barrack block a large fire was crackling, the flames and sparks leaping skywards despite the efforts of the heavens to extinguish them. He could see a few men lounging under the overhanging roof of this block, and the blackening carcass of a deer being roasted on spits, but from his vantage point he could see little else. The garrison, however, seemed a small one and the governor doubtless lived in one of the log cabins, for Drinkwater could just make out a square of yellow light close to the gate, as though a lamp burned behind a crude window. Cautiously he returned to the others, whispering to Quilhampton: 'Damned if I can see what we're looking for.'

'Oh. What now, sir?'

'We'll edge round the place.'

They began to move forward again, a pall of dejection falling on the miserable little column. They became careless, snapping twigs and letting branches fly back into the faces of the men behind them. They lost touch with the stockade on their right, moving into dense brushwood that tore at them, aggravating their tempers and unsettling them. Drinkwater began to question the wisdom of proceeding further. Then he stopped, so abruptly that Quilhampton bumped into him. Not five yards ahead of them a tall figure had risen from the bracken, hurriedly knotting the cords of his breeches. Drinkwater knew instantly it was the mountain-man.

To what degree the man's preoccupation had prevented his hearing the approach of the party, Drinkwater could only guess. Such a *voyageur*, at once a hunter, tracker, trapper and forest dweller, must have possessed instincts keen as any stag, but at that moment they had been somnolent, intent on more fundamental physical needs. Their surprise was mutual and as they stared at each other in silence, Drinkwater could just see the gleam of the foreshortened rifle barrel.

'Another step and you're dead, Mister. I thought you bastards might be back . . .'

So, the mountain-man had not been taken in by the disguise of the morning, and with that realisation Drinkwater sought to temporise, capitalising on that brief confidence of the forenoon.

'I've come for those Englishmen you spoke of.'

The mountain-man gave a short, dry laugh. 'You won't find 'em here.'

'Where then?'

'Why the hell should I tell you?'

'You told the Russians . . . said they knew about the matter.' The mountain-man seemed to hesitate and Drinkwater added, 'I'm surprised you want the Russians on your doorstep.'

'I sure as hell don't want you British. We got rid of you back a-while and I aim to keep it that way . . .'

'And the Russians?' Drinkwater persisted.

'Ain't no trouble at all . . .'

'Bring you vodka for furs and whatever Indian women you can sell 'em I daresay,' said Drinkwater.

'What's that to you, Mister? I've been expecting you ever since

I found your damned men wanderin' about the back-country behind Bodega Bay.'

'So you knew we weren't Spanish?'

'I've been expecting the British a-lookin' for their deserters, Mister. You didn't even come close to convincin' me. You see I know Rubalcava, Mister.'

'And you're on friendly terms with the Russians too, eh? Do I take it you've sold my deserters to that cold-eyed bastard that commands here?'

'What makes you think I'm hugger-mugger with the damned Russkie, eh? I ain't particularly friendly with anybody, especially the bloody British.'

'But . . .'

'But . . . I can't shoot the lot of you so just turn about and walk back to your boat . . .'

'I doubt you can shoot anyone in this damned rain . . .'

'You ain't heard of a Chaumette breech, Mister, or a Goddamned Ferguson rifle? I could blow the shit out of you right now and pick off another of you before you got into those trees . . .'

The click of the gun-lock sounded ominously above the drip and patter of the rain.

'If you don't want the British here, why don't you tell me where those men are?'

'Ain't answering any more questions. You get goin'. *Vamos, Capitán* . . .'

Drinkwater turned and the men parted for him. He looked back once. The rain had eased a little and the cloud thinned. The mountain-man stood watching their retreat, his long gun slung across his arm, the noise of laughter muffled by his huge beard. At the same instant the man threw back his head and loosed an Iroquois war-whoop into the night. The alarm stirred noises from the direction of the stockade and the crack of the man's rifle was swiftly followed by a cry and the crash of a man falling behind him, sprawling full length.

'Back to the boat!' Drinkwater hissed, waving them all past him and stopping only Mr Quilhampton as the two of them bent over the felled seaman. It was Lacey and he was past help; the mountain-man had been as good as his word. The ball had made a

428

gaping hole in Lacey's neck, missing the larynx, but severing the carotid artery. The wound was mortal and Lacey was close to death, his blood streaming over Drinkwater's probing hands.

'Come, James, there's nothing to be done . . .'

There was no sign of the mountain-man but from the fort came the shouts of men answering an alarm. Somewhere to their right they could hear their own party crashing through the undergrowth accompanied by a stream of oaths and curses.

'Go *on*, James!'

'Not without you, sir.'

'Don't be a bloody fool . . .'

Between them Lacey rattled out his life and fell limp. Drinkwater wiped his hands on Lacey's gory jacket.

'Poor devil,' he said, wondering if the ball had been intended for himself.

'Come on then.'

They both began to run.

In the rain and confusion they reached the boat unmolested, but the Russians were already pouring out of the fort towards the landing place. By the time Drinkwater reached the cutter with Quilhampton most of his party had mustered, but two were missing, stumbling about near the fort.

'Where's Hughes?' called Quilhampton.

'Fuck knows, he was behind Tregembo . . .'

'Tregembo?' Drinkwater spun round. 'Is he missing?'

'Seems so, sir . . .'

'God's bones!' Drinkwater swore. 'Get that boat off into the water, hold off the beach. You take command, James.' He raised his voice, 'Tregembo!' He roared, 'Tregembo!'

He began to run back the way he had come. Somewhere to the right he could see the shapes of men running and then the flash and crack of a musket, soon followed by a fusillade of shot as the approaching Russians fired wildly into the night. There was a harsh order screeched out and it stopped. Drinkwater recognised the voice of the governor and then, clearly above the hiss of the rain, he could hear the awful slither and snick of bayonets being fixed. He caught up the sabre he had looted from the schooner and hefted it for balance.

'Tregembo!'

He spat the rain from his mouth and almost retched on the sudden, overpowering stench of pigs. Somewhere close by was a sty and he heard the ruminant grunts of its occupants change to a squealing. Two men and the dull gleam of steel were approaching and must have disturbed the swine.

'Tregembo!'

How many shots had the mountain-man fired? Was Tregembo lying out there dying like Lacey, while he had run for his life?

The two men were nearer and he swung round to defend himself.

'Tregembo!' he roared in one last desperate attempt to locate his servant. Suddenly a third man was upon him, risen, it appeared, from the very ground itself.

'Clap a stopper on the noise, zur . . .'

'God damn you, Tregembo . . .'

Drinkwater slashed wildly at the first assailant and felt his sabre knock aside the bayonet thrust. Whirling the blade he caught the second man as he tried to work round Drinkwater's rear, driving both off for a second. He began to fall back, waving Tregembo behind him, '. . . Why the devil didn't you answer me?'

'I fell among swine,' Tregembo called as he moved towards the boat behind his commander.

'Then run, man, *run!*'

Drinkwater saw an opportunity and slashed again, slicing in above the thrusting bayonet as the Russian infantryman lunged forward. The man's face was a pale blur and Drinkwater saw the dark splotch of blood against his cheek as the point of the sabre caught it, and then he turned and began to run, leaping the tussocks of grass and then slithering through soft sand and mud. He tripped and fell full length in the shallows, hard on Tregembo's heels. The Cornishman turned and helped him to his feet.

'God! What a damned farce!'

They scrambled into the boat amid a confusion of limbs and bodies, dominated by Quilhampton's voice calling above the rain and the tumult, 'Where's the captain? Has anyone seen Captain Drinkwater?'

'Here . . . I'm here, Mr Q . . . now get this festerin' boat under way!'

'Thank God! Aye, aye, sir . . . out oars! Come on there . . . for Christ's sake! Give way!'

As the boat pulled out into the estuary, a storm of small shot whined over their heads and all they could see were a few shapes splashing about in the shallow water in almost as much confusion as themselves.

'Let's sort this boat out.' Drinkwater's own sense of dignity and his innate hatred of disorder surfaced in the rout. 'Be silent there,' he ordered for the noise of swearing continued unabated and it suddenly dawned on him that it was no longer his own men who were responsible.

'What the deuce?'

Drinkwater looked round, thinking for an instant he was going out of his mind for the noise came out of the night ahead of them and the oaths were unmistakably English. Then he saw the looming bulk of one of the anchored brigs athwart whose hawse the current was sweeping them.

'It's the English prisoners, sir,' shouted Quilhampton in a moment of comprehension, 'they must have heard us . . .'

Drinkwater considered the odds. How many Russians were aboard the brig? But the current had committed him.

'Catch a-hold then . . . come, lads, quickly . . . up and board her! Come on there, lads, those are your festerin' shipmates aboard there, prisoners of the Russians . . .'

A groundswell of anger stirred the occupants of the boat and she rocked dangerously as men reached out at the passing hull. Then the cutter jarred against the brig with a crash and they found themselves jammed under her forechains and were swarming up over her ample tumblehome. Driven by their recent defeat and now finding themselves among the familiar surroundings of a ship, they swept the length of her deck within a minute. At her stern, the watch of a dozen men, confused by the noises ashore, suddenly attacked by desperate assailants and mindful that below decks a score of rebellious prisoners only awaited liberty before cutting their gaolers to pieces, soon capitulated. Most jumped over the taffrail to save their lives by swimming ashore, though three were taken prisoner. Drinkwater realised he was in possession of a Russian brig at the same

431

moment that he caught a glimpse of the unsecured cutter drifting away downstream.

'What is it, Mr Derrick?'

There was an odd formality about those left aboard the *Virgen de la Bonanza*. Mr Marsden, the *Patrician*'s carpenter but the most experienced seaman on board, hurried to answer Derrick's summons. The Quaker's innate dignity, his literacy and his position as the captain's secretary almost gave him the status of a gentleman, while his tenacious hold on his faith had elevated him from a mere curiosity to something of a sage among the hands.

'I believe it to be the cutter, Friend Marsden, and it appears to be empty.'

Marsden took up the offered glass and levelled it. The dawn was heavy with the night's rain, the sea a sluggish undulating plain of uniform grey. No wind above the whisper of a breeze ruffled its surface, as though the sea was suppressed beneath the sheer weight of the sky's bequest. Every rope and spar, every sail and block was sodden with water. Rain had run below through cracks and companion-ways, scuttles and ports and, though it was not actually falling at that moment, more was threatened and the coming of day was only a lightening of the tone of the gloom. Their visible horizon was bounded by mist, a murky perimeter into which the grey, unoccupied shell of the cutter rocked, not above six cables away, borne seawards by the inexorable current of the Columbia River.

Fifteen minutes later the thing lay not thirty yards off and they could clearly see it was empty. There were disorderly signs of hurried evacuation. Several of the oars were missing, one stuck up, its blade jammed in the thole pins. Another was broken, the jagged loom indicating it had struck hard against something.

The remnants of rags hung down from the rowlocks, where, the night before, they had muffled them. Oddly the painter lay neatly coiled in the bow.

'Damned if I understand the meaning o' this,' muttered Marsden.

'I think we are alone, Friend, left to our own resources,' said Derrick, his sonorous tone carrying the dreadful implication to Marsden.

432

'Streuth! What's to be done? And the cap'n gone, an' all ... .'

'Could we fetch San Francisco?'

Marsden shrugged. 'God knows . . . I suppose we could . . . ain't my trade, nor yours neither . . . hell and damnation take it!'

'Come, Friend, such language availeth nothing.' Derrick turned away from the rail and looked along the schooner's deck. Their handful of a crew would be hard-pressed to bring the schooner back to San Francisco.

'Oh, my fuckin' oath,' moaned Marsden and Derrick turned. The carpenter was staring to starboard where, out of the mist, the grey shape of a ship was emerging. 'We be sunk good an' proper now, Mister Derrick, that's one o' them Russian brigs we saw yesterday. Reckon they know all about us an' what's happened to the Cap'n.'

'Shall we run then?' Derrick suggested querulously.

'Is that a Russkie?' asked one of the seamen, coming up to the two men while behind him the remainder stood and stared despairingly to leeward. Marsden looked at first Blixoe and then Derrick. He was not given to quick thinking.

'Run? Where to?'

'Anywhere . . . we're faster than a brig, can sail closer to the wind . . .'

Marsden looked at the Quaker with something akin to respect. 'I suppose running ain't fighting,' he said, rubbing his chin and considering the matter.

'Of course we'll run,' snapped the seaman, shouting for them to start the headsail sheets and cast loose the lashings on the helm.

'Wait!' Derrick was staring through the telescope. 'I'd swear that was Mr Quilhampton on the knightheads . . .'

'Seems a shame, zur, to burn a prize like that,' Tregembo muttered, watching Quilhampton's firing party at work and the flames take hold of the brig.

'She stank near as bad as you when you emerged out of that swine-midden,' remarked Drinkwater. 'I have never seen so slovenly maintained a ship.'

'You damned near had me finished with all that shouting,' said Tregembo.

'That's as maybe, Tregembo. Would you have had me abandon you? By God, Susan would never have let me forget it . . .'

They smiled at each other relieved, both aware that they had enjoyed a lucky escape. They withdrew from the stern window of the schooner, Drinkwater to pour himself a glass of the Spanish commander's excellent *oloroso*, Tregembo to fuss the elegant little cabin into something more befitting a British naval captain. The stink of smoke came in and Drinkwater waited for Quilhampton's party to get aboard. A moment or two later Quilhampton knocked on the door. He entered, grimy but smiling. He held out a rolled chart.

'A glass, James, you've earned it . . . what d' you have there?'

'The answer to the riddle, sir . . . yes, thank you.' Quilhampton took the glass from Tregembo, who gave him an old-fashioned, sideways look.

'How did they behave?' asked Drinkwater, unrolling the chart and staring at it.

'The men, sir?'

'Yes.'

'Like lambs, all eagerness to please. Never seen a firing party so eager to destroy a prize, couldn't do enough for me . . . would have burnt the damn thing twice over if it'd been a fit plea for mitigation . . .'

Drinkwater looked up from the chart and eyed the lieutenant speculatively. 'You think it should be, James?'

'We've little choice, sir. In any case, they outnumber us and I'm not sure about the men that were with me. It was only circumstances and self-preservation that kept us together . . . Marsden's all right, Derrick's a canting neutral and I suppose we can rely on old Tregembo . . .'

'Less of the "old", Mr Quilhampton, zur, if you please,' growled the Cornishman.

Quilhampton grinned and downed his glass, winking at Drinkwater.

'Let's hope they all appreciate which side their bread's buttered on now,' said Drinkwater, finishing his own glass, 'even so, I'll have to read 'em the riot act.'

'I'll muster them, then, sir.'

'Yes, if you please, and try not to look so damned pleased with yourself.'

'I think you'll find something to smile about, sir, if you study that chart.'

'Why?'

'I think it shows us where we may find *Patrician*.'

Drinkwater looked down at the chart with its unfamiliar script and mixture of incomprehensible Russian characters and French names favoured by more aristocratic hydrographers. 'Anyway,' went on Quilhampton, pausing by the cabin door, 'I'm uncommon pleased to be given a fighting chance again.'

'Yes,' agreed Drinkwater, 'it was quite a turn up for the books, eh?'

'Well, "fortune favours the brave", sir,' Quilhampton remarked sententiously.

'I think,' replied Drinkwater drily, 'that last night, fortune was merely inclined to favour the least incompetent.'

Quilhampton left with a chuckle, but Drinkwater exchanged a glance with Tregembo.

'I'll let 'ee know if I hear anything, zur, have no fear o' that.'

'Very well, Tregembo,' Drinkwater nodded, 'only I've a notion to set eyes on my family again.'

'You ain't the only one, zur.'

Drinkwater poured himself a second glass of the *oloroso* and, while he waited for the men to be mustered on deck, he studied the chart. The brig's Russian master was an untidy navigator; the erasure of her track was imperfectly carried out. It was quite obvious that Captain Rakitin had a nearer rendezvous than Sitka and, studying the features of the inlet, it was the very place he himself would have chosen to hide a prize. Delighted, he tossed off the glass and composed his features. He was going to have to scold the men, but by all accounts they had quite a tale to tell.

Quilhampton gathered the details, noting them down on a page torn from the schooner's log-book. The men who had absconded from Drake's Bay had found the same village that Quilhampton had been driven from and met the same reception from its inhabitants. Although a body of opinion sought revenge on the local *peons*, wiser councils prevailed and the deserters moved further inland, reducing the chances of being retaken by any parties sent out by Drinkwater. For a day or two they remained together until they reached the great sequoia woods where game, water and freedom had split them into groups and they had lost their discipline. For a few days they wandered happily about and then one party found an Indian village. Their attempt to establish friendly relations with the native women met a hostile rebuttal. Another party roamed into a Franciscan mission and were driven off by angry *mestizos* who had been told they were devils. Within a week the country was raised against them and several were killed or left to the mercies of the natives as the manhunt spread. Eventually twenty-two of them found themselves rounded up and turned over to a strange, English-speaking man in fringed buckskins whom the local people held in some awe.

To the British deserters he promised, with complicit winks and other indications of racial superiority, that if they played along, he would accomplish their rescue. There were prolonged parleys, exchanges of some form of gifts or money and then they were led off on the promise of good behaviour, by the mountain-man whom they knew by the obvious alias of 'Captain Mack'. Since the alternative was inevitable death at the hands of either Indians, half-caste Spanish or the tender ministrations of what they thought was the Inquisition, they shambled off in the wake of their rescuer.

After a march of three days, Captain Mack led them down to the sea, on the shores of Bodega Bay where, to their astonishment, they found soldiers who spoke a language they could not understand, but was clearly not Spanish. It did not take them long to find out that they had unwittingly become the serfs of the Russian-American Company, and that they were to be shipped in one of the filthy brigs that lay in the bay to the Company's more secure post on the Columbia River. Captain Mack had gone with them to strike his bargain with the commandant there, and had been waiting to return to the mountain forests of California when Drinkwater had arrived in the schooner. As for the men, they were to be employed refitting or serving in Russian ships in the Pacific.

'The hands are mustered, Captain.'

Drinkwater came out of his reverie to find Derrick confronting him. 'Eh? Oh, thank you, Derrick. I shall be up directly.'

There was something piratical about the assembly amidships. Whether it was the lean, dishevelled and indisciplined appearance of the men, or whether the character of the schooner under its false colours, or simply the crawling uncertainty that nagged at Drinkwater that contributed to this impression, he was not sure as they stared back at him. Despite his titular right to lead them, his tenure of command had never rested on such insubstantial foundations. Among the men confronting him were almost certainly those who had attempted to sabotage the *Patrician*.

'Very well,' he began, silencing them and studying their faces for traces of guilt, defiance, insolence or contrition. 'Fate has literally cast us in the same boat . . .' he slapped the rail beside him, 'and I intend to discover the whereabouts of the *Patrician* and free our shipmates from the kind of bestial treatment some of you have just subjected yourselves to. Make no mistake about it, there are worse forms of existence than service in the King's Navy.' He paused, to let the point sink in.

'I can offer you little beyond hardship and the possibility of retaking our ship from the Russians, clearing our name as a company and destroying our enemies.'

He paused again, clambering up on the carriage of a 6-pounder. 'Well, what d'you say? Are you for or against? Do we keep that rag aloft,' he pointed up at the red and gold ensign of Spain still at the main peak, 'or are we going to take this little hooker into Plymouth to be condemned as a prize to *Patrician*?'

There was a second's hesitation and then they were yelling stupidly and throwing their arms in the air in acclamation. Drinkwater got down from the gun carriage.

'Very well, Mr Q. Lay me a course of nor'-nor'-west. Happily their experiences as subjects of the Tsar have taught them that there are degrees even of injustice.'

437

19   The Trojan Horse

July–August 1808

Drinkwater tapped the dividers on the chart and looked up, gauging his prisoner.

Vasili Zhdanov, one of the three men captured with the Russian brig, spoke English of a kind, having been in attendance upon his one-time master when that worthy had served as an officer with the Anglophile Seniavin. However, Zhdanov had been caught stealing and after a sound whipping had been sold to the Russian-American Company, so that he had found a kind of life as seaman in one of the company's trading brigs. Now the reek of him, and particularly of his Makhorka tobacco, filled the cabin.

'How do you know that the British ship *Patrician* is here?' Drinkwater pointed to the bay which lay far to the northward, on the south coast of distant Alaska. There were a thousand anchorages amid the archipelagos of islands that extended northwards from the Strait of Juan de Fuca, not least that of Nootka Sound, but this remote spot . . .

'I see . . . she come . . . *Suvorov* come . . .' replied Zhdanov, haltingly.

'Who is captain of *Suvorov*?'

'*Barin* Vladimir Rakitin . . .'

'How many guns?'

Zhdanov shrugged; he was clearly not numerate. 'Do you wish to serve King George of Great Britain?'

'I fight with Royal Navy,' Zhdanov said with some dignity, but whether he referred to Drinkwater's proposed change of allegiance or to his own past history he was unable to make clear. Drinkwater looked up at Quilhampton.

'Split the three of them up, try and make them understand they can join us and swear 'em in. If they protest, you'll have to put 'em back in the bilboes . . .'

'Aye, aye, sir.' Quilhampton led the Russian out. Drinkwater opened a stern window to clear the air. The man reminded him of a strange cross between a feral animal like a bear, and a child. Yet there was something impressive about him, reminding Drinkwater of those vast numbers of such men he had seen encamped about the Lithuanian town of Tilsit a year earlier. Like patient beasts they had awaited their fates with an equanimity that struck him as stoic. Zhdanov had responded to his own autocratic proposal with the simple obedience that made the Tsar's armies almost invincible.

He looked again at the chart. There was logic in secreting a ship in such a place. It was well-surveyed, compared with the adjacent coast, a strange opening into the surrounding mountains, like a fiord except that its entrance, instead of being open, was almost closed off by rocky promontories. Between them, Drinkwater guessed, the tide would rip with considerable ferocity.

Inside, the fiord was deep, a single steep islet rising in its middle, beyond which there was a sudden, abrupt bifurcation, the bay's arms swinging north and south and terminating in glaciers. If Vasili Zhdanov was right, somewhere within those enclosing pincers of promontories lay *Patrician*.

Drinkwater opened the dividers and stepped off the distance, laying the steel points of the instrument against the latitude scale; more than a thousand miles lay between their present position and the lone bay which nestled under the massive shoulder of Mount Elias and the great Alaskan Range. He stared unseeing from the stern windows. So much depended upon their success. Where were Fraser, and Frey, the punctilious Mount or Midshipman Wickham? Were they prisoners aboard their own ship, or had they been held at San Francisco?

If providence granted success to this venture, he would return thither and force those corrupt time-servers, the Arguello brothers, to release his men. And force some measure of expiation out of that dishonourable dog, Rubalcava!

He felt his pulse beat with the mere thought of revenge and a wave of anger swept over him as he recalled the humiliation he had suffered at the hands of Prince Vladimir Rakitin.

If, if only providence had turned her face upon him again, he might yet do something to retrieve the ragged flag of honour.

No matter how assiduously one studied a chart, the reality never quite conformed to the imagination. Assessment of the present landscape had not been helped by the unfamiliar topographical terms *Zaliu*, *Mys* or *Bukhta* rendered incomprehensible by the Cyrillic script. Neither was Drinkwater's familiarity with French sufficiently proficient to determine whether it was La Perouse or the Russian Kruzenstern who had named the places on the chart. What impressed him was the quality of the thing, manufactured as it had been half a world away in the Russian hydrographic office in St Petersburg.

He raised the glass again and raked the shore, seeking the narrow, half-hidden entrance and avoiding the scenic seductions of the mountain range that seemed to beetle down upon the littoral. It was stunningly magnificent, this chain of mighty peaks, shining with the sunlit glitter of permanent ice, like the *nunataks* of Greenland. And then he saw her, the black tracery sharp in the crisp, cool air which sharpened every image with more intensity than the most cunningly wrought lens. He knew instantly that the ship anchored beyond the low headland was indeed *Patrician*.

He shut his glass with a snap. 'Hoist Spanish colours, if you please, and call all hands to their stations.'

He had assumed the worst and formed his ruse accordingly. *Patrician*, he theorised, would be well manned by the enemy, despite his inclination to believe the contrary due to her remote location. Her own people would have been removed in San Francisco, so there would be no spontaneous rising to assist; art and cunning must, therefore, be his chief weapons. He sent below for the Spanish uniforms and saw to his side-arms long before the approach to the entrance. When he was ready he turned the *Virgen de la Bonanza* to the north-east and, ascending to the foretop, spied out the narrow strait between the guardian headlands. From that elevation he saw at once why the entrance was so difficult to locate from the deck. The island, which he knew lay within the bay, lay directly upon the line of sight when peering through the gap, so appearing to form one continuous coastline. Turning, he called down to Quilhampton by the helm, the course was altered and the bowsprit below him swung towards the narrows.

The schooner heeled, turning to larboard and bringing the wind fine on that bow and Drinkwater, surveying the entrance from his perch, felt the fine thrum of wind through the stays and the halliards that ran past him. The water ran suspiciously smooth in the gut, with darker corrugations rippling out from either side, corrugations which tore off into whorls and rips of gyrating turbulence, where unseen rocks or sudden treacherous shifts of current manipulated the violent motion of an ebbing tide.

'Deck there!'

'Sir?' Quilhampton looked aloft.

'I want a steady hand on the helm . . . there's a deal of broken water ahead . . .'

'Aye, aye, zur.'

Drinkwater smiled as Tregembo took the helm and then turned his attention to the narrows again. Their progress was becoming slower, as they felt the increasing opposition of the tide. The schooner crabbed sideways under its influence, unable to point closer to the wind. Drinkwater bestowed a quick glance at the anchored ship.

She was alone, alone beneath those great slabs of mountains which lifted into the heavens behind her, their snow caps sliding into scree and talus, tussocked grass and low, stunted trees which, on the lower ground that fringed the fiord, changed to a dark, impenetrable mantle of firs. And she was most certainly the *Patrician*.

'Steady there . . .'

He felt the schooner lurch and looked below to see Tregembo anticipate the tide-rip's attempt to throw the vessel's head into the wind. The sea was slick with the speed of the tide, almost uninfluenced by the effect of the breeze as it rushed out into the ocean beyond the confines of the bay. Those dark corrugations resolved themselves into standing waves, foaming with energy as the mass of water forced itself out of the bay so that the schooner slowed, stood still and began to slip astern.

The heads of curious seals, impervious to the viciously running

441

ebb, popped out of the grey water to stare like curious, ear-less dogs, their pinched nostrils flaring and closing in exaggerated expressions of outrage at the intrusion.

For an hour they hung, suspended in this fashion until, almost suddenly, the tide slacked, relented and the power of the wind in their sails drove them forwards again. The low roar of the rush of water eased, the corrugations, the rips and eddies diminished and slowly disappeared. For a while the strait was one continuous glossy surface of still water, and then they were through, brought by this curious diminishing climax into sudden proximity with their quarry.

'And now,' said Drinkwater regaining the deck, 'we must play at a Trojan Horse.'

'After Scylla and Charybdis 'twill be little enough, sir,' remarked Quilhampton with unbecoming cheerfulness.

'Belay the classical allusions, Mr Q,' snapped Drinkwater, suddenly irritated; 'belay the loud-mouthed English and lower the boat, then you may carry out your instructions and fire that salute . . .'

The bunting of the Spanish ensign tickled Drinkwater's ear as he was rowed across the dark waters of the inlet towards the *Patrician*. The schooner's boat, hoisted normally under her stern, was smaller than the cutter they had lost in the Columbia River. But he hoped his approach was impressive enough and he was aware, from a flash of reflected light, that he was being scrutinised through a glass by one of the half-dozen men he could see on his own quarterdeck.

Behind him came the dull thud of the 6-pounder, echoing back after a delay to mix its repetition with the sound of the next signal-gun so that the air seemed to reverberate with the concussion of hundreds of guns as the echoes chased one another into the distance in prolonged diminuendo.

No answering salute came from the fo'c's'le of the *Patrician*, no answering dip of her diagonally crossed ensign. He stood up, showing off the Spanish uniform with its plethora of lace, and holding out the bundle of papers that purported to be despatches.

He noted a flurry of activity at the entry with a sigh of mixed relief and satisfaction.

'How far is the schooner, Potter?' he asked the man pulling stroke-oar.

'She's just tacked, sir,' replied Potter, staring astern past Drinkwater, 'an' coming up nicely . . . they're tricing up the foot of the fores'l now, sir and the outer jib's just a-shivering . . . 'bout long pistol shot an' closing, sir.'

'Very well.' Drinkwater could smell the rum on the man's breath as he made his oar bite the water. Off to starboard an unconcerned tern hovered briefly, then plunged into the water and emerged a second later with a glistening fish in its dagger-like beak.

'We're closing fast, lads, be ready . . .' He paused, judged his moment and, in a low voice, ordered the oars tossed and stowed. Beside him Tregembo put the tiller over. Amid a clatter of oars coming inboard the bowman stood up and hooked onto *Patrician*'s chains.

Drinkwater looked up. A face stared down at him and then he began to climb, not daring to look around and ascertain the whereabouts of Quilhampton and the schooner. At the last moment he remembered to speak bastard-French, considering that it was not unreasonable for a Spanish officer to use that language when addressing a French-speaking ally. The fact that he spoke it barbarously was some comfort.

Stepping onto the deck he swept off his hat and bowed.

'*Bonjour, Señores,*' he managed, looking up with relief into the face of an officer he had never seen before, '*ou est votre capitaine, s'il vous plait?*'

'*Tiens! C'est le capitaine anglais!*'

Drinkwater jerked round. To his left stood one of the midshipmen he had last seen in Don José's Residence at San Francisco. Hands flew to swords and he knew that his ruse had failed utterly. He flung the paper bundle at the young man's face and drew the cavalry sabre before either of the Russian officers had reacted fully. Letting out a bull-roar of alarm he swiped the heavy, curved blade upwards in a vicious cut that sent the senior officer, a lieutenant by his epaulettes, reeling backwards, his hands to his face, his dropped sword clattering on the deck.

'Come on, you bastards!' Drinkwater bellowed into the split second's hiatus his quick reaction had brought him. 'Board!'

Would they come, those disloyal quondam deserters, or would they leave him to die like a dog, hacked down by the ring of steel that was forming about him? What would Quilhampton do? Carry out the plan of getting foul of the *Patrician*'s stern in a histrionic display of incompetence which was to have cut Drinkwater's inept French explanation and turned it into a farce of invective levelled by him at Quilhampton, under whose cover the *Virgen de la Bonanza* was to have been run alongside the frigate. During this ludicrous performance his men were supposed to have come aboard . . .

Armed seamen with pikes from the arms' racks around the masts and marines with bayonets, men with spikes and rammers and gun-worms were closing, keeping their distance until they might all rush in and kill him.

'Board, you bastards!' he shouted again, his voice cracking with tension, his eyes moving from one to another of his enemies, seeking which was the natural leader, whose muscles would first tense for the kill and bring down Nemesis upon his reckless head . . .

It seemed he waited an age and then a shuffling of the midshipman's feet told him what he wanted to know. He thrust left, pronating his wrist and driving his arm forward so that the mangled muscles cracked with the speed of his lunge. The *pointe* of his sabre struck the young man on the breast-bone, cracked it and sent him backwards, gasping for breath in an agony of surprise. As he half-turned he sensed reaction to his right, a movement forward to threaten his unprotected back. He cut savagely, reversing the swing of his body, the heavy weapon singing through the air and cutting with a sickening crunch into the upper arm of a bold seaman whose cannon-worm dropped from nerveless hands and who let out a howl of pain and surprise. And then he lost the initiative and was fighting a dozen assailants for his very life.

'Frey, I think you are an infatuated fool. That must be the twentieth portrait of La Belladonna you have done,' quipped Wickham, looking down at the watercolour, 'and they do not improve. Besides they are a waste of the dip . . .' He reached out with dampened fingers to pinch out the miserable flame that lit the thick air of the cold gunroom and received a sharp tap on the knuckles from Frey's brush.

'Go to the devil, Wickham! I purchased that dip out of my own funds . . .'

Wickham sat and put his head in his hands, staring across the grubby table at Frey. 'What d'you suppose they intend to do with us?'

'I don't know,' replied Frey without looking up, 'that's why I paint, so that I do not have to think about such things . . .' He put the brush in the pot of water and stared down at the face of Doña Ana Maria. Then, in a sudden savage movement, his hand screwed up the piece of paper and crumpled it up.

Wickham sat back with a start. 'Shame! It wasn't that bad!'

'No, perhaps not, but . . .'

'Was she really handsome?'

'Quite the most beautiful woman I have ever seen,' Frey waxed suddenly lyrical.

'How many women *have* you seen, Frey? You've been aboard here since . . .'

'What was that?' asked Frey sharply, sitting upright.

'One of the men cursing those bastard Russians for being too free with their knouts, I expect,' said Wickham in a bored tone.

'No! Listen!'

It came again, an agonised bellow of command and there was something vaguely familiar about the voice. Frey's eyes opened wide.

'It can't be . . .'

'Can't be what . . . ?'

The shout came again and then there were the screams and bellows of a fight somewhere above them. Both midshipmen stood. Their sentry, a slovenly Russian marine, stirred uneasily, hefting his neglected musket, his thumb poised on its hammer.

There was a sudden buzz throughout the ship as other men, confined in irons or about their imposed duties realised something momentous was happening on deck. For too many days now they had rotted in a regime of inactivity, required only occasionally to turn out and pump the bilges, or tend the cable. For the most part they had languished in almost total darkness, separated from their

445

officers, uncertain of their future, toying with rumours that, when the *Suvorov* returned, many of them would be drafted into her, or into other Russian ships or settlements. For Prince Rakitin such a draft of healthy labour seemed like a blessing from heaven, sufficient to restore the fortunes of the Russian-American Company after the loss of Rezanov.

Frey stood cautiously, not wishing to alarm the sentry. He had learned enough about their gaolers to realise that the man would display no initiative, did not dare to, and would remain at his post until someone came down and relieved or shot him.

'What the devil is going on?' Frey asked in an agony of uncertainty.

'Damned if I know . . .'

Then there was an outburst of the most horrible noise, a howling ululation that reminded the two youths of stories of Iroquois massacres they had heard old men tell from the Seven Years War. It was much closer than the upper deck, and provoking responses even nearer as the captive British seamen joined in with whoops and shouts of their own. The two midshipmen could hear shouts of joyful recognition, the clank of chains and the thud-thud of axes, the sharp clink as they struck iron links, more shouts and then, to compound the confusion, *Patrician* lurched as something large and heavy struck her.

'Come on, Wickham!' Frey's hand scooped the water-pot from the table and hurled it in the face of their sentry. Momentarily blind the man squeezed the trigger of his musket and the confined space reverberated with the crack of the shot. The ball buried itself in the deck-head and the Russian stabbed out with his bayonet but the thing was unwieldy in the small space, and the two midshipmen dodged nimbly past him.

Out on the gun-deck the scene was like a painting of the Last Judgement. Russians lay dead or writhing in agony, like the damned on their way to hell-fire. A handful of piratical British seamen led by Captain Drinkwater's coxswain Tregembo were turning up the hatchways like avenging angels and out of the hold poured a starveling rabble of pale and ragged bodies, corpses new-released from their tombs, some dragging irons, some half-free of them so that they held the loose links and went howling after their

446

captors, swinging the deadly knuckle-dusters in a whirlwind of vengeful pursuit.

'Tregembo, by all that's holy!' Frey stood for an instant, taking in the scene, then ran to a still-writhing Russian, tore the cutlass from his dying grasp and hurried on deck.

Lieutenant Quilhampton lost his cheerfulness the instant Captain Drinkwater left in the schooner's boat. All his attention had to be paid to split-second timing, to bring the *Virgen de la Bonanza* up under *Patrician*'s stern, to fail in an attempt to tack and fall alongside the frigate in a display of Hispanic incompetence that, if he was a yard or two short, would condemn Captain Drinkwater to an untimely death.

His throat was dry and his heart thudded painfully as he sought to concentrate, gauging the relative angle of approach, his speed, and the set of a tide that was already flooding in through the narrows behind him.

'A point to larboard, if you please,' he forced himself to say, feigning complete mastery of himself and seeing Drinkwater ascend the *Patrician*'s side by the man-ropes.

What would happen if Quilhampton failed and Drinkwater died? For himself he knew that he could never return and press his suit for the hand of Catriona MacEwan. Somehow such a course of action would be altogether dishonourable, knowing that he had failed the one man who had ever shown him kindness. And what of Drinkwater? Quilhampton knew of his distant devotion to his family, for all the estrangement imposed by the naval service, and this particular commission. Did Drinkwater expect him to fail? Would Drinkwater rather die in this remote and staggeringly beautiful corner of the world, attempting to recapture his own ship, rather than live with the knowledge of having lost her? If so the responsibility he bore was even heavier, the bonds of true friendship imposing a greater burden than he felt he had skill to meet.

And then he felt the tide, flooding in with increasing strength. *Patrician* was already lying head to it, his own course crabbed across; another point to larboard perhaps . . .

'Larboard a point.'

'Larboard a point more, sir.' There was warning in the helmsman's voice. Quilhampton looked up; the luff of the mainsail was just lifting.

'She's a-shiver, sir,' Marsden said from amidships.

Quilhampton did not answer, he was watching the schooner's bowsprit, watching it cross the empty sky until . . .

'Down helm!'

The *Virgen de la Bonanza* turned slowly into the wind.

'Midships!'

He stole a quick look along the deck. Apart from the half-a-dozen men at the sheets, the remainder, armed to the teeth, lay in the shadow of the starboard rail or crouched under the carelessly thrown down tarpaulin amidships.

The *Virgen de la Bonanza* lost way. The quarter of the *Patrician* loomed over them. They could see marks of neglect about the frigate, odds and ends of rope, scuffed paintwork . . .

A terrible bellow of range came from the deck above. With mounting anxiety Quilhampton suddenly knew he had now to concentrate more than ever before. Such a howl had not been planned, something was wrong, very wrong. He could abandon all pretence.

'Up helm! Shift the heads'l sheets!'

He checked the swing. 'Steady there, lads, not yet, not yet . . .'

The schooner began to swing backwards. He looked over the side. The boat, bobbing under the main chains of the *Patrician*, was already empty. He saw the last pair of heels disappear in through an open gun-port with relief. Drinkwater had at least the support of Tregembo and his boat's crew. A moment later the boat was crushed between the schooner and the frigate as the two hulls jarred together.

'Now!'

There was an ear-splitting roar from amidships. The big carronade, trained forward at maximum elevation and stuffed with langridge, ripped through the rigging of the forechains and, in the wake of that iron storm, Quilhampton loosed his boarders.

Drinkwater parried the first wave of the attack. There was a curious life in the cavalry sabre; centrifugal force kept it swinging in a wide and dangerous swathe though it tore mercilessly at the wrecked muscles of his wounded right shoulder. How long he could keep such a defence going he did not know, but he knew that he would have been a dead man already had he been armed only with his old hanger. He had fired two of the three pistols he had carried and foolishly thrown them down, intending to draw the third, but he could not free it from his belt, and it ground into his belly as he twisted and dodged his assailants.

He did not escape unscathed. He was cut twice about the face and received a deep wound upon his extended forearm. A ball galled his left shoulder and a pike thrust from the rear took him ignominiously in the fleshy part of the right buttock. He began to feel his strength ebb, aware that one last rally from his opponents would result in his death-wound, for he could fight no more.

His vision was blurring, though his mind retained that coolness that had saved him before and fought off the weakness of his reactions for as long as possible. A man loomed in front of him, he swung the sabre . . . and missed. Tensing his exposed stomach he waited for the searing pain of the pike thrust.

'Fuck me! It's the Cap'n!'

The pike-head whistled past his face as the wielder put it up. Suddenly all opposition melted away, there were friendly faces round him, men he had known once, long ago, long ago when he had commanded the *Patrician* . . .

But it was not Valhalla he woke to, nor had it been the faces of the dead he had seen. Some intelligence beyond mere consciousness had allowed him to faint at last, recognising his part in the fight need no longer be sustained. His men had followed him, wiping out the stain of their desertion.

Somewhere far above him voices were discussing him. Impertinent voices that spoke as though he was nothing more than a blood-horse whose health was uncertain.

'Will he pull through, Mr Lallo?'

'Of course, Mr Q, 'tis only a drop of blood he's lost. He'll save me the trouble of prescribing a remedy. There's nothing serious, though that cut in his *gluteus maximus* will embarrass him . . .'

'His *what*?'

'Arse, Mr Q. He'll not sit for a week without it reminding him of its presence.'

Quilhampton laughed. 'I'll go and see about some food . . .'

'Go and find him a bottle of port. Nothing reconstitutes the blood better than a fortified wine.'

'There's some excellent *oloroso* aboard the *Virgen* . . .'

'What a damnably blasphemous name . . . go and get some then . . .'

'You're a pair of impertinent dogs,' Drinkwater muttered, fully conscious.

'There, Mr Q, I told you recovery would be complete . . . welcome aboard, sir.'

'Thank you, Mr Lallo, how many men do we muster?'

20   Dos de Mayo

August 1808

'I believe they call you "Captain Mack",' Drinkwater said. His wounded buttock still troubled him and he preferred to stand, his back to the stern-windows, a grim imperturbable silhouette regarding his prisoner. Mack's eyes were defiant, truculent. He nodded, but held his tongue.

'I understood you did your hunting further south, amid the barrens of California.'

'They ain't barrens,' said Mack shortly, with a half-smile that was at once menacing and secretive.

'Perhaps not,' replied Drinkwater dismissively; he had learned the term in the American War and its precise meaning was unimportant now.

'You are a citizen of the United States of America, are you not?'

'I suppose I am . . .'

'You *suppose*?'

'In so far as I'm under any man's jurisdiction. I reckon to be born free, Mister, I respect it in others, I expect it from them.'

'Meaning you could have shot to kill me when we disturbed you at your office?'

'Sure. I can hit a running moose . . .'

'You didn't respect the freedom of my men, you turned them over to the Russians.'

'Hell, Cap'n, that's bullshit. You didn't respect their freedom either, an' that's supposing they was free in the first place, instead of run from this here ship.'

Drinkwater smiled. 'But you didn't turn 'em over to the Russkies for love of Old England . . .'

'Sure as hell I didn't.'

'Then why?'

'They was trespassin', Cap'n.'

'So were you, on Spanish territory. Did you sell 'em?'

'What the hell would I want with roubles, Cap'n?' the mountain-man answered contemptuously.

'I presume you require powder and shot,' Drinkwater replied coolly, 'and gold is always gold . . .'

A spark of something flared in the mountain-man's eyes, hostility, malice perhaps, Drinkwater could not be sure beyond knowing he had touched a nerve.

'You are a solitary, Captain Mack. A man apart. I do not pretend to understand your motives and my men would have you hang for your treachery.'

'I promised them nothing!'

'Maybe not. Would you have me hand you over to the Spanish authorities at San Francisco . . . ?'

Patrician lifted to the swell and leaned gently over to the increasing breeze as, on deck, Lieutenant Fraser crowded on sail. Drinkwater smiled with grim satisfaction, for a wave of nausea passed visibly over Mack's features.

'You will do as you please, I reckon,' he said with some difficulty. Drinkwater jerked his head at Sergeant Blixoe.

'Take him below, Sergeant.'

He could afford clemency. It was good to have them all back together. Fraser, Lallo, Mount, Quilhampton, even the lugubrious chaplain, Jonathan Henderson. He looked astern through the cabin windows where, under Hill and Frey, the *Virgen de la Bonanza* danced in their wake. Perhaps best of all was to see little Mr Belchambers's cheerful smile, for Drinkwater did not think he could have brought himself to have written to explain the boy's loss to his trusting parents. It was true that there were still men missing, men who had been pressed by the Spaniards to labour on the wharves of San Francisco, but for the great majority the raid on the outpost on the Columbia River had reunited them in spirit, wiping out memories of discontent, disloyalty and desertion. It was less easy for Drinkwater to forget the depths to which he had sunk, of how near he had been to suicide; less easy to forget the risks he had run in his desperation, but the raid had had its effect, paltry enough though it had been in terms of military glory. They had landed by boat in the mist of early morning in a brief and bloody affair in which all the advantage had been with the assailants. They had carried off all that they had not destroyed, even Tregembo's swine, setting fire to the fort with the same enthusiasm they had burnt the first brig.

Drinkwater turned from the stern windows and glanced down at the chart on his table. They would do the same to the Russian outpost at Bodega Bay, where the mysterious mountain-man had first enslaved his own deserters. His men would enjoy that and he could set free Captain Mack, leave him to his damnable wilderness. Then he would return to San Francisco. His heartbeat quickened at the thought of confronting the Arguello brothers. How unexpected were the twists of fortune and how close he had come to ending his own life in the cell below the *Commandante*'s residence. If it had not been for Doña Ana Maria . . .

He forced his mind into safer channels. His first consideration was the destruction of the second Russian post at Bodega Bay.

Lieutenant Quilhampton jumped into the water of Bodega Bay and led the men ashore. They splashed behind him, Mount leading the marines, Frey with his incendiary party. They met only token resistance. A couple of shots were fired at them out of bravado, but the two grubby wretches immediately flung down their muskets and surrendered. Surprise had been total and the British party entered the now familiar stockade with its stink of urine, grease and unwashed humanity, to set about its destruction.

Only when he saw the flicker of flames did Drinkwater leave the ship in the boat. In the stern-sheets, escorted by two of Mount's marines, sat Captain Mack. Wading ashore with the mountain-man's long rifle, Drinkwater indicated that the marines were to follow him with their prisoner. As they walked towards the blazing pine logs that exploded and split in great upwellings of sparks as the resin within them expanded and took fire, they met Quilhampton's party escorting a pathetic collection of bearded *moujiks* back to the boats.

'Where's the commandant?'

'No one seems to be in command, sir, just this handful of peasants.'

'He's a-fucking Indian women, Cap'n, or lying dead-drunk under a redwood tree,' drawled Captain Mack.

'Very well. Let him go.' Drinkwater motioned to the marines and they stood back. He jerked his head at the mountain-man. '*Vamos!*'

Mack half-smiled at the irony, but held out his hand. 'My gun, Cap'n.'

'You get out of my sight now. When my boat pulls off the beach I'll leave your rifle on that boulder. You can get it then.'

'You don't trust me?'

'Somebody once told me the Cherokees called you people Yankees because they didn't trust you.'

'Ah, but others called us English then . . .'

Mack grinned, reluctantly acknowledging an equal and stalked away. He did not look back and his buckskins were soon as one with the alternate light and shade that lay beneath the trees. Drinkwater turned back to the incendiary roar and crackle of the burning fort when there came a shout, the snap of branches and a roar of anger. Drinkwater spun round.

Mack was running back towards them, pursued by a dark figure in an odd, old-fashioned full-length waistcoat. The man had lost his wig and hat but he held out a pistol and, as he took in the sight of the burning fort, he fired it screaming some frightful accusation after Mack. The mountain-man fell full length, his spine broken by the ball, and Drinkwater ran up to him as he breathed his last. Behind Drinkwater the marines brought down the wigless Russian.

Drinkwater bent over the dying Mack. '. . . Thought . . . I'd betrayed . . .' he got out through clenched teeth, and Drinkwater looked at the Russian, rolling beneath the bayonets of the marines. It must have been the returning commandant, misinterpreting the mayhem before him as his post blazed and Mack walked insouciantly away from the scene.

Drinkwater watched as life ebbed from the tumbled goliath, shot so ignominiously by a debauched ne'er-do-well, and felt that sharp pang of regret, that sense of universal loss that accompanied certain of the deaths he had witnessed. He was about to stand when his eye fell upon something bright.

Half a dozen huge nuggets of the purest gold had rolled out of the mountain-man's leather pouch.

'Bury 'em both,' he called to the marines, and scooping up the treasure he swept them into his pocket.

Gold.

It threw off the reflections of the candle flames leaping and guttering as *Patrician* worked her way off shore in the first hours of the night. Tomorrow she would appear off Point Lobos, but tonight she would hide herself and her prize in the vastness of the Pacific.

Gold.

A king's ransom lay before him. No wonder Mack had scorned the idea of payment for passing *Patrician*'s deserters to the Russians, and no wonder he had not wanted those same men wandering over wherever it was he found the stuff, for that was the only implication that fitted his deed and his character. He would not encourage the Spaniards, for their tentacles would spread inexorably northwards, while the Russians could supply him with those necessities he was compelled to get from civilisation. Powder, shot, steel needles, flints . . . Drinkwater had no idea how many natural resources the wilderness contained.

But it contained gold.

And what the devil would such an unworldly man as 'Captain Mack' do with such a treasure? That was a mystery past his divining.

'Cleared for action, sir!'

'Very well, Mr Fraser.'

Above their heads the white ensign snapped in the breeze from the north that had blown fresh throughout the night and was only now losing its strength as they came under the lee of the land. From his post on the gun-deck, Quilhampton tried to locate the little cove where he and the cutter's crew had holed up and from where he had seen the *Patrician* carried off into captivity. Suppose the *Suvorov* was waiting for them under the protection of the

Spanish battery on Point Lobos? What would be the outcome of the action they were about to fight?

He found he dare not contemplate defeat, and felt the atmosphere aboard the ship imbued with such a feeling of renewal that defeat must be impossible, no matter what the odds. Those two raids, little enough in themselves, had patched up morale, made of them all a ship's company again, a ship's company that had endured much. There was talk of going home after the job was done, after the Spanish and the Russians had been made to eat their own shit, and the gun-captains kneeled with their lanyards taut in their fists in anticipation of this event.

'Thou art my battle-axe and weapons of war,' the Reverend Jonathan Henderson had declaimed at Divine Service that morning, 'for with Thee I will break in pieces the nations, and with Thee I will destroy kingdoms,' he had railed, and if no one understood the finer theological points of his subsequent deductions, all made the blasphemous connection between Jeremiah's imputed words and themselves.

'Stand ready, sir,' Mr Belchambers squeaked at the companionway, 'maximum elevation,' he went on repeating Drinkwater's orders from the quarterdeck, 'no sign of the Russian ships. Target to be the battery, starboard broadside.'

Quilhampton grinned. The boy had the phrases arse-about-face, but he was cool enough. He stooped and peered through the adjacent gun-port. He saw the smoke suddenly mushroom from the end cannon, wafting outwards in a great smoke-ring, but no fall of shot followed.

'Make ready!' Belchambers's squeak came again.

'Make ready there, starbowlines!' Quilhampton roared with mounting excitement.

A second smoke-ring mushroomed from the embrasures of Point Lobos.

'They're bloody well saluting us,' muttered Quilhampton, frowning.

'Hold your fire, sir! There's a flag of truce putting off from the shore.'

A groan of disappointment ran along the gun-deck.

*

'*Capitán*, my brother, Don José Arguello de Salas, *Commandante* of His Most Catholic Majesty's city of San Francisco, extends his most profound apologies for this most unfortunate mistake.'

'Damn you, Don Alejo. Where *is* your brother? I demand to know more of this affair, this so-called *mistake* which I.know to be nothing short of a towering fabrication, a . . . a . . .' words failed to express Drinkwater's angry sense of outrage.

So many half-guessed-at truths had found their answers in the hour since the flag-of-truce had first been seen. But Don Alejo was not a man to concede a thing. As Drinkwater faltered, the wily Spaniard rammed home his counter-stroke.

'We are both guilty, *Capitán*. You, please, you steal our schooner, *La Virgen de la Bonanza*.'

'That is an outrageous allegation . . .'

'*Capitán*, please, it is one of the confusions of this war.'

'If you had informed me, as you were duty bound to do, that she brought news of our new alliance, I should not have been forced to capture her. You, Don Alejo, acted outside all international law by selling, yes sir, *selling* His Britannic Majesty's ship *Patrician* to the Russian power in the person of Prince Rakitin *after* you had heard that your country was once again an ally of mine. Such an action is the basest and most dishonourable that I have ever heard of.'

'A little mistake, *Capitán* Drinkwater,' snapped Don Alejo, 'a little . . . what did your English papers say, eh? Ah, *sí*, a quibble, like when your ships come under your Admiralty orders and attack Bustamente's frigates and blow up the *Mercedes* and send *women* to God before you have a declaration of war! It is nothing! Nothing!' Don Alejo made a gesture of contemptuous dismissal.

'But you traded, Don Alejo, *sold* my ship. You have been trading with the Russians ever since Rezanov came, eh? Your Most Catholic Master does not approve of his servants trading in his monopolies.'

'It was for my country that I remove your ship. You too-much disturb trade. Now we are at peace and allies, you have your ship back.' Don Alejo spoke in a lower key. 'Perhaps, *Capitán* Drinkwater, you should be a little obliged to me . . .'

'Upon my soul, why?' asked Drinkwater aback.

'When you first take me prisoner, *Capitán*, Don Jorge Rubalcava, he want to tell you to go to Monterey. There you not escape. There you lose your ship. Here in San Francisco . . .' He shrugged, a gesture full of implications, and Drinkwater understood that Don Alejo was beyond his comprehension in cunning. Whatever the venal sins of his brother, Don Alejo would emerge on the winning side. If he knew of the presence of gold in California, as that shrewd observation of Quilhampton's suggested, Don Alejo was not the man to make the knowledge public. Had he in some subtle way suggested to Doña Ana Maria that honour was at stake and so ensured Drinkwater's escape through her action? Looking at him, Drinkwater thought the thing at least a possibility. And Don Alejo had nothing to lose by it, for Drinkwater might have failed, lost in some obscure and savage *fracas* on the coast. He shuddered at the mere recollection of the night raid on the Columbia River.

'Now, *Capitán*, as to the matter of your men . . .' said the Spaniard smoothly.

Drinkwater frowned. 'I shall expect them returned instantly.'

'As soon as Don Jorge takes possession of the *aviso*, *Capitán*.' Don Alejo smiled victoriously. Drinkwater opened his mouth to protest the injustice of losing their prize. Then he remembered the gold and felt the weight of those nuggets dragging down the tails of his full-dress coat. When the time came, he thought, he could purchase comforts enough to compensate his men for the loss of their paltry share in the schooner. Perhaps they were better off, for the matter might lie before a prize-court for years, and only the attorneys would benefit. Besides, he had other matters to attend to. There were despatches, brought weeks earlier, carried overland to Panama with the news of the rising against the French, then up the coast in *La Virgen de la Bonanza*. Don Alejo swore he had intended to pass them to Drinkwater on his release, the very day Drinkwater had succeeded in escaping. And there was still the Russian power to destroy.

Don Alejo was holding out a glass.

'A toast to our new alliance, *Capitán* . . . to *Dos de Mayo* . . . the second day of May, the day Madrid rose against the French. It is a pity good news travels so slow, eh?'

*

458

He knew he was not supposed to see her, that she broke some imposition of her father's or her uncle's to contrive this clumsy meeting on the path. She was as lovely as ever and yet there was something infinitely sad about the cast of her features, despite her smile. She held two books out to him. They were his log and journal and he took them, thanking her and tucking them under his arm with the bundle of despatches Don Alejo had at last given him. He smiled back at her.

'*Señorita*, I am indebted to you for ever for my freedom, even,' he added, the smile passing from his face, 'for my very life.' He paused, recalling how close he had come to the ultimate act of despair and her face reflected her own grief. Then he brightened. 'And thank you for your kindness in retrieving my books.'

'It was nothing . . .'

'You knew about the changes in your country's circumstances?' She nodded. '*Sí.*'

'And disobeyed your father?'

'My father is sometimes deceived by Don Alejo.' Drinkwater remembered her obvious dislike of Don Alejo.

'He was engaged in some illegal traffic with the Russians?' She shrugged. 'All would have been well had Nicolai lived.'

'It was fated otherwise, *Señorita*.'

'*Sí. Qué será será*,' she murmured.

'Why did you release me?'

She looked him full in the face then. 'Because you told the truth about Nicolai.'

'It was a small thing.'

'For me it was not. It has changed my life. I am to go into a convent.'

He remembered the Franciscan. 'It is the world's loss, *Señorita*.'

'I prayed for your wife and family . . . *Adiós*, *Capitán*.'

'*Adiós*, *Señorita*.' He bowed as she turned away.

Drinkwater watched through his glass as Hill brought *La Virgen de la Bonanza* to her anchor under Point Lobos that evening. He watched Don Jorge Rubalcava board her and wished he could shoot the treacherous dog with Mack's long rifle that now lay below in his cabin. Then he swung his glass to see if the rest of the

459

bargain was being kept. He watched the boat approach, returning the ragged remnants of his men from the chain gang of servitude. By the time Hill and Frey came back from the schooner, *Patrician*'s anchor was a-trip.

'I would not stay in this pestilential spot another moment,' he remarked to Hill as the sailing master made his report. The knot of officers within hearing nodded in general agreement. Only Mr Frey stood pensively staring astern.

'She intends to become a nun, Mr Frey,' he snapped, an unwonted harshness in his voice.

21 The Night Action

September 1808

Drinkwater stared at the empty bulkhead. The paint was faintly discoloured where the portraits of Elizabeth and the children used to hang. Before him, on the table, were scattered the contents of the despatch brought weeks ago by the *aviso*. It had been a day of explanations, not least that of the most perplexing of his worries, one that had concerned him months earlier at the time of their departure from the Nore.

Some departmental inefficiency had delayed it and now it had been sent out after him to the West Indies, overland to Panama by mule and shipped up the Isthmus, to be opened and scrutinised by Don Alejo Arguello, no doubt, before finding its way to him. It was months old, so old, in fact, that its contents were rendered meaningless by the train of events, except that they heartened him, gave him some insight into his apparent abandonment by the head of the Admiralty's Secret Department Lord Dungarth. He read the relevant passage through again.

I write these notes for your better guidance, my dear Drinkwater, for I find upon my return from Government business elsewhere, that Barrow has sent you out insufficiently prepared. Seniavin declined to serve against us after his Imperial master succumbed to the seductions of Bonaparte, having seen service with us at an earlier period in his career. Rakitin is a less honourable man, untroubled by such scruples and well-known to some of your fellow officers. I would have you know these things before you reach the Pacific, for it reaches me that he is to command a ship of some force, perhaps a seventy-four, and capitalise upon the work done by Rezanov . . .

Drinkwater folded the letter. So, Dungarth had been absent on

461

Government business elsewhere. Drinkwater was intrigued as to where that business might have been. Had his Lordship been back to France? He had made some vague allusions to Hortense Santhonax having become the mistress of Talleyrand. She had turned her coat before, might she not do so again?

He thrust the ridiculous assumption aside. That was altogether too fanciful. What advantage could either Hortense Santhonax or the French Foreign Minister derive from betraying such an unassailably powerful man as the Emperor Napoleon? It was a preposterous daydream. He picked up another letter. The superscription was familiar, but he could not place it. Then he recollected the hand of his friend, Richard White. Drinkwater slit the seal, anticipating his old shipmate must be writing to inform him he had hoisted a rear-admiral's flag.

A deck below Captain Drinkwater, Lieutenant Quilhampton was also reading a letter.

I am sure you meant no unkindness, Catriona had written, *but I assure you that if the necessity to which you were put was painful to you, it was doubly so to me. You had the benefit of long consideration, I had only the most profound of shocks. I have burned those letters you returned but, sir, circumstanced as I am, I must risk all reputation and request you repent yourself of so rash an act.*

'God bless my soul,' he muttered, 'what a surprise! What a marvellous, bloody surprise!'

Drinkwater read White's letter with a profound sense of horror. Following so soon upon the last he could scarce believe its contents and compared the dates. But White's was written a full fortnight after Lord Dungarth's and he had no reason to doubt its accuracy.

My main purpose in writing, my dear Nathaniel, is to acquaint you of the event of Thursday last when, on a lonely stretch of the Canterbury road near Blackheath, an incendiary device exploded beneath the coach of Lord Dungarth and his lordship's life is feared for . . .

He ruffled through the remaining papers (some routine communications from the Navy Office and an enquiry from the Sick and Hurt Board) for a later letter informing him of Dungarth's death, but could find nothing. A feeling of guilt stole over him; he had condemned a friend without cause and now Dungarth might be dead. And there was not even a letter from Elizabeth to console him. He looked up at the bare patches on the forward bulkhead and shook off the omen.

'Is she gaining on us, Mr Hill?' Drinkwater looked astern at the big, dark hull with the bow wave foaming under her forefoot and her pale patches of sails braced sharp up in pursuit of them. There was no doubt of her identity, she was the Russian seventy-four *Suvorov*.

'Gaining steadily, sir,' reported the sailing master.

'Good,' said Drinkwater, expressing satisfaction. He swung to the west where the day was leaching out of the sky and banks of inkily wet cumulus rolled menacingly against the fading light. The pale green pallor of the unclouded portion of the sky promised a full gale by morning. For the time being the wind was fresh and steady from the north-west. 'It'll be dark in an hour, that'll be our time. So you ease that weather foretack, Mr Hill, slow her down a little, I don't want him to lose sight of us, keep him thinking he has all the advantages.'

'Aye, aye, sir.'

'Mr Fraser!'

'Sir?'

'Have you inspected all the preparations?'

'Aye, sir, and your permission to pipe the men below for something to eat, if you please.'

'Most certainly; and a tot for 'em, I want devils tonight.'

'Aye, aye, sir.' Fraser touched the fore-cock of his hat and turned. Drinkwater went below himself, leaving the deck to Hill. In his cabin Mullender poured him a glass of rum and mixed it with water.

'There's some cold pork, sir, sour cabbage and some figgy duff. Tregembo's put a keen edge on your sabre, sir, and your pistols are in the case.'

Mullender indicated the plates and weapons laid in readiness along the sill of the stern windows where the settee cushions had been removed. Drinkwater had lost the privacy of his cabin bulk-heads, since *Patrician* was cleared for action and only a curtain separated him from the gun-deck beyond.

'And I found the portraits, sir, they're all right.'

'Good. Where were they?'

'Tossed in the hold.'

Drinkwater nodded and stared through the windows astern. 'Put out the candles, Mullender, I'll eat in the dark.'

He did not want to lose his night vision and the extinguishing of even so feeble a light would indicate some form of preparation was being made aboard *Patrician*. Drinkwater fervently hoped that Prince Vladimir Rakitin's opinion of him remained low. It had wounded him at the time it had been expressed, but Drinkwater sought now to fling it in the Russian's face.

But he must not tempt providence. She was a fickle deity, much given to casting down men in the throes of over-weening pride.

On deck again it was completely dark. They were near the autumnal equinox and already an approaching winter was casting its cold shadow over the water of the North Pacific. They pitched easily over the great swells, thumping into the occasional waves so that the spray streamed aft after every pale explosion on the weather bow.

'Very well, Mr Hill, pass word for all hands to stand to. Divisional officers to report when ready.'

When he received word that the ship was ready for action and every man at his station he gave his next order.

'Shorten sail!'

They were prepared for it. The lieutenants, midshipmen and mates took up the word and *Patrician* lost the driving force of her main and foresails. Men ran aloft to secure the flogging canvas. Neither sail had been set to much advantage, but not to have carried them would have alerted Rakitin. Now, with the onset of night, Drinkwater doubted the Russian officers would be able to see the reduction in sail. From the *Suvorov*, *Patrician* would be a grey blur in the night, and spanker and topsails would convey that impression just as well.

'Tack ship, Mr Hill.'

The master gave the routine orders with his usual quiet confidence. *Patrician* turned, passing her bow through the wind so that the wind and the spray came over the larboard bow and she stood back to the north-east, slightly across the *Suvorov*'s track, but in an attempt to elude her heavy pursuer's chase. It was precisely, Drinkwater argued, what Rakitin would assume he would do in an attempt to escape. It crossed Drinkwater's mind to wonder what exactly had passed between Rakitin and the Arguellos by way of a purchase price for his ship. He chuckled to himself in the darkness. This time there would be no humiliation, no *superior sailing* with which to reproach himself. This time, he felt in his bones, his ship's company had come through too much to let it go to the devil for want of a purpose.

'Ahhh . . .'

He could just see the *Suvorov*, swinging to starboard having seen the *Patrician* tack. He raised his speaking trumpet. 'Let fall!'

With a thunderous shudder bunt and clew-garnets were let go. Ropes whistled through the blocks and the great sails dropped from the yards, their clews drawn up to chess-tree and bumpkin as they were hauled taut. Drinkwater could almost feel *Patrician* accelerate, an illusion that was confirmed by the sudden change in relative bearing as the two ships closed in the darkness, *Patrician* rushing across the bow of the swinging Russian as she jibbed in stays, taking her wind as she sought to outwit her quarry.

'Hoist your lantern, Mr Belchambers! Mr Q, starboard battery as they bear!'

The noise of the wind and the tamed thunder of the sails gave way to something more urgent. The rushing of the sea between the two hulls, shouts of alarms from the Russian and, beneath their feet, the sinister rumbling of the guns as they were run out through the ports.

They were on top of her now, the range was point-blank, and no sooner were they run out than the gun-captains jerked their lanyards. On the fo'c's'le the heavy calibre carronades fired first and the smoke and concussion rolled aft with an awful and impressive rolling broadside that lit the night with the flames of its lethal explosions, yellow tongues of fire that belched their iron vomit into the heart of the enemy.

Above and behind Drinkwater Mr Belchambers succeeded in hoisting the battle lantern that was to illuminate the ensign straining from the peak of the gaff. It reached its station just as Drinkwater looked up at the spanker.

'Brail up the spanker! Up helm! Shorten sail!'

Patrician turned again, cocking her stern up into the wind, shortening sail again to manoeuvre alongside her shattered victim. The *Suvorov* lay in irons, her head yards aback and gathering sternway. Drinkwater had no time to assess the damage for they had yet to run the gauntlet of her starboard broadside where she mounted a greater weight of metal than her opponent.

'For what we are about to receive . . .' someone muttered the old blasphemy but Quilhampton's gunners were equal to the challenge. As a row of orange flashes lit the side of the *Suvorov* the bow guns of *Patrician*, reloaded and made swiftly ready by the furious exertions of their crews, returned fire. *Patrician* shook from the onslaught of shot. Beside him Hill reeled, spinning round and crashing into him with a violent shock, covering him with gore. Drinkwater grabbed him.

'My God, Hill!' he called, but the old man was already dead and Drinkwater laid him on the deck. Somewhere close by someone was shrieking in agony. It was a marine whose head had been pierced by langridge.

'Silence there!' roared Lieutenant Mount, but the man was beyond the reach of discipline and Blixoe discharged his musket into the man's back. He too fell to the deck. Drinkwater recovered himself, spun round and looked at his enemy.

The *Suvorov* had broached. He could see much of her foremast had gone, and her fo'c's'le was a mass of shattered spars and canvas.

'Down helm! Braces there . . . !'

He brought *Patrician* back towards his enemy and raked her stern from long pistol shot. She was almost helpless, firing hardly a gun in retaliation. Nothing but her stern-chasers would bear now and their ports were too low to open in such a rising sea.

For two hours Drinkwater worked his frigate back and forth, ranging up under the *Suvorov*'s stern, hammering her great black hull with impunity from his position of undisputed advantage. A rising moon shone fitfully between curtains of scud and the vast ocean heaved beneath the two labouring ships. The Russians fought back with small arms and those quarter guns they could bring to bear, but it was only later that Drinkwater learned that their complement was much weakened by the length of their cruise and that Rakitin's eagerness to acquire pressed recruits from the British Navy was to make good these deficiencies. But Russian tenacity was to no avail, for *Suvorov* wallowed unmanageable, a supine victim of *Patrician*'s hot guns whose captains had the range too well and whose 24-pound balls crashed into her fabric with destructive precision. For those two hours they played their fire into their quondam pursuer, rescuing their reputation and the honour of their commander.

Towards four bells in the first watch the pace of *Patrician*'s fire slackened and Drinkwater drew off, heaving-to under easy sail until daylight. Men lay exhausted at their guns and Drinkwater dozed, jammed against the mizen rigging, wrapped in his cloak.

It was Belchambers's excited squeal that woke him. Dawn was upon them and the wallowing hull of the Russian lay less than a mile away. A shred of smoke was drifting away on the wind, for the predicted gale was upon them, the sea rolling down from the north-west, its surface streaked by spume and shredded to leeward in a mist of spray through which the dark shape of a frigate-bird slipped on swept-back wings. The *Suvorov* had rolled all her masts overboard, but a second defiant shot followed the first and the dark, diagonal cross of the Tsar still flew from the stump of her mainmast. In the rough sea she was incapable of further manoeuvre and awaited only the *coup-de-grâce*.

Drinkwater roused his ship and the men stood to their guns again. There was a curiously intent look about them now as they stared over the heaving waste of the grey seas at the wallowing Russian.

'Larboard battery make ready!'

All along the deck the hands went up. 'Ready, sir!'

'Fire!'

Fully half their shot hit the sea, sending up plumes of white which were instantly dissipated by the gale, but clouds of splinters erupted in little explosions along the line of the Russian's hull.

'Ready, sir!'

'Fire!'

They timed it better that time. The concussion of the guns beat at Drinkwater's brain as his eyes registered the destruction their iron was causing to their enemy. He wondered if Rakitin was still alive and found he no longer cared.

'Ready, sir!'

'Fire!'

He raised his glass. They were reducing the *Suvorov* to a shambles; as she rolled helplessly towards them he could see the havoc about her decks. Under the fallen wreckage of her masts and spars a fire had started, a faint growing flicker that sent a rapidly thickening pall of smoke over the sea towards them.

'She's struck, sir!'

Belchambers pointed eagerly at the enemy ship. The boy was right. The Tsar's ensign was being hauled down. 'Cease fire, there! Cease fire!'

'Congratulations, sir,' said Fraser, coming aft.

Drinkwater shook his head. 'Pass my thanks to the ship's company,' he said tersely. Fraser drew back and left Drinkwater staring down at the body of Hill. He had executed the Admiralty's instructions, carried out his particular service to prevent a Russian incursion south of the coast of Alaska.

As he bent over the body of the old sailing master he felt the heavy nuggets in the tail pockets of his coat touch the deck. It came to him that he might be a wealthy man and he wondered if the presence of gold in California was known to anyone in London. He thought of Lord Dungarth and the infernal device. Reaching out his hand he touched Hill's face, then stood and stared to windward, mourning his friends.

Author's Note

Russian penetration of the Pacific coast of North America extended as far south as Fort Ross, on Bodega Bay. The posts of the Russian-American Company are assumed to have been founded in 1811, but Nicolai Rezanov attempted a lodgement in 1806 which apparently failed, perhaps for the reasons here revealed. Conditions under the Company were notoriously poor, even by contemporary Russian standards, and Indian raids were frequent. Had he lived, Rezanov would undoubtedly have achieved much needed reforms, but his tragic death in March 1807, in the obscure Siberian town of Krasnoiarsk, prevented this. He had been on his way to obtain the Tsar's ratification of a treaty to trade with the Spanish colonies which he had agreed in principle with Don José Arguello, *Commandante* at San Francisco. Prior to his landing at San Francisco, Rezanov had headed an embassy to the Japanese capital at Yedo as part of Kruzenstern's circumnavigation. This, too, ended in failure.

Don Alejo is my own invention, for Don José seems to have been a man of honour, unwilling to trade against the wishes of Madrid, although he had reached some form of accommodation with Rezanov. It seemed reasonable to assume his daughter had inherited her father's high-minded character and that she should be attracted to that of Rezanov, for she too existed, famed for her extraordinary beauty. She first met the Russian in April 1806, they fell in love and announced their betrothal. When she finally learnt of his untimely death, the Spanish beauty became a nun.

Descriptions of Russian merchant ships may be found in the pages of Dana, who met them in San Francisco in the 1840s, shortly before the abandonment of the posts at Bodega Bay (Fort Ross) and the Columbia River, and some twenty-odd years before the sale of Alaska to the United States. Several countries laid a spurious claim to this wild and lovely coast in the early years of the last century and it is fascinating to speculate upon the turn of events had the presence of gold been known forty years earlier than it is generally thought to have been. It is not inconceivable that its presence was known to a few who, for reasons of their own, wished it to remain secret.

A Private Revenge

For J.P.B.S

Contents

PART ONE: THE DAMOCLEAN SWORD   475

     The Typhoon   477

1   The Brig   485

2   New Orders   501

3   Whampoa   509

4   The Dragon's Roar   520

5   The Matter of Morale   527

6   The Concerns of a Convoy   539

7   Morris   549

8   Fair Winds and Foul Tempers   559

9   Infirmities of Character   571

10   A Small Victory   582

11   Blood and Rain   590

PART TWO: NEMESIS   601

12   A Council of War   603

13   A Round Robin   616

14   The Winds of Fortune   625

15   The Bronze-bound Chests   634

16   Blow-pipe Creek   641

17   The Gates of the Fortress   652

18   Pursuit   660

PART THREE: A PRIVATE REVENGE   669

19   The Tripod   671

20   A Forlorn Hope   681

21   A Private Revenge   691

22   Penang   696

     Author's Note   702

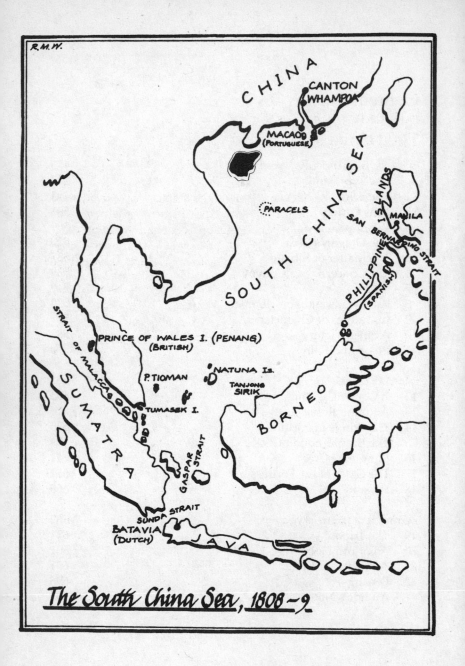

The South China Sea, 1808~9.

PART ONE
The Damoclean Sword

'Seamen are neither reckoned among the living, nor the dead, their whole lives being spent in jeopardy. No sooner is one peril over, but another comes rolling on, like the waves of a fullgrown sea.'

SAMUEL KELLY
An Eighteenth-Century Seaman, 1786

The Typhoon

November 1808

Captain Nathaniel Drinkwater gave up trying to sleep. His cot rocked and jerked so violently on its lanyards that his body was never still. He kicked the twisted blankets aside with a sudden spurt of furious annoyance.

His Britannic Majesty's frigate *Patrician* pitched violently, her bow flung into the air as if her twelve hundred tons were of no consequence, for all her massive timbers. Drinkwater was driven to consider her fabric as a sum of many small and separate parts which, God alone knew, were now subjected to stresses and strains beyond the computation of his tired brain. All that he could consider at that moment was a vivid image of his ship flying to pieces from the pounding she was now undergoing. There was something alarmingly new about this present motion, and the thought led him to conclude that he must have been dozing. Anger had been born out of this interruption of his rest. The knock at the cabin door only increased his resentment.

'Yes?' His voice was sharp and strained.

'Captain, sir, if you please, Mr Fraser's compliments and would you step on deck, sir?'

Midshipman Belchambers's face was grey with fatigue and fright, reminding Drinkwater that he was not alone in his exhaustion.

'What is it?' He raised himself on a precarious elbow and quizzed the midshipman as the cot lanyards alternately slackened and snapped taut so that his awkwardly prone body was feather-light one second and leaden the next. The ship's stern was lifted rapidly as a sea slammed viciously under her transom and against her stern windows over which the dead-lights had been dropped.

Water drove in round the sashes, squirting over the settee before running to join the mess slopping back and forth across the chequer-painted canvas on the deck.

Midshipman Belchambers grabbed a corner of the sideboard, his Adam's apple bobbing uncertainly above his grubby stock.

'I can't say, sir,' he gabbled and, clapping a hand over his mouth, fled from the captain's presence.

Drinkwater stared after the boy. The grey gleam of water, mixed with fragments of biscuit from the shattered china barrel, flowed in miniature torrents round the legs of the lashed table, and over-turned chairs slid back and forth, back and forth . . .

'God's bones!' Drinkwater blasphemed through clenched teeth, hoisting himself carefully out of his cot and seeking a footing in his stockinged feet amid the cold swirl of the water. The shards of porcelain grated across the deck like shingle on a beach as he felt his stockings take up the water. Drinkwater's shins were already criss-crossed with bruises, his old shoulder wound ached abom-inably, his mouth was foul with the taste of bile and his eyes ground grittily in their sockets, sure evidence of lack of sleep.

He clung upright with difficulty, drawing on coat and cloak, despite the stuffiness of the air. Outside his cabin the marine sentry slithered towards him and they collided amid a confused and embarrassed explosion of apology and profanity. *Patrician*'s motion was unpredictably irregular, a bucking, scending, rolling caused by the seas which slammed her sides and ran below by a hundred leaky routes. A rancid stench rose from the crowded berth-deck below and was given seeming embodiment by the creaks and groans of the labouring ship. Grasping the companionway man-ropes, Drinkwater climbed carefully on deck.

He reached the quarterdeck surprised that it was full daylight. Fraser stood clinging to the starboard hammock cranes.

'What is it, Mr Fraser?'

The first lieutenant shook his head, concern etched in his drawn expression.

'I cannot tell precisely, sir . . . the confusion of the sea . . . 'tis the worst thing I've seen.'

Drinkwater was suddenly attentive and looked about him, the stupor of exhaustion flung away. Was it a matter of Scots caution, or did a shoal lurk beneath this monstrous confusion of water? He could not tell; his charts were totally inadequate and he had no precise knowledge of their whereabouts. For four days they had run before the storm without a stitch of canvas set and their topgallant masts struck. Two men had been killed getting the heavy lower yards lashed a-portlast so that *Patrician* offered as little top-hamper as possible to the fury of the wind. The decks were cluttered with lowered spars, yet the big frigate still steered downwind with the speed of a cantering horse.

On the second night of the storm the lower masts had glowed with St Elmo's fire, the corposant running hither and thither in the rigging until their baffled compass had, in the hours that followed, circled gently in a kind of bewilderment that confused Drinkwater. He had lost his old sailing master, killed in the action with the Russian line-of-battle-ship *Suvorov*, and had no one to turn to for advice, as Fraser had now turned to him.

For those four days they had run square to leeward with great seas heaping up astern, their foaming crests breaking and running after the fleeing ship. They had been pooped twice, sluiced from taffrail to knightheads by an avalanche of green water that tore coils of rope from the fife-rails, swept men off their feet and dashed them into the guns. In this deluge arms had been broken, an elbow shattered and a leg snapped so cleanly that it lay like a carpenter's angle. Worst of all two men had been washed overboard. One, Midshipman Wickham, they had not seen again; the other, the marine quarter-guard, had been found clinging to the heads, his feet dragging in the water in the last extremity of distress. The experience made the ship's company more cautious and the second pooping caused less damage.

But this morning the sea no longer drove from astern and the wind no longer roared through the standing rigging to tear the slack stays of the upper masts in great bights to leeward. Nor was the air filled with salt and spray driving downwind like buckshot. Instead, the surface of the ocean rose up in heaps; waves slopped with malignant power against each other, flinging dark columns of water high into the air, from which they fell back in a vast welter of confusion.

In this lashing of the sea *Patrician* was caught helplessly, the violence of her motion whipping her truncated masts so that blocks flew about aloft with sufficient energy to brain a man sent to secure them. Abrupt enough to throw an incautious man from his feet as she lay down to a roll, *Patrician*'s hull would be thrust back by a wave running in opposition to the first. This conflict of forces assailed her simultaneously, sending racking stresses through her straining hull while the tortured bodies of her company met the onslaught with instinctive and tiring muscular exertions.

If the air no longer boomed with the sound of the great wind, it was now filled with the huge slop and hiss of the aimless sea, and the desperate cries of exhausted birds. The deck was covered with their pathetic, flapping forms, a variety of species including brilliantly coloured land-birds.

Looking upwards Drinkwater saw the explanation for his surprise at the daylight. For the duration of the storm they had run under a low and oppressive overcast of thick scud. Now the sky was inexplicably clear and the last stars were fading against the blue of the morning, though the horizon that ringed them was still dull under a rim of encircling fractus.

'I tried a cast o' the lead, sir, but nae bottom . . .' said Fraser, suddenly thrusting out an arm. Drinkwater grasped it, and clawed his way uphill towards the starboard rail, then immediately found himself cannoned into Fraser by the frigate's lurch.

'Devil take it! Obliged, Mr Fraser . . .'

Drinkwater caught his breath and looked about him again. He had, he realised now, known instinctively that this terrible motion was not due to shoal water; the extraordinary funnel of clear and windless sky stirred something else in his tired brain. He fought to clear it, buying time with a pathetic joke.

'Belchambers bid me "step" on deck, Mr Fraser. If it was your choice of phrase you could have bettered it.'

A thin, respectful grin spread briefly across the Scotsman's worried face.

'Aye, sir, 'twas ill-chosen.'

'No matter.' Drinkwater jerked his head at the sky. 'This present lull will not last. I mind some instruction on the matter, 'tis the same as a West India hurricane, though known differently in these seas. Do you look again to the breeching of the guns. I wish we had struck some of them down into the hold, but it is too late now. I'll take the deck.'

'Aye, aye, sir. We've beckets on the wheel and clapped lashings on the tiller. All she'll do is lie a-hull.'

'That's well done.'

Fraser skidded off, shouting names at the duty bosun's mate, and Drinkwater jammed his body against the starboard mizen pin-rail, feeling the sore places on his back where the ropes had abraded him earlier. He looked after his first lieutenant: poor Fraser, as first luff he should have enjoyed the privilege of being exempt from watch-keeping. But with Lieutenant Mylchrist and Mr Hill dead, only he and Quilhampton remained of the lieutenants and senior officers, though Drinkwater had written out an acting commission for Mr Midshipman Frey.

Fraser's predicament led Drinkwater's thoughts to a review of his hard-pressed command. In addition to her present plight there were other concerns that drove his mind into a remorseless circle of worry. The presence of over a hundred Russian prisoners placed strains upon the domestic arrangements of a ship and company already stretched by a long and dangerous voyage. *Patrician*'s own people were worn out with the war, transferred from one ship to another at the whim of the almighty Admiralty and now fighting for their very existence in this dismal corner of the north-west Pacific.

Captain Drinkwater stared bleakly ahead, noting the relative shift in the shrinking patch of blue sky and weighing up the chances of a glimpse of the sun before the cloud lowered over them again.

The squawks of the birds drew his thoughts inboard once more as a handful of seamen, clinging on to any handhold, strove to clear the decks of some of the hundreds of dying creatures. He watched them, trying to judge their temper for though they had fought well against a Russian battle-ship in the Pacific, their mood had been uncertain off the Horn and they had been near-mutinous off California, several of them deserting at San Francisco.

In his heart, Drinkwater knew he could expect no less. Some of them had been at sea since the turn of the century, had served as volunteers in the Peace of Amiens and had then been swept up in the turbulence of the renewed war with France.

Drinkwater cursed the chain of events that had led them to this day, for he too suffered, suffered as personally as his men, for the secret he and they had brought back from the Baltic in the late summer of 1807. That overwhelming need for secrecy had led Their Lordships to despatch him to the Pacific to head off Britain's quondam ally Russia, whose Tsar had abandoned his alliance with the Court of St James in favour of a shoddy opportunist accommodation with Napoleon Bonaparte. This allowed Tsar Alexander to meddle with Sweden and Turkey and lend his British-trained fleet to the Emperor of the French. Had Drinkwater, despite the odds, succeeded in crushing the Russian presence in the Pacific? He had fought the *Suvorov* to a standstill, as the state of his frigate testified, but his cruise to locate the *Juno* had failed. She had slipped from him, and his nature would not allow him the reasonable excuse of having the whole Pacific to search to comfort him in his failure.

Perhaps she was at Canton, perhaps not . . .

A watery gleam caught his attention to larboard. He turned and lifted his eyes. As the circle of clear sky moved over them a shredding of the cloud on its eastern rim exposed for a second a pale yellow disc. The sun!

'Mr Belchambers! My sextant and the chronometer! Upon the instant, sir!'

Transfixed, Drinkwater watched the face of the sun darken as, like dense smoke, cloud trailed across it, then lighten again. Impatiently he waited for the boy's return. The sun swam clear of cloud, hurting his eyes, and he thought its warmth struck him, though afterwards it seemed a mere illusion. Suddenly the confusion of the sea held less terrors and flashed friendly fire back at them in reflections. Amidships a man smiled and raised a low cheer. All about him there was a spontaneous outburst of relief. The watch, huddling in the lee of the boats on the booms, struggled to their feet, other seamen stopped throwing the birds overboard and even, it seemed, the birds themselves ceased their death struggles to bask in the sunlight.

Drinkwater's patience snapped. 'Where the devil's that boy?'

'Beg pardon, sir . . .'

His sentry's head was poked up the companionway level with the deck.

'Eh? What is it?' Drinkwater asked the marine.

'Begging your pardon, sir, but Mr Belchambers 'as 'ad a fall, sir.'

'What? God-damn! What about my sextant?' Drinkwater was already crossing the deck and exchanging the ineffable sweetness of sunshine for the stygian gloom of the gun-deck. Shoving aside the sentry, he entered his cabin. By the grace of God Belchambers had not reached the Hadley sextant, nestling in its baize-lined box and lashed atop his locker. Instead the boy lay amid the swirl of biscuit and china with a sprained ankle. His small, frightened face was twisted with agony.

'I . . . I'm sorry, sir . . . I acted with haste . . . *festina lente*, sir,' the boy added gamely.

'No matter, Mr Belchambers, are you all right?' Drinkwater bent over the midshipman.

'Apart from my ankle, sir . . .'

Drinkwater turned to the marine. 'Get a couple of hands to carry Mr Belchambers to his berth.'

Drinkwater reached across the midshipman who was drawing himself up against the locker. 'You must excuse me, I have urgent matters to attend to.'

Lifting the sextant from its box he caught the strap of the chronometer case with his left hand. Sticking his elbows out for balance he gingerly made for the bottom of the companionway and shouted up for assistance.

'Here, zur, let me . . .'

Old Tregembo, his coxswain, shouldered past him and took the chronometer box.

'Mind how you go, damn it,' snapped Drinkwater as both men grabbed the man-rope at the same instant.

'Up you goes, zur, an' I'll follow . . .'

But it was too late. Already the sun had been swallowed by cloud and the eye of the storm was passing over them. Fractus again curtained the sky and the confusion of the sea was abating. Streaks of spume were appearing upon its surface which was heaping once more in regular ridges. The calm of the dawn had vanished. *Patrician*, with her lashed tiller and locked rudder, was paying off to lie beam on to the rising wind that came at them now from the contrary direction. Drinkwater bit off his disappointment at failing to get a sight. As the deck steadied to a roll, he crossed it swiftly and peered into the binnacle. He had at least a notion of their heading and now, as it blew with swiftly increasing strength, the direction of the gale. That brief glimpse of the sun had fed his starved seaman's instinct with a morsel of information.

The compass had steadied and the wind blew now from the west-nor'-west.

But it was precious little comfort. An hour later *Patrician* was assailed again by the violence of the storm. It no longer screamed with the malevolent harpy-shriek of a strong gale, but had risen to the mind-numbing boom of a mighty wind, and the spray tore at the very eyes in their sockets, forcing their heads away.

'It's blowing great guns, sir,' shouted Fraser as he clawed his way towards Drinkwater on completion of his rounds.

'A great wind, Mr Fraser. I mind now the captain of an Indiaman once telling me it was called *tai-fun* by the Chinese.'

1 The Brig

November 1808

Drinkwater closed the log-book. Knowledge of his position at last gave him a measure of contentment. The inadequacy of his chart sent a flutter of apprehension through his belly, to conflict with the realisation that he had been extraordinarily lucky. He recalled memories of talks with Captain Calvert nearly thirty years earlier, dredging up facts imparted to the impressionable young Midshipman Drinkwater by the old East India commander. Calvert had told him of the curious revolving storms of the China Seas which were comparable with the hurricanes of the West Indies or the feared cyclones of the Bay of Bengal.

From what his sextant and chronometer had revealed he was now able to make an informed guess at *Patrician*'s track in a long curve that had brought her from the Pacific Ocean into the eastern margins of the South China Sea. The typhoon's eye, or centre, that funnel of clear sky in which they had experienced the severest thrashing of the sea, had passed over them, subjecting them to the violent winds beyond. They had been fortunate that their ordeal had lasted only another two days, for though the wind remained fresh and a heavy residual swell still lifted and rolled the frigate, the sea was no longer vicious. A measure of its moderation could be gauged by the smell of smoke and salt pork that was percolating through the ship. The thought of hot food, however rudimentary, brought a glow of satisfaction to Drinkwater's spirits as surely as the knowledge of his ship's position.

In this mood Drinkwater, tired though he was, finished his self-imposed task of writing up his private journal. As he did so his cabin was suddenly filled with the delicious bitter smell of what passed for coffee aboard His Britannic Majesty's frigate *Patrician*. Drinkwater looked up.

'Coffee, sir?'

Mullender poured from the pot he had brought from the pantry and Drinkwater sipped the scalding liquid gratefully. Mullender stood, balancing himself against the heave of the ship which was pronounced here, at the stern.

'Hot food today, sir,' Mullender remarked. Such things assumed a rare importance on board a storm-damaged ship and Drinkwater looked keenly at his steward. How long had Mullender attended him? To his shame he had forgotten; and he had forgotten whether Mullender was married or had children. The man stood patiently, holding the coffee-pot, waiting for Drinkwater to ask for more, a grubby rag of a towel over his bare arm with its sparse flesh and pallid skin. Drinkwater caught the steward's eye and smiled.

'That's good news, Mullender, good news . . .'

'Aye, sir.'

Mullender's impassivity, the expressionless look to his eyes and face struck Drinkwater, and it occurred to him that he had taken Mullender so for granted that he was guilty in some way he could not quite comprehend. He held out his cup and watched the brown liquid gurgle into it.

'We have all been sorely tried, Mullender,' he said as he swallowed the second cupful.

'Aye, sir.'

Drinkwater handed the emptied cup back to the steward. 'That was most welcome, thank you.'

He watched Mullender retreat to the pantry. Was there something odd about the man's demeanour, or was he himself mildly hallucinating from the effects of exhaustion? He did not know. What was important was to secure for them all a period of rest. Wearily he rose from the table and left the cabin.

There was more to hearten him on deck, for it was one of the minor miracles of the sea-service that the sum of a ship's company's efforts could produce spectacular results from meagre resources. And *Patrician* and her people had indeed been sorely tried in the preceding months.

She had taken a buffeting entering the Pacific by way of Cape Horn the previous year; she had been deliberately sabotaged by someone in her own company and refitted on the coast of California; and she had fought two actions, the second against heavy odds. The brutal combat with the Russian line-of-battle-ship *Suvorov* had left her a battered victor with the added responsibility of prisoners amongst her own disaffected crew. Now, bruised by the long passage across the North Pacific and the terrible onslaught of a typhoon, it was still possible to set her to rights, to turn out of her hold sufficient material to make good the worst ravages of the elements, to rouse out of her sail-room enough spare sails to replace her rent canvas, or hoist from her booms a permutation of spars which allowed her to carry topgallants on all three masts. It was true she was no longer the lofty sail-carrier that had left the Nore amid the equinoctial gales of the autumn of 1807, but despite shortages of powder and shot, despite a desperate depletion of her stores and victuals, she remained a King's ship, an arm of British policy in these distant waters.

'Good morning, sir.'

Lieutenant James Quilhampton touched the forecock of his battered hat, his tall, gangling frame familiarly out-at-elbows, his wooden fist by his side and a wide grin upon his face.

'Good to see a little sunshine, Mr Q,' remarked Drinkwater.

'Indeed it is, sir. Frey told me you were active with sextant and chronometer an hour since, sir. Dare I presume a longitude?'

'You may. And it crossed tolerably with yesterday's meridian altitude. If it remains clear, I shall get another at noon and be happy as a prentice-boy on pay-day.'

It was another minor miracle, Drinkwater thought, that neither of his instruments had suffered damage in the typhoon. It was true there were two other quadrants on the ship, but the loss of the chronometer would have been catastrophic.

'We shall have to maintain a masthead look-out, Mr Q, day and night, for we have passed the outer islands and are presently amid the reefs of the China Sea.'

The two men exchanged glances. Both were thinking of the brig *Hellebore* and her wrecking on a reef in the Red Sea.

'God forbid that we should be caught twice like that,'

Quilhampton said fervently, expelling his breath with a shake of his head.

Drinkwater caught the faint whiff of the lieutenant's breath and was reminded of another problem, for the unfortunate taint, increasingly common to them all, was an early sign of scurvy.

'We must wood and water, and seek fresh fruit and vegetables, Mr Q. I've a mind to beat up for the China coast. There's the Portuguese colony of Macao, or the East India Company's establishment at Canton where we may also find word of the *Juno*. It is still possible that she has escorted Russian ships there from Alaska with the season's furs.'

'Will you exchange our prisoners there, sir?' Quilhampton nodded forward to where, under a marine guard, a group of bearded Russians exercised round and round the fo'c's'le.

'If I can. They are a damned liability on board.'

'And their officers, sir?'

It was Drinkwater's turn to expel breath, a signal of exasperation borne with difficulty. 'I doubt they'll go, God damn 'em. My only consolation is that I do not have to suffer them day and night.'

The deaths of Lieutenant Mylchrist and the Master, Mr Hill, had left empty cabins aboard. Acting Lieutenant Frey had been ordered to stay in the gunroom while the cabins of the dead officers were turned over to the most senior of the Russians. At least Captain Prince Vladimir Rakitin did not have to share Drinkwater's own cabin, though he ate at his table. On such a long commission Drinkwater prized his privacy above all else.

'Talk of the devil,' muttered Quilhampton, drawing himself up as officer-of-the-watch to give the paroled prisoners formal permission to exercise on the quarterdeck.

'Good morning, Captain.'

The tall, heavily built figure of the Russian nobleman crossed the deck towards Drinkwater, staring about curiously. Rakitin was pale from his enforced confinement below decks for the duration of the typhoon.

'Good-day.'

Drinkwater was icily polite to his prisoner.

'You have refitted your ship in good time.'

Rakitin's excellent English was unnerving. The Russian had

served with the Royal Navy before the Tsar had turned his coat and succumbed to Napoleon's blandishments at Tilsit. Drinkwater found this familiarity as repulsive as the man himself.

'My men know their duty, Captain,' he replied softly.

The two commanders stood side by side, united in rank, divided by hostility and yet compelled by convention to maintain a degree of amity. Considering them from the other side of the quarterdeck, Quilhampton thought them an odd pair. Tall and powerful, Rakitin's broad shoulders stretched the cloth of his high-collared uniform, an à la mode outfit that stank of Parisian fashion. Beside him, half a head shorter, his soft undress uniform coat lapels fluttering in the breeze, Captain Drinkwater balanced himself against the *Patrician*'s motion.

Quilhampton could see the inequality of Drinkwater's shoulders, the result of two wounds that even padding and the heavy bullion epaulettes could not disguise. The hair, receding slightly from the high forehead, still hung in a thick, ribboned queue down Drinkwater's back, an old-fashioned affectation that conveyed an impression of agelessness to the loyal and devoted Quilhampton. As if sensing this scrutiny Drinkwater turned, catching Quilhampton's eye. The thin scar on the left cheek showed livid after the weathering of recent weeks, and the powder burns about Drinkwater's eye puckered the soft skin to give him a curious, quizzing appearance.

'Mr Q!' Drinkwater called. 'Have the kindness to arrange for Captain Rakitin's officers to attend the purser and supervise an issue of grog to their men in compliment to their labours at the pumps.'

'Aye, aye, sir.'

Rakitin turned, an expression of surprise on his face. 'My men have been pumping?' he asked.

'Yes,' replied Drinkwater smoothly, 'in order that mine might repair the ship.'

Drinkwater felt a contempt for Rakitin's ignorance of what his men had been doing. It seemed for a moment that Rakitin might protest, but he held his tongue. The Russian seamen had proved tireless and dogged workers, as conscientious at pumping as they had been serving the *Suvorov*'s guns. But indomitable as they had been in action, they had been ravaged by scurvy, reduced in numbers by sickness, and the high sea running during the battle had made it difficult for Rakitin to use his lower-deck guns . In the end *Suvorov* had been at the mercy of *Patrician*'s 24- and 18-pounder cannon which had cut up her rigging and masts, hulled her repeatedly, and swept her decks with a hail of canister and langridge. By the time Rakitin struck his colours, *Suvorov*'s powers of resistance were as shattered as her hull and when, in the moderating sea of the following day, they had taken off all those that they could, she had settled so low in the water that the fire they had started aboard her had barely caught. As for Drinkwater, he had lost more men in the rescue than in the action.

Rakitin, left to a sullen contemplation of his fate, had persuaded himself that his ship had been wantonly sacrificed by the British acting under Drinkwater's orders. The fact that Drinkwater possessed neither the resources nor the men to take the *Suvorov* as a prize did not enter into the Russian commander's bitter reflections. Aware that he had failed in his mission, Rakitin sought among his officers men of like opinion, cultivating them assiduously in this assumption, until they had convinced themselves of its accuracy. It was an understandable enough attitude, Drinkwater reflected, aware of the undercurrent of hostility. Rakitin would have to account for the loss of his ship to the Admiralty at St Petersburg, and the difference in force between a seventy-four and a frigate, albeit a heavy one, was going to be difficult to explain.

Rakitin had seized eagerly on the intelligence that the British ship had been built twenty-four years earlier as a 64-gun line-of-battle ship, insinuating this into his persuasive argument and glossing over the fact that she had been cut down to her present establishment in 1795. Somehow Rakitin had mitigated his defeat, at least in his own mind.

Despite this, Drinkwater could not deny an underlying sympathy with Rakitin's plight. He knew what it was to lose a ship. The loss of self-confidence alone could sink a man's spirits beyond revival. Nor did Drinkwater forget other matters concerning Russia; his brother Edward was serving with the Russian army, an agent of Great Britain now, nominally at least, an enemy. So

Drinkwater cultivated Rakitin with an icy reserve, not knowing, in this long and bitter war, when Tsar Alexander might turn his coat again, or when some obligation towards himself might not prove of advantage.

'Our men work well together, Captain. We should not be enemies. I believe Admiral Seniavin feels this.'

'Seniavin?' Rakitin looked at Drinkwater in astonishment, his mind plucked from the narrow contemplation of his misery to the speculative castle-building that officers called 'strategy'.

'Yes,' went on Drinkwater, 'I am advised that he is opposed to the Tsar's alliance with Napoleon Bonaparte.'

'I have my orders, Captain. It is my duty to obey them,' Rakitin growled.

'But,' said Drinkwater, suddenly brightening at the prospect of a little innocent bear-baiting, 'you also have your opinion, *n'est-ce que pas?*'

Rakitin turned and drew himself up. 'The alliance with the Emperor Napoleon is one offering great advantages to Russia. It is impossible that the French should rule Europe from Paris, but Europe ruled from Paris and St Petersburg must be,' he shrugged, '*très formidable . . .*'

'Until the Emperor Napoleon wishes otherwise, eh?'

'Captain Drinkwater, you cannot hold out the hand of friendship to Russia. Your army abandoned ours in the Netherlands, your Nelson threatened our ships in our own Baltic Sea. You still have a fleet there blockading our coasts, you tell us we can only trade with you . . .'

'You sailed in our ships, Prince Vladimir, you learned much from us and supported us in the North Sea. We pressed gold and arms on you, even refitted your ships; was not this proof of our friendship?'

Rakitin flushed with anger and was about to launch into a tirade on Britain's perfidy when there came a cry from the masthead.

'Deck there! Sail to leeward!'

Quilhampton reacted instantaneously, leaping into the lee mizen shrouds and yelling back: 'Where away?'

'Three points on the lee bow, sir . . . looks like a vessel under jury-rig!'

491

Quilhampton scanned the horizon and could see nothing. He jumped to the deck and held his glass out to Midshipman Dutfield.

'Up you go, cully, and see what you make of her.'

Drinkwater and Rakitin, their interest aroused, dropped their conversation instantly and stood watching the nimble boy ascend the rigging of the main mast. Dutfield reached the topgallant yard and threw a leg over it, hooking himself steady and releasing his two hands to raise the glass. His body arced against the sky for what seemed an eternity as everybody on deck waited for his opinion of the stranger.

They saw him lower the glass and look down, expecting any moment to hear news, but, apparently unsure, the midshipman raised the telescope again. The waist was filled with a murmur at the delay.

'Bosun's mate! Keep the men busy there!' Quilhampton ordered, adding, 'Watch your helm there, quartermaster,' as the petty officer at the con inattentively let the ship's head pay off.

At last Dutfield's voice hailed them from aloft.

'Brig, sir, and seen us by the colours reversed in her rigging!'

'What colours?' bellowed Drinkwater through cupped hands.

'British, sir . . .'

'Up helm a trifle, Mr Q, let's bear down on this fellow. Call all hands to stand by to reduce sail . . .'

Patrician lay hove-to, her main-topsail billowed back against the mast and her fore and main courses flogging sullenly in the buntlines as they brought the brig under their lee and prepared to hoist out a boat. Drinkwater studied the craft through his Dollond glass. She was a brig all right, and lying low in the water with both masts gone by the board. Her crew had managed to fish a yard to the stump of her foremast and had a leg-of-mutton sail hoisted, just, Drinkwater judged, giving her master command of his vessel.

'Ah, Mr Frey,' Drinkwater turned to the young man at his elbow, 'do you be kind enough to go over and offer what assistance is in our power. Find out her port of destination and her master's name. If she requires it, we can get a line aboard.'

'Aye, aye, sir.'

'And Mr Frey . . .'

'Sir?'

'Ask if she has any charts of the China coast.'

Drinkwater watched the boat bob over the swell, the oar-blades catching the brilliant sunshine, then disappearing in the deep troughs. As the boat rose again he recalled himself and turned suddenly, casting an incautious eye skywards and receiving the solar glare in his face.

'How bears the sun, Mr Q?' he asked urgently.

Quilhampton grasped Drinkwater's meaning and covered the three yards' distance to the binnacle. 'Close to the meridian, sir.'

'Damn!' With the agility of a younger man, Drinkwater made for the companionway and dropped below, startling Mullender as he fussed about the cabin. Grabbing the sextant from its lashed box and crooking it in his arm, he hastened back on deck. He flicked down the shades and clapped it to his right eye. To his relief he saw the sun was still increasing its altitude, climbing slowly to the meridian, and he waited for the ascent to slow.

'Watch the glass, there!' he called.

The quartermaster of the watch moved aft to heave the log as Quilhampton stood ready to turn the sand-glass. Forward the lookout on the knightheads walked aft and stood beside the belfry. Drinkwater caught the culmination of the sun on the meridian. He could compute their latitude exactly now and by a piece of legerdemain determine, to a reasonable accuracy, their longitude as well. Knowledge of their position would be invaluable both to himself and, he suspected, the beleaguered master of the wallowing brig

'Eight bells!' he called, lowering the sextant. The log was streamed, the glass turned and eight bells struck. The watch was called and yet another day officially began on board the *Patrician*.

An hour later he was bent over the cabin table, comparing his calculations with the reckoning of Captain Ballantyne, Master of the Country brig *Musquito* of Calcutta. Ballantyne was a short, red-faced man in a plain blue coat and tall boots, a tired man who had wrestled gamely with the typhoon for ten days and been forced to sacrifice his masts in order to preserve his ship.

Sunlight reflected off the swell beyond the windows and danced upon the white paintwork of the cabin, filling it with flickering lights as the frigate rolled easily.

'Well, sir,' said Drinkwater straightening up, 'will you serve us as pilot? If we are to bring both our ships safely to an anchor our need of each other is mutual.'

He was aware of continuing suspicion in Ballantyne's face. The merchant shipmaster remained obviously circumspect. To Ballantyne, Drinkwater was something of an enigma, for he was no youthful popinjay like so many of the young sprigs that came out in sloops and frigates to press men like carcasses from Country ships. In fact his appearance in these eastern seas was something of a mystery to a man like Ballantyne who, in common with all the trading fraternity, liked to keep his fingers on the pulse of Government business. Drinkwater's request for a pilot and charts confirmed him in one suspicion.

'I am indeed under an obligation to you, Captain Drinkwater, and one that I would not willingly shirk, but I am surprised to find you here. Are you not part of Drury's squadron?'

It was Drinkwater's turn to show surprise. 'Drury's squadron . . .? No, sir, I am not. I am from the coast of Spanish America. Furthermore I understood Admiral Pellew to be commanding the East India station . . .'

'Pellew still commands, but Drury has a squadron at Macao . . .'

The welcome news that British men-of-war were at hand, that he might speedily obtain spare spars and canvas, perhaps fresh victuals too, besides making good other deficiencies in his own stores from Drury's ships, seemed to lift a massive burden from Drinkwater's weary shoulders.

'Then let us make for Macao, Captain Ballantyne . . .'

'No, sir! That I must urge you not to . . .'

Drinkwater was surprised and said so.

'Captain Drinkwater,' Ballantyne said as patiently as he could, 'you are clearly unacquainted with the situation in these seas. Drury has been empowered by the Governor-General of India to offer what Lord Minto is pleased to call "protection" to the Portuguese Governor at Macao. This is nothing more nor less than coercion, for the Portuguese colonists there are friendly to us, the more so since the damned French have designs on both Portugal

494

herself and her overseas settlements. There are already stories of a French army coming overland through Persia and of an enemy squadron bound for these waters. If they take Macao then our China trade would be ended at a stroke . . .'

Ballantyne stopped, his serious expression adding emphasis to his speech. 'It would mean ruin for many of us in Country ships and the end of the East India Company.'

Drinkwater regarded this information with some cynicism. He held no brief for the India monopoly, but he acknowledged the influence of those who did. Ballantyne seemed to sense some of this indifference.

'Consider, sir,' he said, 'what the alliance between the Dutch and French has already achived: the Sunda Strait is closed to our ships and it has been necessary to convoy the trade through the Strait of Malacca. I do not think you can be aware of the numbers of French cruisers, both privateers and men-o'-war frigates, that the French have operating out of the Mauritius. One, the *Piemontaise*, a National ship, was taken by the *San Fiorenzo* off Cape Comorin, but at appalling cost, and that is our *only* success! That damned rogue Surcouf plundered our shipping right off the Sand Heads with complete impunity . . .'

'The Sand Heads . . .?' queried Drinkwater, aware of his ignorance and the apparent hornet's nest that he was blundering into.

'Aye, off the entrance to the Calcutta river, Captain, plumb under the noses of the Hooghly merchants and Admiral Pellew himself!' Ballantyne's tone was incredulous.

'Pellew cannot have liked that,' observed Drinkwater drily, 'he used to enjoy the boot being on the other foot.'

'You know him then?' aked Ballantyne.

'A long time ago, when he commanded the *Indefatigable*. But this does not explain your reluctance to allow me to take you to Macao. You must undertand that now I have learned of a British flag-officer in the area it is my plain duty to report to him.'

'By all means do so, sir, but *after* you have towed me into the Pearl River. It will delay you perhaps a day, two at the most.'

'You have a reluctance to go to Macao, Captain Ballantyne? A commercial one, perhaps?'

Ballantyne nodded. 'Yes. I have a cargo, sir, a valuable cargo and a mortgage on the ship. Opium for the mandarins makes me damned anxious to take your offer of assistance. Mind you,' Ballantyne added forcefully, 'no salvage claim, by God, or I'll counter-claim on the basis of these charts and my services to bring you into the Pearl River . . .'

'Or Macao . . .'

Ballantyne's eyes suddenly narrowed. 'No, *not* Macao, Captain. My services are not available for Macao.'

'Very well, sir,' said Drinkwater coldly, 'then I shall order the preparations for passing the tow discontinued and make up the numbers of my complement from your ship. While being indebted to you for your elucidation of the mysteries of Oriental politics, I believe that I may find my own way to Macao . . .'

'Hold fast, sir,' Ballantyne snapped back, 'if I lose *Musquito* I am a ruined man. If I go direct to Macao with my ship in her present condition I shall not get her up to Whampoa, nor will I avoid incurring crippling tariffs payable to the Portuguese.' Ballantyne paused. 'I am willing to compensate you for your trouble; an *ex gratia* payment, perhaps . . .'

Drinkwater was indignant. 'I am not to be bribed, damn you!' he said sharply, and Ballantyne met his outrage, raising his own voice.

'An *ex gratia* payment is not a bribe, damn it, it is a legitimate payment for actual services! God damn it, Captain Drinkwater, you have my fate in your hands, sir; it is not easy for me to beg . . .'

Drinkwater considered the man before him. Exhaustion was perhaps making them both over-hasty. Above their heads and floating down through the open skylight came the noise of men heaving a hawser aft, ready to pass across to the stricken brig. Drinkwater needed a few minutes to reflect. He was desperate for those stores, yet there might be problems over having them allocated to *Patrician*, since she was not under Drury's orders. On the other hand the Honourable East India Company's ships at Canton would almost certainly hold stocks of spars and canvas which he could requisition. Judging from Ballantyne's jittery anxiety the spectre of his pressing men would be lever enough for him to have his own way.

'Has Admiral Drury power to take over the dockyard at Macao?' he asked in a more conciliatory tone.

'I think not. The last I heard was that the matter was at an impasse. Drury commands the ships, but his troops are mainly sepoys in the Company's service. *They* are under the direction of a Select Committee acting in the Company's interest. If you ask me there will be trouble with the Portuguese and, after that, trouble with the Chinese.'

'Which is why you are anxious to get your cargo to Canton?'

'Aye. I want to break bulk before the trade is stopped. There are already rumours that the Emperor at Peking wants it permanently terminated. That would not be in the interest of the Viceroy at Canton, it's his principal source of income, both by way of customs duties and chop . . .'

'Chop ?' queried Drinkwater.

'*Cumshaw*, *baksheesh*, bribes . . .'

Abruptly Drinkwater made up his mind. He and his ship needed a brief respite. If he proceeded to Macao doubtless Drury, a man whose reputation he did not know and who in turn owed Drinkwater nothing, might press further duties upon him. He wanted to work his ship homewards and had no wish to have her detained in eastern waters on arduous service that would end up with half his crew dead of scurvy or malaria. He could tow the *Musquito* towards Canton as Ballantyne desired, pretending ignorance of Drury's presence and arguing his urgent need of fresh victuals. He would be certain of finding stores at the Company's depot and might recruit his ship before finding Drury. In addition he might persuade Drury to send another vessel after the *Juno*. He felt desperately tired, overwhelmed by lassitude and, in reality, only too happy to accommodate Ballantyne's entreaty. He felt that sometimes a post-captain might play for advantage like a politician.

'Very well, Captain Ballantyne, the matter is agreed. You will pilot us into the Pearl River and provide me with charts necessary to take me to Penang. I shall take your brig under tow and endeavour to take off as much of your cargo as possible if she shows signs of foundering.'

'Damn it, thank you, sir!' Ballantyne held out his hand, his sudden smile evidence of his relief and the stress under which he had been labouring. Drinkwater wondered how much money rode upon the successful discharge of *Musquito*'s cargo. 'I will put my second officer aboard you, sir,' Ballantyne went on, 'to act as your pilot. He is as familiar as myself with the navigation of the Pearl River.'

'You have perfect confidence in him?'

'Absolute, Captain Drinkwater, and he may stand surety for my good conduct – he is my son.'

'I had not exactly wanted a hostage,' Drinkwater said wryly. 'Come,' he added, 'let us drink to our resolve.'

He summoned Mullender from the pantry and the two men sipped their wine while the companies of their ships passed a towline.

Drinkwater could only guess at what Ballantyne's son's mother had been. A Begum, perhaps, or a Rani? Or did such noble ladies refuse to cohabit with the likes of Ballantyne? With the tow passed, he stood now with the younger man as he had his father, consulting the charts. Possibly he was merely the bastard offspring of a nautch-girl, for he was clearly a man of colour. Drinkwater had yet to test his abilities, though he hoped he had inherited some of his father's skill, for Ballantyne had saved *Musquito* after a fight of ten days against the worst weather a mariner could encounter in these seas. Yet was it possible that so prosaic-looking a man could have sired so exotic a son?

Jahleel Ballantyne was taller than his father, his skin a light coffee colour, his hair jet-black and loosely flowing to his shoulders. He wore a blue broadcloth coat like his father, but his trousers were thin cotton pyjamas, baggy in the leg and caught at the waist by a wide scarlet cummerbund from which a pair of pistol-butts protruded. His low-crowned hat sported an elaborate aigrette and the man smoked long, thin cheroots. He spoke perfect English with a clipped, slightly nasal accent, emphasising his words with eloquent movements of his hands. *Patrician* already had a crop of exotics among the inhabitants of her lower deck. Only time would tell what the wardroom would make of such an addition to its number.

'It is perhaps unnecessary to warn you, sir, of the dangers ahead, because you have many guns and are a ship of force. But we will be proceeding slowly, and we might be mistaken by the Ladrones for an India ship . . .'

'Pardon my interrupting, Mr Ballantyne, but who, or what, are the Ladrones?'

'Chinese pirates, sir. They usually take ships off the Ladrones Islands here.' Ballantyne laid the point of the dividers upon a small archipelago, one of several which lay scattered about the huge estuary of the Pearl River. 'They have numerous junks armed with cannon.'

'Don't the Chinese authorities take a dim view of these people?'

Ballantyne smiled, a peculiarly engaging smile, accompanied by a gentle rocking of his head. 'To the mandarins these people are poor fishermen . . .' he paused, seeing Drinkwater's expression of mystification. 'There is much to understand about these parts, sir.' Jahleel Ballantyne smiled again.

'Indeed, so it would seem, Mr Ballantyne.'

They were interrupted by Mullender.

'Beg pardon, sir, Mr Fraser's compliments and he says he'll have to turn Mr Chirkov out of Mr Mylchrist's cabin, sir, to accommodate . . .'

Mullender nodded in Ballantyne's direction and Drinkwater sensed an amusing antipathy to the presence of the half-caste officer.

'That will be very satisfactory.'

'Mr Chirkov won't like it, sir, he's a very particular young gentleman.'

Drinkwater turned. 'He's a prisoner-of-war, damn it, Mullender, not a maid to be cosseted over her mooning . . . my apologies, Mr Ballantyne, come, let us go on deck . . .'

Tregembo, Drinkwater's coxswain, emerged from the pantry grinning at the discomfited steward who stood in the centre of the suddenly empty cabin.

'What did you stand up for that Russian booby for?' he growled at Mullender. '*Particular* gennelmen aren't exactly the Cap'n's cup o' tea.'

Mullender shrugged, a man of proprieties more than words and deeds.

'Ain't proper . . . Count Chirkov's a gentleman . . .'

'Count Chirkov's a damned bugger, you old toss-pot,' said Tregembo dismissively.

'But he's a gentleman,' persisted Mullender doggedly.

2 New Orders

November 1808

Midshipman Count Anatole Vasili Chirkov of the Imperial Russian Navy found captivity amusing rather than irksome. A proclivity for indolence helped, together with a rather fetchingly cultivated languor. Chirkov had discovered that a certain type of lady in the salons of St Petersburg found the affectation attractive, combined as it was with a biting sarcasm about the endeavours of others. It was a pretension peculiarly adapted to a rich adolescent. The conceit had also proved surprisingly useful aboard ship where, he had realised, a dearth of variety gave him a natural advantage over the dullards on board and provided him with innumerable targets. In fact, captive or not, Midshipman Count Chirkov found himself rather more popular than otherwise.

An exception to this general rule was Captain Drinkwater who proved impervious to Chirkov's charm. The Russian regretted he had not killed the British captain when he had had the chance in Lituya Bay. The momentary advantage he had enjoyed over Captain Drinkwater had enlarged itself in Chirkov's fertile imagination and he would have boasted about it, but for the fact that losing it so swiftly argued against himself. Drinkwater, Chirkov reluctantly had to admit, was no fool. But then neither was he a gentleman, for Chirkov had felt Drinkwater's contempt as long ago as their first encounter in San Francisco and was happy to shrug him off as a curiosity of the British navy. His own captain, Prince Vladimir, had more or less confirmed this, calling Drinkwater 'a tarpaulin', to be tolerated, when he could not be avoided, whilst Chirkov's present inconvenient circumstances persisted.

Chirkov, fluent in the French of his class, had had only a

rudimentary knowledge of English when he had been taken prisoner. Recent association with *Patrician*'s 'young gentlemen', particularly since his transfer from a cabin to the gunroom, had brought them into a greater intimacy. Chirkov had assumed a casual ascendancy over the youthful Belchambers, and formed a loose friendship with Frey who, although rated acting lieutenant, remained accommodated in his former quarters due to the overcrowding of the ship.

Although Chirkov had some duties, they were nominal. He was supposed to supervise a division of the Russian sailors who had their hammocks slung in the cable tiers, but this irksome responsibility was easily delegated to a petty officer. This allowed him to indulge his apparently limitless capacity for doing nothing. At the present moment he was leaning on *Patrician*'s fo'c's'le rail, halfpropped on the breech of the foremost larboard chase gun while Mr Comley, *Patrician*'s bosun and another amusing tarpaulin, hove a cable up outside the ship from the hawse pipe and bent it on to one of the sheet anchors.

Astern of them and, remarkably, still afloat, the brig *Musquito* stretched her towline. It had taken almost a fortnight to beat up into the mouth of the Pearl River among the blue hills and myriad islands of the Kwangtung coast. The bat-winged sails of the big fishing junks that had loomed out of the dawn mist two days earlier were here replaced by hundreds of small sampans. Under sail, fishing or being patiently sculled by short Chinese who tirelessly manipulated their long stern scull, or *yuloh*, they dotted the waters of the estuary. Ahead Chirkov could see that the banks of the river came together and pale marks against the grey-green of the distant hills betrayed the embrasures of forts.

Far above Chirkov's indolent head the lookout reported the presence of 'sails', by which all on the quarterdeck assumed he meant he had sighted the heavy crossed yards of European vessels.

'They will be the Indiamen loading, I suppose,' remarked Drinkwater to Mr Ballantyne who stood next to him on the quarterdeck. A warm afternoon was producing a sea breeze, giving them their first favourable slant since they had picked up the tow, and under all the sail she could set, the British frigate was working slowly inshore.

This fair breeze had produced a mood of contentment in Captain Drinkwater. Ballantyne's fears of pirates had proved groundless. Though two big junks had closed with them in the morning's mist, they had sheered off when they ranged up close, and there was no evidence to suspect their motives had been sinister.

'No, sir . . . they cannot be Indiamen or Country ships,' replied Ballantyne. He raised his glass and studied the masts and spars of the distant ships at anchor. Then he lowered it and pointed ahead of them. 'See, there are the forts at the Bogue, sir, what is sometimes called the Bocca Tigris. Those are the Viceroy's war-junks, three of them anchored under the cannon of the forts. The Indiamen are inside the Narrows, beyond the Bogue at Whampoa. They should already be discharging. Some of those ships *may* be Indiamen but . . .' Again he raised his glass and stared at the anchored vessels, some two points to larboard.

'They're men-o'-war, sir,' shouted Quilhampton suddenly. He had hoisted himself into the mizen rigging and had been looking at the ships himself. 'And flying British colours . . .'

'They must be Admiral Drury's ships, sir,' said Ballantyne.

Drinkwater sensed a rivalry existing between the two young men. He turned to Fraser, standing beside the binnacle and watching anxiously as they crept into Chinese waters.

'What's your opinion, Mr Fraser?'

Fraser borrowed Quilhampton's proffered glass and clambered on to the larboard rail. At last he jumped down.

'No doubt, sir. A British seventy-four, two frigates and two sloops . . .'

'A seventy-four!' exclaimed Drinkwater, unable to contain his surprise. The presence of a powerful third-rate argued it was, at the very least, a force under a senior captain flying a commodore's broad pendant. And that meant an officer senior to Drinkwater. Now his plan to recruit his ship before reporting his presence to his seniors was impossible. He fished irritably in his tail-pocket for his Dollond glass and, stepping up on a carronade slide, half-hoped to confound the experts beside him. To his intense annoyance he found they were correct.

There was something familiar about the seventy-four. She lay with her head to the eastward, riding to a weather tide, and he had a good view of her. He was certain he had seen her before. Then he recognised her. He shut his glass with a snap and jumped down to the deck.

'She's the *Russell*, gentlemen, unless I am greatly mistaken.' But he was confident of her identity. She had been part of Onslow's division at Camperdown and had stood in the line at Copenhagen where, punished for her mistake in following the *Bellona*, she had taken the ground under the Danish guns. 'And she flies a flag at her mizen . . .'

There was no doubt in Drinkwater's mind that he had discovered the squadron under Rear-Admiral Drury.

He had his barge called away as soon as he had saluted Drury's flag, leaving Fraser to anchor *Patrician* and *Musquito*. He could only clearly identify one of the two frigates, the *Dedaigneuse*, for a fine rain had begun to fall and a damp chill filled the air so that the oarsmen bent to their task over a smooth sea, blowing the trickling rain from their mouths. Drinkwater sat wrapped in his thoughts. He watched the big two-decker loom over them as they approached, remembering her on a grey, gun-concussed October afternoon off Camperdown eleven years earlier. Eleven years! Where had the time gone? He wondered if Tregembo, sitting beside him at the tiller, entertained himself with such gloomy thoughts. Eleven years! They were both worn out in the King's Service, grown grey in the harness of duty like their ships.

'Boat ahoy!'

'*Patrician*!' Tregembo's quick response gave no indication of such day-dreaming. On board *Russell* they were already aware of *Patrician*'s identity, for they had exchanged the private signal as they approached, but Tregembo's short reply to the challenge indicated that *Patrician*'s captain sat in the boat. A few minutes later Drinkwater stood on the deck of the line-of-battle-ship listening to the apologies of *Russell*'s first lieutenant who was excusing the absence of her captain.

'He is in conference with the Admiral and the other captains of the squadron, sir,' the lieutenant explained, 'and they have been joined by the Select Committee.'

'And what precisely is that, sir?' asked Drinkwater, feigning a deliberate obtuseness.

'The Select Committee?'

'Yes.'

'A body appointed by Lord Minto, the Governor-General, sir . . .'

'The Governor-General of *India*?' interrupted Drinkwater.

'Why, yes, of course, sir.' A faint note of exasperation was creeping into the lieutenant's voice. 'We have occupied Macao and are now making demands of the Chinese.'

'What the devil for? I had some notion that Macao was Portuguese territory.'

'Why, sir, we have to protect our trade.'

'To protect our interest, more like it.'

'If you say so, sir,' said the lieutenant with ill-concealed disdain. The arrival of His Britannic Majesty's frigate *Patrician* may have taken the flagship by surprise, but it was easy to see that this Captain Drinkwater was a curmudgeon of the old school. The first lieutenant did not think that such an officer would pose much of a threat to the promotion stakes on the East Indies station. Drinkwater appeared to possess the intelligence of an ape! Captain Drinkwater's next remark plucked him out of his smug reverie.

'Be so kind as to tell me the names of the squadron, if you please. I remarked the *Dedaigneuse*; who commands her?'

'Captain Dawson, sir . . .'

'Never heard of him,' snapped Drinkwater.

'A promising young officer,' replied the first lieutenant, laying too facetious an emphasis on the word 'young' and attracting a hard stare from Captain Drinkwater. The lieutenant blushed and hurried on. 'The other is the *Phaeton*, Captain Pellew . . .'

'Sir Edward's son?' asked Drinkwater.

'Yes, sir, Captain Fleetwood Pellew. She's just in from Nangasakie, been trying to discover what the Dutch send two ships to Japan for every year.'

'Is this part of protecting our trade too?' asked Drinkwater drily. 'And the sloop?'

'The *Diana*. The *Jaseur*, sloop, is cruising in the offing. The Indiamen', he went on, gesturing to two Company ships anchored inshore, 'are the *David Scott* and the *Alnwick Castle*, they were taken up to transport five hundred sepoys and some European artillery . . .'

'To occupy Macao.'

'Exactly, sir.'

'Are we at war with Portugal? Or merely doing in the East Indies what we are fighting the French for doing in Europe?'

It amused Drinkwater that such heresy silenced the lieutenant. The uneasy conversation was brought to an abrupt conclusion by a group of men spilling out on to the quarterdeck from the admiral's cabin. Three were obviously the civilians of the Select Committee, the others were the captains of the squadron. Drinkwater wondered what contribution Fleetwood Pellew could make to Admiral Drury's deliberations. He seemed little more than a boy, scarcely older than his own midshipmen.

'Captain Drinkwater?' The admiral's secretary was at his elbow. 'Admiral Drury will see you now, sir.'

'I don't like it, sir, damned if I do. Don't know why Pellew's got us into this damned scrape, running round at the behest of the Governor-General when his lordship represents the Company's fiscal interest with no thought of policy. God damn it, Drinkwater, all I've heard since I came out is "the Company this", and "the Company that". Begin to think the sun rises and sets out of the Company's arse, God damn me if I don't!'

Drury paused, venting his spleen and clearly glad to be rid of the role of courtier.

'Help yourself to a glass.' He indicated a decanter and the sparkle of lead crystal glasses on a tray.

'Thank you, sir.'

'Well, Captain Drinkwater, where the deuce have you sprung from? When this business is over I'm to relieve Pellew, but I'm damned if my briefing mentioned you or your frigate.'

'I'm under Admiralty orders, sir, discretionary instructions concerning the deployment of a Russian line-of-battle-ship . . .'

'A *Russian* battle-ship! Good God, this matter has more complications than a witch's brew!'

'She is destroyed, sir. I have her commander and her survivors aboard *Patrician*.'

506

'You took a line-of-battle-ship with your forty?'

'Her people were much debilitated by scurvy, sir.'

'By heaven, sir, your report will make more interesting reading than most of the paper on my desk!' Drury waved his hand over the litter of correspondence before him. 'I see you brought in a brig.'

'Yes, sir. The *Musquito*; Captain Ballantyne master. She's a Country ship, damaged in the recent typhoon.'

'It missed us here. You'd better get her up the Bocca Tigris and into shelter . . .'

'Very well, sir.'

'Send your written report as soon as possible.'

'Aye, aye, sir. My ship is in want of repairs . . .'

'Is she fit for service, sir? If not you may have a week. No more.'

'A week will be ample, sir.'

'Very well. Thank you, Captain.'

It was rather an inconclusive dismissal, thought Drinkwater as he regained *Russell*'s quarterdeck. Despite his assurance to Drury, a week seemed quite inadequate for what needed to be done. The continuing rain only added to his depression. Later he was to regard the interview as fateful. For the time being he wanted only to sleep.

Rear-Admiral Drury regarded the arrival of an additional frigate as providential. The fact was that the East Indies command was like no other in the long list of the Royal Navy's responsibilities. It had already been the victim of intrigue, formerly being divided between two officers who, admirable individually, reacted like poison when requested to co-operate. Pellew had won the contest and Troubridge had been recalled, to die when the *Blenheim* foundered through old age, rot and the use of 'devil-bolts' in her hull. Now Drury was to inherit the edifice that Pellew had erected, and Drury did not like it. Pellew was universally acknowledged as a fine seaman. As a frigate captain he had been without equal, receiving the reward of a knighthood for the destruction of a French frigate early in the war. But honours had dried up after a decade of conflict, and Pellew had ruined his reputation by shameless nepotism. His boys Fleetwood and Pownall were barely old or fitted enough to be lieutenants in charge of the deck, never mind post-captains!

Drury cursed as he bent over the papers on his desk. As for grand strategy, all that mattered to Lord Minto and the damned Selectmen was the China trade, the India trade, and the self-interest of the merchants of Madras, Bombay and Calcutta. The scum had already written to London with their opinion of no confidence in Pellew and his measures to protect their confounded commerce! Drury wished the Honourable East India Company to the devil.

It was a damned irony, Drury mused. How could anything associated with mercantile transactions be honourable? The very notion was preposterous! He snorted indignantly and while his secretary waited with the patience of a tried and beaten man, the admiral scribbled his signature on a dozen letters and notes.

But William O'Brien Drury was a pragmatist brought up in a hard school. He had not yet inherited Pellew's command and he acknowledged the influence of India House and its Court of Directors. The Select Committeemen hung on his coat tails, eternally muttering about loss and demurrage and half a hundred other insignificant notions that were bound up with their infernal and corrupt business. It was bad enough having to coerce the Portuguese, for it *was* just conceivable that a French squadron from the Mauritius, or a Dutch squadron from Batavia might occupy Macao and strangle the Canton approaches with a blockade, but the idea of bullying the hapless Chinese was quite contrary to Admiral Drury's idea of duty!

At last he sighed, and put down his pen. He rubbed his hand wearily across his face.

'Bring me Captain Drinkwater's report when it is delivered,' he remarked to his secretary, reaching out for the neck of the decanter.

'Do you have any orders for him, sir, that I may be drafting in the interim?'

Drury thought for a moment. 'Yes, I'm going to send him to Penang with those few ships that are completing their lading. They will need an escort and I cannot spare young Pellew or Dawson. Besides,' the admiral added, 'with French cruisers about I'd rather have an experienced officer in command of a convoy than one of those young popinjays.'

'Not to mention the pirates,' muttered the secretary as he scooped up the signed letters for which he had been waiting.

3   Whampoa

November 1808

'Steady as you go, sir.'

Drinkwater lowered his glass and nodded at Lieutenant Fraser. 'Mr Ballantyne has the con . . . sheets and braces to the Master's helm, if you please.'

'Aye, aye, sir.'

Drinkwater held Fraser's eyes, searching for a flicker of resentment. Had Fraser hesitated out of deference to Drinkwater's presence? Or was there a taint of bad blood in the air? Surely not, though God alone knew the undercurrents of discontent that ran beneath the decks of his precious command. Ballantyne was a newcomer, a cuckoo in the uncomfortable nest of *Patrician's* wardroom.

Drinkwater dismissed the morbid train of thought. The Narrows known as the Bogue were closing in, the embrasured forts clearly visible as the breeze blew the ship steadily inshore, with the Chinese Viceroy's war-junks closing in on either quarter like huge, primordial birds of prey. The little *Musquito*, tugging and dragging at the dripping towline, rolled in their wake.

'Very well, Mr Fraser, you may send the men to quarters. In silence, if you will.'

Ballantyne turned and, to avoid his eyes, Drinkwater raised his glass again, studying the curious rig of the closing junk to larboard. He did not want the rat-a-tat-tat of the marine drummer's snare alarming the unpredictable Chinese, despite Admiral Drury's assurances that a bold front would secure him a safe anchorage with the Indiamen above the Second Bar.

'Sir,' implored Ballantyne, 'I most earnestly entreat you not to compromise my father.'

Hissed at by Comley's mates who were deprived of their pipes at the hatchways, the watch below were pouring up from the berth-deck to take their stations at the quarterdeck guns with the low slap-slap of their bare feet.

'And I entreat *you*, Mr Ballantyne, to attend to your duty. You are a King's officer now.' Drinkwater looked quickly at Fraser, but the first lieutenant appeared to derive no satisfaction from his rebuke to the newcomer. Chastened, Ballantyne turned away. There were always problems arriving off a foreign coast, Drinkwater reflected, matters of propriety, of the correct number of guns to fire a salute; of the number to expect in return and of the action to be taken if one did not receive them. He had gathered enough from Drury and Ballantyne himself to realise the delicacy of the balance maintained by the Honourable East India Company and the satellite shipping houses of Calcutta, Madras and Bombay in their relationship with the Celestial Empire of the Son of Heaven.

'The Emperor in Peking, sir, regards King George as a vassal chieftain,' Ballantyne had explained, highly amused, 'such is his ignorance . . .'

Drinkwater raised his telescope and studied the junk to the west of them. There would be no exchange of gun-salutes, Drury had said, not until he had concluded his negotiations with the Viceroy.

'Mr Ballantyne,' said Drinkwater, without lowering the glass, 'there is a gentleman aboard that junk who appears to be a man of some importance.'

'He's the *hoppo*, sir, the mandarin charged with the duty of collecting the customs revenue, the *chop*. I imagine he will board *Musquito* when we bring her to anchor. We should take in the forecourse now, sir . . .'

'Very well.'

'Fore clew-garnets! Rise fore-tacks and sheets!'

Drinkwater turned his attention to the forts. Brilliant-hued banners fluttered over ramparts of pale stone and he could see the muzzles of heavy cannon.

'Antique guns, sir,' reassured Ballantyne.

'What are those things beside the banners?' Drinkwater pointed to coloured shapes bobbing up and down behind the parapet.

'Tiger masks, sir, intended to intimidate us.'

'I see . . .' replied Drinkwater uncertainly.

But the Chinese cannon did not dispute their passage, though the war-junks hung on their flanks until they had passed beyond the Bogue and the First Bar. Under topsails, *Patrician* forced her ponderous way upstream against the yellow ebb of the Pearl River. To starboard the hills rolled away to the east, echoing the jagged peaks of Lin Tin Island offshore, but to larboard a flat alluvial plain stretched westwards, intersected by convoluted channels and formed from marshy and insubstantial islands that altered as the river altered. The hills to the east were bare of trees, stripped by the hand of man, terraced here and there to form fields which fell away from the walled villages on their summits.

With sharply braced yards and the jibs and spanker to assist, *Patrician* rounded a long bend, finding the main stream divided by low islands. Although the layered spire of a pagoda broke the skyline, it was the tall masts and yards of the East Indiamen that dominated the anchorage.

'Whampoa, sir, and that is Danes Island, and that is . . .' Ballantyne aired the knowledge of a dragoman while Drinkwater studied the shipping through his Dollond glass. Most of the Indiamen seemed to be discharging, though there were smaller 'Country' ships, Indian owned, loading from the mass of junks, sampans and lorchas that crowded round them. One or two of these seemed ready for sea.

An hour later *Patrician* had cast off *Musquito* and anchored beside her. From her quarterdeck Ballantyne senior waved his gratitude. Drinkwater turned to the son. The man was well pleased with himself, puffing contentedly on a cheroot.

'Well, sir, you acquitted yourself with credit. If you still wish it I shall request Admiral Drury confirm your acting warrant as master. In the meantime we shall further test your abilities in a refit.'

'I am honoured, sir, to accept.'

'In that case, Mr Ballantyne, be so good as to obtain the services of a tailor and extinguish that confounded cheroot!'

Drinkwater gestured at Ballantyne's exotic figure, and this time Fraser could not repress a smile.

*

'Sentry!'

Drinkwater's exasperated voice rose to a querulous pitch and he dragged himself to his weary feet. He half opened the cabin door to bawl again at the sentry.

'For God's sake, man, do your duty and keep these hawkers quiet!'

His attempt to close the door failed. Instead the mortified marine, his shako missing and his ported musket pressed impotently across his own chest, fell backwards into the captain's arms.

'Beg pardon, sir . . .'

The sight of *Patrician*'s commander, his blue, white and gold uniform marking him as a personage of supreme importance to the people of the Pearl River, only fuelled their desire to secure some patronage from him, the reason for their besieging his quarters. If Drinkwater had entertained any reservations about Ballantyne's ability to find a tailor, they were now swiftly dispelled. Ballantyne could obtain the services of a tailor, a washerwoman, a boot-maker, an ice-seller, a vendor of chickens, eggs or cabbages, a barber, a fortune-teller, a servant or a whore, though, at that moment, they all seemed to be attempting to claim the attention of Captain Drinkwater.

'Tregembo! Mullender!' Drinkwater bellowed, putting his weight behind the broad shoulders of the marine; but no reinforcements came from the pantry and Drinkwater's tired brain realised that similar scenes were being enacted throughout the ship.

'I'm sorry, sir,' mumbled the compressed bootneck.

Drinkwater grunted acceptance of the unfortunate marine's apology. Doubtless the poor fellow expected a dozen at the gratings tomorrow and would likely get them if nothing mollified Drinkwater's rising temper.

'Fire your damned musket, man!' he bellowed in the marine's grubby ear. The sudden report gained them the necessary second's initiative and the throng of supplicating Chinese was pushed beyond the doorway.

'Pass word for Mr Mount!' Drinkwater called through the closed door, leaning his back upon it and wiping his forehead. Catching his breath after the unaccustomed exertion he stared through the stern windows. It was a grey, drizzly late November day, yet the broad waters of the river swarmed with sampans and junks. Somewhere just out of sight on their larboard quarter, *Musquito* lay aground on the fringes of Danes Island. Here, where the Europeans were allowed by the Chinese authorities the concession of a place to repair and refit their ships, Captain Ballantyne was discharging his cargo of opium in order to survey his ship. Low sheds had been erected on the island, under the roofs of which the crews of the Indiamen repaired masts and spars, reminding Drinkwater of the pressing needs of his own ship.

'Sir? Sir? Are you all right?'

Drinkwater recovered himself and opened the door a trifle. The crowd outside had subsided, clearly concluding that admittance to the great man's cabin was impossible. Most had gone in search of more accessible prey.

'Mount, come in, come in. Of course I am all right, but what of the rest of the ship?'

Mount grinned. 'Taken lock, stock and barrel by boarders, sir.'

'Get your men aft, then, and clear 'em. We've got work to do!' Drinkwater noticed the crestfallen look in Mount's eyes. 'Damn it, Mount, you know as well as I do what will happen if liquor vendors get among the people. We will have a species of anarchy aboard.'

'Aye, sir, but the men know there are women available and even I have need of a new shirt . . .'

Drinkwater eyed the marine officer; Mount had served with him for five years and Drinkwater knew him for a steady, reliable man. The plea was eloquent, Drinkwater's testiness a reaction after the long weeks of lonely strain. They had a day or two . . .

'Very well, Mr Mount, clear the ship, then have the goodness to request Mr Ballantyne to arrange for two tradesmen of each kind to come aboard. He and the Purser are to issue passes, you are to put Sergeant Blixoe on the entry and double the sentinels.'

'Aye, aye, sir.'

'And send Fraser aft, I want a guard rowed round the ship. And your men are to fix bayonets and load powder only. I want no unnecessary blood shed on our account.'

'What about women, sir?'

Drinkwater stared at the marine, hesitating. He could allow women on board in accordance with the usage of the Service. It was common in Spithead where men-of-war at anchor frequently assumed a frantic and degenerate appearance, aswarm with whores who were fought over and coupled with by men denied outlet for their natural urges for months at a time. It dispensed with the awkward business of shore-leave and reduced the risk of desertion. One thing could be relied upon if women were allowed on board, and that was the exhaustion of the seamen in a violent excess of promiscuity. It had its merits, if strictly controlled.

Against it was the threat of further rumblings among the men. They were not a happy crew, compounded of volunteers, pressed men, Quota men and the sweepings of British gaols. Many of them had been at sea now for years, hardly stepping ashore except on remote beaches to wood and water the ship. The sight of women would inflame the men, denial of access to them might precipitate serious disaffection and even desertion.

Hovering over this delicate equation was the ever-present spectre of disease. Release of libidinous pressure now might result in an epidemic of clap or worse, the lues. The venereal list already bore eighteen cases of the former acquired in California in addition to the decrepit and decomposing luetic whose appearance served as a ghastly warning to them all and whose shambling figure kept *Patrician*'s heads clean. Surgeon Lallo had reported two more cases of the disease already in the second stage. How many more would be acquired here at Whampoa? He felt irresolute, exhausted.

'You may allow the tradesmen, Mount.' He hesitated, his eyes meeting those of the marine officer who remained expectantly in the cabin.

'Very well . . . women as well, but not until this evening . . .'

Mount departed and soon the frigate was filled with the shouts and squeals of disruption as his mustered marines forced the Chinese back into their boats at the point of the bayonet. If the unfortunate vendors had earlier mistaken *Patrician* for a run-of-the-mill East Indiaman, they were now learning their mistake.

For the next two days Drinkwater kept himself to himself, taking a turn on deck shortly after dawn and again in the evening. The chance to sleep undisturbed while his charge swung to her cable in a safe anchorage was too luxurious an opportunity to forgo after the relentless months of service he had endured. He was overwhelmed with a soporific lethargy, dozing off over his charts like an old man, even after sleeping the clock round, eating erratically, to the despair of Mullender who had purchased fresh vegetables, and drinking little. On the first evening at anchor he had barely been able to keep awake as Captain Ballantyne eloquently expressed his gratitude and sought to introduce Drinkwater to the commanders of the East India Company's ships at Whampoa. Drinkwater excused himself, pleading the disorder of his ship, but in fact the plain truth was that he was utterly exhausted and had no stomach for socialising.

Mullender and Tregembo, his coxswain, crept in and out of the cabin while Derrick, the pressed Quaker who did duty as the captain's clerk, silently maintained the ship's books without the dozing Drinkwater ever being aware of his presence.

'Don't you wake him,' the solicitous Tregembo had said as Derrick passed through the pantry to collect the muster books.

'I am sufficiently acquainted with the virtues of silence, Friend,' replied the Quaker drily.

But their protection was broken by the still-limping Belchambers who nervously, but over-loud, tapped upon the cabin door.

'Sir . . . sir . . . Sir! If you please, sir . . . there's a boat that's brought orders from the flagship, sir.'

'Specie, Captain, my clerk will give you the details. At one per cent its carriage should compensate you a little for the inconveniences attendant upon my diverting you . . .'

It had been a long pull in the barge, though they had sailed much of it, and Drinkwater still felt a mild irritation that Drury had summoned him in person to acquaint him of something as easily conveyed in a letter.

'And the *Juno*, sir? I had hopes of finding her here.'

'Damn the *Juno*, Captain. These matters that I have in hand supersede that preoccupation. I have read your report, read it with interest, Captain Drinkwater, and not a little admiration. I think I may relieve you of the discretionary part of your orders . . .'

Drinkwater looked at the admiral; this was a different Drury. It was obvious to Drinkwater why he had been chosen to relieve Pellew: there was a clear-thinking and obviously principled mind concealed behind the ram-damn seaman's exterior. He warmed to the man, forgiving the admiral the tedium and risk of the long boat journey. He was suddenly pricked with conscience, aware that Admiral Drury might be able to answer a question that had been bothering him for months now.

'Please, do be seated, Captain, and take a glass . . .'

The admiral's servant proffered the tray and then Drury waved him out, seating himself. 'Y'r health, Captain Drinkwater.'

'Your servant, sir.' The fine *bual* reminded Drinkwater of a long dead Welsh commander, and also of the question that begged resolution.

'Sir, forgive the presumption, but I am anxious to know the fate of Lord Dungarth. You will be aware from my orders that I have some knowledge of his Lordship's office . . .'

Dungarth was the obscure head of the British Admiralty's Secret Department, the very centre of its intelligence network and a man who, along with the formidable figure of John Barrow, the Second Secretary, was instrumental in forming Admiralty policy. Drinkwater had known him since he had been a midshipman, even held him as his patron and friend. The last news he had had of the earl was that he had been blown up by an explosive device which had destroyed his carriage somewhere near Blackheath.

'You heard . . .'

'By the hand of Rear-Admiral White, sir . . . an old messmate.'

'Dicky White, eh?' smiled Drury. 'Had the sense to hang up his sword and take his seat in Parliament for a Pocket Borough . . .' Drury sipped his madeira. 'As for Dungarth, he still breathed when last I heard . . . what, eight months ago.'

'But the prognosis . . . ?'

'Was not good.'

Drinkwater nodded and they sat in silence for a moment. 'You had some expectation of preferment by his hand, did you?' asked Drury.

Drinkwater smiled ruefully. 'I fear I am a little long in the tooth to entertain such thoughts, sir.'

'We are of one mind, Captain.'

'I beg your pardon, sir . . .? Drinkwater looked up in surprise. Drury was mocking him!

'I am aware that you are an officer of experience, Captain. I have here,' Drury patted a folded bundle of papers, 'your written orders which, loosely summarised, instruct you to take under convoy those ships ready to proceed. Our presence here in force has disrupted the trade and most of the India ships will not be ready. The Viceroy in Canton has been ordered by his Emperor to evict us from Macao and halt all intercourse with us. This interdict is contrary to the private ambitions of the Viceroy and will inconvenience him in the collection of his revenues. The Son of Heaven at Peking will expect the same tribute from his proconsul in Canton irrespective of its origin. I have come here to stop the French or Dutch from seizing Macao and ruining our trade, but I am also hounded by a mercenary pack of Selectmen to compel the Viceroy to continue trade through Canton and Whampoa and disobey the Emperor. The Indiamen have only just begun to break their outward bulk. There are fourteen large Indiamen, fifteen large Bombay vessels, six from Bengal, five from Penang and a brace from Negapatam and Madras. They have all yet to load. A boom and a fleet of war-junks could seal them above the Bogue and they could be forcibly discharged without any payment for their loading.

'Such a threat has the Selectmen quivering in their boots! That's why I want you to get out whatever specie the Chinese merchants have already collected, and, together with the two Indiamen and eight or nine Country ships that *have* managed to load, see them safe to Penang. If you ain't doing a service to the merchants, you'll be doing one for old Sir Edward.'

'I see, sir. And you think my grey hairs will help me . . .'

'Damn it, Drinkwater, you've *seen* these boy captains! What the hell use d'you think Fleetwood Pellew is without I have a steady first luff to stay his impetuous helm. Such arrant nepotism will ruin the Service, to say nothing of prohibiting the promotion of worthy men who must be shackled in subordinate stations. Between us, magnificent seaman though he be, Pellew's made a ninny of himself on behalf of those two bucks of his.' Drury paused to drain his glass. 'All these young blades think about is prize money; prize money before duty . . .

'Have you heard about young Rainier? No? Last year he was a snot-nosed midshipman; pulled the strings of influence and got himself command of a sloop; begged a cruise off the Commander-in-Chief and went a-skulking in the San Bernardino Strait. Took the Spanish Register ship *San Raphael*, pocketed fifty thousand sterling and sent Sir Edward his share of twenty-six. Yes, that stings, don't it, eh?

'And Fleetwood; sent up to Nangasakie to reconnoitre? Reconnoitre, my arse! Old Daddy Pellew wanted another slice of eighth-pie. Young Fleetwood, the valiant captor of Batavia, was to take one of the two Dutch ships that visit those parts every year and relieve them of the silk or spices, or whatever they go up there for and buy off the Mikado.

'That's why I want *you* to see these ships safe to Penang, Captain. There are several powerful French frigates working out of the Ile de France. Surcouf has raided the doorstep of Calcutta with impunity in a letter-of-marque called the *Revenant* that sails like a witch; word has it that he's at the Mauritius now, but he's quite likely to take another look into the Hooghly or the Malacca Strait.'

'I see, sir . . .'

'Apart from the French National frigates, their privateers and the Dutch ships of war, you've pirates . . . oh yes, sir, pirates. The Ladrones are infested with 'em and they'll take Country ships, knowing them lighter armed than the Company's regular vessels. Get south of the Paracels reefs and you can forget the Ladrones. What you'll have to worry about then are the Sea-Dyaks from Borneo. Fall into a calm and they'll paddle their *praus* up under your transom and cut out whatever they fancy . . . that's why I want a man who knows his duty, Captain Drinkwater, so your one per cent will be well earned if you get a chest or two of silver dollars to India safely.'

Drinkwater put out his hand for the packet of orders. Already his head was formulating the likely signals for his convoy. How the devil could he extend comprehensive protection with a single ship?

'Will you send a sloop with me in support, sir?'

'I doubt I can spare one,' Drury said bluntly. 'When will you be ready for sea?'

'You promised me a week, sir, of which five days yet remain.'

'Very well. And now to a more immediate business . . .'

'Sir?' Drinkwater frowned, puzzled.

'I want to hoist my flag in *Patrician*, Captain Drinkwater, just for a day or two.'

4   The Dragon's Roar

November 1808

Captain Drinkwater looked across the strip of grey water between his barge and that of the *Dedaigneuse*, and met Dawson's eye. He smiled encouragingly at the young post-captain. Dawson smiled back, a trifle apprehensively.

The two captains' barges were leading a flotilla of the squadron's boats, their crews bending to their oars and leaving millions of concentric circles expanding in their wakes to mark the dip, dip, dip of the blades. In each boat sat a small detachment of marines, muskets gleaming between their knees.

Dawson was in command, for Drury had ordered him to proceed the twelve miles upstream from Whampoa to obtain stores (in particular liquor) from the European factories at Canton and to determine the whereabouts of the specie. Drinkwater, out of a sense of curiosity and the realisation that his presence aboard *Patrician* was frustrating Fraser in his attempts to refit the ship, had volunteered his own services and those of a midshipman and his barge. The whiff of action had persuaded Mount to come with a file of his marines and Drury himself had, at the last minute, hailed Dawson's passing boat and climbed aboard. Perhaps it was the admiral's presence that rattled Dawson.

Or perhaps it was the situation that was rapidly deteriorating and that promised trouble ahead of them, that caused the young captain's anxiety. Drinkwater did not know. To be truthful, he did not much care. The whole sorry business seemed utterly incomprehensible and as distant from his pursuit of Russian warships and defeating the French as if he were engaged at single-stick practice on Hadley Common.

The fact was that he was a mended man; his physical collapse had given him time to recover his faculties and his vigour. He wanted to be off with the convoy, to get out of the Pearl River and headed, if not for home, then for the staging post of Penang. He had vague thoughts of persuading Pellew to take ship in *Patrician* when he handed over the chief command to Drury, as a guarantee of their destination. That, he thought, would make a fine Christmas gift to his ship's company. But the silver specie had yet to come down from Canton and *Patrician* was not ready to proceed; so when Drury announced his intention of sending Dawson upstream with the squadron's boats, Drinkwater had found the suggestion of adventure irresistible.

And so, judging by their efforts, had his men. They were all volunteers, all save Tregembo, who followed his captain out of affection, though he would never admit it was more than duty. Drinkwater looked at the men closely as they plied their oars. They looked well enough on their diet of, what had they christened it? Ah yes, he recalled the crude jest, the coarse synonymous phrase for coition, bird's nest pie.

'River's more or less deserted, sir,' remarked Acting Lieutenant Frey beside him.

It was true. Though sampans and a few small junks moved up and down the river, the normal volume of traffic with which they had become familiar was no longer visible.

'I suppose they know what we're up to, Mr Frey.'

'I suppose so, sir.'

It was all an appalling tangle, Drinkwater mused. At Macao an affronted Portuguese population were suffering the occupation of the Company's sepoys, anxious to see the British gone. In the European 'factories' at Canton an increasingly beleaguered group of merchant agents were anxious to get out of China at least *some* of the huge deficit owed by the native merchants. The mandarins and Viceroy, organs of the Imperial civil service, had to maintain their own 'face' and power, while at the same time obeying the orders of the Emperor in Peking who, celestially indifferent to the fate of Canton, wanted all contact with the *fan kwei*, the barbarian 'red-devils', broken off. Meanwhile at Whampoa the ship-masters and the Select Committee wanted to use Drury's armament to force the Chinese to pay up and the Viceroy to permit trading to continue. Drury, declaring the whole thing a 'complex, crooked, left-handed, winding mode of proceeding', had himself joined the boat operation to stop the matter getting entirely out of hand.

Beside Drinkwater, Frey suddenly craned his neck and stared ahead. Drinkwater followed his gaze. The roofs of Canton were coming into view. The tall, narrow-fronted buildings of the factories, marked by the flag-poles and the flaunting foreign colours, lay downstream from the more distant pagodas and the yellow walls of the city which rose from a higgledy-piggledy mass of scratch-built housing clustered about its buttresses.

'Canton . . .', muttered Frey, speaking without knowing it. Drinkwater smiled inwardly. He must remember to call in the midshipmen's journals in a week or two, and see what Mr Frey's skill with brush and water-colour made of the scene.

'Boats ahead, sir!' The call came from the barge's bow. Drinkwater stood up, steadying his knee against a thwart. In the next boat Dawson did the same.

They were strung across the river, lying to a boom of ropes, eight or nine heavy junks, and just below them, sampans which appeared to be full of armed men, men with what looked like medieval hauberks of heavy cloth or leather over their robes, and small metal caps with horsehair plumes.

'They've got bows and arrows, sir!' reported the bowman, and the sailors and marines burst out laughing with good-natured contempt.

Drinkwater, appraising the cordon of junks, judged the passage of the river effectively barred, unless they were going to break Drury's injunction not to open fire. He cast a quick look at either bank. There were cavalry drawn up and though they would be seriously hampered by the multitude of people that stood curiously along the margin of the river, the entire mass was a formidable barrier to their progress.

'Easy there, Mr Frey, easy . . .'

'Pull easy, lads . . .'

The oarsmen slackened their efforts and Drinkwater heard Drury hailing him.

'Cap'n Drinkwater! I'm pushing on ahead . . . do you hang back in my support. My interpreter tells me one of the junks bears an admiral.'

'Very well, sir. And good luck.'

Drury waved his hand and sat down again. Drinkwater saw him lean forward and exchange remarks with the interpreter. Dawson's face was set grimly.

'Oars, Mr Frey.' He turned and waved to the boats astern. As Dawson's barge pulled forward, the flotilla followed Drinkwater's example, their oars lifting horizontally, silver drops of water running along the looms, while the boats slowed, gliding in the admiral's wake.

Drinkwater watched as a perceptible ripple of excitement seemed to transmit itself from one bank to the other via the armed junks, at the sight of the single boat detaching itself from the others.

'What the devil's the admiral trying to do?' muttered Mount.

'Negotiate, Mr Mount,' said Drinkwater, 'and I'll trouble you not to open fire without my express authority.' Drinkwater repeated the order to the lieutenant in the adjacent boat, with instructions to pass it along the line. Drury had been explicit upon the point.

'Why the devil did he bring us then?'

'Something the celestials call "face" I believe, Mr Mount,' said Drinkwater, still watching Dawson's barge as he closed the hostile junks. 'A kind of ritual posturing to decide who shall have the upper hand in a matter. Ask Ballantyne to enlarge on the point . . .'

'Admiral's standing up, sir,' reported the bowman.

'Eyes in the boat,' snapped Frey as the idle and curious oarsmen turned their heads to see what was happening.

'Bloody hell!'

A ground swell of voices like the stridulation of cicadas had accompanied their approach to the cordon. Against it they quite clearly heard Drury's voice and the shrill interpretation. The remarks had been cut short by a dense volley of stones that sent up tiny plumes of water all round Drury's boat.

'Advance!' signalled Drinkwater, and the assorted gigs and cutters, spreading out in a long line, pulled forward once more, closing the admiral whose oarsmen held water not twenty yards from a large, three-masted junk upon whose deck a knot of richly robed mandarins could be clearly seen.

Drury continued expostulating, moving his hands, though they

523

could hear no more than the drone of his voice above the rising chatter of the vast crowd.

More stones plopped about him, some skimming across the placid river or falling alongside the supporting boats. Then suddenly it was not a volley. A sharp cry from the commanding junk and the jerk of a baton launched a hail of well-aimed missiles against the British. Ten yards away Drinkwater saw a marine drop his musket and clap his hands to his nose as blood gushed brightly through his fingers. Men moved dangerously in the boats as knocks and shouts told where others took blows and the boats received damage.

'Up marines, and present!'

Mount's order rang across the water and the marines in all the boats stood up and levelled their muskets. The sudden elevation of the soldiers further rocked the boats and Drinkwater realised they were blocking his view and that he had himself been standing for some moments.

'Hold your fire, damn you!' Drinkwater bellowed, suddenly seeing Dawson's face turn and blench at the proximity of the other boats. Drury turned too, took in the situation at a glance and bent to consult his interpreter.

He straightened up again and looked round. Astern of the admiral's barge the boats had drawn up in line abreast, their oarsmen dabbing at the river to maintain station against the current. Stones continued to fall about them. One concerted volley seemed flung with concentrated viciousness, hitting several men in *Russell*'s longboat. Stung by this furious assault her men suddenly dug in their oar-blades and, with a bending of looms, the marines in her were standing up again, cocking their muskets. Other men in other boats were being hit and cries followed one another with mounting rapidity. Men were shouting now; another boat moved forward and more marines, no longer hesitating like their officers, were flicking off their frizzens and snapping back the hammers of their flintlocks.

'Hold your fire!' roared Drinkwater. Drury had been adamant upon the point, this was to be a *show* of force only. To defy this mob with lead would call down a vengeful horde and the only result would be death for all of them, and a particularly senseless death at that.

'Hold your fire!' Drinkwater shouted again.

'Back-water and hold your fire, damn your eyes!' Drury, frustrated in his attempt to communicate with the Chinese admiral, was himself bull-roaring at his men. His pugnacious spirit was held in admirable check amid a crescendo of noise as cymbals and gongs now enhanced the cries of the Chinese and the curses and mutterings of the British. The marines lowered their muskets irresolutely, and sat down to lessen the target area they presented to the hundreds of Chinese who, leaning from the junks and sampans, seemed provided with an endless supply of pebbles and stones.

'They are driving us out as devils, sir,' volunteered Frey, 'that is why they are beating the gongs . . .'

'Your intelligence is ill-timed, sir,' snapped Drinkwater. 'Sit down, damn you!' he shouted at a midshipman who, in the *Dedaigneuse's* cutter, was standing in her stern sheets, waving his dirk and uttering a stream of obscene invective at the obdurate Chinese.

'Sit down at once and hold your tongue, sir!'

Even in such extreme circumstances the incongruity of the boy's torrent of filth annoyed Drinkwater. They were all over-wrought and he was aware that his silencing of the midshipman was a vent for his own pent-up feelings.

Then suddenly it seemed as if a dark cloud had passed over them and their eyes were assailed by a sibilant vibration that rent the air above them. The volley of arrows splashed into the river astern of them, clearly aimed over their heads in intimidation. And then came a mighty roar, so sudden after the unnerving noise of the arrows that men's faces paled in fear, and so close that the wave of concussion and heat that seared them sizzled hair and added the sharp stink of its frizzing to the blast of powder. Their boats rocked dangerously. The huge bell-mouthed cannon, concealed until that moment by rush matting draping the sides of a war-junk, vomited a red and yellow tongue of fire.

No shot or langridge came from the dragon's mouth, but the message from its black muzzle was potent enough: the Chinese were not open to negotiations. Admiral Drury was waving the boats back. Dawson's barge was crabbing round, swinging her bow downstream. Willingly now the others followed suit and, helped by the current, dropped swiftly down towards the refuge of their ships.

Astern of them the clamour of the Chinese and their gongs rose to a victorious crescendo to which was now added the snap of fire-crackers. Banners waved and the huge dragon gun spat tongues of fire at their retreat. Aboard the greatest of the junks, the Viceroy of Canton received the congratulations of his court.

On either bank cavalry kept pace with them for a mile or so, then fell back, and their last sight of the citizens of the great city was a single draped palanquin that watched them from a low rise on the levee.

The red curtains fluttered a little as the brass ferrule of a tele-scope was withdrawn, and a few minutes later the bearers, obeying some command from within, swung it round and headed back towards Canton. Alongside it trotted a little Indian boy with an impish face and almost pointedly prominent ears.

5 The Matter of Morale

November 1808

'. . . A red flag from the foremasthead of the escort shall signify the convoy to form line ahead, to clear such armament as shall be borne by each ship and to maintain station until such time as the said red flag shall be struck.'

Drinkwater ceased dictating and stared over Derrick's shoulder as the Quaker clerk finished writing.

'I think that is all, Derrick. Now we must have fourteen copies, one each for our charges and two for ourselves, one of which is to be kept in the binnacle. You have my authority to impress the midshipmen on the duty of copy-clerks.'

'Aye, Captain.'

'And Derrick . . .'

The Quaker, gathering pens and ink-pot, looked up at Drinkwater.

'Ensure they make no mistakes . . .'

'Very well, Captain Drinkwater.'

A knock came at the door and Midshipman Belchambers's face peered round it. 'Beg pardon, sir, but Mr Quilhampton's compliments and there's a boy asking to see you.'

'A *boy*?' Drinkwater frowned.

'A native boy, sir . . .'

'A Chinese boy?'

'Looks more like an Indian boy to me, sir.'

Something about his assumption of mature judgement on the part of the youthful Belchambers brought a smile to Drinkwater's face. There had been an atmosphere of something like farce attendant upon the affairs of the British ships at Whampoa following Admiral Drury's 'humane retreat' from Canton.

Drinkwater, in receipt of his orders, wanted only to be out of the river and on his way to Penang. Fortunately Drury had hauled down his flag from *Patrician*'s main-masthead and had returned to *Russell*, pondering his next move and reading the riot act to the dithering Selectmen.

'If neither peace nor commerce is to be had by an act of war, I never will sanction the slaughter of those defenceless multitudes,' Drury had said to them in Drinkwater's cabin before his departure. 'We have trampled under foot every moral law of man and nations, and the poor defenceless Chinese have been infuriated to a frenzy . . .'

Something of the fighting-cock had had to explode from this exemplary lecture and poor Drury, having been humiliated personally in his attempt to act to the satisfaction of all parties, suddenly reacted angrily, perhaps contemplating how fortunate the boat expedition had been in avoiding real casualties.

'However, gentlemen, if one of my seamen had been, or *is* killed, I will destroy Canton. Therefore recollect what *you* will have to answer for. I gave you quiet possession of Macao, but I tell you no hostile act shall be committed against the Chinese, unless a man is killed, which nothing but the most singular accident has prevented. The seamen under my control have borne to be fired at, but once let loose,' the admiral finished dramatically, 'no power on earth can stop 'em!' Out of tact or embarrassment no one mentioned Drury's failure to bring off a single piece of silver specie.

The Select Committee had been packed off to finish negotiations with the mandarins from the luxurious quarters of the *Stirling Castle*, East Indiaman, while Drinkwater gathered the few ships that were ready to proceed and prepared to depart with this small convoy.

And now a boy was asking for him.

'What does he want, Mr Belchambers, have you ascertained that?'

'Well, sir, beg pardon, sir, to see you.'

'You had better bring him down then.'

Belchambers seemed to hesitate.

'What is the matter now?'

'Well, sir, Mr Quilhampton voiced an opinion that the boy might be an, er, assassin, sir . . .'

Drinkwater laughed. 'That's most solicitous of Mr Q, Mr Belchambers. It does not occur to you that the lad is doubtless a servant from one of the Indiamen.'

'That's unlikely, sir . . .'

'Oh?' Drinkwater's temper was shortening. He had other matters to consider and a final letter of instruction to draft for the masters and commanders of the convoy.

'Yes, sir, he came down river in a sampan.'

'Bring him below,' Drinkwater snapped, meeting Derrick's eye as the clerk, penned in the cabin by this odd exchange, now slipped out to co-opt the midshipmen as copy-clerks.

Drinkwater bent over the chart that lay on his table. It was a survey by Huddart, and Ballantyne had laid off the best course for them to follow, south and then south-westward towards the tip of the long Malay peninsula. Such was his preoccupation that he had almost forgotten the announced visitor when the hobbling Belchambers showed the boy in.

He was shorter than the midshipman, and possibly two or three years younger. His feaures were neat and small, almost feminine, with huge brown eyes outlined with a hint of kohl. He bowed, displaying a jewelled turban, and drew from his loose sleeve a letter.

Drinkwater took the letter, an amused smile playing about his mouth, for in the shadows beyond the diminutive exotic, Mr Midshipman Belchambers stood anxiously, his hand on a half-drawn dirk.

Drinkwater slit the wafer, half turning to the window to read the message.

Canton
20th November 1808

To the Officer Commanding the Convoy Bound for India

Honoured Sir,
      Knowing your Imminent Preparations for Departure and the Frustrations your Party has Suffered in its Attempt to recover

the Silver owed the British Merchants by the Rascally Hong, I have
it in my Power to carry off most of the Specie at the time of your
sailing if, in the First Part you Signify at what time this will occur
and, in the Second Part you allow Myself and a Servant to Embark
in your Frigate. The Matter to be Secret between ourselves.

Please convey your Answer to the Bearer. He is dumb but
understands English. I am, Honoured Sir,
Your most humble and obedient Servant,
A Friend.

Drinkwater read the letter through twice. It could be a ruse, of
course. Information as to the convoy's sailing could be passed to
the forts at the Bogue, or to the pirates of the Ladrones. But that
information could as easily be signalled, for it would take several
hours for the convoy to drop down river and they could scarcely
do so unnoticed. In any case Drury had promised them the escort
of the *Phaeton* until they were clear of land.

On the face of it this unknown 'friend' was obviously anxious to
buy his way out of what might prove a dangerous place for a
European, and had the decency to attempt to recover what the
British merchants most desired. Yet why should the man insist on
secrecy when he was proposing to achieve what the British merchants wanted?

To cheat them? Perhaps, and that was why he wanted passage
in a frigate rather than a merchant ship. Drinkwater looked at the
boy. He was dumb, yet the face was intelligent, and it watched
Drinkwater with the passive observance of something feral. He
thought for a moment of calling away his barge and consulting
Drury, but he knew this boy would take news of his indecision
back to his unknown master.

Besides, Drury had employed Drinkwater on the task for his
experience, and he had a mind to get to the bottom of what would
doubtless turn out to be no mystery at all.

'Tell your master . . . no, wait, I'll write.'

He turned to his desk and picked up his steel pen, searching for
the ink-pot that Derrick had moved.

The boy was suddenly beside him, the smell of scent wafting
from his small body. Drinkwater felt a small brown hand on his

arm and the dark, liquid eyes were staring up at his face. Behind them there was a shuffling movement, and the evening light glancing off the river gleamed on the naked blade of Belchambers's dirk.

But these were details on the periphery of Drinkwater's perception. Afterwards he considered the value of the stones in the boy's turban and the oddity of his prominent and pixie ears. In the moment of arrest, as the boy strove to prevent Drinkwater committing anything to paper, he was aware principally of the hollow of the boy's mouth, and the insistent grunts that filled its tongueless monstrosity.

He dreamed that night; a restless half-sleep full of terrors. He was flung down and drowning, drowning in waves of Elizabeth's hair that caught and clung to his struggling body, drowning in the laughter and shouts and smiles of thousands upon thousands of Chinese whose narrow eyes and loose, gaudy clothing seemed to have displaced his wife's tresses and moved with the overwhelming restlessness of the sea. Then he was fighting for air, surfacing in this very cabin, dark, lonely and cold. But there was a sweet and seductive laughter beyond the door and he struggled towards it in anticipation of all the delights of the flesh that he had for so long lived without.

But the woman beyond the door was ghastly; a horror of all the nameless, haunting horrors that mocked a man out of the darkness of his own desire. He drew back, pursued. The hag metamorphosed into the little Indian messenger who, mouth open, came to engulf him with his tongueless hole from which, Drinkwater fancied, the very sulphureous stink of hell itself seemed to emanate. And all about him laughter rang in his ears, laughter from Chinese and Indian and European faces . . .

He jerked awake, the sweat pouring from him, the thin laughter coming from beyond the cabin door. It was high-pitched and piping, and combined with the dream to bring him leaping from his cot, his heart thundering in his chest, his night-shirt sticking to his body and the lank locks of his loosely bound hair plastered to his scalp.

Pulling on breeches and tucking the tails of his night-shirt into them, he yanked his cloak from the hook by the door and stepped

531

precipitately out on to the gun-deck. The dozing marine sentry sprang upright with a click of musket against buckles.

The giggling laughter came again, resolving itself into the now familiar sounds of pre-dawn coition from the berth-deck. His confusion clearing from his fogged mind, Drinkwater ran up the quarterdeck ladder, announcing his presence by a discreet cough.

Mr Meggs, the gunner, appeared from beyond the mizen mast. 'Sir?'

'What day is it?'

'Why, er, Sunday, sir.'

'And the time?'

'A little before three bells, sir,' and then added, as if sensing the captain's distraction, 'in the morning watch, sir.'

'Pipe all hands.'

'All hands, sir?'

'You heard me, damn it, and clear the ship. No showing of legs, Spithead style, I want the lower deck cleared fore and aft and the people mustered.'

'Ship's company to muster, sir, aye, aye.'

Somewhat bemused at this extraordinary behaviour, the elderly Meggs shuffled forward, hesitated, looked back at the captain, then called for the bosun's mate of the watch.

'Mr Meggs!'

The gunner turned at the captain's shout. He began to shuffle aft again.

'Mr Meggs,' said Drinkwater quietly, 'I am aware that only the recent casualties force you to keep watch on deck, but be so kind as not to appear on the quarterdeck in your slippers.'

Meggs looked down at his erring feet. Habitual use of felt slippers in *Patrician*'s magazine, where the wearing of leather soles might rasp and ignite the coarse grains of spilt gunpowder, probably rendered it instinctive that the poor fellow put them on at the call of the watch. Perhaps, thought Drinkwater, catching a smell of the man, he slept in the festering things!

'I beg your pardon, sir.' Meggs looked crestfallen.

'Be a good fellow and have something more suitable on when you muster.'

'Very well, sir . . .' Meggs looked hard at his captain and Drinkwater suddenly looked down at his own appearance.

'Perhaps,' he said, recovering himself at last, 'that had better stand for both of us, eh? You may wait until four bells before turning up the ship.'

Fully awake and aware of the ludicrous appearance he would cut even in the pre-dawn gloom, Drinkwater hurried below. As he turned for his cabin above the companionway, he was aware of a face staring up at him. For a second he stopped, his heart beating as though this was some impish visitation from his dream, and then it was gone, the young Chinese girl vanishing into the stygian darkness.

'Pass word for my steward,' he growled at the marine, and the whisper went around the ship that Captain Drinkwater was awake and something was afoot.

Sluicing his face after the harsh ministrations of the razor, Drinkwater called for a clean ahirt. It occurred to him that the few days of relatively relaxed routine might prove fatal to the delicate matter of morale. He was aware that he had left the refitting of the ship to Fraser and though he could find little to fault with the first lieutenant's arrangements, only time would prove their thoroughness.

Drinkwater was unhappily conscious that any loosening of the bonds of discipline was a risky matter, and that mumblings of discontent had accompanied *Patrician* from the moment the crew of *Antigone* had been turned wholesale into her, topped up with the scum of a hot press and sent round Cape Horn to absent them all from European waters.

The long-service volunteers had had their willingness to serve eroded by lack of shore leave and the association of landsmen, lubbers, thieves and petty felons; men whose proper habitat was a gaol, but whom the Admiralty saw fit to pour into men-of-war to fill their impossible complements. It was for prime seamen to tolerate them, but to be reduced to their level was something that proud men, jealous of their expertise, could not submit to.

Drinkwater's greatest enemy was desertion. Jack had a simple understanding of the world and to him the foreign shore of China offered escape from the endless round of grinding labour expected of him aboard a King's ship. Drinkwater knew and understood all this, and before *Patrician* had sailed for the Pacific he had had to hang a man at the fore-yardarm for desertion, *pour encourager les autres*.

He shook the awful image from his mind's eye and summoned more cogent reasons for his attitude. He could not afford to lose a single man. Ballantyne had told him the Indiamen were often short of hands on a China voyage, of how they embarked Chinese to make up their complements, and how their commanders would be keen to secure the services of a dozen active topmen, even to the extent of hiding them until they were out of sight of land. To this must be added the potent inducement of the high and guaranteed wages paid on Company ships.

In short, Drinkwater mused as he tied his stock and reached behind him for the coat that Mullender held out, he would not be at all surprised if he was short of men. The question was, how many?

Beyond the cabin door the pipes squealed as four bells struck. Drinkwater stood before his mirror, head a-cock, listening to the sounds of reaction, judging by the inevitable sluggishness, the little shrieks of the whores and the suppressed oaths the temper of his men.

Midshipman Count Vasili Chirkov felt his hammock shake.

'Come on, Vasili, get out . . . uniform . . . muster . . .' Midshipman Dutfield was climbing into his breeches, rousing the indolent Russian between grunts of effort as he and his colleagues sought the neglected items of their uniform in the gloomy chaos of the gunroom.

'*Non* . . . no . . .'

The girl stirred in the crook of his arm and nestled comfortably up to him.

Dutfield shook the hammock violently and then Frey was standing close, holding up a glim so that it shone unequivocally over the exposed bodies.

'Come on, you lubber!' the acting lieutenant urged. 'Or the Captain will marry you to the gunner's daughter.'

'No . . .' Chirkov peered over the edge of the hammock. 'I have girl first . . .'

Dutfield and Frey exchanged glances. Frey winked and shrugged. He felt his new-found authority inadequate to the task. The midshipmen left the gunroom and joined the rush to the upper deck.

The ship was a babel of confusion. Everywhere along the berth-deck men were hurriedly drawing on clothes and unlashing arid rolling hammocks. Small brown Tanka women, their usefulness now past and to whom the sudden shrill of the pipes and flurry of activity must have been beyond all comprehension, were being roughly shoved aside. In one place two men were busy thrusting their paramours through an open gun-port into a waiting sampan, in another one of these unfortunate creatures was crying like a child, her ankle badly sprained from too sudden a descent from a hammock.

'Clear lower deck! Out! Out! Out!' Bosun Comley was bawling, urging his mates to use their starters, and lashing about him with his cane.

'Get these whores over the side! This is a King's ship, not a kennel!'

'Bloody hypocrite!' remarked a Quota-man who had once entertained social expectations but had been found guilty of embezzlement.

'Clear lower deck!'

Lieutenant Mount appeared, buttoning his tunic and shouting.

'Ser'nt Blixoe! Pass word for Ser'nt Blixoe . . .'

'Here, sir!'

'Give the Bosun a hand to get these trollops into their boats . . . not too roughly, Ser'nt.'

Meanwhile, in the gunroom, Midshipman Count Vasili Chirkov was reaching the climax of his urgent love-making.

His sword hitched and his hat ready in his hand, Drinkwater half sat on the edge of his table, one leg swinging, awaiting the summons to the deck. When it came at last he affected not to notice the inordinate delay, not to enquire from Mr Belchambers, who had been sent limping down to inform him the muster was complete, why he had heard noises below decks that indicated a party of marines sent twice through the ship. He knew already what *that* signified.

It was growing light as he climbed to the quarterdeck. The men were massed amidships, over the booms and along the gangways, in the lower rigging and, still distracted by the departing women, craning over the rails. Beyond the hammock nettings he could see the trucks of masts as three or four score sampans rocked away from their sides.

'Eyes in the ship there!' Fraser touched his hat. 'Ship's company mustered, sir.'

'Very well, Mr Fraser.'

There was something wrong. He could see instantly the lack of symmetry in the ranks of marines who rigidiy lined the sides of the quarterdeck. He caught Fraser's eye and raised an eyebrow.

'Four men missing, sir,' hissed the first lieutenant in a low, tense voice.

'How many marines?'

'None, sir. Corporal Grice is still searching the ship.'

'Any boats missing?'

'No, sir. Too many sampans . . .'

Drinkwater nodded a curt acceptance of what he had already guessed. Affecting to ignore the report he stepped forward.

'Well, my lads,' he began, staring at the bleary faces that were taking shape in the growing light, 'the Chinese consider us barbarians, I'm told, and looking at the present state of the ship's company, I'm not entirely surprised . . .'

A collectively sheepish grin seemed to spread across the more tractable members of the crew.

'You have all enjoyed a little relaxation and the ship is almost ready to proceed . . .'

'Where are we bound, Cap'n?'

The voice was unidentifiable, but it might have asked for all except the Russian prisoners, for the light of interest kindled in their washed-out faces.

'We are escorting a convoy to Prince of Wales Island and then . . . then I think it time that we took ourselves home . . .'

He was aware that few of them knew where Prince of Wales Island was, and fewer cared, but they all wanted to hear their final destination. He was cut short by a spontaneous burst of cheering, cheering that only died away when Corporal Grice and his detail emerged from the after companionway half dragging, half shoving an able seaman named Ward, and escorting the protesting Chirkov and his half-naked flower-girl in to the amphitheatre of unoccupied deck before the captain.

Chirkov shrugged off the rough hands of the marines and turned as though to join his fellow prisoners, gathered about Prince Vladimir.

'Stand still, sir!' rapped Mount, pleased with his men.

'Make your report, Grice,' said Drinkwater quietly, nodding first at Ward.

'Caught him going out through a gun-port, sir. Into a sampan under number three gun, sir.'

Drinkwater nodded. 'Anything to say, Ward?'

The unhappy man shook his head. 'Put him in the bilboes, Corporal.' Drinkwater had no intention of marring the present moment with a flogging. On the other hand . . .

He turned to the sulking Russian. Not taking his eyes off the young nobleman, Drinkwater said, 'Captain Rakitin, this officer is under duty to you. He is responsible for a division of your men and has been publicly taken with this woman. Have you anything to say on his behalf?'

It gave Drinkwater a grim satisfaction to see the big Russian nonplussed, even if only for a moment.

'If it was one of my midshipmen he would be made to kiss the gunner's daughter!'

'No . . . no, that would be most irregular . . .'

'I shall punish him tomorrow, Captain,' Drinkwater said, 'when I deal with my own defaulters. Kindly be answerable for his behaviour until then.' He turned to Fraser. 'Pipe the men down, Mr Fraser, I want to be ready to weigh at first light tomorrow.'

'What about the deserters, sir? asked Fraser as the muster dispersed.

'No more sampans alongside, Mr Fraser, and a better guard-boat tonight. Forget the deserters and let the men enjoy the anticipation of seeing Midshipman Chirkov's matrimony.'

Touching his hat, Drinkwater left the deck. Behind him Fraser and Mount exchanged glances.

'Forget the deserters,' muttered Fraser, 'that's no' wise . . .'

'I think,' mused Mount quietly to the worried first lieutenant, 'that we are more concerned with morale at the moment.'

6   The Concerns of a Convoy

December 1808

'Well, gentlemen, that concludes matters . . .'

Drinkwater looked round at the faces of the dozen men gathered in his cabin. Most wore plain cloth coats, some sported brass buttons or a strip of gold leaf about their cuffs, but two wore the brass-bound uniform of the East India Company's livery.

'If there are no more questions I wish you all good-night and would be obliged if you would heave a-peak the instant you see my signal at daylight. We will make the best of our way beyond the Bogue and I will signal a boat from each of you before forming the order of sailing.' In this way Drinkwater could allow for any idiosyncrasies he noticed in the passage downstream.

There was a chorus of 'good-nights' and mutual exchanges between these masters of the convoy who all knew each other. An undercurrent of relief had permeated their gathering for Drinkwater's briefing: he knew that indecision had sent the Select Committee into a catalepsy and that these men, at least, were fortunate to have completed their cargoes and be homeward bound.

Drinkwater nodded dismissal to Ballantyne who, attired in the more-or-less regulation dress of a warrant officer, had cleared away the copies of Huddart's charts that had been his passport to *Patrician*'s wardroom. Fraser, too, was about to leave the cabin, but Drinkwater stepped forward and restrained him with his hand.

'Captain Callan,' Drinkwater called, and one of the East India commanders turned in the doorway. 'Might I have a word, sir?'

'Of course, Captain . . .' Callan, a tall, slightly red-faced man with bushy eyebrows above deep-set eyes, was commander of the Indiaman *Guilford*, and senior of the two John Company men.

'I will be blunt with you, sir,' began Drinkwater, 'I am short of men.'

Callan nodded. 'I wondered when you would turn poacher.' He nodded at Fraser. 'We acceded to your first lieutenant's requests for spars from our stores in the bankshalls on Danes Island in the pious hope that we might assuage the Navy's rapacious appetite. It seems that, having plundered our stores, you now want our men.'

'It seems that you do not quite understand . . .' replied Drinkwater coolly.

'Oh, I *quite* understand, Captain Drinkwater. In fact I understand very well and that is why we, the masters in the convoy, have agreed a confederation united to oppose you if you send any men on board our ships with the intention of removing our people. Just attempt it, sir, just attempt it, by God!'

Drinkwater raised an eyebrow. 'You know my rights in the matter, Captain Callan . . .'

'Aye,' Callan retorted swiftly, 'such as they are this far from home and with the sworn affidavits of my colleagues to counter you. Besides, many of my men hold exemptions and it is a matter of record that we too are under-manned.'

'Captain, I do not submit to intimidation. Perhaps you need not threaten me if I assure you that I have no intention of pressing your men. I will give you my word of honour upon the point, if it pleases you.'

'Then, why . . .?'

'But,' Drinkwater pressed on, 'might I ask you how you feel about the boot being on the other foot?'

Callan's mouth was still open and it was clear that Drinkwater's remark had caught him at a disadvantage.

'If I am not to poach from you, sir, you should not poach from me.'

'You heard?' frowned Callan.

'Three prime topmen. I guessed.'

A reluctantly appreciative smile hovered about the corners of Callan's mouth. Drinkwater wondered if Callan knew to what degree he had been bluffing. The commanders of Indiamen were no fools. A fortune of £20,000 was nothing to them, trading as they did on their own account. They were often part-owners of their ships, for the Honourable Company chartered rather than owned the great argosies, expecting them to make four or five voyages before they were worn out. The thought amused Drinkwater, making him smile in return. By Company standards *Patrician* was a hulk!

'I will return them in the morning, Captain Drinkwater.'

'No. Oblige me by holding them until I send for them. I do not want my own people disturbed by a flogging until we are out of soundings.'

'Very well.'

'A glass to warm the temperature of our meeting?'

'Obliged.'

'Pray sit down . . . Fraser, will you join us?'

'Thank you, sir.'

'My first lieutenant has done wonders to repair the damage wrought by the typhoon, Captain Callan, the least we can offer him is a drink . . .'

Fraser blushed and mumbled something as Drinkwater served from the decanter.

'I see you have taken on the younger Ballantyne, Captain Drinkwater,' remarked Callan conversationally.

'Yes. I lost my own master in action. You know him?'

Callan nodded. 'He's illegitimate, of course, Ballantyne has a wife in Lambeth. Rather a colourful fellow, the son . . .'

'He seems competent enough. I do not know that a little colour hurt a man of its own accord.'

'I meant in terms of manner rather than blood, Captain, though there are those who would dispute the matter.'

'Well, I am not versed in these contentions. Let him serve until he proves himself one way or another.'

'Or a ball carries off his head.'

'You think that likely?'

Callan shrugged. 'You heard the opinion aired here tonight that the protection of the trade is inadequate. Pellew has a few frigates on station, but these are too well-known now and the Dutch and French have both got formidable ships in these seas.'

'You havena mentioned pirates, sir,' prompted Fraser, relaxing with his glass.

'Don't be a doubting Thomas, Lieutenant. The Ladrones will not touch us, but the Sea-Dyaks of Borneo are a different matter. They have taken four Country ships this last quarter, and all were richly laden, almost as if they knew . . . I tell you it's been a damned bad year for our trade, without this farce between the Selectmen, the Viceroy and our dear friend Admiral Drury.'

'You refer to the failure to extract the specie?' asked Drinkwater, refilling the glasses.

'Aye. The Chinese merchants of the Hong are a damnable tricky lot. The Viceroy wants the trade, the *Hoppo* of the Imperial Customs wants the trade and the European merchants want the trade, but if they can get it for nothing by hiding behind the Emperor's proscription they will, that's why we're so damned anxious to get our ships out of the river.'

'Captain Callan,' said Drinkwater, rising and walking round behind his writing-table to produce the mysterious letter he had received from Canton, 'what d'you make of this?'

He watched Callan frown over the thing, holding it to the candelabra to read it. He shook his head and looked up.

'I don't recognise the hand. Have you heard further from this Friend ?'

'No . . . I made it clear that we would sail at dawn on the second, but we have heard nothing since his messenger departed.'

Drinkwater thought briefly of the boy and the dream, but dismissed the silly obsession.

'Did you mention it to your admiral?'

Drinkwater shook his head. 'No, he had already rejoined the *Russell* beyond the outer bar. Besides, if the thing had happened I could have sent word that we had got the specie via the *Phaeton*; she is due to drop down river with us tomorrow.'

Callan shrugged and appeared to dismiss the matter. 'I heard you took a Russian seventy-four, Captain,' he said, rising and holding out his hand.

Drinkwater nodded. 'We've a few of her people to prove it.'

'Here's my hand, Captain. I confess your escort is providential. Before your arrival the best we could hope for was Pellew's whipper-snapper Fleetwood. Perhaps we can dine during the passage, Captain, and with you, Lieutenant . . .'

Fraser saw Callan over the side and into his waiting boat. It was quite dark and Drinkwater stared out over the leaden surface of the great river. The mysterious letter seemed to signify nothing beyond some poor European thwarted in his efforts to get out of the beleaguered factories. Whatever its source it was beyond his power to do anything about it.

But thought of the letter worried Drinkwater now that he sat alone in his cabin. It resurrected the image of the tongueless child and the hideous dream. He knew the dream of old. With infinite variations the spectre and the sensation of drowning had accompanied him since the days when he had endured the tyranny of the sodomite bully of the frigate *Cyclops*. He had been an impressionable midshipman then, thirty years earlier, but the dream had come to mean more than the random nocturnal insecurities of his psyche; it had become an agent of premonition.

The thought stirred his imagination. He stopped staring out of the window, turned and picked up the candelabra. The halo of its light fell on the portrait of Elizabeth. Almost unconsciously his hand touched the carmine paint that formed the curve of her lips. Had the premonition served warning of the deserters? Or potential trouble with the Russian prisoners? Somehow neither seemed important enough to warrant the appearance of the spectre. Was the nightmare significant of anything corporeal?

He stood for several minutes willing his head to clear of these foolish megrims, cursing his loneliness and isolation, aware of the half-empty bottle on the table behind him.

That was too easy. He placed the candelabra beside it, paused, then resolutely took his cloak from its peg by the door and made for the blessed sweetness of fresh air.

Pacing up and down the deck he lost track of the time, though the watch, conscious of his presence among them, struck the half-hours punctiliously on the bell, while the sentries' assiduous calls were echoed by the guard-boat rowing round the ship. It was not long before his mind was diverted, preoccupied by anxieties about the forthcoming convoy duty.

Below him the ship stirred slowly into life, prompted in part by the rhythms of her routine, in part by his own orders in preparation for departure. The first symptom of the coming day was the

543

rousing of the 'idlers', those men whose duties lay outside the watch-bill. They included Drinkwater's personal staff, his steward, clerk and coxswain. This trio enjoyed the privilege of brewing what passed for coffee in the sanctum of the captain's pantry, a ritual that reduced itself to a formality of grunts and mutual acceptance as they went on to perform the tasks that bound them not to the ship, but to the person of Captain Drinkwater.

The Quaker Derrick had the lightest duties, clearing the captain's desk and ruling the ledgers and log-book. Tregembo, the old Cornish coxswain who had been with Drinkwater since the captain had been a midshipman aboard *Cyclops*, attended to Drinkwater's personal kit, to his razor, sword and pistols. It was to Mullender that fell the lot of the menial. The captain's steward was a self-effacing man who possessed no private life of his own, nor any personality to awaken him to the deprivation. He had been born to servitude and never questioned his lot, content with the tiny privileges that accrued to his rating.

The trio was dominated by Tregembo, for Tregembo was a man of forthright stamp, whose wife Susan was cook to the Drinkwater ménage in distant Hampshire. Long service and Cornish cunning had ensured Tregembo exercised influence, even in the wardroom, and his protection of his master was legendary throughout the ship. It was Tregembo who first sensed danger.

'What means this 'ere?' he asked Derrick, holding out the letter from Canton that Drinkwater had left upon his desk.

'Thou should'st not read the captain's correspondence . . .'

'*Thou* knows I can't read, that's why I'm asking *thee*!' snapped Tregembo at the Quaker. 'Tis what that boy brought . . .'

'Yes . . . 'tis only a request for a passage,' said Derrick dismissively, taking the sheet of paper and slipping it into the ship's letter book.

'I didn't like the cut o' that boy . . .' ruminated Tregembo, 'he put me in mind o' something . . .'

'Thou seest knots in a bullrush, Friend,' muttered Derrick and Tregembo, staring through the stern windows at the emerging grey of the Pearl River, growled uncharitably.

'He put me in mind of a boy who used to be a whatsit to Captain Allen o' the *Rattler*.'

'And what does that signify?' asked Derrick.

'Nothing,' said Tregembo, 'but that Captain Allen was hanged for buggery.'

Lieutenant Quilhampton was called with the news that the captain was already on deck. James Quilhampton had suffered the agonies of sexual temptation while *Patrician* had swung to her anchor. He was near despair, for it was months earlier that he had received a letter already half a year old, that Catriona MacEwan would not repulse his advances if he pressed his suit. To the thin, one-handed young man, such a prospect offered a happiness that he had once despaired of, and the Captain's announcement that they were homeward bound only made their present tardiness the more reprehensible. He was suddenly, expectantly awake on this dawn of departure, eager to get the anchor atrip and loose off the gun that, with a shaking topsail, would signal the convoy to weigh. Waving aside the offered coffee he pulled on shirt and breeches, rasped his cheeks and wound a none-too-clean stock about his neck. Kicking his feet into pinchbeck-buckled shoes he strapped his wooden forearm in place, pulled on coat and hat, and hurried on deck.

His arrival coincided with the midships sentry's challenge.

'Boat 'hoy!'

In a frenzy of efficiency he hurried to the entry and peered over the side. 'It's only a junk, man,' he snapped at the marine, waving at the score or so of batwinged sails that moved slowly over the almost windless river.

'Aye, sir, but she's been standing towards us since she came through the Indymen . . .'

'She does appear to be approaching us, Mr Q,' remarked Drinkwater, coming up.

'Morning, sir.'

'Mornin',' replied Drinkwater, turning to the marine. 'Give her another hail.' Drinkwater raised his glass and levelled it at the junk. Quilhampton spotted activity about the mast, one of the three sails beginning to collapse, flattening the row of battens one on top of the other as the halliard was let go.

'Boat, 'hoy!' bellowed the marine.

'Ah, I thought so . . .' Drinkwater lowered his glass and

Quilhampton could himself see the flash of colour in the grey dawn, like the blue of a jay's wing, where the gaily coloured figure of the little Indian boy stood at the junk's ungainly bow.

'I think we have a passenger or two, Mr Q, and a whip at the main yardarm might prove useful.'

'Aye, aye, sir.' Quilhampton turned away just as the bosun's pipes began squealing at the hatchways to turn up *Patrician*'s company. It did not seem to matter that they had thirteen or fourteen thousand miles of ocean to cross before a sight of the English coast would greet them: there was nothing so exciting as the final moment of homeward departure!

Behind him, watched by the marine and Captain Drinkwater, the junk rounded to under the *Patrician*'s quarter and dropped alongside.

Tregembo watched the junk from the starboard quarter-gallery. Something in the appearance of that boy and the mention of sodomy had brought back unpleasant memories of the berth-deck of His Britannic Majesty's frigate *Cyclops* and the unpleasant coterie that had held sway under the leadership of a certain Midshipman Morris. Morris had been the evil genius who had presided over the cockpit and whose authority the young Drinkwater had challenged. Tregembo too had been mixed up in the dark and unacknowledged doings of the lower deck that had ended the tyranny by the quiet murder of one of Morris's confederates. Not that Tregembo possessed a conscience over the matter, rather that the disturbing influence had dominated an unhappy period of his hard life and the unbidden memory had made him introspective, in the manner of all elderly men. That is why for several moments he could not believe his eyes and thought himself victim of a trick of the light.

'It be impossible,' he muttered, for the figure was too gross, too robed in fantastical costume and too given to fat to be anything other than someone else. But just for a moment, as the mandarin hoisted himself up *Patrician*'s tumblehome by way of the man-ropes, Tregembo fell victim to the fanciful notion that he was the man Morris.

It was Quilhampton who first recognised the stranger stepping down on to *Patrician*'s deck. Quilhampton had known Morris when that officer had briefly commanded the brig *Hellebore* and Drinkwater had served as his first lieutenant. Unlike Tregembo he knew little of the man's history or his appearance as a younger man. Quilhampton recalled him already running to seed, though not as gross or disguised as he now appeared. Quilhampton had half forgotten the sick commander they had left in hospital at the Cape of Good Hope, forgotten the rumours that the ship's surgeon had been poisoning him, forgotten even the few facts from his own past that Captain Drinkwater had let slip. To Quilhampton recognition came most easily, though he too was surprised at the extravagant appearance of this quondam naval officer.

Drinkwater, his mind ranging from the forthcoming details of ordering his charges under weigh to the potential securing of the specie he anticipated off the junk's deck, saw only a large, obese man in the yellow silk robe of a mandarin. Recognition of the man as a European was incidental to the sudden flurry of activity about the deck. Fraser was alongside him, as was Ballantyne, and Acting Lieutenant Frey had his yeoman of signals bending flags on to halliards.

Reports flooded aft: the capstans were manned and the nippers in place, below in the cable tiers the Russians prepared to coil the huge, wet and heavy cable. Mr Comley had his fo'c's'le men at their stations and the topsail sheets and halliards were manned. On the quarterdeck a party of marines were tailing on to the main topsail halliards and a quarter-gunner, lanyard in hand, had a carronade charged and ready to fire as the signal for the convoy to weigh.

Gradually a calm settled over *Patrician*. Men stood expectantly at their stations; Fraser told off the acknowledged reports as they came in; Ballantyne stood by the wheel. Only Quilhampton seemed party to the drama at the embarkation point.

'Are you the gentleman from Canton?' asked Drinkwater, giving the newcomer his full attention now. 'D'you have that specie ready to heave aboard?'

The Indian boy stood beside his master, contrasting his bulk.

'I am he, Captain Drinkwater, and the specie wants only a tackle to secure it.'

It was the voice, the voice and the malignant and venomous inflection of hatred laid upon his own name that awoke Drinkwater to the stranger's identity. Suddenly the nightmare's premonition came to him.

And recognition slid beneath Drinkwater's rib-cage with the white-hot agony of a sword-thrust.

7 Morris

December 1808

It was clear from the self-possession of Morris's smile that he was not surprised at the presence of Nathaniel Drinkwater in the Pearl River. The solicitations of the unknown 'friend' suddenly assumed a sinister aspect and the infallibility of the nightmare was proved once again, for here, at last, Drinkwater knew, was the cacodemon presaged by his dream. This realisation steadied him and he met again the eyes of his enemy.

Morris's gross figure was largely hidden under the yellow silk robe but his hooded eyes seemed to complete his strange oriental transformation.

'Captain Drinkwater, what a pleasure!' Morris bowed, the smile wider as he sensed Drinkwater's uncertainty. 'Please be so kind as to have my traps, and in particular the two bronze-bound chests, hoisted aboard.'

'Mr Q!' Quilhampton, casting a suspicious eye in Morris's direction, crossed the deck. 'Have the goodness to escort this gentleman and his . . . his servant to my cabin.' Drinkwater paused, then added, 'And look lively with those chests.'

'Mr Quilhampton, I do recall you too . . . still with Captain Drinkwater, eh?' Something offensive in Morris's tone lingered after he had left the deck and the boom of the signal gun made Drinkwater start, even though he had absently nodded his permission for its discharge, for he had been watching the heavy chests swing aboard. He disguised his exposure with a barked order: 'Lively with those halliards now!'

The topsail yards rose on freshly slushed masts. The braces were manned and trimmed so that, as the anchor tripped from the mud of the river-bed, *Patrician*'s head fell off downstream in a languid turn that carried her perilously close to the *Guilford* before her long raking jib-boom pointed at the forts of the Bogue and the open sea beyond.

Drinkwater left the management of his ship to his officers and levelled his glass at the big Indiaman's quarterdeck. He could see Callan, arm outstretched as he got his own ship under weigh. A junk still lay alongside her and was being cast off as *Patrician* drew clear of *Guilford*'s quarter.

'Leggo and haul!'

The foretopsail swung on its parrel, flogged, then bellied out to the favourable air that, with the current, swept them southwards. Astern other ships were blossoming canvas, including Fleetwood Pellew's *Phaeton*, and beyond the convoy the remaining ships lay idle, awaiting the outcome of the negotiations with the Chinese. Among them Drinkwater could just make out the half-repaired masts of *Musquito*.

Beside the binnacle, his dark face working with anxiety, the younger Ballantyne ordered the helm eased a spoke or two, while Fraser, speaking-trumpet in hand, supervised the setting of more sail.

As *Guilford* fell astern, Callan raised his hat and bellowed something across the widening gap of water. Drinkwater was not sure of what he said, though his gesture indicated something of success.

'Pleased to be going, sir,' remarked Quilhampton, who had returned to the deck, nodding at the *Guilford*.

'So it would seem,' acknowledged Drinkwater, fixing Quilhampton with a stare. 'You have secured our guest, have you?'

'Aye, sir . . . he is Commander Morris, isn't he? I mean I didn't expect to see *him* here . . .'

'Neither did I, Mr Q, believe me, neither did I, and I doubt he still holds naval rank.' And then another thought struck him. 'Is Tregembo aware of his identity?'

'Yes, sir . . . leastways I think so, for he looked shocked when I entered the cabin . . .'

'Tregembo was in my cabin?'

'Aye, sir; with Derrick and your steward . . .'

'God's bones!'

Tregembo was a factor in the complex train of thought that

assailed him with renewed force. It was clear that he could no longer avoid giving the matter of Morris his full attention. He looked about him. The convoy stretched astern of *Patrician*, each ship setting more canvas and with a red ensign at the peak, for Drinkwater had insisted they show a unity of national colours and that the East Indiamen forsake the grid-iron ensign the Company flew east of St Helena.

It seemed his orders were being followed to the letter and he grunted his satisfaction. Ballantyne and Fraser had the conduct of the ship well in hand and he anticipated no trouble when they passed the Bogue; he could absent himself from the quarterdeck for a while.

'Mr Fraser! Do you call me if you need me.'

Drinkwater went below. Enveloped by the gloom of the gun-deck he paused, rubbing his eyes as a worm of apprehension writhed in his gut. Should he send for Quilhampton as a witness, or keep this stinking matter to himself?

The rousing click of the marine sentry's musket against his webbing buckles stirred him. He must show none of the weakness he felt. Morris was the lowest kind of creature that crawled upon the face of the earth. God rot him.

Drinkwater nodded perfunctorily at the marine and passed into his cabin.

Morris was sitting at the table. The boy knelt beside him bare-headed and the pair were almost in silhouette, backed by the expanse of the stern windows. The bright picture of the following convoy, the teeming river and the green hills of China lent a mesmeric effect to the confrontation. There was no sign of Drinkwater's staff and the door to the pantry was closed. Morris's hand stroked the boy's head, his fingers playing with a pixie ear as though it belonged to a spaniel. The concupiscent gesture uninterrupted by Drinkwater's arrival appalled him. It was Morris, in perfect possession of his wits, who broke the silence.

'Necessity makes strange bedfellows, Nathaniel.'

The *double entendre*, the use of his Christian name, even the sound of Morris's voice seemed to strangle any reply from Drinkwater and, for a gasping moment, he felt the sensation of drowning revive from the memory of his dream.

'So . . . they gave you a frigate, eh? I always marked you for a coming man, did I not? In New York, I recall . . . and later . . . oh, I remember everything, Nathaniel, everything . . . the humiliations I suffered at your hands, the termination of my career, my illness and abandonment at the Cape . . .'

There was no whining in this catalogue of grievance, but the sincere belief in a corrupt truth. Morris's tone brought Drinkwater to himself and swept aside the spectral remnants of his own fears.

'Hold your tongue, damn you! You cut no ice here, sir! I shall have you put aboard an Indiaman directly we . . .'

'No! No, you will not do that, Nathaniel, consider the matter of the specie . . .'

'D'you think I care a fiddler's damn for one per cent of anything that *you've* had a hand in?'

'Tch, tch, Nathaniel . . .'

'God damn you, sir, but desist from using my name!'

'We are excessively prejudiced, I fear, eh?' Morris was almost purring, his bloated face expanded laterally by a smile, his hand ever fondling the head and ears and nape of the boy. 'Come, come, then, *Captain*, shed your tired old hypocrisy; make known what arrangements you have provided for my accommodation. You will not transfer me to an Indiaman, no, nor to one of those pestilential Country ships. For a start they will likely refuse me, for a second reason, if you need further persuasion, the specie, whether you wish to claim your percentage or not, will be at greater risk aboard another ship . . . the pirates are dangerously active in these seas, my dear fellow . . . Come, reconsider and do not be intemperate, you always were the very devil for duty, even as a tight-arsed little midshipman.'

'Morris, as God is my witness . . .'

'Oh, silence! And stop that prating cant before you start! What use would I have for *you* now, eh?' The sly, archly languid tone was shed in an instant. It had come upon Morris lately, like his fat. Remembered was the sharp trading of insult for insult, of venom flecking the very spittle round his mouth in the malignant outbursts that had first alerted Midshipman Drinkwater to the presence of an envious and inept rival. Later, the horrified young Drinkwater dicovered the bully was a sodomite who dominated a faction among the weaker members of the lower deck of the frigate *Cyclops*.*

Morris's forbidden passion had awakened sympathetic lusts elsewhere on board, to become not a secret cabal which might have existed undetected by authority, but a hell's kitchen that dealt in intimidation and murder. It was whispered that sodomy was as old as the Bible; that some men deprived of any outlet for physical passion would inevitably be seduced by its specious attractions to relieve the misery of their lives aboard a man-of-war. Some such men might be forgiven the aberration if it impinged on no one unwillingly, whatever the raillings of the Articles of War. But Morris had made of his vice a weapon with which to terrorise, a means by which to indulge and fulfil a cruel megalomania. At the end of the affair, when he had been tactfully dismissed from the ship to avoid scandal, Morris had laid the blame on unrequited love. The thought still appalled Drinkwater.

'You sired siblings on your Elizabeth then.' Morris nodded at the portraits on the forward bulkhead. The indelicate remark presumed the familiarity of old friendship.

'You presume too much. Hold your tongue here!'

'Ah, I forgot. Captain Drinkwater *commands* here.' The sarcasm was as smooth as the yellow silk robe Morris wore. 'But *I* am beyond your orders, *muy Capitán*. I am no longer in your navy. I resigned my commission from His Britannic Majesty's illustrious service. I am passed far beyond you and your lash.'

'Two boxes of specie do not purchase you immunity from authority,' Drinkwater cautioned, a horrible thought occurring to him of Morris and Rakitin in some unholy confederacy, combining with the disaffected elements of his tired and impatient crew. Morris smiled, unconcerned at Drinkwater's attitude.

'I have taken some insurance. More specie went aboard *Guilford*. Odious though it may seem to you, my arrival at Calcutta will be expected. You will have to attend to your duty most assiduously in respect of the *Guilford*, my dear fellow. As for me, I will not insist that you pander to my *every* whim; I doubt, candidly, that you would be able to . . .'

---

* See *An Eye of the Fleet*.

Drinkwater stood stock-still, half listening to Morris's baiting sarcasm. He could see, beyond the rim of the table, the lip of the half-opened drawer where, prior to his arrival, it was clear Morris had been inspecting the contents of his journal. He opened his mouth to inveigh further, but thought better of it. A knock sounded on the cabin door. Midshipman Dutfield announced Lieutenant Fraser's compliments and the intelligence that they were approaching the Bogue.

'Very well, Mr Dutfield, I will be up directly.'

'A handsome young man, Captain.' Morris's laughter followed Drinkwater in his retreat to the quarterdeck.

Lieutenant Quilhampton flung his hat on his cot and wrenched at the stock about his thin neck. He turned to find Tregembo at the door of his tiny cabin. 'May I speak with 'ee, zur?'

'What the devil is it, Tregembo?'

'Do 'ee know who's come aboard, zur?'

'You mean that fat mandarin is, or was, Commander Morris? Aye, I know, and I doubt the captain is much pleased about the matter . . . why?'

Quilhampton stared at the old Cornishman. He had never seen the weather-beaten face seamed with so much anxiety.

'Zur, forgive me for saying so, 'tis more than a fancy, but you only remember that bugger from the Hellebore . . .'

'I mind enough that he was an evil sod with one of the midshipmen there . . .'

'No,' interrupted Tregembo urgently and lowering his voice, 'I mean more'n that, zur; I mind him from way back on the old *Cyclops*, zur. 'E swore then as how he'd spavin the Cap'n, zur, and I know, zur, I feels it now as he's come to do just that.'

Quilhampton frowned. 'Spavin? You mean *ruin* Captain Drinkwater? How can he do that? You ain't suggesting this counterfeit mandarin fellow *knew* who commanded this ship? Come, come, Tregembo, I understand your dislike of matters as they stand, but he's clearly been engaged in trade and wants to leave Canton . . . anything else is sheer foolish conjecture.'

Tregembo opened his mouth, shut it and stared at the lieutenant.

'Beg pardon for troubling you, zur.' And he left Quilhampton staring at the closed door.

Morris had been put in command of the brig *Hellebore* at Mocha, at the end of 1799, or beginning of 1800, he could not quite recall. He had superseded Commander Griffiths, killed in action, and had relieved Lieutenant Drinkwater of his temporary command. Quilhampton remembered Morris getting the step in rank that properly belonged to Drinkwater. Surely that fact would atone for any earlier disagreement between the two men? Doubtless so partisan a champion of Drinkwater as Tregembo would see such a miscarriage of justice in an unfavourable light as far as Morris was concerned. But he remembered other things too; those rumours about Morris that concerned allusions of sodomy with one of the midshipmen, and the scuttlebutt that the surgeon and his woman, a convict they had rescued from an open boat, had been poisoning Morris.* He had dismissed it at the time; young Midshipman Quilhampton had not then learnt the extent of the perfidy of ordinary mortals.

Was there something in Tregembo's alarum? Or was the old man a victim of senility, of over-anxiety on behalf of his master?

Of course, that was it! He was known to be jealous of his assumed influence over the captain. So what if he remembered the petty squabbles between a pair of midshipmen in an ancient and long-rotten frigate? Lieutenant Quilhampton shrugged off the matter and bellowed at the wardroom messman to fetch him a basin of warm water from the galley. While he waited he fell to calculating how long it would be before he might present himself in the Edinburgh drawing-room of Mistress Catriona MacEwan and whether, after so long a commission, he had accrued sufficient funds to take a wife.

Drinkwater's thoughts were hardly on the convoy he was marshalling off the Bogue. *Patrician* lay with her sails clewed up, only her mizen topsail still sheeted home and backed against its mast. Above his head a flutter of bunting tested his signalling system and already, in conformity with his orders, boats from the various ships

* See *A Brig of War*.

were converging on the frigate. First to arrive was *Phaeton*'s, to collect his final despatch to Admiral Drury. Her midshipman was of the same age as her commanding officer.

'Tell Captain Pellew that I'd be obliged if he would stand to the southward in company until sunset tomorrow.'

'Very well, sir.'

'And that I shall discharge him from his obligation at that time by a gun and the union at the foremasthead.'

'Union at the foremasthead . . . aye, aye, sir.'

Drinkwater turned to greet Callan. 'I did not expect you would come in person, Captain Callan,' he remarked, surprised.

'I do not think you understood my hail in the river, Captain Drinkwater, but I loaded several chests of specie from a junk, sent by order of the Hong without guard to avoid rousing the suspicions of the Imperial Customs. I counted the amount, ten thousand taels less a few score, some three and a half thousand sterling at seven shillings the *liang*. I think Drury and the Selectmen should be informed.'

'I agree. I have sent the substance of your news by *Phaeton*'s boat.'

'You have?'

Drinkwater nodded. 'I also shipped specie, though I have not counted it, two chests.'

Callan's eyes lit up. 'By God, Captain, we've done it! The Hong must be under diabolical pressure . . .'

'Captain Callan,' Drinkwater broke in, 'I'm not certain you are correct. It is my understanding that the removal of the specie may not necessarily have been with the full approbation of the Hong. It was brought off by a European, a man in mandarin costume named, I believe, Mister Morris . . .'

Callan's expression darkened and his forehead furrowed. 'Morris? You say "brought off", is he here, on board?'

'In my cabin,' Drinkwater nodded.

'I must speak with him . . .'

'One moment,' Drinkwater reined Callan. 'What d' you know of him?'

Callan reflected a moment. 'He is a man of irregular habits, Captain, not approved of by society in Calcutta, but not unknown in these parts. He was ostracised to Canton but was undeniably successful as a man of business, holding high influence over certain of the native houses in Calcutta, Rangoon and now, here, in China.'

'If by "irregular habits" you refer to the sin of Sodom, I take it you forgive him on the grounds that you and your colleagues find his acumen of use to you.'

The veiled sarcasm in Drinkwater's voice stung Callan, who flushed. 'This is the east, Captain, things are not ordered here the way they are in England.'

'Come, come, sir,' said Drinkwater acidly, relieving himself of some of the bile formed by the encounter with Morris, 'it is unfair to suggest that Mr Morris's pederasty is unique to the orient. You find him useful, that I understand . . .'

'Captain, you are under a misapprehension if you consider men of trade to be inferior to men of your warlike stamp . . .'

'I infer no such imputation, Captain Callan. I simply remark upon your tolerance. Mr Morris does not strike me as a man upon whom, sodomite or not, I would put the least reliance.' Drinkwater paused, he did not want to give Callan the information that he and Morris were old acquaintances. 'Well, perhaps I am wrong. He brought off the silver and has redeemed the trade for this year, at least. Tell me, whence did he come? Is he Country born?'

'No . . . he came out in an Indiaman from the Cape, found employment in the Marine at Bombay, but shortly afterwards resigned. There was a whiff of scandal, I believe. I first knew him some six years ago when he arrived at Calcutta. He caused a flutter then for appearing in native costume. Shortly afterwards he moved to Rangoon on behalf of some Parsee interests, and then here, to Canton. But I must see him . . .'

Callan went below, escorted by Belchambers to admit him past the marine sentry. Drinkwater was fully occupied himself as officers, mates and a master or two came aboard from the merchant ships. Patiently he answered their questions and issued his last-minute orders. Chiefly he impressed upon them the necessity of keeping in company and of not passing the Rhio archipelago without escort, for which purpose he named Pulo Tioman the rendezvous. Few demurred, only an officer off the *Ligonier*, with *Guilford* the only other Indiaman, objecting on the grounds of delay, while the second mate of a Country brig, the *Hormuzeer*, claimed his ship was swift enough to outrun even the fastest cruiser the French could send against them.

'Well, sir,' Drinkwater replied testily, 'the responsibility for his vessel lies undisputedly with your master, but if I were he I would prefer the company of others to the risk of isolation.'

The man went off grumbling and Drinkwater turned away, only to be confronted with Callan. 'Have you answered the purpose of your visit?' he asked the India officer.

'Yes, thank you. I am not certain *I* trust him, Captain Drinkwater, but he has shown me accounts which indicate the money is indeed from the Hong in just and equitable payment of debts. I would *like* to believe him . . .'

'What possible advantage could he derive from the matter, his having admitted the sums to you?'

Callan shrugged. 'That is what makes me uneasy; on the face of it I cannot see any.'

'Then perhaps he will be content with a commission. Did you ask him from what he was running?'

'Why he abandoned his post at Canton?'

'Yes.'

'He volunteered that he was in danger of his life after the repulse of Admiral Drury and on account of the disfavour in which the native Chinese presently hold Europeans . . . but that will pass,' Callan added, 'the minute their supply of opium is throttled.'

'Nevertheless, he himself may well be in fear of some retribution.' Drinkwater did not know why he sprang thus to Morris's defence. Perhaps, he thought, as Callan summoned his boat, because at the back of his mind was a suspicion forming that was too dark, too terrible and too preposterous to be anything other than the invented phobia of a disturbed mind.

8   Fair Winds and Foul Tempers

December 1808

It was symptomatic of the confusion in Drinkwater's mind caused by the presence of Morris that he forgot the matter of the deserters during Callan's visit. Fraser reminded him later that day, asking also if he felt well.

'Quite well, thank you,' Drinkwater replied tartly, 'do I give you the impression otherwise?'

Fraser almost visibly quailed: 'I had it in mind that you were not yourself, sir . . .'

'Then who the devil should I be, eh?'

'I beg your pardon, sir . . .'

'Damn it, Fraser, I beg yours. Yes, I'm deuced distempered and out at all elbows with a festering passenger occupying my cabin. Needs must when the devil drives and the ship is so overcrowded, but tell Marsden I want the place screened . . . decently too, no parish-rigging, but a decent slat-and-canvas job.' Drinkwater paused, judging how far he could take Fraser into his confidence. 'That man is to be allowed as little liberty as possible. His boy-servant will attend his needs and he will be permitted the freedom of the quarterdeck only when I give my permission and at no time in the hours of darkness. He will dine at my table, damn it, and I shall be consulted in all matters concerning him. Mount is to advise his sentries of this. The invitation of the wardroom is not to be extended to him.'

'Aye, aye, sir . . . er, may I ask why you . . .?'

'No, sir, you may not. You have your orders, now attend to them.'

'Very well, sir . . . and what about Chirkov?'

Drinkwater swore. 'We are down by the head with idlers, damn it! Send Mr Comley to the gunroom, Fraser, and in the presence of all its inhabitants have him administer a dozen stripes of his cane. Let's have done with that young gentleman once and for all!'

'And the deserters, sir? Word has it that the people know their whereabouts and . . .'

'And . . .?'

'Begging your pardon, sir, but that you do too.'

Drinkwater stared at his first lieutenant. Fraser was a good, competent officer. Drinkwater had taken him as a favour to Lord Keith and though there was not the intimacy that existed between the captain and Quilhampton, there was a strong sense of mutual regard between them. He had never known Fraser attempt to meddle with his own method of command before, yet here was a direct, if obscure, inference.

'Go on, Mr Fraser, and do stop begging my pardon; you are, after all, the first lieutenant.'

Fraser's diffidence seemed to slip from him, and Drinkwater mentally reprobated himself for his cross-grainedness. He sometimes forgot the age difference between himself and his officers and the intimidating effect it could have on their confidences.

'Well, sir, I got wind o' scuttlebutt that the people had heard you knew the whereabouts o' the deserters . . .' (How? Drinkwater asked himself. Not Tregembo, certainly; perhaps Mullender or the Quaker Derrick, whose loyalty lay closer to his moral creed than any imposed regulations of the Admiralty.) '. . . and that you wouldn't reclaim them on account o' the fact that you didna' want trouble.'

'I see. But such an assumption of weakness might provoke trouble nevertheless.'

'Aye, sir, that's true,' said Fraser, relieved that the captain took his point.

Drinkwater recalled his remark to Callan about not wanting to disaffect the men when the ship was idle. Misinterpretation of such a speech was not surprising. He still had *Phaeton* in company, he could alter course for Macao and arraign the recaptured deserters before a court martial which would assuredly hang them. Or he could affect to ignore the matter a while longer, and deal with it when he judged proper.

'I shall recover the deserters tomorrow, Mr Fraser, if the sea permits it. In the meantime deal with Midshipman Chirkov and get Marsden to rig up those screens.'

In the gloom of the gunroom, lit by the grease-dips' guttering flames, the *Patrician*'s midshipmen stood alongside their Russian counterparts. In the main they had got on well together. Frey, partly by virtue of his personality, partly by his acting rank, was the acknowledged senior, and there was some evidence that Chirkov was not liked by the other Russians on account of his overwhelming idleness. There was, therefore, no particular objection to the first lieutenant's announcement of the punishment, nor any move to release Chirkov when he struggled, protesting the indignity of being held by two of Comley's mates. It was no fault of the other midshipmen, British or Russian, if Chirkov failed to understand that he was being let off lightly, given what amounted to a private punishment on a crowded man-of-war, rather than the spectacular public humbling of being beaten over the breech of a quarterdeck carronade.

Comley laid on over Chirkov's breeched backside to the count of twelve, and when he marched his mates out of the cockpit he respectfully touched his hat to them all. 'Gentlemen . . .' he said.

'There, sir,' Frey remarked reasonably to the straightening Chirkov who was choking back tears of rage, pain and humiliation, 'you have had the honour of a thrashing from one of His Britannic Majesty's bosuns, he is senior to you and therefore your submission is without prejudice to your character as an officer.'

Grins greeted this droll speech, but its humour was lost on Chirkov.

'A *Mister* Bosun is not superior to a Russian *Count*,' he hissed.

'Perhaps not, sir,' replied Frey quickly, 'but he is most assuredly superior to a midshipman.'

'Particularly a *Russian* midshipman,' added Belchambers, boldly.

Enraged, Chirkov turned on the diminutive Belchambers, but the boy adroitly dodged him and the sudden movement sent agonies of pain through Chirkov's buttocks. As Belchambers slipped past his would-be assailant and made for the companionway to the deck, Frey, Dutfield and the rest barred his retreat. Chirkov was faced with an unsmiling wall of bodies.

'You deserved it, Count Chirkov,' said Frey, 'recall you are a prisoner of war. You would do best to forget the matter. I can assure you that Captain Drinkwater has dismissed it from his mind.'

'What do I worry about your Captain Drinkwater's mind? Captain Drinkwater can go to the devil! I am insulted. I cannot call for satisfactions from Mister Bosun but I can from you!' Chirkov rammed a finger into Frey's face. 'You are only *acting* lieutenant, you are challenged!'

A stillness fell on the gunroom. The midshipmen swayed amid the creaks and groans of the ship's fabric as it worked easily in the quartering sea. They watched Frey's reaction.

'Duelling is forbidden on board ship, sir, but I shall be pleased to meet you ashore upon our arrival at Prince of Wales Island.'

'Pistols,' snarled Chirkov, and stumbled unhappily from the circle of onlookers.

Captain Drinkwater looked about him. He knew he ought to be contented. The convoy was dosed up in good order, spread over some five square miles of the China Sea, not in columns but a loose formation centred on *Guilford* and *Ligonier*, the big Indiamen, both of which had lanterns in their mizen tops that glowed weakly in the failing daylight. Clouds covered the sky, outriders of the northerly monsoon that drove them southwards with a fair wind for the Malacca Strait. In accordance with his Standing Orders the ships were taking in their topgallants for the night, snugging down to avoid the separation that might make one of them a vulnerable hen for any marauding French *reynard* cruising on the horizon. Drinkwater looked at the main crosstrees from which Midshipman Dutfield was just then descending. When the midshipman reached the deck he made his report.

'Two junks in the north-east quarter, sir, otherwise nothing in sight beyond the convoy.'

Acknowledging the intelligence, Drinkwater was peeved that the news brought him no satisfaction. He nodded and turned to Frey.

'You may fire the chaser, Mr Frey, and make *Phaeton*'s number . . .'

Drinkwater looked astern. Fleetwood Pellew's crack frigate

dipped her ensign in farewell, hauled her yards and, on a taut bowline, stood to windward, returning to the coast of China. *Patrician* was in sole charge now and Drinkwater could go below.

But he lingered. There was no solace in the cabin, divided as it was and with Morris inert and inscrutable behind the canvas screen. So far Drinkwater had avoided all contact with his enemy, unwilling to stir any memory or allow Morris the slightest grounds for reawakening old enmities. Drinkwater did not know how Morris had got word of his presence in the Pearl River, though it was not hard to imagine in the circumscribed circle of gossip attached to the trading fraternity at Canton, but he was convinced Morris had some ulterior motive for selecting *Patrician* as his means of reaching India. And it went beyond the customary carriage of specie in His Majesty's ships, as witness the chests put aboard *Guilford*.

No, Morris had personal reasons for seeking passage with Nathaniel Drinkwater, and the quondam naval officer had once sworn he would professionally ruin the man who had displaced him on a quarterdeck.

Coxswain Tregembo lay in his hammock and stared at the dimly visible deck beam a few inches above his nose. During the night the sea had risen and *Patrician* was scending before the quartering waves. On either side of him the hammocks of other men pressed against his own in the fourteen inches allowed each man. Tregembo was part of a suspended island of humanity that moved almost independently of the ship, adding its own creaks and rasps and rub of rope and ring and canvas to the aching groan of the working timbers of the frigate.

To a less inured nose than Tregembo's, the stench would have been overpowering, for all Lieutenant Fraser's sedulous swabbing with vinegar, airing and burning of loose powder. Ineffectually washed bodies, the exhalations of men on an indifferent diet that whistled through badly maintained teeth and the night-loosening of wind combined with the effluvia of the bilge that rose from below. Rat droppings and the residual essences of the myriad store concealed in the storerooms and hold added to the decomposing mud and weed drawn inboard on the cables so lately laid on the bed of the Pearl River. Flakes of green and noxious matter gave off gases as they broke down into dust, to be carried into the limbers of the ship by the trickling rivulets of leaks that found their inexorable way below.

Scarcely noticing this mephitic miasma that cast yellow haloes round the guarded lanterns by the companionways and dully illuminated the dozing sentries, Tregembo lay unsleeping. He too considered the presence of Morris in their midst.

Unlike his captain, Tregembo's intellect did not flirt with notions of providence or fate. Considerations of coincidence in Morris's resurrection aboard *Patrician* were quite absent from his thoughts. To Tregembo the world was not a vast, wondrous mystery in which his life held some fraction of universal implication; but a confined, tangible microcosm of discomfort, tolerable if one occupied the office of captain's coxswain under a man of Drinkwater's stamp. It was not that Tregembo lacked the intelligence to cast his mind beyond the compressing tumblehome of *Patrician*'s planking, nor that he was incapable of regarding the star-strewn sky with awe. It was just that his firmament was limited by the deck beam above him and that such considerations as Drinkwater could indulge in, for Tregembo bordered on the effete and were beyond the sensible limits of practical men. That Morris had turned up in China was, to Tregembo, not to be wondered at. He had been left half-way there, at the Cape of Good Hope some years ago, and it did not surprise the old Cornishman that he had made a new life for himself beyond the Indian Seas.

Listening to the noises of the night around him, to the soft, abrasive whisper of a hundred swinging hammocks and the labouring of the ship, the audible hiss of the sea beyond the double planking of the hull, the thrum of wind in the rigging far above him and the mumbles and grunts of dreaming men, Tregembo thought back to a gale-lashed night nearly thirty years earlier when he and another had sprung a man from a foot-rope when reefing a sail, flinging him into the sea, to disappear into the blackness astern of the hard-pressed frigate *Cyclops*.

It had been a judicial murder, secretly sanctioned by the tacit approval of most of the members of the lower deck, and it had put an end to the bullying and the tyranny of a certain Midshipman Morris and his sodomitically inclined cronies. Tregembo smiled to himself.

He recalled the young Drinkwater seeking guidance when the same Morris turned upon his messmates for amusement. The eventual confrontation had matured the promising young midshipman, and had been the beginning of Tregembo's service to Drinkwater.

What worried Tregembo now, and kept him from sleeping, was the certainty that Morris would seek in some way to discredit the captain. When the young Drinkwater had sought out Tregembo for a confidant, the Cornishman had advised him that he had nothing to lose by opposing the cockpit bully. Now things were different; Captain Drinkwater had everything to lose, and the thought made Tregembo uneasy.

Morris too was awake, listening to the breathing of Drinkwater beyond the canvas screen. The captain was asleep now, Morris knew, though it had been a long time before he had dropped off. Morris had heard also the revealing tinkle of glass and bottle after Drinkwater had come below.

Never, in his most extreme fantasies, had Morris imagined that Drinkwater would ever be delivered up to him so perfectly. In the days when, after his ousting from the *Cyclops*, he had smarted over his rival's luck, he had continued his pursuit of a naval career. He had been helped by petticoat influence, of course, but there was nothing unusual in that. Then had come the time when he had been appointed to the brig *Hellebore* and, delectably, had Drinkwater as his first lieutenant.

Only the onset of chronic illness had prevented him from fully exploiting that opportunity, and in his long convalescence at the Cape Drinkwater had slipped from his grasp. News had come to Morris there of the death of his sister by whose influence he had formerly gained employment, and a letter refusing to ratify his promotion to Master and Commander had left him high and dry at the tip of Africa. He could have gone home, but a welter of debts and creditors decided him against it. Besides, the frequent passage of Indiamen and the consequent society of one or two men of oriental taste induced him to try his luck in India.

Morris smiled to himself. He felt immensely benign, as good and calm as when the opium fumes took his soul and wafted it through paradise. Even in the gloom he could see the pale face of the sleeping boy. He had not paid much for the tongue-tied child, more for the services of the surgeon of the European infantry battalion in Madras whose fourchette had not simply sliced the frenum, but had excavated the child's mouth to make an apolaustic orifice for his master.

There was no abatement of the wind at dawn. Cloud obscured the sky and a touch of mist hazed the horizon. The convoy remained in tolerably good order but Drinkwater, early on deck from an unsatisfactory night's rest, was frustrated in his plans to lower a boat and recover his deserters.

Tregembo had more success, entering the captain's cabin soon after Drinkwater had gone on deck and before either Mullender or Derrick was about. Slipping round the canvas screen he woke the corpulent mass of Morris by hauling his catamite off him. It was the first time Morris had knowingly laid eyes on the old Cornishman for ten years.

'What the . . .?'

'Remember me, do ye?'

'You . . .' Morris's face creased with fear and the struggle to recall a name. The old man had been in Drinkwater's cabin when he had first entered it. Now he shook Morris with a horrid violence.

'Tregembo, Cap'n's cox'n. *I* remember *you*, an' I want words to tell 'ee that I'll see 'ee in hell before ye'll touch the Cap'n!'

Morris, still supine in the tossing cot, quailed under the venom of Tregembo's words. The boy had shrunk into a crouch, whimpering against the carriage of a gun.

'Tregembo . . .' muttered Morris, his eyes fixed on the glowering, over-zealous old man, recalling memories of Tregembo's past and how, like Drinkwater's, they lay like the strands of a rope, woven with his own. It was clear that Tregembo had come to threaten, not to murder. This realisation emboldened Morris. He eased his bulk on to an elbow.

'Ah, yes, Tregembo . . . yes, I recall you now. You are Captain Drinkwater's lickspittle, his tale-bearer. Yes, I recall you well, *and* your part in certain doings aboard *Cyclops* . . .'

'Aye. And you'd do well to keep your memories in your mind, *Mister* Morris, for I'm not afeared of you and know what you'd do if ye had the chance. Just you recollect that old Tregembo will be watching you, and your dandy-prat there.' Tregembo gestured at the boy.

'Is that a threat, Tregembo?'

But the Cornishman had said his piece and retired beyond the canvas screen. The boy whimpered fearfully and, as *Patrician* dipped suddenly into the trough of a wave, vomited over the deck. The sharp stink assailed Morris's nostrils and from pique he clouted the frightened and abject creature.

Tregembo felt satisfied with his mission of intimidation. He had hoped for an ally in Mr Quilhampton and had been disappointed. There was, however, one further thing to be done to complete the execution of the plan he had made during the night.

He found Drinkwater at the weather hance, wrapped in his boat-cloak.

'Beg pardon, zur . . .'

'What is it, Tregembo? . . .'

'That Morris, zur.' Tregembo's eyes met the Captain's.

'Well?'

''E knows me, zur . . . I spoke to him this morning.'

'You announced your presence, you mean . . . advised him to mind his manners, is that it?'

'Something o' the sort, zur.'

Drinkwater smiled. 'Be careful of him, Tregembo. Unfortunately we must bear with him . . .'

'*You* be careful o' him, zur,' Tregembo broke in, 'he's not forgotten nothing, zur . . . be assured o' that.'

'Thank you for your advice.'

Tregembo bridled at the faintly patronising air of Drinkwater's reply. 'He weren't never a gennelman, zur; he'm no longer quality.'

'No, you're right . . .'

'You shouldn't leave your pistols in your cabin, zur, I don't know that he's got any himself, but . . .'

'I've been thinking about that. I've decided to take over poor Hill's cabin and put Prince Vladimir in to share with Morris.'

Tregembo considered the proposition and a twinkle in his eyes caught an answering glimmer in Drinkwater's.

'I'll see to it, zur.'

'If you please.'

'Beg pardon, sir.' Lieutenant Quilhampton touched the fore-cock of his hat.

'Yes? What is it?'

'Weather's tending to thicken, sir.'

Drinkwater cast a look about the frigate, quickly counting his scattered charges. Two of the Country ships, small, round bilged brigs, were wallowing, dropping astern and fading into the encroaching mist that had dissolved the horizon, reducing the visible circle of sea on which the ships of the convoy drove southwards.

'Very well. Make the signal to shorten sail.'

Quilhampton acknowledged the order and the hitched bundles of coloured bunting soared aloft to break out at the main masthead. From forward an unshotted gun boomed to leeward, drawing attention to the signal. While the *Patrician*'s men leapt into the shrouds and lay aloft, Drinkwater watched the evolutions of the merchant ships. He knew the Indiamen were reluctant to crack on apace, believing in a leisurely progress as least wearing on cargo, company and passengers. If the convoy were being shadowed, now would prove an opportune occasion for an attack. But the convoy behaved itself. The Indiamen shortened down and the cluster of Country ships followed suit, the rearward sluggards sensibly holding on until they had come up with the majority.

'Bring the ship close to the starboard quarter of the rearmost brig, Mr Q.'

'On the wind'd quarter of the *Courier*, aye, aye, sir.'

If they were to be attacked, Drinkwater wanted *Patrician* to windward and able to crack on sail to support any part of his little fleet. He watched as the helm was put down and the men manned the braces, swinging the yards a point or two, easing the sheets and leading the weather tacks forward. The convoy drew out on *Patrician*'s larboard bow and then, yards swung again, she came back before the wind, reined in upon the quarter of the inappropriately named brig *Courier*, slowest vessel in the convoy.

Aware of someone beside him, Drinkwater turned, expecting

Quilhampton to report the adjustment to the frigate's station, but it was Rakitin.

'I have had a report, Captain Drinkwater, from one of my officers, that you have ordered him to be beaten. Count Chirkov is most . . .' Rakitin sought the right word for the humiliation of his subordinate with no success. 'Count Chirkov has . . . I protest most strongly.'

Drinkwater fixed the Russian with a glare and tried with difficulty to keep his temper. Morris, the Russians, such petty matters; relatively trivial when compared to the importance of the convoy and the dangers inherent in the latent disaffection of his crew. He knew that in the circumscribed limits of a ship such trifling irritations assumed an importance scarcely to be conceived by those on land, an importance that the rigid enforcement of naval discipline defused, but which grew and festered among those not held in such thrall with, moreover, the time and opportunity to dwell upon them. He rounded on the Russian.

'Captain Rakitin, if you did me the courtesy of maintaining order among your officers, a situation requiring punishment would not have arisen. As it was I ordered your officer punished according to the usage of the British service in which he is now a prisoner. He was not publicly humiliated in front of the ship's company and should not, therefore, complain. However,' Drinkwater continued, a mischievous idea occurring to him, 'I have made arrangements for you to transfer into my own cabin, vacating the one you presently occupy. I also deliver Midshipman Count Chirkov into your especial charge. He is to live and mess with you and not to contaminate my own young men any more. Good-day to you!'

Drinkwater strode purposefully across the deck, bent over the binnacle to check the course and took station with Lieutenant Quilhampton.

'For God's sake, James, talk some sense to me before I am constrained to do something I shall regret.'

Quilhampton turned, cast a glance beyond Drinkwater's shoulder and muttered, 'He's in pursuit, sir . . .'

'God's bones,' said Drinkwater through clenched teeth.

'Captain Drinkwater,' began Rakitin who had taken a moment

to digest the import of Drinkwater's remarks, 'Captain Drinkwater, it is not . . .'

'Deck there!' came the lookout's shrill cry. 'Ship to loo'ard bearing up! Gunfire to the s'uth'ard!'

The dull boom of a gun rolled over the water and the sharp point of fire from a second discharge caught their eyes as the ships of the convoy began to swing to starboard across the bows of those behind them. Strict order seemed about to dissolve into chaos.

'Hands to the braces! Starboard your helm, Mister! Don't run aboard that damned brig! Call all hands!'

Drinkwater dodged Rakitin, hauled himself up into the mizen rigging and strove to make out what was happening ahead. He hesitated only a second as another stab of yellow gunfire flashed through the mist.

'Beat to quarters!'

9   Infirmities of Character

December 1808

'Hold your course!'

Drinkwater moved beside the binnacle, steadying the helms-men and countering a sudden and distressing nervousness on the part of Ballantyne, the new sailing master. *Guilford* loomed past a pistol-shot distant, her yards triced hard-up to avoid plunging into *Ligonier* under her lee. The latter, foul of the *Hormuzeer*, had broached and a brief glance showed men running out along her jib-boom, hacking at the mess of broken spars, torn canvas and tangled ropes where it had jammed in the Country ship's main rigging.

As *Patrician*'s stern lifted, Drinkwater could see ahead. Only two more ships lay to leeward, and both were clearing from lar-board, their heads laid on the starboard tack. Raising his glass he swept it across the misty horizon expecting to see the pale squares of enemy topsails taking substance above the low hull of a French frigate.

'Ship cleared for action, sir,' Fraser reported, and Drinkwater nodded. He had been so occupied with conning *Patrician* through the convoy that he had scarcely noticed the rattle of the marine drummer's snare, or the rushing preparations round the deck. Mount's marines lined the hammock nettings and the quarterdeck and fo'c's'le gunners knelt expectantly by their pieces. Midshipmen stood at their stations, little Belchambers, his ankle near normal, in the main-top. Drinkwater thought of Morris, suddenly exposed to the vulgar gaze of the people as the cabin bulkheads were removed and the eighteen-pounder beneath his cot was manned by a dozen barefoot seamen. Drinkwater wondered if he was still fondling his pathic.

They were crossing the stern of the leeward-most ship now and Ballantyne was gesticulating.

'Please, sir! Something is not correct!'

'Eh? What's that?'

'They are waving, sir, on the ship to starboard . . .'

Drinkwater strode to the rail and peered over the hammock nettings. The square stern of the heavily laden *Carnatic* presented itself to his gaze. Two men were waving frantically from her rail and then a belch of smoke rolled from her waist as she discharged another gun.

'By God, it's an alarm!'

Drinkwater spun round. He had already detected the danger ahead by the sudden increase in the pitch of the deck.

'Braces, there! Lively now! Start 'em for your lives! Down helm! Down helm!'

There was no enemy frigate waiting to leeward of the convoy ready to snap up a prize; only an uncharted reef upon which the sea broke in sudden, serried ranks of rollers which exploded upwards, filling the air with an intense mist.

Mount saved them, slashing through the standing part of the main brace with his hanger, then cutting back into the strands of the topsail brace. As the yards flew round *Patrician* lay over assisting the helmsmen as they palmed the wheel-spokes rapidly through their hands. A member of the afterguard was already at the mizen braces while others started the main sheet at the chesstree. The heavy frigate lurched to leeward, running her larboard gun-ports under water and taking gouts of streaming sea-water below as Lieutenant Quilhampton, in charge of the main batteries and suddenly aware of something amiss, ordered the ports secured.

'Jesus Christ . . .' someone blasphemed. The steady stern breeze seemed, now that they reached obliquely across it, to blow with the ferocity of a gale. The extra canvas, shaken out again as they had overtaken the convoy, now pressed them over. To windward the seas assumed a new and forbidding aspect, heaping sharply into breaking peaks as they felt the rising sea-bed beneath them.

Drinkwater turned to leeward. He was beyond the heart-thumping apprehension of anxiety, his mind perfectly cool with that detachment that feared the worst. At any moment, driven by his own impetuosity, he expected *Patrician*'s keel to strike the reef in a sudden, overwhelming shock that would carry her masts and yards over the side.

Beyond the narrow beam of the frigate's hull the seas downwind bore a different look. Their precipitate energy was spent, they crashed and foamed and flung themselves in a thundering welter of white and green water upon the invisible obstacle of the reef.

'Hold her steady!' he ordered, his voice level as every man upon the upper deck who was aware of their danger held his breath.

For a minute . . . two . . . *Patrician* skimmed, heeling along the very rim of the reef, held from dashing herself to pieces only by the unseen, submarine run-off where the broken waves, spending themselves above, poured back whence they had come.

Ten minutes later they were in clear water and the white surge of foaming breakers with its cap of wafting spume lay fine on the weather quarter.

'I'm obliged to you, Mr Mount.'

'Your servant, sir,' replied Mount, still amazed at his own prescience.

'A damned close thing . . .' Drinkwater's heart was thumping vigorously now. Reaction had set in; he felt a wave of nausea and a weakling tremble in his leg muscles. 'Secure the guns and pipe the men down,' he said to Fraser between clenched teeth.

And then Morris was there, standing upon the quarterdeck watching Comley hustling a party along to reeve off a new mainbrace; his loose, yellow silk robe flapping in the wind, the Indian, decorously turned out in coat, turban and aigrette, hanging by his side.

Men were nudging each other and staring at the bizarre sight. When Morris and Drinkwater confronted each other, the latter was still pale from his recent experience.

'You alarmed us, Captain,' Morris said smoothly, 'we thought you were going into action, but I see that, like Caligula, you had declared war on the ocean.'

The smug, urbane transition of remark into insult struck Drinkwater. He was reminded of how dangerous a man Morris was, that he was not without education, and came from a class that accepted privilege as a birthright. It had formed part of Morris's original enmity that the youthful Drinkwater was an example of an upstart family.

But Drinkwater's nausea was swiftly overcome by a rising and revengeful anger. He recalled something of the detached coolness that sustained him in moments of extreme stress.

'The bulkheads will shortly be re-erected. You will be able to return to your quarters very soon.' The words were polite, the tone sharp.

'But it is remarkably refreshing here on deck, Captain. You have a fine set of men . . . handsome fellows . . .'

The remark was loud enough to be overheard, on the face of it harmless enough, but tinged with notice of intent, judging by the amusement in Morris's deep-set, hooded eyes.

'Go below, sir,' Drinkwater snapped, facing his old enemy, and between them crackled the brittle electricity of dislike. Morris smiled and then turned to go. Drinkwater found himself confronted by Ballantyne. The master stood open-mouthed and Drinkwater thought of his earlier nervousness. He appeared to have a coward upon his quarterdeck.

'What the devil *is* it, Mr Ballantyne? Come, pull yourself together, the danger's past. Be kind enough to work out an estimate of our position so that we can amend the charts . . .'

'No, no, sir. It is that man.' Ballantyne's head shook from side to side. 'I know him . . .'

It occurred to Drinkwater that Ballantyne had not previously seen their passenger. For all Drinkwater knew, Morris had traded under a pseudonym.

'I knew him in Rangoon, sir,' Ballantyne persisted, 'he was up to mischief. He made much money.'

Mischief seemed a very mild word for what Drinkwater knew Morris was capable of.

'I should not believe all you hear, Captain Drinkwater, especially from a man of mixed blood.'

Overheard, Ballantyne paled, while Morris's head disappeared for the second time below the lip of the companionway coaming.

For two days nothing of note occurred. The wind eased, clearing the air so that the horizon became again the clear rim of visibility beloved by seamen. The convoy remained in good order and Drinkwater, immeasurably relieved by his move into the master's cabin, felt his spirits lighten. He dismissed his earlier fears of interference from Morris as foolish imaginings, recollections of the past when he had been a circumstantial victim of Morris's vicious and capricious nature. Now he had the upper hand; Morris was held aft under guard yet in the comparative freedom of the great cabin. His officers were loyal. The morale of his men was much improved by the news that their return home was now only a matter of time, and the convoy was well disciplined.

Privately, too, the move was beneficial. He had had Mullender take down the portraits, his journal was secure and his personal effects were removed from the defiling presence of Morris. What Morris did behind the canvas screen was his own affair, so long as it did not impinge upon the life, public or private, of Captain Drinkwater and his ship.

As Drinkwater's mood lifted, James Quilhampton's was damped by growing apprehension. The first excitements of departure from Whampoa had worn off, and the drudgery of watch-keeping imposed its own monotonous routines which combined with the demands of the ship and convoy to rouse dormant worries. It was Quilhampton who had, months ago, suppressed an incipient mutiny before its eruption. These were the same men, he thought as he paced the quarterdeck daily, observing them about their duties, the same unpaid labourers who were sorely tried by the hard usage of the King's Service. To Quilhampton, the spectre of mutiny assumed a new danger now that they were homeward bound; the danger that it might destroy any possibility of him marrying Mistress MacEwan. Part of his cavalier reception of Tregembo's warning was not so much because he did not believe in it, but because he did not want to contemplate any additional factor that might threaten or destroy his expectations.

Beyond the screen bisecting the captain's cabin Morris heard Captain Rakitin leave his indolent young companion while he took his exercise on deck. Morris, wrapped in his silk robe, touched the shoulder of his Ganymede and pointed at the screen. Impassively the boy rose and slipped past the end of the partition where, at the stern windows, communication between the divided cabin was possible. Morris waited, composing his face to its most benign expression, smoking a long, thin Burmese cheroot.

'Good morning,' he said as Chirkov, summoned by curiosity, followed the turbaned pixie. 'Please sit down. I hear you speak excellent English. Would you care for a glass . . .?'

The boy produced a porcelain bottle and poured *samsu* into one of Drinkwater's glasses. Standing, Chirkov tossed back the glass, the raw rice spirit rasping his throat with a fire reminiscent of vodka. The glass was refilled. The Russian seemed reluctant to sit.

'We are both prisoners of Captain Drinkwater . . .' Morris began experimentally, pleased with the contemptuously dismissive gesture made by Chirkov.

'You do not like Captain Drinkwater?' Morris asked.

'No! He is doing me dishonour, great dishonour. I will fight and shoot one of his officers soon.'

'A duel, eh? Well, well.' Morris motioned the boy to produce more *samsu*. 'And what is this great dishonour the ignoble Captain has done you?' Morris's voice had a soothing, honeyed tone.

'He ordered me to be beaten!' Chirkov spluttered indignantly.

'Beaten?' Morris's tongue flickered pinkly over his lips in a quicksilver reaction of heightened interest. He flickered a commanding glance at the Indian boy and more *samsu* tinkled into Chirkov's glass to be tossed back by the impetuous Russian. 'How barbaric,' Morris muttered sympathetically. 'And it is still painful, eh?'

Chirkov nodded, watching the boy pour yet more *samsu*. '*Oui* . . . yes.'

'I have a salve . . . a medicine, specific against such a wound. If it is not treated it may fester.' Morris smiled, reassuringly. 'You do not want gangrene, do you?' Abstractedly Morris touched the glowing end of his cheroot to a bundle of sticks by his elbow.

'Gangrene?' Chirkov frowned.

'Mortification . . .'

Chirkov understood and the dull gleam of alarm deliberately kindled by Morris appeared in his fuddled eyes.

'Would you like me to . . .?' Morris's hands made a gesturing of massage and he addressed a few words of Hindi to the Indian boy.

Samsu and sympathy and the strange scent that wafted now about the cabin from joss-sticks burning in a brass pot beside Morris dissolved the young man's suspicions. The turbanned boy returned to his master's side with a pot of unguent. Morris made a sign for Chirkov to expose himself. Morris smiled a complicit smile and Chirkov, drunk and of sensuous disposition, did as he was bid. Morris dipped his hands in the salve and began to apply it as Chirkov, holding on to the edge of the table, stood before him.

For a few seconds a heavy silence filled the cabin. Morris felt the fierce triumph of discovery as Chirkov's compliance revealed his own hedonistic nature and then the Russian too was aware of the most pleasurable and undreamed of sensations flooding through him as the tongueless boy obeyed his master's instructions.

'A glass, Mr Ballantyne?'

'Er, thank you, Mr Quilhampton.' Ballantyne struggled with the awkward surname. In the post-daylight gloom of the wardroom Quilhampton pushed the glass across the table, taking two fingers off its base as Ballantyne seized it. Then, holding the neck of the decanter in one hand, his own glass in the other, he tipped his chair back against the heel of the ship and with the unthinking ease of long practice, threw both feet on to the edge of the table. Ballantyne watched with fascination, for the hand in which Quilhampton held his glass, his left, was of wood.

'A rum thing, ain't it?' remarked the unabashed lieutenant.

'I beg your pardon, Mr Q . . .' Ballantyne's overwhelming predilection for formality was one of his characteristic features. 'You lost it in action, I believe?'

'Yes. Damned careless of me, wasn't it? Have a biscuit. No? Then pass the barrel, there's a good fellow.'

'Have you had much experience of action?' There was an eagerness in Ballantyne's question that, together with other remarks he had made, had provoked a character analysis from Mount that suggested the new sailing master nurtured a desire to distinguish himself. 'To prove himself,' Mount had explained, with a knowing look that attributed Ballantyne's desire for glory to his coloured skin.

'Action?' remarked Quilhampton. 'Yes, I've seen enough. And you, have you had much experience with women, Mr Ballantyne, for I'm woefully ignorant upon the subject.'

'Women?' A faint light of astonishment filled Ballantyne's eyes. 'But you talk often of your woman, Mr Q . . .'

'Because I am a besotted fool,' Quilhampton said in an attempt at flippancy, 'but I want to know of *women*, of the gender as a whole, not one in particular.'

'What is it you want to know?'

'Have you known many women?'

'Of course. Many, *many* women.' Ballantyne rolled his head in his quaint, exotic manner.

'Can a woman love a man with a wooden hand?'

'Now you are asking about one woman, Mr Q, and I am not comprehending you.'

'But to answer honestly you need to have known many women,' Quilhampton replied, a faint edge of desperation entering his voice.

'That is true. But I cannot answer for the particular . . .'

'No.' Quilhampton's face fell. In the silence the messman entered with a lantern.

'But . . .' said Ballantyne as the man retired, 'but I think it would be easier for a woman to love a man with a wooden hand than for a man to love a woman with a wooden leg.'

Quilhampton paused in the act of refilling his glass and stared at Ballantyne. The master was deadly serious and suddenly Quilhampton burst into laughter, giggling uncontrollably so that he only got all four chair legs and both his feet back on the deck with difficulty.

'What the devil is this rumpus?' asked Mount, emerging from his cabin, unfamiliarly attired in shirt-sleeves.

'Ballantyne,' gasped Quilhampton, 'Ballantyne is making up riddles . . .'

Mount leaned against the door frame of his cabin and looked upon the young lieutenant indulgently as Quilhampton recounted the conversation. Switching his glance to the master Mount was aware that Quilhampton's unbridled mirth had irritated Ballantyne. He was bristling with affront, unable to see anything beyond Quilhampton's ridicule of his remark. Mount was quick to retrieve the situation.

'Perhaps, Mr Ballantyne, you would favour me with an answer to a more serious question than a young jackanapes like James is capable of framing.'

'What is it, Mr Mount?' Ballantyne asked, suspicious now that the two Englishmen were going to bat him back and forth like a shuttlecock.

'I heard you remark to the Captain that you knew something of our somewhat unusual passenger. Who, or what exactly is he?'

Quilhampton was still giggling, but Mount's question almost silenced him for he could make his own contribution to its answer. Almost, for his amusement was sustained by the sudden over-whelmingly serious cast that Ballantyne's swarthy features assumed. It seemed to Quilhampton that this gravity of its own accord drew Mount to a vacant chair, and his amusement only subsided slowly, for his sensibilities still lingered on Catriona MacEwan, the point from which his question arose.

'He is a bad man, Mr Mount. It is said that he was formerly a naval officer, but he was in Calcutta for some years and then moved to Rangoon where he traded with a Parsee. My father had some business with their house and they cheated him. My father has never divulged the particulars of their transactions, for I believe the loss was too shameful for him. Some time after this the Parsee was found dead, and although nothing could be proved against this man he moved on to Canton where he had considerable influence with the Hong in the interest of the opium trade. It is said that he had connections with the Viceroy and these enabled him to travel outside the normal limits imposed by the authorities on the foreign devils . . .'

'Foreign devils?' queried Mount, frowning.

'The Europeans in the factories . . .'

'Ah . . . please go on . . .'

'I cannot tell you much more, except that I know of his dishonest connections with my father and that when, on one or two occasions I saw him in Canton, my father warned me against him.'

'But you are not going into trade, are you, Mr Ballantyne? You have volunteered for King George's service, at least for the time being.'

'I should like to serve His Majesty,' said Ballantyne. 'Is it true that by being master I cannot obtain a commission?'

'It is unusual, certainly, unless you distinguish yourself in action against the enemy. I suppose if you earned Captain Drinkwater's approbation and were mentioned in the *Gazette*, a commission might be forthcoming.'

There was a dry edge to Mount's voice that only Quilhampton recognised as faintly mocking. Now all suspicion was gone from Ballantyne's mind.

'And do you think we shall see action on a convoy escort?' Ballantyne asked.

Mount shrugged. 'One can never tell . . .'

The noise of the fo'c's'le bell rang through the ship and the frigate stirred to the call of the watch. 'On the other hand the call of duty is remorseless,' he added. 'Your watch, Mr Ballantyne . . .'

'You should not bait him, James,' remarked Mount, stretching himself and yawning.

'I didn't . . .'

'Then keep your love-sickness to yourself.'

'It ain't contagious.'

'No, but misery is and a long commission's fertile ground for that.' Mount rose. 'Good-night, James, and sweet dreams.'

Quilhampton sat alone for a few moments. Soon Fraser would come below demanding a glass and the remains of the biscuit barrel. Quilhampton threw off his thoughts of Catriona, for the image of Morris had intruded. He wondered why he had not added his own contribution to the pooling of knowledge about Morris. Was it because he could not admit that such a man had once held a commission as a naval officer?

He would confide in Mount. He would trust Mount with his life, but Ballantyne . . .? Ballantyne was not quite one of them; a merchant officer, a man of colour, a man for whom the grey seas of Ushant and the Channel were a closed book. Was Drinkwater truly going to confirm his appointment as master?

Quilhampton shrugged, drained his glass and made for his cabin. He did not want to socialise with Fraser, only to thrust his mind back to the pleasurable agony of dreaming of Catriona MacEwan.

*

On deck Mr Ballantyne paced up and down and dreamed of glory. He had set down upon Captain Drinkwater's chart the estimated position of the reef upon which the *Patrician* and her convoy had so nearly met disaster and earned a word of approval. He had modestly demurred from appending his own name to the shoal and now he fantasised about earning a more durable reward from the taciturn Captain Drinkwater. A commission as a lieutenant in the Royal Navy could lead him to social heights denied him on the Indian coast, for his mother had not been the Begum of Drinkwater's fancy, but a nautch-girl stolen from a temple by his lusty father, a beauty, true, but a woman of no consequence in Indian society. His father cared little for the conventions of the coast and had set his heart on an estate in the English shires if fortune smiled on him. But Ballantyne the son had a sharper perception of values, forced upon him by bastard birth, a tainted skin and opportunities that had raised him from the gutter in which an Indian Brahmin had once suggested he belonged. Something of a subconscious resentment of his father for the predicament in which he had been placed prevented him from accepting a life in merchant ships, and the turn of events which took him from the labouring hull of the dismasted *Musquito* and placed him aboard the puissant mass of *Patrician* had awakened a sentiment of predestination in him.

It was this happy mood, combined with a lack of appreciation of the exact status of Midshipman Chirkov, that led him to indulge the Russian prisoner when he requested to take the air on deck.

Mr Ballantyne, Master of His Britannic Majesty's frigate *Patrician*, felt a certain lofty condescension to Count Anatole Vasili Chirkov, and indulged the young and apparently interested Russian officer in a dissertation on their navigational position in the South China Sea.

10   A Small Victory

January 1809

In the stuffy hutch that had formerly been inhabited by *Patrician's* sailing master Drinkwater sat writing his journal. For a few moments he reflected before dipping his pen. Then he carefully scribed the date, forming the numerals of the new year with care.

> *We are now south of the twelfth parallel in less misty weather and lighter winds. My apprehensions of attack by Spanish cruisers from the Philippines seem unfounded and I assume their recent loss added to the knowledge of Drury's squadron in the area has made them more concerned for their own register ships than the plunder of our India trade.*
>
> *The convoy continues to behave well. The discipline of the Indiamen is excellent and the Country ships seek to emulate them to the extent of making the throwing out of recriminatory signals unnecessary. This good behaviour is not consistent with the conduct of all convoys . . .*

Drinkwater paused. While he allowed himself a certain latitude in personal asides, he was conscious of a desire to scribble all his random thoughts on to paper. He knew it was a consequence of his loneliness and the thought usually stopped him short of such confessions. Besides, they were too revealing when read later. But the urge to place something on record about Morris was strong, though the nature of the words he would employ eluded him. All he had written to date was a brief entry that Morris, *formerly Master and Commander in His Majesty's Service, now a merchant at Canton, has come aboard for the passage with a quantity of specie.*

It was a masterpiece of understatement, making no allusion to their previous acquaintance. Drinkwater knew the omission begged the question of for whom he wrote his journals. He had been ordered to destroy them, but had refused, considering them personal and not public property. In accordance with John Barrow's instructions his ship's logs had been dumped, so that no record of her activities in the Baltic existed; but even a man in the public employ was not to be utterly divested of personal life at the whim of another so employed.

He knew that, in truth, he wrote his journals for himself, an indulgence taken like wine or tobacco. It was unnecessary for him to have written anything about Morris beyond the fact that, like a phoenix, the man had risen from the ashes of the past. Out of the uncertainties and passions of adolescence when their antipathy had first found form, to the hatred of maturity aboard the brig *Hellebore* where Morris had indeed been 'Master and Commander', they had come now to a snarling and wary truce.

'Like two senescent dogs,' Drinkwater muttered, half lifting his pen as if to write down the words. But he laid the pen aside and closed his journal.

'We are too old now, too interested in feathering nests for our old age to disturb our lives with the revival of former passions.'

He spoke the words to himself, a low mumble that at least satisfied him in their formation, even though they failed to find their way on to the written page.

The improvement in the weather, the convoy's discipline in maintaining station and the apparently resigned behaviour of Morris persuaded Drinkwater that, subject to a degree of vigilance, his *bête noire* might be permitted the occasional freedom of the quarterdeck. The incongruous sight of Morris, corpulent under the shimmering silk of his robe, pacing beside Rakitin, became familiar to the other occupants of the quarterdeck during the first dog watch. As the hour of tropical sunset approached, Drinkwater also kept the deck, maintaining his own watch upon the two men. Little appeared to pass between them beyond the odd word, and the Russian seemed to have shrunk beside the obscene bulk of Morris. No longer filling his elegant uniform, Rakitin paced with hunched shoulders next to his enforced companion. The relentless nature of the ship's routine soon removed the novelty of this odd, morose promenade.

Midshipman Chirkov was also more in evidence, showing active signs of growing interest in professional matters and receiving instruction from Mr Ballantyne in a most gratifying manner. Drinkwater hoped the young man was taking advantage of the opportunity to increase his knowledge and that, reconciled to his fate, circumstances had wrought a sea-change in him.

The lighter winds slowed their southward progress and allowed fraternising between the ships so that, late one afternoon, Drinkwater found himself aboard the *Guilford*, dining at Callan's ample table.

Throughout the meal Drinkwater felt a sense of detachment. It was partly due to the fact that he was an outsider and not one of the small band of intimates who had grown wealthy in the service of the Honourable East India Company. Among the diners, four of Callan's own officers and an equal number from the *Ligonier*, including her commander, had been joined by several of the masters of the Country ships, men who considered themselves equal to, if after, the lordly Company captains. Drinkwater found the overt and artificial social posturing rather amusing, though their knowledge of the trade and navigation of the eastern seas, expressed in an argot with which he was unfamiliar, increased his sense of being an outsider.

The assumed superiority on the part of the East India commanders, whose wealth and power conferred on them a cachet that found its greatest expression in these remote oriental waters, seemed to Drinkwater a bubble ripe for pricking. He had accepted Callan's invitation, he privately admitted to himself, for motives other than the anticipation of a good meal. Looking down the table, however, he could see James Quilhampton entertained no such ulterior considerations for the meal was sumptuous, served on crisp, white linen, eaten off splendid porcelain with fine silver cutlery and accompanied by wines drunk from glittering crystal glasses.

Drinkwater enjoyed the luxury of the meal. He played up to Callan's efforts to engage him in conversation, but both men knew that unfinished business lay between them and only the convention of good manners prevented its open and indelicate discussion before the other guests. Quilhampton and a handful of his own subordinates were being entertained by the Indiamen's. Drinkwater's attention was engaged by the senior men about him, portly men for the most part, fleshy and rubicund from the climate and its alcoholic antidotes. They were men of strong opinion, products of almost unbridled licence and power, and although this fell short of the life-and-death power of a post-captain in the Royal Navy, it was clear that the opportunities their commands gave them for making money had given them confidence of another kind.

It occurred to Drinkwater that Callan might have assembled these men as allies to shame him into passing over the matter of the deserters. He smiled inwardly. He was quite capable of enjoying the fruits of Callan's table with as much insouciance as was Callan in accepting the protection of his frigate's cannon.

"Twas a trifle of a near-run thing t'other-day, Captain Drinkwater,' remarked one of the masters of a Country ship. 'We were firing alarm guns and you took 'em for shots at an enemy, eh?'

A silence had fallen and faces turned towards him. A conspiracy to embarrass him seemed in the air, or was it a remark provoked by over-much liquor? At the lower end of the table, too, there was a stir of interest and Drinkwater was gratified at the sudden irritation in Quilhampton's loyal eyes. Deliberately Drinkwater drained his glass.

'I took 'em, sir, for what you say they were, alarm guns. I would have been failing in my duty had I ignored them. Had you perused your instructions you would have observed a signal to indicate the convoy was standing into danger . . .'

Drinkwater watched the face of his interlocutor flush. The company shifted awkwardly in its chairs and he was persuaded that there *was* at best some practical joke afoot to throw him in a foolish light, for another spoke as though trying to regain the initiative.

'I don't think there was time for the hoisting of flags, Captain Drinkwater . . .'

The diners sniffed agreement, as though implying such niceties were all very well for a well-manned frigate, but a tightly run merchant ship could not afford the luxuries of signal staff.

'You were damned lucky to get away with it,' remarked the commander of the *Ligonier*.

'Now there I *would* agree with you, sir,' Drinkwater said smoothly, 'but a miss is as good as a mile, they say . . .'

'And we were fortunate not to lose your services,' said Callan soothingly.

'Yes,' agreed Drinkwater drily. 'What bothers me, gentlemen, is how such experts in the navigation of these seas as yourselves came to be so misled in your navigation.' He paused, gratified by a suggestion of embarrassment among them.

'I take it,' he went on, 'that we nearly ran ashore upon a hitherto uncharted spur of the Paracels? I trust you have all amended your charts accordingly . . .'

Drinkwater looked the length of the table. It had been a foolish attempt to mock him, of that he was now certain, and unwittingly they had given him a means to get his own back.

'A delightful meal, Captain Callan, and one in which the humour of the company induces me to ask you for the return of my men.'

There was only the briefest of pauses and then Callan urbanely agreed.

'Of course, Captain Drinkwater, of course . . .'

Was there the merest twinkle in Callan's eye? Drinkwater could not be certain, but he hoped so, for they had measured blade for blade and Drinkwater was fencer enough to know he had the advantage.

Contrary to expectations aboard *Patrician*, Drinkwater did not punish the deserters immediately. He had, he admitted to himself as he sat wooden-faced in the stern of his barge, fully intended to, but the sullen faces of his barge crew as, eyes averted, they rocked back and forward, half-heartedly pulling at the knocking oar-looms, dissuaded him. Not that he was afraid of the consequences of the flogging as he had earlier been. Indeed his mood was almost one of light-heartedness, so clumsy had been the efforts of the merchant masters to disconcert him, but Drinkwater possessed a strong, almost puritanical sense of propriety born of long service, and he would have despised himself if, after a magnificent dinner, he had viciously flogged the deserters.

It was impossible that he could excuse or exculpate them, for he had hanged a man for the same crime before leaving for the Pacific and such unheard-of leniency would, by its inconsistency, lead others into the same path. But their downcast misery as they sat in the stern sheets of the barge, in such close proximity to their captain, filled Drinkwater with an odd, angering compassion that, by the time he reached the ship, had dispelled his good humour.

'Put those men in the bilboes,' he curtly ordered Fraser as the first lieutenant stood with the rigid side-party, 'and prevent anyone approaching them,' he said to Mount, before hurrying below, only just catching himself in time to turn aside for the master's cabin and not walk, seething, into the main cabin. Suddenly the confines of his self-imposed prison oppressed him, and he as quickly returned to the deck, to pace up and down, up and down along the line of quarterdeck guns until he had mastered himself.

'He doesn't want to hang 'em,' said Quilhampton to the lounging officers in the wardroom.

'He'll have to. A court martial at Prince of Wales Island will condemn them without a thought . . .' remarked Fraser.

'Not if he punishes 'em now, quickly . . .'

'You mean flogs them?' asked Fraser.

'Yes,' replied Quilhampton, ''twill serve as an example to the rest.'

'Good God, man, we were hanging people before! D'you think their blessed Lordships'd approve of a mere flogging? They want stiffs for desertion, not red meat. He'll no' flog them, but keep them in irons until he can have them courtmartialled by a full board at Penang.'

'But he doesn't *want* to hang 'em,' persisted Quilhampton.

'Och, you presume on your knowledge o' the man, Jamie. I sympathise but not even Captain Drinkwater can get awa' from the fact that desertion's a hanging offence.'

'Tomorrow will tell who's right. If he hasn't flogged 'em by seven bells in the forenoon watch I'm not James Quilhampton.' Quilhampton rose, yawning. 'I've the middle tonight, and I'm weary . . .'

'What do you think, Mister Lallo?' Fraser asked of the surgeon who had sat silently through this exchange.

Lallo shrugged. 'I've no idea. Mr Q's solution seems the most humane, yours the most in conformity with the regulations . . .'

'And the easiest for you,' added Fraser drily.

'Ah yes.' Lallo's tone was unenthusiastic. 'Mr Fraser,' he said, suddenly shifting in his chair and reaching for the decanter on the wardroom table, 'there are other problems that confront us, you know.'

'Oh . . .?' Something in Lallo's voice caught Fraser's attention. 'What?'

'I thought I had three cases of lues as a legacy of California, now I have five, maybe six.'

'And is that so unusual? I saw the venereal list myself only this morning.'

'Two of the cases I'm certain are syphilitic, but the others . . .'

'You are not sure?'

'No, I mean, yes, I'm sure.' Lallo rubbed his hand across his forehead in a gesture of extreme exhaustion. 'But it isn't the pox.'

'Well, what is it?' snapped Fraser, a sudden fearful cramp contracting the muscles of his belly.

'Button-scurvy . . .'

'Scurvy?'

'No! *Button*-scurvy, Mr Fraser, framboesia, the yaws . . .'

'The yaws!'

'Aye, and it's contagious.'

Midshipman Chirkov's quarterdeck appearances had begun to assume a semblance of normality, so much so that the flattered Ballantyne remarked upon his regular interest to Quilhampton when handing over the deck to him at midnight. Together with the details of the course steered and the bearings of the merchantmen, the information made no impression upon the still sleep-dulled Quilhampton until he had been on watch for some time and had dismissed the more immediate preoccupations of his duty. It occurred to him then that Midshipman Chirkov's sudden enthusiasm was singularly uncharacteristic and that, for reasons of his own, he was currying favour with the vulnerable and somewhat pathetic Ballantyne. Had Quilhampton also known the state of hostility that existed between Chirkov and Frey, he might have associated Chirkov's sudden interest in navigation with something more sinister. But that was a matter of honour, a matter of honour forbidden on board ship, and so a closely guarded secret of the gunroom. As it was, his conversation with Ballantyne led him to make other assumptions, blinding him to what was going on almost under his very nose.

Morris had made no attempt to convert the indolent and sensual Russian to his own particular vice. Indeed, age, jaded appetite and excessive corpulence had rendered him less active himself in its pursuit. Besides, his seduction of the Russian youth had aims other than the fulfilment of his own overt desires; what Morris meditated was something infinitely more pleasurable than the mere gratification of lust, something that still appealed to a man far gone in lechery, holding out the budding promise of the most exquisite pleasure.

The boy he had had fashioned for his unique and effortless delight could be employed with equal facility to enrapture the libidinous Chirkov without too much arousing the young man's disgust at himself. Morris was delighted for the gift of so compliant an accomplice as Chirkov.

Nor did the lounging Chirkov, half drunk, half drugged by *samsu* and Malwa opium during the nights in which Rakitin slept and he and Morris held their unholy court, realise the extent to which he was being used. Morris had explained the dislike Drinkwater felt for them both as an unmannerly prejudice, offering Chirkov a spiteful little revenge upon the British captain by finding out the location of the frigate from the log and traverse board so that he, Morris, might be kept abreast of events that Drinkwater, out of malice, denied him. In return, the extravagant pleasures of Morris's half of the cabin amused the young man as an acceptable alternative to the gypsies who had first introduced him to the gratification of the flesh.

And unbeknown to anyone, even his helpless catamite, Morris plotted the southward progres of the convoy on a chart of his own.

11   Blood and Rain

January 1809

'One!'

Spread-eagled against the triced-up grating the man's body jerked in reflexive response to the first stroke of the cat. The flesh of the back was surprisingly pale, turning bronze at the nape of the neck. As he watched, his face a grim mask, Drinkwater saw the red weals begin to streak the skin . . .

'Two!

As the second weals emerged beneath the unruptured skin, the first were rising in sharp relief. Drinkwater watched the man's face, the mouth distorted by the leather pad upon which he bit. The deserter had his eyes screwed tight-shut and Drinkwater knew he was bracing himself for the dreadful assault on his body . . .

'Three!'

The stretched skin, pressed upwards from below by the bleeding tissues beneath, began to break. At first the stretched pores exuded suppurations of blood and plasma, giving the impression of a rosy sweat that spread in bands across the man's back . . .

'Four!'

Was this better than hanging? Was this man's life confined in the wooden bulwarks of His Britannic Majesty's frigate *Patrician*, in which even the ship's very name emphasised the subordination of her company, better than a swift and final agony at the end of a yard-rope? Was there, Drinkwater wondered as the bosun's mate laid on the tailed whip again, not one sublime second of freedom before the awful darkness of oblivion? One infinitesimal fragment of time and space where the spirit was free of obligation, of duty, of subservience?

'Six!'

His own freedom to think such thoughts suddenly overcame him. He wanted to ask whether, in that conjectural moment, a man would be free too of the awful obligation to have another man whipped; as if, in some way, the recipient of those lacerations should feel grateful to him for the moderation of the punishment his crime had merited. Drinkwater's eyes flickered to the mass of the ship's company gathered in the waist. Were they, could they fail to be aware of the condign nature of this thrashing? Did they not see in it a spirit of leniency, of sympathy, almost? Or did they see in it a weakness in himself, a weakness, perhaps, to be exploited?

They watched without expression. They had watched such punishments before and those that were intelligent enough to realise knew he *had* been lenient. Three dozen lashes was more than he normally administered, but it was downright *soft* on four bloody fools who had run in a place like China and had then been discovered in the very convoy the bloody ship was escorting!

'Twelve!'

Mr Comley intoned the strokes like those of a bell. The bosun's mate stopped and handed over the cat to another that the thrasher might not ease the violence of his stripes through fatigue. Their Lordships thought of everything . . .

'Thirteen!'

Old Tregembo watched, sensing the mood of his fellows as vaguely contemptuous of the four men for having been caught so easily. Quilhampton watched full of the knowledge that Drinkwater had agonised over the decision and confident that he had come to the right, the only decision open to a reasonable man. Fraser, the cares of first lieutenant weighing upon him, felt a stirring of disapproval. He would have preferred the matter handed over to the admiral at Madras, or Calcutta or wherever he was, removing the stigma of it from the ship. Sometimes he envied Drinkwater's impeccable, irreproachable acceptance of his responsibilities, sometimes he disapproved of it. Like every second-in-command in history, Fraser knew what *he* would have done in the circumstances, and that it would have been diametrically opposite to what was now happening . . .

'Twenty!'

It never occurred to Fraser that he would have handed the

matter over through weakness, for there were half a dozen good reasons why, in his heart, he felt his own decision would have been the right one. Nor did it occur to him that Drinkwater had given more than the most superficial consideration to the matter.

'Twenty-four!'

The bosun's mates changed again for the last dozen. The man's back was laid open now. The cat bit into one vast bruise that had burst into a flayed mass of dark, bloody flesh. Lallo, the surgeon, stared at it, only half seeing more toil for him and his mates, his eyes fixed with a greater calculation on the men amidships, computing, or attempting to compute, how many had already taken the infection of the yaws . . .

'Thirty!'

He had heard someone mutter the words 'humane punishment' as they had assembled on the quarterdeck in response to the cry for all hands to muster. It seemed a sophisticated conceit to run words like that together in justification of so barbaric a ritual. Not that Lallo condemned the flogging from any lofty principle; he was too old to think the world would ever set itself to rights, but to talk of 'humane punishment' was almost as stupid a thing to do as to run away from a man-o'-war; almost deserving of the same treatment too, he thought morosely . . .

'Thirty-one!'

Derrick made himself watch, though revulsion rose in his throat on hardly suppressed upwellings of bile. He had seen this evil so often now, perpetrated on the whim of a man he both liked and respected. Intellectually he understood all Drinkwater's motives, both official and unofficial. But the inherent brutalising of them all he condemned as utterly evil. It reaffirmed his pacifism, revived his faith, for without war there would not be this grim, so-called necessity . . .

'Thirty-two!'

The deserter was hanging by his wrist lashings now, unconscious like some early martyr. Blood ran down to the deck and trickled from his mouth where the leather pad had become dislodged. Senseless he hung there in the sunshine upon the golden, scrubbed timber of the grating so that Midshipman Chirkov was reminded of an icon, the glittering uniforms of the marines an encrustation of rubies, the naval officers a semi-circle of sapphires. Fumes of opium still whirled in his brain, enhancing his hearing so that he heard the involuntary exhalations of the man's lungs as the sodden cat thrashed its final strokes upon the rib-cage. Chirkov felt nothing for the victim. All sensations were inwards The flogging did not even remind him of his own humiliation. He saw only the strange beauty of the agonised body.

'Thirty-five!'

Midshipman Belchambers waited to faint. To his eternal shame he had fainted several times when witnessing punishment and, although he had since that humiliating period seen action and distinguished himself, he still feared that irresistible loss of control . . .

'Thirty-six! Water! Cut him down!'

The man's body twitched as the green-white water slopped not ungently over his bloodied back, but he was unconscious as the bosun's mates sliced the lashings at his wrists and dragged him to one side where his messmates took him. Midshipman Belchambers took a deep breath. He was rather pleased with himself . . .

'Next!'

Like Chirkov, Morris's hearing was acute. A pipe of opium made it so and the sounds from the quarterdeck revived old memories in Morris's mind, memories that the drug uncoiled in lascivious scrolls drawn in graphically slow motion across the mind's eye.

He fondled the boy's ear, realising that these were days of sublime happiness. Not only was he basking in the anticipation of personal success, but that was heightened by the unexpected bonus of encompassing the ruin of a man he had once attempted to love. To the expectation of revenge he now found added the knowledge that that youthful paragon had been brought low in the world, low enough to have his delicate nature sullied by the grim necessity of ordering floggings.

'Ah, my fine friend, how has the bloom withered upon the stalk, eh?' He chuckled, pleased, seeing in his mind's eye that it was Drinkwater's back that received the thrashing of the cat.

His grip suddenly tightened on the boy's ear, turning the puckish face towards his own bloated and puffy flesh.

'Tonight! Tonight we will do it. It will have to be tonight. And then, my little imp, we shall see, oh, yes, we shall see . . .'

The boy grunted, the spittle in his throat, his mouth opening.

But Morris had averted his own hooded eyes, for above his head he heard more noises of punishment . . .

'One! Two!'

And he smiled.

Despite his conviction of the rightness of Drinkwater's decision to mete out swift and humane justice to the deserters, Lieutenant Quilhampton did not share the captain's analysis of the people's collective attitude. For one thing he was less accustomed than Drinkwater to thinking of the ship's company as one amorphous mass. Rather, to him they were a sum of many separate parts, some of whom, those who fulfilled their duties in his division, were well known to him. But part of this disagreement was attributable to his own involvement in the stilling of their mutinous spirit in the Baltic. He knew that for a while he had sat on a powder keg and alone had snuffed out an already sputtering fuse. He was, therefore, upon his guard in the hours following the floggings. Loyalty, this apprehension about the explosive mood of the hands and his eager longing to return home, stopped him from sleeping, and men nudged each other from mess-table to mess-table and hammock to hammock as Quilhampton prowled about the ship on one pretext or another.

But the mood of the ship was not threatening, for with that swift change that occurs at sea like the lifting of cloud shadows or a shift in the wind, the reported sight of blue islands to the south of them set their minds on a new tack, dispelling the gloom of the morning and setting their imaginations on anticipation of arrival at Prince of Wales Island, Pulo Penang, first stage on their homeward track.

'Where away?' asked Drinkwater with boyish eagerness, glad of some image to feast on after the shambolic succession of raw backs that had imprinted itself on his consciousness.

'Three points to larboard, sir. The Natunas,' replied Ballantyne confidently. The Dutch name alerted Drinkwater to the possibility of the presence of Dutch cruisers. He swung round and examined the convoy: still in good order, only one ship a trifle too far to leeward.

'Make to *Hindoostan*, "Keep better station".'

'The *Carnatic*'s run a little ahead of her station, sir,' offered Ballantyne helpfully.

'No matter. She's in the grain of the convoy and another pair of eyes up ahead saves us a little trouble.'

'We may encounter a Dutchman or two, sir.'

'Yes,' Drinkwater said shortly, still peering through his glass, once more levelled at the serried blue summits of the Natuna Islands. He would almost welcome an action with the enemy, welcome it as being his proper business, as purging to his blood and cathartic to his ship. And if he died during it he could hug the satisfaction of duty well done to his crushed bosom as he enjoyed that vital, sparking moment of ineffable knowledge of freedom . . .

Bloody stupid thought!

He snapped the Dollond glass shut. 'Very well, Mr Ballantyne. Send the men to quarters, we'll exercise the great guns!'

Drinkwater stayed on deck long after they had resecured their brutish artillery and the men, delighted with their exertions and the pulverising they had given the three beflagged casks, raced aloft and made sail to catch up with the convoy from which they had become separated in their manoeuvring. They had resumed their station long before the red sun reached down and touched the green horizon on its strange, tropical setting. It seemed quenched by the lambent rim of the visible world, cutting the sun in two so that a lenticular fragment of it lingered, gradually changing from fire to ice and then facing and etiolating the sky in the suddenness of the tropic night.

There was a magic in the moment and Drinkwater lingered to savour it, so unlike the attenuated twilight of the grey northern seas with which he was more familiar. One by one the heavily brilliant stars began to appear, those near the horizon coruscating with sudden apparent changes of fiery colour so that he fell into the simple game of identification, cudgelling his wits to remember their names and sad that command removed him from the daily necessity of knowing what he had once been adept at.

Beside him Ballantyne performed the mysteries of navigation, grunting figures to Midshipman Dutfield who read the corresponding times on the chronometer and noted the altitudes on a tablet. Drinkwater indulged his game and noted the disappearance of

Canopus, half-alarmed that a squall would reach treacherously down and strike them.

'Wind's falling away, sir,' Acting Lieutenant Frey remarked as he took over the deck for the first watch.

'Yes.'

Having regained their station they were snugged down under easy sail, watching over the convoy as they had since leaving the Pearl River. One was tempted to call it an uneventful passage, setting aside the intrusion of Morris; but even that seemed contained since his judicious move to the master's cabin.

'I shall be below if you require me, Mr Frey.'

'Aye, aye, sir.'

He read for a little, but the cabin was stuffily hot despite the wind-sails rigged amidships. He turned to his journal but the threat of megrims brought on by over-long introspection on the morning's floggings led him to conclude the task in as concise a form as decency allowed. In the end he amused himself with a letter to Elizabeth. If they were not sent home from Prince of Wales Island then he could forward the letter and, in any case, it was better written now, while his mood was light, than when he learned, pledges to his men notwithstanding, that *Patrician* formed a welcome addition to the East Indies squadron.

He must have dozed, for he found himself shaken awake with no idea of the time and the candle burnt low. He blew it out and, in his shirt-sleeves, went on deck.

The watch were busy, attentive to the shouts of Frey and his subordinate petty officers as they braced round the slatting sails. It was not a strong squall, but it had struck them from out of nowhere and the topsails and their blocks were flogging wildly.

'Lively there, damn it!' Frey cannoned into him. 'Get out of my . . . Oh! Beg pardon, sir!' Frey drew back, hand to hat barely perceptible in the sudden impenetrable blackness. 'Taken aback, sir, damned squall hit us without warning.'

'It's uncommon dark,' replied Drinkwater. 'Have a mind for the convoy, Mr Frey.'

'Aye, sir.'

Frey turned and bawled for Mr Belchambers, sending him forward with the night-glass to keep a sharp lookout.

Drinkwater scrambled up the heaving deck to the starboard hance, went to fish in his pocket for his glass and then realised he was coatless. Not only was the night dark, it was damnably warm too.

'Only to be expected in four degrees north, I suppose . . .'

'Beg pardon, sir?' It was Frey again, looming up and staring forward at men working at the midships pinrail. Drinkwater was not conscious of having spoken and the revelation of talking to himself startled him.

'Black as the Earl of Hell's riding boots.'

'Yes, sir.' Drinkwater heard the grin in Frey's voice. 'There're the lights of the convoy, sir, fine to starboard . . . see?'

Drinkwater stared. Yes, he could see the faint glimmer of stern lanterns to the southward. And *Patrician* was steadying on course now, her yards braced round as the wind picked up, suddenly cold. Seconds later they were leaning to the pressure of it and rushing through the water at a rate of knots. Then with an equally bewildering suddenness the night was riven by lightning, a flash of intense brilliance that showed the dark spots of the convoy ahead and to starboard of them, leaving an almost indelible image on the retina so that it seemed nature had obliged them with a brief spectral revelation to ease their anxieties.

The next minute they were soaking from the deluge of rain that poured upon them, blotting out all but a narrow silver-slashed circle of sea around them, their heads split with the thunderous assault of the exploding cloud above them.

In the confusion of steadying on their course Drinkwater bumped into another body. It recoiled, half apologetically, and in a further, less brilliant flash of lightning which seemed to strike the sea with a sizzling alongside them, he recognised the startled face of Midshipman Chirkov.

'What happens if lightning strikes the ship, sir?' asked Frey anxiously, the cocks of his hat spewing water like gutter-pipes, his face a pale gash in the darkness.

'I should think it'd consume our masts . . . possibly set us on fire . . .'

Drinkwater tried to think. He had heard of such a thing, surely? But there was nothing they could do to avert it. 'Steady on south by west, Mr Frey,' he said coolly. It was the only thing to do in this shivering cold. The rain fell so heavily that he felt the weight of its volume upon his head and shoulders.

'Binnacle light's out, sir . . .' he heard one of the helmsmen report.

'Well, get below and fetch a light,' Frey snapped.

'Keep her full and bye, Mr Frey. Steer by the luff of the main tops'l.'

'Aye, aye, sir.'

A note of weary tolerance had crept into Frey's voice. Drinkwater peered upwards, water pouring into his eyes. The main topsail was a pale, almost imperceptible ghost seen as through a rain-beaten window.

'Do your *best*, Mr Frey,' he said with asperity.

In the hiatus that followed, as they waited for the rekindled light for the binnacle that, to judge by the curses muttered from the companionway, was extinguished as soon as it reached the deck, Drinkwater remembered Chirkov.

'Was that Mr Chirkov on deck?' he asked Frey in a more intimate, conversational tone.

'Chirkov? Oh, yes, sir, I expect so. He's taken to coming on deck. Ballantyne says he's interested in the navigation of the ship.'

'Well, keep the lubber below after dark. You know my orders.'

'Aye, aye, sir,' replied Frey, thoroughly peeved, and ready to shoot Chirkov any moment the Russian gave him opportunity.

Going below, Drinkwater found the ship in a state of disruption. The two Chinese pigs kept in the manger forward of the breakwater were terrified by the over-charged atmosphere and had begun squealing. Men below in the berth-deck were grumbling and Corporal Grice had turned out some of his men, so that a foot patrol in cross-belts and drawers had emerged from the orlop deck and were just then going below again to the hoots and jeers of those able to see the fools they had made of themselves. There was something chaotic about the ridiculous scene as it met Drinkwater's eyes, reminding him of one of the seditious drawings he had seen by Mr Gillray. For, at the foot of the ladder, a little pool of light was formed by half a dozen purser's glims from which an obscenely swearing quartermaster was trying to relight the binnacle lamp. It was this bizarre source of illumination that drew attention to Corporal Grice's folly. Drinkwater stepped over the hunched and cursing backs, leaving them to their task without his presence being known. Rain was streaming over the coaming of the companionway and he was chilled to shuddering by it.

He found Tregembo waiting for him with a towel. 'Thank you, Tregembo.'

'Zur . . .'

The remains of the candle he had extinguished earlier guttered on its holder. As he dried himself he felt the heel of the deck ease and a few moments later little Belchambers came below to report normality established on deck.

'Is the convoy in sight?'

'No, sir, the rain is still obscuring it, though it's much lighter now than it was, but Mr Frey says he had a good look at the convoy's bearing in the lightning, sir, and he's quite happy.'

'Very well, Mr Belchambers. Thank you.'

'Good-night, sir.'

'Good-night.'

'Thank you, Tregembo. You may get your own head down now.'

'Aye, zur . . . G'night, zur.'

Outside the cabin Tregembo bumped into the surgeon.

'Cap'n's just turning in,' he said defensively, standing in Lallo's way.

'Very well,' said Lallo. The surgeon had been meditating all day when to tell Drinkwater about the epidemic of yaws that he might anticipate and had turned in irresolute. Woken by the general agitation of the ship and the clap of thunder he had resolved to act immediately. Now he felt a little foolish, and not a little relieved. A night would make no difference.

'I'll see him first thing in the morning,' he said, turning away.

But Mr Lallo was not the first officer to report to Drinkwater next morning; he was beaten by Mr Ballantyne who, head shaking and excited, burst in to Drinkwater's cabin with such violence that he fetched up against the rim of the bunk. Drinkwater started from sleep as if murder was in the wind.

'Sir! Oh, sir, calamity, sir!'

'What the devil is it? Why have you left the deck, Mr Ballantyne?' Drinkwater spluttered.

'The convoy, sir, it is not in sight!'

PART TWO
Nemesis

'The only thing necessary for the triumph of evil is for good men to do nothing.'

EDMUND BURKE

12   A Council of War

January 1809

A sickeningly empty horizon greeted Drinkwater's eyes as he cast about the ship. In a despairing movement he looked aloft to where, astride the main royal yard, Midshipman Dutfield scanned the sea. Looking down, Dutfield shook his head.

'God's bones!' Drinkwater swore, then strode to the binnacle and stared at the compass. The lubber's line pointed unerringly at south by west. Drinkwater looked aloft again, the sails were drawing, all seemed well. He stood, puzzling. Some instinct was rasping his intelligence, telling him something was wrong, very wrong, though he was totally at a loss to understand what. Full daylight was upon them; the rising sun, above the horizon for fully half an hour, remained below a bank of wet and coiling cumulus to the east. For a long moment he stared at that cloud bank, as though seeking an answer there, cudgelling his brain to think, *think*.

Both he and Frey had seen the convoy last night. The cluster of ships had been quite distinct, to leeward of them, perhaps a little too far off the starboard bow for absolutely perfect station-keeping, but . . .

Had that squall, local and intense, affected only *Patrician*? It was possible, but it had not lasted long enough to carry the frigate beyond the visible horizon of the group of ships.

A slanting shaft of sunlight speared downwards from a rent in the clouds. A moment later it was joined by another, and another. Three patches of glittering sea flared where the sunbeams struck, scintillating intensely.

'Bloody hell!'

Drinkwater's eye ran up the beams, seeking their theoretical intersection where, still hidden, the sun lurked behind the bank of cloud. In a stride he was beside the binnacle, sensing something was definitely wrong, electrified by suspicion.

He could not be sure. It was difficult to take an azimuth in such a way . . .

He fumed, impatient for a sight of the sun. Not one of the three patches seemed to move nearer to them, then one disappeared.

'Is there something . . .?' Ballantyne's voice was nervously hesitant.

'Get an azimuth the moment the sun shows, get my sextant and chronometer up here upon the instant!'

It had to be the lightning, a corposant perhaps, that had run unobserved in all that black deluge the previous night. There was no other explanation . . .

'Look, sir, the sun!'

Neither sextant nor chronometer had arrived but Drinkwater did not need to work out the calculation. It was too blindingly obvious. Though they crawled across the face of the globe and altered the bearing of the sun at any given time of the day, and although the sun was almost imperceptibly moving towards them as it orbited further and further north towards the equinoctial and the vernal equinox of the northern spring, he could see that an error existed in their compass; an error of perhaps thirty or forty degrees, sufficient to have misled them into sailing on a diverging course from the convoy. It was with something like relief that he offered the worried faces on the quarterdeck an explanation.

'Our compass is thirty or forty degrees in error, gentlemen. We have been sailing more nearly south-east than south all night. It must have been disturbed by the lightning.'

A murmur of surprise, mixed with wonder and relieved suspense, crossed several faces. Drinkwater looked at the dog-vane and made a hurried calculation, a rough estimate in triangulation that he would work out more carefully in a moment when he had the leisure to do so. For the time being a swift alteration of course and speed were needed.

'Lay me a course of south-west, Mr Ballantyne, and have the watch set all plain sail!'

'Sou' west and all plain sail, sir, aye, aye, sir!'

Drinkwater looked about him again. The wind was a light but

steady breeze. God alone knew what the convoy commanders would think when they realised *Patrician* was absent, but he could imagine well enough! A creeping anxiety began to replace the feeling of relief at having discovered the cause of the navigational mystery.

The Natunas were astern; suppose they had concealed a Dutch cruiser, or even a French one? He rubbed his chin, feeling the scrubby bristles rough against the palm of his hand.

Canvas flogged above him and the cries of 'Let fall! Clew down!' and 'Sheet home!' accompanied the sudden bellying of the fore and main courses. Above the topsails the topgallants and royals were spreading *Patrician*'s pale wings in the morning sunlight. His eye was caught by a sudden movement lower down. Midshipman Chirkov was on deck. Drinkwater recollected the presence of the young Russian the night before. He suddenly vented all his bile on the good-for-nothing young man.

'Mr Chirkov! Damn you, sir, but my orders are explicit! You are forbidden to be on deck at this hour!'

There seemed something vaguely dreamy about the young man, something weird that Drinkwater had neither the time nor the patience to investigate. Doubtless the young devil had got his hands on liquor, probably Rakitin gave him access to it . . .

'Go below, sir, at once!'

'All plain sail, sir,' reported Ballantyne, recalling Drinkwater to normality.

'Very well, Mr Ballantyne, thank you.'

'Sir?'

'Well, what is it? Hurry man, for I want to set the stuns'ls.'

'Would not the lightning have affected other ships? We were, by all accounts, no distance from the convoy.'

'What?' Drinkwater looked sharply at the master. Did Ballantyne have a valid point, or did that single, fateful glimpse of the convoy argue that it had been immune from the lightning? He recalled the bolt hitting the sea quite close. Surely *that* was what had disturbed the magnetism in the needles suspended on their silken threads below the compass card. It had all been something of a nightmare, Drinkwater thought, recalling vignettes of evidence, lit by flashes of lightning or the unholy gathering of men round the binnacle light on the gun-deck.

'No. I think not,' he said with assumed certainty. 'There was a thunderbolt struck the sea quite close to us, Mr Ballantyne, I think it was that that mazed our compass . . .'

And so he came to believe for the time being.

'Trouble never comes in small bottles, does it, Mr Lallo?'

'No, sir.'

'What should we do? Quarantine 'em?'

'We may be too late for that, sir,' Lallo cautioned.

'Is it as contagious as the Gaol Fever?' Gaol fever they called it aboard ship, and ship fever they called it ashore, ascribing its spread to the least desirable elements of each of the societies in which, amid the endemic squalor, it spread like wildfire.

'It's hard to say, sir. I'm not over-familiar with the yaws, but typhus . . .'

We've contained outbreaks of *that* before . . .' Drinkwater said hopefully. It was true. Clean clothes and salt-water douches seemed, if not to cure typhus, at least to inhibit its spread. Perhaps the same treatment might stay this present unpleasant disease. He suggested it. Lallo nodded gloomily.

'We must *try*,' said Drinkwater encouragingly, bracing himself as *Patrician* leaned to a stronger gust under the press of canvas she was now carrying. Suddenly Drinkwater longed for the luxury of his own cabin; to be watching the white-green wake streaming astern from below the open sashes of the wide stern window, and the sea-birds dipping in it.

Lallo coughed, aware of Drinkwater's sudden abstraction. He stared at the surgeon's lined face. Was he going out of his mind to be thinking such inane thoughts? How could he stare delighting in the swirling wake when Lallo was here, bent under the weight of his message of death?

'Quarantine 'em,' he said, suddenly resolute, 'station 'em at the after guns; to be issued with new slops at the ship's expense (we've widows' men to cover the matter), ditch their clothing. They're to be hosed down twice daily and dance until they're dry. Keep their bodies from touching anything . . .'

Lallo nodded and rose. 'I'll tell Fraser to re-quarter them. You said after guns, sir?'

Drinkwater nodded. Yes, he thought, after guns, close to Morris . . .

'Sail ho!'

Drinkwater stirred from his doze, fighting off the fog of an afternoon sleep.

'Two sails! No three-ee! Point to starboard! 'Tis the convoy!'

He was on deck before the hail was finished, up on the rail and motioning for the deck glass. Someone put it into his hand and he watched the sails of a brig climb up over the rim of the world, saw them foreshorten as she altered course towards them and then he jumped down on deck and felt like grabbing both Fraser's hands and dancing ring-a-roses with him for the sheer joy of finding the lost ships. Instead he said:

'Put your helm down a touch, Mr Fraser, let's close with 'em as fast as possible and offer our apologies . . .'

The two vessels came up hand over fist. On the horizon to the south-west they could see the rest of the convoy close together.

'Odd, sir, they seem to be hove-to.'

'Shows they've been waiting for us. They've been buzznacking.'

Drinkwater's cheerful tone was redolent of the relief he was feeling at overtaking the convoy before dark. It was *Hormuzeer* that approached them, a trim little brig that had once been a privateer and now ran opium to China under the command of an elderly but energetic Scotsman named Macgillivray. Through their glasses they could see her come into the wind with a large red flag flying at her foremasthead.

'That's a damned odd signal for her to be flying,' someone said among the curious little knot of officers who had gathered on deck.

'Into action?'

'They're hoisting out a boat . . .'

'Get the stuns'ls off her, Mr Fraser, if you please,' snapped Drinkwater, his face suddenly grim. 'If that's the convoy over there, we've two ships missing.'

'Aye, sir, we sorely missed you. Your absence, sir, was ill-timed. Dolorous, sir, damned dolorous.' Macgillivray's face was thin, hollow-cheeked and pitted by smallpox. A hooked nose that belonged to a larger man jutted from between two deep-set and rheumy eyes that fixed Drinkwater with a piercing glitter. Across the nose and cheeks, red and broken veins spread like the tributaries of a mapped river, contrasting with dead-white skin that seemed to have been permanently shaded by a broad-brimmed hat. As if to augment the ferocity of his expression, grey whiskers, sharply shaved below the cheekbone, grew upon his face below his eyes.

'I have explained, Captain Macgillivray, why I failed to keep station last night. The matter is done, sir, and the time for recriminations is past . . .'

'No, sir! Damn no, sir! We shall have time for recriminations at Penang, you mark my words. We demand the navy protects us, sir, and you are missing. We lost two ships, sir . . .'

'Captain Macgillivray, you have told me three times that two ships are missing and I have told you twice why we lost contact with you.' Drinkwater was almost shouting down the furious Scotsman, bludgeoning him into silence with his own anger. 'Now, sir, will you do me the courtesy of telling me *which* two ships and how they were lost?'

Macgillivray subsided, then he opened his thin mouth as though diving for more air. 'Pirates, sir, pirates. Sea-Dyaks from Borneo forty *praus* strong, sir, forty! Pirates with gongs and shrieks and stink-pots and blow-pipes in red jackets. T Straight for the *Guilford* they came, took *Hindoostan* as well, swarmed aboard and carried her off before you knew it.'

'When?'

'At dawn.'

'Did you attempt to drive them off?'

'Aye, we opened fire, but the wind was light . . .'

'And you were spread out?'

'Aye, maybe a little . . .'

'Ah . . .'

'Not for reasons of slackness, Captain, oh, no, not for that, I assure you. We had spread out to seek yourself. Some of us saw you struck by lightning, like you said, but we were mistaken, for you are here, now.'

That 'now' seemed like an accusation of a crime.

'And they carried the *Guilford* off, from under your noses? You didn't pursue . . . ?'

'It's *your* job to pursue, Captain, not ours to lose our cargoes. We did what we could. I followed a little myself. They went sou' b' west, for the Borneo coast . . .'

The two men fell silent. After a while Drinkwater looked up. 'I will make the signal for all commanders in an hour, Captain Macgillivray. Then I shall decide what to do.'

'There's damn all you can do – now.'

Drinkwater looked up into the undisguised contempt in the Scotsman's eyes.

He had wanted the hour to work *Patrician* into the main body of the convoy. That was the reason he gave out on the quarterdeck. In reality he wanted the time to re-establish himself, albeit temporarily, in the more impressive surroundings of his cabin, to remove the screen and evict Morris and Rakitin. In the event it was noon before the last indignant master was pulled alongside and the ships rocked gently upon the now motionless sea. The wind had died and the calm was glassy, as though the ocean lacked the energy to move under the full heat of the brazen sun. Drinkwater had fended off the verbal assaults of each and every one of the merchant captains, reiterating the circumstances of *Patrician*'s separation until he was only half-convinced of its accuracy. It was too extravagant a tale to be wholly believable, particularly by men with little faith and large axes to grind.

The cabin, as he called the meeting to order, seemed to heave with indignation and Drinkwater himself was very close to losing his temper. Only the thought that an outburst of anger would carry to Morris on the quarterdeck held him in check.

'Gentlemen! Gentlemen!' He managed at last to quieten them. 'What has happened is a matter of regret to us all. Both you and I are incredulous at aspects of events, you that my frigate was absent, I because your pursuit seems to have been non-existent . . .'

'There were forty *praus*, damn you, and poisoned darts all over the place and cannon . . .'

'And bugger-all wind . . .'

'There was sufficient of a wind to return me to station . . . but let that all pass . . .'

They subsided again. Drinkwater pressed doggedly on. 'What we must now decide is how to proceed.'

'Proceed?' queried one voice. 'Why to Penang, of course.'

'Aye!' A chorus of voices rose in assent.

Drinkwater frowned. Did they intend to abandon Callan? Was the motivation of these men solely and wholly governed by profit? So different from his own thinking was this conclusion that he stood for a moment nonplussed.

'Captain Drinkwater, I think you misunderstand us.' Drinkwater looked at the speaker, glad at last that one reasonable voice spoke from the hostile group before him. It was that of Captain Cunningham, commander of the *Ligonier*.

'I rather hope I do,' replied Drinkwater curtly.

'It is not that we wish to abandon Captain Callan; in all likelihood he will be repatriated by the Dutch, for this kind of thing has happened before. The Sea-Dyaks are interested only in booty. They will strip *Guilford* of all that they require or can trade with the Dutch; powder, small arms, shot, plus cargo. Since hostilities with the Batavians began, the wily squareheads have sought out the princes of the Sarawak tribes and offered them bribes for the capture and surrender of any of our Indiamen. I doubt Callan or his officers will come to any *personal* harm . . .' Cunningham paused and a stillness filled the hitherto noisy cabin. Drinkwater sensed the compliance of the other masters: Cunningham was poised for the *coup de grâce*. 'Your own predicament, Captain, is perhaps even less certain of its outcome than Captain Callan's.'

A further pause, pregnant with opprobrium, let the implied threat sink in. Macgillivray, a man of little subtlety, could not let the matter rest on so insubstantial a foundation; besides, he had concocted a phrase of such obscurity that he flung it now like an accusation of untruth.

'The fulmineous intervention of nature you *say* you experienced, Captain Drinkwater, offers poorly against the loss of two ships.'

'One of which carried specie,' put in another.

They were the kicks of a cowardly mob, delivered after a man was in the gutter.

Drinkwater stood before his accusers. Inwardly he felt crushed. Fate had dealt him a cruel blow! To be singled out by Macgillivray's 'fulmineous intervention of nature' seemed so cruelly unjust as to anger some primitive inner part of him so that, although silent, he raked their faces with a baleful glare. He mastered the inner seething with the realisation that he wanted a drink. He would have one in a minute, immediately he had disposed of these men, bent to their wishes.

'Very well, gentlemen. I shall accede to your request and escort you to Penang.'

'Well, let us hope you *do*, Captain,' said Macgillivray, as the downcast company turned for the cabin door. Drinkwater stood stock-still as they filed out. Then, almost out of habit, he turned towards the pantry and bawled for his steward. The cathartic bellow did him good and Mullender, by some small miracle of intuition, appeared with a bottle and glasses.

Drinkwater took a glass. As he stood impatiently waiting for Mullender to fill it with blackstrap, unannounced Morris reentered the cabin. His expression bore witness to the fact that he had gleaned knowledge of Drinkwater's discomfiture.

'Where is Captain Rakitin?' Drinkwater asked, delaying his need to swallow the cheap port.

'On the quarterdeck, zur.'

It was Tregembo who answered, stooping at the pantry door, ancient, worn, like a futtock of the ship itself. It seemed oddly appropriate that Tregembo, like Mullender, should have mustered in the pantry, for all that his occupation of the cabin was to be short-lived.

'Thank you.'

Drinkwater fixed both steward and coxswain with the stare of dismissal. Mullender put down the bottle and the pantry door closed behind them, though their listening presence beyond the mahogany louvres was almost visible.

'Your health, Nathaniel.' Morris helped himself to a glass, an ironical smile about his hooded eyes. 'And, of course, your damnation.'

Drinkwater merely glared, then seized gratefully on the excuse to gulp his drink, making to leave the cabin.

'Don't go,' said Morris, divining his purpose, 'we have been so little together. Intolerably little for such old shipmates . . .'

'Morris, we never made the least pretence at friendship. We fought, if I recollect, some kind of duel, and you made numerous threats against my person. You behaved abominably to members of the *Cyclops*'s company and, if there was such a thing as natural justice in the world, you should have been hanged.'

He tailed off. Morris was laughing at him. 'Oh, Nathaniel, Nathaniel, you are still an innocent I see. Still dreaming of a "natural justice" and other such silly philosophies . . . How much have you missed, eh? You and I are old men now and here you are beset by worries, buggered upon the altar of your duty . . . You left me at the Cape a sick man . . . I hungered for the destiny you had before you and hated you for seeming to command fate. That was ten years ago, before Bonaparte burst upon us all . . .'

'Bonaparte?' Drinkwater frowned, bemused by this drivel of Morris's.

'Yes, Bonaparte, blazing like a comet across the imaginations of men. "Do as you will," he screamed at the world. "Do as you will . . ."'

There was something about Morris that was not quite drunkenness, but nevertheless reminded Drinkwater of intoxication. There was also, now he came to think of it, a faint, unfamiliarly sweet aroma in the cabin, gradually reasserting itself after the sweaty stink of the convoy masters. Of course! A man of Morris's disposition, influenced by every sensuous inclination of the human body, would be an opium eater. Drinkwater poured himself another drink.

'So I forsook my duty,' went on Morris, 'she was a raddled whore that had nothing to offer me but the pox of responsibility that now consumes you. I counted myself lucky to have found my destiny half-way to India, and took ship to find what I knew to exist if prudish knaves like you did not stand in my way . . .'

'You charm me by your tale, sir,' said Drinkwater unmoved. 'No doubt your little Indian Ganymede approves wholly of tearing out his tongue for your unnatural pleasure! I doubt even the monstrous genius of Bonaparte would approve of that!'

Drinkwater half turned away but his arm was caught by Morris.

Both the speed and the force of the grip surprised Drinkwater and he felt himself pulled back to face his enemy.

'D'you dream, Nathaniel? Eh? Of course you do – unholy dreams here, on your cot, eh? Coiled by the legs of . . . of whom, eh? Your Elizabeth, or other, secret women? Well, I dreamed my own dreams . . .'

With a violent gesture Drinkwater shook himself free. The compulsion to run, to escape the cabin and Morris's contaminating company was strong in him, but some dreadful fascination kept him rooted to the spot. As abruptly as he had advanced, Morris fell back. The intense, almost complicit tone vanished and he spoke again in his arch, mocking manner.

'Do you know,' Morris said, 'they say in Peking that the Son of Heaven finds the most exquisite pleasure in impaling a goose who, at the appropriate moment, is strangled . . .?'

'Damn you . . .'

Sickened, Drinkwater turned away. As he made for the door he caught sight of the boy. He was asleep, had slept, it seemed, all through the noisy council and its revolting aftermath, half-naked, a brown curl in the corner of Drinkwater's quondam cabin.

There was nothing he could bring himself to do in the remaining hours of that disastrous day but pace up and down the quarterdeck, biliously angry as the convoy stood for the entrance of the Malacca Strait. Great clouds reared on the horizon, huge anvil-shaped thunderheads that rose over the steaming tropical rain forests of the distant land. As night fell these huge, billowing clouds were illuminated from within, possessed by flickering demons as lightning, too far away to crackle with thunder, sparked and flashed tremendously within their charged and coiling vapours. The sight tormented Drinkwater as he continued his lonely, self-imposed vigil, recalling over and over again Macgillivray's facetious phrase: 'fulmineous intervention of nature'.

In deference to his savage mood, men moved quietly about the upper decks and the officers, alternating as the ship's routine ground its remorseless way into time, gave their orders in low voices. It seemed, as he gradually emerged from the depths of introspection, that they were humouring him, like a child. The thought made him unreasonably angry and he cast about for some weapon of chastisement. Was that Frey on watch? No, Quilhampton.

'Mr Quilhampton.'

'Sir?'

'Have we established, sir,' spat Drinkwater, with unbending formality, 'why the binnacle lamp was extinguished last night?'

'Er . . . I . . . I've no idea, sir . . . was it not the rain, sir?'

Drinkwater's temper fed deliciously on such foolishness. 'The lamp has a chimney, sir, is set in a binnacle for the purpose of protecting it from the weather. Its wick may have become soaked when it was removed from such protection, but that was not the reason for its extinguishing. May I suggest a lack of oil as a plausible explanation, eh? I recognise it as one out of favour with the officers as bespeaking a slackness on their part, but . . .', he faltered. He was going to say something about a lack of oil providing a natural explanation, but it smacked so of Macgillivray's phrase that it cut his tirade dead.

'Oh, for God's sake check the damned thing now!'

He cast Quilhampton aside and stalked off into the night, ashamed of himself. God! How he hated this commission! Ever since that poor devil had been swung to the yard-arm at the Nore there had been ill-luck aboard. Now they even had to compensate for a compass deviating thirty-eight degrees, at least until the effects of the thunderbolt wore off . . .

'Sir!'

Something urgent in Quilhampton's tone brought him up. Any peevishness Quilhampton might have felt at his commander's unspeakable behaviour was absent from the imperative note in the lieutenant's voice. Drinkwater turned. Quilhampton was advancing towards him. The binnacle lamp had been extinguished to check the reservoir, but in the gloom Drinkwater could just make out the faint sheen of the glass door of the locker and something in Quilhampton's hand.

'What is it?'

'This, sir.' Drinkwater was aware that Quilhampton was holding out his hand.

'I can't see a damned thing.' Then he was vaguely aware of a dark shape like an irregular musket ball darkening Quilhampton's palm.

'Bit of metal, sir,' said Quilhampton in a low voice, 'half filling the oil reservoir. Could have put the lamp out prematurely . . .'

'God's bones!'

An act of sabotage? The thought was in both their minds, for it would not be the first that had occurred. A similar event had happened on the coast of California when the ship was found to have developed a persistent and elusive leak.

'Say nothing more,' Drinkwater whispered urgently, then raised his voice to a normal level. 'Very well, Mr Q, relight the lamp.'

Drinkwater walked across the gently leaning deck and stopped beside the wheel. In such light winds only two men stood beside it, staring aloft at the main topsail, steering by the wind until the light was re-established in the binnacle. It was all clear to him now. It was no mere reduction of the volume of the reservoir that had been sought, it was something far more sinister. In a few moments the lamp would come back on deck and prove him correct, but the metallic lump he held in his hand was no melted leaden musket ball poured molten into the base of the lamp. It resisted the imprint of his thumb-nail with an almost crystalline stubbornness.

'Here, sir . . .'

Drinkwater stood aside. The lamp was placed back between the two copper grooves that held it in place, throwing a gentle radiance across the neatly inscribed compass card.

'What course, sir?' asked the puzzled helmsman, sure that he had held the ship's head steady relative to the wind during the last quarter of an hour.

'You may steer sou' west a-half west.'

'Sou' west a-half west, aye, aye, sir.' There was a brief pause, then the helmsman said, 'She's that now, sir.'

'Yes,' replied Drinkwater quietly, 'I know she is.'

'Sir?' In the dim glow the rumple of a frown creased Quilhampton's forehead.

Drinkwater held up the small nugget. 'It's a piece of magnetic lodestone, Mr Q, perfect for deliberately inducing a deviation in the compass.'

13　A Round Robin

January 1809

'What d'you intend to do, sir?'

Fraser's voice was tight with anxiety. Ever since the flogging of the deserters he had been half expecting some such outbreak among the people.

'What the devil can I do, Mr Fraser, except abjure you and all the officers to be on their guard?'

'Could be the quarantined men, sir,' suggested Fraser.

'What? Some kind of collective revenge for their misfortune?'

Fraser shrugged. 'Ye canna let it pass, sir.'

'No. But they all know we discovered the thing, 'tis common gossip throughout the ship. Such scuttlebutt spreads like wildfire . . .'

'Could you not . . .' Fraser looked conspiratorially about the deck, to make sure that no one was within earshot of the pair of them, '. . . ask Tregembo to . . .?'

'Spy, you mean? Carry lower-deck tittle-tattle?'

'Aye, sir.' Fraser seemed rather relieved that Drinkwater grasped his meaning.

'If it was known, I'm damned certain Tregembo would have told me. The trouble is Tregembo don't know.'

Fraser subsided into unhappy silence. Drinkwater was aware that Midshipman Dutfield was trying to catch his eye.

'Beg pardon, sir, but Mr Ballantyne's compliments and the entrance to the strait is in sight.'

'Very well, Mr Dutfield, thank you.'

They had, for the past two days, been aware of the presence of land. At first they had seen the electric storms above the distant, jungle-covered mountains, then the clusters of islands forming the

Anambas archipelago lifted over the horizon. Odd tangles of floating vegetation, bound by the roots and stumpy remnants of mangroves, drifted past. 'Floating islands' Ballantyne called them, recounting how sometimes they reached astonishing size and had once concealed a host of Dyak canoes from which he and his father had only escaped with difficulty and the prompt arrival of a breeze.

Of Dyaks they had seen nothing, gliding over a smooth, empty sea, and now picking up their landfall with gratifying precision. Rank upon rank of hills were emerging blue and low from the clouds hovering over them, a seemingly impenetrable barrier whose nearer bastions were turning slowly green as they approached. Stretching away into the northern distance the long finger of the Malay peninsula crept round almost a third of the horizon, its distal point Pulo Tumasek. To larboard rose a wild jumble of islands, the Rhio archipelago, which, from this distance, retained the impression of a continuous, if indented coastline. Beyond, indicated as yet by clouds, lay the vast island of Sumatra, parallel to the Malay coast and containing, between the two, the Malacca Strait, highway to Prince of Wales Island, as Penang was then more familiarly known. Beyond all lay the Indian Seas.

Drinkwater strained his glass further to larboard. Somewhere to the southwards, beyond the Rhio islands, lay the Gaspar and Sunda Straits, shortest route to the Cape of Good Hope, and barred to the China fleet by Dutch and French cruisers. But today he could see nothing, nothing but an empty blue sea, glittering beneath a brazen sky. And, curiously, it brought him no pleasure. Somehow he would rather have seen an enemy, been faced with a task; somehow the very emptiness of the ocean seemed ominous.

'Beg pardon, sir.'

Belchambers's face, poked round the door of the tiny cabin, was more readily seen in his shaving mirror, thought Drinkwater, as he rasped the razor upwards over the stretched skin of his throat.

'What is it?'

He forced the query through the clenched teeth of a jutting jaw.

'This, sir.' Drinkwater swivelled his eyes a little. The image of Belchambers's hand could be seen in the cracked mirror. The fingers unfolded to reveal a crushed scrap of paper.

Drinkwater had seen one before and the shock made him nick himself. It was a round robin, a message from the ship's company, and it cast his mind uneasily back to the days of ninety-seven, the year of the great mutinies. They had been a common thing then, demands, protests, both reasonable and unreasonable, sent aft to the officers in this anonymous, yet neatly demotic way.

'What does it say?'

Affecting a *sang-froid* he did not feel, Drinkwater dabbed at his bleeding throat and completed his shave. 'Read it,' he commanded, a little more forcefully.

Belchambers cleared his throat. The self-conscious gesture relaxed Drinkwater. 'Are they going to cut my throat, or should I complete the matter myself, Mr Belchambers? Eh? Give the thing here, thank you.'

He took the crumpled and grubby paper and the boy fled gratefully. Captain Drinkwater's mood had been dangerously unpredictable of late.

Drinkwater smoothed the sheet and stared at it. In all justice to the midshipman, it was not easy to read, almost obscured by the creases into which it had been balled, the easier to be thrown on to the quarterdeck. It would have been tossed at Quilhampton's feet, no doubt, with not a man on deck anywhere near it as the lieutenant bent to pick it up. Or, of course, it would have been dropped during the night. No matter now; here it was, in the hands for which it was intended, and the writing was well formed, legalistic and educated – a bad sign. Drinkwater frowned; he was seeing ominous signs in everything these days. He read:

> To Captain Drinkwater, Esquire
>> Y'r Honour,
>
> We, the Ship's Company, with our Humble Duty beg to Acquaint Your Honour of our Reprobation of the Events of this Day. Knowing Your Honour's Mind to be of Lofty Principles, we, the Ship's Company, Entreat you not to be Misled by former Occurrences. We Solemnly Swear that no Malice Aforethought attaches to the Heinous and Hideous Interference with the Binnacle Lantern that Must be Contemptible to the Minds of British Seamen.

We, the Ship's Company, Desire to Inform Your Honour
of our Loyalty to Our Duty and Our Country
Signed,
By Us all,
One and Indivisible.

It was a concoction worthy of the most appalling Patriotic Club, but its outrage rang with sincerity. Its very vehemence suggested a wiping out of the shameful acts off California. These were men, quite capable of outrageously mutinous behaviour, angrily repudiating any suggestion of its initiation in this case.

'They want to go home,' muttered Drinkwater, smiling at himself in the battered glass, and crushing the round robin in his hand.

But it offered little peace of mind, merely diverting his suspicion elsewhere. Morris he knew to be too motivated by self-interest to have attempted such a stupid thing. Morris had nothing to gain by diverting *Patrician* and could not possibly have known of the Dyak presence. Drinkwater was tempted to seek its motivation in mischief rather than malice. He recalled Midshipman Chirkov's sudden interest in navigational matters, and the suspicion, once it crossed his mind, seemed a reasonable one, redolent of idle folly and petulant resentment over earlier humiliation.

Dangerously stupid and consequentially disastrous as the matter had been, he realised his suspicions were circumstantial and unprovable. He knew only that his own vigilance must increase, and that the burden of his responsibilities weighed even heavier upon him. When later that day, as the sun dipped crimson towards the thunderheads above the blue mountains of Sumatra, the masthead reported two sails, Captain Drinkwater could not have cared whether or not they were enemies.

They made contact with the two ships just before daylight finally vanished from the tropic sky, two sloops from Penang sent questing down the Malacca Strait after reports of enemy cruisers off the Rhio archipelago. They were not naval ships, but belonged to the East India Company's Bombay Marine, the *Arrow* and the *Dart*, nattily smart twenty-two-gun ship-rigged sloops aswarm with lascars and a commander not much older, or so it seemed to Drinkwater's jaundiced eye, than Fleetwood Pellew.

Convoy, escort and new arrivals lay to in a calm through the night. The continuing windlessness of the following morning with the sea like blue steel, pricked here and there by the lifting spear-heads of flying fish, allowed much boat-trafficking between the ships. Drinkwater, watching the masters rowed about the wallowing fleet, knew that tittle-tattle was being plied about, mostly pejorative to his reputation, a fact confirmed by the boats' avoidance of the *Patrician*.

After an hour or so of this feeling of having been sent to Coventry, Drinkwater ordered the signal hoisted for 'all captains'. In the event only two boats pulled towards the frigate, one from the *Ligonier*, bearing an embarrassed Cunningham, the other from the *Arrow*. Cunningham made the introductions and Drinkwater was aware that, in the Company's service, the commander of an Indiaman outweighed an officer of the Marine. For this he was profoundly grateful, for the young prig seemed ready to read Drinkwater a lecture.

'. . . And so, sir,' concluded Cunningham with a decent preamble about Drinkwater's able, though unfortunate, escort, 'Captain Hennessey here . . .', Hennessey footed the meagrest of bows by way of identification, 'is of the opinion that he should take over the escort.'

'And what is *your* opinion, Captain Cunningham, might I ask?'

'Why, sir, that you continue to accompany us to Penang; only a fool would opine that your guns are not valuable.'

There was the slightest emphasis on the word 'fool'. Clearly Hennessey was attempting to arrogate command of the escort against Cunningham's inclination. The young commander flared his nostrils in a spiritedly equine fashion, registering well-controlled indignation.

'Well, sir, since I am *ordered* by Admiral Drury to command and escort this convoy, I shall continue to do so until I see it safe at anchor at Penang. Captain Hennessey and his colleagues are welcome to join us, subordinate to my command, of course.'

It did not gratify Drinkwater to argue about such matters. The thing was plain as the nose on one's face if one took the trouble to look at it.

'Might I ask what Captain Hennessey's orders are?'

The young man spoke for the first time, a nasally superior voice, just as Drinkwater had expected, wondering, in an errant moment, if the salons or withdrawing rooms, or whatever they called them in Calcutta, made a point of turning out such stuffed shirts.

'I am ordered upon a cruise, sah, reports having reached Fort Cornwallis that Dutch and French cruisers were active in the Rhio Strait. Captain Cunningham informs me that you saw nothing and passed safely through. Therefore I shall consider it my duty, there being, according to Captain Cunningham, no further trade coming down from Canton, to see these ships back to Prince of Wales Island.'

'Are you apprehensive of attack between here and Penang, sir?' asked Drinkwater.

'I have no reason to be, but one never knows, and the Company cannot stand the loss of a second of its own ships . . .'

'*Ligonier* will be the only Company ship to get through from Canton, Captain Drinkwater,' broke in Cunningham, as though to add a reasonable weight to Hennessey's plan.

'It occurs to me, gentlemen, that Captain Hennessey, with his local knowledge of these waters, might double that score and recover *Guilford*.' Cunningham and Hennessey exchanged glances; it was clear they had already discussed the matter and Cunningham's anxiety had prevailed.

'I would go myself, but for a lack of charts,' Drinkwater added quickly. Hennessey shot him a swift glance. Was the young dandy subtle enough to spot the gauge flung at his feet? 'Is Admiral Pellew at Penang?'

'He is expected, sah,' drawled Hennessey, speculatively, adding, 'I have charts, Captain Drinkwater, Dutch charts . . . ! '

'Perhaps you will allow me the use of them. Now I shall escort the convoy to Prince of Wales Island and then we shall see . . . '

He ushered the two men to the rail. Hennessey left first, Cunningham hanging back a little.

'I am sorry for the outcome of all this, Captain Drinkwater. I am aware that you have done your utmost.'

'You imply repercussions, sir. I am conscious of having done my duty. There may be a little more I can do. At any event I shall make my report to Admiral Pellew in due course.'

'Pellew will stand by you. He is himself under attack by the merchant houses of Calcutta as well as the Company.'

Drinkwater was close to grinning. With Dungarth dead and John Barrow hostile at the Admiralty, he expected little further employment. What did it matter if providence had made his name smell in the noses of the Court of Directors in Leadenhall Street? The baying of the Calcutta merchants could touch him very little. He longed to be home with Elizabeth and the children. 'Let us hope poor Callan survives,' he added, as Cunningham shook out the man-ropes that lay down the curve of *Patrician's* tumblehome.

'Indeed,' said Cunningham, 'but I fear 'tis not Callan that will upset the Directors, but his thirty thousand sterling . . .'

'I beg your pardon?' Drinkwater's sharp interrogative held Cunningham one-footed at the rail.

'The specie, aboard *Guilford* . . .'

'*How much*, though, sir? *How much* did you say?'

'Thirty thousand sterling.'

'God's bones, the man told me three!'

Cunningham frowned. 'Three? Three thousand? Good heavens, no. Mind you Callan was a thoughtful fellow, perhaps he did not wish to worry you.'

Drinkwater stared after the boat as it pulled Cunningham back to the massive bulk of the Indiaman. What a bootless concern, Drinkwater thought ironically, as if anything could stop him from worrying.

It took some eight days to work their way northwards in the capricious winds of the land-locked strait, eight days of bracing yards and tacking, of easing sheets and hauling tacks, of setting studdingsails and dousing them when they began to outrun their charges. And for Drinkwater eight days of brooding introspection. He had decided to return and make a sweep along the Borneo coast; perhaps his luck might come back and he would catch a sleeping Dutchman in a river mouth – he hardly dared hope for the recapture of *Guilford*. At any rate Pellew would approve, he had no need to report to the Admiral in person, merely to send in his written account via Cunningham and then turn south off Pulo Penang.

The green and lush island hove into view at last, and the cluster of ships, steadied finally before a westerly breeze, stood north along its west coast to avoid the shoals to the south of the island.

They bore away round Muka Head and Drinkwater stood in until he could see the low, embrasured ramparts of Fort Cornwallis commanding the anchorage on the eastern flank of the heights, between Prince of Wales Island and the mainland. Here he anchored, hoisted out all boats and divested himself of his Russian prisoners. Pellew was not at the anchorage, but a frigate was, commanded by an officer far junior to himself, who grudgingly obeyed the order by the hand of Acting Lieutenant Frey to hold the prisoners against his return. Three of the *moujiks*, Lithuanians from the old Duchy of Kurland, swore their oaths to King George and remained aboard *Patrician*.

Drinkwater bade a civil farewell to Rakitin. The man was far gone in lethargy, a catalepsy tending, according to Lallo, to suicide and common among the Slavic peoples. Rakitin had eaten Morris's opium, but it was not the white poppy that killed him, nor remorse over his defeat. He died within a week of leaving *Patrician* of a cancer undiagnosed by Lallo.

Midshipman Count Vasili Chirkov left under protest, swearing that when *Patrician* returned, he and Frey must settle their affair of honour. It was perhaps fortunate that Frey was employed upon his errand in another boat at the time, for Drinkwater was impatient to be gone. Frey had secured the promised charts, poor enough things by the look of them, and had filled them a few stummed casks of fresh water.

All day Drinkwater was active on deck, aware that below Mullender and Tregembo were clearing his cabin, dislodging Morris from it and burning gunpowder within, to stum it like the water-casks of any impurities.

'Mr Fraser, do you see the launch? Damn it, but I want to be under weigh within the hour, before sunset at the latest . . .'

Both men strained their eyes to locate the launch amid the anchored ships and bum-boats, *praus* and *tonkangs* that teemed in the sheltered waters.

'Beg pardon, zur.'

Distracted, Drinkwater turned. Tregembo stood before him.

'Well? What the devil is it now?'
'It's Morris, zur . . . he won't leave your cabin.'

14   The Winds of Fortune

January–February 1809

'I can help you, Drinkwater.'

This was a different Morris. Gone was the overt hedonist, the flaunting amoral character that sought to discomfit his old enemy. This was the wily man who had succeeded in trade, swindled or earned his enviable position at Canton and wherever else the winds of fortune had blown his perverted and unlovely carcase. Drinkwater saw, to his surprise, flashes of the old Morris he had first known, the tyrannical bully but also the seaman and officer, the man of gentle birth whose sexual excesses, had they been discreet, might not have disturbed the outward life of a gentleman of substance and quality.

Drinkwater thrust aside Morris's blandishments. 'I do not want you on my ship a moment longer than necessary,' Drinkwater stated bluntly.

'But you want that Indiaman back, don't you?' Morris stood his ground. 'You are returning to search for her and have, I'll warrant, not the slightest idea where to look . . .'

'What interest can you have in the matter? You and your silver are safely here in Penang; you can leave for Calcutta with the trade, my orders were only that I should see it safely this far . . .'

'Do you think I have no interest in the specie aboard *Guilford* . . .?'

'You showed precious little interest in the matter at the time . . .'

'My dear Nathaniel, how you misunderstand and misjudge me. Of course I relished your embarrassment. I do not hold your values, I seek my amusements where I may find them. I do not offer my help out of friendship, you know me too well for that . . . no, no . . . But I *do* have an interest in the fate of that silver . . .'

'Well, of what help can you be? broke in Drinkwater impatiently. 'Do you know where *Guilford* is now? How can you? Do you know anything of this coast? And what motivates this sudden about-face, this, this impetuous urge to assist?'

'Nathaniel, Nathaniel, your questions are too fast. Listen, I have told you, I have some interest in the silver; I alone brought it out of Canton in defiance of the Viceroy, its loss alone may be held against me, my business interests will suffer from its loss; my "face", my standing, my good name will be diminished. As to the coast, let me tell you I know both the estuaries of the Sekrang and the Sarebas Rivers, for I travelled on two Dutch ships and know them for haunts of the Sea-Dyaks.

'But why . . .?' Doubts assailed Drinkwater, but Morris pressed on.

'When the *Guilford* was taken I was more amused by your discomfiture than the loss. Recollect how long I have waited for your humiliation. But now you are determined to return. That is a different matter. For a while we have something in common . . .'

'You are offering me . . .'

'Terms . . . an alliance.'

'God's bones . . .'

'Furthermore,' Morris persisted, 'I have charts, better charts than those there . . .' Morris pointed to the half-unwound rolls of Hennessey's charts flung upon the cabin table until, later, Drinkwater could study them.

'See . . .'

Morris turned, drawing the top off a leather tube that he took from a fold of his robe. He drew a tightly rolled paper and held it out. Drinkwater took it and opened it. It was remarkably detailed, annotated with neatly pencilled notes. He moved across to hold it in the light from the stern windows but Morris took it from him, rolling it up again with his pudgy, beringed fingers.

'A sprat, Nathaniel, to catch the mackerel of your good favour . . .'

Drinkwater looked at Morris. The odium of him! He was almost wheedling in that mincing mode the seamen called nancying.

'You will let me have access to those charts?' Drinkwater asked.

'I will pilot you, using them. You need them only for the

estuaries, your boats may search the edges of the swamps and mangroves.' Morris paused and Drinkwater hesitated.

'You need me, Nathaniel,' Morris said softly, almost seductively, 'you need me to rescue your reputation . . .'

It was true. Despite the doubt and uncertainties, it was true.

'Do you think we have the slightest chance?' Drinkwater asked.

Morris noted the plural pronoun. He had hooked his prey. He forced his features into a grave, counselling expression.

'A good one . . . with a little luck . . .'

Drinkwater prevaricated a moment longer, though both men knew his mind was made up. 'How much specie was aboard *Guilford*?' he asked guilelessly.

Morris shrugged. 'Oh, ten, twenty thousand perhaps, certainly ten.'

Was the imprecision of Morris's reply sinister? And why had Callan himself lied about the amount of specie aboard his ship? For a moment or two Drinkwater stood indecisively, gauging the intentions of the man before him. He was already determined to turn back in quest of the lost ships, but he knew that he was without resources and that, intolerable though it was, Morris might be able to help. If, as he claimed, the good name of Morris himself would be impugned, then for a while they might hold something in common. Repugnant though the consideration might be to Drinkwater, honour and duty compelled him to submit to this personal humiliation in the hope of recovering the captured ships.

Drinkwater sighed. 'Very well, I'll give the order to weigh.'

By the light of the candles Drinkwater studied Hennessey's charts. They were not comparable with Morris's, but adequate for strategic planning . . .

Strategic planning!

The whole business was a mockery, a wild goose chase of the utmost folly, an attempt to save his . . . what was it Morris called it? His 'face'. That barometer of a man's standing in the world. 'You need me to rescue your reputation,' Morris had said, and Drinkwater ground his teeth at being so beholden. There was a knock at the cabin door. 'Enter!'

'You sent for me, zur?'

'Aye, Tregembo . . . what is the temper of the men? This is a testing time. Today they saw Penang and know it for an English post, now we sail south-east and only a fool knows that ain't for home.'

'Like you said, zur, I've given out that you've to clear the Dutchies out o' the strait, zur; said you'd orders for a month's cruise and that after that the Admiral's promised to hoist his flag aboard us for passage to the Cape.'

'Damn it, Tregembo, I didn't ask you to embroider my intention. Now you've made me a liar!'

'I've bought ye a month, zur.'

'Damn me!' Drinkwater's eyes met those of the old Cornishman. 'Yes, you have, and I thank you for it.' Drinkwater smiled. 'A month to keep us out of the Comptor, eh?'

'It'll not come to that, zur.'

'No.' No, it would not come to that. He no longer feared poverty, but there were other things. 'Thank you, Tregembo.' He bent over the chart, but the old Cornishman did not budge.

'Zur . . .'

'Well, what is it?'

'Morris, zur, don't trust him.'

'I don't . . . only I must, just a little.'

'Zur, I knows how you judged it were that young devil that played hokey with the compass.'

'Chirkov? Yes . . . though I can prove nothing.'

'No, zur. Mullenderl tell 'ee, though it took me long enough to get it out of him, he's the wits of a malkin, but he's certain sure it were the Russian. Mullender was in an' out, tendin' to 'em all in here.' Tregembo waved a hand about the cabin, disturbing the candle flames and making shadows leap like the spectres he invoked. 'You know 'ow 'e comes and goes silent like. He says how he saw 'em all smoking and drinking together, right little hell's kitchen they made o' this place, zur, beggin' your pardon . . .'

'Go on.'

'The boy too, zur, that little Turk. You know what he's for?'

'I can guess, Tregembo. Morris hasn't changed his habits.'

''Tis worse than a Portsmouth knocking shop . . . Mullender

628

didn't say much. Learnt to keep his mouth shut, I s'pose, or didn't want to start Derrick a-Quakering at him . . .'

'If all he saw was Morris and Chirkov . . .'

'Not buggering, zur, though I daresay they did that too, but in conversation, zur . . .'

'Conversation?'

'And Morris gave Chirkov a lump o' something . . .'

'A lump of opium, perhaps?'

'Only if opium's hard enough to rattle on the deck when it's dropped, zur.'

'The lump of lodestone?'

'Aye . . .'

Both men looked at each other, recalling the web of intimidation and cruelty that Morris had once cast over the helpless seamen aboard *Cyclops* thirty years earlier.

'So, the leopard hasn't changed his spots, has he?'

'No, zur.'

But why had Morris engineered such an act? The question tormented him after Tregembo had gone, and he sat slumped at the cabin table, toying with an empty glass and staring at Hennessey's charts. There was no reasonable explanation. Even though personal revenge was a powerful motive, particularly to a man as amoral as Morris, Drinkwater was convinced that Morris's pecuniary interests would have outweighed any other considerations during their passage from Canton.

As Drinkwater wrestled with the problem he felt a rising tide of panic welling in his gut. His loneliness seemed to crush him and in his weakness he reached out for the bottle. From forward, beyond the barrier of the cabin door, came the tinny, quadruple double strikes of eight bells and he heard the ship stir as the watch changed. He withdrew his hand from the bottle and swore. He commanded a fine ship, he had sufficient fire-power at his fingertips to bolster his courage better than any damned bottle! And he had Morris close by, damned near mewed up under lock and key.

Drinkwater rose and, leaning forward on his hands, stared unseeing down at Hennessey's charts. He was a fool and Tregembo an alarmist. Certainly Morris had put Chirkov up to the stupid act of tampering with the compass, but they had been drunk, or drugged, befuddled to an act of gross irresponsibility. Their jape had misfired and gone disastrously wrong. It was not Drinkwater who needed Morris, but Morris who needed Drinkwater! Surely *that* was the explanation, for not even the malevolent Morris could have foreseen that the convoy would be attacked by piratical Sea-Dyaks the following dawn and that the treasure aboard *Guilford* would be spirited away.

Thirty thousand sterling!

No wonder Morris had been imprecise about the amount, for its enormity was a measure of his consummate folly. Morris had wished to make trouble, to discredit Drinkwater and, like a good puppet-master, pull strings to rob his enemy of influence in London. Recovering his spirits, Drinkwater thought there was an ironical satisfaction in this line of reasoning, a grimly humorous if somewhat chilly comfort. Providence, it seemed, had failed them both.

'Devil take it,' he murmured reaching for his hat, 'but it argues powerfully for the bugger's co-operation.'

And with that conclusion, Captain Drinkwater went more cheerfully on deck.

'Red cutter's in sight, sir.'

Drinkwater looked up from Hennesey's chart pinned to a board a-top the binnacle and covered the three yards to Quilhampton's side in an instant. The lieutenant had his eye screwed to the long-glass, bracing its weight against a mizen backstay as *Patrician*, her main topsail backed to the mast, lay hove to off the Borneo coast. It was the second week of their search and January was already over. Another hot and almost windless day had dawned. There was barely enough movement in the air to press the heavy canvas against the main-top and the sea was flat, metallic and seemingly motionless, reflecting the refulgence of the sun.

Drinkwater stared in the direction of Quilhampton's telescope. He could just make out the wavering quadrilateral of the red cutter's lugsail as she cleared the Sarebas River. The estuary was invisible from this distance.

'Damn coast looks all the same,' Drinkwater muttered. 'Is she signalling?'

'Not at the moment . . . I think they're trimming the sheets, sir.'

Even from the mastheads the entrance of the creeks and obscure rivers that wound their way into the interior were impossible to make out. There seemed no appreciable difference in the endless miles of coastline they had patiently worked along. Endless vistas of ragged-edged blue-green swamp formed an indeterminate littoral. Distant hills rose blue-green, climbing into rolling cloud, evidence of firm footing beyond the sub-aqueous morass of the swamp which lay steaming under the sun.

'Cutter's signalling, sir . . .'

A tiny bubble of expectation formed in the pit of Drinkwater's stomach: perhaps this time . . .?

Drinkwater knew their chances of finding *Guilford* and *Hindoostan* had diminished to the point of impossibility. They would have been burnt or disposed of by now.

'Nothing to report.' Quilhampton lowered and closed the glass with a snap. The tiny, half-formed bubble in Drinkwater's gut burst. He felt the sun hot upon his shoulders. With every day that passed it had climbed further up the sky as it approached the equinox. Its relentless heat paralysed his will.

'Make the signal for recall.'

'Aye, aye, sir.'

The bark of the carronade drawing attention to the numeral flag jerking aloft drew Morris on deck. With him came his helot, small and brown, near-naked, but for a loin-cloth and the jewelled turban.

'No luck?' Morris asked.

'No,' Drinkwater answered flatly.

Morris met Drinkwater's eyes. The sight of Drinkwater's wilting resolve brought a thrill of both pleasure and sudden alarm to Morris. He had intended torture, but he must not lose the initiative. Drinkwater must not be driven to give up the search. Besides, he was as eager to reach the location of that mighty haul of specie as was Drinkwater! He bent over the chart, his fat, fleshy and glittering finger indicating a headland where the coast swung sharply east.

'Tanjong Sirik, Captain,' he said, drawing Drinkwater's attention to the point. 'Our last hope is here, Sumpitan Creek, Blow-pipe

Creek we called it, naming it for the ferocity of its inhabitants and their use of poisoned darts.'

Drinkwater stared at the pointing finger. It was beautifully manicured and reminded Drinkwater of a fat Duchess's digit. More significantly, it pointed to a white blank on Hennessey's chart. Where the coast swung round Tanjong Sirik, a gap appeared, an area of unsurveyed coastline unknown to the Dutch hydrographers.

'Into uncharted waters,' Drinkwater said ruminatively: a last chance. Morris had played his fish with infinite cunning. Drinkwater had will enough for one last throw.

'Not quite, Captain,' Morris said in a low voice, 'perhaps uncharted, but not quite unknown.'

Beyond Tanjong Sirik there was no mystery. The endless jungle of mangroves dipped south and seemed to disappear in an inlet beyond which it curved north and then eastward as far as the keenest eye at the masthead could discern. They passed small native *praus* and men fishing, and the smoking fires and *atap*-roofed huts on stilts which emerged like excrescences of the jungle itself. Small strips of sand with beached dugouts gave indications of firmer ground and the reason for these remote habitations, but of the mighty war-*praus*, the sea-going assault craft of the Sea-Dyaks called *bankongs*, there was no sign.

Drinkwater had originally nursed some vague plan of coasting this wasteland in the hope of attracting attack, of appearing sufficiently like an Indiaman to mislead whatever lookout the putative pirates employed. But they were either nonexistent or knew full well that *Patrician* was no Indiaman, but a man-of-war. Not even the subterfuge of hoisting Dutch colours, resorted to two days ago, had made the slightest difference. Apart from the fisherfolk, the coast had remained obdurately uninhabited.

As *Patrician* stood inshore, coasting slowly to the east of Tanjong Sirik, Drinkwater allowed Morris on the quarterdeck. The sun was westering and the blessed cool of evening was upon them. Morris scanned the line of the shore through his glass, his silk robe fluttering about his obese form.

'Blow-pipe Creek lies to the southward,' Morris remarked.

Drinkwater raised his glass and stared at the impenetrable barrier of the mangroves. He would give the game one last throw of the dice; one last opportunity to see if providence would change his luck. He had nothing to lose by sending the boats away for a final search before he admitted himself beaten. His only satisfaction was the knowledge that Morris, too, had failed.

'You may bring the ship to an anchor here. It is good holding ground, if I recall correctly.'

Drinkwater grunted assent and gave the requisite orders.

Before the last of the daylight was leached out of the sky the launch and both cutters lay alongside, stores aboard and crews told off. The sentinels stood vigilant, their muskets loaded, primed and with fresh flints new-fitted, and the officers had been ordered to maintain a keen-eyed watch. Drinkwater was too old an officer, and too good a fencer, to sleep well with his guard down.

He was very tired, tired beyond what the exertions of the day justified. Perhaps it was age, or the strain of rubbing shoulders with Morris in this quotidian way. Morris had proved an expert pilot for the place and, Drinkwater was reluctantly compelled to admit, appeared to have justified all his claims made at Penang. If only this were the place . . .

Drinkwater closed his eyes. The last thing he heard before sleep claimed him was the gentle knock of oars on thole pins as a guard-boat rowed watch about the ship.

He slept as he rarely slept, deeply. The near-silence of the anchored ship released his nerves so that nature overcame his seaman's instincts. He did not hear the sudden roar of torrential rain that abruptly opened like the sluice gates of heaven. It drowned the watch, the heavy drops bouncing off the wooden decks so that a ghostly mist seemed to rise a foot from the planking. It pummelled the toiling oarsmen in the guard-boat that laboured the small hours through under Midshipman Dutfield's command, beating them into inactivity and forcing them to crouch, dull-witted, in the drifting boat.

It stopped almost as suddenly as it had begun. Those on duty gasped with the relief, blew the droplets off their noses and scraped back the hair from their foreheads, shivering in the chill. It was some time after the air cleared before anyone discovered what had happened under the cover of the downpour.

It took Frey a further five full minutes to coax Drinkwater into wakefulness.

'What is it?' Drinkwater was dazed by the depth of his sleep.

'Sir, the boats, the launch and cutters . . .'

'What about them?'

'They are missing!'

15   The Bronze-bound Chests

February 1809

'*What?*'

Drinkwater was awake now, scrambling out of his cot and reaching for his breeches. 'Where's the guard-boat? How the devil did the boats break adrift?'

'They didn't, sir,' said Frey unhappily, 'they were cut adrift.'

'*Cut?*' He paused, thinking furiously. There was little doubt but what *that* meant. 'Turn up the hands, muster the ship's company at once, and pass word for my coxswain!'

Drinkwater finished dressing as *Patrician* came alive to the shouts and pipings of the duty bosun's mate. Two hours before dawn her people were hustled unceremoniously out of their hammocks.

'Pass word for my coxswain!' Drinkwater roared the command at the bulkhead and heard it taken up by the sentry beyond. He cast angrily about for a lost shoe. Mullender answered the summons.

'I sent for Tregembo, man, not you!'

Mullender's face seemed to tremble in the lantern light. The cares of endless servitude had removed all traces of individuality from its customary mien so that Drinkwater took his distress for a trick of the guttering flame he held up.

'S . . . sir . . .' Mullender was stuttering, a blob of saliva gleaming wetly on his stubbled chin.

'What the hell is it?' Drinkwater spotted the lost shoe and bent to pull it on.

'Tregembo, sir . . .'

Drinkwater stood. The ship was growing quiet again, evidence that her company were standing shivering on deck.

'Well?'

In a moment Frey or Dutfield would come down and report the lower deck cleared.

'He's missing, sir.'

'What d'you mean he's missing? How the devil d'you know?'

Cut boat-painters, deserters, Tregembo missing . . . what the deuce did it mean? They were taking a damned long time to count heads. How many had run?

Suddenly he had no more patience to wait the conventional summons. Shoving poor Mullender aside he made for the ladder.

He met Fraser in the act of turning from the last divisional report.

'Ship's company all accounted for, Sir, except Mullender and Tregembo.'

'Mullender's in my cabin . . .'

The dark pits of Fraser's eyes stared from the pale oval of his face. Was Fraser implying Tregembo had absconded? Slashed the painters of the boats and disappeared? What was it the orientalists called it? Running *amok* . . . had Tregembo run *amok*?

'Are you certain you have accounted for every man? In this darkness one could answer for another.'

'Certain, sir. I've had the divisional officers check each man individually.'

That accounted for the delay. But Drinkwater was too dumbfounded to accept Tregembo was responsible. He opened his mouth to inveigh against the inefficiency of the guard-boat when Fraser pre-empted him.

'He must have gone in the rain, sir. Frey said you couldn't see the hand in front o' your face, and the noise and wind were terrific.'

Drinkwater noticed the sodden decks and dripping ropes for the first time. But not Tregembo . . .

And then a thought struck him.

'Morris! Has Morris been called?'

'Er . . .'

No one had called the passenger, but he could not have failed to have heard the noise, nor have resisted the impulse to see what had provoked it. And even if he had not turned out himself, he would certainly have sent his catamite to spy.

'Mr Frey!'

'Sir?'

'Check the master's cabin. See if Mr Morris is there!'

'Yes, sir.'

Drinkwater paced across the quarterdeck. The entire ship's company waited, the men forward, heaped in a great wide-eyed pile across the booms, indistinguishable as individuals, but potent in their mass. Beside and behind him stood the rigid lines of marines and more casual grouping of the officers. Only Drinkwater moved, measuring his paces with the awful feeling that he was on the brink of something, without quite knowing what it was . . .

Frey's returning footsteps pounded on the ladder and Drinkwater already knew he was right in his suspicions.

'Gone, sir . . . taken his effects and gone . . .'

'What about those chests?'

'Didn't see them, sir, but,' Frey gasped from his exertion, 'I didn't search his cabin properly . . .'

'No matter. Mr Mount!'

'Sir?' The marine lieutenant stepped forward. He was in his night-shirt but wore baldric and hanger.

'Which of your men was on duty at Morris's door?'

'I . . .' Mount drew a step forward and lowered his voice. 'I withdrew the sentry there, sir . . . I had not thought him to be necessary after the cordiality you showed Mr Morris and he was removed from the presence of Captain Rakitin. I beg your pardon . . .'

'God damn it, Mount, *cordiality*? God's bones, you had no authority! No orders to . . . to do such a thing!' Drinkwater met Mount's confidential tone with his own muted fury. 'You have let me down, sir . . .'

'Sir, I beg your pardon . . .' The agony of Mount's sincerity twisted the stock phrase. 'I merely thought . . .'

Recriminations were of no avail now and in his heart Drinkwater perceived the logic of Mount's misplaced initiative. It was not really the marine officer's fault. How could he have communicated his worst fears when he had not admitted them to himself? In any case the time for dithering was past. He raised his voice: 'Get your men to turn the ship inside out. I want every store and locker thoroughly searched. I want to know if any clue exists as to where the three missing men have gone . . .'

He called for the purser and surgeon to get their keys and assist. What he did not say was that he sought the body of his coxswain.

'Mr Frey, get a fresh crew told off for the barge. The minute you can see what you are doing I want you to carry out a search for those boats. Mr Fraser, you will remain here with the people until Mount's search is completed. Then you may pipe 'em below.' He paused, considering addressing the patient multitude that still waited, then thought better of it. Instead he caught sight of Ballantyne's figure in the gloom.

'Mr Ballantyne, you attend me. Do you get a lantern upon the instant.'

'Aye, aye, sir.'

He waited for Ballantyne to return, remarking to Fraser, 'Tregembo's a victim, Mr Fraser, not a causative factor in this mystery. Morris is a man of consummate evil. Tregembo and I knew him thirty years ago. We may find Tregembo on board, in which case he will be dead. But we may yet find him alive, for Morris could not have got far in a cutter with only a boy to help him . . .'

'I don't understand, sir, are you suggesting . . .?'

But Fraser was denied a word of explanation, for Drinkwater, seeing Ballantyne with a lantern, disappeared below. He led the master to the cabin Ballantyne himself should rightfully have occupied, had the accommodation aboard *Patrician* not been so disrupted.

'Hold the lantern up.'

Drinkwater examined the louvred door, then pushed it open. There were no signs of struggle. Morris's cot was rumpled, a single sheet thrown aside. The boy's bedroll almost bore the curled, foetal shape of the creature. A robe, a heavy brocaded mantle of crimson silk, lay in a crumpled heap, the only sign of hurried departure, but the heavy leather portmanteau with which Morris had come aboard was empty, its lid flung back and its interior void. The smell of opium, which was for Drinkwater the very scent of Morris's corruption, filled the stale air in the tiny cabin.

'Lower,' Drinkwater commanded, bending and wrenching open

the lockers built below the cot. The lantern light fell on the dull gleam of brass locks and bronze banding.

'Ahhh . . .' Ballantyne could hold his tongue no longer.

'D'you have a pistol, Mr Ballantyne?'

'In my cabin, sir . . .'

'Get it,' Drinkwater snapped, adding 'loaded . . . here, give me the lantern.'

He set the lantern on the deck as Ballantyne scrambled off excitedly in search of his pistol. Reaching into the locker Drinkwater's hand found the corner of a chest and dragged it out of the locker beside the lantern. It was heavy, very heavy. He struggled with the second and was panting slightly as Ballantyne returned. He had Mount with him.

'I've found nothing, sir,' said the marine officer.

'It's loaded and primed, sir. Shall I?'

'Yes.'

Drinkwater drew back into the doorway and felt Mount's breath on his neck. Ballantyne squeezed himself into a corner of the cabin and held the pistol with both hands, arms extended. It was a heavy, double-barrelled weapon. Ballantyne's thumbs cocked the hammers. He braced himself. Drinkwater saw for the first time that the bronze bands on the chests were low reliefs of fantastically writhing dragons. Each lock was shaped in the head of a Chinese lion, their hasps of steel.

Ballantyne squeezed the trigger of the first barrel. The hammer struck the frizzen and the brief flash became a sharp bang that momentarily deafened them in the confined space. The small discharge of smoke cleared to reveal the first lock shattered. Shifting his aim Ballantyne blew the second apart.

'Reload,' commanded Drinkwater. 'Your hanger, Mount.'

Drinkwater took the marine officer's sword and inserted its point under the bent hasp of the lock and twisted it. Mount drew his breath in at the outrageous use of his prized weapon.

Damn Mount! Half of this was his fault!

The lock fell to the deck and Drinkwater attacked the second; it too gave way.

'Ready, sir.' Ballantyne raised the pistol to repeat the process on the second chest.

'Wait!'

Drinkwater gave a final jerk with Mount's sword and passed it backwards without turning. He felt a mean satisfaction at the damage he had inflicted to the perfection of its *pointe*. Then, with both hands, he lifted the curved lid of the chest. He had expected the glitter of silver or even the soft gleam of gold.

'What the hell . . . ?'

Drinkwater ignored the comments of the impatiently watching officers and put out a hand. The dull metallic sheen resolved itself into irregular lumps of mineral. As he lifted one and half turned to show it to Mount and Ballantyne he felt his hand move under a curious impulse.

It was irresistibly drawn towards the blued steel barrels of Ballantyne's pistol.

'Lodestone, gentlemen,' he said, standing and tossing the lump of magnetic ore back where it came from.

16   Blow-pipe Creek

February 1809

'It's pointless going any further, Belchambers, put your helm down.' Frey turned aft from his position in the bow of the barge. 'This is a cul-de-sac.' He slapped the insect stabbing his cheek and swore as the mosquito buzzed away unharmed. The dry leaves of the mangroves plucked at him, like the claws of hideous succubi in a nightmare.

'Backwater larboard, pull starboard.' Belchambers was having difficulty turning the barge in the root-choked gullet, a green and slimy inlet that wound out of the bay and into the jungle. It was one of the innumerable such creeks that they had attempted to penetrate since dawn.

Already the sun was lifting above the shelter of the overhanging branches, and the coils of mist that had clung like samite to the water were evaporating. Occasional birds, bright flashes of brilliant hue, whirred across the thin finger of water, shrieking or rasping alarm with a noise that had, at first, frightened them with its raucous suddenness. When they rested upon their oars they could hear the strange burp of trumpet fish coming to them through the planking of the boat and the distant chatter of monkeys was once interrupted by the sullen roar of a tiger cheated of its prey.

'It's no use . . . there's nothing here . . .'

The heat was filling the air with a weight of its own. The men were sodden with their own sweat and Frey's shirt clung to him like the dress of a Parisian courtesan. The effects of the early breakfast and the Spanish *aguardiente* with which the boat's crew had broken their fast were wearing off.

'Give way . . .'

'Look, sir!'

Belchambers's order, parially obeyed but ignored by two men who had seen the same thing, caused a moment's confusion.

'What is it?' Frey asked sharply, starting round.

'There, sir. Under that branch . . .'

Frey and Belchambers stared in the indicated direction. It was almost submerged. Just the upper curve of it, with the notch cut for a sculling oar, showed vermilion above the murky water. It might have been a dead bough but it was the scarlet transom of the red cutter, its stern painted for easy identification at a distance. It was no more than ten yards from them, sunk beneath the overhanging branches of a mangrove bush.

'We'll need kegs to refloat it . . . this bottom's so damned soft . . .' said Frey, probing with a boat-hook.

'Might work a spar underneath, sir, and jack 'er up on this 'ere root, like . . .'

'Damned good idea, Carey,' remarked Belchambers eagerly, 'let's try with the boat-mast, Frey . . .'

'*Mister* Frey, if you don't mind,' said Frey archly. 'Very well . . .'

'Hey, sir . . . look!'

They could see the tip of a pair of thole pins just breaking the surface a few yards further into the swamp.

'It's the launch!' Frey and Belchambers chorused simultaneously.

'But *why*, sir?'

Fraser waved his hands, pacing about the cabin, unable to keep the seat Drinkwater had provided for him. Quilhampton and Mount sat watching, while Drinkwater stood silhouetted against the stern windows, staring moodily at the green curtain of jungle that stretched across their field of view. Ballantyne was supervising the rigging of a spring upon the anchor cable, sounds of which came from beyond the head.

Drinkwater appeared to ignore Fraser's question. Mount, still smarting from his own idiocy, sat silent. Quilhampton knew better than to speak. He guessed something of what Drinkwater was thinking; he had been aboard *Hellebore*.

'I don't understand why this man Morris . . .' Fraser began again, jerking his hands like a hatter with the shakes. But it was not mercurial poisoning that motivated the first lieutenant, it was the incomprehension of an unimaginative man. This time Drinkwater responded. Turning from the windows, he cut Fraser short.

'*I* don't understand precisely *why* this man Morris chooses to act the way he does, Mr Fraser.' He lowered his voice which was strained with a tension that Quilhampton knew to be fear for the life of old Tregembo. 'Sit down, sit down . . . you see, gentlemen, I have cause now to believe that this man Morris quite deliberately engineered the separation of *Patrician* from her station on the night of the storm of thunder and lightning. In short I have been fooled – mightily fooled.' Drinkwater paused, inwardly seething.

'Oh yes,' he went on, looking round at their astonished faces, 'believe me, he is quite capable of such an act, for I knew him many years ago. We were midshipmen together. There is no need for details, except to tell you that we formed a mutual dislike; he affected a grievance against me for some imagined advantage I possessed over him. I was, it is true, briefly preferred before him . . .'

Drinkwater broke off. It was impossible to tell these men who stared at him with rapt attention that Morris had, in his twisted and perverse way, declared a desire for the young Drinkwater. The thought was repulsive to him even now.

But he had to tell them something of the man's character, if only to prepare them for what they were up against.

'He was, is, also a sodomite, a sodomite of a particularly cruel disposition. Mr Q may recall conduct aboard *Hellebore*, for we had the misfortune to meet again in ninety-nine. Morris corrupted a midshipman who was later drowned.'

The sceptical Fraser turned to look at Quilhampton who gave a corroborative nod.

'Prior, however, to this, while still aboard *Cyclops*, Morris was involved in a cabal of similarly inclined men. One of them was later tossed overboard. Tregembo was involved in this rough justice. I don't know whether Morris knew that, I suspect not, but Tregembo knew enough about Morris and was loyal enough to me to have risked his life . . .'

Drinkwater paused and drew a hand across his perspiring brow.

643

'Perhaps Morris simply took him to man a pair of oars . . . I don't know . . .'

'You say Morris took *him*, sir,' said Fraser, 'suppose Tregembo took Morris.'

'That is possible, sir,' added Quilhampton hurriedly, 'Tregembo might well have done that. He came to me once, sir, weeks ago . . .' he faltered.

'Go on,' snapped Drinkwater, 'you interest me.'

'Well, sir, he came to me,' Quilhampton frowned, trying to recall the circumstances, 'asking if I had recognised Morris when he came aboard at Whampoa. I said yes, and Tregembo reminded me of the character he had assumed aboard the *Hellebore*. Then he told me something about your earlier association . . .'

'Aboard *Cyclops*?'

'Exactly. He seemed to want to enlist me in some way.'

'Enlist you?'

'Yes. He said he knew Morris would – what was the word? Spavin you.' Quilhampton paused and looked down. 'I'm afraid I told him the whole thing was nonsense. Rather let him down, sir.'

'Was there anything else?' Drinkwater quizzed.

'No, sir, only that I believe words to have passed between Tregembo and Morris. Perhaps Tregembo chose last night to act, to protect you.'

'It makes a kind of sense,' said Mount, speaking for the first time, an edge of sarcasm in his voice, 'but it begs a lot of questions.'

'What questions?' Quilhampton asked defensively.

'Why Tregembo should choose last night; why, if he contemplated some violent act, he had to make off in a boat which he could hardly have handled alone; and why he should cut all the others adrift. It makes no sense for Tregembo to run off into the jungle denying us our boats.'

'But it is exactly what Tregembo *would* do, Mount, don't you see?' argued Quilhampton. 'Precisely to prevent us from following . . .'

'That's too fantastical,' Mount said dismissively, the pragmatic soldier routing the quixotic young lieutenant. They fell silent.

'Is it too fantastical, gentlemen,' said Drinkwater slowly, 'to suggest that Morris separated *Patrician* from the convoy out of more than mere malice aforethought towards me? Is it too fantastical to suggest that . . .'

Drinkwater paused at the knock on the door. 'Enter! Ah, Mr Ballantyne, I trust the spring is now clapped on the cable?'

'Yes, sir.'

'Very well. Please take a seat. I am theorising, please bear with me.' Drinkwater continued. 'As I say, is it not possible that Morris knew of our progress? He was a seaman, remember, and could, knowing our position, detach us from the convoy when he wished.'

'You mean he knew the convoy was to be attacked?' asked an incredulous Fraser.

'I mean he caused it to be attacked.'

'Well done, lads.'

Frey grinned appreciatively at the gasping men. Two hours of furious activity had refloated the red cutter. By dint of hard levering they had got her stem on a mangrove root and, by lacing the barge's bottom boards underfoot, managed with much awkwardness to find a footing themselves sufficient to work the boat so that its entire gunwhale was lapping the surface of the viscid water.

By jamming a thole pin into the empty bung-hole, they had been able to bale and now she floated not quite empty and low in the water, astern of the barge. Sodden and mud-besplattered, the men tumbled back into the barge and got out their oars.

'Give way, Mr Belchambers, back to the ship for reinforcements, some kegs and lashings, and we'll have that launch up in a trice.'

With renewed hope the seamen bent to their oars.

'I'll see you get a tot for your trouble, lads,' said Frey magnanimously, raising grins of anticipation.

'I never thought I'd say it, sir,' said Carey, the man who had spotted the scuttled boat, 'but I'd rather have a tumbler o' water . . .'

A silence greeted Drinkwater's hypothesis. Fraser crossed then recrossed his legs in an unconscious gesture of disbelief. Eventually Mount spoke.

'That's rather unlikely, sir.'

'Is it?' Drinkwater looked at Ballantyne. 'Mr Ballantyne, how familiar were you with Midshipman Chirkov?'

Ballantyne, a little mystified at the direction of the discussion, rose like a fish to a fly. 'Count Chirkov did me the honour of requesting instruction upon navigation, sir.'

'And you discussed such matters as the navigation of the ship?'

'Yes.' Ballantyne's head shook slightly, a note of uncertainty in his voice.

'To the extent of disclosing our position?'

'Well, to the extent of illustrating my talks about the day's work, the traverse and so forth, yes . . .' He stared about him. The faces of the other officers were turned towards him, their eyes hardening as he spoke. 'Have I committed some indiscretion?'

'Unwittingly, I think you have. Chirkov, by your own admission, was able to keep Morris informed of our position. We follow a predictable route, it was only necessary for Morris to detach us near the Natunas for his allies to attack. You see Morris had a most detailed chart of this area. I caught only a glimpse of it, and accepted his assurance that Hennessey's was adequate enough for our navigation.'

'And Chirkov interfered with the compass too?' asked the embarrassed Ballantyne.

Drinkwater nodded. 'I believe so, he too was capable of such a thing. Then Morris, knowing of my intention to return and search for the *Guilford*, persuaded me to accept his own offer of assistance . . .'

And led us here?' said Mount, only half-questioningly. 'But why?'

'Because somewhere out there in that wilderness is, if not *Guilford*, then the fruit of a long matured plan . . .'

'I don't understand,' puzzled Fraser.

'*Guilford* was carrying thirty thousand sterling.'

Whistles of wonder came from his listeners. '*Thirty* thousand . . .!'

'A prodigious sum, you'll allow, and Morris had planned to seize it at a time when the naval command on the East Indies station was changing, when the Selectmen were making such a racket in Macao and Canton that Admiral Drury was distracted and had no spare frigates to escort the small and vulnerable convoy that Morris *knew* would get out of the Pearl River before the negotiations reached stalemate. That is why the arrangements were made for the specie to travel aboard the Indiaman and not a warship, why Callan was reluctant to admit he had a large sum in case I was jealous and insisted on carrying it for my percentage.

'*Our* arrival threatened Morris's plan but *my* arrival gave him an opportunity for personal vengeance. He knew the point at which the convoy would be attacked, it was only necessary to detach us from it to accomplish both his basic plan and my own professional ruin.' He looked round, watching their faces for acceptance of his theory. 'And very soon,' he added, 'I expect an attack.'

'Who by, sir? asked Fraser, still unconvinced 'And who are these allies you speak of?'

'Sea-Dyaks,' snapped Quilhampton with a sharp air of impatience at the first lieutenant's obtuseness.

'As the hoplites,' agreed Mount with greater perception, 'but by what power does this Morris bend them to his will?'

'Sir, look!'

Mount's rhetorical question went unanswered, for Quilhampton was pointing excitedly through the stern windows to which Drinkwater had his back. He turned. Frey was standing in the bow of the barge, waving his arms above his head. Even at that distance they could see his shirt was torn to the waist and the thighs of his breeches were dark with mud. Behind the barge, towing on its painter and still somewhat waterlogged, followed the red cutter.

Drinkwater pulled himself laboriously over the last of the futtock shrouds and into the main-top. He paused for a minute, unseen from the deck, and caught his breath. He was exposed fully to the noonday glare of the sun, and the heat and exertion made him dizzy. The heavy cross timbers of the semicircular fighting top were warm to the touch, the iron eyebolts and fittings that secured the dark hemp rigging burnt his fingers when he touched them. Across the after side of the platform ran a low barricade terminating in mountings for two small swivel guns. He pulled the telescope from his belt, levelled it along a swivel crutch and painstakingly surveyed the surroundings.

Beyond the indentation of the coast, the sea was vast and empty, reflecting the blue of the sky and rippled here and there by catspaws of wind. To the west the prominence of Tanjong Sirik lay blue on the horizon, its distal point curled upwards as if shrivelling in the heat, a blue tongue shimmering below it – the effect of refraction, a mirage, giving the illusion of the cape being elevated above the horizon.

To the north-east the coast continued, jungle lapping the ocean with its scalloped edge of swamp. To the east and south the horizon was bounded by a spine of hills and mountains above which white coils of cloud drifted lazily upwards. Here and there spurs ran off this distant range, light green and with intervening blue furrows where, Drinkwater presumed, hidden rivers poured from the uplands. These streams with their suggestions of plashing waterfalls and cool, silver torrents sliding over smooth pebbles brought a sudden longing to him. But his shirt stuck clammily to his skin and the rivers vanished below the dark mantle of the jungle. It was not all mangroves. He could see some five miles away the different foliage of higher, more majestic species: banyan, tamarind and peepul trees, and the fronded heads of nipah palms. But in the end the mangrove swallowed everything, obscuring the streams, now become sluggish rivers that capitulated to inlets of the salt sea, to mix in the creeks and islets below Tanjong Sirik in a complex tangle of nature that defied penetration.

But Morris *had* penetrated it. Somewhere in that green desert Morris waited expectantly with Tregembo as his prisoner. Drinkwater knew with the clarity of absolute certainty that Tregembo had been taken not merely as an oarsman, but as a lure. Morris had cut loose and sunk the boats simply to delay Drinkwater, for he knew Drinkwater's character well enough to depend upon him following, just as he had worked upon old Tregembo with subtle cunning. Drinkwater could not guess with what ploy Morris had tempted Tregembo, but he knew that the Cornishman would have gone with Morris and his catamite, not in fear of Morris's pistol at his brain, but in the foolish conviction that he could save Drinkwater and that he could turn the tables on

Morris before Drinkwater himself was lured to his death. But Tregembo could not have known that the rain and the squall would have covered the approach of Morris's Dyak allies and aided their retreat with all the boats so that the presence of an oarsman was barely necessary.

And now Drinkwater scanned the jungle, aware that angry pursuit would be a trap, that his seamen would flounder up every blind alley of a creek, hot, tired, bitten and, in a day or so, utterly demoralised, easy targets for the deadly blow-pipes of the Dyaks.

He was aware of a quickening feeling of panic and forced his mind to concentrate on other matters, matters that might legitimately justify him in sending his boats into that hostile and unfamiliar wilderness. But there was no sign of *Guilford*. Carefully, fighting down the impatient urge to be impotently active, he re-scanned the jungle, systematically working over it. Pausing occasionally to wipe and rest his straining eye, he studied every exposed inch of jungle . . .

Nothing . . .

He blew out air and settled back against the mast. He used to sit in *Cyclops*'s top like this, learning how to make a carrick bend and a stuns'l sheet bend, and how to whip and point a rope, while Tregembo, a red-faced topman of near thirty summers, good-naturedly corrected his fumbling fingers. This had been his battle station and he had fought his first action from such a place, in Rodney's Moonlight Battle off Cape St Vincent.

January 1780.

It was all so long ago. Tregembo and then Elizabeth . . . and then Tregembo and his Susan, waspish Susan who was now cook to the Drinkwater ménage . . .

God! He had to do something! Something for Susan and something for Elizabeth. He could not sit here and let the sun burn him up, no matter what the odds Morris had stacked against him.

He drew the sleeve of his shirt across his forehead, blinked his eyes and stared again over the undulating plain of tree-tops.

Suddenly he clapped his glass to his eye. Damn! The bloody thing had become unfocused. He twisted the two tubes, muttering at his own ineptitude, his sweaty hands slipping on the warm brass.

'Yes!' He felt the sudden surge of his heart. He had been hoping, hoping for the sight of an ill-concealed mast, or the thin blue column of cooking smoke, but they were too cunning for that!

He felt like laughing, so great was his sensation of relief, but the thought of Tregembo sobered him. He lowered the glass, his head unmoving. Could he see them without the glass . . . ?

Yes.

He leaned over the edge of the top. 'Mr Dutfield! In my cabin, next to the chronometer you'll find my pocket compass . . .'

He waited, fixing his eyes upon the vague and distant shapes, so tiny, so indicative . . .

He felt the faint vibration of Dutfield's ascent.

'Here, sir.'

Drinkwater took the offered brass instrument, snapped up the vanes and sighted through the slits. Yes, he could see them quite well now . . .

'Beg pardon, sir, may I ask what you have seen?'

Carefully Drinkwater adjusted his head and made sure of the bearing.

'What I can see, Mr Dutfield, is . . . is . . .' he floundered for a phrase worthy of the occasion. 'What I'd call an intervention of nature, yes, that's it, an avifaunal intervention of nature.'

Dutfield's blank look made him grin as he threw his leg over the edge of the top and sought with his foot for the top futtock shroud.

'Steady . . . keep still, Carey . . . that's it . . . bail some more.'

The launch just floated. The slop of water in it made its motion sluggish under the influence of free-surface effect and occasionally it lurched so that water poured back in over the gunwhale. The quick righting movement exerted by the nimble Carey corrected this, resta-bilising the thing, and, as it rolled the other way, Carey steadied it, feet spread apart, arms outstretched, like a circus rope-walker.

Men floundered alongside, half swimming, half walking in the soft, insubstantial ooze, working the rope net beneath the launch's keel as it stirred itself an inch off the bottom.

'Pull it tight!' Frey held a corner and waved to the barge, lying ten yards away. 'Let's have those kegs, and lively, before we're stuck in this shit!'

They lashed the kegs, already haltered, as low as they could force them, fighting their buoyancy until at last the thing was done. The waterlogged launch lay within the net which in turn was buoyed up by the hard-bunged kegs.

'Right. All aboard!'

They floundered back to the barge where they clambered in over the transom. Frey was last aboard. He took the launch's painter from his teeth and handed it to Belchambers. The midshipman took a turn round the barge's after thwart.

'Very well . . . give way!'

It was a hard slog. The weight of the launch was terrific and, unless they maintained a steady drag, the water in the launch slopped into her stern, reducing her after freeboard.

Leaves brushed them, dead branches tore at them as they dragged their burden out into the wider stream. Already the sun was dropping fast.

'Back by sunset, lads, come on,' Frey urged. 'A steady pull.'

There was a sudden clatter forward. Frey leant over the side and tried to grab the oar that slid past them.

'Carey! What the fucking hell . . .?'

'He's dead, sir! Got a fuckin' arrer stuck in 'im!'

But only Belchambers saw the gleam of brown flesh as an arm was withdrawn, and a sudden fear chilled him to silence.

17   The Gates of the Fortress

February 1809

'Yes, I know what it is . . . do not touch the point, it may still bear poison. It is a dart from a *sumpitan*, a blow-pipe.'

'Thank you, Mr Ballantyne,' said Drinkwater.

'It is very effective, sir, and dangerous. The Dyaks use them. This man Carey was killed by Dyaks. They also carry the *parang*, a sword with which they are able to inflict a terrible wound, and they are famed for their skill with the *kris*, a knife with an undulating blade.'

'Have you fought them before, Mr Ballantyne?'

'In a hand-to-hand action only once, though I have been attacked by them more often. They will not press an attack if met with resolution, but resort to cover and strategies.'

'Stratagems, Mr Ballantyne,' corrected Mount with military punctiliousness.

'Stratagems then,' said Ballantyne, petulant at this humiliation.

'We are indebted to you, Mr Ballantyne,' Drinkwater soothed. He looked down at the chart spread before him and the pencilled line of his bearing: it petered out in a vast blank area. 'Now oblige me by listening carefully . . .'

It was that period of the crepuscular hour that nautical astronomists call 'nautical twilight', when the sun is twelve degrees below the horizon, rising to 'civil twilight' at six degrees and the full splendour of the dawn. Already the world had lost its monotones, the first shades of green were emerging from the variant greys, dull as slate still, but discernible to the acutely trained sailor's eye. Drinkwater reached the main-top.

'Morning, sir.' Belchambers greeted him with a whisper and his damp party stirred, three seamen and four marines who had slept at their action stations.

'Mornin', Mr Belchambers. Pray let me rest my glass . . .'

The whole ship's company had slept on their arms. Below, the boats were hoisted out of the water, though ready provisioned and prepared after their adventure of the previous day. Boarding nettings stretched upwards from the rail triced out to the yard-arms ready to catch any attempts to sneak aboard *Patrician* while the ship herself, her guns loaded though withdrawn behind closed ports, lay with her broadside facing the land, a spring tensioned upon her anchor cable.

Drinkwater peered southwards in the direction of his bearing. The landscape was shrouded by thin veils of mist that lay more densely in long, pale tendrils, winding across the lower parts of the swamps. In this light they seemed to stretch into infinity. Somewhere in the jungle a tribe of monkeys stirred with a sudden chattering.

'Morning, Belchambers.' Frey clambered up after Drinkwater who was already busy with his compass. Frey produced his drawing block and conferred with the captain. Drinkwater pointed out the wider streaks of fog that lay in definite lines over the mangroves.

'Those fog-banks,' Drinkwater explained, 'lie most densely over the channels of the waterways through this morass. See there,' he pointed, 'how that one leads south, then swings slightly east, bends sharply and runs to . . . here, look . . .'

Frey bent to stare through the vanes of the pocket compass.

'Runs to intersect with a bearing of south-east a-quarter south . . .'

'Got it, sir.'

'Then sketch it!'

Only the scratch of Frey's pencil could be heard. Drinkwater, holding the compass so that Frey could see it, put out his free hand to lean on the mast. Where yesterday the iron-work had burned his hand, it was now cold with condensation.

'Sir . . .'

'Pray be quiet, Mr Belchambers, and allow . . .' Drinkwater broke off and followed Belchambers's pointing hand. He could see the dark shapes detach from the jungle, see the faint white rings along their sides where the Dyaks plied their paddles.

'I'll go, sir!' The topman had reached out for the backstay even before Drinkwater had opened his mouth. Silently he lowered himself hand-over-hand to the deck. Looking down, Drinkwater saw him alert Fraser and the news galvanised the first lieutenant. He saw men radiate outwards to warn the ship, heard the low, urgent voice of the Scotsman and someone below shush another into silence.

'In the event of an alarm I want absolute silence preserved,' Drinkwater had ordered. He wondered how much of his own idle chatter the Dyaks had heard, for sound carried for miles over still water.

As if to echo his thoughts another burst of chattering came from the distant jungle. More Dyaks, or the cries of wakening monkeys?

'Finished, sir . . .'

Frey straightened up. Drinkwater shut his compass with an over-loud snap. He pointed at the approaching *praus*. Frey nodded and Drinkwater jerked his head. Frey swung himself over the edge of the top.

'Good luck, Mr Belchambers,' Drinkwater hissed, and followed Frey.

'Thank you, sir,' replied the boy. He was thinking of Carey slumped forward in the barge and the smooth muscled flesh of the brown arm that had dealt the stealthy blow.

Drinkwater reached the deck and turned. He was almost certain his movements would have been seen and had been conscious, in his descent, that his body offered a target for the deadly *sumpitan*.

'Here, sir . . .'

Mullender held out sword and pistols.

'Thank you,' he muttered; it had been Tregembo's duty. The thought filled him with a fierce desire for action. He joined Fraser by the hammock nettings.

All along the barricade the dull white shapes of men in breeches and shirts told where Mount's marines stood to, their loaded muskets presented. They were to fire the fusillade that gave the signal for fire at will.

'Your privilege, Mount,' Drinkwater hissed.

'Sir . . . they seem to be hesitating . . .' Mount's head was raised, watching the boats as they stilled and gathered together. Then Drinkwater saw the sudden flurry of energy. White whirled along their sides as, after a brief pause, the Dyaks dug their paddles into the water and their boats seemed to leap forward.

At the same moment there burst forth an ululating chant as each man wailed simultaneously, the sharp exhalation adding power to his effort. In addition to this outburst of noise, shrieks and the crashing reverberations of gongs disturbed the tranquillity of the anchorage. The air was filled too with brief whirring sounds and the clatter of darts as a battery of blow-pipes were employed. Most struck the rigging and fell harmlessly to the deck with a rattle.

'Fire!'

Mount's voice exploded with pent-up force. The spluttering crackle of musketry illuminated the rail. Above their heads the vicious roar of the swivel guns in the tops spat langridge at the attackers and then the wildly aimed, depressed muzzles of *Patrician*'s main batteries trundled out through their ports and added their smoke and fire and iron to the horrendous noise.

The air was filled with the sharp smell of powder and white columns of water rose a short distance off the ship, but Drinkwater was aware that the boats still came on. He could see details clearly now in the swiftly growing light; the red jackets of the warriors, the men at the paddles and the faces of men with blow-pipes to their mouths. Others stood, whirling slings about their heads, and he was assailed by a foul, acrid stench as the stink-pots flew aboard. They were lobbed over the rail and came to rest, giving off choking fumes of dense, sulphureous gases which stung eyes and skin. The *praus* were closing in now and the marines were standing, leaning outboard to fire down into them.

'Drop shot into 'em!' roared Drinkwater, hefting heavy carronade balls out of the adjacent garlands and hoping to sink the *praus* as their occupants sought a foothold on *Patrician*'s side.

'Won't press an attack, eh?' Mount called, turning to snap orders at Corporal Grice. A marine fell back with a dart protruding from his throat. The poor man's hand tried to tear it free but its venom acted quickly and he fell, twitching on the deck. 'Don't expose your men, Grice,' Mount bellowed above the shrieks and gongs. 'You too, Blixoe.'

A fire party ran aft attempting to deal with the noxious stink-pots; a second marine fell back, crashing into Drinkwater. He caught the man, then laid him gently on the deck. A short spear protruded from his chest. Drinkwater took up the man's musket and tried, through the smoke, to take stock of the situation.

Below, their cannon now useless, the *Patricians* stabbed at the Dyaks with boarding pikes, rammers and worms. One by one Quilhampton got his guns inboard and the ports closed. But something was wrong.

'Mr Ballantyne!'

'Sir?'

The master's eyes were wild with excitement, the whites contrasting vividly with his dusky skin.

'We're swinging. They've cut the spring. And look!'

The Dyaks were swarming over the bow, where the ship was easiest to board.

'Reinforce the fo'c's'le!'

'I understand, sir!'

God! Did the man have to be prolix at a moment like this? Drinkwater tugged at Mount's shoulder, but Mount was already swinging some men into line and Fraser had seen them too.

Drinkwater was still holding the dead marine's musket. The thing was unloaded, but its weight and the wickedly gleaming bayonet recommended it. He ran forward.

'Come on!'

The party defending the fo'c's'le had been beaten back. They were in disarray and retiring along the gangways. Drinkwater, Fraser and Mount rushed forward yelling, as though the noise itself formed some counter-attack to the awful hubbub of the Dyaks.

Their enemy were lithe and strong, men with short, powerful limbs and gracefully muscled bodies who swung their terrible *parangs* to deadly effect. This was no fencing match but a hacking, stabbing game and Drinkwater was grateful for the heavy musket as he leaned forward, stamping his leading foot and lunging.

There was blood on his arm from somewhere and he felt a blow strike his shoulder, but the glimpse of a bared chest received the full power of his driving body and he felt the terrible jar as the bayonet struck bone, scraped downwards and entered the Dyak's belly. Drinkwater wrenched free with the prescribed twist, stamped back, swung half right and thrust again. This time the musket met the heavy weight of a long *parang*. The sword struck it a second time and forced it down. Drinkwater had a sudden glimpse of the *parang* withdrawn, pulled back over the assailant's head as the man prepared for a mighty cut, a curving slash . . .

Drinkwater slewed to the left, following the fall of the musket. But his right arm straightened, the twisted muscles in his shoulder cracking with the speed and strain of the effort. The butt of the musket rose as its muzzle dropped, the heavy wooden club flying up to catch the Dyak's elbow as he cut, forcing the bent arm into its owner's face and crushing the delicate articulation of the joint. The Dyak retreated a little, and Drinkwater swung, swivelling his body as fast as he could, withdrawing his arms parallel to his right flank and then driving the musket forward again. The bayonet entered beneath the Dyak's ribs so that it pierced the heart at its junction with the aorta.

Drinkwater was snarling now, howling with the awful savagery of the business. He stepped forward. He wanted more of this, more to assuage the guilt he felt at Tregembo's disappearance, more to vent the pent-up anger of months, more to remove the obloquy of humiliation he had felt at losing two ships, more to cleanse his soul of the taint of Morris . . .

'They're in full flight now!' It was Ballantyne's voice, Ballantyne covered in blood, his sword-arm sodden with red gore, his face streaked with it where he had wiped his forehead.

Drinkwater leaned on the breech of a chase gun and panted. Turning, he could see the *praus* paddling away from them. A few Dyaks swam, shouting after them. Looking back along *Patrician*'s deck he could see his own dead. Already the wounded were being carried below.

Only on the fo'c's'le had the enemy lodged a footing and now they had gone. He wanted a drink badly.

'You're going to follow 'em, aren't you, sir?' Mount came running up. 'Fraser's already getting the boats down.'

'Yes, of course, Mount. No victory's complete without pursuit.'

They grinned at each other and Mount blew his cheeks out. 'Quite, sir.'

'Very well, Mr Fraser, you know what to do.'

'Aye, sir, but I still think . . .'

'I know you do, and I appreciate it, but I am resolved. We would not be here had not a personal element been involved. Good luck.'

'And you, sir.'

'James . . .' He nodded farewell to Quilhampton who was even more furious than Fraser at being left behind. But with Tregembo gone and he himself thrusting his impetuous head into the lion's den there had to be someone to go home to Hampshire.

'Sir.'

He slid down the man-ropes, found the launch's gunwhale with his feet and made his way aft. Acting Lieutenant Frey looked expectantly from the barge.

'Lead the way!'

The two boats lowered their vertical oars and gave chase after the blue cutter. Drinkwater settled the tiller under his arm and sat back against the transom. Fraser had every right to complain; as first lieutenant any detached operation was his by right to command. It provided him with a chance to distinguish himself, to obtain that step in rank to master and commander and then, if he were lucky, to post-captain. Well, Drinkwater had denied him that right and this was not going to be one of those glorious events that made the pages of the *Gazette* glow with refulgent patriotism. It was going to be a nasty, bloody assault and Drinkwater knew he would be damned lucky to get back at all, let alone unscathed.

That was why he had also left Quilhampton behind. Quilhampton would have followed him and risked himself unnecessarily just as Tregembo had done. If he was killed Drinkwater wanted James Quilhampton to stand protector to Elizabeth and his children, not to mention Susan Tregembo and the legless boy Billy who also formed a part of his private establishment. Besides, Fraser needed adequate support in case he was attacked separately.

In any case Ballantyne seemed eager enough for glory. Let the coxcomb bear the brunt of the attack. Drinkwater stared ahead; it was too soon to see the stern of Ballantyne's cutter, but he did not want the master rushing ahead on his own. He had sent Ballantyne on to try and keep contact with the Dyaks, delaying only long enough to get the boat carronade rigged on its slide in the bow of the launch. Midshipman Dutfield was sorting out cartridges for it at that moment.

Drinkwater tried to calculate how many men he had with him. He had left Mount in support of the ship, but a handful of marines in each boat, their oarsmen and the carronade crew . . .

Perhaps fifty, at the most. He would be limited to a reconnaissance . . . a reconnaissance in force.

The mangroves had closed round them now and he had lost sight of the ship. Ahead of him the barrier of jungle seemed impenetrable. They passed the spot where Frey had recovered the lost boats. Branches snapped astern. The men struggled at the oars as the channel petered out, then they were through. A large white-painted tree reared a huge and twisted bole at an angle out of the ooze. A block hung from it, through which a rope, old and festooned with slimy growth, sagged into the water and lay across perhaps three fathoms of its surface like a snake, then fastened itself to the branches through which they had just forced their way. A cunningly hidden contrivance, thought Drinkwater.

'I think we have just forced the gates of the fortress,' Drinkwater said for the benefit of his toiling boat's crew.

18 Pursuit

February 1809

Drinkwater tried to calculate the distance they were travelling, but found it difficult. Though he had a compass he had no watch and therefore, though his men pulled with a steady stroke, no accurate means of charting the seemingly endless corridors of smooth water which led deeper into the jungle. At a rough estimate, he guessed, they must be some four or five miles from *Patrician*, and should be overhauling Ballantyne's boat.

He was increasingly concerned about the master, a feeling that was heightened by the sense of entrapment caused by the surrounding jungle. The white-painted tree and the concealed entrance told him they were on the right trail, confirming, if he glanced at his compass, his observations from the main-top. But the oppressive silence of the vegetation, the increasing density of the mangroves and the brazen heat which increased as the sun climbed into the sky weighed on him.

Only once had he seen a sign of life. A bright-eyed monkey had peered suddenly and shockingly at him and his cry of alarm was only stifled by the chattering retreat made by the animal. Instead he coughed, to cover his confusion.

Occasionally he stood, peering ahead and seeking evidence of Ballantyne, but the oily water ran on through the overhanging foliage, trailing creepers and burping gently from the unseen activities of the trumpet fish. The sense of oppression, of being watched, was omnipresent. The men pulled obediently, but their eyes were downcast or stared apprehensively at the passing blur of leaves and shadows. If their eyes met Drinkwater's they looked quickly away. He knew they were as nervous as kittens. In a little while they would rest on their oars and he would stoke up their courage from the spirits keg.

Drinkwater was certain now that he would not find *Guilford* or *Hindoostan* hidden here. They had probably been burnt and were lying beneath the waters of the anchorage, stripped of whatever this nest of devils could find useful. He did not like to contemplate what reserves of powder and shot the Dyaks might have accrued by such means. The question was, did they need it for their attacks, for the manufacture of stink-pots and so on, or had they fortified their stronghold? And if they had access to powder, they also had access to firearms, for *Guilford* had had an arms chest and all her officers had had sporting guns. The sense of being lured into the mangrove jungle fastened more firmly on Drinkwater's imagination. The morning's attack, though it *might* have succeeded and delivered him a prisoner to Morris, was a feint, a further stratagem designed to draw Drinkwater in pursuit.

Should he go on?

He could not now abandon Ballantyne.

'Is your gun loaded, Mr Dutfield?' he asked, breaking the almost intolerable silence at last.

'Yes, sir. Langridge shot.'

'Very well, pull a little harder, my lads, I want to come up with the other boat.'

Frey saw his intention, pulled to one side and rested his men at their oars. Drinkwater's launch drew alongside, and as both crews refreshed themselves and the two boats glided onwards under their own momentum, he and Frey conferred.

'He's got a long way ahead, sir.'

'My own thoughts exactly. I think we may have lost him . . .'

'I've seen no other channels, sir . . .'

'No; I don't mean in that way, Mr Frey . . .' Drinkwater left the sentence unfinished. Frey grasped his meaning and nodded glumly. But they could not abandon the master, although Drinkwater's instinct told him to return to the ship, to work out a better strategy and recruit his strength. He looked at the sky. He could see what he was looking for now in the almost white heat above the jungle.

'We'll continue a little further, Mr Frey. Give way.'

661

Grunting and sullen, the boats' crews pushed out their oars and bent once more to their task. Fifteen minutes later they discovered Ballantyne.

The creek had opened out into a wide pool into which three other inlets appeared to debouch. Ballantyne's cutter was at the far end, adrift, its oars oddly disposed, some trailing, others sticking upwards, as though their looms were jammed in the bottom boards.

The oarsmen appeared exhausted, slumped over their bristling oars while Ballantyne sat upright in the stern. As the barge and launch came into line abreast, spreading over the greater width of the pool, Drinkwater and Frey both urged their men to greater efforts. Something about the attitude of the cutter's crew combined with the oppressive silence of their surroundings to restrain joyous shouts of recognition. That, and the realisation that it was pointless.

The cutter's crew were dead, dead from a volley of air-blown darts that had silently struck them in their pursuit. Ballantyne's body had endured the added mutilation of throat-slitting; a distinction reserved for the officer whose implication was not lost on Drinkwater.

Horror-struck, the gasping crews of barge and launch lay across their own oar looms, white-faced. Someone threw up, the yellow vomit coiling viciously in the water. For a long moment Drinkwater too fought down the gall rising in his throat, a bilious reaction compounded of revulsion and fear.

'We can't go on, sir,' said Frey, with a sense of relief, 'we don't know which channel to take.' He nodded at the three creeks that wound out of the pool and lost themselves in a tangle of trailing vegetation.

Drinkwater looked up. He could still see that fortuitous manifestation he had first spotted from *Patrician*. It was less than a long cannon shot away and it was not difficult to guess which creek led to it.

'I wonder how long they towed Ballantyne's boat after they ambushed it?' he said. 'A long way . . . long enough to lure us here, and then they released it when we were confronted with a confusing choice . . .'

'Yes, sir,' Frey agreed hastily, staring round, wondering how many unseen eyes were watching them, waiting to employ their deadly blow-pipes. His eagerness to be off was obvious, as was that of all the others.

With what he knew would be infuriating deliberation, Drinkwater picked up his glass and, focusing it, raked the shadows beneath the overhanging trees for any sign of an enemy. He did not expect to see very much, but a hidden boat or canoe would signal extreme danger. The silence of the jungle remained impenetrable. He closed the glass with a click.

'I believe we are supposed to be scared off, Mr Frey . . . but that channel there,' he pointed to a gap in the grey-green tangle of leaves, 'leads to . . .'

To what?

He did not know, had no means of knowing beyond the simple and obvious deduction that somewhere beyond that opening in the dense vegetation lay the answer to the riddle of Morris and the whereabouts of Tregembo.

'To the bastards that did *this*!'

His vehemence raised a grunting response from a few of the more impetuous men.

'How d'you know, sir?'

Frey was ashen-faced, aware that he was, for the first time in his life, confronting authority. Fear had made him suddenly bold, fear and the revelation that Captain Drinkwater was not here the gold-laced and puissant figure whose will directed the *Patrician* and her company. To his keen and artistically responsive intelligence, Drinkwater's sharp, vehement outburst only underlined the captain's weakness. To young Frey, Drinkwater at that moment was a rather pathetic man driven on by guilt at the loss of a faithful servant and an obsession with their peculiar passenger. He had learned about Morris from Quilhampton and, as he challenged Drinkwater, he fancied the captain's wounded shoulder sagged more than usual, as though, divested of coat and bullion epaulettes, it was unequal to the weight it bore.

Just as Drinkwater's outburst had stirred a response, so too did Frey's, a buzz of agreement from men who could see no point in going on. Drinkwater's eyes met those of his lieutenant. He knew Frey was no coward, but he also knew that Frey's confrontation was deliberate. For a moment he sat in an almost detached contemplation, his eyes remaining locked on to those of his subordinate. Frey was sweating, the sheen of it curiously obvious on his pale face. Drinkwater grinned suddenly and he was gratified at Frey's astonishment.

'How do I know, Mr Frey? Look!' Drinkwater pointed at the sky. 'An intervention of nature,' he said, deliberately self-mocking.

'Those . . . birds?' The crews of both boats were staring after Drinkwater's pointing arm and Drinkwater could sense the incredulity in all their minds, voiced for them by Acting Lieutenant Frey.

'Yes, Mr Frey, those birds . . . D'you perceive what they are, sir? Eh?' There were nine of them, large, dark birds with wide wings that terminated in splayed pinions and broad, forked tails. They wheeled effortlessly round and round so limited an axis that they betrayed the Dyak stronghold, even from the distance of *Patrician*'s anchorage.

'They're kites, sir,' answered Frey with dawning comprehension.

'Yes, Mr Frey, that's exactly what they are, kites giving away the position of our enemy.' The silence that followed was filled only with the hum of flies that were already blackening the bodies in the adjacent cutter.

'We've got our own, sir,' said one of the launch crew. They looked directly above their heads.

A single kite soared in a tightening spiral, seeing and scenting the mortifying carrion in the drifting cutter.

'Very well,' said Drinkwater with sudden resolution. 'I want six volunteers to take the oars; five marines, also volunteers, with ten muskets. I will exchange these men into the cutter as being handier upstream. You, Mr Frey, will take the launch and tow the barge back to the ship. You will put the bodies of our shipmates into the barge. Mr Dutfield, I'd be obliged of your company, but I want only volunteers.'

'Of course, sir, I'll come.'

'Obliged. Now, the rest of you. Who's with me?'

'I'll come with you, sir!'

They lashed the three boats together and, rocking madly, gunwhale banging against gunwhale, effected the transfers. When they had sorted themselves out and he had disposed the marines as he wanted them in the cutter, each with two muskets and a double supply of powder and shot, Drinkwater looked at Frey.

'Well, Mr Frey, we've left you a little water, and you take our best wishes back to the ship. Be off with you.'

Frey seemed to hesitate. 'I'll exchange with Dutfield, sir,' he said. .

'No, you won't,' replied Drinkwater, 'give way, lads.'

'And then he disappeared?' Quilhampton asked.

'Leaving no orders?' added Fraser.

Frey nodded unhappily at Quilhampton and answered the first lieutenant upon whom the imminent burden of command was settling like a sentence of death. 'No, none.'

'Bluidy hell!' Fraser ran the fingers of his right hand through his sandy hair with a gesture of despair. 'Has the man taken leave of his senses?' He sought consolation in the faces of Frey, Quilhampton and the silent Mount. 'This is taking a vendetta too bluidy far . . .'

'No,' Mount broke in sharply, his tone cautionary and his eye catching that of Fraser. 'No. I understand your feelings, Fraser, but Captain Drinkwater is not a fool. There is the matter of two captured ships and thirty thousand sterling.'

'And Tregembo,' said Quilhampton.

The four officers were silent for a moment, then Mount went on. 'If Captain Drinkwater issued no orders, then he wants nothing done. Nothing, that is, beyond maintaining our vigilance here.'

Drinkwater stirred and sat up. He was stiff and bruised from the hard thwarts, aware that he had dozed off. His movement rocked the boat and other men stirred, groaning faintly.

'Shhh . . .'

Those awake pressed their shipmates into silence and Drinkwater looked enquiringly at Dutfield. The midshipman, left with half the cutter's crew on watch, shook his head. Both 'halves' of the volunteer crew had dossed down in the boat as best they could for an hour or so each. Now the afternoon was far advanced and Drinkwater meditated taking them back into the stream, out of the cover of the mangroves that hung close overhead. They had heard and seen nothing in the period they had rested.

'Splice the mainbrace,' Drinkwater whispered. The raw spirits animated the men and he watched them as they drank or impatiently awaited their turn. Most of the men were members of his own barge crew, strong hefty fellows with some sense of identification with himself. He was glad to see, too, Corporal Grice among the marines. Grice had a wife and family to whom he was said to be devoted and Drinkwater had not expected him to volunteer. He smiled bitterly to himself; he also had a wife and family. Not for the first time he thought that war made fools of men . . .

'Muffle your oars now . . . perfect silence from now on . . .'

They pulled out into the stream. The kites had gone, forsaking their aerial vantage point as the air cooled a little. Or perhaps they had settled themselves on whatever it was that attracted them.

The narrow corridor of green seemed interminable. From time to time the foliage met overhead, shutting out the sky and filtering the increasingly slanting sunlight so that well-defined shafts of it formed illuminated patches, contrasting with the shadowed gloom of the leafy tunnel.

There was a difference in the vegetation now, Drinkwater noticed. No longer was the mangrove ubiquitous; there were an increasing number of nipah palms and heavy trunked trees like beeches, he thought, suggesting a firmer foundation for their roots. His theory found confirmation almost immediately as a low clearing came into view, a semi-circle of ferns and grass that surrounded a low slab of rock. He noticed, too, that about the broken branches that lay in the shallows, the creek ran with a perceptible stream, indicating a faster current than lower down. This was not merely an indented coast; it was indeed, as he had guessed from his masthead observations, fed by rivers. He strained his eyes ahead. Judging by his last sighting of the kites they could not have far to go now. His heart beat crazily in his chest. They had seen no sign, no indication of hostility, of being watched, if one discounted the creeping feeling along the spine.

A bend lay ahead. There was a break in the trees . . .

'Oars!' he hissed urgently. The blades rose dripping from the water and waited motionless, the men craned anxiously round. In the bow, muskets ready, two marines nervously fingered their triggers.

Through the break in the trees, brief though it was, he could just see, not more trees as he had expected, but a rising green bluff and the grey, sunlit outcrops of rock. What appeared to be too straight a line for nature ran across the summit of the eminence. This line was nicked by small gaps: an embrasured rampart, its guns commanding the creek up which they now glided.

Had they been seen?

He thought he detected a man's head above the line of the parapet. Then he was sure of it. As the boat silently advanced out of the shadows with the setting sun behind it, the light fell upon the stronghold of the Sea-Dyaks.

Above a wooden jetty, alongside which a number of the heavy *praus* were moored, numerous huts dotted the hillside and stretched higher upstream in a veritable township. More huts stood out over the river on stilts with another group of *praus* tied to stakes and smaller dugouts bobbing alongside them. Men and, he guessed, women moved about, the colours of their sarongs a brilliant contrast to the unrelieved green of the jungle. Here and there he spotted the scarlet jackets that he had observed on the attackers of that dawn. The lazy blue of cooking smoke rose from a single fire and a low, mellifluous song was being sung somewhere.

The whole scene was one of tranquil and arresting beauty. The still evening air was now filled with the stridulations of cicadas and the faint scent of roasting meat came to them, stirring the pangs of hunger in their empty, deprived bellies.

'Hold water!'

Jerked from meditation the oars bit the water, arresting the gentle forward motion of the cutter. It slowed to a stop under the last overhanging branches of a gigantic peepul tree, concealed in the growing pool of shadow. Drinkwater could see the place was cunningly fortified. Several batteries of cannon covered the approach, and a palisade of stakes seemed to be arranged in some way that protected the hill itself. Off the river bank he could see the water streaming past the pointed spikes of an estacade. He would need more than a boat gun to force a landing, unless he could take the place by subterfuge.

As he stood making his reconnaissance he was aware of the dull mutters of men being eaten by insects, and the sudden flutter of a giant fruit-bat made him jerk involuntarily. For a moment the boat rocked and Drinkwater expected a shout and the roar of a cannon to signal they had been seen, but nothing happened. He raked the parapet with his telescope and then stopped, feeling his heart leap with shock.

A yellow-robed figure stood against the sky staring through a glass directly at him. They were observed!

For a moment he seemed paralysed, the realisation that the man was Morris slowly dawning on him. As he lowered his glass Drinkwater saw Morris turn and move an arm, giving an obvious signal.

Drinkwater's guts contracted, expecting the well-aimed shot to smash the boat and end his life in a sudden bone-crushing impact. But instead there came a scream, a scream of such intense agony that it made their flesh creep and their very blood run cold.

PART THREE

A Private Revenge

'A man does not have himself killed for a few halfpence a day . . .
you must speak to the soul in order to electrify the man . . .'

NAPOLEON

19 The Tripod

February 1809

It seemed to Quilhampton an act of *lèse-majesté* to be thus conferring in Drinkwater's cabin. Behind him, in silent witness, the portraits of Elizabeth and her children seemed pathetic effects. He was too stunned, too mystified to pay much attention to what Fraser and Mount were saying and he stood obedient to whatever decision they made as, with Dutfield, they bent over the chart laid on the table and the scrap of paper the midshipman had brought back. The group monopolised the candles, leaving Quilhampton and a disconsolate Frey in umbral shadow.

'And that is all?' asked Fraser, his sandy features furrowed by concern and confusion, turning the scrap of paper over and over, first looking at one side, then the other.

'Yes, sir, beyond urging me to insist that you adhered to the instruction.'

'Adhere to it! 'Tis little enough to go on . . .'

Frey had arrived back at the ship towing his grisly cargo, bringing the news that the captain had penetrated deeper into the jungle. Frey's mood had been brittle, a product of the weight of guilt he bore at not supporting Drinkwater. He now stood silently moody, his eyes downcast.

Dutfield's arrival two hours after dark had plunged the waiting officers into still deeper gloom. The sense of having been abandoned filled Fraser with an unreasonable, petulant, but understandable anger. He knew of no precedent for the captain's conduct and sensed only personal affront. Fraser lacked both imagination and initiative, competent though he was at the routine duties of a first lieutenant.

But to Quilhampton's relief, Mount regarded the matter in a different light. A more thorough professional, none of Mount's considerations were influenced by the possibility, or in this case difficulty, of advancement. It was to Drinkwater that Fraser and the sea-officers looked for the creation of their professional openings and opportunities. Drinkwater's irregular conduct had denied Fraser any discernible advantages, and yet his rank compelled him to undertake responsibilities for which he had little liking and less aptitude.

The marine officer, however, regarded the task in a different light. Perhaps fortunately, it was a military rather than a naval problem. He leaned over and with the most perfunctory 'By y'r leave, Fraser . . .' gently removed the scrap of paper from the first lieutenant's dithering hand. Meditatively he read again Drinkwater's scribbled instruction:

Storm the place at dawn. Dutfield knows. Do not fail. N.D.

'Do not fail, Nathaniel Drinkwater,' he said aloud, then turned the thing over, staring at the rough, pencilled sketch-map of the river passage. 'Tis a simple enough matter, Fraser. We shall need all the men we've got and, as 'tis now near midnight, we have not a moment to lose.'

Fraser confined himself to an unhappy grunt.

'And you were not followed?' Mount asked Dutfield.

'I . . . I am not certain . . . at first I thought we were, but no shot followed us and, after the business of the captain, we pulled like . . . like . . .'

'Devils?' prompted Mount.

'Yes, sir,' Dutfield hesitated, swallowed and then, foundering under the earnest scrutiny of the anxious faces, added, 'though I will not admit to fear, sir, once the captain had gone . . .'

'It was as though the witch Nannie was after your horse's tail, eh?' Mount's literary allusion was as much to encourage Fraser as Dutfield. But Fraser did not appear familiar with the obscure poet and Mount let the matter drop. 'Do you tell off the men, Mr Fraser. Small arms, pikes, cutlasses, as many and as much as you can spare from the ship, with water and spirits, aye, and biscuit in the boats . . .'

'And food before we go,' put in Quilhampton, stirring at last from his catalepsy.

'We?' said Fraser suddenly in the prevailing mood of coming to. 'You, sir, will stay with the ship . . .'

'But . . .'

'I command, Mr Quilhampton . . . but you may see to the boats by all means. You are to plan the assault, Mount; Frey, you will second Mr Mount . . .'

'Aye, aye, sir.' Frey brightened a little.

'Dutfield will be our guide . . .'

While Fraser grasped at straws obvious and expedient, Mount bent his attention to details. 'Now, Mr Dutfield, please be seated, help yourself to a glass there, and cast your mind back to the sight of the Dyak fortification. I want you to recollect calmly every little detail of the place . . .'

'I wish to God I knew the captain's mind,' said Fraser, voicing his thoughts out loud and earning from Mount a recriminatory glare.

'Now, Dutfield, be a good fellow and *think*.'

Drinkwater lay on his back and stared at the stars beyond the darkly indistinct shapes of the leaves overhead. Although the stridulations of cicadas rasped incessantly about him, it was the persistent echo of that terrible scream that seemed to fade and swell, fade and swell in his brain.

There was no doubt in his mind but that a man within the precincts of the fortress was undergoing torture, and that that man was Tregembo.

The absolute certainty of this fact seemed enshrined in that provocative gesture of Morris's: Tregembo had been made to scream to Morris's order, made to scream to communicate Morris's power in this terrible place.

As the cutter had been swung short-round amid a furious splashing of tugging and back-watering oars, no shot had splintered them, no *sumpitan* had spat its venomous darts after their retreat. They had been defeated by that chilling, heart-rending cry, echoed and amplified by their primitive fear.

It had been the conviction of the source of the scream that had thrust into Drinkwater's mind the impetuous notion of remaining. He had had few moments to plan beyond scribbling the urgent need for an attack in force, before ordering Dutfield, ashen-faced over the tiller, to swing the cutter into the bank, trail his oars and

673

allow Drinkwater to leap clear. He had landed among the ferns and grass of that first low clearing they had spotted shortly before the Dyak fortress came into view. He still lay there, waiting to order his thoughts, summon his courage; waiting for the night . . .

The night had come now with the swiftness characteristic of the tropical latitudes and still he lay supine, like a dead man fearful of the predicament his folly had led him into.

But he knew it was not simply impetuosity that had made him jump. It was something far less facile, a complex mixture of obligation, hatred and loathing, wounded pride, a ludicrous sense of justice and, God help him, that raddled whore duty. Stern, inflexible and dutiful, Drinkwater's inner self was capable of excoriating self-criticism. If that leap from the cutter had been the compound product of largely virtuous qualities, he knew inwardly such virtue was a product of deep-seated fear. And that fear now had his heart in its cold clutch, immobilising him on the damp ground.

He recalled Mount's unanswered question: what power did Morris exert over these remote and warlike people? He supposed it must lie rooted in the silver. A Dyak prince's confederation could be purchased, no doubt, and he had learned that silver was the principal currency in these waters. But Morris must have more influence than that, for he had trusted them with thirty thousand sterling! It remained a mystery, though he was no longer in doubt that it had been Morris who had abducted Tregembo, though by what means he had no idea. A message, perhaps, through the boy, a luring to his cabin, the application of a drug . . . Guiltily, Drinkwater remembered his own exhaustion that night. He had dismissed Tregembo early . . .

It was as dark as the tomb now but for the stars. He wished he had one of Ballantyne's cheroots to ward off the mosquitoes that sought his flesh in droves. Eventually it was this irritating attack that brought him to himself. He stretched, fighting off the cramp that lying on the damp earth had induced. He had no clear idea of what he was going to do, or even attempt to do. He had vague ideas of reconnoitring the fortress, or attempting a diversion when Fraser launched his attack . . .

Or freeing Tregembo.

How could a man survive the pain inherent in that scream?

He rose to his feet. He had a marine's water-bottle, a cartouche box with powder and shot, two pistols and a sword. At the last second of his hurried departure Dutfield had hurled his dirk as enhancement to Drinkwater's armoury. It was of an unfashionable design, round-hilted, a lion's head snarling up the arm of its wielder. Drinkwater picked it up and stuck it into his belt. His eyes were accustomed to the dark now and the river threw off a weird light. Cautiously he took a draught of water, corked and slung the flask. No boats had followed the retreating cutter. Morris was damnably confident . . .

He had not gone a hundred yards before he discovered his first obstacle, a secondary creek separating the clearing where he had landed from the rising ground upon which the Dyak stronghold was located. Some trick of the twists of the creeks obscured the point at which he came upon it from the main landing, though he could see clearly the hard line of the parapet set dimly against the velvet sky.

It took him half an hour to work his way slowly and as silently as possible upstream over the tangle of roots, fallen trees and hang-ing vines that strung themselves like malevolent ropes across his path. The night was filled with the steaming of the rain forest, the stink of rich blooms, of humus and decay, of fungus and the ran-cidly sharp stench of excrement. Rustlings and sudden, startling flappings marked his disturbance of the unseen denizens of this foliated habitat. He thrust his mind away from thoughts of ser-pents. Ballantyne had spoken of the hamadryad cobra, of enormous lizards, of bats that drew blood from men . . .

But the second scream turned his thoughts to Morris waiting for him on the hill beyond the creek.

He made the crossing at a spot where overhanging branches obscured him from all but an observer opposite. The slime of the muddy banks covered the white linen of his shirt and the calico of his breeches. Taking his shoes from between his teeth and rear-ranging the parcel of powder and arms he had held above his head, he found his bearings and moved slowly uphill.

In the direction of Morris.

*

Ever since his boyhood when his father had been thrown from a bolting horse and killed, Nathaniel Drinkwater had believed in fate. His thirty years' service as a sea-officer, subject to the vicissitudes of wind and weather, of action, of orders, of disaster, victory and defeat, had only confirmed his belief. Although paying formal respect to the Established Church and owning a vague acknowledgement of God, he privately considered fate to be the arbiter of men's destinies. Fate was the Almighty's agent, prescribing the interlocking paths which formed the lives of the men and women he had known. These men and women had marked him for better and for worse: the gentle constancy of Elizabeth, the friendship of Quilhampton, the haunting loveliness of the Spanish beauty at San Francisco, the patronage of Lord Dungarth and the devoted loyalty of Tregembo who now endured God knew what horrors on his behalf . . .

And the enmity of Morris . . .

Drinkwater only half acknowledged that it was perverse love that bound him to Morris. The passion, unrequited by himself, had twisted the heartless young Morris into a cruel, vicious and domineering character whose forbidden vice gained greater satisfaction from the infliction of pain upon those who came under his influence. Unresolved emotions, unsatiated lusts, lay like unseen strands of circumstance between them, exerting their own ineluctable influence like lunar gravity upon the sea.

A third scream froze the sweat on Drinkwater's back as he stumbled suddenly into the edge of a small, steeply inclined plantation. It was Tregembo's fate to have drawn these men together.

Drinkwater moved with infinite caution now. Hunger sharpened his awareness and he dug from his body the reserves that the sea-service had laid there. Movement stimulated an irrational, feral thrill, a compound of fear and nervous reaction that acted on his spirit like a drug.

Making his way round the perimeter of the standing crops, he knew himself to be climbing, climbing up the northern or left flank of the stronghold as viewed from the river. It was the shoulder of the hill and he guessed, from the rising vastness of the sky ahead of him, that he was nearing the summit. Somewhere hidden beyond the crops and the shoulder of the hill, the rampart projected.

Behind and below him, the dense jungle stretched in a monotonous grey, partly hidden under its nocturnal mantle of mist.

On the hillside a faint breeze stirred, striking his damp body with a chill, and bearing too the bark of a dog, suddenly near, and the sound of men's voices.

The small cultivated patch gave way to a steepening of the gradient where an outcrop of rock thrust through the soil. He edged under its cover and took stock. If there were guards they watched the river, for below him rolled the jungle running north to the sea, south and east interminably, a grey, mist-streaked wilderness under the stars, impassable to all but the Malay Dyaks who were bred to its secrets.

Cautiously he edged round the rock.

The elevation he had achieved surprised him. He had supposed the rampart was constructed on the hill's highest point and knew now that this was incorrect. The rampart was formed on a natural level commanding the river; the summit, hidden from the observation of an attacker, was set back a little.

But there was someone on the rampart below him, a long figure, dark against the lighter tone of the river. The man moved, a leisurely, unhurried gesture like a stretch. Drinkwater considered the wisdom of attempting his murder and decided so positive a proof of his presence would do him little good. Instead he was distracted by laughter, a rising cadence of voices and then again, only much louder now, loud enough for him to hear it start with a series of sobs and end in the terrible gasps of a man fighting for air, came the scream.

Withdrawing behind the summit Drinkwater wriggled backwards then moved to his left, eastwards and upstream so that when he next crossed the skyline he should, he estimated, have a view of the native village, for the scent of wood smoke was strong in his nostrils, mixing with the subtle-sweet reek of humanity.

He had not miscalculated. The flattening of the hill, that had formed a narrow terrace behind the rampart before rising to the rocky summit, was here wider and further widened by the artifice of man. Beyond his sight the *atap* roofs of the huts stepped down the hillside to the landing place he had seen earlier. But immediately below him, on the flattened area, the low wooden *istana* stood, the palace of the chieftain, thatched with the *atap* leaves of the nipah palm. Before the *istana* extended an area of beaten earth illuminated by four blazing fires. Men wearing sarongs hitched like breech clouts squatted around the flames, eating and drinking. Some wore short, red jackets and head-dresses of bright cloth. The flickering light reflected from the sweat on their brown bodies and glanced off the rings they wore in their ears. Outside the gaping entrance of the *istana* were three chairs. In these sat the leaders of these men: a native chieftain dressed in yellow silk; a lesser Dyak conspicuous, even at fifty yards, by the quantity and size of the rings in the pendant lobes of his ears; and Morris.

Morris too wore yellow silk, and sat like the jade and soapstone images of the Buddha Drinkwater had seen offered for sale at Whampoa. So vivid was the firelight and so animated the scene below him that it was some seconds before Drinkwater noticed the three timbers of the tripod that rose above the area, its apex in the dark.

As he directed his attention to this central contrivance, allowing his pupils to adjust, he saw something square hanging from a heavy block. It seemed to sway slightly of its own volition, though the light from below made it hard for his tired eyes to see . . .

A wave of excited chatter rose and Drinkwater was distracted from his speculation by a group of women emerging from the *istana*. Their arrival was accompanied by a sudden drumming and they moved amongst the men in an undisciplined but arousing dance that induced the warriors to stamp their feet in time with the pounding rhythm. One or two leapt to their feet and joined the women, others did the same and a jostling throng of wild and lasciviously abandoned Dyaks was soon dancing to the insistent drum. Cries and whoops came from the mob and Drinkwater was aware that this was no native ritual and that many of the men below him were not Sea-Dyaks but half-breeds, Tamils and Chinese, *mestizo* Spaniards from Manila, miscegenate Portuguese from Macao, bastard Batavians and degenerate Britons from God knew where.

Morris had his own Praetorian guard amongst the sea-pirates of the Borneo coast, deserters, escaped prisoners, drunks and opium-eaters, a rag-bag of riff-raff and scum that the lapping tide of European civilisation had cast up like flotsam on this remote shore.

Here were the means to attack Company and Country ships, here were the means to work them, to infiltrate their crews, to rise in co-ordinated piracy that needed only the Dyaks for cover and the expertise of their skills in handling their *praus*. The cleverness of the thing astonished Drinkwater; how perfectly they had been fooled, he thought.

His deductions were confirmed by shouts of abuse in recog-nisable English and Spanish. Several men were arguing over women, and the drum-beats died away as, aroused to an erotic frenzy, the purpose of the Bacchanalia reached its climax. Frantic coupling was already in progress, less uninhibited pairs melting into the shadows or seeking privacy in the huts lower down the slopes.

A rustling in the undergrowth below him impelled Drinkwater to retreat, moving sideways into brush and ferns as a libidinous couple burst over the ridge, flinging themselves on to the ground vacated by himself. Within seconds they were engrossed in an urgent and grunting embrace; Drinkwater took advantage of their preoccupation and shifted his position.

When he again looked down on to the beaten earth before the *istana* he was closer to the seated leaders. They remained after the departure of their men, seemingly impassive to the arousing frenzy of the dance. A few guards stayed in attendance on the triumvirate, who appeared to be puffing on pipes.

Suddenly Morris heaved himself to his feet and, like a crouching familiar, Drinkwater saw the turbanned boy scuttle from the shadow of his robe. In the dying flames of the now neglected fires the yellow silk seemed to shimmer and the guards cringed as Morris shot out an imperative arm. The Dyaks seemed galvanised, moving to the tripod. The dark square was lowered, revealing itself as a small cage of bamboo. A prescient cramp seized Drinkwater's gut, contracting it sharply. His heart thundered in his chest. The Dyaks opened a rickety door and dragged out a bundle which they quickly hitched to the lowered rope.

In a trice they were dancing back, tallying on to the rope and hoisting the bundle up again, leaving the cage dragged to one side.

Drinkwater could see what it was now, though there was some-thing oddly liquid about its movement as it left the ground feet first. Suspended upside down was the naked body of a man. As he rose he emitted a low gurgling moan.

Still standing, Morris shouted: '*Arria-a-ah!*'

With the gorge rising uncontrollably in his throat Drinkwater could hear the anticipatory pleasure in those last attenuated syllables. The Dyaks released the rope. The low moan rose to a brief and awful shriek which stopped as the body struck the hard earth beneath the tripod.

It was Tregembo.

20   A Forlorn Hope

February 1809

Tregembo, or what had once been Tregembo, lay oddly crumpled and without form. The earlier liquidity of the body was clear to Drinkwater now, clear as the piercing of those agonised shrieks, for the tripod had done its terrible work. Tregembo, though still living, had been broken into pieces, his bones fractured by repeated impact with the ground.

Drinkwater vomited, his empty stomach producing little but the slimy discharge of bodily disgust.

'There, sir!'

Dutfield's arm was outstretched, a pale line of rigidity above the swaying grey shapes of the oarsmen.

'Hold water!' hissed Fraser, and the gentle knock-knock of the rag-muffled oars ceased, the turgid water swirled with dull stir-rings of phosphorescence and the boat slewed to a stop.

Dutfield's keen eye had detected the only landmark within the creek, the captain's landing place. They lay on their oars and gath-ered themselves for the final assault. Mount was aware that they were already late, for the edges of the overhanging trees were darker against the lightening sky. But a canopy of vapour hung above them, cold on their skin and dampening the priming powder in the pans.

'Cold steel,' he whispered, 'if your firelocks fail, cold steel . . .'

He heard the words passed along, the sibilant consonant thrilling Mount with its menace. The slide of steel from scabbards, the last tiny clicks and rattles of men turning pistols in their hands and thumbing hammers and frizzens, an occasional grunt, the papist whisper of a prayer, passed like a breeze over dry grass.

'Ready, Mount?' Fraser's voice came low over the flat water that was assuming a faint yellow in response to the dawn sky.

'Aye,' the marine officer replied.

'Frey?'

'Aye, sir.'

'Pater?'

'Yes . . .'

Even the purser, Mount thought, the warrant officer's unusual presence indicative of just how desperate a hope rested with them. *Patrician*'s officers were spread very thinly indeed, and if their assault failed, if it was bloodily repulsed as, Mount privately thought, by all the laws of military science it should be, the ship would inevitably fall.

'Take station then . . .'

There was a back-watering, a twisting of the boats' alignments. Oars became briefly entangled in the narrow channel. A man cursed, stung beyond toleration by yet one more mosquito.

'Silence!'

'*Vestigia nulla retrorsum*,' muttered Mount, 'no retreat from the lion's den,' and in a louder voice, 'Cold steel and a steady arm, my lads . . .'

'Stand by!' commanded Fraser, and the oarsmen leaned forward, their blades hovering above the water.

'Give way!'

'Thank the Lord for this mist,' muttered Mount as the stern thwart of the launch pressed his calf with the impetus of acceleration.

Taking station on the launch, the *Patrician*'s boats swept forward to the attack.

Morris passed the pipe to the boy, exhaling the last fumes of the drug. An utter peace descended upon his mind swimming in a pool of the most perfect tranquillity. His body seemed to float, satiated as it was by the most exquisite of lusts. No Celestial Emperor had ever enjoyed more perfect a sequence of sensations and now his mind rolled clear of every earthly inhibition, filling with a light more intense than the yellow dawn that flooded the eastern sky. He seemed elevated, lifted to the eminence of a god. Far, far below him lay the broken, used body of Tregembo. After so many years, revenge was infinitely sweet . . .

And there was yet one pleasure to enjoy . . .

His hearing, tuned to an unnatural acuity by the opium, detected the approaching boats. Swaying slightly he looked down at the upturned face of his catamite.

'Here they come!' he said, and the boy ran fom the *istana* with the news while Morris waited for the moment of consummation he had first thought of when he saw Nathaniel Drinkwater from the curtained secrecy of his palanquin beside the Pearl River.

Drinkwater woke with a start. He had no idea how long he had passed out, but a lemon yellow light already flooded the eastern sky. With quickening anxiety he lifted his head, half expecting to have been discovered, but the lovers had vanished and he was suddenly cold and lonely. The sharp stink of his spew stung his nostrils and, in a sudden wave of self-recrimination, he recalled the events of the night. It had been no nightmare that he had witnessed, though when he sought Tregembo's smashed body it was no longer there.

As he gathered his thoughts, the hill below him erupted in an explosion of fire and smoke. Hesitating only long enough to gather his arms he was up and running at a low lope, gaining height and flinging himself down in the shelter of the rocky outcrop at the summit of the hill. Here, not daring to look below before he was ready, he drew the charges from his pistols and, with shaking hands, poured fresh powder into the barrels and pans.

He had come here to reconnoitre and create a diversion and what had he done? Thrown up like a greenhorn midshipman and fainted! Now Fraser was launching his attack, Mount would be storming ashore at the head of his boot-necked lobsters in sure and certain faith of some diversion carried out by the ever resourceful Captain Drinkwater – and he was cowering behind a rock . . .

Christ, he had even abandoned Tregembo!

The thought brought him to his feet. He drew in a great gulp of air, filling his lungs with the sharpness and scent of the morning. Beyond the rock, on the hillside, the rattle of musketry had augmented the desultory thunder of artillery. Devoid of plans but filled with a desperate determination, Drinkwater emerged from cover.

He stood against the sky looking down upon the scene below. Heavy wraiths of mist lay over the creek and it was clear the gunners had no better a view of the approaching boats than he had, but they were working the six cannon with a regular determination that argued they had predetermined the trajectory of their shots. Drinkwater dropped below the skyline and ran to the right, towards the plantation through which he had laboriously climbed. Before he reached it he dodged down and worked his way round the hill. He had a better view here, although he was slightly below the level of the rampart. Gun-smoke hung in a dense pall over the palisade, but the plumed spouts rose from the mist where the plunging shot fell in the creek.

Below the six-gun battery on the summit the hill was terraced with earthworks, parallels of defence behind which Morris's polyglot army levelled their muskets at the pool before the landing place.

Drinkwater tried to gauge numbers. Perhaps two hundred men, perhaps two hundred and fifty, and they were supported by more cannon, smaller pieces but quite capable of decimating any assault force that stormed the hill.

There was the sudden reverberating bark and flash of a wide-muzzled gun that showed through the low veil of mist. A carronade! Fraser's boat gun, by God! The hot cloud that it belched seemed to burn a hole in the mist, though the small shot it fired did little damage beyond peppering a *prau* and cutting up the ground around the landing.

To Drinkwater's left came a shout and he looked round. A man, the yellow-robed chieftain, stood on the parapet of the upper battery and drew his gunners' attention to the presence of the launch's gun.

Quickly Drinkwater levelled his pistol. It was a long shot, too long for a man in his condition but . . .

He squeezed the trigger, then quickly rolled away beyond the edge of the escarpment, out of sight. He did not wait to reload but climbed quickly, returning to the overhang nearer the stone outcrop of the summit. Here he reloaded, then edged forward. The chieftain appeared unscathed, but he no longer leapt gesticulating on the parapet. Resting his hand on the ground and propping the heavy barrel of the pistol on a stone, Drinkwater laid the weapon on the same man. As the ragged discharge of the battery ripped the morning apart again, he too let fly his fire. At twenty-five yards the ball went home, spinning the Dyak to the ground. Drinkwater ducked down to reload.

He had begun to create a diversion.

Ten yards from the landing the blue cutter struck the stakes of the estacade. Such was the pace of her advance that the bow was stove in by the impact. Frey was equal to the moment.

'Over the bow!' he shouted and leapt from the tiller. Stepping lightly on the thwarts, he touched a toe on the stem and, waving his cutlass, plunged into the water. An outraged sense of having been misunderstood had possessed Frey from the moment he had abandoned Drinkwater. Already privately convinced the captain was dead, Frey sought to expiate his guilt. With a foolish gallantry his men followed him, cutlass-bearing seamen, half a dozen with boarding pikes, few of whom could swim in the deep water. They floundered, found the oars they had so precipitately abandoned and, wrenching them free of their thole-pins, kicked their legs as they supported their bodies on the ash looms.

The mist mercifully covered their confusion. Virtually unopposed, they dragged their way gasping ashore.

Fraser's launch had by good fortune forced the gap left in the estacade. Dutfield, in command of the carronade, wrenched clear the wedges as his crew plied sponge and rammer.

'Fire!'

The boat bucked and the short, smoking black cannon napped taut its breechings as it recoiled on the greased slide.

'In my wake!' Fraser screamed at the other boats, seeing the fate of Frey's cutter. 'Come on!' He was waving as Mount leaned on the tiller of the red cutter and led Pater's boat past the launch that stood off and pounded the landing. Fraser's men were trailing their oars, making room for Mount and Pater whose boats were almost gunwhale under with their load of armed men. The pale glint of bayonets showed purposefully and then a plunging shot dropped on the launch. The sudden dark swirl of water ran red with the blood of an oarsman whose leg was shattered by the iron ball.

'Cease fire and give way! Don't shoot our fellows in the back!'

Tearing off his hat Fraser thrust it into the hole and then felt the boat's bow rise as it grounded.

The sun emerged above the eastern tree-line, its slanting rays striking through the swirling vapour. Both attackers and defenders had, as yet, no very clear view of the opposition. The upper battery continued to fire, blindly dropping its shot beyond the boats where the plunging balls threw fountains of mud and water harmlessly into the air. As Mount and Frey stumbled gasping ashore, they forced their men into a rough line and peered about them. The hill rose upwards, scarred by the barred lines of the earthworks and palisades, while to their right the higgledy-piggledy gables of the *atap*-roofed houses tumbled down the hillside.

The brief flashes and eruptions of smoke lining the lower defences marked their objective. The musketry fire struck its first victims and Mount sensed his men waver. He shook his sword and took a deep breath.

'Forward!'

The ragged line of sodden men began to advance: seamen in the centre with boarding pikes in their hands, cutlasses swinging on their hips from canvas baldrics; on the flanks the steadying influence of Mount's marines, stripped of their red coats, but in close order. Bayonets and cutlasses caught the rays of sunlight and gleamed wickedly as, with every foot of elevation, the attackers came clear of the clinging river-mist.

Above, Drinkwater saw them clearly, recognised Mount and Frey, caught the evil sparkle of the light on the weapons. Directly below him two of the gunners were bent over the wounded chieftain. They did not seem to have considered the possibility that the shot had come from behind them, for the noise of gongs and the war-shrieks of the Dyaks, the heavy powder smoke and their own high excitement dulled their wits to this unlikely event. Despite the fact that their shot was now useless, the boats having passed the fixed line of its fall, they continued to load and fire, unable to depress their guns to command the slope of the hill. Emboldened, Drinkwater struck two of them with pistol balls, rolling backwards to reload.

The sunlight cleared his head of the cataleptic horrors seen in the night. His nerve was sharply steady, his brain functioned with that cool clarity that operated beyond the threshold of fear, when desperation summoned up the most primitive of instincts, that of the aggressive survivor.

When he looked at the battery again, he was aware of some confusion; a debate seemed to be in progress, some of the gunners favouring joining their brethren in the defences below, two pointing to their right, clearly considering some attack was coming up from the plantation. They had not yet realised that those shots had come directly from their rear. He saw the gunners split their forces. Suddenly the battery was empty!

Drinkwater hesitated only long enough to see that the wavering line of the attackers seemed to have reached the first line of earthworks, then he was bounding down the hill, his sword bouncing on his hip, Dutfield's dirk digging into the small of his back.

At the rear of the gun platform lay half a dozen powder kegs. An astonished man, a Portuguese or Spaniard by the look of him, sat quietly filling cartridges with a scoop, hidden from view by the angle of the slope above him. Drinkwater was no more than three yards from him, and only the indrawn breath of surprise alerted Drinkwater to the man's existence. For a split second the two stared at each other, then Drinkwater discharged the pistol in his right hand. The impact of the ball smashed the man's skull hard against the rock behind him. Copper scoop and cotton cartridge bag fell with a surreal slowness from his grip. Powder cascaded in a tiny stream off the man's saronged lap.

Grabbing an already filled bag, Drinkwater split it and continued the trail, scuffling backwards and drawing the grey line in the direction of the plantation. Running back to the sagging body of the cartridge-filler he overturned the broached powder cask with his foot, then ran to the battery. Piles of shot lay by the guns. Bending, he lobbed them, bowl-like, back under the overhang, aiming them at the stack of powder kegs.

Picking up a linstock carelessly thrown down by the departing gunners, he blew on the foot of slow match that smouldered in its end, walking smartly to the end of his powder trail and stepping over the body of the chieftain.

He was about to touch the slow match to the powder when he heard voices, the shouts of the searching gunners returning from the plantation. Somewhere below the rampart the gongs rose to a crescendo and shouts, screams and cheers told of savage hand-to-hand fighting. Drinkwater touched the slow match to the powder and flung himself into the upright crops in the plantation.

The voices were quite near, raised in some urgent expectation. Had they seen him? Had they seen the powder train sputtering away? He lifted his head. Someone crashed through the stems a yard away, turned and saw the prone Drinkwater. The pistol misfired, too hurriedly loaded . . . The gunner shouted something and raised a *parang*. Drinkwater gathered his legs, tossed the useless pistol aside and drew Dutfield's dirk. The *parang* swung, biting earth, its owner staggered back with the dirk buried in his loin, Drinkwater's shoulder thrust into his chest. They crashed into the gunner's confederate, the three of them falling. Drinkwater struggled to withdraw the dirk; his sword hilt dug painfully into his side, both the men were on top of him now, one vomiting blood and bile, the other yelling with rage, recovering himself and preparing to retaliate.

There was a sudden roar, blasting hot air out of the hillside in a hellish, roasting exhalation. Drinkwater heard, or fancied he heard, the crinkle of frizzing hair and skin as the gunner's yell turned to an agonised shriek. The searing force of the explosion rolled over them, pounding them with shards of rock and gobbets of earth. Only their position in the plantation saved them from the falling shot and the landslip as the rampart exploded outwards, cascading rock, stones, earth, cannon shot and two dislodged guns over the parapet on to the third defensive line immediately below it.

Badly shaken, quivering like a wounded animal, Drinkwater dragged himself from beneath the two gunners. Both were near death and he turned his head sharply from the horror of the sight. To his right as he stood facing uphill, a dense cloud of dust still hung over the site of the explosion, but a great scar of exposed earth and rock was gradually emerging beneath it.

The muscles in his thighs still shuddering, Drinkwater moved forward.

Shot, debris, rock and, quite recognisable, a man's leg, fell on the launch in which Fraser and his oarsmen, and Dutfield and his carronade crew, were theoretically covering the landing. Fraser's main preoccupation had been in stemming the leak with something more effective than his hat and, at the moment of the explosion, he had just succeeded. His coat, stretched underneath the boat by its arms and tails on light ropes, had reduced the inflow. Further insertions of shirts made it possible to reduce the amount to a trickle. As the launch crew found themselves afloat amid widening circles of disturbed water, they looked up at the brown cloud still hanging over the hillside.

'Sir!' shouted Dutfield, pointing excitedly. 'It's the captain!'

He stood at the edge of the great scar, staring down on the brief hiatus in the savage fight below. Then he turned and vanished from their sight.

'Thank God . . .' breathed Fraser with a heartfelt blasphemy.

Mount caught a sight of Drinkwater while he fought to keep his footing. As the explosion had rolled rock, cannon shot and earth down on them Mount had roared his anger, meeting a *parang* thrust and riposting before turning on a second assailant. The indiscriminate avalanche bore down on them, though the wild trajectory of the heavier debris flew over their heads. Mount was already aware of losing many of his men. Muskets the enemy might possess, but they did not disdain the deadly *sumpitan*. The struggle uphill had cost them dear, for forty of the hundred and twenty men committed to it were lying behind them killed or wounded.

But the sliding earth had caused more havoc to the defenders, unnerving them, shaking their already fragile discipline and raining debris on their backs, filling their entrenchments. The hardened *Patrician*s recovered first. Waving his sword Mount thrust forward, shouting a manic encouragement to his men.

On the flank Frey was also rallying the attack. He had not seen the captain, and the strength of the fortification and the determination of the enemy had surprised him. His sense of having betrayed Drinkwater lay heavily upon him and he fought with a sullen, dogged and careless energy.

'Look out, sir!' He heard Corporal Grice's warning and turned, his cutlass half-raised to parry, but Grice had spotted a new movement by the enemy. To their right, along the lower slope from the direction of the village, red jackets bright and the light gleaming on their *parangs* and blow-pipes, advanced a column of Dyaks.

'Right face, Corporal!'

But Fraser had seen them from the launch.

'Mr Dutfield . . .' Fraser pointed at the ragged column threatening Frey's flank. Dutfield nodded his comprehension and busied himself round the carronade.

'Hold water starboard, one stroke larboard.' Fraser swung the launch. 'Hold water all . . . a short pull larboard bow.' The bow oarsman dabbed at the water and Dutfield, sighting along the stubby barrel, held up his hand, then stood back and jerked his lanyard. The carronade roared and a swathe of langridge cut into the Dyaks, sending them reeling. The counter-attack broke and fled.

Looking again at the hill, Fraser was aware that the resistance was crumbling. His men were everywhere triumphant, putting to death the last fragmented pockets of opposition.

'By heaven,' he said, his voice almost reverential, 'I believe we've done it!'

21 A Private Revenge

February 1809

Drinkwater left the struggle for the hill in the balance. Whatever the outcome he had unfinished business to attend to and he wanted it over with, even if afterwards he had to tumble ignominiously into a retreating boat.

Half sliding, half scrambling, he descended to the area before the *istana*. The high framework of the tripod dominated the place and the smell of ashes mixed here with the tang of powder smoke. Despite the raucous noise of battle, it was deserted, the Dyaks involved in their attack on Frey's men. Pausing only to check his weapons, Drinkwater ran up the steps into the wooden *istana*.

It was dark inside and it took his eyes a moment to adjust. The entrance chamber was floored with intricately woven matting, and hung with bright-coloured cloth. Beyond, a partition with a door led to the inner *balai*, or audience hall. A pale shape lay in the centre of the matting and Drinkwater knelt beside it.

'Tregembo . . . Tregembo, forgive me . . . I was too late . . .'

There was the faintest respiration in the thing, for it was no longer a body but a shapeless mass, blotched with pale areas from which the broken blood vessels had emptied themselves, and dark with suggilations where, like some foul and swollen bladder, it spread upon the flooring. Uncontrolled, the bowels wept.

Shaking with disgust and rage, Drinkwater pressed the barrel of his pistol against Tregembo's skull and pulled the trigger. The swollen body subsided as a red and white mass fanned out across the matting.

'Goodbye, old friend . . .'

'What a touching sight . . .'

His eyes blurred with tears, Drinkwater looked up. Morris stood before him, a pair of heavy pistols in his hands.

'The faithful retainer . . .'

'Hold your tongue, you bastard.' Drinkwater made to rise.

'Stay where you are!' Morris commanded sharply. 'Your kneeling posture is, how shall we say, most appropriate, eh?

'You do not approve of the pursuit of pleasure, my dear Nathaniel, do you? You cannot understand it, can you? You and your ridiculous preference for *duty*!' Morris spat the word contemptuously. 'You are a fool, a willing tool of your masters, an instrument of policy, hiding yourself under your epaulettes and trumpery nonsense, knowing *nothing*!'

'Damn you . . .'

'Oh, damnation, my dear Nathaniel, is a condition figuring largely in *your* calendar. There is nothing after death and in life we are free to pursue pleasure. It is a more acceptable way of employing power than your own and I imagine I have caused less deaths than you . . .'

'You . . .'

'Disarm yourself . . .' Morris jerked his head and the turbanned catamite emerged from the inner chamber. 'Don't lecture me on the perversity of my philosophy, Nathaniel, surrender your weapons to Budrudeen.' Morris moved the pistols, emphasising Drinkwater's weakness.

Drinkwater threw his own on the matting, pulled the second from his waist and dropped that, the boy skipping as the heavy pistol skidded towards his bare toes. Budrudeen bent to recover them and Drinkwater jerked the sword free from his scabbard and offered the hilt to him.

Budrudeen took it. The red stub of his tongue clacked in his wet mouth. Drinkwater felt the comforting hardness of Dutfield's dirk nestling in the small of his back. Budrudeen retreated with his trophies.

'No, don't lecture me . . . I have waited a long time for this moment. Ever since you took a dislike to me . . .'

'Damn you, Morris, you wanted buggery . . .'

'Among other things, yes. Do you know a Sikh fortune-teller in Calcutta told me I was blessed among men, that I should have everything I desired and when he asked what was it I desired most, he put his hands upon my head then wrote your name on a paper.' Morris smiled. 'Most remarkable, eh?' He chuckled. The noise of gongs had ceased and screams and shouts came from somewhere below them.

'I had planned to take the specie, of course. That had long been in my mind, but seeing you in that foolish demonstration at Canton . . .'

The noise of retreat was now obvious. Morris's composure began to waver.

'Stand up!'

Drinkwater obeyed.

'Precede me into the inner chamber . . .'

Drinkwater met Morris's eyes and as the other made way he stepped forward, gauging the distance . . .

'No tricks.'

Throwing his full weight behind his left shoulder, Drinkwater charged.

'Dog's turd!'

Morris fired. A searing heat burnt across Drinkwater's left forearm, the ball grazed his thigh and struck harmlessly into the wooden floor. The other shot went wide as Morris fell back, stumbling on his robe, his mind still under the residual effect of opium, his reactions slowed. He crashed into the partition and made to jab one pistol into his assailant's ribs. Drinkwater's fist had already closed round the hilt of Dutfield's dirk. He slashed Morris's wrist.

In a reflex of pain, Morris dropped both weapons. Drinkwater drove the foot-long blade hard into Morris's gut.

'Bastard!' he roared, wrenching the blade upwards so that his wounded muscles cracked.

Morris crashed to his knees as Drinkwater withdrew the blade. He was red to the wrist. Morris looked down, his hands going to his belly. Something blue and shiny dipped through his fumbling fingers.

'Drinkwater . . .' Morris looked up, his voice reaching a crescendo of agony, his mouth twisting, his veiled eyes now wide with disbelief.

Drinkwater stood back horrified. Morris fell forward, caught his weight on his right hand. His eviscerated entrails slithered on to the matting. A faintly offensive smell rose from them on waves of vapour. Morris raised his slashed wrist in a terrible gesture of supplication.

'Nathaniel . . .!'

Drinkwater felt a terrible pity rising like vomit in his throat.

'Nathaniel . . .'

'Christ damn you!' Drinkwater screamed, slashing the dirk across Morris's face. His frenzy ebbing, Drinkwater stepped backwards, gasping. Morris remained supported by one hand. His lower jaw and cheek showed white through the fallen flesh, but his eyes remained on Drinkwater. Then suddenly a dark hole appeared in his forehead. It was a small hole, Drinkwater noted, though the impact of it threw Morris rearing backwards. Drinkwater had not heard the pistol and it was only gradually that he turned his head and saw the smoking muzzle in the hands of the boy Budrudeen.

With the assistance of the boy, Drinkwater found a lamp and spilled its oil, setting it on fire with powder and a spark. It caught quickly, flames racing across the dry matting of the *istana*. Still dazed, Drinkwater backed out into the sunshine. Within the *istana* the flames were already licking up the columns, curling the cloth hangings. He caught a last glimpse of Morris stretched under his robe of yellow silk in a pool of gore. He lay beside Tregembo's poor bruised and bloated corpse. Then thick coils of smoke and the racing flames hid them from his view. The boy was tugging at him, clacking urgently and indicating that they should run. Something in his face set Drinkwater in motion, releasing him from his archarnement.

He began to run, to run and run, leaving the foul place far behind him in a blind panic. The hot blast of the explosion thrust him in the back. He fell skidding forward, aware of earth and filth in his mouth and the tumbling form of the boy whirling through the air, some trick of the blast tossing him high. A force seemed to squeeze behind Drinkwater's eyeballs; all he could see was a lake of blood.

And then it was raining!

The silvery droplets fell about him. He looked round for

Elizabeth and the children. They would get wet, for the rain was heavy, beating down, striking his bare flesh.

'Sir? Sir? Can you hear me, sir? Are you all right, sir?'

'Elizabeth . . .?'

'It's Frey, sir . . . Frey . . . It's all over, sir . . .'

And he opened his eyes to see silver coins falling from the sky.

22 Penang

March 1809

It was ironic that he should have been saved by the boy
Budrudeen. In that final confrontation with Morris the boy might
have saved his master instead, but mutilation and degradation
had, in the end, turned him against his persecutor. The shot was
probably the only act Budrudeen had performed uncoerced in his
short life. It was, too, a refutation of Morris's appalling creed.

The boy had not survived long, expiring soon after they brought
his abused body back to *Patrician* in the flotilla of boats pulled by
exhausted oarsmen. The losses they had sustained had been fearful
and they had burnt the *kampong* as an act of corporate vengeance
while the Dyaks melted into the jungle. And yet they returned
with an air of triumph, for they had discovered a hoard of silver,
much of it picked up on the hillside by men induced to be honest
on the promise of legitimate reward, though there were undoubtedly private sums hidden about *Patrician*. Over forty thousand
pounds worth, by the best calculations, the proceeds of years of
depredations against the merchant trade in the South China Sea.
Some of this booty had been held near the powder magazine below
the *istana* and so had been blown spectacularly into the air.

But even this justification, satisfactory though it seemed to the
profit-mesmerised survivors, failed to gratify Drinkwater. He was
seized by the most profound doubts about his conduct, plunged
into the blackest of depressions as *Patrician*, under the easy sail
manageable by her depleted company, rounded Tumasek Island
and headed north-west into the Strait of Malacca.

'All men murder their own innocence, sir,' said Derrick as he sat,
pen poised, awaiting the captain's dictation. Drinkwater looked at
the Quaker; it was the first time Derrick had called him 'sir'.

'Why do you say that?' he asked guiltily, as though caught in a culpable act.

'It is part of the human condition.'

'That is damned cold comfort.'

'The truth is rarely comfortable, especially when it touches ourselves.'

Drinkwater opened his mouth to damn the canting and sanctimonious prattler, but acknowledged the other as an equal. 'Does your creed prohibit you rendering assistance?'

'My creed tells me to be guided by the inner spirit . . .'

'I had no time for such deep considerations,' said Drinkwater with a hint of returning spirit. 'A course of events initiated and guided by an amoral hand will find little to inhibit it. The most outrageous evil can be perpetrated with bewildering ease, especially if directed by a cool mind . . .' And Morris had possessed that, he thought morosely. He stared fixedly at Derrick who lowered his eyes to the paper.

'It has not been my lot, sir, to come face to face with such things.'

The ghost of a smile crept across Drinkwater's mouth. 'No; you have been fortunate,' he hesitated, 'or wise . . .'

Had he had innocence left to murder? Yet something had died in him as he slashed Morris in his frenzy, and the realisation robbed him of all sense of having avenged Tregembo.

'Perhaps that is why the Almighty reserved the right to vengeance,' said Derrick with disarming prescience.

'Damn it, don't preach at me,' snapped Drinkwater, 'bend your attention to my report,' and he began to dictate.

'Penang, sir.'

Quilhampton was smiling as Drinkwater came on deck and they exchanged salutes. The high-peaked island was still distant, still remote and blue. Beyond it and stretching away on the starboard beam lay the line of the Malay coast.

'We shall be at anchor by noon, sir.'

'Yes.'

'How is the wound, sir?'

'The wound is nothing, James. Lallo's curettage removed the morbid tissue and there is no inflammation. I assure you I am quite well. It is not yet time for you to step into my shoes.'

'Sir, I never . . .'

'No, of course you didn't. You are certainly more cheerful than you have been, no, hear me out. It was a bloody business, James, not an affair of much honour. To be candid I did not expect to survive it and, damn me, considered you owed me obligation enough to attend to Elizabeth and the children . . .'

'Sir, of course . . .'

'Well, sir, enough said about the matter then. I apprehend,' went on Drinkwater, diverting the conversation with an obvious hand, 'you will be disappointed again today.'

'Why so, sir?'

'Your high spirits are evidence of expectations, ain't they?'

'Er, well, I, er . . .'

'You will receive no word from Mistress McEwan, James, because, despite the foolish inventions of your imagination, no one in England knows where we are, beyond the fact that we were last ordered to the Pacific.'

'But we are homeward bound, sir, are we not?'

Drinkwater turned, lifted his glass and scrutinised the island as it loomed over the horizon.

'God and Admiral Sir Ed'd Pellew permitting.'

'Captain Drinkwater, pray take a seat . . . a glass, sir?'

'Your servant, Sir Ed'd.'

'I collect we've met before, sir?'

'In ninety-four, sir, a night action on the French coast with the flying squadron. I was in *Kestrel* . . .'

'Ah, yes, the cutter . . . a gallant scrap, eh?'

'Indeed, sir.'

'May I present Captain Frederick Torrington of the *Polyphemus*, the latest teak frigate from the Parsee yard at Bombay.'

Drinkwater recalled the elegant, over-painted thirty-six-gun cruiser his boat had passed pulling to the flagship.

'Sir. A fine-looking ship, a credit to the Service . . .'

Drinkwater nodded to the thin-lipped boy who wore the single epaulette of a junior post-captain, then turned again to the pock-marked, balding admiral whose tall frame still seemed to possess the energy of a young man.

'Sir, my report . . .' he handed over the papers. 'May I enquire, Sir Ed'd, if those two ships in the roads are from Canton or Calcutta?'

'You refer to the Indiaman and the Country-wallah?' drawled Torrington.

'I do, yes . . .' Drinkwater was aware of an amused glance passing between Pellew and Torrington.

'Why do you ask, Captain Drinkwater?'

'The Indiaman seemed familiar, sir . . .'

'She should do, sir, she was part of your convoy.' It was Torrington who spoke, the tone of his voice impertinent, even insolent.

'Is she *Guilford*?'

'Yes . . . I took her . . .'

'Torrington had the good fortune, Captain Drinkwater, to be sent on a cruise by myself . . .'

'Hoisted Dutch colours and lay to in the Gaspar Strait. Took those two fellows two days later . . . damndest piece of luck. Taken by pirates don't you know; got 'em back without a shot being fired.'

'Damndest luck, sir. I congratulate you. Captain Callan is in health?'

'Positively so, sir, *absolument* . . .'

'Leadenhall Street will be most gratified, Captain Torrington. I had despaired of ever finding them again.'

'*Nil desperandum*, Captain Drinkwater.'

'It is difficult to avoid it sometimes, sir,' said Drinkwater ruefully, 'but doubtless the experience will affect you one day . . .'

Pellew coughed, a trifle pointedly. 'I expect Captain Torrington will be rewarded by the Court of Directors with a present of plate,' he said.

'I do most assuredly hope so, Sir Ed'd.' Drinkwater stood.

'Sit down, sit down. Captain Torrington was just leaving . . .'

There was a twinkle in Pellew's eyes as the door closed behind Torrington. 'Forgive him, Drinkwater, he's a bear cub.'

'That is the trouble, sir.' Drinkwater stopped, thinking he had gone too far with such a shameless nepotist as Pellew, for all his reputation as the finest seaman of his age.

'Now tell me, when will Drury be back? Did you see my son Fleetwood? I am damnably weary of this station and long to follow you home.'

'Sir?' Drinkwater looked sharply at the admiral.

'You are a person of some standing, Captain Drinkwater, though I admit the fact is not known to Captain Torrington.'

'How so, sir?'

Pellew shuffled his papers on his desk, failed to find what he was looking for and tinkled a hand-bell. While they waited for his secretary he added, 'I have received specific instructions about you if, as the Admiralty has it, you "appear in these seas", a quaint turn of phrase, you'll allow.'

'Indeed, sir.' Drinkwater suppressed his revivifying curiosity. Somehow it was enormously stimulating to find that life went on.

'His Lordship requires you in England.'

'His Lordship?'

'Lord Dungarth who, as we both know, attends to matters of some delicacy.'

'He is not dead, Sir Ed'd?'

'I think, sir, it was intended that his enemies should think he was.'

'It deceived his friends . . . then he is quite well?'

'He is hulled, but serviceable. He lost a leg, but his reasoning parts are unaffected.'

'I am sorry for his leg, but that is good news.'

'Now your report . . . the matter of the silver is serious.' Pellew dropped his avuncular attitude and was, remorselessly, the Commander-in-Chief, East Indies Station. 'Those damned *traders* in Calcutta have a powerful lobby . . .'

'The silver is safe, sir. I recovered it. And a little more besides.'

'Ahhh, that *is* good news . . .' And Pellew's well-known cupidity was interrupted by the arrival of his secretary. 'Have the goodness to find the Admiralty's instructions regarding Captain Drinkwater, if you please.'

'And so, sir, after consultations with Sir Edward's physician I am persuaded they offer no threat and that my regime of salt-bathing has been efficacious. I apprehend that there will be no further outbreaks of button-scurvy, sir.'

Drinkwater nodded at the surgeon indulgently. 'Ah, Mr Lallo, I am delighted to hear it. Your remedy', he said, with a touch of irony, 'does you credit.'

'Thank you, sir. I also learned from Sir Edward's man that Captain Rakitin lately succumbed to a quotidian fever induced by a carcinoma.'

'I am sorry to hear that, Mr Lallo, indeed I am. I do not believe the Russians will long bear arms against us.'

'Let us hope you are right, sir. We have few friends in the world.' Lallo rose to take his leave, then seemed to hesitate.

'There is something else, Mr Lallo?'

'Sir . . . there is wild talk of a duel, sir.'

'A duel?' snapped Drinkwater incredulously. 'By God, is the appetite for blood insatiable? Between whom, pray?'

'Between young Midshipman Chirkov who is still here in Penang and . . .'

'Go on, sir, go on, I demand to know!'

'Frey, sir.'

'God's bones, has the young jackanapes lost his reason, send for him upon the instant.'

Drinkwater sat immobilised while he waited for Frey. What the deuce was the matter with the lad?

'You sent for me, sir?'

'Indeed, Mr Frey, I did. I hear you are engaged to meet Midshipman Chirkov upon a matter of . . . of . . .'

'Honour, sir.'

'Have you any explanation to offer me? You know the practice to be forbidden, a rule I most strictly enforce.'

'You forbid me to meet Midshipman Chirkov, sir, even in our capacities as private gentlemen?' Frey's manner was prickly.

'I most certainly do, Mr Frey.'

'But my honour, sir?'

'Damn your honour, sir! You will oblige me by your obedience.'

'Sir, I protest!'

'Hold your tongue, sir! I have just obtained for you ratification of your commission as lieutenant from the Commander-in-Chief! I have just persuaded Admiral Pellew that it is unnecessary for you to take the formal examination. I have just descanted upon your abilities, praised your steadiness, recommended your proficiency as a watercolourist, as being an officer ideally fitted for surveying. I have, in short, Mr Frey, enlarged on every segment of your character that I might adduce in your favour to procure this preferment. You will therefore attend to my own orders in preference to your foolish notion to demand satisfaction.'

'Sir,' said Frey unhappily, 'I had no idea of your high opinion.'

'Mr Frey,' said Drinkwater grimly, 'I have lost too many friends to allow you to put your life to the hazard for a trifling notion of honour.'

'But, sir . . .'

'I forbid it!'

Drinkwater's voice cracked with anger. He paused, then added in a quieter tone, 'Your talk of honour and the compulsive need for satisfaction are foolish principles . . .' The captain lapsed into an introspective silence. An awkwardness hung in the air, broken in the end by Frey.

'Very well, sir, I submit. And thank you for your efforts on my behalf.'

'Eh? Oh, yes . . . yes, very well.' Drinkwater recovered himself, coughing to clear his throat. 'You will be glad to know,' he seated himself, 'that we are ordered home. The rigours of your duty will demand more courage than facing Mr Chirkov's pistols, a thing quickly done, but it's courage of a different sort, Mr Frey.'

Frey left the cabin. For a moment Drinkwater stared after the young man, then he buried his head in his hands.

Author's Note

The British occupation of Macao and Admiral Drury's extraordinary demonstration before Canton are a sideshow of the Napoleonic War largely ignored by standard histories. Drury, the first of several British naval officers to appear in the Pearl River during the nineteenth century, was unique for his sympathetic attitude to the Chinese. I have largely used his own words to express his sentiments. The Chinese regarded his 'humane treatment' as a victory of their own. Pellew too, though a shameless nepotist, was no imperialist, and Drinkwater's view of British policy in India was also expressed by Sir Edward. Both Pellew and Drury were harassed by Company and Country mercantile interests who considered the convoy arrangements of the former inadequate, and said so publicly. To some extent their criticisms of the Navy's preference for seeking prizes were justified.

Few, if any, merchant ships got out of the Pearl River during the 1808 season, but Drury did send a frigate up to Whampoa to secure a quantity of specie owed by the Chinese merchants. Rumours of a French overland expedition via Persia were current at the time (and considered by Napoleon), while the depredations of French corsairs continued in the Indian Ocean. I am chiefly indebted to Captain Eastwick's memoirs for a contemporary picture of the Canton trading scene and in particular the Country ships.

Piracy in the South China Sea continues to be a problem in the present century. Raffles's acquisition of the island of Tumasek broke much of the power of the pirates when he founded Singapore in 1819, but at that time, as his own Malay tutor, Abdullah bin Abdul Kadir, wrote: 'no mortal dared to pass through the Straits . . . Jinns and satans even were afraid, for that was the place the pirates made use of . . . There also they put to death their captives . . . All along the beach there were hundreds of human skulls, some of them old, some fresh . . . in various stages of decay.' Shortly after the end of the Napoleonic War the British Admiralty sent Captain Henry Keppel to extirpate these nests of pirates. Doubtless they were influenced by Drinkwater's report on the subject. Nor were naval vessels immune from what Raffles called 'an evil of ancient date', for in 1807 the Dutch warship *De Vrede* was captured and her officers and crew treated with characteristic barbarism.

Although unseasonal, typhoons are not unknown as late in the year as November. Finally, the origin of the enmity between Drinkwater and Morris may be found detailed in *An Eye of the Fleet* and *A Brig of War*; the presence of the Russian prisoners in *In Distant Waters*.

THE SHADOW
OF THE EAGLE

Richard Woodman

It is 1814. Napoleon had abdicated and the 'Great War' is at an end. As King Louis XVIII is escorted back to France by an Allied squadron, and Europe prepares to celebrate the return of legitimate monarchy, tensions remain. The Tsar of Russia has grand designs of his own, while, from the ashes of defeat, Bonapartists plot to restore the eagle whose shadow still lies across the continent. Attending King Louis, Captain Nathaniel Drinkwater receives secret intelligence of an imminent threat to peace, and seizing an opportunity only he can exploit, risks his life and reputation to prevent disaster befalling his country . . .

EBB TIDE

Richard Woodman

It is 1843, and Captain Sir Nathaniel Drinkwater embarks on the paddle-steamer *Vestal* for an inspection of lighthouses on the west coast of England. Bowed with age and honours, the old sea-officer has been drawn out of retirement on half-pay to fulfil his public duty. The following day, however, tragedy strikes, and Drinkwater, the punctilious seaman and sympathetic libertarian, is suddenly confronted with the spectre of his past life: the sins and follies, valour and heroics, triumphs and disasters.

SIXTY MINUTES FOR ST GEORGE

Alexander Fullerton

On St George's Day, 23 April 1918, the Royal Navy launched
a desperate assault on the German base at Zeebrugge. In the sixty
minutes from touchdown to withdrawal, eleven VCs were won
and hundreds lay dead or wounded. Churchill said the raid
"may well rank as the finest feat of arms of the Great War".

Alexander Fullerton's descriptions of minelaying
operations, coastal patrols in foul Channel weather and the
savagery of clashes with enemy destroyers are heightened by his
outstanding ability to recreate the war as it was felt and lived.

INTO THE FIRE

Alexander Fullerton

Summer 1943, and Rosie Ewing is leaving on her second
mission to German-occupied France. She's a Special Operations
Executive agent and a 'pianist' – Resistance slang for a radio
operator – and with pianists' average life in the field currently six
weeks, it's hardly surprising she's shaking.

Her brief is to set up a new network in Rouen, where
the one agent still at large is suspected of having betrayed his
colleagues. She's to be landed from a gunboat in a remote cove
on the Brittany coast, then has to get to Paris by train, carrying
forged papers, a radio transceiver and more than a million francs
in cash. Terrifyingly vulnerable, she knows the dangers of a
second's carelessness or treachery, and the consequences of
crumbling under the force of Gestapo torture . . .

Time Warner Paperback titles available by post:

☐	The First Nathaniel Drinkwater Omnibus	Richard Woodman	£9.99
☐	The Second Nathaniel Drinkwater Omnibus	Richard Woodman	£9.99
☐	Death or Damnation: The Fourth Nathaniel Drinkwater Omnibus	Richard Woodman	£9.99
☐	Distant Gunfire: The Fifth Nathaniel Drinkwater Omnibus	Richard Woodman	£9.99
☐	Into the Fire	Alexander Fullerton	£5.99
☐	Sixty Minutes for St George	Alexander Fullerton	£5.99

The prices shown above are correct at time of going to press. However, the publishers reserve the right to increase prices on covers from those previously advertised without prior notice.

TIME WARNER PAPERBACKS
P.O. Box 121, Kettering, Northants NN14 4ZQ
Tel: 01832 737525, Fax: 01832 733076
Email: aspenhouse@FSBDial.co.uk

POST AND PACKING:
Payments can be made as follows: cheque, postal order (payable to Time Warner Books) or by credit cards. Do not send cash or currency.

All U.K. Orders	**FREE OF CHARGE**
E.E.C. & Overseas	25% of order value

Name (Block Letters) _____

Address_____

_____

Post/zip code:_____

☐ Please keep me in touch with future Time Warner publications

☐ I enclose my remittance £_____

☐ I wish to pay by Visa/Access/Mastercard/Eurocard

Card Expiry Date

☐☐☐☐☐☐☐☐☐☐☐☐☐☐☐☐☐☐☐

_____